Great Expectations

Charles Dickens

THE EMC MASTERPIECE SERIES

Access Editions

SERIES EDITOR

Robert D. Shepherd

EMC/Paradigm Publishing
St. Paul, Minnesota

Staff Credits:
For **EMC/Paradigm Publishing**, St. Paul, Minnesota

Laurie Skiba
Editor

Eileen Slater
Editorial Consultant

Shannon O'Donnell Taylor
Associate Editor

Jennifer J. Anderson
Assistant Editor

For **Penobscot School Publishing, Inc.**, Danvers, Massachusetts

Editorial

Robert D. Shepherd
President, Executive Editor

Christina E. Kolb
Managing Editor

Sara Hyry
Editor

Allyson Stanford
Editor

Sharon Salinger
Copyeditor

Marilyn Murphy Shepherd
Editorial Advisor

Design and Production

Charles Q. Bent
Production Manager

Diane Castro
Compositor

Janet Stebbings
Illustrator

ISBN 0-8219-1641-6

Published by EMC/Paradigm Publishing
875 Montreal Way
St. Paul, Minnesota 55102

Printed in the United States of America.
10 9 8 7 6 5 4 3 2 xxx 08 07 06 05 04 03 02

Table of Contents

Miss Havisham

ILLUSTRATION **V**

THE LIFE AND WORKS OF

Charles Dickens

Charles Dickens (1812–1870). Charles Dickens was born at Portsea near Portsmouth, England, the second of eight children. His early childhood seems to have been a happy one. Charles's father, however, was unwise with his money and went deeply into debt. The family moved to London when Charles was eleven, and soon after, his father was sent to debtor's prison. At that time Charles had to leave school and support himself working at a factory labeling bottles for four months before his father was released and the family reunited. Afterward, Charles Dickens never spoke of this experience, but the pain of it shaped his writing, particularly in his descriptions of the sufferings of poor children, orphans, and other victims of injustice. This experience also created in Dickens a grim determination to succeed.

Charles Dickens

After leaving school again at age fifteen, Dickens worked as a clerk in the law firm of Ellis and Blackmore at Gray's Inn. His diligent study of court matters and of shorthand soon led to a career as a journalist, which Dickens began by reporting on events in criminal court. By 1832 he was a general reporter for the *True Sun* and a parliamentary reporter for the *Mirror of Parliament*. In his free time, he began to write short fictional character sketches, which he published in various magazines under the pseudonym *Boz*. After attracting considerable attention for their lively humor, these early writings were published in book form in 1836 as *Sketches by Boz*.

The following year proved pivotal for Dickens. Just weeks after *Sketches by Boz* was issued, the first monthly installment of his first novel, *The Pickwick Papers*, appeared. At this time Dickens also married Catherine Hogarth, the daughter of the editor of the *Evening Chronicle*. His much beloved sister-in-law Mary Hogarth came to live with the young couple, but contracted a sudden illness and died in Charles's arms. Her loss was a deep blow from which Dickens does not seem to have ever recovered.

Nearly all of Dickens's major works of fiction were first published in serial form, appearing in weekly or monthly magazines, sometimes with hundreds of thousands of readers waiting eagerly for each new installment. *The Pickwick Papers* had a slow start but quickly became a publishing phenomenon, and Dickens enjoyed a lavish social life and friendships with many celebrities of the day. However, his social life did not keep him from writing prodigiously. In the following twelve years, his major works included *Oliver Twist*,

A Christmas Carol, Nicholas Nickleby, The Old Curiosity Shop, and *Dombey and Son.* During this time, Dickens's writings moved from humor to increasingly complex social criticism of a world ruled by the business interests of the industrial revolution rather than human feeling.

David Copperfield, published in 1849, was Dickens's most autobiographical novel, marking the point in his career at which he had come to a more mature view of himself and the intricate workings of society. In the next decade, he published some of his greatest works, including *Hard Times, Bleak House,* and *A Tale of Two Cities.* During this time Dickens also founded and edited two magazines, *Household Words* and *All the Year Round,* in which he serialized some of his essays and fiction.

In 1859, after years of increasing marital tension, Dickens separated from his wife and moved with most of his ten children to a country house at Gad's Hill, near his childhood home in Chatham. There he wrote *Our Mutual Friend* and *Great Expectations.* In 1867 he left England for a successful reading tour of the United States. The traveling took a tremendous physical toll on him and he returned to England the following year in declining health. Even so, he insisted on making a tour of England in 1869. A physical collapse forced him to suspend the tour, but did not keep him from giving a farewell series of lectures in London in the winter of 1870. On June 8, after a full day of work on his last novel, *The Mystery of Edwin Drood,* Dickens had a fatal stroke and died the following day.

In addition to his novels and work as an editor, Dickens loved the theater, and led an amateur company for many years. His enthusiasm for amateur theater is reflected in the novel *Great Expectations* in the character of Mr. Wopsle. Dickens's theatrical flair also contributed to the success of his reading tours in England and the United States.

Dickens did more than write: he worked hard to rectify many of the social injustices he described in his novels, involving himself in welfare projects including the cleaning up of slums, schools for poor children, and homes for unwed mothers. Dickens's social concerns emerged as an important theme in *Great Expectations,* particularly in the descriptions of the mistreatment of children, with whom Dickens sympathized immensely; descriptions of England's legal system; and his sympathetic portrayal of the convict Magwitch. Dickens developed the character of Magwitch to reflect someone who was inevitably led to a life of crime because of society's indifference to the plight of poor orphans. Dickens's writings were a powerful call for social reform, and have proved prophetic of the continuing efforts to humanize industrial society in our own era.

Time Line of Dickens's Life

Feb. 7, 1812 — Charles Dickens is born in Portsea near Portsmouth, England, to John and Elizabeth Dickens.

1817–1821 — Family resides at Chatham, Kent; Dickens reads voraciously and flourishes in the quiet country setting.

1822 — Dickens's family moves to London.

1824 — Dickens's father jailed for failing to pay his debts. Dickens takes a factory job for four months, before his father is released from prison.

1827 — Dickens leaves school again to work for Ellis and Blackmore, a Gray's Inn law firm.

1828 — Dickens begins work as a freelance court reporter.

1833 — Dickens begins publishing a popular series of character studies in magazines under the title *Sketches by Boz*.

1834 — Dickens begins work as a reporter for the *Morning Chronicle*.

1836 — Dickens marries Catherine Hogarth.

1836–1837 — Dickens's first novel, *The Pickwick Papers,* is published in serial form and quickly finds unprecedented success.

1837 — *Oliver Twist* is published. Dickens's sister-in-law, Mary Hogarth, dies suddenly at age seventeen.

1838–1839 — *Nicholas Nickleby* is published.

1840–1841 — *The Old Curiosity Shop* sells 100,000 copies.

1841 — *Barnaby Rudge* is Dickens's first commercial failure.

Dickens travels in the United States for six months; despite success, he leaves disillusioned by American democracy and appalled by the practice of slavery.	1842
A Christmas Carol is published.	1843
Dombey and Son is published.	1846–1848
David Copperfield, Dickens's most autobiographical novel, is published. In 1850, he founds *Household Words,* a weekly magazine which he also edits.	1849–1850
Bleak House is published.	1852–1853
Dickens publishes *Hard Times* in *Household Words.*	1854
Little Dorrit is published.	1855–1857
Dickens publishes *A Tale of Two Cities* in *All Year Round,* which he founds in the same year to succeed *Household Words.* After years of marital problems, Dickens separates from his wife and moves with his younger children to his country house at Gad's Hill in Kent.	1859
Dickens publishes *Great Expectations.*	1860–1861
Our Mutual Friend, the last of Dickens's fourteen major novels, is published.	1864–1865
Dickens conducts a successful but physically exhausting reading tour in the United States. His health never returns.	1867–1868
Dickens begins his last novel, *The Mystery of Edwin Drood,* but never completes it.	1870
Dickens dies of a stroke at Gad's Hill.	June 9, 1870

Great Expectations

The Victorian Era

Charles Dickens wrote during the Victorian Era, which takes its name from Queen Victoria (1819–1901), whose reign from 1837 to 1901 was the longest in British history. Throughout her reign, she maintained a sense of dignity and decorum that restored the average person's high opinion of the monarchy after a series of dissolute, ineffectual leaders. Today, the term Victorian is often associated with extreme or hypocritical prudery; however, that fact probably has more to do with middle-class attitudes in Victorian England than with the character of Victoria herself. In 1840, Victoria married a German prince, Albert of Saxe-Coburg-Gotha, who became prince consort of England. Although England was ruled by prime ministers and the elected members of Parliament, Victoria and Albert set a standard of national pride and optimism that influenced their subjects to bring about enormous changes in the world.

The Growth of the British Empire

During the Victorian Era, England became the most powerful nation on earth, ruling a vast empire. Its dominions included the relatively independent and self-governing countries of Canada, Australia, and New Zealand, as well as imperial colonies in Hong Kong, Singapore, South Africa, Rhodesia (modern Zimbabwe), Kenya, Cyprus, British Guyana, Ceylon (now Sri Lanka), and India (modern India, Pakistan, and Bangladesh).

The origins of British Imperialism lay in the defeat of the Spanish Armada during the Elizabethan Era (1558–1603). During the centuries that followed, England built a large navy and merchant fleet for purposes of trade and colonization. By the mid-eighteenth century, England was the largest exporter and importer, the primary manufacturer, and the wealthiest country in the world. British dominion over much of the globe led to tendencies of excessive optimism, smugness, and arrogance among well-to-do English people. Many came to believe that it was their country's destiny and duty to bring English values, laws, customs, and religion to poor "savage races."

The Industrial Revolution and Its Consequences

The Industrial Revolution that led to the modern era began in the late 1700s with the invention of machines for weaving. Gradually, a factory system emerged in England that supplied much of the rest of the world with finished goods. English textile factories had to be supplied with coal and iron, so mining increased and the canal and railway systems were developed. The coming of factories meant a dramatic shift in the English economy away from agriculture and toward the production of manufactured goods. Millions of people crowded into factory and mill towns. With this exodus, the old, landed gentry lost power and political power shifted almost completely into the hands of factory owners and merchants.

England made great progress during this period in the development of the tools and techniques of mass production, which were brilliantly displayed in the Great Exhibition of 1851. The exhibition was organized by Prince Albert and housed in a marvel of modern architecture, a Crystal Palace of glass and iron. Visitors to the exhibition had a chance to see firsthand the machines that were making over the modern world, such as hydraulic presses, locomotives, machine tools, power looms, reapers, and steamboats.

Despite such advances, industrialization in England was also attended by great social evils. Vast wealth was concentrated in a few hands. Most laboring people lived in poverty. Children as young as five years old worked sixteen-hour days in factories and mines. Cities grew beyond their means, and sprawling, rat-infested slums appeared. Clean drinking water was scarce, and cholera epidemics killed hundreds of thousands of people. Hunger was common. Such conditions bred crime and moral license. One writer who comprehensively and sympathetically documented and described the lives of those at the lowest stratum of London society was journalist Henry Mayhew (1812–1887). In his work *London Labour and the London Poor,* Mayhew focused on the lives and economic and social realities of children and adults who swept streets, gathered rags and bones, sold oranges, and performed acrobatic tricks to eke out a meager living in the sordid and fetid lodging houses and slums they called home. Mayhew's work profoundly influenced Dickens, who knew poverty first-hand. As writers like Dickens turned to portraying social ills in their work, they shocked a comfortable and complacent middle class and sowed the seeds of reform.

Social and Political Reform

The terrible conditions among the working poor in England during the Victorian Age were addressed by a series of social and political reforms. Acts passed in the 1830s extended the vote to most middle-class men, abolished slavery in British colonies, and regulated child labor in factories. Poverty continued to be a major social problem, despite the Poor-Law-Amendment Act of 1834, which created a system of workhouses for indigent people. Prime Minister Robert Peel, reacting to the hunger and social unrest, pushed through legislation repealing the so-called Corn Laws that placed high tariffs on imported grain and kept the price of bread artificially high. Other Reform Bills passed by 1885 extended the vote to almost all English men. In 1869, debtors' prisons were abolished, and nearly universal primary education was instituted. In 1871, the Trade Union Act made it legal for laborers to organize to protect their rights. Throughout the period, various laws were passed regulating food, drugs, and sanitation. One important force for social change was the Chartist Movement, begun in 1837. The Chartists took their name from a document called the People's Charter, which called for widespread political reforms, including universal male suffrage and vote by ballot. The Evangelical Movement, which emphasized a Protestant faith in personal salvation through Jesus Christ, led to an enormous outpouring of philanthropic and charitable work and to the foundation of the Salvation Army and the Young Men's Christian Association, or YMCA. While Dickens himself was involved with a number of social projects, he also used his writings as a way to comment on the path reform was taking in Victorian England, satirizing those who were concerned with educating and converting those in foreign lands while ignoring the poor in their own streets, as well as those who lectured the English poor about morality but did nothing to educate the poor or raise their quality of life.

Currents of Victorian Thought

The Victorian Age was a time of vigorous, intense intellectual activity in England. Leading thinkers of the period included the following:

Philosopher and social critic John Stuart Mill (1806–1873) popularized the Utilitarianism of the philosopher Jeremy Bentham, arguing that the object of moral action was to bring about "the greatest good for the greatest number" of people. Mill also championed Liberalism, arguing that governments had the right to restrict the actions of individuals only when those actions harmed others and that society should use its collective resources to provide for the basic welfare of its members. In *The Subjection of Women*, Mill argued that women should be treated as equals under the law and provided with opportunities for education.

Charles Darwin (1809–1882) advanced in his book *On the Origin of Species* the not-entirely-new idea that the many species of animals and plants on the planet had evolved from common ancestors. Darwin's chief contribution to evolutionary theory was the mechanism that he provided to explain it. Darwin based his explanation on the writings of Thomas Malthus (1766–1834), who argued in his *Essay on the Principle of Population* that populations naturally increase geometrically, while available resources increase only arithmetically, leading to fierce competition for resources and inevitably to famine, disease, and war. According to Darwin, species change as a result of such competition. In every generation of individuals, there were random variations. Darwin stated that competition for limited resources led to the selective survival of the fittest—those creatures best suited to take advantage of available resources.

Herbert Spencer (1820–1903) attempted to apply the ideas of Darwin to many areas of human endeavor and thought. Proponents of Spencer's Social Darwinism held that in human society, as in nature, survival properly belonged to the fittest—those most able to survive. Social Darwinism was used by many Victorians to justify social inequalities based on race, social or economic class, and gender. The Social Darwinists championed not only the ideas of Spencer, but also those of the eighteenth-century economist Adam Smith, who held that the best government economic policy was to follow a laissez-faire or "let it be" policy of little or no government intervention. Followers of Mill and other Liberals argued that government did have a proper role in protecting the weak against the strong, the poor against the wealthy. Still more radical thinkers, the Socialists, believed in far-reaching government control and in the abolition of private property in favor of publicly or communally owned lands and businesses.

Class in Victorian England

Class distinctions in England shifted as the economy changed from an agricultural to a manufacturing focus and factory owners and merchants became more powerful. Moving up in class was difficult. In Dickens's novel *Great*

Expectations, Pip's expectations are to allow him to be a gentleman. To the Victorians, the word *expectations* meant legacy as well as anticipation. In that closed society, one of the few ways in which a lower or lower-middle class person could rise socially was to receive or inherit valuables, including land, money, and jewelry. One of the first sums Pip receives is spent on clothing, an outward sign of his status as a gentleman. *Great Expectations* examines the psychological and ethical implications of advancing in the social system by acquiring wealth from the labors of others.

Crime and Punishment in Victorian England

Dickens is arguably the author of the period most associated with crime and punishment. To understand Dickens's works, including *Great Expectations*, it is important to note some aspects of the legal and penal systems of Victorian England. While present-day Americans enjoy the right to be considered innocent until proven guilty, and the legal guarantee to a speedy trial, such rights were not granted in Victorian England. In fact, in some areas of England, trials were only held once a year when traveling judges arrived. There was also no system of appeal; once found guilty, a convict's only hope was a royal pardon.

Prisons during Dickens's time were overcrowded, dirty, miserable places. Ventilation and sanitation were not adequately maintained, and illness was rampant. People of varying ages and degrees of crime were kept together. Corruption and bribery of prison workers was commonplace. Because of crowded conditions, as an alternative to prison many criminals were shipped to British colonies—after a time almost exclusively to Australia. Crimes ranging from shoplifting to murder were punishable by death. The condemned were often publicly hanged as a warning to others to abide by the law.

Victorian Literature

In response to the difficult conditions in many of England's cities during the Victorian Era, a new style of literary expression was born: Realism. Realism is the attempt to render in art or literature an accurate portrayal of reality. Although the development of the novel in the eighteenth century, with its detailed descriptions of characters and settings, could be considered Realist, literary historians usually apply the term to works of the late nineteenth century that dealt with the harsher details of ordinary lives. As literacy became more common among the middle class, the popularity of the novel soared to its greatest height. Realistic, detailed descriptions of everyday life, and especially of its darker aspects, appealed to many readers disillusioned by the "progress" going on around them.

Charles Dickens, perhaps the most famous of the Victorian novelists, was wildly popular in his day. Many of his novels were published in serial form in monthly installments or in magazines. This form of publication, and his comic and sentimental descriptions of the lives of people of diverse occupations and social classes, gave Dickens an exceptionally large and varied audience. Novels such as *A Christmas Carol* (1843), *David Copperfield* (1850), and *Great Expectations* (1861) are typical of Dickens's fiction in their attacks on social indifference to poverty and injustice, their comic invention, and their call on charity and love to resolve, or at least to alleviate, the troubles of the Victorian Age.

Characters in *Great Expectations*

Main Characters

Pip (Philip Pirrip). Pip, the narrator and main character of the novel, is an orphan who is raised by his ill-tempered sister and her husband. His ambition in life is to improve his social position.

Joe Gargery. Joe is a skilled blacksmith and Pip's long suffering brother-in-law and father figure. A simple, kind, and gentle man, Joe is a good and loyal friend.

Mrs. Joe. Pip's sister, Mrs. Joe is more than twenty years older than he and raises him "by hand." She is physically rough in her discipline and has a fierce temper.

Biddy. Pip's first teacher, Biddy comes to live with Joe, Mrs. Joe, and Pip in the Gargery household. Generally forgiving, kind, and patient, Biddy is also not afraid of pointing out flaws in Pip's behavior. She recognizes that Joe is a worthy man.

Abel Magwitch (alias Provis). Magwitch is a criminal Pip meets down by the marshes. Magwitch later makes his fortune in Australia. Although he has a crude exterior, he is a generous, loyal man.

Miss Havisham. The spoiled daughter of a wealthy brewer, Miss Havisham is abandoned on her wedding day. She spends the rest of her life raising Estella, her adopted daughter, to wreak revenge on men for the rejection and humiliation she suffered.

Estella Havisham. Estella is the adopted daughter of Miss Havisham. Although she is beautiful and intelligent, Estella grows up with a heart of ice because of the training of her benefactress.

Mr. Jaggers. Jaggers is a shrewd, aggressive, and intelligent lawyer who manages Pip's affairs until he is twenty-one. He is also Miss Havisham's lawyer.

John Wemmick. Wemmick is a clerk in Jaggers's office who befriends Pip. He leads two separate lives—one at the office, and one at his home in Walworth. There, he dotes on his "Aged Parent" and feels tender love for Miss Skiffins.

Herbert Pocket. Herbert, a relative of Miss Havisham, is Pip's closest friend and confidant in London. He is a kind, honest, and gentle young man with ambitious dreams for himself.

Minor Characters

Mr. Wopsle. A friend of the Gargerys, Wopsle leaves his position in the church of Pip's village to head for London and pursue his dream of becoming a great actor. His abilities, however, are questionable.

Orlick. Orlick is an employee of Joe Gargery and is one of Pip's enemies. He is strong and swarthy and has a mean temper.

Uncle Pumblechook. Pumblechook is Joe's uncle and a seed merchant. He is pompous, arrogant, and treats Pip badly.

The Aged Parent. The Aged Parent is Wemmick's father.

Miss Skiffins. Miss Skiffins is Wemmick's beloved. Her relationship with Wemmick is one of the few positive, loving relationships that Pip witnesses.

Mr. Matthew Pocket. Mr. Pocket is Herbert's father. He refuses to compete for the favor of Miss Havisham and lives by tutoring young gentlemen like Pip. He feels helpless in his chaotic household but proves a capable teacher for Pip.

Mrs. Pocket. Mrs. Pocket is the wife of Mr. Pocket and Herbert's mother. She is obsessed with social status, constantly bemoaning the fact that her grandfather narrowly missed being a baronet and that her social standing lowered when she married Mr. Pocket.

Bentley Drummle. Bentley Drummle is a student at the Pocket residence. He is a brutish fellow whom Pip dislikes, especially when he discovers that Drummle also harbors an affection for Estella.

Startop. Startop is another student of Matthew Pocket. He is kind, gentle, and good-natured, and befriends Pip and Herbert.

Clara. Clara is Herbert Pocket's beloved. She lives with her father by the river.

Compeyson. Compeyson is the fiance who deserts Miss Havisham on their wedding day. He is the second convict in the marshes.

Molly. Molly is Jaggers's housekeeper. Wemmick warns Pip that she once had a violent streak in her. Pip later makes surprising discoveries about her past.

Camilla and Raymond. These two are a couple who flatter Miss Havisham, hoping to make their fortune after her death. They resent Pip.

Miss Sarah Pocket. A relative of Herbert's, she also seeks to please Miss Havisham so that she will receive a large settlement in Miss Havisham's will. She also has a very negative attitude about Pip.

Echoes:

Quotations from Charles Dickens

"There are strings," said Mr. Tappertit, " . . . in the human heart that had better not be wibrated." *—Barnaby Rudge*

This is a London particular . . . A fog, miss. *—Bleak House*

It is a melancholy truth that even great men have their poor relations. *—Bleak House*

"God bless us every one!" said Tiny Tim, the last of all. *—A Christmas Carol*

"It was as true," said Mr. Barkis, " . . . as taxes is. And nothing's truer than them." *—David Copperfield*

If there were no bad people, there would be no good lawyers. *—Great Expectations*

Oliver Twist has asked for more! *—Oliver Twist*

He had used the word in its Pickwickian sense. . . . He had merely considered him a humbug in a Pickwickian point of view. *—Pickwick Papers*

"I am ruminating," said Mr. Pickwick, "on the strange mutability of human affairs."
"Ah, I see—in at the palace door one day, out at the window the next. Philosopher, sir?"
"An observer of human nature, sir," said Mr. Pickwick. *—Pickwick Papers*

It was the best of times, it was the worst of times, it was the age of wisdom, it was the age of foolishness, it was the epoch of belief, it was the epoch of incredulity, it was the season of light, it was the season of darkness, it was the spring of hope, it was the winter of despair, we had everything before us, we had nothing before us, we were all going direct to Heaven, we were all going direct the other way. . . . *—A Tale of Two Cities*

It is a far, far better thing that I do, than I have ever done; it is a far, far better rest that I go to than I have ever known. *—A Tale of Two Cities*

CHAPTER 1

My father's family name being Pirrip, and my Christian name Philip, my infant tongue could make of both names nothing longer or more <u>explicit</u> than Pip. So I called myself Pip, and came to be called Pip.

I give Pirrip as my father's family name on the authority of his tombstone and my sister—Mrs. Joe Gargery, who married the blacksmith. As I never saw my father or my mother, and never saw any likeness of either of them (for their days were long before the days of photographs), my first fancies regarding what they were like were unreasonably <u>derived</u> from their tombstones. The shape of the letters on my father's gave me an odd idea that he was a square, stout, dark man, with curly black hair. From the character and turn of the inscription, *"Also Georgiana Wife of the Above,"* I drew a childish conclusion that my mother was freckled and sickly. To five little stone lozenges,[1] each about a foot and a half long, which were arranged in a neat row beside their grave, and were sacred to the memory of five little brothers of mine— who gave up trying to get a living exceedingly early in that universal struggle—I am indebted for a belief I religiously <u>entertained</u> that they had all been born on their backs with their hands in their trousers pockets, and had never taken them out in this state of existence.

Ours was the marsh country, down by the river, within, as the river wound, twenty miles of the sea. My first most vivid and broad impression of the identity of things seems to me to have been gained on a memorable raw afternoon towards evening. At such a time I found out for certain that this bleak place overgrown with nettles[2] was the churchyard; and that Philip Pirrip, Late of this Parish, and Also Georgiana Wife of the Above, were dead and buried; and that Alexander, Bartholomew, Abraham, Tobias, and Roger, infant children of the aforesaid, were also dead and buried; and that the dark flat wilderness beyond the churchyard, intersected with dikes and mounds and gates, with scattered cattle feeding on

Margin notes:

◄ How did Pip get his name?

(handwritten) Couldn't say name correctly

◄ Why has Pip never seen his parents?

(handwritten) They died

◄ What is Pip's earliest memory?

---

1. **lozenges.** Diamond-shaped slabs; here, the children's gravestones
2. **nettles.** Stinging, spiny plants

Words For Everyday Use

ex • plic • it (eks plis´it) *adj.*, clearly stated
de • rive (di rīv´) *vt.*, trace from a source
en • ter • tain (en´tər tān´) *vt.*, hold

it, was the marshes; and that the low leaden line beyond was the river; and that the distant savage <u>lair</u> from which the wind was rushing was the sea; and that the small bundle of shivers growing afraid of it all and beginning to cry was Pip.

"Hold your noise!" cried a terrible voice, as a man started up from among the graves at the side of the church porch. "Keep still, you little devil, or I'll cut your throat!"

► *What kind of man comes upon Pip in the churchyard?*

A fearful man, all in coarse gray, with a great iron[3] on his leg. A man with no hat, and with broken shoes, and with an old rag tied round his head. A man who had been soaked in water, and smothered in mud, and <u>lamed</u> by stones, and cut by <u>flints</u>, and stung by nettles, and torn by briars; who limped, and shivered, and glared, and growled; and whose teeth chattered in his head as he seized me by the chin.

"Oh! Don't cut my throat, sir," I pleaded in terror. "Pray don't do it, sir."

"Tell us your name!" said the man. "Quick!"

"Pip, sir."

"Once more," said the man, staring at me. "Give it mouth!"[4]

"Pip. Pip, sir."

"Show us where you live," said the man. "Pint[5] out the place!"

I pointed to where our village lay, on the flat in-shore among the alder trees and pollards,[6] a mile or more from the church.

► *What does the man do that frightens Pip?*

The man, after looking at me for a moment, turned me upside down, and emptied my pockets. There was nothing in them but a piece of bread. When the church came to itself—for he was so sudden and strong that he made it go head over heels before me, and I saw the steeple under my feet—when the church came to itself, I say, I was seated on a high tombstone, trembling, while he ate the bread <u>ravenously</u>.

"You young dog," said the man, licking his lips, "what fat cheeks you ha'[7] got."

I believe they were fat, though I was at that time undersized for my years, and not strong.

"Darn me if I couldn't eat 'em," said the man, with a threatening shake of his head, "and if I han't[8] half a mind to't!"

---

3. **iron.** Shackle or chain
4. **Give it mouth.** Speak loudly
5. **Pint.** Point
6. **pollards.** Trees with the top branches cut back
7. **ha'.** Have
8. **han't.** Haven't

Words For Everyday Use	
lair (ler) *n.,* hiding place; den	
lamed (lāmd) *adj.,* made lame or injured	
flint (flint) *n.,* hard, sharp stone	
rav • e • nous • ly (rav´ə nəs lē) *adv.,* hungrily	

I earnestly expressed my hope that he wouldn't, and held tighter to the tombstone on which he had put me; partly to keep myself upon it; partly to keep myself from crying.

"Now lookee here!" said the man. "Where's your mother?"

"There, sir!" said I.

He started, made a short run, and stopped and looked over his shoulder.

"There, sir!" I timidly explained. "Also Georgiana. That's my mother."

"Oh!" said he, coming back. "And is that your father alonger[9] your mother?"

"Yes, sir," said I; "him, too; late of this parish."

"Ha!" he muttered then, considering. "Who d'ye live with—supposin' ye're kindly let to live, which I han't made up my mind about?"

"My sister, sir—Mrs. Joe Gargery—wife of Joe Gargery, the blacksmith, sir."

"Blacksmith, eh?" said he. And looked down at his leg.

After darkly looking at his leg and me several times, he came closer to my tombstone, took me by both arms, and tilted me back as far as he could hold me, so that his eyes looked most powerfully down into mine, and mine looked most helplessly up into his.

◀ *What else does the man do to intimidate Pip?*

"Now lookee here," he said, "the question being whether you're to be let to live, you know what a <u>file</u> is?"

"Yes, sir."

"And you know what wittles[10] is?"

"Yes, sir."

After each question he tilted me over a little more, so as to give me a greater sense of helplessness and danger.

"You get me a file." He tilted me again. "And you get me wittles." He tilted me again. "You bring 'em both to me." He tilted me again. "Or I'll have your heart and liver out." He tilted me again.

◀ *Why does the man want a file?*

I was dreadfully frightened, and so giddy that I clung to him with both hands, and said, "If you would kindly please to let me keep upright, sir, perhaps I shouldn't be sick, and perhaps I could attend[11] more."

---

9. **alonger.** Alongside
10. **wittles.** Vittles, food. The *v* is often pronounced like a *w* in the dialect of these characters.
11. **attend.** Help

Words For Everyday Use	
ear • nest • ly (ur´nist lē) *adv.,* sincerely; with urgency	
file (fīl) *n.,* steel tool with rough, ridged surface for grinding	

He gave me a most tremendous dip and roll, so that the church jumped over its own weathercock.[12] Then he held me by the arms in an upright position on the top of the stone, and went on in these fearful terms:

► What does the man make Pip promise?

"You bring me, tomorrow morning early, that file and them wittles. You bring the lot to me at that old battery[13] over yonder. You do it, and you never dare to say a word or dare to make a sign concerning your having seen such a person as me, or any person sumever,[14] and you shall be let to live. You fail, or you go from my words in any partickler, no matter how small it is, and your heart and your liver shall be tore out, roasted, and ate. Now, I ain't alone, as you may think I am. There's a young man hid with me, in comparison with which young man I am a angel. That young man hears the words I speak. That young man has a secret way pecooliar[15] to himself of getting at a boy, and at his heart, and at his liver. It is in wain[16] for a boy to attempt to hide himself from that young man. A boy may lock his door, may be warm in bed, may tuck himself up, may draw the clothes over his head, may think himself comfortable and safe, but that young man will softly creep and creep his way to him and tear him open. I am a-keeping that young man from harming of you at the present moment with great difficulty. I find it wery hard to hold that young man off of your inside. Now, what do you say?"

► Who does the stranger say is with him?

I said that I would get him the file, and I would get him what broken bits of food I could, and I would come to him at the battery, early in the morning.

"Say, Lord strike you dead if you don't!" said the man.

I said so, and he took me down.

"Now," he pursued, "you remember what you've undertook, and you remember that young man, and you get home!"

"Goo-good night, sir," I <u>faltered</u>.

"Much of that!" said he, glancing about him over the cold wet flat. "I wish I was a frog. Or a eel!"

At the same time, he hugged his shuddering body in both his arms—clasping himself, as if to hold himself together—

---

12. **weathercock.** Weather vane in the shape of a rooster, which turns with the wind and shows its direction
13. **battery.** Place where military equipment, such as artillery, is kept
14. **sumever.** Whatsoever
15. **pecooliar.** Peculiar
16. **wain.** Vain

Words For Everyday Use

fal • ter (fôl´ter) *vi.*, speak haltingly; stammer

and limped towards the low church wall. As I saw him go, picking his way among the nettles, and among the brambles that bound the green mounds, he looked in my young eyes as if he were <u>eluding</u> the hands of the dead people, stretching up cautiously out of their graves to get a twist upon his ankle and pull him in.

When he came to the low church wall, he got over it like a man whose legs were numbed and stiff, and then turned round to look for me. When I saw him turning, I set my face towards home, and made the best use of my legs. But presently I looked over my shoulder, and saw him going on again towards the river, still hugging himself in both arms, and picking his way with his sore feet among the great stones dropped into the marshes here and there for stepping-places when the rains were heavy, or the tide was in.

The marshes were just a long black horizontal line then, as I stopped to look after him; and the river was just another horizontal line, not nearly so broad not yet so black; and the sky was just a row of long angry red lines and dense black lines intermixed. On the edge of the river I could faintly make out the only two black things in all the <u>prospect</u> that seemed to be standing upright; one of these was the <u>beacon</u> by which the sailors steered—like an unhooped cask upon a pole—an ugly thing when you were near it; the other a gibbet,[17] with some chains hanging to it which had once held a pirate. The man was limping on towards this latter, as if he were the pirate come to life, and come down, and going back to hook himself up again. It gave me a terrible turn when I thought so, and as I saw the cattle lifting their heads to gaze after him, I wondered whether they thought so, too. I looked all round for the horrible young man, and could see no signs of him. But now I was frightened again, and ran home without stopping.

◀ Whom does it seem the man is trying to elude?

◀ Do you think Pip feels some sympathy toward the stranger? Why, or why not?

◀ What two things does Pip see on the edge of the river? What might each represent?

---

17. **gibbet.** Gallows used to hang criminals

Words For Everyday Use

e • lude (ē loōd´) vt., avoid; escape
pros • pect (präs´pekt) n., broad view
bea • con (bēk´'n) n., lighthouse

My sister, Mrs. Joe Gargery, was more than twenty years older than I, and had established a great reputation with herself and the neighbors because she had brought me up "by hand." Having at that time to find out for myself what the expression meant, and knowing her to have a hard and heavy hand, and to be much in the habit of laying it upon her husband as well as upon me, I supposed that Joe Gargery and I were both brought up by hand.

She was not a good-looking woman, my sister; and I had a general impression that she must have made Joe Gargery marry her by hand. Joe was a fair man, with curls of flaxen hair on each side of his smooth face, and with eyes of such a very undecided blue that they seemed to have somehow got mixed with their own whites. He was a mild, good-natured, sweet-tempered, easy-going, foolish, dear fellow—a sort of Hercules[1] in strength, and also in weakness.

My sister, Mrs. Joe, with black hair and eyes, had such a prevailing redness of skin that I sometimes used to wonder whether it was possible she washed herself with a nutmeg-grater instead of soap. She was tall and bony, and almost always wore a coarse apron, fastened over her figure behind with two loops, and having a square, <u>impregnable</u> bib in front that was stuck full of pins and needles. She made it a powerful <u>merit</u> in herself, and a strong <u>reproach</u> against Joe, that she wore this apron so much. Though I really see no reason why she should have worn it at all: or why, if she did wear it at all, she should not have taken it off every day of her life.

Joe's forge[2] adjoined our house, which was a wooden house, as many of the dwellings in our country were—most of them, at that time. When I ran home from the churchyard, the forge was shut up, and Joe was sitting alone in the kitchen. Joe and I being fellow-sufferers, and having <u>confidences</u> as such, Joe <u>imparted</u> a confidence to me the moment I raised the latch of the door and peeped in at him opposite to it, sitting in the chimney-corner.

---

1. **Hercules.** Greek hero known for his strength
2. **forge.** Blacksmith's furnace for heating metal

► What does it mean to be brought up "by hand"?

► Compare and contrast the physical appearances of Joe and his wife. Why does Pip think his sister got Joe to marry her "by hand"?

► What draws Joe and Pip together?

Words For Everyday Use

im • preg • nable (im preg′ nə bəl) *adj.*, incapaple of being pierced; impenetrable

mer • it (mer′ it) *n.*, mark of excellence

re • proach (ri prōch′) *n.*, blame; disgrace

con • fi • dence (kän′ fə dəns) *n.*, something told as a secret

im • part (im pärt′) *vt.*, make known; reveal

"Mrs. Joe has been out a dozen times, looking for you, Pip. And she's out now, making it a baker's dozen."

"Is she?"

"Yes, Pip," said Joe; "and what's worse, she's got Tickler with her."

At this dismal intelligence, I twisted the only button on my waistcoat round and round, and looked in great depression at the fire. Tickler was a wax-ended piece of cane, worn smooth by collision with my tickled frame.

◄ What is "Tickler"? To what use does Mrs. Joe put it?

"She sot[3] down," said Joe, "and she got up, and she made a grab at Tickler, and she ram-paged out. That's what she did," said Joe, slowly clearing the fire between the lower bars with the poker, and looking at it; "she ram-paged out, Pip."

"Has she been gone long, Joe?" I always treated him as a larger species of child, and as no more than my equal.

"Well," said Joe, glancing up at the Dutch clock, "she's been on the ram-page, this last spell, about five minutes, Pip. She's a coming! Get behind the door, old chap, and have the jack-towel[4] betwixt you."

◄ What does Joe do to try to protect Pip from Mrs. Joe?

I took the advice. My sister, Mrs. Joe, throwing the door wide open, and finding an obstruction behind it, immediately <u>divined</u> the cause, and applied Tickler to its further investigation. She concluded by throwing me—I often served as a <u>connubial</u> missile—at Joe, who, glad to get hold of me on any terms, passed me on into the chimney and quietly fenced me up there with his great leg.

"Where have you been, you young monkey?" said Mrs. Joe, stamping her foot. "Tell me directly what you've been doing to wear me away with fret and fright and worrit,[5] or I'd have you out of that corner if you was fifty Pips, and he was five hundred Gargerys."

"I have only been to the churchyard," said I, from my stool, crying and rubbing myself.

"Churchyard!" repeated my sister. "If it warn't[6] for me, you'd have been to the churchyard long ago, and stayed there. Who brought you up by hand?"

"You did," said I.

---

3. **sot.** Sat
4. **jack-towel.** Rack for hanging objects attached to the back of a door
5. **worrit.** Worry
6. **warn't.** Wasn't

Words For Everyday Use

di • vine (də vīn´) vt., guess or find out
con • nu • bi • al (kə no͞o´bē əl) adj., of marriage

► How does Mrs.
Joe feel about being
a wife and Pip's
caretaker?

► Why is Pip
worried?

"And why did I do it, I should like to know?" exclaimed my sister.

I whimpered, "I don't know."

"*I* don't!" said my sister. "I'd never do it again! I know that. I may truly say I've never had this apron of mine off, since born you were. It's bad enough to be a blacksmith's wife (and him a Gargery) without being your mother."

My thoughts strayed from that question as I looked <u>disconsolately</u> at the fire. For the fugitive out on the marshes with the ironed leg, the mysterious young man, the file, the food, and the dreadful pledge I was under to commit a <u>larceny</u> on those sheltering premises rose before me in the avenging coals.

"Hah!" said Mrs. Joe, restoring Tickler to his station. "Churchyard, indeed! You may well say churchyard, you two." One of us, by-the-bye, had not said it at all. "You'll drive *me* to the churchyard betwixt[7] you, one of these days, and oh, a pr-r-recious pair you'd be without me!"

As she applied herself to set the tea-things, Joe peeped down at me over his leg, as if he were mentally casting me and himself up, and calculating what kind of pair we practically should make, under the <u>grievous</u> circumstances foreshadowed. After that, he sat feeling his right-side flaxen curls and whisker, and following Mrs. Joe about with his blue eyes, as his manner always was at squally[8] times.

My sister had a <u>trenchant</u> way of cutting our bread-and-butter for us that never varied. First, with her left hand she jammed the loaf hard and fast against her bib—where it sometimes got a pin into it, and sometimes a needle, which we afterwards got into our mouths. Then she took some butter (not too much) on a knife and spread it on the loaf, in an apothecary[9] kind of way, as if she were making a plaster—using both sides of the knife with a slapping <u>dexterity</u>, and trimming and molding the butter off round the crust. Then she gave the knife a final smart wipe on the edge of the plaster, and then sawed a very thick round off the loaf; which she finally, before separating from the loaf, hewed into two halves, of which Joe got one, and I the other.

---

7. **betwixt.** Between
8. **squally.** Stormy; difficult
9. **apothecary.** Pharmacist; person who prepares medicines

Words For Everyday Use

dis • con • so • late • ly (dis kän'sə lit lē) *adv.*, unhappily

lar • ce • ny (lär'sə nē) *n.*, theft

griev • ous (grēv'əs) *adj.*, severe; serious

trench • ant (trench'ənt) *adj.*, forceful

dex • ter • i • ty (deks ter'ə tē) *n.*, skill

On the present occasion, though I was hungry, I dared not eat my slice. I felt that I must have something in reserve for my dreadful acquaintance and his ally, the still more dreadful young man. I knew Mrs. Joe's housekeeping to be of the strictest kind, and that my larcenous researches might find nothing available in the safe. Therefore I resolved to put my hunk of bread-and-butter down the leg of my trousers.

◄ Why doesn't Pip eat his bread?

The effort of <u>resolution</u> necessary to the achievement of this purpose I found to be quite awful. It was as if I had to make up my mind to leap from the top of a high house, or plunge into a great depth of water. And it was made the more difficult by the unconscious Joe. In our already-mentioned freemasonry[10] as fellow-sufferers, and in his good-natured companionship with me, it was our evening habit to compare the way we bit through our slices by silently holding them up to each other's admiration now and then—which stimulated us to new exertions. Tonight, Joe several times invited me, by the display of his fast-diminishing slice, to enter upon our usual friendly competition; but he found me, each time, with my yellow mug of tea on one knee and my untouched bread-and-butter on the other. At last, I desperately considered that the thing I contemplated must be done, and that it had best be done in the least improbable manner consistent with the circumstances. I took advantage of a moment when Joe had just looked at me, and got my bread-and-butter down my leg.

◄ What game do Joe and Pip often play together as they eat? Why does this game make Pip's plan difficult? What does he do with his bread?

Joe was evidently made uncomfortable by what he supposed to be my loss of appetite, and took a thoughtful bite out of his slice, which he didn't seem to enjoy. He turned it about in his mouth much longer than usual, pondering over it a good deal, and after all gulped it down like a pill. He was about to take another bite, and had just got his head on one side for a good purchase on it, when his eye fell on me, and he saw that my bread-and-butter was gone.

The wonder and <u>consternation</u> with which Joe stopped on the <u>threshold</u> of his bite and stared at me were too evident to escape my sister's observation.

"What's the matter now?" said she smartly, as she put down her cup.

---

10. **freemasonry.** Brotherhood

Words For Everyday Use	**res • o • lu • tion** (rez´ə lo͞o´shən) n., determination
	con • ster • na • tion (kän´stər nā´shən) n., great fear that makes one feel helpless
	thresh • old (thresh´ōld) n., beginning point

"I say, you know!" muttered Joe, shaking his head at me in very serious remonstrance. "Pip, old chap! You'll do yourself a mischief.[11] It'll stick somewhere. You can't have chawed[12] it, Pip."

"What's the matter *now*?" repeated my sister more sharply than before.

"If you can cough any trifle on it up, Pip, I'd recommend you to do it," said Joe, all <u>aghast</u>. "Manners is manners, but still your 'elth's[13] your 'elth."

► Why does Mrs. Joe hit her husband's head against the wall?

By this time, my sister was quite desperate, so she pounced on Joe, and, taking him by the two whiskers, knocked his head for a little while against the wall behind him—while I sat in the corner, looking guiltily on.

"Now, perhaps you'll mention what's the matter," said my sister, out of breath, "you staring great stuck pig."

Joe looked at her in a helpless way, then took a helpless bite, and looked at me again.

► What does Joe think Pip has done?

"You know, Pip," said Joe solemnly, with his last bite in his cheek, and speaking in a confidential voice, as if we two were quite alone, "you and me is always friends, and I'd be the last to tell upon you, any time. But such a"—he moved his chair, and looked about the floor between us, and then again at me—"such a most uncommon bolt[14] as that!"

"Been bolting his food, has he?" cried my sister.

"You know, old chap," said Joe, looking at me, and not at Mrs. Joe, with his bite still in his cheek, "I bolted, myself, when I was your age—frequent—and as a boy I've been among many bolters; but I never seen your bolting equal yet, Pip, and it's a mercy you ain't bolted dead."

► Why does Mrs. Joe dose Pip? What does she use?

My sister made a dive at me, and fished me up by the hair: saying nothing more than the awful words, "You come along and be dosed."[15]

Some medical beast had revived tar-water[16] in those days as a fine medicine, and Mrs. Joe always kept a supply of it in the cupboard, having a belief in its virtues correspondent to its

---

11. **do yourself a mischief.** Make yourself sick
12. **chawed.** Chewed
13. **'elth's.** Health's
14. **bolt.** Gulp
15. **dosed.** Given medicine
16. **tar-water.** Unpleasant liquid thought to have medicinal value

Words For Everyday Use

a • ghast (ə gast´) *adj.,* horrified

nastiness. At the best of times, so much of this <u>elixir</u> was administered to me as a choice restorative that I was conscious of going about smelling like a new fence. On this particular evening, the urgency of my case demanded a pint of this mixture, which was poured down my throat, for my greater comfort, while Mrs. Joe held my head under her arm, as a boot would be held in a bootjack.[17] Joe got off with half a pint, but was made to swallow that (much to his disturbance, as he sat slowly munching and meditating before the fire), "because he had a turn."[18] Judging from myself, I should say he certainly had a turn afterwards, if he had had none before.

Conscience is a dreadful thing when it accuses man or boy, but when, in the case of a boy, that secret burden cooperates with another secret burden down the leg of his trousers, it is (as I can testify) a great punishment. The guilty knowledge that I was going to rob Mrs. Joe—I never thought I was going to rob Joe, for I never thought of any of the housekeeping property as his—united to the necessity of always keeping one hand on my bread-and-butter as I sat, or when I was ordered about the kitchen on any small errand, almost drove me out of my mind. Then, as the marsh winds made the fire glow and flare, I thought I heard the voice outside of the man with the iron on his leg who had sworn me to secrecy, declaring that he couldn't and wouldn't starve until tomorrow, but must be fed now. At other times, I thought, What if the young man who was with so much difficulty restrained from <u>imbruing</u> his hands in me should yield to a constitutional impatience, or should mistake the time, and should think himself <u>accredited</u> to my heart and liver tonight, instead of tomorrow! If ever anybody's hair stood on end with terror, mine must have done so then. But, perhaps, nobody's ever did?

It was Christmas Eve, and I had to stir the pudding for next day with a copper-stick, from seven to eight by the Dutch clock. I tried it with the load upon my leg (and that made me think afresh of the man with the load on *his* leg), and found the tendency of exercise to bring the bread-and-butter out at my ankle quite unmanageable. Happily I slipped away, and deposited that part of my conscience in my garret bedroom.

◄ *Why doesn't Pip feel guilty about taking food from Joe?*

◄ *What does Pip fear?*

---

17. **bootjack.** Forked device for holding a boot while it is being taken off of the foot
18. **had a turn.** Suffered a shock or surprise

Words For Everyday Use

e • lix • ir (i lik´sər) *n.*, medicinal potion
im • brue (im brᴏᴏ´) *vt.*, soak or stain, especially with blood
ac • cred • it (ə kred´ it) *vt.*, authorize

► *Why are the guns fired?*

"Hark!" said I, when I had done my stirring, and was taking a final warm in the chimney-corner before being sent up to bed; "was that great guns, Joe?"

"Ah!" said Joe. "There's another conwict[19] off."

"What does that mean, Joe?" said I.

Mrs. Joe, who always took explanations upon herself, said snappishly, "Escaped. Escaped," administering the definition like tar-water.

While Mrs. Joe sat with her head bending over her needle-work, I put my mouth into the forms of saying to Joe, "What's a convict?" Joe put *his* mouth into the forms of returning such a highly elaborate answer that I could make out nothing of it but the single word, "Pip."

► *How do you know how many convicts have escaped?*

"There was a conwict off last night," said Joe, aloud, "after sunset-gun. And they fired warning of him. And now it appears they're firing warning of another."

"*Who's* firing?" said I.

► *What does Mrs. Joe want Pip to do?*

"Drat that boy," interposed my sister, frowning at me over her work, "what a questioner he is. Ask no questions, and you'll be told no lies."

It was not very polite to herself, I thought, to imply that I should be told lies by her, even if I did ask questions. But she never was polite, unless there was company.

At this point, Joe greatly <u>augmented</u> my curiosity by taking the utmost pains to open his mouth very wide, and to put it into the form of a word that looked to me like "sulks." Therefore, I naturally pointed to Mrs. Joe, and put my mouth into the form of saying "her?" But Joe wouldn't hear of that at all, and again opened his mouth very wide, and shook the form of a most <u>emphatic</u> word out of it. But I could make nothing of the word.

"Mrs. Joe," said I, as a last resort, "I should like to know— if you wouldn't much mind—where the firing comes from?"

"Lord bless the boy!" exclaimed my sister, as if she didn't quite mean that, but rather the contrary. "From the Hulks!"

"Oh-h!" said I, looking at Joe. "Hulks!"

Joe gave a <u>reproachful</u> cough, as much as to say, "Well, I told you so."

"And please, what's Hulks?" said I.

---

19. **conwict.** Convict

Words For Everyday Use	aug • ment (ôg ment´) *vt.*, increase
	em • phat • ic (em fat´ik) *adj.*, expressed with emphasis
	re • proach • ful (ri prōch´fəl) *adj.*, expressing blame

"That's the way with this boy!" exclaimed my sister, pointing me out with her needle and thread, and shaking her head at me. "Answer him one question, and he'll ask you a dozen directly. Hulks are prison-ships, right 'cross th' meshes." We always used that name for marshes, in our country.

"I wonder who's put into prison-ships, and why they're put there?" said I, in a general way, and with quiet desperation.

It was too much for Mrs. Joe, who immediately rose. "I tell you what, young fellow," said she, "I didn't bring you up by hand to <u>badger</u> people's lives out. It would be blame to me, and not praise, if I had. People are put in the Hulks because they murder, and because they rob, and forge, and do all sorts of bad; and they always begin by asking questions. Now, you get along to bed!"

◀ What are the Hulks?

I was never allowed a candle to light me to bed, and, as I went upstairs in the dark, with my head tingling—from Mrs. Joe's thimble having played the tambourine upon it, to accompany her last words—I felt fearfully sensible[20] of the great convenience that the Hulks were handy for me. I was clearly on my way there. I had begun by asking questions, and I was going to rob Mrs. Joe.

◀ Why does Pip think he might end up on the Hulks?

Since that time, which is far enough away now, I have often thought that few people know what secrecy there is in the young, under terror. No matter how unreasonable the terror, so that it be terror. I was in mortal terror of the young man who wanted my heart and liver; I was in mortal terror of my <u>interlocutor</u> with the iron leg; I was in mortal terror of myself, from whom an awful promise had been <u>extracted</u>; I had no hope of deliverance through my all-powerful sister, who repulsed me at every turn; I am afraid to think of what I might have done on requirement, in the secrecy of my terror.

If I slept at all that night, it was only to imagine myself drifting down the river on a strong spring-tide, to the Hulks; a ghostly pirate calling out to me through a speaking-trumpet, as I passed the gibbet-station, that I had better come ashore and be hanged there at once, and not put it off. I was afraid to sleep, even if I had been inclined, for I knew that at the first faint dawn of morning I must rob the pantry. There was no doing it in the night, for there was no getting a light by

◀ Why is it easier for Pip to steal food in the morning?

---

20. **sensible.** Aware

Words For Everyday Use

badg • er (baj´ər) *vt.,* pester

in • ter • loc • u • tor (in´tər läk´yo͞o tər) *n.,* person taking part in conversation

ex • tract (ik strakt´) *vt.,* pull out by force

easy friction then; to have got one, I must have struck it out of flint and steel, and have made a noise like the very pirate himself rattling his chains.

As soon as the great black velvet <u>pall</u> outside my little window was shot with gray, I got up and went downstairs; every board upon the way, and every crack in every board, calling after me, "Stop thief!" and "Get up, Mrs. Joe!" In the pantry, which was far more abundantly supplied than usual, owing to the season, I was very much alarmed by a hare hanging up by the heels, whom I rather thought I caught, when my back was half-turned, winking. I had no time for <u>verification</u>, no time for selection, no time for anything, for I had no time to spare. I stole some bread, some rind of cheese, about half a jar of mincemeat (which I tied up in my pocket-handkerchief with my last night's slice), some brandy from a stone bottle (which I decanted into a glass bottle I had secretly used for making that intoxicating fluid, Spanish-licorice-water, up in my room, diluting the stone bottle from a jug in the kitchen cupboard), a meat bone with very little on it, and a beautiful round compact pork pie. I was nearly going away without the pie, but I was tempted to mount upon a shelf, to look what it was that was put away so carefully in a covered earthenware dish in a corner, and I found it was the pie, and I took it, in the hope that it was not intended for early use, and would not be missed for some time.

▶ *What does Pip take?*

There was a door in the kitchen, communicating with[21] the forge; I unlocked and unbolted that door, and got a file from among Joe's tools. Then I put the fastenings as I had found them, opened the door at which I had entered when I ran home last night, shut it, and ran for the misty marshes.

---

21. **communicating with.** Leading to

Words For Everyday Use

pall (pôl) *n.*, covering of dark clouds

ver • i • fi • ca • tion (ver´ə fi kā´shən) *n.*, confirmation; making sure

CHAPTER 3

It was a rimy[1] morning, and very damp. I had seen the damp lying on the outside of my little window, as if some goblin had been crying there all night, and using the window for a pocket-handkerchief. Now, I saw the damp lying on the bare hedges and spare grass, like a coarser sort of spiders' webs, hanging itself from twig to twig and blade to blade. On every rail and gate, wet lay clammy, and the marsh-mist was so thick that the wooden finger on the post directing people to our village—a direction which they never accepted, for they never came there—was invisible to me until I was quite close under it. Then, as I looked up at it, while it dripped, it seemed to my oppressed conscience like a phantom devoting[2] me to the Hulks.

◄ What kind of weather does Pip encounter? What is his reaction to it?

The mist was heavier yet when I got out upon the marshes, so that instead of my running at everything, everything seemed to run at me. This was very disagreeable to a guilty mind. The gates and dikes and banks came bursting at me through the mist, as if they cried as plainly as could be, "A boy with somebody else's pork pie! Stop him!" The cattle came upon me with like suddenness, staring out of their eyes, and steaming out of their nostrils, "Halloa, young thief!" One black ox, with a white <u>cravat</u> on—who even had to my awakened conscience something of a clerical air—fixed me so <u>obstinately</u> with his eyes, and moved his blunt head round in such an accusatory manner as I moved round, that I blubbered out to him, "I couldn't help it, sir! It wasn't for myself I took it!" Upon which he put down his head, blew a cloud of smoke out of his nose, and vanished with a kick-up of his hind legs and a flourish of his tail.

◄ What do the cattle seem to say to Pip? Why does he speak to the ox?

All this time I was getting on towards the river, but however fast I went, I couldn't warm my feet, to which the damp cold seemed <u>riveted</u>, as the iron was riveted to the leg of the man I was running to meet. I knew my way to the battery, pretty straight, for I had been down there on a Sunday with Joe, and Joe, sitting on an old gun, had told me that when I

---

1. **rimy.** Frosty
2. **devoting.** Dooming

Words For Everyday Use

cra • vat (krə vat´) n., necktie or scarf
ob • sti • nate • ly (äb´stə nət lē) adv., stubbornly
riv • et • ed (riv´it əd) adj., firmly fixed or held

was 'prentice[3] to him, regularly bound, we would have such larks[4] there! However, in the confusion of the mist, I found myself at last too far to the right, and consequently had to try back along the riverside, on the bank of loose stones above the mud and the stakes that staked the tide out. Making my way along here with all dispatch,[5] I had just crossed a ditch which I knew to be very near the battery, and had just scrambled up the mound beyond the ditch, when I saw the man sitting before me. His back was towards me, and he had his arms folded, and was nodding forward, heavy with sleep.

I thought he would be more glad if I came upon him with his breakfast, in that unexpected manner, so I went forward softly and touched him on the shoulder. He instantly jumped up, and it was not the same man, but another man!

► In what ways is this man similar to the one Pip is seeking?

► What does the man do when he sees Pip?

And yet this man was dressed in coarse gray, too, and had a great iron on his leg, and was lame, and hoarse, and cold, and was everything that the other man was; except that he had not the same face, and had a flat, broad-brimmed, low-crowned felt hat on. All this I saw in a moment, for I had only a moment to see it in: he swore an oath at me, made a hit at me—it was a round, weak blow that missed me and almost knocked himself down, for it made him stumble—and then he ran into the mist, stumbling twice as he went, and I lost him.

"It's the young man!" I thought, feeling my heart shoot as I identified him. I dare say I should have felt a pain in my liver, too, if I had known where it was.

► Describe the "right man."

I was soon at the battery, after that, and there was the right man—hugging himself and limping to and fro, as if he had never all night left off hugging and limping—waiting for me. He was awfully cold, to be sure. I half expected to see him drop down before my face and die of deadly cold. His eyes looked so awfully hungry, too, that when I handed him the file and he laid it down on the grass, it occurred to me he would have tried to eat it, if he had not seen my bundle. He did not turn me upside down, this time, to get at what I had, but left me right side upwards while I opened the bundle and emptied my pockets.

"What's in the bottle, boy?" said he.

"Brandy," said I.

He was already handing mincemeat down his throat in the most curious manner—more like a man who was putting it away somewhere in a violent hurry than a man who was

---

3. **'prentice** Apprentice, person learning a skill from a craftsperson
4. **larks.** Carefree adventures; fun times
5. **dispatch.** Efficient speed

eating it—but he left off to take some of the liquor. He shivered all the while so violently that it was quite as much as he could do to keep the neck of the bottle between his teeth without biting it off.

"I think you have got the ague,"[6] said I.

"I'm much of your opinion, boy," said he.

"It's bad about here," I told him. "You've been lying out on the meshes, and they're dreadful aguish. Rheumatic[7] too."

"I'll eat my breakfast afore they're the death of me," said he. "I'd do that if I was going to be strung up to that there gallows as there is over there, directly arftferwards. I'll beat the shivers so far, *I'll* bet you."

He was gobbling mincemeat, meatbone, bread, cheese, and pork pie all at once, staring distrustfully while he did so at the mist all round us, and often stopping—even stopping his jaws—to listen. Some real or fancied sound, some clink upon the river or breathing of beast upon the marsh, now gave him a start, and he said suddenly:

"You're not a deceiving imp? You brought no one with you?"

"No, sir! No!"

"Nor giv' no one the office to follow you?"

"No!"

"Well," said he, "I believe you. You'd be but a fierce young hound indeed, if at your time of life you could help to hunt a wretched warmint,[8] hunted as near death and dunghill as this poor wretched warmint is!"

Something clicked in his throat as if had works in him like a clock, and was going to strike. And he smeared his ragged rough sleeve over his eyes.

Pitying his desolation, and watching him as he gradually settled down upon the pie, I made bold to say, "I am glad you enjoy it."

"Did you speak?"

"I said I was glad you enjoyed it."

"Thankee, my boy. I do."

I had often watched a large dog of ours eating his food; and I now noticed a decided similarity between the dog's way of eating and the man's. The man took strong sharp sudden bites, just like the dog. He swallowed, or rather snapped up, every mouthful, too soon and too fast; and he looked sideways here and there while he ate, as if he thought there was danger in every direction of somebody's coming to take the pie away. He was altogether too unsettled in his mind

◄ What does the man do as he eats?

◄ How does Pip feel about this man?

◄ To what does Pip compare the man's eating habits?

---

6. **ague.** Fever
7. **Rheumatic.** Causing rheumatism; disorder characterized by pain and stiffness
8. **warmint.** Varmint; troublesome person or animal

over it to appreciate it comfortably, I thought, or to have anybody to dine with him, without making a chop with his jaws at the visitor. In all of which particulars he was very like the dog.

▶ To whom does Pip refer?

"I am afraid you won't leave any of it for him," said I timidly, after a silence during which I had hesitated as to the politeness of making the remark. "There's no more to be got where that came from." It was the certainty of this fact that <u>impelled</u> me to offer the hint.

"Leave any for him? Who's him?" said my friend, stopping in his crunching of pie crust.

"The young man. That you spoke of. That was hid with you."

"Oh, ah!" he returned, with something like a gruff laugh. "Him? Yes, yes! *He* don't want no wittles."

"I thought he looked as if he did," said I.

▶ What does Pip reveal?

The man stopped eating, and regarded me with the keenest <u>scrutiny</u> and the greatest surprise.

"Looked? When?"

"Just now."

"Where?"

"Yonder," said I, pointing; "over there, where I found him nodding asleep, and thought it was you."

He held me by the collar and stared at me so that I began to think his first idea about cutting my throat had revived.

"Dressed like you, you know, only with a hat," I explained, trembling; "and—and"—I was very anxious to put this delicately—"and with—the same reason for wanting to borrow a file. Didn't you hear the cannon last night?"

"Then there *was* firing!" he said to himself.

"I wonder you shouldn't have been sure of that," I returned, "for we heard it up at home, and that's further away, and we were shut in besides."

▶ Why is the convict not certain whether he heard shots?

"Why, see now!" said he. "When a man's alone on these flats, with a light head and a light stomach, perishing of cold and want, he hears nothin' all night but guns firing and voices calling. Hears? He sees the soldiers, with their red coats lighted up by the torches carried afore, closing in round him. Hears his number called, hears himself challenged, hears the rattle of the muskets, hears the orders 'Make ready! Present! Cover him steady, men!' and is laid hands on—and there's nothin'! Why, if I see one pursuing

Words For Everyday Use	**im • pel** (im pel´) *vt.,* urge or compel **scru • ti • ny** (skro͞ot´ nē) *n.,* close examination

party last night—coming up in order, damn 'em, with their tramp, tramp—I see a hundred. And as to firing! Why, I see the mist shake with the cannon, arter it was broad day. But this man"—he had said all the rest as if he had forgotten my being there—"did you notice anything in him?"

"He had a badly bruised face," said I, recalling what I hardly knew I knew.

◄ What does the convict want to know?

"Not here?" exclaimed the man, striking his left cheek mercilessly with the flat of his hand.

"Yes, there!"

"Where is he?" He crammed what little food was left into the breast of his gray jacket. "Show me the way he went. I'll pull him down, like a bloodhound. Curse this iron on my sore leg! Give us hold of the file, boy."

I indicated in what direction the mist had shrouded the other man, and he looked up at it for an instant. But he was down on the rank[9] wet grass, filing at his iron like a madman, and not minding me or minding his own leg, which had an old chafe upon it, and was bloody, but which he handled as roughly as if it had no more feeling in it than the file. I was very much afraid of him again, now that he had worked himself into this fierce hurry, and I was likewise very much afraid of keeping away from home any longer. I told him I must go, but he took no notice, so I thought the best thing I could do was to slip off. The last I saw of him, his head was bent over his knee and he was working hard at his fetter,[10] muttering impatient <u>imprecations</u> at it and his leg. The last I heard of him, I stopped in the mist to listen, and the file was still going.

◄ What does the convict do? How does Pip feel about him now?

◄ What is Pip's last image of the convict?

9. **rank.** Overgrown
10. **fetter.** Shackle or chain for the feet

Words For Everyday Use

im • pre • ca • tion (im′pri kā′shən) *n.,* curse

► *What does Pip expect to find when he returns home? What does he find instead?*

I fully expected to find a constable[1] in the kitchen, waiting to take me up. But not only was there no constable there, but no discovery had yet been made of the robbery. Mrs. Joe was <u>prodigiously</u> busy in getting the house ready for the festivities of the day, and Joe had been put upon the kitchen doorstep to keep him out of the dustpan—an article into which his destiny always led him, sooner or later, when my sister was vigorously reaping the floors of her establishment.

"And where the deuce ha' *you* been?" was Mrs. Joe's Christmas <u>salutation</u>, when I and my conscience showed ourselves.

I said I had been down to hear the carols. "Ah! well!" observed Mrs. Joe. "You might ha' done worse." Not a doubt of that, I thought.

"Perhaps if I warn't a blacksmith's wife, and (what's the same thing) a slave with her apron never off, *I* should have been to hear the carols," said Mrs. Joe. "I'm rather partial to carols myself, and that's the best of reasons for my never hearing any."

► *What mood is Mrs. Joe in? What sign do Joe and Pip use to notify each other of her mood?*

Joe, who had ventured into the kitchen after me as the dustpan had retired before us, drew the back of his hand across his nose with a <u>conciliatory</u> air, when Mrs. Joe darted a look at him, and, when her eyes were withdrawn, secretly crossed his two forefingers, and exhibited them to me, as our token that Mrs. Joe was in a cross temper. This was so much her normal state that Joe and I would often, for weeks together, be, as to our fingers, like monumental Crusaders as to their legs.[2]

We were to have a superb dinner, consisting of a leg of pickled pork and greens, and a pair of roast stuffed fowls. A handsome mince pie had been made yesterday morning (which accounted for the mincemeat not being missed), and the pudding was already on the boil. These extensive arrangements occasioned us to be cut off unceremoniously in respect to breakfast; "for I ain't," said Mrs. Joe, "I ain't

---

1. **constable.** Police officer
2. **Joe and I . . . legs.** Joe and Pip had their fingers crossed. The comparison refers to an erroneous belief that, if the legs of a statue were crossed, the subject had been on a Crusade.

Words For Everyday Use

pro • di • gious • ly (prō dij´əs lē) *adv.,* amazingly

sal • u • ta • tion (sal´yo͞o tā´shən) *n.,* greeting

con • cil • i • a • to • ry (kən sil´ē ə tôr´ē) *adj.,* tending to reconcile; overcoming another's distrust a-going to have no formal cramming and busting and washing up now, with what I've got before me, I promise you!"

So, we had our slices served out, as if we were two thousand troops on a forced march instead of a man and boy at home; and we took gulps of milk and water, with apologetic <u>countenances</u>, from a jug on the dresser. In the meantime, Mrs. Joe put clean white curtains up, and tacked a new flowered flounce across the wide chimney to replace the old one, and uncovered the little state parlor across the passage, which was never uncovered at any other time, but passed the rest of the year in a cool haze of silver paper, which even extended to the four little white crockery poodles on the mantelshelf, each with a black nose and a basket of flowers in his mouth, and each the <u>counterpart</u> of the other. Mrs. Joe was a very clean housekeeper, but had an exquisite art of making her cleanliness more uncomfortable and unacceptable than dirt itself. Cleanliness is next to Godliness, and some people do the same by their religion.

My sister having so much to do, was going to church <u>vicariously</u>; that is to say, Joe and I were going. In his working clothes, Joe was a well-knit characteristic-looking blacksmith; in his holiday clothes, he was more like a scarecrow in good circumstances than anything else. Nothing that he wore then fitted him or seemed to belong to him; and everything that he wore then grazed[3] him. On the present festive occasion he emerged from his room, when the <u>blithe</u> bells were going, the picture of misery, in a full suit of Sunday penitentials.[4] As to me, I think my sister must have had some general idea that I was a young offender whom an accoucheur[5] policeman had taken up (on my birthday) and delivered over to her, to be dealt with according to the outraged majesty of the law. I was always treated as if I had insisted on being born in opposition to the dictates of reason, religion, and morality, and against the dissuading arguments of my best friends. Even when I was taken to have a new suit of clothes, the tailor had orders to make them like a kind of reformatory, and on no account to let me have the free use of my limbs.

◄ In what way does Joe change when he is in his Sunday clothes? How does Pip feel about his own Sunday clothes?

---

3. **grazed.** Scraped, rubbed
4. **penitentials.** List of rules detailing the steps to take for forgiveness of sin
5. **accoucheur.** Specially trained person who assists in the birth of children

Words For Everyday Use

coun • te • nance (koun´tə nəns) n., look on a person's face that shows his or her feelings

coun • ter • part (koun´tər pärt´) n., thing that goes with something else to make a set

vi • car • i • ous • ly (vī ker´ē əs lē) adv., as a shared participation in another's experience

blithe (blīth) adj., cheerful; carefree

► What inner suffering does Pip experience? What does he consider doing?

Joe and I going to church, therefore, must have been a moving spectacle for compassionate minds. Yet, what I suffered outside was nothing to what I underwent within. The terrors that had <u>assailed</u> me whenever Mrs. Joe had gone near the pantry, or out of the room, were only to be equaled by the <u>remorse</u> with which my mind dwelt on what my hands had done. Under the weight of my wicked secret, I pondered whether the Church would be powerful enough to shield me from the vengeance of the terrible young man, if I <u>divulged</u> to that establishment. I conceived the idea that the time when the banns[6] were read and when the clergyman said, "Ye are now to declare it!" would be the time for me to rise and propose a private conference in the vestry. I am far from being sure that I might not have astonished our small congregation by resorting to this extreme measure, but for its being Christmas Day and no Sunday.

► What are the plans for Christmas day?

Mr. Wopsle, the clerk at church, was to dine with us; and Mr. Hubble, the wheelwright, and Mrs. Hubble; and Uncle Pumblechook (Joe's uncle, but Mrs. Joe <u>appropriated</u> him), who was a well-to-do corn-chandler[7] in the nearest town, and drove his own chaise-cart.[8] The dinner hour was half-past one. When Joe and I got home, we found the table laid, and Mrs. Joe dressed, and the dinner dressing, and the front door unlocked (it never was at any other time) for the company to enter by, and everything most splendid. And still, not a word of the robbery.

The time came, without bringing with it any relief to my feelings, and the company came. Mr. Wopsle, united to a Roman nose and a large shining bald forehead, had a deep voice which he was uncommonly proud of; indeed it was understood among his acquaintance that if you could only give him his head,[9] he would read the clergyman into fits; he himself confessed that if the Church was "thrown open," meaning to competition, he would not despair of making his mark in it. The Church not being "thrown open," he was, as I have said, our clerk. But he punished the amens tremendously; and when he gave out the psalm—always giving the

---

6. **banns.** Proclamations made in church
7. **corn-chandler.** Merchant who sells corn
8. **chaise-cart.** Horse-drawn carriage
9. **give him his head.** Give him his way

Words For Everyday Use	
	as • sail (ə sāl´) vt., attack with force
	re • morse (ri mors´) n., deep sense of guilt
	di • vulge (də vulj´) vt., reveal
	ap • pro • pri • ate (ə prō´prē āt´) vt., take for one's own use

whole verse—he looked all round the congregation first, as much as to say, "You have heard our friend overhead; <u>oblige</u> me with your opinion of this style!"

I opened the door to the company—making believe that it was a habit of ours to open that door—and I opened it first to Mr. Wopsle, next to Mr. and Mrs. Hubble, and last of all to Uncle Pumblechook. N.B.[10] *I* was not allowed to call him uncle, under the severest penalties.

"Mrs. Joe," said Uncle Pumblechook—a large hard-breathing middle-aged slow man, with a mouth like a fish, dull staring eyes, and sandy hair standing upright on his head, so that he looked as if he had just been all but choked, and had that moment come to—"I have brought you as the compliments of the season—I have brought you, mum, a bottle of sherry wine—and I have brought you, mum, a bottle of port wine."

◄ What does Uncle Pumblechook bring? What exchange occurs between Pumblechook and Mrs. Joe?

Every Christmas Day he presented himself, as a <u>profound</u> novelty, with exactly the same words, and carrying the two bottles like dumbbells. Every Christmas Day, Mrs. Joe replied, as she now replied, "Oh, Un—cle Pum—ble—chook! This *is* kind!" Every Christmas Day, he retorted, as he now retorted, "It's no more than your merits. And now are you all bobbish, and how's sixpenn'orth of halfpence?"[11] meaning me.

We dined on these occasions in the kitchen, and <u>adjourned</u>, for the nuts and oranges and apples, to the parlor; which was a change very like Joe's change from his working clothes to his Sunday dress. My sister was uncommonly lively on the present occasion, and indeed was generally more gracious in the society of Mrs. Hubble than in other company. I remember Mrs. Hubble as a little curly sharp-edged person in sky-blue, who held a conventionally juvenile position,[12] because she had married Mr. Hubble—I don't know at what remote period—when she was much younger than he. I remember Mr. Hubble as a tough high-shouldered stooping old man, of a sawdusty fragrance, with his legs extraordinarily wide apart; so that in my short days I always saw some miles of open country between them when I met him coming up the lane.

◄ How does this meal differ from usual meals?

---

10. **N.B.** *Nota bene,* or note well; expression used to call attention to something important
11. **sixpennorth of halfpence.** Small amount of money; nickname for Pip
12. **conventionally juvenile position.** Relationship in which she was always considered a child

Words For Everyday Use

o • blige (ə blīj´) *vt.,* do a favor for
pro • found (prō found´) *adj.,* deeply or intensely felt
ad • journ (ə jurn´) *vt.,* move from one place to another

▶ Why is Pip uncomfortable?

Among this good company I should have felt myself, even if I hadn't robbed the pantry, in a false position. Not because I was squeezed in at an acute angle of the tablecloth, with the table in my chest, and the Pumblechookian elbow in my eye, nor because I was not allowed to speak (I didn't want to speak), nor because I was regaled with the scaly tips of the drumsticks of the fowls, and with those obscure corners of pork of which the pig, when living, had had the least reason to be vain. No; I should not have minded that if they would only have left me alone. But they wouldn't leave me alone. They seemed to think the opportunity lost if they failed to point the conversation at me, every now and then, and stick the point into me. I might have been an unfortunate little bull in a Spanish arena, I got so smartly touched up by these moral goads.[13]

It began the moment we sat down to dinner. Mr. Wopsle said grace with theatrical <u>declamation</u>—as it now appears to me, something like a religious cross of the ghost in *Hamlet* with Richard the Third[14]—and ended with the very proper <u>aspiration</u> that we might be truly grateful. Upon which my sister fixed me with her eye, and said, in a low reproachful voice, "Do you hear that? Be grateful."

▶ What do the adults think of Pip? How do they treat him?

"Especially," said Mr. Pumblechook, "be grateful, boy, to them which brought you up by hand."

Mrs. Hubble shook her head, and contemplating me with a mournful <u>presentiment</u> that I should come to no good, asked, "Why is it that the young are never grateful?" This moral mystery seemed too much for the company until Mr. Hubble <u>tersely</u> solved it by saying, "Naterally wicious."[15] Everybody then murmured "True!" and looked at me in a particularly unpleasant and personal manner.

▶ What does Joe do to try to comfort Pip?

Joe's station and influence were something feebler (if possible) when there was company than when there was none. But he always aided and comforted me when he could, in some way of his own, and he always did so at dinner-time by giving me gravy, if there were any. There being plenty of gravy today, Joe spooned into my plate, at this point, about half a pint.

---

13. **goads.** Sharp, pointed sticks used to drive cattle
14. **ghost . . . Richard the Third.** Characters in plays by William Shakespeare
15. **Naterally wicious.** Naturally vicious; wicked by nature

---

Words For Everyday Use

dec • la • ma • tion (dek´lə mā´shən) *n.*, loud and showy way of speaking

as • pi • ra • tion (as´pə rā´shən) *n.*, hope; strong desire

pre • sen • ti • ment (prē zent´ə mənt) *n.*, prediction that something unfortunate is about to take place

terse • ly (tʉrs´lē) *adv.*, concisely; using as few words as possible

A little later on in the dinner, Mr. Wopsle reviewed the sermon with some severity, and <u>intimated</u>—in the usual hypothetical case of the Church being "thrown open"—what kind of sermon *he* would have given them. After favoring them with some heads of that discourse, he remarked that he considered the subject of the day's <u>homily</u> ill-chosen; which was the less excusable, he added, when there were so many subjects "going about."

"True again," said Uncle Pumblechook. "You've hit it, sir! Plenty of subjects going about, for them that know how to put salt upon their tails.[16] That's what's wanted. A man needn't go far to find a subject, if he's ready with his salt-box." Mr. Pumblechook added, after a short interval of reflection, "Look at pork alone. There's a subject! If you want a subject, look at pork!"

"True, sir. Many a moral for the young," returned Mr. Wopsle; and I knew he was going to lug me in, before he said it; "might be deduced from the text."

("You listen to this," said my sister to me, in a severe parenthesis.)

Joe gave me some more gravy.

"Swine," pursued Mr. Wopsle, in his deepest voice, and pointing his fork at my blushes, as if he were mentioning my Christian name; "Swine were the companions of the prodigal.[17] The gluttony of swine is put before us as an example to the young." (I thought this pretty well in him who had been praising up the pork for being so plump and juicy.) "What is detestable in a pig is more detestable in a boy."

◀ *To what do the adults compare Pip?*

"Or girl," suggested Mr. Hubble.

"Of course, or girl, Mr. Hubble," <u>assented</u> Mr. Wopsle, rather irritably, "but there is no girl present."

"Besides," said Mr. Pumblechook, turning sharp on me, "think what you've got to be grateful for. If you'd been born a squeaker—"

"He *was,* if ever a child was," said my sister, most emphatically.

Joe gave me some more gravy.

"Well, but I mean a four-footed squeaker," said Mr. Pumblechook. "If you had been born such, would you have been here now? Not you—"

---

16. **put salt upon their tails.** Make a subject interesting
17. **prodigal.** Mr. Wopsle is referring to a parable found in Luke 15:11–32, whch tells of a prodigal, or wasteful and extravagant, son who comes to no good.

Words For Everyday Use	in • ti • mate (in′tə māt′) *vt.,* hint or imply
	hom • i • ly (häm′ə lē) *n.,* sermon
	as • sent (ə sent′) *vi.,* agree

"Unless in that form," said Mr. Wopsle, nodding towards the dish.

"But I don't mean in that form, sir," returned Mr. Pumblechook, who had an objection to being interrupted; "I mean, enjoying himself with his elders and betters, and improving himself with their conversation, and rolling in the lap of luxury. Would he have been doing that? No, he wouldn't. And what would have been your destination?" turning on me again. "You would have been disposed of for so many shillings according to the market price of the article, and Dunstable the butcher would have come up to you as you lay in your straw, and he would have whipped you under his left arm, and with his right he would have tucked up his frock to get a penknife from out of his waistcoat pocket, and he would have shed your blood and had your life. No bringing up by hand then. Not a bit of it!"

Joe offered me more gravy, which I was afraid to take.

"He was a world of trouble to you, ma'am," said Mrs. Hubble, <u>commiserating</u> my sister.

▶ What trouble does Mrs. Joe say Pip has caused her?

"Trouble?" echoed my sister, "trouble?" And then entered on a fearful catalogue of all the illnesses I had been guilty of, and all the acts of sleeplessness I had committed, and all the high places I had tumbled from, and all the low places I had tumbled into, and all the injuries I had done myself, and all the times she had wished me in my grave, and I had <u>contumaciously</u> refused to go there.

I think the Romans must have aggravated one another very much, with their noses. Perhaps they became the restless people they were in consequence. Anyhow, Mr. Wopsle's Roman nose[18] so aggravated me during the recital of my <u>misdemeanors</u> that I should have liked to pull it until he howled. But all I had endured up to this time, was nothing in comparison with the awful feelings that took possession of me when the pause was broken which <u>ensued</u> upon my sister's recital, and in which pause everybody had looked at me (as I felt painfully conscious) with indignation and <u>abhorrence</u>.

▶ What does Pip wish to do as the others recount his failings?

"Yet," said Mr. Pumblechook, leading the company gently back to the theme from which they had strayed, "pork—regarded as biled[19]—is rich, too; ain't it?"

---

18 **Roman nose.** A nose with a high, prominent bridge
19. **biled.** Boiled

Words For Everyday Use

com • mis • er • ate (kə miz′ ər āt′) vt., express pity for

con • tu • ma • cious • ly (kän′tyoo mā′shəs lē) adv., disobediently

mis • de • mean • or (mis′di mēn′ ər) n., minor offense

en • sue (en soo′) vi., follow immediately

ab • hor • rence (ab hôr′əns) n., loathing;

"Have a little brandy, Uncle," said my sister.

O Heavens, it had come at last! He would find it was weak, he would say it was weak, and I was lost! I held tight to the leg of the table under the cloth, with both hands, and awaited my fate.

◄ Why is Pip afraid of Pumblechook taking a sip of brandy?

My sister went for the stone bottle, came back with the stone bottle, and poured his brandy out: no one else taking any. The wretched man trifled with his glass—took it up, looked at it through the light, put it down—prolonged my misery. All this time Mrs. Joe and Joe were briskly clearing the table for the pie and pudding.

I couldn't keep my eyes off him. Always holding tight by the leg of the table with my hands and feet, I saw the miserable creature finger his glass playfully, take it up, smile, throw his head back, and drink the brandy off. Instantly afterwards, the company were seized with unspeakable <u>consternation</u>, owing to his springing to his feet, turning round several times in an appalling <u>spasmodic</u> whooping-cough dance, and rushing out at the door; he then became visible through the window, violently plunging and <u>expectorating</u>, making the most hideous faces, and apparently out of his mind.

I held on tight, while Mrs. Joe and Joe ran to him. I didn't know how I had done it, but I had no doubt I had murdered him somehow. In my dreadful situation, it was a relief when he was brought back, and, surveying the company all round as if *they* had disagreed with him, sank down into his chair with the one significant gasp, "Tar!"

I had filled up the bottle from the tar-water jug. I knew he would be worse by-and-by. I moved the table, like a medium of the present day, by the vigor of my unseen hold upon it.

◄ What is in the stone bottle? How did it get there?

"Tar!" cried my sister, in amazement. "Why, how ever could tar come there?"

But, Uncle Pumblechook, who was <u>omnipotent</u> in that kitchen, wouldn't hear the word, wouldn't hear of the subject, <u>imperiously</u> waved it all away with his hand, and asked for hot gin-and-water. My sister, who had begun to be alarmingly meditative, had to employ herself actively in getting the gin, the hot water, the sugar, and the lemon-peel, and mixing them. For the time at least, I was saved. I still held on to the leg of the table, but clutched it now with the fervor of gratitude.

◄ What happens to Pip?

Words For Everyday Use

con • ster • na • tion (kän´stər nā´shən) n., great fear or shock

spas • mod • ic (spaz mäd´ik) adj., like a spasm; sudden and irregular; fitful

ex • pec • to • rate (ek spek´tə rāt´) vt., cough up and spit out

om • nip • o • tent (äm nip´ə tənt) adj., all powerful

im • pe • ri • ous • ly (im pir´ē əs lē) adv., urgently; in a domineering way

By degrees, I became calm enough to release my grasp, and partake of pudding. Mr. Pumblechook partook of pudding. All partook of pudding. The course terminated, and Mr. Pumblechook had begun to beam under the genial influence of gin-and-water. I began to think I should get over the day, when my sister said to Joe, "Clean plates—cold."

I clutched the leg of the table again immediately, and pressed it to my bosom as if it had been the companion of my youth and friend of my soul. I foresaw what was coming, and I felt that this time I really was gone.

▶ How do the guests respond to the idea of having pork pie? How does Pip feel at the mention of the pork pie?

"You must taste," said my sister, addressing the guests with her best grace, "You must taste, to finish with, such a delightful and delicious present of Uncle Pumblechook's!"

Must they! Let them not hope to taste it!

"You must know," said my sister, rising, "it's a pie—a savory pork pie."

The company murmured their compliments. Uncle Pumblechook, sensible of having deserved well of his fellow-creatures, said—quite <u>vivaciously</u>, all things considered— "Well, Mrs. Joe, we'll do our best endeavors; let us have a cut at this same pie."

My sister went out to get it. I heard her steps proceed to the pantry. I saw Mr. Pumblechook balance his knife. I saw reawakening appetite in the Roman nostrils of Mr. Wopsle. I heard Mr. Hubble remark that "a bit of savory pork pie would lay atop of anything you could mention, and do no harm," and I heard Joe say, "You shall have some, Pip." I have never been absolutely certain whether I uttered a shrill yell of terror, merely in spirit, or in the bodily hearing of the company. I felt that I could bear no more, and that I must run away. I released the leg of the table, and ran for my life.

▶ Why doesn't Pip get past the house door?

But I ran no further than the house door, for there I ran head foremost into a party of soldiers with their muskets, one of whom held out a pair of handcuffs to me, saying, "Here you are, look sharp, come on!"

Words
For
Everyday
Use

vi • va • cious • ly (vī va′shəs lē) *adv.*, in a lively way

CHAPTER 5

The <u>apparition</u> of a file of soldiers ringing down the butt-ends of their loaded muskets on our doorstep caused the dinner-party to rise from table in confusion, and caused Mrs. Joe, reentering the kitchen empty-handed, to stop short and stare in her wondering <u>lament</u> of "Gracious goodness gracious me, what's gone—with the—pie!"

The sergeant and I were in the kitchen when Mrs. Joe stood staring; at which crisis I partially recovered the use of my senses. It was the sergeant who had spoken to me, and he was now looking round at the company, with his handcuffs invitingly extended towards them in his right hand, and his left on my shoulder.

"Excuse me, ladies and gentleman," said the sergeant, "but as I have mentioned at the door to this smart young shaver"—which he hadn't—"I am on a chase in the name of the king, and I want the blacksmith."

◀ Whom does the sergeant seek?

"And pray, what might you want with *him?*" retorted my sister, quick to resent his being wanted at all.

"Missis," returned the gallant sergeant, "speaking for myself, I should reply, the honor and pleasure of his fine wife's acquaintance; speaking for the king, I answer, a little job done."

This was received as rather neat in the sergeant; insomuch that Mr. Pumblechook cried audibly, "Good again!"

"You see, blacksmith," said the sergeant, who had by this time picked out Joe with his eye, "we have had an accident with these, and I find the lock of one of 'em goes wrong, and the coupling don't act pretty. As they are wanted for immediate service, will you throw your eye over them?"[1]

◀ What does the sergeant ask Joe to do?

Joe threw his eye over them, and pronounced that the job would necessitate the lighting of his forge fire, and would take nearer two hours than one, "Will it? Then will you set about it at once, blacksmith?" said the off-hand sergeant, "as it's on his Majesty's service. And if my men can bear a hand anywhere, they'll make themselves useful." With that he called to his men, who came trooping into the kitchen one after another, and piled their arms in a corner. And then they stood about, as soldiers do; now with their hands loosely

---

1. **throw your eye over them.** Take a look at them; inspect them

Words For Everyday Use

ap • pa • ri • tion (ap´ə rish´ən) *n.,* unexpected appearance

la • ment (lə ment´) *n.,* outward expression of sorrow

clasped before them; now resting a knee or a shoulder; now easing a belt or a pouch; now opening the door to spit stiffly over their high stocks, out into the yard.

► Why is Pip relieved?

All these things I saw without then knowing that I saw them, for I was in an agony of <u>apprehension</u>. But, beginning to perceive that the handcuffs were not for me, and that the military had so far got the better of the pie as to put it in the background, I collected a little more of my scattered wits.

"Would you give me the time?" said the sergeant, addressing himself to Mr. Pumblechook, as to a man whose appreciative powers justified the <u>inference</u> that he was equal to the time.[2]

"It's just gone half-past two."

"That's not so bad," said the sergeant, reflecting; "even if I was forced to halt here nigh two hours, that'll do. How far might you call yourselves from the marshes, hereabouts? Not above a mile, I reckon?"

"Just a mile," said Mrs. Joe.

"That'll do. We begin to close in upon 'em about dusk. A little before dusk, my orders are. That'll do."

"Convicts, sergeant?" asked Mr. Wopsle, in a matter-of-course way.

► For whom are the soldiers searching? What does the sergeant ask? Why is Pip able to conceal what he knows?

"Aye!" returned the sergeant, "two. They're pretty well known to be out on the marshes still, and they won't try to get clear of 'em before dusk. Anybody here seen anything of any such game?"

Everybody, myself excepted, said no, with confidence. Nobody thought of me.

"Well!" said the sergeant, "they'll find themselves trapped in a circle, I expect, sooner than they count on. Now, blacksmith! If you're ready, his Majesty the King is."

Joe had got his coat and waistcoat and cravat off, and his leather apron on, and passed into the forge. One of the soldiers opened its wooden windows, another lighted the fire, another turned to at the bellows, the rest stood round the blaze, which was soon roaring. Then Joe began to hammer and clink, hammer and clink, and we all looked on.

► In what way does Mrs. Joe's behavior change?

The interest of the <u>impending</u> pursuit not only absorbed the general attention, but even made my sister <u>liberal</u>. She drew a pitcher of beer from the cask for the soldiers, and invited the sergeant to take a glass of brandy. But Mr. Pumblechook

2. **whose appreciative powers . . . time.** Whose ability to grasp a problem led one to conclude that he was able to tell the time

Words For Everyday Use	
ap • pre • hen • sion (ap´rē hen´shən) n., dread	**im • pend • ing** (im pend´iŋ) adj., about to take place
in • fer • ence (in´fər əns) n., conclusion arrived at by reasoning	**lib • er • al** (lib´ər əl) adj., generous

said, sharply, "Give him wine, mum. I'll engage there's no tar in that!" So the sergeant thanked him and said that, as he preferred his drink without tar, he would take wine, if it was equally convenient. When it was given him, he drank his Majesty's health and compliments of the season, and took it all at a mouthful and smacked his lips.

"Good stuff, eh, sergeant?" said Mr. Pumblechook.

"I'll tell you something," returned the sergeant; "I suspect that stuff's of *your* providing."

Mr. Pumblechook, with a fat sort of laugh, said, "Aye, aye? Why?"

"Because," returned the sergeant, clapping him on the shoulder, "you're a man that knows what's what."

"D'ye think so?" said Mr. Pumblechook, with his former laugh. "Have another glass!"

"With you. Hob and nob," returned the sergeant. "The top of mine to the foot of yours—the foot of yours to the top of mine—Ring once, ring twice—the best tune on the musical glasses! Your health. May you live a thousand years, and never be a worse judge of the right sort than you are at the present moment of your life!"[3]

The sergeant tossed off his glass again and seemed quite ready for another glass. I noticed that Mr. Pumblechook in his hospitality appeared to forget that he had made a present of the wine, but took the bottle from Mrs. Joe and had all the credit of handing it about in a gush of <u>joviality</u>. Even I got some. And he was so very free of the wine that he even called for the other bottle, and handed that about with the same liberality, when the first was gone.

◀ How do Pumblechook and the sergeant behave toward one another?

As I watched them while they all stood clustering about the forge, enjoying themselves so much, I thought what terrible good sauce for a dinner my fugitive friend on the marshes was. They had not enjoyed themselves a quarter so much before the entertainment was brightened with the excitement he furnished. And now, when they were all in lively anticipation of "the two villains" being taken, and when the bellows seemed to roar for the fugitives, the fire to flare for them, the smoke to hurry away in pursuit of them, Joe to hammer and clink for them, and all the murky

◀ Why are the adults so animated?

---

3. **Hob and nob . . . life!** Toast, or statement of good wishes made just before drinking

► What is Pip's reaction to the situation? Why does his reaction differ from that of the adults?

► Why does Mrs. Joe allow Joe and Pip to accompany the soldiers?

► How do Joe and Pip feel about finding the convicts?

shadows on the wall to shake at them in menace as the blaze rose and sank and the red-hot sparks dropped and died, the pale afternoon outside almost seemed in my pitying young fancy to have turned pale on their account, poor wretches.

At last, Joe's job was done, and the ringing and roaring stopped. As Joe got on his coat, he mustered courage to propose that some of us should go down with the soldiers and see what came of the hunt. Mr. Pumblechook and Mr. Hubble declined, on the plea of a pipe and ladies' society;[4] but Mr. Wopsle said he would go, if Joe would. Joe said he was agreeable, and would take me, if Mrs. Joe approved. We never should have got leave to go, I am sure, but for Mrs. Joe's curiosity to know all about it and how it ended. As it was, she merely <u>stipulated</u>, "If you bring the boy back with his head blown to bits by a musket, don't look to me to put it together again."

The sergeant took a polite leave of the ladies, and parted from Mr. Pumblechook as from a comrade; though I doubt if he were quite as fully sensible of that gentleman's merits under <u>arid</u> conditions, as when something moist was going. His men resumed their muskets and fell in. Mr. Wopsle, Joe, and I received strict charge to keep in the rear, and to speak no word after we reached the marshes. When we were all out in the raw air and were steadily moving towards our business, I <u>treasonably</u> whispered to Joe, "I hope, Joe, we shan't find them." And Joe whispered to me, "I'd give a shilling if they had cut and run, Pip."

We were joined by no stragglers from the village, for the weather was cold and threatening, the way dreary, the footing bad, darkness coming on, and the people had good fires indoors and were keeping the day. A few faces hurried to glowing windows and looked after us, but none came out. We passed the finger-post, and held straight on to the churchyard. There, we were stopped a few minutes by a signal from the sergeant's hand, while two or three of his men <u>dispersed</u> themselves among the graves, and also examined the porch. They came in again without finding anything, and then we struck out on the open marshes, through the gate at the side of the churchyard. A bitter sleet came rattling against us here on the east wind, and Joe took me on his back.

---

4. **on the plea . . . society.** With the excuse that they wanted to smoke pipes and enjoy the company of the women

Words For Everyday Use

stip • u • late (stip´yōō lāt) *vt.*, specify as an essential condition

ar • id (ar´id) *adj.*, dry

trea • son • a • bly (trē´z'n ə blē) *adv.*, like a traitor helping the enemy

dis • perse (dis purs´) *vt.*, scatter

Now that we were out upon the dismal wilderness where they little thought I had been within eight or nine hours, and had seen both men hiding, I considered for the first time, with great dread, if we should come upon them, would my particular convict suppose that it was I who had brought the soldiers there? He had asked me if I was a deceiving imp, and he had said I should be a fierce young hound if I joined the hunt against him. Would he believe that I was both imp and hound in treacherous earnest, and had betrayed him?

◀ What concern does Pip have?

It was of no use asking myself this question now. There I was, on Joe's back, and there was Joe beneath me, charging at the ditches like a hunter, and stimulating Mr. Wopsle not to tumble on his Roman nose, and to keep up with us. The soldiers were in front of us, extending into a pretty wide line with an interval between man and man. We were taking the course I had begun with, and from which I had <u>diverged</u> into the mist. Either the mist was not out again yet, or the wind had <u>dispelled</u> it. Under the low red glare of sunset, the beacon, and the gibbet, and the mound of the battery, and the opposite shore of the river were plain, though all of a watery lead color.

With my heart thumping like a blacksmith at Joe's broad shoulder, I looked all about for any sign of the convicts. I could see none, I could hear none. Mr. Wopsle had greatly alarmed me more than once by his blowing and hard breathing; but I knew the sounds by this time, and could <u>dissociate</u> them from the object of pursuit. I got a dreadful start when I thought I heard the file still going; but it was only a sheep bell. The sheep stopped in their eating and looked timidly at us; and the cattle, their heads turned from the wind and sleet, stared angrily as if they held us responsible for both annoyances; but except these things, and the shudder of the dying day in every blade of grass, there was no break in the bleak stillness of the marshes.

◀ What does Pip think he hears?

The soldiers were moving on in the direction of the old battery, and we were moving on a little way behind them, when, all of a sudden, we all stopped. For there had reached us, on the wings of the wind and rain, a long shout. It was repeated. It was at a distance towards the east, but it was long and loud. Nay, there seemed to be two or more shouts raised together—if one might judge from a confusion in the sound.

◀ What do the sergeant and his men hear?

Words For Everyday Use	
	di • verge (dī vʉrj´) *vi.,* depart
	dis • pel (dis pel´) *vt.,* drive away
	dis • so • ci • ate (di sō´shē āt´) *vt.,* separate

To this effect the sergeant and the nearest men were speaking under their breath, when Joe and I came up. After another moment's listening, Joe (who was a good judge) agreed, and Mr. Wopsle (who was a bad judge) agreed. The sergeant, a decisive man, ordered that the sound should not be answered, but that the course should be changed, and that his men should make towards it "at the double." So we started to the right (where the east was), and Joe pounded away so wonderfully that I had to hold on tight to keep my seat.

It was a run indeed now, and what Joe called, in the only two words he spoke all the time, "a winder."[5] Down banks and up banks, and over gates, and splashing into dikes, and breaking among coarse rushes: no man cared where he went. As we came nearer to the shouting, it became more and more apparent that it was made by more than one voice. Sometimes it seemed to stop altogether, and then the soldiers stopped. When it broke out again, the soldiers made for it at a greater rate than ever, and we after them. After a while, we had so run it down that we could hear one voice calling "Murder!" and another voice, "Convicts! Runaways! Guard! This way for the runaway convicts!" Then both voices would seem to be stifled in a struggle, and then would break out again. And when it had come to this, the soldiers ran like deer, and Joe too.

► What do the soldiers do?

The sergeant ran in first, when we had run the noise quite down, and two of his men ran in close upon him. Their pieces were cocked and leveled when we all ran in.

"Here are both men!" panted the sergeant, struggling at the bottom of a ditch. "Surrender, you two! And confound you for two wild beasts! Come asunder!"

Water was splashing, and mud was flying, and oaths were being sworn, and blows were being struck, when some more men went down into the ditch to help the sergeant; and dragged out, separately, my convict and the other one. Both were bleeding and panting and execrating and struggling; but of course I knew them both directly.

► What does Pip's convict ask the sergeant to remember? What is the sergeant's reaction?

"Mind!" said my convict, wiping blood from his face with his ragged sleeves, and shaking torn hair from his fingers; "*I* took him! *I* give him up to you! Mind that!"

---

5. **winder.** One that takes one's breath away

Words For Everyday Use	a • sun • der (ə sun ´dər) *adv.*, apart
	ex • e • crate (ek´si krāt´) *vi.*, speak abusively; curse

"It's not much to be particular about," said the sergeant; "it'll do you small good, my man, being in the same plight yourself. Handcuffs there!"

"I don't expect it to do me any good. I don't want it to do me more good than it does now," said my convict, with a greedy laugh. "I took him. He knows it. That's enough for me."

The other convict was <u>livid</u> to look at, and, in addition to the old bruised left side of his face, seemed to be bruised and torn all over. He could not so much as get his breath to speak until they were both separately handcuffed, but leaned upon a soldier to keep himself from falling.

"Take notice, guard—he tried to murder me," were his first words.

◀ *What conflict exists between the two men?*

"Tried to murder him?" said my convict, disdainfully. "Try, and not do it? I took him, and giv' him up; that's what I done. I not only prevented him getting off the marshes, but I dragged him here—dragged him this far on his way back. He's a gentleman, if you please, this villain. Now, the Hulks has got its gentleman again, through me. Murder him? Worth my while, too, to murder him, when I could do worse and drag him back!"

The other one still gasped, "He tried—he tried—to—murder me. Bear—bear witness."

"Lookee here!" said my convict to the sergeant. "Single-handed I got clear of the prison-ship; I made a dash and I done it. I could ha' got clear of these death-cold flats likewise—look at my leg: you won't find much iron on it—if I hadn't made discovery that *he* was here. Let *him* go free? Let *him* profit by the means as I found out? Let *him* make a fool of me afresh and again? Once more? No, no, no. If I had died at the bottom there"—and he made an emphatic swing at the ditch with his manacled[6] hands—"I'd have held to him with that grip, that you should have been safe to find him in my hold."

The other fugitive, who was evidently in extreme horror of his companion, repeated, "He tried to murder me. I should have been a dead man if you had not come up."

"He lies!" said my convict, with fierce energy. "He's a liar born, and he'll die a liar. Look at his face; ain't it written there? Let him turn those eyes of his on me. I defy him to do it."

---

6. **manacled.** Handcuffed

Words For Everyday Use

liv • id (liv´id) *adj.*, grayish-blue from bruising

The other, with an effort at a scornful smile—which could not, however, collect the nervous working of his mouth into any set expression—looked at the soldiers, and looked about at the marshes and at the sky, but certainly did not look at the speaker.

► How do the two convicts know one another?

"Do you see him?" pursued my convict. "Do you see what a villain he is? Do you see those <u>groveling</u> and wandering eyes? That's how he looked when we were tried together. He never looked at me."

The other, always working and working his dry lips and turning his eyes restlessly about him far and near, did at last turn them for a moment on the speaker, with the words, "You are not much to look at," and with a half-taunting glance at the bound hands. At that point, my convict became so frantically exasperated that he would have rushed upon him but for the <u>interposition</u> of the soldiers. "Didn't I tell you," said the other convict then, "that he would murder me, if he could?" And anyone could see that he shook with fear, and that there broke out upon his lips curious white flakes, like thin snow.

"Enough of this parley,"[7] said the sergeant. "Light those torches."

► Why does Pip want to get the attention of his convict? What does he notice when his convict looks at him?

As one of the soldiers, who carried a basket in lieu[8] of a gun, went down on his knee to open it, my convict looked round him for the first time, and saw me. I had alighted from Joe's back on the brink of the ditch when we came up, and had not moved since. I looked at him eagerly when he looked at me, and slightly moved my hands and shook my head. I had been waiting for him to see me, that I might try to assure him of my innocence. It was not at all expressed to me that he even comprehended my intention, for he gave me a look that I did not understand, and it all passed in a moment. But if he had looked at me for an hour or for a day, I could not have remembered his face ever afterwards as having been more attentive.

The soldier with the basket soon got a light, and lighted three or four torches, and took one himself and distributed the others. It had been almost dark before, but now it seemed quite dark, and soon afterwards very dark. Before we departed

---

7. **parley.** Conference with an enemy
8. **in lieu.** Instead

Words For Everyday Use

grov • el • ing (gräv´ʹl iŋ) *adj.*, cringing; lowly

in • ter • po • si • tion (in´tər pə zish´ən) *n.*, intervention; placing between from that spot, four soldiers standing in a ring fired twice into the air. Presently we saw other torches kindled at some distance behind us, and others on the marshes on the opposite bank of the river. "All right," said the sergeant. "March."

We had not gone far when three cannons were fired ahead of us with a sound that seemed to burst something inside my ear. "You are expected on board," said the sergeant to my convict; "they know you are coming. Don't straggle, my man. Close up here."

The two were kept apart, and each walked surrounded by a separate guard. I had hold of Joe's hand now, and Joe carried one of the torches. Mr. Wopsle had been for going back, but Joe was resolved to see it out, so we went on with the party. There was a reasonably good path now, mostly on the edge of the river, with a divergence here and there where a dike came, with a miniature windmill on it and a muddy sluice-gate.[9] When I looked round, I could see the other lights coming in after us. The torches we carried dropped great blotches of fire upon the track, and I could see those, too, lying smoking and flaring. I could see nothing else but black darkness. Our lights warmed the air about us with their pitchy blaze, and the two prisoners seemed rather to like that, as they limped along in the midst of the muskets. We could not go fast because of their lameness; and they were so spent that two or three times we had to halt while they rested.

◄ In what manner does the group travel to the ship?

After an hour or so of this traveling, we came to a rough wooden hut and a landing-place. There was a guard in the hut, and they challenged, and the sergeant answered. Then we went into the hut, where there was a smell of tobacco and whitewash, and a bright fire, and a lamp, and a stand of muskets, and a drum, and a low wooden bedstead, like an overgrown mangle[10] without the machinery, capable of holding about a dozen soldiers all at once. Three or four soldiers who lay upon it in their greatcoats were not much interested in us, but just lifted their heads and took a sleepy stare, and then lay down again. The sergeant made some kind of report, and some entry in a book, and then the convict whom I call the other convict was drafted off with his guard, to go on board first.

My convict never looked at me, except that once. While we stood in the hut, he stood before the fire looking thoughtfully at it, or putting up his feet by turns upon the hob, and looking thoughtfully at them as if he pitied them for their recent adventures. Suddenly, he turned to the sergeant, and remarked:

9. **sluice-gate.** Opening in an artificial channel for water used to control the flow
10. **mangle.** A machine that irons cloth, especially sheets, by passing it through rollers

"I wish to say something respecting this escape. It may prevent some persons laying under suspicion alonger me."

"You can say what you like," returned the sergeant, standing coolly looking at him, with his arms folded, "but you have no call to say it here. You'll have opportunity enough to say about it, and hear about it, before it's done with, you know."

"I know, but this is another pint, a separate matter. A man can't starve; at least *I* can't. I took some wittles, up at the willage over yonder—where the church stands a'most out on the marshes."

"You mean stole," said the sergeant.

"And I'll tell you where from. From the blacksmith's."

"Halloa!" said the sergeant, staring at Joe.

"Halloa, Pip!" said Joe, staring at me.

"It was some broken wittles—that's what it was—and a dram of liquor, and a pie."

"Have you happened to miss such an article as a pie, blacksmith?" asked the sergeant confidentially.

"My wife did, at the very moment when you came in. Don't you know, Pip?"

"So," said my convict, turning his eyes on Joe in a moody manner, and without the least glance at me; "so you're the blacksmith, are you? Then I'm sorry to say I've eat your pie."

"God knows you're welcome to it—so far as it was ever mine," returned Joe, with a saving remembrance of Mrs. Joe. "We don't know what you have done, but we wouldn't have you starved to death for it, poor miserable fellow-creatur. Would us, Pip?"

The something that I had noticed before clicked in the man's throat again, and he turned his back. The boat had returned, and his guard were ready, so we followed him to the landing-place made of rough stakes and stones, and saw him put into the boat, which was rowed by a crew of convicts like himself. No one seemed surprised to see him, or interested in seeing him, or glad to see him, or sorry to see him, or spoke a word, except that somebody in the boat growled as if to dogs, "Give way, you!" which was the signal for the dip of the oars. By the light of the torches, we saw the black Hulk lying out a little way from the mud of the shore, like a wicked Noah's ark. Cribbed and barred and moored by massive rusty chains, the prison-ship seemed in my young eyes to be ironed like the prisoners. We saw the boat go alongside, and we saw him taken up the side and disappear. Then, the ends of the torches were flung hissing into the water, and went out, as if it were all over with him.

To what does the convict confess?

What is Joe's response to the confession?

What happens when the convict arrives on the boat?

CHAPTER 6

My state of mind regarding the pilfering[1] from which I had been so unexpectedly <u>exonerated</u> did not <u>impel</u> me to frank disclosure; but I hope it had some dregs of good at the bottom of it.

I do not recall that I felt any tenderness of conscience in reference to Mrs. Joe, when the fear of being found out was lifted off me. But I loved Joe—perhaps for no better reason in those early days than because the dear fellow let me love him—and as to him my inner self was not so easily <u>composed</u>. It was much upon my mind (particularly when I first saw him looking about for his file) that I ought to tell Joe the whole truth. Yet I did not, and for the reason that I mistrusted that if I did, he would think me worse than I was. The fear of losing Joe's confidence, and of thenceforth sitting in the chimney-corner at night staring drearily at my forever lost companion and friend, tied up my tongue. I <u>morbidly</u> represented to myself that if Joe knew it, I never afterwards could see him at the fireside feeling his fair whisker without thinking that he was meditating on it. That if Joe knew it, I never afterwards could see him glance, however casually, at yesterday's meat or pudding when it came on today's table without thinking that he was debating whether I had been in the pantry. That if Joe knew it, and at any subsequent period of our joint domestic life remarked that his beer was flat or thick, the conviction that he suspected tar in it would bring a rush of blood to my face. In a word, I was too cowardly to do what I knew to be right, as I had been too cowardly to avoid doing what I knew to be wrong. I had had no intercourse[2] with the world at that time, and I imitated none of its many inhabitants who act in this manner. Quite an untaught genius, I made the discovery of the line of action for myself.

As I was sleepy before we were far away from the prison-ship, Joe took me on his back again and carried me home. He must have had a tiresome journey of it, for Mr. Wopsle, being knocked up,[3] was in such a very bad temper that if the

◀ *Why does Pip love Joe? How does Pip feel about not telling Joe the truth?*

◀ *Why doesn't Pip tell Joe the truth?*

---

1. **pilfering.** Stealing
2. **intercourse.** Interaction or communication
3. **knocked up.** Exhausted

Words For Everyday Use	**ex • on • er • ate** (eg zän´ər āt´) *vt.*, free from a charge **im • pel** (im pel´) *vt.*, force; urge	**com • pose** (kəm pōz´) *vt.*, make calm **mor • bid • ly** (môr´bid lē) *adv.*, gloomily

Church had been thrown open, he would probably have excommunicated[3] the whole expedition, beginning with Joe and myself. In his lay capacity, he persisted in sitting down in the damp to such an insane extent that, when his coat was taken off to be dried at the kitchen fire, the <u>circumstantial</u> evidence on his trousers would have hanged him if it had been a capital offense.[4]

By that time, I was staggering on the kitchen floor like a little drunkard, through having been newly set upon my feet, and through having been fast asleep, and through waking in the heat and lights and noise of tongues. As I came to myself (with the aid of a heavy thump between the shoulders, and the restorative exclamation "Yah! Was there ever such a boy as this!" from my sister), I found Joe telling then about the convict's confession, and all the visitors suggesting different ways by which he had got into the pantry. Mr. Pumblechook made out, after carefully surveying the premises, that he had first got upon the roof of the forge, and had then got upon the roof of the house, and had then let himself down the kitchen chimney by a rope made of his bedding cut into strips; and as Mr. Pumblechook was very positive and drove his own chaise-cart—over everybody—it was agreed that it must be so. Mr. Wopsle, indeed, wildly cried out "No!" with the feeble <u>malice</u> of a tired man; but as he had no theory, and no coat on, he was <u>unanimously</u> set at nought[5]—not to mention his smoking hard behind, as he stood with his back to the kitchen fire to draw the damp out: which was not calculated to inspire confidence.

This was all I heard that night before my sister clutched me, as a slumberous offense to the company's eyesight, and assisted me up to bed with such a strong hand that I seemed to have fifty boots on, and to be dangling them all against the edges of the stairs. My state of mind, as I have described it, began before I was up in the morning, and lasted long after the subject had died out, and had ceased to be mentioned saving on exceptional occasions.

▶ What is Pumblechook's theory about the convict? Why is it accepted?

---

3. **excommunicated.** Excluded or cut off from the church
4. **he persisted . . . capital offense.** He stubbornly sat on a wet surface—so much so that if having wet trousers had been a hanging crime, his pants were wet enough to convict him.
5. **nought.** Nothing

Words For Everyday Use

cir • cum • stan • tial (surˊ kəm stanˊshəl) *adj.,* based on circumstances or evidence

mal • ice (malˊis) *n.,* desire to harm another

u • nan • i • mous • ly (yo͞o nanˊə məs lē) *adv.,* in complete agreement with

Responding to the Selection

If you were in Pip's position, how would you feel toward the different adults in your life? Why?

Reviewing the Selection

Recalling and Interpreting

1. **R:** What do you know about Pip's background by the end of chapter 1? What unusual event does he experience?

2. **I:** Dickens had this novel published in monthly installments. What has he done in the first chapter to capture and sustain the reader's interest and sympathy, and to make him or her want to keep reading?

3. **R:** Who are Pip's caretakers?

4. **I:** Why is there a special bond between Joe and Pip? In what ways is this bond demonstrated?

5. **R:** What does Pip promise to bring back to the stranger? What difficulties does Pip have in fulfilling his promise? What events make Pip fear that his actions have been discovered?

6. **I:** What motivates Pip to fulfill his promise? How does he feel after he has fulfilled his promise?

7. **R:** What happens to the convict? What does the convict confess after he is caught?

8. **I:** What does Pip say and do that shows sympathy and generosity toward the convict? Why do you think the convict makes his confession? In what way is Joe's reaction to the convict's apology similar to Pip's attitude toward the convict?

Synthesizing

9. What do Mrs. Joe's behavior and language reveal about her, and the feelings she holds for Joe and Pip?

10. What does the way others treat both the convict and Pip reveal about the social order at the time when the novel is set?

Understanding Literature (QUESTIONS FOR DISCUSSION)

1. Setting. The **setting** of a literary work is the time and place in which it occurs, together with all the details used to create a sense of particular time and place. What is the setting of this novel? What details does Dickens provide to establish the setting?

2. Characterization. Characterization is the use of literary techniques to create a character. Writers use three major techniques to create characters: direct description, portrayal of characters' behavior, and representations of characters' internal states. Dickens uses each of these techniques to describe the characters who have thus far been introduced. Find an example of each technique. Be sure to identify the character being described. Then explain what the narrator reveals about each of the following characters: Pip, Joe, Mrs. Joe, the adults at the dinner party, and Pip's convict. What are each character's (or group of characters') major personality traits?

3. Satire. Satire is humorous writing or speech intended to point out errors, falsehoods, foibles, or failings. It is written for the purpose of reforming human behavior and institutions. Explain why Dickens's description of the Christmas dinner can be considered an example of satirical writing. What types of people and notions is the author satirizing? Explain why Pip's assumption that the soldiers have come to arrest him is both humorous and sad. In what way does Pip's assumption comment upon adult behavior? In what way is Dickens hinting that society should be reformed?

CHAPTER 7

At the time when I stood in the churchyard, reading the family tombstones, I had just enough learning to be able to spell them out. My <u>construction</u> even of their simple meaning was not very correct, for I read "Wife of the Above" as a complimentary reference to my father's <u>exaltation</u> to a better world; and if any one of my deceased relations had been referred to as "Below," I have no doubt I should have formed the worst opinions of that member of the family. Neither were my notions of the theological[1] positions to which my catechism[2] bound me at all accurate, for I have a lively remembrance that I supposed my declaration that I was to "walk in the same all the days of my life" laid me under an obligation always to go through the village from our house in one particular direction, and never to vary it by turning down by the wheelwright's[3] or up by the mill.

◄ *Describe Pip's education. What mistakes does he make because of it?*

When I was old enough, I was to be apprenticed to Joe, and until I could assume that dignity I was not to be what Mrs. Joe called "pompeyed," or (as I render it) pampered. Therefore, I was not only odd-boy about the forge, but if any neighbor happened to want an extra boy to frighten birds, or pick up stones, or do any such job, I was favored with the employment. In order, however, that our superior position might not be compromised thereby, a money-box was kept on the kitchen mantel-shelf, into which it was publicly made known that all my earnings were dropped. I have an impression that they were to be contributed eventually towards the <u>liquidation</u> of the national debt, but I know I had no hope of any personal participation in the treasure.

◄ *What does Pip do to earn money? Does Pip expect to receive any of it?*

Mr. Wopsle's great-aunt kept an evening school in the village; that is to say, she was a ridiculous old woman of limited means and unlimited <u>infirmity</u> who used to go to sleep from six to seven every evening in the society of youth who paid twopence per week each for the improving opportunity of seeing her do it. She rented a small cottage, and Mr. Wopsle had the room upstairs, where we students used to overhear

---

1. **theological.** Having to do with religious study
2. **catechism.** Handbook for teaching the fundamentals of religion
3. **wheelwright's.** Shop or home of person who makes and repairs wheels

Words For Everyday Use

con • struc • tion (kən struk´shən) n., interpretation

ex • al • ta • tion (eg´zôl tā´shən) n., being raised in status

liq • ui • da • tion (lik´wə dā´shən) n., payment of a debt

in • fir • mi • ty (in fʉr´mə tē) n., weakness; feebleness

him reading aloud in a most dignified and terrific manner, and occasionally bumping on the ceiling. There was a fiction that Mr. Wopsle "examined" the scholars once a quarter. What he did on those occasions was to turn up his cuffs, stick up his hair, and give us Mark Antony's oration over the body of Cæsar.[4] This was always followed by Collins's Ode on the Passions, wherein I particularly <u>venerated</u> Mr. Wopsle as Revenge, throwing his blood-stained sword in thunder down, and taking the war-<u>denouncing</u> trumpet with a withering look. It was not with me then, as it was in later life, when I fell into the society of the Passions,[5] and compared them with Collins and Wopsle, rather to the disadvantage of both gentlemen.

Mr. Wopsle's great-aunt, besides keeping this educational institution, kept—in the same room—a little general shop. She had no idea what stock she had, or what the price of anything in it was; but there was a little greasy memorandum-book kept in a drawer which served as a catalogue of prices, and by this oracle[6] Biddy arranged all the shop transactions.

► Who is Biddy? What similarities does she share with Pip?

Biddy was Mr. Wopsle's great-aunt's granddaughter; I confess myself quiet unequal to the working out of the problem, what relation she was to Mr. Wopsle. She was an orphan like myself; like me, too, had been brought up by hand. She was most noticeable, I thought, in respect of her extremities; for her hair always wanted[7] brushing, her hands always wanted washing, and her shoes always wanted mending and pulling up at heel. This description must be received with a weekday limitation. On Sundays she went to church elaborated.[8]

► Who helps Pip with his studies? What does Pip struggle to learn?

Much of my unassisted self, and more by the help of Biddy than of Mr. Wopsle's great-aunt, I struggled through the alphabet as if it had been a bramble bush, getting considerably worried and scratched by every letter. After that, I fell among

---

4. **Mark Antony's oration . . . Cæsar.** Julius Cæsar (100–44 BC) was a Roman general and statesman and dictator of the Roman Empire. On March 15, 44 BC, Cæsar was murdered in the senate by a group of opponents. In Shakespeare's *Julius Cæsar*, Mark Antony (83–30 BC), a Roman general, gives a stirring speech over the body of Cæsar.
5. **fell into . . . Passions.** Met a group dedicated to dramatic works
6. **oracle.** Something believed to possess great knowledge
7. **wanted.** Needed; lacked
8. **elaborated.** Carefully fixed

Words For Everyday Use

ven • er • ate (ven´ər āt´) *vt.*, look upon with deep respect
de • nounc • ing (di nouns´ iŋ) *adj.*, condemning openly

those thieves, the nine figures, who seemed every evening to do something new to disguise themselves and baffle recognition. But, at last I began, in a purblind[9] groping way, to read, write, and cipher on the very smallest scale.

One night, I was sitting in the chimney-corner with my slate, expending great efforts on the production of a letter to Joe. I think it must have been a full year after our hunt upon the marshes, for it was a long time after, and it was winter and a hard frost. With an alphabet on the hearth at my feet for reference, I contrived in an hour or two to print and smear this epistle:[10]

"MI DEEr JO i OPE U r KRWITE WELL i OPE i SHAL SON B HABELL 4 2 TEEDGE U JO AN THEN WE SHORL B SO GLODD AN WEN i M PRENGTD 2 U JO WOT LARX AN BLEVE ME INF XN PIP."

There was no <u>indispensable</u> necessity for my communicating with Joe by letter, inasmuch as he sat beside me and we were alone. But I delivered this written communication (slate and all) with my own hand, and Joe received it as a miracle of <u>erudition</u>.

"I say, Pip, old chap!" cried Joe, opening his blue eyes wide, "what a scholar you are! Ain't you?"

"I should like to be," said I, glancing at the slate as he held it—with a misgiving that the writing was rather hilly.

"Why, here's a J," said Joe, "and a O equal to anythink! Here's a J and a O, Pip, and a J-O, Joe."

I had never heard Joe read aloud to any greater extent than this monosyllable, and I had observed at church last Sunday, when I accidentally held our prayer book upside down, that it seemed to suit his convenience quite as well as if it had been all right. Wishing to embrace the present occasion of finding out whether, in teaching Joe, I should have to begin quite at the beginning, I said, "Ah! But read the rest, Joe."

"The rest, eh, Pip?" said Joe, looking at it with a lowly searching eye, "One, two, three. Why, here's three Js, and three Os, and three J-O, Joes, in it, Pip!"

I leaned over Joe, and, with the aid of my forefinger, read him the whole letter.

◀ *What clues reveal that Joe is unable to read?*

---

9. **purblind.** Partly blind
10. **epistle.** Long, formal, instructive letter; here used ironically

Words For Everyday Use

in • dis • pen • sa • ble (in′dis pen′sə bəl) *adj.*, essential

er • u • di • tion (er′yo͞o dish′ən) *n.*, learning acquired by reading and study

"Astonishing!" said Joe, when I had finished. "You ARE a scholar."

"How do you spell Gargery, Joe?" I asked him, with a modest patronage.[11]

"I don't spell it at all," said Joe.

"But supposing you did?"

"It *can't* be supposed," said Joe. "Tho' I'm oncommon fond of reading, too."

"Are you, Joe?"

"Oncommon. Give me," said Joe, "a good book, or a good newspaper, and sit me down afore a good fire, and I ask no better. Lord!" he continued, after rubbing his knees a little, "when you *do* come to a J and a O, and says you, 'Here, at last, is a J-O, Joe,' how interesting reading is!"

I derived from this last that Joe's education, like steam,[12] was yet in its infancy. Pursuing the subject, I inquired:

"Didn't you ever go to school, Joe, when you were as little as me?"

"No, Pip."

"Why didn't you ever go to school, Joe, when you were as little as me?"

▶ What was Joe's life like as a boy?

"Well, Pip," said Joe, taking up the poker, and settling himself to his usual occupation when he was thoughtful, of slowly raking the fire between the lower bars, "I'll tell you. My father, Pip, he were given to drink, and when he were overtook with drink, he hammered away at my mother most onmerciful. It were a'most the only hammering he did, indeed, 'xcepting at myself. And he hammered at me with a wigour[13] only to be equaled by the wigour with which he didn't hammer at his anwil.[14] You're a-listening and understanding, Pip?"

"Yes, Joe."

" 'Consequence, my mother and me we ran away from my father several times; and then my mother she'd go out to work, and she'd say, 'Joe,' she'd say, 'now, please God, you shall have some schooling, child,' and she'd put me to school. But my father were that good in his hart that he couldn't a-bear to be without us. So, he'd come with a most tremenjous crowd and make such a row[15] at the doors of the houses where we was that they used to be obligated to have no more to do with us and to give us up to him. And then he took us home and hammered us. Which, you see, Pip,"

▶ Why is Joe uneducated?

---

11. **patronage.** Courtesy shown to one considered inferior
12. **like steam.** Like the invention of steam engine technology
13. **wigour.** Vigor
14. **anwil.** Anvil
15. **row.** Noisy disturbance

said Joe, pausing in his meditative raking of the fire, and looking at me, "were a drawback on my learning."

"Certainly, poor Joe!"

"Though mind you, Pip," said Joe, with a <u>judicial</u> touch or two of the poker on the top bar, "rendering unto all their doo,[16] and maintaining equal justice betwixt man and man, my father were that good in his hart, don't you see?"

I didn't see, but I didn't say so.

"Well!" Joe pursued, "somebody must keep the pot a-biling,[17] Pip, or the pot won't bile, don't you know?"

I saw that, and said so.

" 'Consequence, my father didn't make objections to my going to work; so I went to work at my present calling, which were his too, if he would have followed it, and I worked tolerable hard, I assure *you*, Pip. In time I were able to keep him,[18] and I kep' him till he went off in a purple 'leptic[19] fit. And it were my intentions to have had put upon his tombstone that whatsume'er the failings on his part, remember reader he were that good in his hart."

Joe recited this couplet[20] with such <u>manifest</u> pride and careful <u>perspicuity</u>, that I asked him if he had made it himself.

"I made it," said Joe, "my own self. I made it in a moment. It was like striking out a horseshoe complete, in a single blow. I never was so much surprised in all my life—couldn't credit my own 'ed—to tell you the truth, hardly believed it *were* my own 'ed. As I was saying, Pip, it were my intentions to have had it cut over him; but poetry costs money, cut it how you will, small or large, and it were not done. Not to mention bearers, all the money that could be spared were wanted for my mother. She were in poor 'elth, and quite broke. She waren't long of following, poor soul, and her share of peace come round at last."

Joe's blue eyes turned a little watery; he rubbed, first one of them, and then the other, in a most uncongenial and uncomfortable manner, with the round knob on the top of the poker.

"It were but lonesome then," said Joe, "living here alone, and I got acquainted with your sister. Now, Pip"—Joe looked

◄ What does Joe claim about his father? Do you agree with Joe? What does this statement reveal about Joe?

◄ What does Joe say that shows that he cared for his father?

◄ What surprises Joe?

---

16. **doo.** Due
17. **a-biling.** Boiling
18 **keep him.** Support him
19. **purple 'leptic.** Epileptic
20. **couplet.** Two lines of poetry; here, Joe's intended inscription for his father's tombstone

Words For Everyday Use	ju • di • cial (jo͞o dish´əl) *adj.*, carefully considering the facts
	man • i • fest (man´ ə fest´) *adj.*, obvious
	per • spi • cu • i • ty (pʉr´spə kyo͞o´ ə tē) *adj.*, clarity of expression

firmly at me, as if he knew I was not going to agree with him—"your sister is a fine figure of a woman."

I could not help looking at the fire, in an obvious state of doubt.

► What is Joe's opinion of Mrs. Joe? How does he feel about her?

"Whatever family opinions, or whatever the world's opinions, on that subject may be, Pip, your sister is"—Joe tapped the top bar with the poker after every word following—"a—fine—figure—of—a—woman!"

I could think of nothing better to say than, "I am glad you think so, Joe."

"So am I," returned Joe, catching me up. "*I* am glad I think so, Pip. A little redness, or a little matter of bone, here or there, what does it signify[21] to me?"

I <u>sagaciously</u> observed, if it didn't signify to him, to whom did it signify?

"Certainly!" assented Joe. "That's it. You're right, old chap! When I got acquainted with your sister, it were the talk how she was bringing you up by hand. Very kind of her, too, all the folks said, and I said, along with all the folks. As to you," Joe pursued with a countenance expressive of seeing something very nasty indeed, "if you could have been aware how small and flabby and mean you was, dear me, you'd have formed the most <u>contemptible</u> opinions of yourself!"

Not exactly <u>relishing</u> this, I said, "Never mind me, Joe."

► When Joe married Pip's sister, what did he tell her about Pip?

"But I did mind you, Pip," he returned with tender simplicity. "When I offered to your sister to keep company, and to be asked in church, at such times as she was willing and ready to come to the forge, I said to her, 'And bring the poor little child. God bless the poor little child,' I said to your sister, 'there's room for *him* at the forge!'"

I broke out crying and begging pardon, and hugged Joe round the neck: who dropped the poker to hug me, and to say, "Ever the best of friends; ain't us, Pip? Don't cry, old chap!"

When this little interruption was over, Joe resumed:

"Well, you see, Pip, and here we are! That's about where it lights; here we are! Now, when you take me in hand in my learning, Pip (and I tell you beforehand I am awful dull, most awful dull), Mrs. Joe mustn't see too much of what we're up to. It must be done, as I may say, on the sly. And why on the sly? I'll tell you why, Pip."

---

21. **signify.** Matter; mean

Words For Everyday Use	sa • ga • cious • ly (sə gā′shəs lē) adv., wisely
	con • tempt • i • ble (kən temp′tə bəl) adj., deserving scorn
	rel • ish (rel′ish) vt., enjoy

He had taken up the poker again—without which I doubt if he could have proceeded in his demonstration.

"Your sister is given to government."

"Given to government, Joe?" I was startled, for I had some shadowy idea (and I am afraid I must add, hope) that Joe had divorced her in favor of the Lords of the Admiralty, or Treasury.[22]

"Given to government," said Joe. "Which I meantersay the government of you and myself."

"Oh!"

"And she ain't over partial to having scholars on the premises," Joe continued, "and in partickler would not be over partial to my being a scholar, for fear as I might rise. Like a sort or rebel, don't you see?"

I was going to retort with an inquiry, and had got as far as "Why—" when Joe stopped me.

"Stay a bit. I know what you're a-going to say, Pip; stay a bit! I don't deny that your sister comes the mo-gul[23] over us, now and again. I don't deny that she do throw us backfalls, and that she do drop down upon us heavy. At such times as when your sister is on the ram-page, Pip," Joe sank his voice to a whisper and glanced at the door, "candor compels fur to admit that she is a buster."

Joe pronounced this word as if it began with at least twelve capital Bs.

"Why don't I rise? That were your observation when I broke it off, Pip?"

"Yes, Joe."

"Well," said Joe, passing the poker into his left hand, that he might feel his whisker; and I had no hope of him whenever he took to that placid occupation; "your sister's a master-mind. A master-mind."

"What's that?" I asked, in some hope of bringing him to a stand. But, Joe was readier with his definition than I had expected, and completely stopped me by arguing circularly, and answering with a fixed look, "Her."

"And I ain't a master-mind," Joe resumed, when he had unfixed his look, and got back to his whisker. "And last of all,

◀ Why doesn't Mrs. Joe want her husband to be literate?

◀ What does Joe admit about his wife?

---

22. in favor . . . Treasury. For the benefit of the British government agencies controlling naval affairs and finances
23. mo-gul. Like a Mogul, one of a group who conquered India

Words For Everyday Use

can • dor (kan′dər) n., honesty; frankness

▶ What reasons does Joe have for accepting the way Mrs. Joe behaves?

Pip—and this I want to say very serous to you, old chap—I see so much in my poor mother, of a woman drudging and slaving and breaking her honest hart and never getting no peace in her mortal days, that I'm dead afeerd of going wrong in the way of not doing what's right by a woman, and I'd fur rather of the two go wrong the t'other way, and be a little ill-conwenienced myself. I wish it was only me that got put out, Pip; I wish there warn't no Tickler for you, old chap; I wish I could take it all on myself; but this is the up-and-down-and-straight on it, Pip, and I hope you'll overlook shortcomings."

▶ How does Pip feel about Joe after learning more about his life?

Young as I was, I believe that I dated a new admiration of Joe from that night. We were equals afterwards, as we had been before; but, afterwards at quiet times when I sat looking at Joe and thinking about him, I had a new sensation of feeling conscious that I was looking up to Joe in my heart.

"However," said Joe, rising to replenish the fire; "here's the Dutch clock a-working himself up to being equal to strike eight of 'em, and she's not come home yet! I hope Uncle Pumblechook's mare mayn't have set a fore-foot on a piece o' ice, and gone down."

Mrs. Joe made occasional trips with Uncle Pumblechook on market-days, to assist him in buying such household stuffs and goods as required a woman's judgment; Uncle Pumblechook being a bachelor and <u>reposing</u> no confidences in his domestic servant. This was market-day, and Mrs. Joe was out on one of these expeditions.

▶ About what does the weather make Pip think?

Joe made the fire and swept the hearth, and then we went to the door to listen for the chaise-cart. It was a dry cold night, and the wind blew keenly, and the frost was white and hard. A man would die tonight of lying out on the marshes, I thought. And then I looked at the stars, and considered how awful if would be for a man to turn his face up to them as he froze to death, and see no help or pity in all the glittering multitude.

"Here comes the mare," said Joe, "ringing like a peal of bells!"

The sound of her iron shoes upon the hard road was quite musical, as she came along at a much brisker trot than usual. We got a chair out, ready for Mrs. Joe's alighting, and stirred up the fire that they might see a bright window, and took a final survey of the kitchen that nothing might be out of its place. When we had completed these preparations, they drove up, wrapped to the eyes. Mrs. Joe was soon landed,

Words For Everyday Use

re • pose (ri pōz´) vt., place trust in someone

and Uncle Pumblechook was soon down too, covering the mare with a cloth, and we were soon all in the kitchen, carrying so much cold air with us that it seemed to drive all the heat out of the fire.

"Now," said Mrs. Joe, unwrapping herself with haste and excitement, and throwing her bonnet back on her shoulders where it hung by the strings, "if this boy ain't grateful this night, he never will be!"

I looked as grateful as any boy possibly could who was wholly uninformed why he ought to assume that expression.

"It's only to be hoped," said my sister, "that he won't be pompeyed. But I have my fears."

"She ain't in that line, mum," said Mr. Pumblechook. "She knows better."

She? I looked at Joe, making the motion with my lips and eyebrows, "She?" Joe looked at me, making the motion with *his* lips and eyebrows, "She?" My sister catching him in the act, he drew the back of his hand across his nose with his usual conciliatory air on such occasions, and looked at her.

"Well?" said my sister, in her snappish way. "What are you staring at? Is the house a-fire?"

"—Which some individual," Joe politely hinted, "mentioned—she."

"And she is a she, I suppose?" said my sister. "Unless you call Miss Havisham a he. And I doubt if even you'll go so far as that."

"Miss Havisham, up town?" said Joe.

"Is there any Miss Havisham down town?" returned my sister. "She wants this boy to go and play there. And of course he's going. And he had better play there," said my sister, shaking her head at me as an encouragement to be extremely light and sportive, "or I'll work him."

◄ *What is expected of Pip?*

I had heard of Miss Havisham up town—everybody for miles round, had heard of Miss Havisham up town—as an immensely rich and grim lady who lived in a large and dismal house barricaded against robbers, and who led a life of seclusion.

◄ *Who is Miss Havisham?*

"Well, to be sure!" said Joe, astounded. "I wonder how she come to know Pip!"

"Noodle!" cried my sister. "Who said she knew him?"

"—Which some individual," Joe again politely hinted,

Words For Everyday Use	se • clu • sion (si klo͞o´zhən) *n.,* isolation

► How does Mrs. Joe treat her husband and his questions?

"mentioned that she wanted him to go and play there."

"And couldn't she ask Uncle Pumblechook if he knew of a boy to go and play there? Isn't it just barely possible that Uncle Pumblechook may be a tenant of hers, and that he may sometimes—we won't say quarterly or half-yearly, for that would be requiring too much of you—but sometimes—go there to pay his rent? And couldn't she then ask Uncle Pumblechook if he knew of a boy to go and play there? And couldn't Uncle Pumblechook, being always considerate and thoughtful for us—though you may not think it, Joseph," in a tone of the deepest reproach, as if he were the most <u>callous</u> of nephews, "then mention this boy, standing prancing here"—which I solemnly declare I was not doing—"that I have forever been a willing slave to?"

"Good again!" cried Uncle Pumblechook. "Well put! Prettily pointed! Good indeed! Now, Joseph, you know the case."

"No, Joseph," said my sister, still in a reproachful manner, while Joe apologetically drew the back of his hand across and across his nose, "you do not yet—though you may not think it—know the case. You may consider that you do, but you do *not,* Joseph. For you do not know that Uncle Pumblechook, being sensible that for anything we can tell, this boy's fortune may be made by his going to Miss Havisham's, has offered to take him into town tonight in his own chaise-cart, and to keep him tonight, and to take him with his own hands to Miss Havisham's tomorrow morning. And Lor-a-mussy me!"[24] cried my sister, casting off her bonnet in sudden desperation, "here I stand talking to mere mooncalfs,[25] with Uncle Pumblechook waiting, and the mare catching cold at the door, and the boy grimed with crock and dirt from the hair of his head to the sole of his foot!"

► What is Mrs. Joe's hope for Pip?

► What does she do to prepare Pip for visiting Miss Havisham?

With that, she pounced upon me, like an eagle on a lamb, and my face was squeezed into wooden bowls in sinks, and my head was put under taps of water-butts,[26] and I was soaped, and kneaded, and toweled, and thumped, and harrowed,[27] and rasped,[28] until I really was quite beside myself.

---

24. **Lor-a-mussy me.** Lord have mercy on me (exclamation)
25. **mooncalfs.** Idiots
26. **butts.** Barrels
27. **harrowed.** Tormented
28. **rasped.** Scraped

Words For Everyday Use

cal • lous (kal´əs) *adj.,* unfeeling

(I may here remark that I suppose myself to be better acquainted than any living authority with the ridgy effect of a wedding-ring, passing unsympathetically over the human countenance.)

When my <u>ablutions</u> were completed, I was put into clean linen of the stiffest character, like a young penitent into sack-cloth, and was trussed up in my tightest and fearfullest suit. I was then delivered over to Mr. Pumblechook, who formally received me as if he were the sheriff, and who let off upon me the speech that I knew he had been dying to make all along: "Boy, be forever grateful to all friends, but especially unto them which brought you up by hand!"

"Good-bye, Joe!"

"God bless you, Pip, old chap!"

I had never parted from him before, and what with my feelings and what with soap-suds, I could at first see no stars from the chaise-cart. But they twinkled out one by one, without throwing any light on the questions why on earth I was going to play at Miss Havisham's, and what on earth I was expected to play at.

◄ What does Pip wonder as he sets out from home for the first time?

ab • lu • tion (ab loo´shən) n., washing of the body

CHAPTER 8

► What is
Pumblechook's trade?

Mr. Pumblechook's premises in the High Street of the market town were of a peppercorny and farinaceous[1] character, as the premises of a corn-chandler and seedsman should be. It appeared to me that he must be a very happy man indeed, to have so many little drawers in his shop; and I wondered when I peeped into one or two on the lower tiers, and saw the tied-up brown paper packets inside, whether the flower-seeds and bulbs ever wanted of a fine day to break out of those jails, and bloom.

It was in the early morning after my arrival that I entertained this <u>speculation</u>. On the previous night, I had been sent straight to bed in an attic with a sloping roof, which was so low in the corner where the bedstead was that I calculated the tiles as being within a foot of my eyebrows. In the same early morning, I discovered a singular <u>affinity</u> between seeds and corduroys. Mr. Pumblechook wore corduroys, and so did his shopman; and somehow, there was a general air and flavor about the corduroys so much in the nature of seeds, and a general air and flavor about the seeds so much in the nature of corduroys, that I hardly knew which was which. The same opportunity served me for noticing that Mr. Pumblechook appeared to conduct his business by looking across the street at the saddler, who appeared to transact *his* business by keeping his eye on the coachmaker, who appeared to get on in life by putting his hands in his pockets and contemplating the baker, who in his turn folded his arms and stared at the grocer, who stood at his door and yawned at the chemist. The watchmaker, always poring over a little desk with a magnifying glass at his eye, and always inspected by a group in smock-frocks[2] poring over him through the glass of his shop-window, seemed to be about the only person in the High Street whose trade engaged his attention.

Mr. Pumblechook and I breakfasted at eight o'clock in the parlor behind the shop, while the shopman took his mug of tea and hunch[3] of bread-and-butter on a sack of peas in

---

1. **farinaceous.** Containing, consisting of, or made from flour or meal
2. **smock-frocks.** Heavy, loose, shirtlike outer garments worn to protect the clothes
3. **hunch.** Chunk

Words
For
Everyday
Use

af • fin • i • ty (ə fin′ə tē) *n.*, similarity

the front premises. I considered Mr. Pumblechook wretched company. Besides being possessed by my sister's idea that a mortifying and penitential character ought to be imparted to my diet—besides giving me as much crumb as possible in combination with as little butter, and putting such a quantity of warm water into my milk that it would have been more candid to have left the milk out altogether—his conversation consisted of nothing but arithmetic. On my politely bidding him good morning, he said pompously, "Seven times nine, boy?" And how should *I* be able to answer, dodged in that way, in a strange place, on an empty stomach! I was hungry but before I had swallowed a morsel, he began a running sum that lasted all through the breakfast. "Seven?" "And four?" "And eight?" "And six?" "And two?" "And ten?" And so on. And after each figure was disposed of, it was as much as I could do to get a bite or a sup before the next came; while he sat at his ease guessing nothing, and eating bacon and hot roll in (if I may be allowed the expression) a gorging and gormandizing[4] manner.

◄ What is breakfast with Pumblechook like? What makes it especially unpleasant for Pip?

For such reasons I was very glad when ten o'clock came and we started for Miss Havisham's; though I was not at all at my ease regarding the manner in which I should acquit[5] myself under that lady's roof. Within a quarter of an hour we came to Miss Havisham's house, which was of old brick, and dismal, and had a great many iron bars to it. Some of the windows had been walled up; of those that remained, all the lower were rustily barred. There was a courtyard in front, and that was barred; so, we had to wait, after ringing the bell, until someone should come to open it. While we waited at the gate, I peeped in (even then Mr. Pumblechook said, "And fourteen?" but I pretended not to hear him), and saw that at the side of the house there was a large brewery. No brewing was going on in it, and none seemed to have gone on for a long long time.

◄ What unusual things does Pip notice about Miss Havisham's house?

A window was raised, and a clear voice demanded "What name?" To which my conductor replied, "Pumblechook." The voice returned, "Quite right," and the window was shut again, and a young lady came across the courtyard, with keys in her hand.

"This," said Mr. Pumblechook, "is Pip."

---

4. **gormandizing.** Eating like a glutton
5. **acquit.** Conduct

Words For Everyday Use

mor • ti • fy • ing (môrt´ ə fī´ iŋ) *adj.*, punishing or controlling by self-denial or fasting

pen • i • ten • tial (pen´i ten´shəl) *adj.*, expressing sorrow for wrongdoing

can • did (kan´did) *adj.*, honest

pom • pous • ly (päm´pəs lē) *adv.*, in a self-important manner

"This is Pip, is it?" returned the young lady, who was very pretty and seemed very proud; "come in, Pip."

Mr. Pumblechook was coming in also, when she stopped him with the gate.

"Oh!" she said. "Did you wish to see Miss Havisham?"

"If Miss Havisham wished to see me," returned Mr. Pumblechook, discomfited.[6]

"Ah!" said the girl; "but you see, she don't."

She said it so finally, and in such an undiscussible way, that Mr. Pumblechook, though in a condition of ruffled dignity, could not protest. But he eyed me severely—as if *I* had done anything to him!—and departed with the words reproachfully delivered: "Boy! Let your behavior here be a credit unto them which brought you up by hand!" I was not free from apprehension that he would come back to pro-pound through the gate, "And sixteen?" But he didn't.

▶ What admonition does Pumblechook give Pip?

My young conductress locked the gate, and we went across the courtyard. It was paved and clean, but grass was growing in every crevice. The brewery buildings had a little lane of communication with it; and the wooden gates of that lane stood open, and all the brewery beyond stood open, away to the high enclosing wall; and all was empty and disused. The cold wind seemed to blow colder there than outside the gate; and it made a shrill noise in howling in and out at the open sides of the brewery, like the noise of wind in the rigging of a ship at sea.

She saw me looking at it, and she said, "You could drink without hurt all the strong beer that's brewed there now, boy."

"I should think I could, miss," said I, in a shy way.

"Better not try to brew beer there now, or it would turn out sour, boy; don't you think so?"

"It looks like it, miss."

"Not that anybody means to try," she added, "for that's all done with, and the place will stand as idle as it is, till it falls. As to strong beer, there's enough of it in the cellars already to drown the Manor House."

"Is that the name of this house, miss?"

"One of its names, boy."

"It has more than one, then, miss?"

---

6. **discomfited.** Made uneasy

Words For Everyday Use

pro • pound (prə pound´) *vt.*, put forth for consideration

"One more. Its other name was Satis; which is Greek, or Latin, or Hebrew, or all three—or all one to me—for enough."

"Enough House!" said I; "that's a curious name, miss."

"Yes," she replied; "but it meant more than it said. It meant, when it was given, that whoever had this house could want nothing else. They must have been easily satisfied in those days, I should think. But don't loiter, boy."

Though she called me "boy" so often, and with a carelessness that was far from complimentary, she was of about my own age. She seemed much older than I, of course, being a girl, and beautiful and <u>self-possessed</u>; and she was as scornful of me as if she had been one-and-twenty, and a queen.

We went into the house by a side door—the great front entrance had two chains across it outside—and the first thing I noticed was that the passages were all dark, and that she had left a candle burning there. She took it up, and we went through more passages and up a staircase, and still it was all dark, and only the candle lighted us.

At last we came to the door of a room, and she said, "Go in."

I answered, more in shyness than politeness, "After you, miss."

To this, she returned: "Don't be ridiculous, boy; I am not going in." And scornfully walked away, and—what was worse—took the candle with her.

This was very uncomfortable, and I was half-afraid. However, the only thing to be done being to knock at the door, I knocked, and was told from within to enter. I entered, therefore, and found myself in a pretty large room, well lighted with wax candles. No glimpse of daylight was to be seen in it. It was a dressing room, as I supposed from the furniture, though much of it was of forms and uses then quite unknown to me. But prominent in it was a draped table with a gilded looking glass,[7] and that I made out at first sight to be a fine lady's dressing table.[8]

Whether I should have made out this object so soon if there had been no fine lady sitting at it, I cannot say. In an armchair, with an elbow resting on the table and her head leaning on that hand, sat the strangest lady I have ever seen, or shall ever see.

---

7. **looking glass.** Mirror
8. **dressing table.** Low table with a mirror for use while grooming

◀ *What does the name* Satis House *mean?*

◀ *What is the atmosphere inside Satis House?*

Words For Everyday Use

self pos • sessed (self pə zesd´) *adj.,* in full control of one's feelings and actions

She was dressed in rich materials—satins, and lace, and silks—all of white. Her shoes were white. And she had a long white veil dependent from her hair, and she had bridal flowers in her hair, but her hair was white. Some bright jewels sparkled on her neck and on her hands, and some other jewels lay sparkling on the table. Dresses less splendid than the dress she wore, and half-packed trunks, were scattered about. She had not quite finished dressing, for she had but one shoe on—the other was on the table near her hand—her veil was but half arranged, her watch and chain were not put on, and some lace for her bosom lay with those trinkets, and with her handkerchief, and gloves, and some flowers, and a prayer book, all confusedly heaped about the looking glass.

▶ What is strange about Miss Havisham's appearance?

It was not in the first few moments that I saw all these things, though I saw more of them in the first moments than might be supposed. But I saw that everything within my view which ought to be white had been white long ago, and had lost its luster, and was faded and yellow. I saw that the bride within the bridal dress had withered like the dress, and like the flowers, and had no brightness left but the brightness of her sunken eyes. I saw that the dress had been put upon the rounded figure of a young woman, and that the figure upon which it now hung loose had shrunk to skin and bone. Once I had been taken to see some <u>ghastly</u> waxwork at the fair, representing I know not what impossible personage lying in state.[9] Once I had been taken to one of our old marsh churches to see a skeleton in the ashes of a rich dress that had been dug out of a vault under the church pavement. Now, waxwork and skeleton seemed to have dark eyes that moved and looked at me. I should have cried out, if I could.

"Who is it?" said the lady at the table.

"Pip, ma'am."

"Pip?"

"Mr. Pumblechook's boy, ma'am. Come—to play."

"Come nearer; let me look at you. Come close."

It was when I stood before her, avoiding her eyes, that I took note of the surrounding objects in detail, and saw that her watch had stopped at twenty minutes to nine, and that a clock in the room had stopped at twenty minutes to nine.

9. **lying in state.** Placed in public view for honors prior to burial

Words For Everyday Use

ghast • ly (gast′ lē) *adj.,* horrible; ghostlike

"Look at me," said Miss Havisham. "You are not afraid of a woman who has never seen the sun since you were born?"

I regret to state that I was not afraid of telling the enormous lie comprehended in the answer "No."

◄ What does Miss Havisham tell Pip about herself?

"Do you know what I touch here?" she said, laying her hands, one upon the other, on her left side.

"Yes, ma'am." (It made me think of the young man.)

"What do I touch?"

"Your heart."

"Broken!"

She uttered the word with an eager look, and with strong emphasis, and with a weird smile that had a kind of boast in it. Afterwards, she kept her hands there for a little while, and slowly took them away as if they were heavy.

"I am tired," said Miss Havisham. "I want diversion, and I have done with men and women. Play."

I think it will be conceded by my most disputatious reader that she could hardly have directed an unfortunate boy to do anything in the wide world more difficult to be done under the circumstances.

"I sometimes have sick fancies," she went on, "and I have a sick fancy that I want to see some play. There there!" with an impatient movement of the fingers of her right hand; "play, play, play!"

For a moment, with the fear of my sister's working[10] me before my eyes, I had a desperate idea of starting round the room in the assumed character of Mr. Pumblechook's chaise-cart. But I felt myself so unequal to the performance that I gave it up, and stood looking at Miss Havisham in what I suppose she took for a dogged manner, inasmuch as she said, when we had taken a good look at each other:

◄ Why is Pip unable to do as he is told?

"Are you sullen and obstinate?"

"No, ma'am, I am very sorry for you, and very sorry I can't play just now. If you complain of me I shall get into trouble with my sister, so I would do it if I could; but it's so new here, and so strange, and so fine—and melancholy—" I stopped, fearing I might say too much, or had already said it, and we took another look at each other.

Before she spoke again, she turned her eyes from me, and looked at the dress she wore, and at the dressing table, and

10. **working.** Beating

Words For Everyday Use

com • pre • hend • ed (käm′ prə hend´ əd) *adj.*, included

di • ver • sion (di vʉr′ zhən) *n.*, something that distracts the mind and entertains

con • cede (kən sēd´) *vt.*, acknowledge

dis • pu • ta • tious (dis′ pyo͞o tā´ shəs) *adj.*, fond of arguing

mel • an • chol • y (mel´ ən käl´ ē) *adj.*, sad

finally at herself in the looking glass.

"So new to him," she muttered, "so old to me; so strange to him, so familiar to me; so melancholy to both of us! Call Estella."

As she was still looking at the reflection of herself, I thought she was still talking to herself, and kept quiet.

"Call Estella," she repeated, flashing a look at me. "You can do that. Call Estella. At the door."

To stand in the dark in a mysterious passage of an unknown house, bawling Estella to a scornful young lady neither visible nor responsive, and feeling it a dreadful liberty so to roar out her name, was almost as bad as playing to order. But she answered at last, and her light came along the dark passage like a star.

Miss Havisham beckoned her to come close, and took up a jewel from the table, and tried its effect upon her fair young bosom and against her pretty brown hair. "Your own, one day, my dear, and you will use it well. Let me see you play cards with this boy."

► What does Miss Havisham suggest?

► How does Estella view Pip?

"With this boy? Why, he is a common laboring-boy!"

I thought I overheard Miss Havisham answer—only it seemed so unlikely, "Well? You can break his heart."

"What do you play, boy?" asked Estella of myself, with the greatest <u>disdain</u>.

"Nothing but Beggar my Neighbor, miss."

"Beggar him," said Miss Havisham to Estella. So we sat down to cards.

► What does Pip realize about this place?

It was then I began to understand that everything in the room had stopped, like the watch and the clock, a long time ago. I noticed that Miss Havisham put down the jewel exactly on the spot from which she had taken it up. As Estella dealt the cards, I glanced at the dressing table again, and saw that the shoe upon it, once white, now yellow, had never been worn. I glanced down at the foot from which the shoe was absent, and saw that the silk stocking on it, once white, now yellow, had been trodden[11] ragged. Without this arrest of everything, this standing still of all the pale decayed objects, not even the withered bridal dress on the collapsed form could have looked so like grave-clothes, or the long veil so like a shroud.

---

11. **trodden.** Worn from walking

Words For Everyday Use

dis • dain (dis dān´) *n.,* scorn

So she sat, corpse-like, as we played at cards; the frillings and trimmings on her bridal dress looking like earthy paper. I knew nothing then of the discoveries that are occasionally made of bodies buried in ancient times, which fall to powder in the moment of being distinctly seen; but I have often thought since that she must have looked as if the admission of the natural light of day would have struck her to dust.

"He calls the knaves jacks, this boy!" said Estella with disdain, before our first game was out. "And what coarse hands he has! And what thick boots!"

I had never thought of being ashamed of my hands before; but I began to consider them a very <u>indifferent</u> pair. Her contempt for me was so strong that it became infectious, and I caught it.

She won the game, and I dealt. I misdealt, as was only natural, when I knew she was lying in wait for me to do wrong; and she denounced me for a stupid, clumsy laboring-boy.

"You say nothing of her," remarked Miss Havisham to me, as she looked on. "She says many hard things of you, yet you say nothing of her. What do you think of her?"

◀ *How does Pip feel about Estella?*

"I don't like to say," I stammered.

"Tell me in my ear," said Miss Havisham, bending down.

"I think she is very proud," I replied, in a whisper.

"Anything else?"

"I think she is very pretty."

"Anything else?"

"I think she is very insulting." (She was looking at me then with a look of supreme <u>aversion</u>.)

"Anything else?"

"I think I should like to go home."

"And never see her again, though she is so pretty?"

"I am not sure that I shouldn't like to see her again, but I should like to go home now."

"You shall go soon," said Miss Havisham aloud. "Play the game out."

Saving for the one weird smile at first, I should have felt almost sure that Miss Havisham's face could not smile. It had dropped into a watchful and brooding expression—most likely when all the things about her had become <u>transfixed</u>—and it looked as if nothing could ever lift it up again. Her chest had dropped, so that she stooped; and her voice had dropped, so

Words For Everyday Use	**in • dif • fer • ent** (in dif´ər ənt) *adj.*, mediocre **a • ver • sion** (ə vʉr´zhən) *n.*, intense dislike **trans • fixed** (trans fiksd´) *adj.*, motionless; fixed in one position

that she spoke low, and with a dead lull upon her; altogether, she had the appearance of having dropped, body and soul, within and without, under the weight of a crushing blow.

I played the game to an end with Estella, and she beggared[12] me. She threw the cards down on the table when she had won them all, as if she despised them for having been won of me.

"When shall I have you here again?" said Miss Havisham. "Let me think."

I was beginning to remind her that today was Wednesday when she checked me with her former impatient movement of the fingers of her right hand.

▶ What are Miss Havisham's instructions for Pip?

"There, there! I know nothing of days of the week; I know nothing of weeks of the year. Come again after six days. You hear?"

"Yes, ma'am."

"Estella, take him down. Let him have something to eat, and let him roam and look about him while he eats. Go, Pip."

I followed the candle down, as I had followed the candle up, and she stood it in the place where we had found it. Until she opened the side entrance, I had fancied, without thinking about it, that it must necessarily be nighttime. The rush of the daylight quite <u>confounded</u> me, and made me feel as if I had been in the candlelight of the strange room many hours.

"You are to wait here, you boy," said Estella, and disappeared and closed the door.

I took the opportunity of being alone in the courtyard to look at my coarse hands and my common boots. My opinion of those accessories was not favorable. They had never troubled me before, but they troubled me now, as <u>vulgar appendages</u>. I determined to ask Joe why he had ever taught me to call those picture-cards jacks which ought to be called knaves. I wished Joe had been rather more genteelly[13] brought up, and then I should have been so, too.

▶ Why does Pip feel humiliated? How does Estella react to his humiliation?

She came back, with some bread and meat and a little mug of beer. She put the mug down on the stones of the yard, and gave me the bread and meat without looking at me, as <u>insolently</u> as if I were a dog in disgrace. I was so humiliated, hurt, <u>spurned</u>, offended, angry, sorry—I cannot hit upon the right

---

12. **beggared.** Beat at "Beggar my Neighbor"
13. **genteelly.** Politely, elegantly

Words For Everyday Use

con • found (kən found´) vt., confuse
vul • gar (vul´gər) adj., common; crude
ap • pend • age (ə pen´dij) n., something that is attached

in • so • lent • ly (in´sə lənt lē) adv., disrespectfully; arrogantly
spurned (spʉrnd) adj., rejected

name for the smart—God knows what its name was—that tears started to my eyes. The moment they sprang there, the girl looked at me with a quick delight in having been the cause of them. This gave me power to keep them back and to look at her: so, she gave a <u>contemptuous</u> toss—but with a sense, I thought, of having made too sure that I was so wounded—and left me.

◄ *What does Pip do when he is finally alone?*

But, when she was gone, I looked about me for a place to hide my face in, and got behind one of the gates in the brewery-lane, and leaned my sleeve against the wall there, and leaned my forehead on it and cried. As I cried, I kicked the wall, and took a hard twist at my hair; so bitter were my feelings, and so sharp was the smart without a name, that it needed counteraction.

My sister's bringing up had made me sensitive. In the little world in which children have their existence, whosoever brings them up, there is nothing so finely perceived and so finely felt as injustice. It may be only small injustice that the child can be exposed to; but the child is small, and its world is small, and its rocking-horse stands as many hands high, according to scale, as a big-boned Irish hunter. Within myself, I had <u>sustained</u>, from my babyhood, a perpetual conflict with injustice. I had known, from the time when I could speak, that my sister, in her <u>capricious</u> and violent <u>coercion</u>, was unjust to me. I had cherished a profound conviction that her bringing me up by hand gave her no right to bring me up by jerks. Through all my punishments, disgraces, fasts and vigils, and other penitential performances, I had nursed this assurance; and to my communing so much with it, in a solitary and unprotected way, I in great part refer the fact that I was morally timid and very sensitive.

I got rid of my injured feelings for the time by kicking them into the brewery wall, and twisting them out of my hair, and then I smoothed my face with my sleeve, and came from behind the gate. The bread and meat were acceptable, and the beer was warming and tingling, and I was soon in spirits to look about me.

To be sure, it was a deserted place, down to the pigeon-house in the brewery yard, which had been blown crooked on its pole by some high wind, and would have made the pigeons think themselves at sea, if there had been any

◄ *What is the evidence of disuse and decay?*

pigeons there to be rocked by it. But, there were no pigeons in the dovecot,[14] no horses in the stable, no pigs in the sty, no malt in the storehouse, no smells of grains and beer in the copper or the vat. All the uses and scents of the brewery might have evaporated with its last reek of smoke. In a by-yard, there was a wilderness of empty casks, which had a certain sour remembrance of better days lingering about them; but it was too sour to be accepted as a sample of the beer that was gone—and in this respect I remember those <u>recluses</u> as being like most others.

Behind the furthest end of the brewery was a rank garden with an old wall: not so high but that I could struggle up and hold on long enough to look over it, and see that the rank garden was the garden of the house, and that it was overgrown with tangled weeds, but that there was a track upon the green and yellow paths, as if someone sometimes walked there, and that Estella was walking away from me even then. But she seemed to be everywhere. For, when I yielded to the temptation presented by the casks, and began to walk on them, I saw *her* walking on them at the end of the yard of casks. She had her back towards me, and held her pretty brown hair spread out in her two hands, and never looked round, and passed out of my view directly. So, in the brewery itself—by which I mean the large paved lofty place in which they used to make the beer, and where the brewing utensils still were. When I first went into it, and, rather oppressed by its gloom, stood near the door looking about me, I saw her pass among the extinguished fires, and ascend some light iron stairs, and go out by a gallery high overhead, as if she were going out into the sky.

It was in this place, and at this moment, that a strange thing happened to my fancy. I thought it a strange thing then, and I thought it a stranger thing long afterwards. I turned my eyes—a little dimmed by looking up at the frosty light—towards a great wooden beam in a low nook of the building near me on my right hand, and I saw a figure hanging there by the neck. A figure all in yellow white, with but one shoe to the feet; and it hung so that I could see that the faded trimmings of the dress were like earthy paper, and that the face was Miss Havisham's, with a movement going over

▶ Whose presence does Pip sense everywhere?

▶ What does Pip imagine that he sees? How does he react?

---

14. **dovecot.** Small house for nesting pigeons

Words For Everyday Use

rec • luse (rek´ lo͞os) *n.*, one who chooses to live alone the whole countenance as if she were trying to call to me. In the terror of seeing the figure, and in the terror of being certain that it had not been there a moment before, I at first ran from it, and then ran towards it. And my terror was greatest of all when I found no figure there.

Nothing less than the frosty light of the cheerful sky, the sight of people passing beyond the bars of the courtyard gate, and the reviving influence of the rest of the bread and meat and beer could have brought me round. Even with those aids, I might not have come to myself as soon as I did but that I saw Estella approaching with the keys, to let me out. She would have some fair reason for looking down upon me, I thought, if she saw me frightened; and she should have no fair reason.

She gave me a triumphant glance in passing me, as if she rejoiced that my hands were so coarse and my boots were so thick, and she opened the gate, and stood holding it. I was passing out without looking at her, when she touched me with a taunting hand.

"Why don't you cry?"

"Because I don't want to."

◄ How does Estella further humiliate Pip?

"You do," said she. "You have been crying till you are half-blind, and you are near crying again now."

She laughed contemptuously, pushed me out, and locked the gate upon me. I went straight to Mr. Pumblechook's, and was immensely relieved to find him not at home. So, leaving word with the shopman on what day I was wanted at Miss Havisham's again, I set off on the four-mile walk to our forge, pondering, as I went along, on all I had seen, and deeply revolving that I was a common laboring-boy; that my hands were coarse; that my boots were thick; that I had fallen into a despicable habit of calling knaves jacks; that I was much more ignorant than I had considered myself last night; and generally that I was in a low-lived bad way.

◄ What does Pip think of himself now?

CHAPTER 9

When I reached home, my sister was very curious to know all about Miss Havisham's, and asked a number of questions. And I soon found myself getting heavily bumped from behind in the nape of the neck and the small of the back, and having my face <u>ignominiously</u> shoved against the kitchen wall, because I did not answer those questions at sufficient length.

If a dread of not being understood be hidden in the breasts of other young people to anything like the extent to which it used to be hidden in mine—which I consider probable, as I have no particular reason to suspect myself of having been a <u>monstrosity</u>—it is the key to many reservations. I felt convinced that if I described Miss Havisham's as my eyes had seen it, I should not be understood. Not only that, but I felt convinced that Miss Havisham, too, would not be understood; and although she was perfectly incomprehensible to me, I entertained an impression that there would be something coarse and treacherous in my dragging her as she really was (to say nothing of Miss Estella) before the contemplation of Mrs. Joe. Consequently, I said as little as I could, and had my face shoved against the kitchen wall.

The worst of it was that that bullying old Pumblechook, preyed upon by a devouring curiosity to be informed of all I had seen and heard, came gaping over in his chaise-cart at tea-time to have the details <u>divulged</u> to him. And the mere sight of the torment, with his fishy eyes and mouth open, his sandy hair inquisitively on end, and his waistcoat heaving with windy arithmetic, made me vicious in my <u>reticence</u>.

"Well, boy," Uncle Pumblechook began, as soon as he was seated in the chair of honor by the fire. "How did you get on up town?"

I answered, "Pretty well, sir," and my sister shook her fist at me.

"Pretty well?" Mr. Pumblechook repeated. "Pretty well is no answer. Tell us what you mean by pretty well, boy?"

Whitewash on the forehead hardens the brain into a state of obstinacy perhaps. Anyhow, with whitewash from the wall on my forehead, my obstinacy was <u>adamantine</u>. I

▶ *Why does Mrs. Joe bump and shove Pip?*

▶ *Why doesn't Pip tell Mrs. Joe all about his experiences?*

Words For Everyday Use

ig • no • min • i • ous • ly (igʹnə minʹ ē əs lē) *adv.*, shamefully; disgracefully

mon • stros • i • ty (män sträsʹə tē) *n.*, something grotesquely abnormal

di • vulge (də vuljʹ) *vt.*, reveal

ret • i • cence (retʹə səns) *n.*, reserve; silence

ad • a • man • tine (adʹə manʹtin) *adj.*, unbreakable; unyielding reflected for some time, and then answered as if I had discovered a new idea, "I mean pretty well."

My sister with an exclamation of impatience was going to fly at me—I had no shadow of defense, for Joe was busy in the forge—when Mr. Pumblechook interposed with "No! Don't lose your temper. Leave this lad to me, ma'am; leave this lad to me." Mr. Pumblechook then turned me towards him as if he were going to cut my hair, and said:

"First (to get our thoughts in order:) Forty-three pence?"[1]

◀ What is unusual about Uncle Pumblechook's questions?

I calculated the consequences of replying "Four hundred pound," and finding them against me, went as near the answer as I could—which was somewhere about eight-pence off. Mr. Pumblechook then put me through my pence-table from "twelve pence make one shilling," up to "forty pence make three and fourpence," and then triumphantly demanded, as if he had done for me, "*Now!* How much is forty-three pence?" To which I replied, after a long interval of reflection, "I don't know." And I was so aggravated that I almost doubt if I did know.

Mr. Pumblechook worked his head like a screw to screw it out of me, and said, "Is forty-three pence seven and sixpence three fardens, for instance?"

"Yes!" said I. And although my sister instantly boxed my ears, it was highly gratifying to me to see that the answer spoilt his joke, and brought him to a dead stop.

"Boy! What is Miss Havisham like?" Mr. Pumblechook began again when he had recovered, folding his arms tight on his chest and applying the screw.

"Very tall and dark," I told him.

"Is she, Uncle?" asked my sister.

Mr. Pumblechook winked assent; from which I at once inferred that he had never seen Miss Havisham, for she was nothing of the kind.

◀ What does Pip infer? Why?

"Good!" said Mr. Pumblechook conceitedly. ("This is the way to have him! We are beginning to hold our own, I think, mum.")

"I am sure, Uncle," returned Mrs. Joe, "I wish you had him always: you know so well how to deal with him."

---

1. **Forty-three pence.** Pumblechook wants Pip to tell him how many shillings (there are twelve pence in one shilling) are in this amount and how many pence are remaining. The answer is three shillings and seven pence.

Words For Everyday Use   grat • i • fy • ing (grat´ə fī´ iŋ) *adj.*, pleasing

"Now, boy! What was she a-doing of, when you went in today?" asked Mr. Pumblechook.

"She was sitting," I answered, "in a black velvet coach."

Mr. Pumblechook and Mrs. Joe stared at one another—as they well might—and both repeated, "In a black velvet coach?"

"Yes," said I. "And Miss Estella—that's her niece, I think—handed her in cake and wine at the coach-window, on a gold plate. And we all had cake and wine on gold plates. And I got up behind the coach to eat mine, because she told me to."

"Was anybody else there?" asked Mr. Pumblechook.

"Four dogs," said I.

"Large or small?"

"Immense," said I. "And they fought for veal cutlets out of a silver basket."

▶ What motivates Pip to create his tale of fancy?

Mr. Pumblechook and Mrs. Joe stared at one another again, in utter amazement. I was perfectly frantic—a reckless witness under the torture—and would have told them anything.

"Where *was* this coach, in the name of gracious?" asked my sister.

"In Miss Havisham's room." They stared again. "But there weren't any horses to it." I added this saving clause, in the moment of rejecting four richly caparisoned coursers,[2] which I had had wild thoughts of harnessing.

"Can this be possible, Uncle?" asked Mrs. Joe. "What can the boy mean?"

"I'll tell you, mum," said Mr. Pumblechook. "My opinion is, it's a sedan chair.[3] She's <u>flighty</u>, you know—very flighty—quite flighty enough to pass her days in a sedan chair."

"Did you ever see her in it, Uncle?" asked Mrs. Joe.

▶ What does Pumblechook admit?

"How could I," he returned, forced to the admission, "when I never see her in my life? Never clapped eyes upon her!"

"Goodness, Uncle! And yet you have spoken to her?"

"Why, don't you know," said Mr. Pumblechook <u>testily</u>, "that when I have been there, I have been took up to the outside of her door, and the door has stood ajar, and she has spoken to me that way. Don't say you don't know *that*, mum. However, the boy went there to play. What did you play at, boy?"

---

2. **richly caparisoned coursers.** Graceful, swift horses covered with fancy trappings

3. **sedan chair.** Enclosed chair for one person, with glass windows, carried on poles by two men, used in the seventeenth and eighteenth centuries

---

Words For Everyday Use

flight • y (flīt´ē) *adj.*, crazy

tes • ti • ly (tes´tə lē) *adv.*, irritably; with annoyance

"We played with flags," I said. (I beg to observe that I think of myself with amazement when I recall the lies I told on this occasion.)

"Flags!" echoed my sister.

"Yes," said I. "Estella waved a blue flag, and I waved a red one, and Miss Havisham waved one sprinkled all over with little gold stars, out at the coach-window. And then we all waved our swords and hurrahed."

"Swords!" repeated my sister. "Where did you get swords from?"

"Out of a cupboard," said I. "And I saw pistols in it—and jam—and pills. And there was no daylight in the room, but it was all lighted up with candles."

"That's true, mum," said Mr. Pumblechook, with a grave nod. "That's the state of the case, for that much I've seen myself." And then they both stared at me, and I, with an <u>obtrusive</u> show of <u>artlessness</u> on my countenance, stared at them, and plaited[4] the right leg of my trousers with my right hand.

If they had asked me any more questions I should undoubtedly have betrayed myself, for I was even then on the point of mentioning that there was a balloon in the yard, and should have hazarded the statement but for my invention being divided between that phenomenon and a bear in the brewery. They were so much occupied, however, in discussing the marvels I had already presented for their consideration that I escaped. The subject still held them when Joe came in from his work to have a cup of tea—to whom my sister, more for the relief of her own mind than for the <u>gratification</u> of his, related my pretended experiences.

◄ Why does the questioning stop?

Now when I saw Joe open his blue eyes and roll them all round the kitchen in helpless amazement, I was overtaken by penitence; but only as regarded him—not in the least as regarded the other two. Towards Joe, and Joe only, I considered myself a young monster, while they sat debating what results would come to me from Miss Havisham's acquaintance and favor. They had no doubt that Miss Havisham would "do something" for me; their doubts related to the form that something would take. My sister stood out for "property." Mr. Pumblechook was in favor of a handsome

◄ How does Pip feel about what he has done? Why?

◄ With what are Mrs. Joe and Pumblechook concerned?

---

4. **plaited.** Pleated; folded

Words For Everyday Use

ob • tru • sive (əb trōō´siv) *adj.,* calling attention to oneself in a displeasing way

art • less • ness (ärt´ lis nəs) *n.,* lack of deceit; innocence; naiveté

grat • i • fi • ca • tion (grat´ə fi kā´shən) *n.,* satisfaction; pleasure premium for binding me apprentice to some genteel trade—say, the corn and seed trade, for instance. Joe fell into the deepest disgrace with both for offering the bright suggestion that I might only be presented with one of the dogs who had fought for the veal cutlets. "If a fool's head can't express better opinions than that," said my sister, "and you have got any work to do, you had better go and do it." So he went.

After Mr. Pumblechook had driven off, and when my sister was washing up, I stole into the forge to Joe, and remained by him until he had done for the night. Then I said, "Before the fire goes out, Joe, I should like to tell you something."

"Should you, Pip?" said Joe, drawing his shoeing-stool near the forge. "Then tell us. What is it, Pip?"

"Joe," said I, taking hold of his rolled-up shirt-sleeve, and twisting it between my finger and thumb, "you remember all that about Miss Havisham's?"

"Remember?" said Joe. "I believe you! Wonderful!"

"It's a terrible thing, Joe; it ain't true."

▶ What does Pip confess?

"What are you telling of, Pip?" cried Joe, falling back in the greatest amazement. "You don't mean to say it's—"

"Yes I do; it's lies, Joe."

"But not all of it? Why sure you don't mean to say, Pip, that there was no black welwet co—ch?" For, I stood shaking my head. "But at least there was dogs, Pip? Come, Pip," said Joe persuasively, "if there warn't no weal cutlets, at least there was dogs?"

"No, Joe."

"A dog?" said Joe. "A puppy? Come!"

"No, Joe, there was nothing at all of the kind."

As I fixed my eyes hopelessly on Joe, Joe contemplated me in dismay. "Pip, old chap! This won't do, old fellow! I say! Where do you expect to go to?"

"It's terrible, Joe; ain't it?"

"Terrible?" cried Joe. "Awful! What possessed you?"

"I don't know what possessed me, Joe," I replied, letting his shirt-sleeve go, and sitting down in the ashes at his feet, hanging my head; "but I wish you hadn't taught me to call knaves at cards jacks; and I wish my boots weren't so thick nor my hands so coarse."

▶ What does Pip admit to Joe about his experiences at Satis House?

And then I told Joe that I felt very miserable, and that I hadn't been able to explain myself to Mrs. Joe and

Words For Everyday Use

pre • mi • um (prē´mē əm) *n.*, reward; payment

Pumblechook, who were so rude to me, and that there had been a beautiful young lady at Miss Havisham's who was dreadfully proud, and that she had said I was common, and that I knew I was common, and that I wished I was not common, and that the lies had come of it somehow, though I didn't know how.

This was a case of metaphysics,[5] at least as difficult for Joe to deal with as for me. But Joe took the case altogether out of the region of metaphysics, and by that means vanquished it.

"There's one thing you may be sure of, Pip," said Joe, after some <u>rumination</u>, "namely, that lies is lies. Howsever they come, they didn't ought to come, and they come from the father of lies, and work round to the same. Don't you tell no more of 'em, Pip. *That* ain't the way to get out of being common, old chap. And as to being common, I don't make it out at all clear. You are oncommon in some things. You're oncommon small. Likewise you're a oncommon scholar."

◀ What does Joe tell Pip about lies?

"No, I am ignorant and backward, Joe."

"Why, see what a letter you wrote last night! Wrote in print even! I've seen letters—ah! and from gentlefolks!—that I'll swear weren't wrote in print," said Joe.

"I have learnt next to nothing, Joe. You think much of me. It's only that."

"Well, Pip," said Joe, "be it so, or be it son't, you must be a common scholar afore you can be a oncommon one, I should hope! The king upon his throne, with his crown upon his 'ed, can't sit and write his acts of Parliament in print, without having begun, when he were a unpromoted prince, with the alphabet—ah!" added Joe, with a shake of the head that was full of meaning, "and begun at A, too, and worked his way to Z. And *I* know what that is to do, though I can't say I've exactly done it."

◀ How does Joe try to encourage Pip?

There was some hope in this piece of wisdom, and it rather encouraged me.

"Whether common ones as to callings and earnings," pursued Joe, reflectively, "mightn't be the better of continuing for to keep company with common ones, instead of going out to play with oncommon ones—which reminds me to hope that there were a flag, perhaps?"

◀ With whom does Joe advise Pip to "keep company" in the future?

---

5. **metaphysics.** Philosophy about the nature of reality; any difficult reasoning

Words For Everyday Use

ru • mi • na • tion (rōō′mə nā′shən) *n.,* thought

"No, Joe."

"(I'm sorry there weren't a flag, Pip). Whether that might be, or mightn't be, is a thing as can't be looked into now without putting your sister on the ram-page; and that's a thing not to be thought of as being done intentional. Lookee here, Pip, at what is said to you by a true friend. Which this to you the true friend say. If you can't get to be oncommon through going straight, you'll never get to do it through going crooked. So don't tell no more on 'em, Pip, and live well and die happy."

"You are not angry with me, Joe?"

"No, old chap. But bearing in mind that them were which I meantersay of a stunning and outdacious[6] sort—alluding to them which bordered on weal cutlets and dog-fighting—a sincere wellwisher would adwise, Pip, there being dropped into your meditations, when you go upstairs to bed. That's all, old chap, and don't never do it no more."

▶ *What does Pip think about?*

When I got up to my little room and said my prayers, I did not forget Joe's recommendation, and yet my young mind was in that disturbed and unthankful state that I thought long after I laid me down, how common Estella would consider Joe, a mere blacksmith: how thick his boots, and how coarse his hands. I thought how Joe and my sister were then sitting in the kitchen, and how I had come up to bed from the kitchen, and how Miss Havisham and Estella never sat in a kitchen, but were far above the level of such common doings. I fell asleep recalling what I "used to do" when I was at Miss Havisham's; as though I had been there weeks or months, instead of hours—and as though it were quite an old subject of remembrance, instead of one that had arisen only that day.

▶ *What significance does the narrator suggest one particular day can have?*

That was a memorable day to me, for it made great changes in me. But it is the same with any life. Imagine one selected day struck out of it, and think how different its course would have been. Pause you who read this, and think for a moment of the long chain of iron or gold, of thorns or flowers, that would never have bound you, but for the formation of the first link on one memorable day.

---

6. **outdacious.** Audacious; bold or daring

CHAPTER 10

The <u>felicitous</u> idea occurred to me a morning or two later when I woke that the best step I could take towards making myself uncommon was to get out of Biddy everything she knew. In pursuance[1] of this <u>luminous</u> conception, I mentioned to Biddy when I went to Mr. Wopsle's great-aunt's at night that I had a particular reason for wishing to get on in life, and that I should feel very much obliged to her if she would impart all her learning to me. Biddy, who was the most obliging of girls, immediately said she would, and indeed began to carry out her promise within five minutes.

The educational scheme or course established by Mr. Wopsle's great-aunt may be resolved into the following synopsis.[2] The pupils ate apples and put straws down one another's backs, until Mr. Wopsle's great-aunt collected her energies, and made an indiscriminate totter at them with a birch-rod. After receiving the charge with every mark of <u>derision</u>, the pupils formed in line and buzzingly passed a ragged book from hand to hand. The book had an alphabet in it, some figures and tables, and a little spelling—that is to say, it had had once. As soon as this volume began to circulate, Mr. Wopsle's great-aunt fell into a state of coma; arising either from sleep or a rheumatic paroxysm.[3] The pupils then entered among themselves upon a competitive examination on the subject of boots, with the view of <u>ascertaining</u> who could tread the hardest upon whose toes. This mental exercise lasted until Biddy made a rush at them and distributed three defaced[4] Bibles (shaped as if they had been unskillfully cut off the chump-end of something), more illegibly printed at the best than any curiosities of literature I have since met with, speckled all over with iron-mold, and having various specimens of the insect world smashed between their leaves. This part of the course was usually lightened by several single combats between Biddy and <u>refractory</u> students. When the fights were over, Biddy gave out the number of a page, and then we all

◄ How does Pip plan to make himself "uncommon"?

◄ Why is Mr. Wopsle's great-aunt's school little help?

---

1. **pursuance.** Pursuit
2. **synopsis.** Condensation of the whole story into a summary
3. **rheumatic paroxysm.** Sudden spasm, cough, or sneeze
4. **defaced.** Made unreadable by damage

► What does Biddy try to do? Is she successful?

read aloud what we could—or what we couldn't—in a frightful chorus; Biddy leading with a high shrill <u>monotonous</u> voice, and none of us having the least notion of, or reverence for, what we were reading about. When this horrible din had lasted a certain time, it mechanically awoke Mr. Wopsle's great-aunt, who staggered at a boy <u>fortuitously</u>, and pulled his ears. This was understood to terminate the course for the evening, and we emerged into the air with shrieks of intellectual victory. It is fair to remark that there was no prohibition against any pupil's entertaining himself with a slate or even with the ink (when there was any), but that it was not easy to pursue that branch of study in the winter season, on account of the little general shop in which the classes were holden[5]— and which was also Mr. Wopsle's great-aunt's sitting room and bedchamber—being but faintly illuminated through the agency of one low-spirited dip-candle and no snuffers.

It appeared to me that it would take time to become uncommon under these circumstances: nevertheless, I resolved to try it, and that very evening Biddy entered on our special agreement by imparting some information from her little catalogue of prices under the head of moist sugar, and lending me, to copy at home, a large old English D which she had imitated from the heading of some newspaper, and which I supposed, until she told me what it was, to be a design for a buckle.

Of course there was a public house[6] in the village, and of course Joe liked sometimes to smoke his pipe there. I had received strict orders from my sister to call for him at the Three Jolly Bargemen[7] that evening, on my way from school, and bring him home at my peril. To the Three Jolly Bargemen, therefore, I directed my steps.

There was a bar at the Jolly Bargemen, with some alarmingly long chalk scores in it on the wall at the side of the door, which seemed to me to be never paid off.[8] They had been there ever since I could remember, and had grown more than I had. But there was a quantity of chalk about our country, and perhaps the people neglected no opportunity of turning it to account.[9]

---

5. **holden.** Held
6. **public house.** Inn or tavern
7. **Three Jolly Bargemen.** Name of the public house; bargemen work on barges, or flat rafts that float on the river.
8. **alarmingly long . . . paid off.** The barkeeper writes how much the customers owe on a chalkboard. These debts seem never to be paid.
9. **turning it to account.** Putting it to good use (in accounting debts)

Words For Everyday Use

mo • not • o • nous (mə nät´ 'n əs) *adj.,* going on in the same tone

for • tu • i • tous • ly (fôr to͞o´ə təs lē) *adv.,* fortunately

It being Saturday night, I found the landlord looking rather grimly at these records, but as my business was with Joe and not with him, I merely wished him good evening, and passed into the common room at the end of the passage, where there was a bright large kitchen fire, and where Joe was smoking his pipe in company with Mr. Wopsle and a stranger. Joe greeted me as usual with "Halloa, Pip, old chap!" and the moment he said that, the stranger turned his head and looked at me.

◄ Why does the "secret-looking" man turn his head?

He was a secret-looking man whom I had never seen before. His head was all on one side, and one of his eyes was half shut up, as if he were taking aim at something with an invisible gun. He had a pipe in his mouth, and he took it out, and, after slowly blowing all his smoke away and looking hard at me all the time, nodded. So, I nodded, and then he nodded again, and made room on the settle[10] beside him that I might sit down there.

But, as I was used to sit beside Joe whenever I entered that place of resort, I said "No, thank you, sir," and fell into the space Joe made for me on the opposite settle. The strange man, after glancing at Joe, and seeing that his attention was otherwise engaged, nodded to me again when I had taken my seat, and then rubbed his leg—in a very odd way, as it struck me.

◄ What does the stranger do to engage Pip and Joe?

"You was saying," said the strange man, turning to Joe, "that you was a blacksmith."

"Yes. I said it, you know," said Joe.

"What'll you drink, Mr.—? You didn't mention your name, by-the-bye."

Joe mentioned it now, and the strange man called him by it.

"What'll you drink, Mr. Gargery? At my expense? To top up with?"

"Well," said Joe, "to tell you the truth, I ain't much in the habit of drinking at anybody's expense but my own."

"Habit? No," returned the stranger, "but once and away, and on a Saturday night, too. Come! Put a name to it, Mr. Gargery."

"I wouldn't wish to be stiff company," said Joe. "Rum."

"Rum," repeated the stranger. "And will the other gentleman originate a sentiment."

"Rum," said Mr. Wopsle.

"Three rums!" cried the stranger, calling to the landlord. "Glasses round!"

"This other gentleman," observed Joe, by way of introducing Mr. Wopsle, "is a gentleman that you would like to hear give it out. Our clerk at church."

---

10. **settle.** Long bench

"Aha!" said the stranger, quickly, and cocking his eye at me. "The lonely church, right out on the marshes, with graves round it!"

"That's it," said Joe.

The stranger, with a comfortable kind of grunt over his pipe, put his legs up on the settle that he had to himself. He wore a flapping broad-brimmed traveler's hat, and under it a handkerchief tied over his head in the manner of a cap, so that he showed no hair. As he looked at the fire, I thought I saw a cunning expression, followed by a half-laugh, come into his face.

"I am not acquainted with this country, gentlemen, but it seems a solitary country towards the river."

"Most marshes is solitary," said Joe.

▶ What is the stranger trying to find out?

"No doubt, no doubt. Do you find any gypsies, now, or tramps, or vagrants of any sort, out there?"

"No," said Joe; "none but a runaway conwict now and then. And we don't find *them,* easy. Eh, Mr. Wopsle?"

Mr. Wopsle, with a majestic remembrance of old <u>discomfiture</u>, assented, but not warmly.

"Seems you have been out after such?" asked the stranger.

"Once," returned Joe. "Not that we wanted to take them, you understand; we went out as lookers on; me and Mr. Wopsle, and Pip. Didn't us, Pip?"

"Yes, Joe."

The stranger looked at me again—still cocking his eye, as if he were expressly taking aim at me with his invisible gun—and said, "He's a likely young <u>parcel</u> of bones that. What is it you call him?"

"Pip," said Joe.

"Christened Pip?"

"No, not christened Pip."

"Surname[11] Pip?"

"No," said Joe, "it's a kind of family name what he gave himself when a infant, and is called by."

"Son of yours?"

"Well," said Joe meditatively—not, of course, that it could be in anywise necessary to consider about it, but because it was the way at the Jolly Bargemen to seem to consider deeply about everything that was discussed over pipes—"well, no. No, he ain't."

---

11. **Surname.** Last name

| Words For Everyday Use | **dis • com • fi • ture** (dis kumˈfi chʉr) *n.,* embarrassment |
| | **par • cel** (pärˈsəl) *n.,* package |

"Nevvy?"[12] said the strange man.

"Well," said Joe, with the same appearance of profound cogitation, "he is not—no, not to deceive you, he is *not*—my nevvy."

"What the blue blazes is he?" asked the stranger. Which appeared to me to be an inquiry of unnecessary strength.

Mr. Wopsle struck in upon that—as one who knew all about relationships, having professional occasion to bear in mind what female relations a man might not marry—and expounded the ties between me and Joe. Having his hand in, Mr. Wopsle finished off with a most terrifically snarling passage from *Richard the Third,* and seemed to think he had done quite enough to account for it when he added, "as the poet says."

And here I may remark that when Mr. Wopsle referred to me, he considered it a necessary part of such reference to rumple my hair and poke it into my eyes. I cannot conceive why everybody of his standing who visited at our house should always have put me through the same <u>inflammatory</u> process under similar circumstances. Yet I do not call to mind that I was ever in my earlier youth the subject of remark in our social family circle but some large-handed person took some such <u>ophthalmic</u> steps to <u>patronize</u> me.

◄ *What does Pip resent?*

All this while, the strange man looked at nobody but me, and looked at me as if he were determined to have a shot at me at last, and bring me down. But he said nothing after offering his blue blazes observation, until the glasses of rum-and-water were brought: and then he made his shot, and a most extraordinary shot it was.

◄ *What "shot" does the stranger make to Pip? What does Pip realize?*

It was not a verbal remark, but a proceeding in dumb show,[13] and was pointedly addressed to me. He stirred his rum-and-water pointedly at me, and he tasted his rum-and-water pointedly at me. And he stirred it and he tasted it: not with a spoon that was brought to him, but *with a file.*

He did this so that nobody but I saw the file; and when he had done it, he wiped the file and put it in a breast-pocket. I knew it to be Joe's file, and I knew that he knew my convict the moment I saw the instrument. I sat gazing at him, spellbound. But he now reclined on his settle, taking very little notice of me, and talking principally about turnips.

12. **Nevvy.** Nephew
13. **dumb show.** Pantomime

Words For Everyday Use

in • flam • ma • to • ry (in flam´ə tôr´ē) *adj.,* rousing excitement or anger
oph • thal • mic (äf thal´mik) *adj.,* visible

pa • tron • ize (pā´trə nīz´) *vt.,* be kind or helpful to in a snobbish way

There was a delicious sense of cleaning up and making a quiet pause before going on in life afresh in our village on Saturday nights, which stimulated Joe to dare to stay out half an hour longer on Saturdays than at other times. The half hour and the rum-and-water running out together, Joe got up to go, and took me by the hand.

"Stop half a moment, Mr. Gargery," said the strange man. "I think I've got a bright new shilling somewhere in my pocket, and if I have, the boy shall have it."

He looked it out from a handful of small change, folded it in some crumpled paper, and gave it to me. "Yours!" said he. "Mind! Your own."

▶ What does the convict give to Pip?

I thanked him, staring at him far beyond the bounds of good manners, and holding tight to Joe. He gave Joe good-night, and he gave Mr. Wopsle good-night (who went out with us), and he gave me only a look with his aiming eye—no, not a look, for he shut it up, but wonders may be done with an eye by hiding it.

On the way home, if I had been in a humor for talking, the talk must have been all on my side, for Mr. Wopsle parted from us at the door of the Jolly Bargemen, and Joe went all the way home with his mouth wide open, to rinse the rum out with as much air as possible. But I was in a manner <u>stu-pefied</u> by this turning up of my old misdeed and old acquaintance, and could think of nothing else.

▶ Why does Joe tell his wife about the evening?

My sister was not in a very bad temper when we presented ourselves in the kitchen, and Joe was encouraged by that unusual circumstance to tell her about the bright shilling. "A bad un,[14] I'll be bound," said Mrs. Joe triumphantly, "or he wouldn't have given it to the boy! Let's look at it."

I took it out of the paper, and it proved to be a good one. "But what's this?" said Mrs. Joe, throwing down the shilling and catching up the paper. "Two one-pound notes?"

▶ What do they find? What does Joe do?

Nothing less than two fat sweltering one-pound notes that seemed to have been on terms of the warmest intimacy with all the cattle markets in the county. Joe caught up his hat again, and ran with them to the Jolly Bargemen to restore them to their owner. While he was gone I sat down on my

---

14. **bad un.** Counterfeit coin

Words
For
Everyday
Use

stu • pe • fied (stōōp´ə fīd) adj., stunned

usual stool and looked vacantly at my sister, feeling pretty sure that the man would not be there.

Presently, Joe came back, saying that the man was gone, but that he, Joe, had left word at the Three Jolly Bargemen concerning the notes. Then my sister sealed them up in a piece of paper, and put them under some dried rose leaves in an ornamental teapot on the top of a press[10] in the state parlor. There they remained a nightmare to me many and many a night and day.

I had sadly broken sleep when I got to bed, through thinking of the strange man taking aim at me with his invisible gun, and of the guiltily coarse and common thing it was to be on secret terms of conspiracy with convicts—a feature in my low career that I had previously forgotten. I was haunted by the file too. A dread possessed me that when I least expected it, the file would reappear. I coaxed myself to sleep by thinking of Miss Havisham's next Wednesday; and in my sleep I saw the file coming at me out of a door, without seeing who held it, and I screamed myself awake.

◄ What does Pip dream about? Why does Pip have a nightmare?

15. **press.** Upright closet in which clothes or other articles are kept

At the appointed time I returned to Miss Havisham's, and my hesitating ring at the gate brought out Estella. She locked it after admitting me, as she had done before, and again preceded me into the dark passage where her candle stood. She took no notice of me until she had the candle in her hand, when she looked over her shoulder, <u>superciliously</u> saying, "You are to come this way today," and took me to quite another part of the house.

The passage was a long one, and seemed to pervade the whole square basement of the Manor House. We <u>traversed</u> but one side of the square, however, and at the end of it she stopped and put her candle down and opened a door. Here the daylight reappeared, and I found myself in a small paved courtyard, the opposite side of which was formed by a detached dwelling-house that looked as if it had once belonged to the manager or head clerk of the extinct brewery. There was a clock in the outer wall of this house. Like the clock in Miss Havisham's room, and like Miss Havisham's watch, it had stopped at twenty minutes to nine.

▶ *What are Pip's instructions?*

We went in at the door, which stood open, and into a gloomy room with a low ceiling, on the ground floor at the back. There was some company in the room, and Estella said to me as she joined it, "You are to go and stand there, boy, till you are wanted." "There" being the window, I crossed to it, and stood "there" in a very uncomfortable state of mind, looking out.

It opened to the ground, and looked into a most miserable corner of the neglected garden, upon a rank ruin of cabbage-stalks, and one box-tree that had been clipped round long ago, like a pudding, and had a new growth at the top of it, out of shape and of a different color, as if that part of the pudding had stuck to the saucepan and got burnt. This was my homely thought as I contemplated the box-tree. There had been some light snow overnight, and it lay nowhere else to my knowledge; but it had not quite melted from the cold shadow of this bit of garden, and the wind caught it up in little <u>eddies</u> and threw it at the window, as if it pelted me for coming there.

Words For Everyday Use	**su • per • cil • i • ous • ly** (so͞o′pər sil′ē əs lē) *adv.*, scornfully; haughtily
	tra • verse (trə vʉrs′) *vt.*, pass over or through
	ed • dy (ed′ē) *n.*, swirling current of air

I divined that my coming had stopped conversation in the room, and that its other occupants were looking at me. I could see nothing of the room except the shining of the fire in the window glass, but I stiffened in all my joints with the consciousness that I was under close inspection.

There were three ladies in the room and one gentleman. Before I had been standing at the window five minutes, they somehow conveyed to me that they were all toadies and humbugs,[1] but that each of them pretended not to know that the others were toadies and humbugs, because the admission that he or she did know it would have made him or her out to be a toady and humbug.

They all had a listless and dreary air of waiting somebody's pleasure, and the most talkative of the ladies had to speak quite rigidly to <u>repress</u> a yawn. This lady, whose name was Camilla, very much reminded me of my sister, with the difference that she was older, and (as I found when I caught sight of her) of a blunter cast of features. Indeed, when I knew her better I began to think it was a mercy she had any features at all, so very blank and high was the dead wall of her face.

"Poor dear soul!" said this lady, with an abruptness of manner quite my sister's. "Nobody's enemy but his own!"

"It would be much more commendable to be somebody else's enemy," said the gentleman; "far more natural."

"Cousin Raymond," observed another lady, "we are to love our neighbor."

"Sarah Pocket," returned Cousin Raymond, "if a man is not his own neighbor, who is?"

Miss Pocket laughed, and Camilla laughed and said (checking a yawn), "The idea!" But I thought they seemed to think it rather a good idea too. The other lady, who had not spoken yet, said gravely and emphatically, "*Very* true!"

"Poor soul!" Camilla presently went on (I knew they had all been looking at me in the mean time), "he is so very strange! Would anyone believe that when Tom's wife died, he actually could not be <u>induced</u> to see the importance of the children's having the deepest of trimmings to their mourning?[2]

◄ *What happens when Pips enters the room? Who is there?*

---

1. **toadies and humbugs.** Flatterers and phonies
2. **deepest . . . mourning.** Camilla is lamenting that this person did not consider it important to buy his children the most impressive mourning clothes.

Words For Everyday Use

re • press (ri pres´) *vt.*, hold back
in • duce (in do͞os´) *vt.*, persuade

'Good Lord!' says he, 'Camilla, what can it signify so long as the poor <u>bereaved</u> little things are in black?' So like Matthew! The idea!"

"Good points in him, good points in him," said Cousin Raymond; "Heaven forbid I should deny good points in him; but he never had, and he never will have, any sense of the <u>proprieties</u>."

"You know I was obliged," said Camilla, "I was obliged to be firm. I said, 'It WILL NOT DO for the credit of the family.' I told him that, without deep trimmings, the family was disgraced. I cried about it from breakfast till dinner. I injured my digestion. And at last he flung out in his violent way, and said, with a D, 'Then do as you like.' Thank goodness it will always be a consolation to me to know that I instantly went out in a pouring rain and bought the things."

"*He* paid for them, did he not?" asked Estella.

"It's not the question, my dear child, who paid for them," returned Camilla. "*I* bought them. And I shall often think of that with peace, when I wake up in the night."

▶ Why are the adults upset with Pip?

The ringing of a distant bell, combined with the echoing of some cry or call along the passage by which I had come, interrupted the conversation and caused Estella to say to me, "Now, boy!" On my turning round, they all looked at me with the utmost contempt, and, as I went out, I heard Sarah Pocket say, "Well I am sure! What next!" and Camilla add, with indignation, "Was there ever such a fancy! The i-*de*-a!"

As we were going with our candle along the dark passage, Estella stopped all of a sudden, and, facing round, said in her <u>taunting</u> manner, with her face quite close to mine:

"Well?"

"Well, miss?" I answered, almost falling over her and checking myself.

▶ What has Miss Havisham revealed to Estella?

She stood looking at me, and of course I stood looking at her.

"Am I pretty?"

"Yes, I think you are very pretty."

"Am I insulting?"

"Not so much so as you were last time," said I.

"Not so much so?"

"No."

She fired when she asked the last question, and she slapped my face with such force as she had, when I answered it.

Words For Everyday Use	be • reaved (bē rēvd′) *adj.*, left in a state of loss and grief
	pro • pri • e • ty (prə prī′ə tē) *n.*, accepted standard of behavior
	taunt • ing (tônt′iŋ) *adj.*, sarcastic; ridiculing

"Now?" said she. "You little coarse monster, what do you think of me now?"

"I shall not tell you."

"Because you are going to tell upstairs. Is that it?"

"No," said I, "that's not it."

"Why don't you cry again, you little wretch?"

"Because I'll never cry for you again," said I. Which was, I suppose, as false a declaration as ever was made; for I was inwardly crying for her then, and I know what I know of the pain she cost me afterwards.

◄ What does Pip declare to Estella? Why is this declaration false?

We went on our way upstairs after this episode, and as we were going up, we met a gentleman groping his way down.

"Whom have we here?" asked the gentleman, stopping and looking at me.

"A boy," said Estella.

He was a burly man of an exceedingly dark complexion, with an exceedingly large head and a corresponding large hand. He took my chin in his large hand and turned up my face to have a look at me by the light of the candle. He was prematurely bald on the top of his head, and had bushy black eyebrows that wouldn't lie down, but stood up bristling. His eyes were set very deep in his head, and were disagreeably sharp and suspicious. He had a large watch chain, and strong black dots where his beard and whiskers would have been if he had let them. He was nothing to me, and I could have had no foresight then that he ever would be anything to me, but it happened that I had this opportunity of observing him well.

"Boy of the neighborhood? Hey?" said he.

"Yes, sir," said I.

"How do *you* come here?"

"Miss Havisham sent for me, sir," I explained.

"Well! Behave yourself. I have a pretty large experience of boys, and you're a bad set of fellows. Now mind!" said he, biting the side of his great forefinger as he frowned at me, "you behave yourself!"

◄ What is the man's advice to Pip? What is his opinion of boys?

With those words, he released me—which I was glad of, for his hand smelt of scented soap—and went his way downstairs. I wondered whether he could be a doctor; but no, I thought; he couldn't be a doctor, or he would have a quieter and more persuasive manner. There was not much time to consider the subject, for we were soon in Miss Havisham's room, where she and everything else were just as I had left them. Estella left me standing near the door, and I stood there until Miss Havisham cast her eyes upon me from the dressing table.

▶ Why is Pip sent into another room?

"So!" she said, without being startled or surprised; "the days have worn away, have they?"

"Yes, ma'am. Today is—"

"There, there, there!" with the impatient movement of her fingers. "I don't want to know. Are you ready to play?"

I was obliged to answer in some confusion, "I don't think I am, ma'am."

"Not at cards again?" she demanded with a searching look.

"Yes, ma'am; I could do that, if I was wanted."

"Since this house strikes you old and grave, boy," said Miss Havisham impatiently, "and you are unwilling to play, are you willing to work?"

I could answer this inquiry with a better heart than I had been able to find for the other question, and I said I was quite willing.

"Then go into that opposite room," said she, pointing at the door behind me with her withered hand, "and wait there till I come."

I crossed the staircase landing, and entered the room she indicated. From that room too, the daylight was completely excluded, and it had an airless smell that was oppressive. A fire had been lately kindled in the damp old-fashioned grate,[3] and it was more disposed to go out than to burn up, and the reluctant smoke which hung in the room seemed colder than the clearer air—like our own marsh mist. Certain wintry branches of candles on the high chimney-piece faintly lighted the chamber, or, it would be more expressive to say, faintly troubled its darkness. It was spacious, and I dare say had once been handsome, but every <u>discernible</u> thing in it was covered with dust and mold, and dropping to pieces. The most prominent object was a long table with a tablecloth spread on it, as if a feast had been in preparation when the house and the clocks all stopped together. An épergne[4] or centerpiece of some kind was in the middle of this cloth; it was so heavily overhung with cobwebs that its form was quite undistinguishable; and, as I looked along the yellow expanse out of which I remember its seeming to grow, like a black fungus, I saw speckled-legged spiders with blotchy bodies running home to it, and running out from it, as if

▶ What does Pip notice about the room?

---

3. **grate.** Metal frame for holding wood or coal in a fireplace or stove
4. **épergne.** Table centerpiece for holding fruits or flowers

Words For Everyday Use	**dis • cern • i • ble** (di zʉrn´ə bəl) *adj.*, recognizable

some circumstances of the greatest public importance had just <u>transpired</u> in the spider community.

I heard the mice too, rattling behind the panels, as if the same occurrence were important to their interests. But the black beetles took no notice of the agitation, and groped about the hearth in a <u>ponderous</u> elderly way, as if they were short-sighted and hard of hearing, and not on terms with one another.

These crawling things had fascinated my attention, and I was watching them from a distance, when Miss Havisham laid a hand upon my shoulder. In her other hand she had a crutch-headed stick on which she leaned, and she looked like the witch of the place.

"This," said she, pointing to the long table with her stick, "is where I will be laid when I am dead. They shall come and look at me here."

◄ *What is Miss Havisham's plan?*

With some vague misgiving that she might get upon the table then and there and die at once, the complete realization of the ghastly waxwork at the fair, I shrank under her touch.

"What do you think that is?" she asked me, again pointing with her stick; "that, where those cobwebs are?"

"I can't guess what it is, ma'am."

"It's a great cake. A bride-cake. Mine!"

She looked all round the room in a glaring manner, and then said, leaning on me while her hand twitched my shoulder, "Come, come, come! Walk me, walk me!"

I made out from this that the work I had to do was to walk Miss Havisham round and round the room. Accordingly, I started at once, and she leaned upon my shoulder, and we went away at a pace that might have been an imitation (founded on my first impulse under that roof) of Mr. Pumblechook's chaise-cart.

◄ *What is Pip's task?*

She was not physically strong, and after a little time said, "Slower!" Still, we went at an impatient fitful speed, and as we went, she twitched the hand upon my shoulder, and worked her mouth, and led me to believe that we were going fast because her thoughts went fast. After a while she said, "Call Estella!" so I went out on the landing and roared that name as I had done on the previous occasion. When her light appeared, I returned to Miss Havisham, and we started away again round and round the room.

Words For Everyday Use

tran • spire (tran spīr´) *vi.,* take place
pon • der • ous (pän´dər əs) *adj.,* very heavy or massive

If only Estella had come to be a spectator of our proceedings, I should have felt sufficiently discontented; but, as she brought with her the three ladies and the gentleman whom I had seen below, I didn't know what to do. In my politeness I would have stopped, but Miss Havisham twitched my shoulder, and we posted on—with a shame-faced consciousness on my part that they would think it was all my doing.

"Dear Miss Havisham," said Miss Sarah Pocket. "How well you look!"

"I do not," returned Miss Havisham. "I am yellow skin and bone."

Camilla brightened when Miss Pocket met with this <u>rebuff</u>; and she murmured, as she <u>plaintively</u> contemplated Miss Havisham, "Poor dear soul! Certainly not to be expected to look well, poor thing. The idea!"

"And how are *you?*" said Miss Havisham to Camilla. As we were close to Camilla then, I would have stopped as a matter of course, only Miss Havisham wouldn't stop. We swept on, and I felt that I was highly obnoxious to Camilla.

"Thank you, Miss Havisham," she returned, "I am as well as can be expected."

"Why, what's the matter with you?" asked Miss Havisham, with exceeding sharpness.

"Nothing worth mentioning," replied Camilla. "I don't wish to make a display of my feelings, but I have habitually thought of you more in the night than I am quite equal to."

"Then don't think of me," retorted Miss Havisham.

"Very easily said!" remarked Camilla, <u>amiably</u> repressing a sob, while a hitch came into her upper lip, and her tears overflowed. "Raymond is a witness what ginger and sal volatile[5] I am obliged to take in the night. Raymond is a witness what nervous jerkings I have in my legs. Chokings and nervous jerkings, however, are nothing new to me when I think with anxiety of those I love. If I could be less affectionate and sensitive, I should have a better digestion and an iron set of nerves. I am sure I wish it could be so. But as to not thinking of you in the night—the idea!" Here, a burst of tears.

The Raymond referred to I understood to be the gentleman present, and him I understood to be Mr. Camilla. He came to

► How do Miss Havisham's guests treat her? How does Miss Havisham treat her guests?

► What does Camilla say is the cause of her "nervous jerkings"?

---

5. **ginger and sal volatile.** Mixture of salts used medicinally

Words For Everyday Use	re • buff (ri buf´) *n.,* abrupt, blunt refusal of help or sympathy
	plain • tive • ly (plān´tiv lē) *adv.,* mournfully; sadly
	a • mi • a • bly (ā´mē ə blē) *adv.,* good-naturedly

the rescue at this point, and said in a <u>consolatory</u> and complimentary voice, "Camilla, my dear, it is well known that your family feelings are gradually undermining you to the extent of making one of your legs shorter than the other."

"I am not aware," observed the grave lady whose voice I had heard but once, "that to think of any person is to make a great claim upon that person, my dear."

Miss Sarah Pocket, whom I now saw to be a little dry brown <u>corrugated</u> old woman, with a small face that might have been made of walnut shells, and a large mouth like a cat's without the whiskers, supported this position by saying, "No, indeed, my dear. Hem!"

"Thinking is easy enough," said the grave lady.

"What is easier, you know?" assented Miss Sarah Pocket.

"Oh, yes, yes!" cried Camilla, whose <u>fermenting</u> feelings appeared to rise from her legs to her bosom. "It's all very true! It's a weakness to be so affectionate, but I can't help it. No doubt my health would be much better if it was otherwise; still, I wouldn't change my disposition if I could. It's the cause of much suffering, but it's a consolation to know I possess it, when I wake up in the night." Here, another burst of feeling.

Miss Havisham and I had never stopped all this time, but kept going round and round the room; now brushing against the skirts of the visitors, now giving them the whole length of the dismal chamber.

"There's Matthew!" said Camilla. "Never mixing with any natural ties, never coming here to see how Miss Havisham is! I have taken to the sofa with my staylace[6] cut, and have lain there hours, insensible, with my head over the side, and my hair all down, and my feet I don't know where—"

◀ *Why is Camilla upset with Matthew?*

("Much higher than your head, my love," said Mr. Camilla.)

"I have gone off into that state, hours and hours, on account of Matthew's strange and inexplicable conduct, and nobody has thanked me."

"Really I must say I should think not!" interposed the grave lady.

"You see, my dear," added Miss Sarah Pocket (a <u>blandly</u> vicious personage), "the question to put to yourself is, who did you expect to thank you, my love?"

---

6. **staylace.** Lace to hold together clothing

| Words For Everyday Use | con • sol • a • to • ry (kən säl´ə tôr´ē) *adj.,* comforting | fer • ment • ing (fər ment´iŋ) *adj.,* bubbling up |
| | cor • ru • gat • ed (kôr´ə gāt´əd) *adj.,* wrinkled | bland • ly (bland´lē) *adv.,* in a dull way |

"Without expecting any thanks, or anything of the sort," resumed Camilla, "I have remained in that state hours and hours, and Raymond is a witness of the extent to which I have choked, and what the total inefficacy of ginger has been, and I have been heard at the pianoforte[7]-tuner's across the street, where the poor mistaken children have even supposed it to be pigeons cooing at a distance—and now to be told—" Here Camilla put her hand to her throat and began to be quite chemical as to the formation of new combinations there.

▶ What does the mention of Matthew's name prompt Miss Havisham to do?

When this same Matthew was mentioned, Miss Havisham stopped me and herself, and stood looking at the speaker. This change had a great influence in bringing Camilla's chemistry to a sudden end.

"Matthew will come and see me at last," said Miss Havisham sternly, "when I am laid on that table. That will be his place—there," striking the table with her stick, "at my head! And yours will be there! And your husband's there! And Sarah Pocket's there! And Georgiana's there! Now you all know where to take your stations when you come to feast upon me. And now go!"

At the mention of each name, she had struck the table with her stick in a new place. She now said, "Walk me, walk me!" and we went on again.

"I suppose there's nothing to be done," exclaimed Camilla, "but comply and depart. It's something to have seen the object of one's love and duty, even for so short a time. I shall think of it with a melancholy satisfaction when I wake up in the night. I wish Matthew could have that comfort, but he sets it at defiance. I am determined not to make a display of my feelings, but it's very hard to be told one wants to feast on one's relations—as if one was a giant—and to be told to go. The bare idea!"

Mr. Camilla interposing, as Mrs. Camilla laid her hand upon her heaving bosom, that lady assumed an unnatural fortitude of manner which I supposed to be expressive of an intention to drop and choke when out of view, and kissing her hand to Miss Havisham, was escorted forth. Sarah Pocket and Georgiana contended who should remain last; but Sarah

---

7. **pianoforte.** Piano

Words For Everyday Use

in • ef • fi • ca • cy (in ef´i kə sē) *n.*, inability to produce the desired effect

for • ti • tude (fôr´tə to͞od´) *n.*, firm courage and strength

con • tend (kən tend´) *vi.*, vie; strive in competition was too knowing to be outdone, and <u>ambled</u> round Georgiana with that artful slipperiness that the latter was obliged to take <u>precedence</u>. Sarah Pocket then made her separate effect of departing with, "Bless you, Miss Havisham dear!" and with a smile of forgiving pity on her walnut-shell countenance for the weaknesses of the rest.

While Estella was away lighting them down, Miss Havisham still walked with her hand on my shoulder, but more and more slowly. At last she stopped before the fire, and said, after muttering and looking at it some seconds:

"This is my birthday, Pip."

I was going to wish her many happy returns, when she lifted her stick.

"I don't suffer it to be spoken of. I don't suffer those who were here just now, or anyone, to speak of it. They come here on the day, but they dare not refer to it."

Of course I made no further effort to refer to it.

"On this day of the year, long before you were born, this heap of decay," stabbing with her crutched stick at the pile of cobwebs on the table, but not touching it, "was brought here. It and I have worn away together. The mice have gnawed at it, and sharper teeth than teeth of mice have gnawed at me."

She held the head of her stick against her heart as she stood looking at the table; she in her once white dress, all yellow and withered; the once white cloth all yellow and withered; everything around in a state to crumble under a touch.

"When the ruin is complete," said she, with a ghastly look, "and when they lay me dead, in my bride's dress on the bride's table—which shall be done, and which will be the finished curse upon him—so much the better if it is done on this day!"

She stood looking at the table as if she stood looking at her own figure lying there. I remained quiet. Estella returned, and she, too, remained quiet. It seemed to me that we continued thus for a long time. In the heavy air of the room, and the heavy darkness that brooded in its remoter corners, I even had an alarming fancy that Estella and I might presently begin to decay.

At length, not coming out of her <u>distraught</u> state by degrees, but in an instant, Miss Havisham said, "Let me see you two play at cards; why have you not begun?" With that,

◄ Why have Miss Havisham's relatives come to visit? How does Miss Havisham feel about this particular day?

◄ For what does Miss Havisham wish?

Words For Everyday Use

am • ble (am´bəl) vi., walk in a leisurely manner
prec • e • dence (pres´ə dəns) n., first place
dis • traught (dis trôt´) adj., very troubled

▶ What does Miss Havisham especially want Pip to notice?

we returned to her room, and sat down as before; I was beggared, as before; and again, as before, Miss Havisham watched us all the time, directed my attention to Estella's beauty, and made me notice it the more by trying her jewels on Estella's breast and hair.

Estella, for her part, likewise treated me as before; except that she did not <u>condescend</u> to speak. When we had played some half-dozen games, a day was appointed for my return, and I was taken down into the yard to be fed in the former dog-like manner. There, too, I was again left to wander about as I liked.

It is not much to the purpose whether a gate in that garden wall which I had scrambled up to peep over on the last occasion was, on that last occasion, open or shut. Enough that I saw no gate then, and that I saw one now. As it stood open, and as I knew that Estella had let the visitors out—for she had returned with the keys in her hand—I strolled into the garden, and strolled all over it. It was quite a wilderness, and there were old melon-frames and cucumber-frames in it, which seemed in their decline to have produced a spontaneous growth of weak attempts at pieces of old hats and boots, with now and then a weedy offshoot into the likeness of a battered saucepan.

▶ Who surprises Pip in the window?

When I had exhausted the garden and a greenhouse with nothing in it but a fallen-down grape-vine and some bottles, I found myself in the dismal corner upon which I had looked out of window. Never questioning for a moment that the house was now empty, I looked in at another window, and found myself, to my great surprise, exchanging a broad stare with a pale young gentleman with red eyelids and light hair.

This pale young gentleman quickly disappeared, and reappeared beside me. He had been at his books when I had found myself staring at him, and I now saw that he was inky.

"Halloa!" said he, "young fellow!"

Halloa being a general observation which I had usually observed to be best answered by itself, I said, "Halloa!" politely omitting young fellow.

"Who let *you* in?" said he.

"Miss Estella."

"Who gave you leave to prowl about?"

"Miss Estella."

Words For Everyday Use

con • de • scend (kän′də send′) *vi.*, lower oneself

"Come and fight," said the pale young gentleman.

What could I do but follow him? I have often asked myself the question since; but what else could I do? His manner was so final, and I was so astonished, that I followed where he led, as if I had been under a spell.

"Stop a minute, though," he said, wheeling round before we had gone many paces. "I ought to give you a reason for fighting, too. There it is!" In a most irritating manner he instantly slapped his hands against one another, daintily flung one of his legs up behind him, pulled my hair, slapped his hands again, dipped his head, and butted it into my stomach.

The bull-like proceeding last mentioned, besides that it was unquestionably to be regarded in the light of a <u>liberty</u>, was particularly disagreeable just after bread and meat. I therefore hit out at him, and was going to hit out again, when he said, "Aha! Would you?" and began dancing backwards and forwards in a manner quite unparalleled within my limited experience.

"Laws of the game!" said he. Here, he skipped from his left leg on to his right. "Regular rules!" Here, he skipped from his right leg on to his left. "Come to the ground, and go through the preliminaries!" Here, he dodged backwards and forwards, and did all sorts of things while I looked helplessly at him.

I was secretly afraid of him when I saw him so <u>dexterous</u>; but I felt morally and physically convinced that his light head of hair could have had no business in the pit of my stomach, and that I had a right to consider it irrelevant when so <u>obtruded</u> on my attention. Therefore, I followed him, without a word, to a retired nook of the garden formed by the junction of two walls and screened by some rubbish. On his asking me if I was satisfied with the ground, and on my replying Yes, he begged my leave[8] to absent himself for a moment, and quickly returned with a bottle of water and a sponge dipped in vinegar. "Available for both," he said, placing these against the wall. And then fell to pulling off, not only his jacket and waistcoat, but his shirt too, in a manner at once lighthearted, businesslike, and bloodthirsty.

Although he did not look very healthy—having pimples on his face, and a breaking out on his mouth—these dreadful

◄ What does the young man want Pip to do?

---

8. **begged my leave.** Asked my permission

Words For Everyday Use	**lib • er • ty** (lib´ər tē) *n.*, action that is too free or too bold
	dex • ter • ous (deks´tər əs) *adj.*, skilled in the use of hands or body
	ob • trude (əb tro͞od´) *vt.*, force upon others unwanted

preparations quite appalled me. I judged him to be about my own age, but he was much taller, and he had a way of spinning himself about that was full of appearance. For the rest, he was a young gentleman in a gray suit (when not denuded[9] for battle), with his elbows, knees, wrists, and heels considerably in advance of the rest of him as to development.

▶ *What surprises Pip?*

My heart failed me when I saw him squaring at me with every demonstration of mechanical nicety, and eyeing my anatomy as if he were minutely choosing his bone. I never have been so surprised in my life as I was when I let out the first blow, and saw him lying on his back, looking up at me with a bloody nose and his face exceedingly foreshortened.

But, he was on his feet directly, and after sponging himself with a great show of dexterity, began squaring again. The second greatest surprise I have ever had in my life was seeing him on his back again, looking up at me out of a black eye.

His spirit inspired me with great respect. He seemed to have no strength, and he never once hit me hard, and he was always knocked down; but, he would be up again in a moment sponging himself or drinking out of the water bottle, with the greatest satisfaction in seconding himself according to form, and then came at me with an air and a show that made me believe he really was going to do for me at last. He got heavily bruised, for I am sorry to record that the more I hit him, the harder I hit him; but, he came up again and again and again, until at last he got a bad fall with the back of his head against the wall.

▶ *What is the outcome of the fight? How does Pip feel about it?*

Even after that crisis in our affairs, he got up and turned round and round confusedly a few times, not knowing where I was; but finally went on his knees to his sponge and threw it up: at the same time panting out, "That means you have won."

He seemed so brave and innocent that, although I had not proposed the contest, I felt but a gloomy satisfaction in my victory. Indeed, I go so far as to hope that I regarded myself while dressing as a species of savage young wolf, or other wild beast. However, I got dressed, darkly wiping my <u>sanguinary</u> face at intervals, and I said, "Can I help you?" and he said, "No thankee," and I said, "Good afternoon," and *he* said, "Same to you."

---

9. **denuded.** Stripped of clothing

Words For Everyday Use

san • gui • nar • y (saŋ´gwi ner´ē) *adj.,* bloodstained

When I got into the courtyard, I found Estella waiting with the keys. But she neither asked me where I had been, nor why I had kept her waiting; and there was a bright flush upon her face, as though something had happened to delight her. Instead of going straight to the gate too, she stepped back into the passage, and beckoned me.

"Come here! You may kiss me if you like."

I kissed her cheek as she turned it to me. I think I would have gone through a great deal to kiss her cheek. But I felt that the kiss was given to the coarse common boy as a piece of money might have been, and that it was worth nothing.

◀ *Does the kiss satisfy Pip? Why, or why not?*

What with the birthday visitors, and what with the cards, and what with the fight, my stay had lasted so long that, when I neared home, the light on the spit of sand off the point on the marshes was gleaming against a black night sky, and Joe's furnace was flinging a path of fire across the road.

CHAPTER 12

▶ Why is Pip
uneasy?

My mind grew very uneasy on the subject of the pale young gentleman. The more I thought of the fight, and recalled the pale young gentleman on his back in various stages of puffy and incrimsoned[1] countenance, the more certain it appeared that something would be done to me. I felt that the pale young gentleman's blood was on my head, and that the law would avenge it. Without having any definite idea of the penalties I had <u>incurred</u>, it was clear to me that village boys could not go stalking about the country, <u>ravaging</u> the houses of gentlefolks and pitching into the studious youth of England, without laying themselves open to severe punishment. For some days, I even kept close at home, and looked out at the kitchen door with the greatest caution and <u>trepidation</u> before going on an errand, lest the officers of the county jail should pounce upon me. The pale young gentleman's nose had stained my trousers, and I tried to wash out that evidence of my guilt in the dead of night. I had cut my knuckles against the pale young gentleman's teeth, and I twisted my imagination into a thousand tangles, as I devised incredible ways of accounting for that damnatory[2] circumstance when I should be hailed before the judges.

▶ When is he most
afraid?

When the day came round for my return to the scene of the deed of violence, my terrors reached their height. Whether myrmidons[3] of justice, specially sent down from London, would be lying in ambush behind the gate? Whether Miss Havisham, preferring to take personal vengeance for an outrage done to her house, might rise in those grave-clothes of hers, draw a pistol, and shoot me dead? Whether <u>suborned</u> boys—a numerous band of mercenaries[4]—might be engaged to fall upon me in the brewery, and cuff me until I was no more? It was high testimony to my confidence in the spirit of the pale young gentleman that I never imagined *him* <u>accessory</u> to these retaliations; they always came into my mind as the acts of injudicious relatives of his, goaded on by

1. **incrimsoned.** Red
2. **damnatory.** Condemning
3. **myrmidons.** Unquestioning warriors
4. **mercenaries.** Soldiers serving for pay in a foreign army

Words For Everyday Use

in • cur (in kʉr´) *vt.*, bring upon oneself
rav • age (rav´ij) *vt.*, destroy violently
trep • i • da • tion (trep´ə dā´shən) *n.*, fearful uncertainty

sub • orned (sə bôrd´) *adj.*, urged to do something illegal; bribed
ac • ces • so • ry (ək ses´ər ē) *adj.*, helping in an unlawful act

the state of his <u>visage</u> and an indignant sympathy with the family features.

However, go to Miss Havisham's I must, and go I did. And behold! nothing came of the late struggle. It was not <u>alluded</u> to in any way, and no pale young gentleman was to be discovered on the premises. I found the same gate open, and I explored the garden, and even looked in at the windows of the detached house; but my view was suddenly stopped by the closed shutters within, and all was lifeless. Only in the corner where the combat had taken place could I detect any evidence of the young gentleman's existence. There were traces of his gore in that spot, and I covered them with garden-mold[5] from the eye of man.

On the broad landing between Miss Havisham's own room and that other room in which the long table was laid out, I saw a garden chair—a light chair on wheels, that you pushed from behind. It had been placed there since my last visit, and I entered, that same day, on a regular occupation of pushing Miss Havisham in this chair (when she was tired of walking with her hand upon my shoulder) round her own room, and across the landing, and round the other room. Over and over and over again, we would make these journeys, and sometimes they would last as long as three hours at a stretch. I insensibly fall into a general mention of these journeys as numerous, because it was at once settled that I should return every alternate day at noon for these purposes, and because I am now going to sum up a period of at least eight or ten months.

As we began to be more used to one another, Miss Havisham talked more to me, and asked me such questions as what had I learnt and what was I going to be? I told her I was going to be apprenticed to Joe, I believed; and I enlarged upon my knowing nothing and wanting to know everything, in the hope that she might offer some help towards that desirable end. But, she did not; on the contrary, she seemed to prefer my being ignorant. Neither did she ever give me any money—or anything but my daily dinner—nor even stipulate that I should be paid for my services.

Estella was always about, and always let me in and out, but never told me I might kiss her again. Sometimes, she would

◀ *What happens when he returns?*

◀ *How does Miss Havisham's behavior toward Pip change? What does he hope for? Does Miss Havisham seem likely to give this sort of help? Why, or why not?*

---

5. **garden-mold.** Soil

Words For Everyday Use

vis • age (vis´ij) *n.,* face
al • lude (ə lo͞od´) *vi.,* refer in an indirect way

coldly tolerate me; sometimes, she would condescend to me; sometimes, she would be quite familiar with me; sometimes, she would tell me energetically that she hated me. Miss Havisham would often ask me in a whisper, or when we were alone, "Does she grow prettier and prettier, Pip?" And when I said Yes (for indeed she did), would seem to enjoy it greedily. Also, when we played at cards, Miss Havisham would look on, with a miserly relish of Estella's moods, whatever they were. And sometimes, when her moods were so many and so contradictory of one another that I was puzzled what to say or do, Miss Havisham would embrace her with lavish fondness, murmuring something in her ear that sounded like, "Break their hearts my pride and hope, break their hearts and have no mercy!"

► What does Miss Havisham encourage Estella to do?

There was a song Joe used to hum fragments of at the forge, of which the burden was Old Clem.[6] This was not a very ceremonious way of rendering <u>homage</u> to a patron saint, but I believe Old Clem stood in that relation towards smiths. It was a song that imitated the measure of beating upon iron, and was a mere lyrical excuse for the introduction of Old Clem's respected name. Thus, you were to hammer boys round—Old Clem! With a thump and a sound—Old Clem! Beat it out, beat it out—Old Clem! With a clink for the stout—Old Clem! Blow the fire, blow the fire—Old Clem! Roaring dryer, soaring higher—Old Clem! One day soon after the appearance of the chair, Miss Havisham suddenly saying to me, with the impatient movement of her fingers, "There, there, there! Sing!" I was surprised into crooning this ditty[7] as I pushed her over the floor. It happened so to catch her fancy that she took it up in a low brooding voice, as if she were singing in her sleep. After that, it became customary with us to have it as we moved about, and Estella would often join in; though the whole strain was so <u>subdued</u>, even when there were three of us, that it made less noise in the grim old house than the lightest breath of wind.

► What does Pip ask the reader to consider?

What could I become with these surroundings? How could my character fail to be influenced by them? Is it to be

---

6. **Old Clem.** Chorus sung in procession on St. Clement's Day, November 23
7. **ditty.** Song

Words For Everyday Use

hom • age (häm´ij) *n.,* action performed to show honor

sub • dued (səb do͞od´) *adj.,* softened; quiet; kept back

wondered at if my thoughts were dazed, as my eyes were, when I came out into the natural sunlight from the misty yellow rooms?

Perhaps I might have told Joe about the pale young gentleman, if I had not previously been betrayed into those enormous inventions to which I had confessed. Under the circumstances, I felt that Joe could hardly fail to discern in the pale young gentleman an appropriate passenger to be put into the black velvet coach; therefore, I said nothing of him. Besides, that shrinking from having Miss Havisham and Estella discussed which had come upon me in the beginning grew much more potent as time went on. I reposed complete confidence in no one but Biddy; but I told poor Biddy everything. Why it came natural to me to do so, and why Biddy had a deep concern in everything I told her, I did not know then, though I think I know now.

◄ *What is special about Pip's relationship with Biddy?*

Meanwhile, councils went on in the kitchen at home, <u>fraught</u> with almost insupportable aggravation to my exasperated spirit. That ass, Pumblechook, used often to come over of a night for the purpose of discussing my prospects with my sister; and I really do believe (to this hour with less penitence than I ought to feel) that if these hands could have taken a linch-pin[8] out of his chaise-cart, they would have done it. The miserable man was a man of that confined <u>stolidity</u> of mind that he could not discuss my prospects without having me before him—as it were, to operate upon—and he would drag me up from my stool (usually by the collar) where I was quiet in a corner, and, putting me before the fire as if I were going to be cooked, would begin by saying, "Now, mum, here is this boy! Here is this boy which you brought up by hand. Hold up your head, boy, and be forever grateful unto them which so did do. Now, mum, with respections[9] to this boy!" And then he would rumple my hair the wrong way—which from my earliest remembrance, as already hinted, I have in my soul denied the right of any fellow creature to do—and would hold me before him by the sleeve: a spectacle of <u>imbecility</u> only to be equalled by himself.

---

8. **linch-pin.** Pin that goes through the end of an axle to keep the wheel from coming off
9. **respections.** Respect

Words For Everyday Use

fraught (frôt) *adj.,* filled

sto • lid • i • ty (stə lid′ə tē) *n.,* emotionlessness

im • be • cil • i • ty (im′bə sil′ə tē) *n.,* stupidity

▶ *What angers Pip about his sister's and Pumblechook's behavior?*

Then he and my sister would pair off in such nonsensical speculations about Miss Havisham, and about what she would do with me and for me, that I used to want—quite painfully—to burst into spiteful tears, fly at Pumblechook, and pummel him all over. In these dialogues, my sister spoke to me as if she were morally wrenching one of my teeth out at every reference; while Pumblechook himself, self-constituted my patron, would sit supervising me with a <u>depreciatory</u> eye, like the architect of my fortunes who thought himself engaged on a very <u>unremunerative</u> job.

▶ *What role does Joe take in the discussion? What does he want for Pip?*

In these discussions, Joe bore no part. But he was often talked at, while they were in progress, by reason of Mrs. Joe's perceiving that he was not favorable to my being taken from the forge. I was fully old enough now to be apprenticed to Joe, and when Joe sat with the poker on his knees thoughtfully raking out the ashes between the lower bars, my sister would so distinctly <u>construe</u> that innocent action into opposition on his part that she would dive at him, take the poker out of his hands, shake him, and put it away. There was a most irritating end to every one of these debates. All in a moment, with nothing to lead up to it, my sister would stop herself in a yawn, and catching sight of me as it were <u>incidentally</u>, would swoop upon me with, "Come! there's enough of *you! You* get along to bed; *you*'ve given trouble enough for one night, I hope!" As if I had besought[10] them as a favor to bother my life out.

We went on in this way for a long time, and it seemed likely that we should continue to go on in this way for a long time, when, one day, Miss Havisham stopped short as she and I were walking—she leaning on my shoulder—and said, with some displeasure:

"You are growing tall, Pip!"

I thought it best to hint, through the medium of a meditative look, that this might be occasioned by circumstances over which I had no control.

She said no more at the time; but she presently stopped and looked at me again; and presently again; and after that, looked frowning and moody. On the next day of my attendance, when our usual exercise was over, and I had landed

---

10. **besought.** Asked

Words For Everyday Use

de • pre • ci • a • to • ry (di prē´shē ə tôr´ē) *adj.,* belittling

un • re • mu • ner • a • tive (un ri myoo´ nə rāt´iv) *adj.,* unprofitable

con • strue (kən stroo´) *vt.,* interpret

in • ci • den • tal • ly (in´si dent´ lē) *adv.,* by chance; as of little importance her at her dressing table, she stayed me with a movement of her impatient fingers:

"Tell me the name again of that blacksmith of yours."

"Joe Gargery, ma'am."

"Meaning the master you were to be apprenticed to?"

"Yes, Miss Havisham."

"You had better be apprenticed at once. Would Gargery come here with you, and bring your indentures,[11] do you think?"

◄ Why does Miss Havisham ask that Joe visit?

I signified that I had no doubt he would take it as an honor to be asked.

"Then let him come."

"At any particular time, Miss Havisham?"

"There, there! I know nothing about times. Let him come soon, and come alone with you."

When I got home at night, and delivered this message for Joe, my sister "went on the rampage" in a more alarming degree than at any previous period. She asked me and Joe whether we supposed she was doormats under our feet, and how we dared to use her so, and what company we graciously thought she *was* fit for? When she had exhausted a torrent of such inquiries, she threw a candlestick at Joe, burst into a loud sobbing, got out the dustpan—which was always a very bad sign—put on her coarse apron, and began cleaning up to a terrible extent. Not satisfied with a dry cleaning, she took to a pail and scrubbing-brush, and cleaned us out of house and home, so that we stood shivering in the backyard. It was ten o'clock at night before we ventured to creep in again, and then she asked Joe why he hadn't married a Negress slave at once? Joe offered no answer, poor fellow, but stood feeling his whiskers and looking <u>dejectedly</u> at me, as if he thought it really might have been a better speculation.

◄ What is Mrs. Joe's reaction to the news?

---

11. **indentures.** Papers to become an indentured servant or apprentice

CHAPTER 13

► What are Pip's thoughts about Joe's appearance?

It was a trial to my feelings, on the next day but one, to see Joe arraying himself in his Sunday clothes to accompany me to Miss Havisham's. However, as he thought his court-suit[1] necessary to the occasion, it was not for me tell him that he looked far better in his working dress; the rather, because I knew he made himself so dreadfully uncomfortable entirely on my account, and that it was for me he pulled up his shirt-collar so very high behind, that it made the hair on the crown of his head stand up like a tuft of feathers.

At breakfast-time, my sister declared her intention of going to town with us, and being left at Uncle Pumblechook's, and called for "when we had done with our fine ladies"—a way of putting the case from which Joe appeared inclined to augur[2] the worst. The forge was shut up for the day, and Joe inscribed in chalk upon the door (as it was his custom to do on the very rare occasions when he was not at work) the monosyllable HOUT, accompanied by a sketch of an arrow supposed to be flying in the direction he had taken.

► Why does Mrs. Joe bring so many items into town?

We walked to town, my sister leading the way in a very large beaver bonnet, and carrying a basket like the Great Seal of England[3] in plaited straw, a pair of pattens,[4] a spare shawl, and an umbrella, though it was a fine bright day. I am not quite clear whether these articles were carried <u>penitentially</u> or <u>ostentatiously</u>; but, I rather think they were displayed as articles of property—much as Cleopatra or any other sovereign lady on the rampage might exhibit her wealth in a pageant or procession.

When we came to Pumblechook's, my sister bounced in and left us. As it was almost noon, Joe and I held straight on to Miss Havisham's house. Estella opened the gate as usual, and, the moment she appeared, Joe took his hat off and stood weighing it by the brim in both his hands, as if he had

---

1. **court-suit.** Fancy or best suit
2. **augur.** Foretell
3. **Great Seal of England.** Design placed on government documents to prove their genuineness; the comparison may refer to the complexity of the pattern on the basket or it may mean Mrs. Joe carried her basket with a purposeful, official attitude.
4. **pattens.** Overshoes raised on rings to keep shoes out of the mud

Words
For
Everyday
Use

pen • i • ten • tial • ly (pen´i ten´shə lē) *adv.*, expressing a sin or regret

os • ten • ta • tious • ly (äs´tən ta´shəs lē) *adv.*, with a showy display of wealth some urgent reason in his mind for being particular to half a quarter of an ounce.

Estella took no notice of either of us, but led us the way that I knew so well. I followed next to her, and Joe came last. When I looked back at Joe in the long passage, he was still weighing his hat with the greatest care, and was coming after us in long strides on the tips of his toes.

Estella told me we were both to go in, so I took Joe by the coat-cuff and conducted him into Miss Havisham's presence. She was seated at her dressing table, and looked round at us immediately.

"Oh!" said she to Joe. "You are the husband of the sister of this boy?"

I could hardly have imagined dear old Joe looking so unlike himself or so like some extraordinary bird, standing, as he did, speechless, with his tuft of feathers ruffled, and his mouth open as if he wanted a worm.

◄ *How does Joe show his discomfort?*

"You are the husband," repeated Miss Havisham, "of the sister of this boy?"

It was very aggravating; but, throughout the interview, Joe persisted in addressing me instead of Miss Havisham.

"Which I meantersay, Pip," Joe now observed, in a manner that was at once expressive of forcible argumentation, strict confidence, and great politeness, "as I hup and married your sister, and I were at the time what you might call (if you was any ways inclined) a single man."

"Well!" said Miss Havisham. "And you have reared the boy, with the intention of taking him for your apprentice; is that so, Mr. Gargery?"

"You know, Pip," replied Joe, "as you and me were ever friends, and it were looked forrard to betwixt us, as being calc'lated to lead to larks. Not but what, Pip, if you had ever made objections to the business—such as its being open to black and sut,[5] or such-like—not but what they would have been attended to, don't you see?"

"Has the boy," said Miss Havisham, "ever made any objection? Does he like the trade?"

"Which it is well beknown to yourself, Pip," returned Joe, strengthening his former mixture of argumentation, confidence, and politeness, "that it were the wish of your own hart." (I saw the idea suddenly break upon him that he would adapt his epitaph[6] to the occasion, before he went on to say) "And there weren't no objection on your part, and Pip it were the great wish of your hart!"

---

5. **black and sut.** Dirt and soot from a blacksmith's forge
6. **epitaph.** Inscription on a tomb in memory of the person buried there

It was quite in vain for me to endeavor to make him sensible that he ought to speak to Miss Havisham. The more I made faces and gestures to him to do it, the more confidential, argumentative, and polite he persisted in being to me.

"Have you brought his indentures with you?" asked Miss Havisham.

"Well, Pip, you know," replied Joe, as if that were a little unreasonable, "you yourself see me put 'em in my 'at, and therefore you know as they are here." With which he took them out, and gave them, not to Miss Havisham, but to me. I am afraid I was ashamed of the dear good fellow—I *know* I was ashamed of him—when I saw that Estella stood at the back of Miss Havisham's chair, and that her eyes laughed mischievously. I took the indentures out of his hand and gave them to Miss Havisham.

▶ How does Pip react to Joe's behavior?

"You expected," said Miss Havisham, as she looked them over, "no premium with the boy?"

"Joe!" I <u>remonstrated</u>; for he made no reply at all. "Why don't you answer—"

"Pip," returned Joe, cutting me short as if he were hurt, "which I meantersay that were not a question requiring a answer betwixt yourself and me, and which you know the answer to be full well No. You know it to be No, Pip, and wherefore should I say it?"

Miss Havisham glanced at him as if she understood what he really was better than I had thought possible, seeing what he was there, and took up a little bag from the table beside her.

▶ Why does Miss Havisham give Joe money?

"Pip has earned a premium here," she said, "and here it is. There are five-and-twenty guineas[7] in this bag. Give it to your master, Pip."

As if he were absolutely out of his mind with the wonder awakened in him by her strange figure and the strange room, Joe, even at this pass, persisted in addressing me.

▶ What is Joe trying to say?

"This is very liberal on your part, Pip," said Joe, "and it is as such received and grateful welcome, though never looked for, far nor near nor nowheres. And now, old chap," said Joe, conveying to me a sensation, first of burning and then of freezing, for I felt as if that familiar expression were applied to Miss Havisham; "and now, old chap, may we do our duty! May you

---

7. **guineas.** Gold coins equal to twenty-one shillings

Words For Everyday Use

re • mon • strate (ri män′strāt) *vi.,* protest

and me do our duty, both on us by one and another, and by them which your liberal present—have—conweyed—to be—for the satisfaction of mind—of—them as never—" here Joe showed that he felt he had fallen into frightful difficulties, until he triumphantly rescued himself with the words, "and from myself far be it!" These words had such a round and convincing sound for him that he said them twice.

"Good-bye, Pip!" said Miss Havisham. "Let them out, Estella."

"Am I to come again, Miss Havisham?" I asked.

"No. Gargery is your master now. Gargery! One word!"

Thus calling him back as I went out of the door, I heard her say to Joe, in a distinct emphatic voice, "The boy has been a good boy here, and that is his reward. Of course, as an honest man, you will expect no other and no more."

◄ What does Miss Havisham's remark to Joe reveal?

How Joe got out of the room, I have never been able to determine, but I know that when he did get out, he was steadily proceeding upstairs instead of coming down, and was deaf to all remonstrances until I went after him and laid hold of him. In another minute we were outside the gate, and it was locked, and Estella was gone. When we stood in the daylight alone again, Joe backed up against a wall, and said to me, "Astonishing!" And there he remained so long, saying "Astonishing" at intervals so often that I began to think his senses were never coming back. At length he prolonged his remark into "Pip, I do assure *you* this is as-TON-ishing!" and so, by degrees, became conversational and able to walk away.

I have reason to think that Joe's intellects were brightened by the encounter they had passed through, and that on our way to Pumblechook's, he invented a subtle and deep <u>design</u>. My reason is to be found in what took place in Mr. Pumblechook's parlor: where, on our presenting ourselves, my sister sat in conference with that detested seedsman.

"Well!" cried my sister, addressing us both at once. "And what's happened to *you?* I wonder you condescend to come back to such poor society as this, I am sure I do!"

"Miss Havisham," said Joe, with a fixed look at me, like an effort of remembrance, "made it wery partick'ler that we should give her—were it compliments or respects, Pip?"

◄ What lies does Joe tell his wife? How does she react to these lies?

"Compliments," I said.

"Which that were my own belief," answered Joe—"her compliments to Mrs. J. Gargery—"

Words For Everyday Use

de • sign (di zīn´) *n.,* plan

"Much good they'll do me!" observed my sister, but rather gratified, too.

"And wishing," pursued Joe, with another fixed look at me, like another effort to remembrance, "that the state of Miss Havisham's 'elth were sitch as would have—allowed, were it, Pip?"

"Of her having the pleasure," I added.

"Of ladies' company," said Joe. And drew a long breath.

"Well!" cried my sister, with a <u>mollified</u> glance at Mr. Pumblechook. "She might have had the politeness to send that message at first, but it's better late than never. And what did she give young Rantipole[7] here?"

"She giv' him," said Joe, "nothing."

Mrs. Joe was going to break out, but Joe went on.

"What she giv'," said Joe, "she giv' to his friends. 'And by his friends,' were her explanation, 'I mean into the hands of his sister, Mrs. J. Gargery.' Them were her words, 'Mrs. J. Gargery.' She mayn't have know'd," added Joe, with an appearance of reflection, "whether it were Joe or Jorge."

My sister looked at Pumblechook, who smoothed the elbows of his wooden armchair, and nodded at her and at the fire, as if he had known all about it beforehand.

"And how much have you got?" asked my sister, laughing. Positively, laughing!

"What would present company say to ten pound?" demanded Joe.

"They'd say," returned my sister, curtly, "pretty well. Not too much, but pretty well."

"It's more than that, then," said Joe.

That fearful impostor, Pumblechook, immediately nodded, and said, as he rubbed the arms of his chair: "It's more than that, mum."

"Why, you don't mean to say—" began my sister.

"Yes I do, mum," said Pumblechook; "but wait a bit. Go on, Joseph. Good in you! Go on!"

"What would present company say," proceeded Joe, "to twenty pound?"

"Handsome would be the word," returned my sister.

"Well, then," said Joe, "It's more than twenty pound."

---

8. **young Rantipole.** Wild and ill-behaved person; possibly a reference to a story in which a woman gives gifts to good children, but gives no reward to the Rantipole children, who act good in her presence but badly while out of it

Words
For
Everyday
Use

mol • li • fied (mäl´ə fīd´) *adj.*, less severe; appeased

That <u>abject</u> hypocrite, Pumblechook, nodded again, and said with a patronizing laugh, "It's more than that, mum. Good again! Follow her up, Joseph!"

"Then to make an end of it," said Joe, delightedly handing the bag to my sister; "it's five-and-twenty pound."

◀ To whom does the money belong? Why does Joe give it to his wife?

"It's five-and-twenty pound, mum," echoed that basest of swindlers, Pumblechook, rising to shake hands with her; "and it's no more than your merits (as I said when my opinion was asked), and I wish you joy of the money!"

If the villain had stopped here, his case would have been sufficiently awful, but he blackened his guilt by proceeding to take me into custody, with a right of patronage that left all his former criminality far behind.

"Now you see, Joseph and wife," said Pumblechook, as he took me by the arm above the elbow, "I am one of them that always go right through with what they've begun. This boy must be bound out of hand.[9] That's *my* way. Bound out of hand."

◀ What decision does Pumblechook make for Pip and Joe?

"Goodness knows, Uncle Pumblechook," said my sister (grasping the money), "we're deeply beholden[10] to you."

"Never mind me, mum," returned that diabolical[11] corn-chandler. "A pleasure's a pleasure all the world over. But this boy, you know; we must have him bound. I said I'd see to it—to tell you the truth."

The justices were sitting in the Town Hall near at hand, and we at once went over to have me bound apprentice to Joe in the magisterial[12] presence. I say, we went over, but I was pushed over by Pumblechook, exactly as if I had that moment picked a pocket or fired a rick;[13] indeed, it was the general impression in court that I had been taken red-handed, for, as Pumblechook shoved me before him through the crowd, I heard some people say, "What's he done?" and others, "He's a young 'un, too, but looks bad, don't he?" One person of mild and benevolent aspect even gave me a tract[14] ornamented with a woodcut of a <u>malevolent</u> young man

◀ What do people think of Pip when they see him pushed into Town Hall by Pumblechook?

---

9. **bound out of hand.** Pip must be formally bound as an apprentice by the courts
10. **beholden.** Indebted
11. **diabolical.** Devilish
12. **magisterial.** Of the magistrates, civil officers who administer the law
13. **fired a rick.** Set on fire a stack of straw
14. **tract.** Pamphlet on a religious subject

Words For Everyday Use

ab • ject (ab´jekt) *adj.,* miserable; wretched

ma • lev • o • lent (mə lev´ə lənt) *adj.,* wishing evil or harm to others fitted up with a perfect sausage-shop of fetters, and entitled, TO BE READ IN MY CELL.

The Hall was a queer place, I thought, with higher pews in it than a church—and with people hanging over the pews looking on—and with mighty justices (one with a powdered head) leaning back in chairs, with folded arms, or taking snuff, or going to sleep, or writing, or reading the newspapers—and with some shining black portraits on the walls, which my unartistic eye regarded as a composition of hardbake and sticking plaster.[15] Here, in a corner, my indentures were duly signed and <u>attested</u>, and I was "bound;" Mr. Pumblechook holding me all the while as if we had looked in on our way to the scaffold to have those little <u>preliminaries</u> disposed of.

When we had come out again, and had got rid of the boys who had been put into great spirits by the expectation of seeing me publicly tortured, and who were much disappointed to find that my friends were merely rallying round me, we went back to Pumblechook's. And there my sister became so excited by the twenty-five guineas that nothing would serve her but we must have a dinner out of that <u>windfall</u> at the Blue Boar, and that Mr. Pumblechook must go over in his chaise-cart, and bring the Hubbles and Mr. Wopsle.

► What does Mrs. Joe do with the money?

It was agreed to be done, and a most melancholy day I passed. For, it <u>inscrutably</u> appeared to stand to reason, in the minds of the whole company, that I was an <u>excrescence</u> on the entertainment. And to make it worse, they all asked me from time to time—in short, whenever they had nothing else to do—why I didn't enjoy myself. And what could I possibly do then but say that I *was* enjoying myself—when I wasn't!

However, they were grown up and had their own way, and made the most of it. That swindling Pumblechook, exalted into the <u>beneficent</u> contriver of the whole occasion, actually took the top of the table; and when he addressed them on the subject of my being bound, and had fiendishly congratulated them on my being liable to imprisonment if I played at cards, drank strong liquors, kept late hours or bad company, or indulged in other vagaries[16] which the form of my indentures appeared to contemplate as next to inevitable, he placed me standing on a chair beside him to illustrate his remarks.

---

15. **hardbake and sticking plaster.** Almond toffee and adhesive for covering a wound
16. **vagaries.** Odd conduct or actions

Words For Everyday Use

at • test (ə test´) *vt.*, certify; declare valid

pre • lim • i • na • ry (pri lim´ ə ner´ē) *n.*, step leading up to the main procedure

wind • fall (wind´fôl) *n.*, unexpected gain

in • scru • ta • bly (in skro͞ot´ə blē) *adv.*, mysteriously; in a way not easily understood

ex • cres • cence (eks kres´əns) *n.*, abnormal or disfiguring outgrowth

be • ne • fi • cent (bə nef´ə sənt) *adj.*, doing good

My only other remembrances of the great festival are that they wouldn't let me go to sleep, but whenever they saw me dropping off, woke me up and told me to enjoy myself; that, rather late in the evening Mr. Wopsle gave us Collins's ode, and threw his bloodstain'd sword in thunder down, with such effect that a waiter came in and said, "The commercials[17] underneath sent up their compliments, and it wasn't the Tumblers' Arms"; that they were all in excellent spirits on the road home, and sang "O Lady Fair!" Mr. Wopsle taking the bass, and asserting with a tremendously strong voice (in reply to the inquisitive bore who leads that piece of music in a most <u>impertinent</u> manner, by wanting to know all about everybody's private affairs) that *he* was the man with his white locks flowing, and that he was upon the whole the weakest pilgrim going.

Finally, I remember that when I got into my little bedroom, I was truly wretched, and had a strong conviction on me that I should never like Joe's trade. I had liked it once, but once was not now.

◄ *How does Pip feel about becoming indentured?*

---

17. **commercials.** Short for commercial travelers; traveling salesmen often had their own gathering rooms at inns.

Words For Everyday Use

im • per • ti • nent (im purt´'n ənt) *adj.*, disrespectful; insolent

Responding to the Selection

If you were in Pip's position and were sent to Miss Havisham's each week, how do you think you would react? What would you think, say, and do the first time you met Miss Havisham and Estella? How would your behavior and thoughts change as you became more familiar with them?

Reviewing the Selection

Recalling and Interpreting

1. **R:** What does Joe reveal about his past when Pip asks him why he never learned to read? What good things does Joe have to say about his father and his wife? How does Pip feel about Joe after hearing his life story?

2. **I:** In what way does Joe's past explain his willingness to tolerate his wife's harshness? What does the fact that Joe tries to see the good in his father and his wife reveal about him as a character? How do you think Pip's life would have been different if Joe had not married Pip's sister?

3. **R:** What is unusual about Miss Havisham and her surroundings? What does she want Pip to do during his visits? Describe how Miss Havisham encourages Estella to behave toward Pip. What does she want Estella to do? What lies does Pip tell his sister and Mr. Pumblechook about his experiences? When Pip reveals the truth to Joe, what advice about being "common" versus "oncommon," does Joe give Pip?

4. **I:** Explain what you think the great tragedy of Miss Havisham's life is. In what way is Miss Havisham using Estella? In what way is she using Pip? Why does Pip tell these lies rather than the truth? What does this reason reveal about his character and the way he is changing? Explain whether Joe's advice is sound.

5. **R:** Whom does Pip meet at the Three Jolly Bargemen? What is the clue to the man's connection to Pip?

6. **I:** Why do you think Pip is upset at seeing this man, even though the man gives him some money?

7. **R:** What expectations do Mrs. Joe and Mr. Pumblechook have about Pip's association with Miss Havisham? What expectations do Camilla, Cousin Raymond, Sarah Pocket, and Georgiana have about Miss Havisham? To what do these people look forward? How does Miss Havisham treat them? What expectations does Joe have about his future with Pip? When Miss Havisham sends Pip back for good

with Joe, what does she give Joe? What does she make very clear to him in private? How does Mrs. Joe feel about this reward? How does Pip feel about it? about his future?

8. **I:** What is Dickens indicating about "Great Expectations" in chapters 7–13? In what way are the expectations, both financial and personal, of various characters undermined? What might Dickens be indicating about counting too much upon expectations?

Synthesizing

9. In what way is Pip changing as a character? What does he hope to become? What is Pip tempted by? How have his feelings toward Joe changed? Explain whether Pip should feel inferior. What good things in his own life is Pip overlooking? Explain which character you think the author believed to be the better person—Joe, Miss Havisham, Estella, or the wealthy relatives who call upon Miss Havisham. What qualities is the author emphasizing as important in a person? What qualities are unimportant?

10. What does the scene at the Three Jolly Bargemen imply about Pip's future? Based on what you know about Pip and his great expectations, predict what kind of relationship might develop between Pip and the convict. Will Pip ever escape the influence of the convict?

Understanding Literature (QUESTIONS FOR DISCUSSION)

1. **Bildungsroman and Archetype.** A *Bildungsroman* is a novel that tells the story of the growth or development of a person from youth to adulthood. *Great Expectations* is commonly considered to be an example of a *Bildungsroman.* An **archetype** is an inherited, often unconscious, ancestral memory or motif that recurs throughout history and literature. One archetypal theme in literature from all places and ages is the fall from a state of innocence to a state of experience. While this loss is sometimes viewed very negatively, as in the story of Adam and Eve's expulsion from the Garden of Eden in the Bible, other times the loss of innocence is viewed as an essential part of the process of growing up. In what way has Pip lost some of his innocence in chapters 7–13? How do you think this experience will affect him as an adult? Explain the attitude Dickens takes toward the loss of innocence. What attitude toward children does he express? toward many adults?

2. **Simile and Foil.** A **simile** is a comparison using *like* or

as. A **foil** is a character whose attributes, or characteristics, contrast with, and therefore throw into relief, the attributes of another character. Dickens describes Estella's approach down the hall in the following manner: "she answered at last, and her light came along the dark passage like a star." Estella's candle (and implicitly Estella herself) is compared to a star. Dickens makes the comparison between Estella and a star even more strongly in this passage because Estella's name means "star." Think about the different attributes of stars. In what way is Estella like one? Biddy's name means "hen." In what way is this name in keeping with her character? In what way is Estella similar to and different from Biddy? In what way do their feelings toward and treatment of Pip differ? Why might these characters be considered foils?

CHAPTER 14

It is a most miserable thing to feel ashamed of home. There may be black ingratitude in the thing and the punishment may be <u>retributive</u> and well deserved; but that it is a miserable thing, I can testify.

Home had never been a very pleasant place to me, because of my sister's temper. But Joe had <u>sanctified</u> it, and I believed in it. I had believed in the best parlor as a most elegant saloon; I had believed in the front door as a mysterious portal of the Temple of State[1] whose solemn opening was attended with a sacrifice of roast fowls; I had believed in the kitchen as a <u>chaste</u> though not magnificent apartment; I had believed in the forge as the glowing road to manhood and independence. Within a single year all this was changed. Now, it was all coarse and common, and I would not have had Miss Havisham and Estella see it on any account.

◄ *What opinion had Pip had of his home? What does he think of it now? Why has his perception of home changed?*

How much of my ungracious condition of mind may have been my own fault, how much Miss Havisham's, how much my sister's, is now of no moment[2] to me or to anyone. The change was made in me; the thing was done. Well or ill done, excusably or inexcusably, it was done.

Once it had seemed to me that when I should at last roll up my shirt-sleeves and go into the forge, Joe's 'prentice, I should be distinguished and happy. Now the reality was in my hold, I only felt that I was dusty with the dust of the small coal, and that I had a weight upon my daily remembrance to which the anvil was a feather. There have been occasions in my later life (I suppose as in most lives) when I have felt for a time as if a thick curtain had fallen on all its interest and romance, to shut me out from anything save dull endurance any more. Never has that curtain dropped so heavy and blank as when my way in life lay stretched out straight before me through the newly-entered road of apprenticeship to Joe.

◄ *What had Pip once thought of the idea of being Joe's apprentice? How does he feel now that he is Joe's apprentice?*

I remember that at a later period of my "time," I used to stand about the churchyard on Sunday evenings, when

---

1. **portal of the Temple of State.** Entrance to a sacred place of worship and ruling
2. **moment.** Importance

Words For Everyday Use

re • trib • u • tive (ri trib´yo͞o tiv) *adj.*, in payment for evil done

sanc • ti • fy (saŋk´tə fī) *vt.*, set apart as holy; purify

chaste (chāst) *adj.*, pure; decent

night was falling, comparing my own perspective with the windy marsh view, and making out some likeness between them by thinking how flat and low both were, and how on both there came an unknown way and dark mist and then the sea. I was quite as <u>dejected</u> on the first working-day of my apprenticeship as in that after-time; but I am glad to know that I never breathed a murmur to Joe while my indentures lasted. It is about the only thing I *am* glad to know of myself in that connection.

▶ What effect does Joe have on Pip?

For, though it includes what I proceed to add, all the merit of what I proceed to add was Joe's. It was not because I was faithful, but because Joe was faithful, that I never ran away and went for a soldier or a sailor. It was not because I had a strong sense of the virtue of <u>industry</u>, but because Joe had a strong sense of the virtue of industry, that I worked with tolerable[3] zeal against the grain.[4] It is not possible to know how far the influence of any amiable honest-hearted duty-doing man flies out into the world, but it is very possible to know how it has touched one's self in going by, and I know right well that any good that intermixed itself with my apprenticeship came of plain contented Joe, and not of restless aspiring discontented me.

▶ What does Pip dread and fear?

What I wanted, who can say? How can *I* say, when I never knew? What I dreaded was that in some unlucky hour I, being at my grimiest and commonest, should lift up my eyes and see Estella looking in at one of the wooden windows of the forge. I was haunted by the fear that she would, sooner or later, find me out, with a black face and hands, doing the coarsest part of my work, and would <u>exult</u> over me and despise me. Often after dark, when I was pulling the bellows for Joe, and we were singing Old Clem, and when the thought how we used to sing it at Miss Havisham's would seem to show me Estella's face in the fire, with her pretty hair fluttering in the wind and her eyes scorning me—often at such a time I would look towards those panels of black night in the wall which the wooden windows then were, and would fancy that I saw her just drawing her face away, and would believe that she had come at last.

---

3. **tolerable.** Fair amount of
4. **against the grain.** Contrary to one's feelings and wishes

---

Words For Everyday Use

de • ject • ed (dē jek′tid) *adj.,* depressed; in low spirits

in • dus • try (in′dəs trē) *n.,* hard work; diligence

ex • ult (eg zult′) *vi.,* rejoice

After that, when we went in to supper, the place and the meal would have a more homely look than ever, and I would feel more ashamed of home than ever, in my own ungracious breast.

◄ Why is Pip even more ashamed upon returning home?

CHAPTER 15

As I was getting too big for Mr. Wopsle's great-aunt's room, my education under that <u>preposterous</u> female terminated. Not, however, until Biddy had imparted to me everything she knew, from the little catalogue of prices, to a comic song she had once bought for a halfpenny. Although the only <u>coherent</u> part of the latter piece of literature were the opening lines,

> When I went to Lunnon[1] town sirs,
>> Too rul loo rul
>> Too rul loo rul
> Wasn't I done very brown sirs?
>> Too rul loo rul
>> Too rul loo rul

—still, in my desire to be wiser, I got this composition by heart with the utmost gravity; nor do I recollect that I questioned its merit, except that I thought (as I still do) the amount of Too rul somewhat in excess of the poetry. In my hunger for information, I made proposals to Mr. Wopsle to bestow some intellectual crumbs upon me;[2] with which he kindly <u>complied</u>. As it turned out, however, that he only wanted me for a dramatic lay-figure,[3] to be contradicted and embraced and wept over and bullied and clutched and stabbed and knocked about in a variety of ways, I soon declined that course of instruction; though not until Mr. Wopsle in his poetic fury had severely mauled me.

Whatever I acquired, I tried to impart to Joe. This statement sounds so well that I cannot in my conscience let it pass unexplained. I wanted to make Joe less ignorant and common, that he might be worthier of my society and less open to Estella's reproach.

The old battery out on the marshes was our place of study, and a broken slate and a short piece of slate pencil were our educational implements: to which Joe always added a pipe of

► *Whom does Pip ask to help him with his studies? What is the result?*

► *What are Pip's motives in teaching Joe?*

---

1. **Lunnon.** London
2. **bestow . . . me.** Teach me a little something
3. **dramatic lay-figure.** Nonprofessional actor

tobacco. I never knew Joe to remember anything from one Sunday to another, or to acquire, under my tuition,[4] any piece of information whatever. Yet he would smoke his pipe at the battery with a far more <u>sagacious</u> air than anywhere else—even with a learned air—as if he considered himself to be advancing immensely. Dear fellow, I hope he did.

It was pleasant and quiet, out there with the sails on the river passing beyond the earthwork,[5] and sometimes, when the tide was low, looking as if they belonged to sunken ships that were still sailing on at the bottom of the water. Whenever I watched the vessels standing out to sea with their white sails spread, I somehow thought of Miss Havisham and Estella; and whenever the light struck aslant, afar off, upon a cloud or sail or green hillside or water-line, it was just the same. Miss Havisham and Estella and the strange house and the strange life appeared to have something to do with everything that was picturesque.

One Sunday when Joe, greatly enjoying his pipe, had so plumed[6] himself on being "most awful dull" that I had given him up for the day, I lay on the earthwork for some time with my chin on my hand, <u>descrying</u> traces of Miss Havisham and Estella all over the prospect, in the sky and in the water, until at last I resolved to mention a thought concerning them that had been much in my head.

"Joe," said I; "don't you think I ought to pay Miss Havisham a visit?"

"Well, Pip," returned Joe, slowly considering. "What for?"

"What for, Joe? What is any visit made for?"

"There is some wisits, p'r'aps," said Joe, "as forever remains open to the question, Pip. But in regard to wisiting Miss Havisham. She might think you wanted something—expected something of her."

"Don't you think I might say that I did not, Joe?"

"You might, old chap," said Joe. "And she might credit it. Similarly, she mightn't."

Joe felt, as I did, that he had made a point there, and he pulled hard at his pipe to keep himself from weakening it by repetition.

◄ *Are the lessons successful?*

◄ *Why doesn't Joe think Pip should visit Miss Havisham?*

---

4. **tuition.** Instruction, teaching
5. **earthwork.** Embankment
6. **plumed.** Prided

Words For Everyday Use

sa • ga • cious (sə gā´shəs) *adj.*, showing sound judgment; wise

de • scry (di skrī´) *vt.*, discover; detect

"You see, Pip," Joe pursued, as soon as he was past that danger, "Miss Havisham done the handsome thing by you. When Miss Havisham done the handsome thing by you, she called me back to say to me as that were all."

"Yes, Joe. I heard her."

"ALL," Joe repeated, very emphatically.

"Yes, Joe. I tell you, I heard her."

"Which I meantersay, Pip, it might be that her meaning were—Make a end on it!—As you was!—Me to the North, and you to the South!—Keep in sunders!"[7]

I had thought of that too, and it was very far from comforting to me to find that he had thought of it; for it seemed to render it more probable.

"But Joe."

"Yes, old chap."

▶ What reason does Pip give for his interest? What does Joe think Pip should do?

"Here am I, getting on in the first year of my time, and, since the day of my being bound I have never thanked Miss Havisham, or asked after her, or shown that I remember her."

"That's true, Pip; and unless you was to turn her out a set of shoes all four round[8]—and which I meantersay as even a set of shoes all four round might not act acceptable as a present in a total wacancy of hoofs—"

"I don't mean that sort of remembrance, Joe; I don't mean a present."

But Joe had got the idea of a present in his head and must harp upon[9] it. "Or even," said he, "if you was helped to knocking her up a new chain for the front door—or say a gross or two of shark-headed screws for general use—or some light fancy article, such as a toasting-fork when she took her muffins—or a gridiron[10] when she took a sprat[11] or such like—"

"I don't mean any present at all, Joe," I interposed.

"Well," said Joe, still harping on it as though I had particularly pressed it, "if I was yourself, Pip, I wouldn't. No, I would *not*. For what's a door-chain when she's got one always up? And shark-headers is open to misrepresentations. And if it was a toasting-fork, you'd go into brass and do yourself no

---

7. **Keep in sunders.** Stay away
8. **turn her out . . . round.** Make her a set of horseshoes
9. **harp upon.** Talk about to an excessive and tedious degree
10. **gridiron.** Framework of metal bars on which to broil meat or fish
11. **sprat.** Small fish

Words For Everyday Use

in • ter • pose (in'tər pōz´) *vt.,* introduce into a conversation credit. And the oncommonest workman can't show himself oncommon in a gridiron—for a gridiron IS a gridiron," said Joe, steadfastly impressing it upon me, as if he were endeavoring to rouse me from a fixed <u>delusion</u>, "and you may haim[12] at what you like, but a gridiron it will come out, either by your leave or again your leave, and you can't help yourself—"

"My dear Joe," I cried, in desperation taking hold of his coat, "don't go on in that way. I never thought of making Miss Havisham any present."

"No, Pip," Joe assented, as if he had been contending for that all along, "and what I say to you is, you are right, Pip."

"Yes, Joe; but what I wanted to say was that, as we are rather slack just now, if you would give me a half-holiday tomorrow, I think I would go uptown and make a call on Miss Est—Havisham."

◄ Why does Pip really want to go?

"Which her name," said Joe, gravely, "ain't Estavisham, Pip, unless she have been rechris'ended."[13]

"I know, Joe, I know. It was slip of mine. What do you think of it, Joe?"

In brief, Joe thought that if I thought well of it, he thought well of it. But, he was particular in stipulating that if I were not received with cordiality, or if I were not encouraged to repeat my visit as a visit which had no <u>ulterior</u> object, but was simply one of gratitude for a favor received, then this experimental trip should have no <u>successor</u>. By these conditions I promised to abide.

◄ To what conditions does Pip agree?

Now Joe kept a journeyman[14] at weekly wages whose name was Orlick. He pretended that his Christian name was Dolge—a clear impossibility—but he was a fellow of that obstinate disposition that I believe him to have been the prey of no delusion in this particular, but wilfully to have imposed that name upon the village as an <u>affront</u> to its understanding. He was a broad-shouldered loose-limbed swarthy fellow of great strength, never in a hurry, and always slouching. He never even seemed to come to his work on purpose, but would slouch in as if by mere accident; and when he went to the Jolly Bargemen to eat his dinner, or went away at night, he would

◄ Who is Orlick? What kind of man is he?

---

12. **haim.** Aim
13. **rechris'ended.** Rechristened; given another name at baptism
14. **journeyman.** Worker qualified to work at his trade after serving his apprenticeship

---

Words For Everyday Use

de • lu • sion (di lo͞oʹzhən) *n.*, false belief

ul • te • ri • or (ul tirʹē ər) *adj.*, beyond what is openly made known

suc • ces • sor (sək sesʹər) *n.*, one that follows another

af • front (ə fruntʹ) *n.*, open insult

slouch out, like Cain or the Wandering Jew,[15] as if he had no idea where he was going, and no intention of ever coming back. He lodged at a sluice-keeper's[16] out on the marshes, and on working-days would come slouching from his hermitage,[17] with his hands in his pockets and his dinner loosely tied in a bundle round his neck and dangling on his back. On Sundays he mostly lay all day on sluice-gates, or stood against ricks and barns. He always slouched, locomotively, with his eyes on the ground; and, when <u>accosted</u> or otherwise required to raise them, he looked up in a half-resentful, half-puzzled way, as though the only thought he ever had was that it was rather an odd and injurious fact that he should never be thinking.

► *Describe the relationship between Pip and Orlick.*

This <u>morose</u> journeyman had no liking for me. When I was very small and timid, he gave me to understand that the Devil lived in a black corner of the forge, and that he knew the fiend very well: also that it was necessary to make up the fire once in seven years with a live boy, and that I might consider myself fuel. When I became Joe's 'prentice, Orlick was perhaps confirmed in some suspicion that I should displace him; howbeit, he liked me still less. Not that he ever said anything, or did anything, openly importing hostility; I only noticed that he always beat his sparks in my direction, and that whenever I sang Old Clem, he came in out of time.

Dolge Orlick was at work and present, next day, when I reminded Joe of my half-holiday. He said nothing at the moment, for he and Joe had just got a piece of hot iron between them, and I was at the bellows; but by-and-by he said, leaning on his hammer:

► *What does Orlick request? Why?*

"Now, master! Sure you're not a-going to favor only one of us. If young Pip has a half-holiday, do as much for Old Orlick." I suppose he was about five-and-twenty, but he usually spoke of himself as an ancient person.

"Why, what'll you do with a half-holiday, if you get it?" said Joe.

"What'll *I* do with it! What'll *he* do with it? I'll do as much with it as *him*," said Orlick.

"As to Pip, he's going uptown," said Joe.

---

15. **Cain or the Wandering Jew.** Cain, oldest son of Adam and Eve who was sent away for murdering his brother; Wandering Jew, Jew condemned by God to wander the earth because of his scornful attitude toward Christ
16. **sluice-keeper's.** Home of the keeper of the watergate
17. **hermitage.** Secluded home or retreat

Words For Everyday Use	
ac • cost (ə kôst´) *vt.*, confront	mo • rose (mə rōs´) *adj.*, sullen

"Well then, as to Old Orlick, *he's* a going uptown," retorted that worthy. "Two can go uptown. Tain't only one wot can go uptown."

"Don't lose your temper," said Joe.

"Shall if I like," growled Orlick. "Some and their uptowning! Now, master! Come. No favoring in this shop. Be a man!"

The master refusing to entertain the subject until the journeyman was in a better temper, Orlick plunged at the furnace, drew out a red-hot bar, made at me with it as if he were going to run it through my body, whisked it round my head, laid it on the anvil, hammered it out—as if it were I, I thought, and the sparks were my spurting blood—and finally said, when he had hammered himself hot and the iron cold, and he again leaned on his hammer:

◀ To what does Joe agree? Why does he wait?

"Now, master!"

"Are you all right now?" demanded Joe.

"Ah! I am all right," said gruff Old Orlick.

"Then, as in general you stick to your work as well as most men," said Joe, "let it be a half-holiday for all."

My sister had been standing silent in the yard, within hearing—she was a most <u>unscrupulous</u> spy and listener—and she instantly looked in at one of the windows.

"Like you, you fool!" said she to Joe, "giving holidays to great idle hulkers like that. You are a rich man, upon my life, to waste wages in that way. I wish *I* was his master!"

"You'd be everybody's master if you durst," retorted Orlick, with an ill-favored grin.

◀ Why is Mrs. Joe upset? What do she and Orlick think of each other?

("Let her alone," said Joe.)

"I'd be a match for all noodles[18] and all rogues," returned my sister, beginning to work herself into a mighty rage. "And I couldn't be a match for the noodles without being a match for your master, who's the dunderheaded[19] king of the noodles. And I couldn't be a match for the rogues without being a match for you, who are the blackest-looking and the worst rogue between this and France. Now!"

"You're a foul shrew,[20] Mother Gargery," growled the journeyman. "If that makes a judge of rogues, you ought to be a good 'un."

---

18. **noodles.** Fools, simpletons
19. **dunderheaded.** Dull-witted
20. **shrew.** Nagging, bad-tempered woman

Words For Everyday Use

un • scru • pu • lous (un skr$\overline{oo}$´pyə ləs) *adj.*, not restrained by ideas of right and wrong

("Let her alone, will you?" said Joe.)

"What did you say?" cried my sister, beginning to scream. "What did you say? What did that fellow Orlick say to me, Pip? What did he call me, with my husband standing by? Oh! Oh! Oh!" Each of these exclamations was a shriek; and I must remark of my sister, what is equally true of all the violent women I have ever seen, that passion was no excuse for her, because it is undeniable that instead of <u>lapsing</u> into passion, she consciously and deliberately took extraordinary pains to force herself into it, and became blindly furious by regular stages. "What was the name he gave me before the base man who swore to defend me? Oh! Hold me! Oh!"

"Ah-h-h!" growled the journeyman, between his teeth, "I'd hold you, if you was my wife. I'd hold you under the pump, and choke it out of you."

("I tell you, let her alone," said Joe.)

"Oh! To hear him!" cried my sister, with a clap of her hands and a scream together—which was her next stage. "To hear the names he's giving me! That Orlick! In my own house! Me, a married woman! With my husband standing by! Oh! Oh!" Here my sister, after a fit of clappings and screamings, beat her hands upon her bosom and upon her knees, and threw her cap off, and pulled her hair down— which were the last stages on her road to frenzy. Being by this time a perfect fury and a complete success, she made a dash at the door, which I had fortunately locked.

▶ Why does Joe fight with Orlick? What is the outcome?

What could the wretched Joe do now, after his disregarded parenthetical interruptions, but stand up to his journeyman, and ask him what he meant by interfering betwixt himself and Mrs. Joe; and further, whether he was man enough to come on? Old Orlick felt that the situation admitted of nothing less than coming on, and was on his defense straightway, so, without so much as pulling off their singed and burnt aprons, they went at one another, like two giants. But if any man in that neighborhood could stand up long against Joe, I never saw the man. Orlick, as if he had been of no more account than the pale young gentleman, was very soon among the coal dust, and in no hurry to come out of it. Then Joe unlocked the door and picked up my sister, who had dropped insensible at the window (but who had seen the fight first, I think), and who was carried into the house and laid down,

Words For Everyday Use

lapse (laps) *vi.,* slip

and who was recommended to revive, and would do nothing but struggle and clench her hands in Joe's hair. Then came that singular calm and silence which succeed all uproars; and then with the vague sensation which I have always connected with such a lull—namely, that it was Sunday, and somebody was dead—I went upstairs to dress myself.

When I came down again, I found Joe and Orlick sweeping up, without any other traces of discomposure than a slit in one of Orlick's nostrils, which was neither expressive nor ornamental. A pot of beer had appeared from the Jolly Bargemen, and they were sharing it by turns in a peaceable manner. The lull had a <u>sedative</u> and philosophical influence on Joe, who followed me out into the road to say, as a parting observation that might do me good, "On the rampage, Pip, and off the rampage, Pip—such is life!"

◀ What do the men do afterward?

With what absurd emotions (for we think the feelings that are very serious in a man quite comical in a boy) I found myself again going to Miss Havisham's, matters little here. Nor how I passed and repassed the gate many times before I could make up my mind to ring. Nor how I debated whether I should go away without ringing; nor, how I should undoubtedly have gone, if my time had been my own, to come back.

Miss Sarah Pocket came to the gate. No Estella.

"How, then? You here again?" said Miss Pocket. "What do you want?"

When I said that I only came to see how Miss Havisham was, Sarah evidently <u>deliberated</u> whether or no she should send me about my business. But, unwilling to hazard the responsibility, she let me in, and presently brought the sharp message that I was to "come up."

Everything was unchanged, and Miss Havisham was alone.

"Well?" said she, fixing her eyes upon me. "I hope you want nothing? You'll get nothing."

"No, indeed, Miss Havisham. I only wanted you to know that I am doing very well in my apprenticeship, and am always much obliged to you."

"There, there!" with the old restless fingers. "Come now and then; come on your birthday. Aye!" she cried suddenly, turning herself and her chair towards me, "You are looking round for Estella? Hey?"

◀ What does Miss Havisham tell Pip? What does she realize?

Words
For
Everyday
Use

sed • a • tive (sed´ə tiv) *adj.,* tending to soothe or quiet

de • lib • e • rate (di lib´ər āt´) *vt.,* consider carefully

I had been looking round—in fact, for Estella—and I stammered that I hoped she was well.

▶ Where is Estella? Why?

"Abroad," said Miss Havisham; "educating for a lady; far out of reach; prettier than ever; admired by all who see her. Do you feel that you have lost her?"

There was such a <u>malignant</u> enjoyment in her utterance of the last words, and she broke into such a disagreeable laugh that I was at a loss what to say. She spared me the trouble of considering by dismissing me. When the gate was closed upon me by Sarah of the walnut-shell countenance, I felt more than ever dissatisfied with my home and with my trade and with everything; and that was all I took by *that* motion.

▶ Why is Pip dissatisfied?

As I was loitering along the High Street, looking in disconsolately at the shop windows, and thinking what I would buy if I were a gentleman, who should come out of the bookshop but Mr. Wopsle. Mr. Wopsle had in his hand the affecting tragedy of George Barnwell,[21] in which he had that moment invested sixpence, with the view of heaping every word of it on the head of Pumblechook, with whom he was going to drink tea. No sooner did he see me than he appeared to consider that a special Providence had put a 'prentice in his way to be read at; and he laid hold of me, and insisted on my accompanying him to the Pumblechookian parlor. As I knew it would be miserable at home, and as the nights were dark and the way was dreary, and almost any companionship on the road was better than none, I made no great resistance; consequently, we turned into Pumblechook's just as the street and the shops were lighting up.

▶ How does Pip spend the evening?

As I never assisted at any other representation of George Barnwell, I don't know how long it may usually take; but I know very well that it took until half-past nine o'clock that night, and that when Mr. Wopsle got into Newgate, I thought he never would go to the scaffold, he became so much slower than at any former period of his disgraceful career. I thought it a little too much that he should complain of being cut short in his flower after all, as if he had not been running to seed, leaf after leaf, ever since his course began. This, however, was a mere question of length and wearisomeness. What

---

21. **affecting . . . Barnwell.** Popular tragedy by George Lillo, based on an old ballad. Barnwell, the apprentice, robs his employer and murders his uncle.

Words For Everyday Use

ma • lig • nant (mə lig´nənt) *adj.*, evil

stung me was the identification of the whole affair with my unoffending self. When Barnwell began to go wrong, I declare I felt positively apologetic, Pumblechook's indignant stare so taxed me with it. Wopsle, too, took pains to present me in the worst light. At once ferocious and <u>maudlin</u>, I was made to murder my uncle with no <u>extenuating</u> circumstances whatever; Millwood put me down in argument, on every occasion; it became sheer <u>monomania</u> in my master's daughter to care a button for me; and all I can say for my gasping and procrastinating conduct on the fatal morning is that it was worthy of the general feebleness of my character. Even after I was happily hanged and Wopsle had closed the book, Pumblechook sat staring at me, and shaking his head, and saying, "Take warning, boy, take warning!" as if it were a well-known fact that I contemplated murdering a near relation, provided I could only induce one to have the weakness to become my benefactor.

It was a very dark night when it was all over, and when I set out with Mr. Wopsle on the walk home. Beyond town, we found a heavy mist out, and it fell wet and thick. The turnpike lamp was a blur, quite out of the lamp's usual place apparently, and its rays looked solid substance on the fog. We were noticing this, and saying how that the mist rose with a change of wind from a certain quarter of our marshes, when we came upon a man, slouching under the lee of the turnpike house.

"Halloa!" we said, stopping. "Orlick, there?"

"Ah!" he answered, slouching out. "I was standing by, a minute, on the chance of company."

"You are late," I remarked.

Orlick not unnaturally answered, "Well? And *you're* late."

"We have been," said Mr. Wopsle, exalted with his late performance, "we have been indulging, Mr. Orlick, in an intellectual evening."

Old Orlick growled, as if he had nothing to say about that, and we all went on together. I asked him presently whether he had been spending his half-holiday up and down town?

"Yes," said he, "all of it. I come in behind yourself. I didn't see you, but I must have been pretty close behind you. By-the-bye, the guns is going again."

"At the Hulks?" said I.

◄ *Whom do they meet on the road?*

Words For Everyday Use

maud • lin (môd´lin) *adj.,* foolishly sentimental

ex • ten • u • at • ing (ik sten´yo͞o wāt´iŋ) *adj.,* serving as an excuse

mon • o • ma • ni • a (män´ō mā´nē ə) *n.,* mental disorder characterized by a preoccupation with one subject

"Aye! There's some of the birds flown from the cages. The guns have been going since dark, about. You'll hear one presently."

In effect, we had not walked many yards further, when the well-remembered boom came towards us, deadened by the mist, and heavily rolled away along the low grounds by the river, as if it were pursuing and threatening the fugitives.

"A good night for cutting off in," said Orlick. "We'd be puzzled how to bring down a jail-bird on the wing tonight."

The subject was a suggestive one to me, and I thought about it in silence. Mr. Wopsle, as the ill-<u>requited</u> uncle of the evening's tragedy, fell to meditating aloud in his garden at Camberwell.[22] Orlick, with his hands in his pockets, slouched heavily at my side. It was very dark, very wet, very muddy, and so we splashed along. Now and then, the sound of the signal cannon broke upon us again, and again rolled sulkily along the course of the river. I kept myself to myself and my thoughts. Mr. Wopsle died amiably at Camberwell, and exceedingly game on Bosworth Field,[23] and in the greatest agonies at Glastonbury.[24] Orlick sometimes growled, "Beat it out, beat it out—Old Clem! With a clink for the stout—Old Clem!" I thought he had been drinking, but he was not drunk.

Thus, we came to the village. The way by which we approached it took us past the Three Jolly Bargemen, which we were surprised to find—it being eleven o'clock—in a state of commotion, with the door wide open, and <u>unwonted</u> lights that had been hastily caught up and put down scattered about. Mr. Wopsle dropped in to ask what was the matter (surmising that a convict had been taken), but came running out in a great hurry.

"There's something wrong," said he, without stopping, "up at your place, Pip. Run all!"

"What is it?" I asked, keeping up with him. So did Orlick, at my side.

▶ What do they learn at the Three Jolly Bargemen?

---

22. **Camberwell.** District of south London
23. **died . . . Bosworth Field.** Mr. Wopsle was playing the role of Richard III in Shakespeare's play. Bosworth Field was the site of the final battle in the Wars of the Roses where Richard III was defeated in 1485.
24. **Glastonbury.** County in Somerset, England where the legendary King Arthur is said to have been buried

Words For Everyday Use

re • quit • ed (ri kwīt′ 'd) *adj.*, paid back
un • wont • ed (un wän′tid) *adj.*, uncommon

"I can't quite understand. The house seems to have been violently entered when Joe Gargery was out. Supposed by convicts. Somebody has been attacked and hurt."

We were running too fast to admit of more being said, and we made no stop until we got into our kitchen. It was full of people; the whole village was there, or in the yard; and there was a surgeon, and there was Joe, and there was a group of women, all on the floor in the midst of the kitchen. The unemployed bystanders drew back when they saw me, and so I became aware of my sister—lying without sense or movement on the bare boards where she had been knocked down by a tremendous blow on the back of the head, dealt by some unknown hand when her face was turned towards the fire—destined never to be on the rampage again while she was the wife of Joe.

◄ *What does Pip find when he arrives home?*

◄ *How will Mrs. Joe's behavior change?*

CHAPTER 16

With my head full of George Barnwell, I was at first disposed to believe that *I* must have had some hand in the attack upon my sister, or at all events that as her near relation, popularly known to be under obligations to her, I was a more legitimate object of suspicion than anyone else. But when, in the clearer light of next morning, I began to reconsider the matter and to hear it discussed around me on all sides, I took another view of the case, which was more reasonable.

Joe had been at the Three Jolly Bargemen, smoking his pipe, from a quarter after eight o'clock to a quarter before ten. While he was there, my sister had been seen standing at the kitchen door and had exchanged good night with a farm-laborer going home. The man could not be more particular as to the time at which he saw her (he got into dense confusion when he tried to be) than that it must have been before nine. When Joe went home at five minutes before ten, he found her struck down on the floor, and promptly called in assistance. The fire had not then burnt unusually low, nor was the snuff of the candle very long; the candle, however, had been blown out.

Nothing had been taken away from any part of the house. Neither, beyond the blowing out of the candle—which stood on a table between the door and my sister, and was behind her when she stood facing the fire and was struck—was there any disarrangement of the kitchen, excepting such as she herself had made, in falling and bleeding. But, there was one remarkable piece of evidence on the spot. She had been struck with something blunt and heavy, on the head and spine; after the blows were dealt, something heavy had been thrown down at her with considerable violence, as she lay on her face. And on the ground beside her, when Joe picked her up, was a convict's leg-iron which had been filed <u>asunder</u>.

Now Joe, examining this iron with a smith's eye, declared it to have been filed asunder some time ago. The hue and cry[1] going off to the Hulks, and people coming thence to examine the iron, Joe's opinion was <u>corroborated</u>. They did not undertake to say when it had left the prison-ships to

► *With what is Mrs. Joe attacked? What can Joe tell about this object?*

---

1. **hue and cry.** Loud outcry or demand; here refers to those loudly going to the prison ships to demand information

Words For Everyday Use

a • sun • der (ə sunʹdər) *adv.,* into parts or pieces

cor • rob • o • rate (kə räbʹə rātʹ) *vt.,* confirm; support which it undoubtedly had once belonged, but they claimed to know for certain that that particular manacle had not been worn by either of two convicts who had escaped last night. Further, one of those two was already retaken, and had not freed himself of his iron.

Knowing what I knew, I set up an inference of my own here. I believed the iron to be my convict's iron—the iron I had seen and heard him filing at, on the marshes—but my mind did not accuse him of having put it to its latest use. For, I believed one of two other persons to have become possessed of it, and to have turned it to this cruel account. Either Orlick, or the strange man who had shown me the file.

◄ Whom does Pip suspect? Why?

Now, as to Orlick; he had gone to town exactly as he told us when we picked him up at the turnpike, he had been seen about town all the evening, he had been in divers[2] companies in several public houses, and he had come back with myself and Mr. Wopsle. There was nothing against him, save the quarrel; and my sister had quarreled with him, and with everybody else about her, ten thousand times. As to the strange man, if he had come back for his two bank notes, there could have been no dispute about them, because my sister was fully prepared to restore them. Besides, there had been no altercation; the assailant had come in so silently and suddenly that she had been felled before she could look round.

It was horrible to think that I had provided the weapon, however undesignedly, but I could hardly think otherwise. I suffered unspeakable trouble while I considered and reconsidered whether I should at last dissolve that spell of my childhood and tell Joe all the story. For months afterwards, I every day settled the question finally in the negative, and reopened and reargued it next morning. The contention came, after all, to this—the secret was such an old one now, had so grown into me and become a part of myself, that I could not tear it away. In addition to the dread that, having led up to so much mischief, it would be now more likely than ever to alienate Joe from me if he believed it, I had a further restraining dread that he would not believe it, but would assert it with the fabulous dogs and veal cutlets as a monstrous invention. However, I temporized[3] with myself, of

◄ What thought bothers Pip? With what does he struggle? Why doesn't Pip reveal what he knows to Joe?

---

2. **divers.** Various
3. **temporized.** Acted according to the occasion, without regard to principle

Words For Everyday Use

al • ter • ca • tion (ôl´tər kā´shən) *n.*, angry quarrel
con • ten • tion (kən ten´shən) *n.*, argument

► What is Pip's final decision?

► How would you characterize the investigators of this crime? Explain whether they are effective.

► What effect does the attack have on Mrs. Joe?

► In what way has the attack "improved" Mrs. Joe?

course—for was I not wavering between right and wrong, when the thing is always done?—and resolved to make a full disclosure if I should see any such new occasion as a new chance of helping in the discovery of the assailant.

The constables, and the Bow Street men[4] from London—for this happened in the days of the extinct red-waistcoated police—were about the house for a week or two, and did pretty much what I have heard and read of like authorities doing in other such cases. They took up several obviously wrong people, and they ran their heads very hard against wrong ideas, and persisted in trying to fit the circumstances to the ideas, instead of trying to extract ideas from the circumstances. Also, they stood about the door of the Jolly Bargemen, with knowing and reserved looks that filled the whole neighborhood with admiration; and they had a mysterious manner of taking their drink that was almost as good as taking the culprit. But not quite, for they never did it.

Long after these constitutional powers had dispersed, my sister lay very ill in bed. Her sight was disturbed, so that she saw objects multiplied, and grasped at visionary[5] teacups and wine glasses instead of the realities; her hearing was greatly impaired; her memory also; and her speech was unintelligible. When at last she came round so far as to be helped downstairs, it was still necessary to keep my slate always by her, that she might indicate in writing what she could not indicate in speech. As she was (very bad handwriting apart) a more than indifferent speller, and as Joe was a more than indifferent reader, extraordinary complications arose between them, which I was always called in to solve. The administration of mutton instead of medicine, the substitution of tea for Joe, and the baker for bacon, were among the mildest of my own mistakes.

However, her temper was greatly improved, and she was patient. A <u>tremulous</u> uncertainty of the action of all her limbs soon became a part of her regular state, and afterwards, at intervals of two or three months, she would often put her hands to her head, and would then remain for about a week

---

4. **Bow Street men.** Group of detectives founded by the novelist Henry Fielding in 1749; this group, of whom Dickens had a poor opinion, wore red waistcoasts and lasted until 1839.

5. **visionary.** Imaginary

Words
For
Everyday
Use

trem • u • lous (trem´yo͞o ləs) *adj.*, trembling

at a time in some gloomy <u>aberration</u> of mind. We were at a loss to find a suitable attendant for her, until a circumstance happened conveniently to relieve us. Mr. Wopsle's great-aunt conquered a confirmed habit of living into which she had fallen, and Biddy became a part of our establishment.

It may have been about a month after my sister's reappearance in the kitchen when Biddy came to us with a small speckled box containing the whole of her worldly effects, and became a blessing to the household. Above all she was a blessing to Joe, for the dear old fellow was sadly cut up by the constant contemplation of the wreck of his wife, and had been accustomed, while attending on her of an evening, to turn to me every now and then and say, with his blue eyes moistened, "Such a fine figure of a woman as she once were, Pip!" Biddy instantly taking the cleverest charge of her as though she had studied her from infancy, Joe became able in some sort to appreciate the greater quiet of his life, and to get down to the Jolly Bargemen now and then for a change that did him good. It was characteristic of the police people that they had all more or less suspected poor Joe (though he never knew it), and that they had to a man <u>concurred</u> in regarding him as one of the deepest spirits they had ever encountered.

Biddy's first triumph in her new office was to solve a difficulty that had completely <u>vanquished</u> me. I had tried hard at it, but had made nothing of it. Thus it was:

Again and again and again, my sister had traced upon the slate a character that looked like a curious T, and then with the utmost eagerness had called our attention to it as something she particularly wanted. I had in vain tried everything producible that began with a T, from tar to toast and tub. At length it had come into my head that the sign looked like a hammer, and on my lustily calling that word in my sister's ear, she had begun to hammer on the table and had expressed a qualified assent. Thereupon, I had brought in all our hammers, one after another, but without avail. Then I bethought me of a crutch, the shape being much the same, and I borrowed one in the village, and displayed it to my sister with considerable confidence. But she shook her head to that extent when she was shown it that we were terrified lest in her weak and shattered state she should dislocate her neck.

◀ Who comes to help and under what circumstances?

◀ In what ways does Joe's life change after Biddy comes to help?

◀ How did the police view Joe? What does this reveal about these police officers?

◀ What unusual thing does Mrs. Joe do time and again?

Words For Everyday Use	**ab • er • ra • tion** (ab´ər ā´shən) *n.*, mental derangement
	con • cur (kən kur´) *vi.*, agree
	van • quish (vaŋ´kwish) *vt.*, defeat

When my sister found that Biddy was very quick to understand her, this mysterious sign reappeared on the slate. Biddy looked thoughtfully at it, heard my explanation, looked thoughtfully at my sister, looked thoughtfully at Joe (who was always represented on the slate by his initial letter), and ran into the forge, followed by Joe and me.

"Why, of course!" cried Biddy, with an exultant face. "Don't you see? It's *him!*"

Orlick, without a doubt! She had lost his name, and could only signify him by his hammer. We told him why we wanted him to come into the kitchen, and he slowly laid down his hammer, wiped his brow with his arm, took another wipe at it with his apron, and came slouching out, with a curious loose vagabond bend in the knees that strongly distinguished him.

I confess that I expected to see my sister denounce him, and that I was disappointed by the different result. She <u>manifested</u> the greatest anxiety to be on good terms with him, was evidently much pleased by his being at length produced, and motioned that she would have him given something to drink. She watched his countenance as if she were particularly wishful to be assured that he took kindly to his reception, she showed every possible desire to <u>conciliate</u> him, and there was an air of humble <u>propitiation</u> in all she did, such as I have seen pervade the bearing of a child towards a hard master. After that day, a day rarely passed without her drawing the hammer on her slate, and without Orlick's slouching in and standing doggedly before her, as if he knew no more than I did what to make of it.

▶ *What does Biddy discover? What does Pip suspect is the reason why Mrs. Joe wishes to see this person? Is he right?*

▶ *To what does Pip compare his sister's manner toward Orlick?*

Words For Everyday Use

man • i • fest (man´ə fest´) *vt.*, reveal; make clear

con • cil • i • ate (kən sil´ē āt´) *vt.*, win over; gain good will of

pro • pi • ti • a • tion (prō pish´ē ā´shən) *n.*, appeasing; winning a person over

CHAPTER 17

I now fell into a regular routine of apprenticeship life, which was varied, beyond the limits of the village and the marshes, by no more remarkable circumstance than the arrival of my birthday and my paying another visit to Miss Havisham. I found Miss Sarah Pocket still on duty at the gate, I found Miss Havisham just as I had left her, and she spoke of Estella in the very same way, if not in the very same words. The interview lasted but a few minutes, and she gave me a guinea when I was going, and told me to come again on my next birthday. I may mention at once that this became an annual custom. I tried to decline taking the guinea on the first occasion, but with no better effect than causing her to ask me very angrily if I expected more? Then, and after that, I took it.

◄ How does Pip characterize his life? What does he do each year?

So unchanging was the dull old house, the yellow light in the darkened room, the faded <u>specter</u> in the chair by the dressing-table glass, that I felt as if the stopping of the clocks had stopped time in that mysterious place, and, while I and everything else outside it grew older, it stood still. Daylight never entered the house, as to my thoughts and remembrances of it, any more than as to the actual fact. It bewildered me, and under its influence I continued at heart to hate my trade and to be ashamed of home.

◄ How does Pip feel about Satis House? Why?

Imperceptibly I became conscious of a change in Biddy, however. Her shoes came up at the heel, her hair grew bright and neat, her hands were always clean. She was not beautiful—she was common, and could not be like Estella—but she was pleasant and wholesome and sweet-tempered. She had not been with us more than a year (I remember her being newly out of mourning at the time it struck me), when I observed to myself one evening that she had curiously thoughtful and attentive eyes; eyes that were very pretty and very good.

◄ Who does change? In what ways does this person change?

It came of my lifting up my own eyes from a task I was poring at—writing some passages from a book, to improve myself in two ways at once by a sort of <u>stratagem</u>—and seeing Biddy observant of what I was about. I laid down my pen, and Biddy stopped in her needlework without laying it down.

Words For Everyday Use

spec • ter (spek´tər) *n.*, ghost
strat • a • gem (strat´ə jəm) *n.*, trick or scheme

"Biddy," said I, "how do you manage it? Either I am very stupid, or you are very clever."

"What is it that I manage? I don't know," returned Biddy, smiling.

She managed our whole domestic life, and wonderfully too; but I did not mean that, though that made what I did mean more surprising.

▶ On what does Pip spend his money?

"How do you manage, Biddy," said I, "to learn everything that I learn, and always to keep up with me?" I was beginning to be rather vain of my knowledge, for I spent my birthday guineas on it, and set aside the greater part of my pocket-money for similar investment; though I have no doubt, now, that the little I knew was extremely dear[1] at the price.

"I might as well ask you," said Biddy, "how *you* manage?"

"No; because when I come in from the forge of a night, anyone can see me turning to at it. But you never turn to at it, Biddy."

"I suppose I must catch it—like a cough," said Biddy, quietly, and went on with her sewing.

▶ What does Pip come to realize about Biddy?

Pursuing my idea as I leaned back in my wooden chair and looked at Biddy sewing away with her head on one side, I began to think her rather an extraordinary girl. For I called to mind now that she was equally accomplished in the terms of our trade, and the names of our different sorts of work, and our various tools. In short, whatever I knew, Biddy knew. Theoretically, she was already as good a blacksmith as I, or better.

"You are one of those, Biddy," said I, "who make the most of every chance. You never had a chance before you came here, and see how improved you are!"

Biddy looked at me for an instant, and went on with her sewing. "I was your first teacher though, wasn't I?" said she, as she sewed.

"Biddy!" I exclaimed, in amazement. "Why, you are crying!"

"No I am not," said Biddy, looking up and laughing. "What put that in your head?"

What could have put it in my head but the glistening of a tear as it dropped on her work? I sat silent, recalling what a drudge[2] she had been until Mr. Wopsle's great-aunt successfully overcame that bad habit of living, so highly desirable to be got rid of by some people. I recalled the hopeless circumstances by which she had been surrounded in the miserable little shop and the miserable little noisy evening school, with that miserable old bundle of incompetence always to be

---

1. **dear.** Expensive, costly
2. **drudge.** Person who does hard and tiresome work

dragged and shouldered. I reflected that even in those unto-ward[3] times there must have been <u>latent</u> in Biddy what was now developing, for, in my first uneasiness and discontent, I had turned to her for help as a matter of course. Biddy sat quietly sewing, shedding no more tears, and while I looked at her and thought about it all, it occurred to me that perhaps I had not been sufficiently grateful to Biddy. I might have been too reserved, and should have patronized her more (though I did not use that precise word in my meditations) with my confidence.

◄ What does Pip resolve about his relationship with Biddy?

"Yes, Biddy," I observed, when I had done turning it over, "you were my first teacher, and that at a time when we little thought of ever being together like this, in this kitchen."

"Ah, poor thing!" replied Biddy. It was like her self-forgetfulness, to transfer the remark to my sister, and to get up and be busy about her, making her more comfortable. "That's sadly true!"

"Well," said I, "we must talk together a little more, as we used to do. And I must consult you a little more, as I used to do. Let us have a quiet walk on the marshes next Sunday, Biddy, and a long chat."

◄ What does Pip ask Biddy to do? Why?

My sister was never left alone now; but Joe more than readily undertook the care of her on that Sunday afternoon, and Biddy and I went out together. It was summertime and lovely weather. When we had passed the village and the church and the churchyard, and were out on the marshes, and began to see the sails of the ships as they sailed on, I began to combine Miss Havisham and Estella with the prospect, in my usual way. When we came to the riverside and sat down on the bank, with the water rippling at our feet, making it all more quiet than it would have been without that sound, I resolved that it was a good time and place for the admission of Biddy into my inner confidence.

"Biddy," said I, after binding her to secrecy, "I want to be a gentleman."

◄ What does Pip reveal? What is Biddy's reaction? How does Pip respond?

"Oh, I wouldn't, if I was you!" she returned. "I don't think it would answer."

"Biddy," said I, with some severity, "I have particular reasons for wanting to be a gentleman."

---

3. **untoward.** Awkward

Words For Everyday Use

la • tent (lāt´'nt) *adj.,* inactive or hidden

"You know best, Pip; but don't you think you are happier as you are?"

"Biddy," I exclaimed impatiently, "I am not at all happy as I am. I am disgusted with my calling and with my life. I have never taken to either since I was bound. Don't be absurd."

"Was I absurd?" said Biddy, quietly raising her eyebrows; "I am sorry for that; I didn't mean to be. I only want you to do well, and be comfortable."

"Well, then, understand once for all that I never shall or can be comfortable—or anything but miserable—there, Biddy!—unless I can lead a very different sort of life from the life I lead now."

"That's a pity!" said Biddy, shaking her head with a sorrowful air.

Now, I too had so often thought it a pity that, in the singular kind of quarrel with myself which I was always carrying on, I was half-inclined to shed tears of vexation and distress when Biddy gave <u>utterance</u> to her sentiment and my own. I told her she was right, and I knew it was much to be regretted, but still it was not to be helped.

► What does Pip say he wishes he could have done?

"If I could have settled down," I said to Biddy, plucking up the short grass within reach, much as I had once upon a time pulled my feelings out of my hair and kicked them into the brewery wall; "if I could have settled down and been but half as fond of the forge as I was when I was little, I know it would have been much better for me. You and I and Joe would have wanted nothing then, and Joe and I would perhaps have gone partners when I was out of my time, and I might even have grown up to keep company with you, and we might have sat on this very bank on a fine Sunday, quite different people. I should have been good enough for *you;* shouldn't I, Biddy?"

Biddy sighed as she looked at the ships sailing on, and returned for answer, "Yes, I am not over-particular." It scarcely sounded flattering, but I knew she meant well.

► What reason does he give for being dissatisfied?

"Instead of that," said I, plucking up more grass and chewing a blade or two, "see how I am going on. Dissatisfied, and uncomfortable, and—what would it signify to me, being coarse and common, if nobody had told me so?"

Biddy turned her face suddenly towards mine, and looked far more attentively at me than she had looked at the sailing ships.

Words For Everyday Use	**ut • ter • ance** (ut´ər əns) *n.,* that which is spoken; expression

"It was neither a very true nor a very polite thing to say," she remarked, directing her eyes to the ships again. "Who said it?"

I was <u>disconcerted</u>, for I had broken away without quite seeing where I was going to. It was not to be shuffled off, now, however, and I answered, "The beautiful young lady at Miss Havisham's, and she's more beautiful than anybody ever was, and I admire her dreadfully, and I want to be a gentleman on her account." Having made this lunatic confession, I began to throw my torn-up grass into the river, as if I had some thoughts of following it.

◄ What is Pip's "lunatic confession"?

"Do you want to be a gentleman to spite her or to gain her over?" Biddy quietly asked me, after a pause.

"I don't know," I moodily answered.

"Because if it is to spite her," Biddy pursued, "I should think—but you know best—that might be better and more independently done by caring nothing for her words. And if it is to gain her over, I should think—but you know best— she was not worth gaining over."

◄ What advice does Biddy give Pip? What does this tell you about Biddy?

Exactly what I myself had thought, many times. Exactly what was perfectly manifest to me at the moment. But how could I, a poor dazed village lad, avoid that wonderful inconsistency into which the best and wisest of men fall every day?

"It may be all quite true," said I to Biddy, "but I admire her dreadfully."

In short, I turned over on my face when I came to that, and got a good grasp on the hair, on each side of my head, and wrenched it well. All the while knowing the madness of my heart to be so very mad and misplaced that I was quite conscious it would have served my face right if I had lifted it up by my hair, and knocked it against the pebbles as a punishment for belonging to such an idiot.

Biddy was the wisest of girls, and she tried to reason no more with me. She put her hand, which was a comfortable hand, though roughened by work, upon my hands, one after another, and gently took them out of my hair. Then she softly patted my shoulder in a soothing way, while with my face upon my sleeve I cried a little—exactly as I had done in the brewery yard—and felt vaguely convinced that I was very much ill-used by somebody, or by everybody; I can't say which.

"I am glad of one thing," said Biddy, "and that is that you have felt you could give me your confidence, Pip. And I am

◄ For what is Biddy grateful? What does she say it is too late to do?

Words For Everyday Use

dis • con • cert • ed (dis´kən sʉrt´əd) *adj.*, upset

glad of another thing, and that is that of course you know you may depend upon my keeping it and always so far deserving it. If your first teacher (dear! such a poor one, and so much in need of being taught herself!) had been your teacher at the present time, she thinks she knows what lesson she would set. But it would be a hard one to learn, and you have got beyond her, and it's of no use now." So, with a quiet sigh for me, Biddy rose from the bank, and said, with a fresh and pleasant change of voice, "Shall we walk a little further, or go home?"

▶ What does Pip say he will always do? How does Biddy say that Pip would change if he were a gentleman? Does Pip think it likely that he will become a gentleman?

"Biddy," I cried, getting up, putting my arm round her neck, and giving her a kiss, "I shall always tell you everything."

"Till you're a gentleman," said Biddy.

"You know I never shall be, so that's always. Not that I have any occasion to tell you anything, for you know everything I know—as I told you at home the other night."

"Ah!" said Biddy, quite in a whisper, as she looked away at the ships. And then repeated, with her former pleasant change, "Shall we walk a little further, or go home?"

I said to Biddy we would walk a little further, and we did so, and the summer afternoon toned down into the summer evening, and it was very beautiful. I began to consider whether I was not more naturally and wholesomely situated, after all, in these circumstances, than playing beggar my neighbor by candlelight in the room with the stopped clocks, and being despised by Estella. I thought it would be very good for me if I could get her out of my head with all the rest of those remembrances and fancies, and could go to work determined to relish what I had to do, and stick to it, and make the best of it. I asked myself the question whether I did not surely know that if Estella were beside me at that moment instead of Biddy, she would make me miserable? I was obliged to admit that I did know it for a certainty, and I said to myself, "Pip, what a fool you are!"

▶ What choices does Pip consider? What does he realize about Estella?

We talked a good deal as we walked, and all that Biddy said seemed right. Biddy was never insulting, or capricious, or Biddy today and somebody else tomorrow; she would have derived only pain, and no pleasure, from giving me pain; she would far rather have wounded her own breast than mine. How could it be, then, that I did not like her much the better of the two?

"Biddy," said I, when we were walking homeward, "I wish you could put me right."

"I wish I could!" said Biddy.

▶ What does Pip want from Biddy? What does Biddy realize?

"If I could only get myself to fall in love with you—you don't mind my speaking so openly to such an old acquaintance?"

"Oh dear, not at all!" said Biddy. "Don't mind me."

"If I could only get myself to do it, *that* would be the thing for me."

"But you never will, you see," said Biddy.

It did not appear quite so unlikely to me that evening as it would have done if we had discussed it a few hours before. I therefore observed I was not quite sure of that. But Biddy said she *was,* and she said it decisively. In my heart I believed her to be right; and yet I took it rather ill, too, that she should be so positive on the point.

When we came near the churchyard, we had to cross an embankment, and get over a stile[4] near a sluice-gate. There started up, from the gate, or from the rushes, or from the ooze (which was quite in his <u>stagnant</u> way), Old Orlick.

◀ Whom do they meet? What makes this person appear threatening?

"Halloa!" he growled, "where are you two going?"

"Where should we be going, but home?"

"Well then," said he, "I'm jiggered[5] if I don't see you home!"

This penalty of being jiggered was a favorite supposititious[6] case of his. He attached no definite meaning to the word that I am aware of, but used it, like his own pretended Christian name, to affront mankind, and convey an idea of something savagely damaging. When I was younger, I had had a general belief that if he had jiggered me, personally, he would have done it with a sharp and twisted hook.

Biddy was much against his going with us, and said to me in a whisper, "Don't let him come; I don't like him." As I did not like him either, I took the liberty of saying that we thanked him, but we didn't want seeing home. He received that piece of information with a yell of laughter, and dropped back, but came slouching after us at a little distance.

◀ What are Biddy's feelings about Orlick? Why does she feel this way?

Curious to know whether Biddy suspected him of having had a hand in that murderous attack of which my sister had never been able to give any account, I asked her why she did not like him.

"Oh!" she replied, glancing over her shoulder as he slouched after us, "because I—I am afraid he likes me."

"Did he ever tell you he liked you?" I asked indignantly.

---

4. **stile.** Set of steps used in climbing over a fence or wall
5. **jiggered.** Mild oath
6. **supposititious.** Hypothetical

Words For Everyday Use

stag • nant (stag´nənt) *adj.,* inactive; sluggish

"No," said Biddy, glancing over her shoulder again, "he never told me so; but he dances at[7] me, whenever he can catch my eye."

However novel and peculiar this testimony of attachment, I did not doubt the accuracy of the interpretation. I was very hot indeed upon Old Orlick's daring to admire her; as hot as if it were an outrage on myself.

"But it makes no difference to you, you know," said Biddy, calmly.

"No, Biddy, it makes no difference to me; only I don't like it; I don't approve of it."

"Nor I neither," said Biddy. "Though *that* makes no difference to you."

"Exactly," said I; "but I must tell you I should have no opinion of you,[8] Biddy, if he danced at you with your own consent."

▶ *What is the relationship between Pip and Orlick?*

I kept an eye on Orlick after that night, and whenever circumstances were favorable to his dancing at Biddy, got before him to obscure that demonstration. He had struck root in Joe's establishment by reason of my sister's sudden fancy for him, or I should have tried to get him dismissed. He quite understood and <u>reciprocated</u> my good intentions, as I had reason to know thereafter.

And now, because my mind was not confused enough before, I complicated its confusion fifty thousand-fold by having states and seasons when I was clear that Biddy was immeasurably better than Estella, and that the plain honest working life to which I was born had nothing in it to be ashamed of, but offered me sufficient means of self-respect and happiness. At those times, I would decide conclusively that my <u>disaffection</u> to dear old Joe and the forge was gone, and that I was growing up in a fair way to be partners with Joe and to keep company with Biddy—when all in a moment some confounding remembrance of the Havisham days would fall upon me, like a destructive missile, and scatter my wits again. Scattered wits take a long time picking up; and often, before I had got them well together, they would be dispersed in all directions by one stray thought, that perhaps after all Miss Havisham was going to make my fortune when my time was out.

▶ *What keeps interrupting Pip's thoughts? What does he try to do?*

---

7. **dances at.** Flirts with
8. **have no opinion of you.** Have a low opinion of you

Words For Everyday Use

re • cip • ro • cate (ri sip´rə kāt´) *vt.,* give, do, feel in return; return in kind or degree

dis • af • fec • tion (dis´ə fek´shən) *n.,* disloyalty; withdrawal of friendship

If my time had run out, it would have left me still at the height of my perplexities, I dare say. It never did run out, however, but was brought to a premature end, as I proceed to relate.

CHAPTER 18

► What is the group assembled at the Three Jolly Bargemen doing?

It was in the fourth year of my apprenticeship to Joe, and it was a Saturday night. There was a group assembled round the fire at the Three Jolly Bargemen, attentive to Mr. Wopsle as he read the newspaper aloud. Of that group, I was one.

A highly popular murder had been committed, and Mr. Wopsle was <u>imbrued</u> in blood to the eyebrows. He <u>gloated</u> over every abhorrent adjective in the description, and identified himself with every witness at the inquest.[1] He faintly moaned, "I am done for," as the victim, and he barbarously[2] bellowed, "I'll serve you out," as the murderer. He gave the medical testimony in pointed imitation of our local practitioner; and he piped and shook as the aged turnpike-keeper who had heard blows, to an extent so very <u>paralytic</u> as to suggest a doubt regarding the mental competency of that witness. The coroner, in Mr. Wopsle's hands, became Timon of Athens;[3] the beadle,[4] Coriolanus.[5] He enjoyed himself thoroughly, and we all enjoyed ourselves, and were delightfully comfortable. In this cozy state of mind we came to the verdict of willful murder.

► Who comes over to speak to the group? How does this person behave?

Then, and not sooner, I became aware of a strange gentleman leaning over the back of the settle opposite me, looking on. There was an expression of contempt on his face, and he bit the side of a great forefinger as he watched the group of faces.

"Well!" said the stranger to Mr. Wopsle, when the reading was done, "you have settled it all to your own satisfaction, I have no doubt?"

Everybody started and looked up, as if it were the murderer. He looked at everybody coldly and sarcastically.

"Guilty, of course?" said he. "Out with it. Come!"

► What verdict does Wopsle pronounce upon the person accused of the crime? What does the stranger point out?

"Sir," returned Mr. Wopsle, "without having the honor of your acquaintance, I do say guilty." Upon this we all took courage to unite in a confirmatory murmur.

---

1. **inquest.** Investigation of a death
2. **barbarously.** Cruelly, brutally
3. **Timon of Athens.** Title character in a play by Shakespeare, a bitter man who hates humankind
4. **beadle.** Messenger of a law court
5. **Coriolanus.** Title character in a play by Shakespeare, a proud aristocrat

Words For Everyday Use

im • brue (im brōō´) vt., soak, especially with blood
gloat (glōt) vi., express malicious pleasure
par • a • lyt • ic (par´ə lit´ik) adj., showing a helpless inability to act

"I know you do," said the stranger; "I knew you would. I told you so. But now I'll ask you a question. Do you know, or do you not know, that the law of England supposes every man to be innocent, until he is proved—proved—to be guilty?"

"Sir," Mr. Wopsle began to reply, "as an Englishman myself, I—"

"Come!" said the stranger, biting his forefinger at him. "Don't evade the question. Either you know it, or you don't know it. Which is it to be?"

He stood with his head on one side and himself on one side, in a bullying <u>interrogative</u> manner, and he threw his forefinger at Mr. Wopsle—as it were to mark him out—before biting it again.

◀ *Describe the stranger's treatment of Mr. Wopsle.*

"Now!" said he. "Do you know it, or don't you know it?"

"Certainly I know it," replied Mr. Wopsle.

"Certainly you know it. Then why didn't you say so at first? Now, I'll ask you another question"; taking possession of Mr. Wopsle, as if he had a right to him. "*Do* you know that none of these witnesses have yet been cross-examined?"

Mr. Wopsle was beginning, "I can only say—" when the stranger stopped him.

"What? You won't answer the question yes or no? Now, I'll try you again." Throwing his finger at him again. "Attend to me. Are you aware, or are you not aware, that none of these witnesses have yet been cross-examined? Come, I only want one word from you. Yes, or no?"

Mr. Wopsle hesitated, and we all began to conceive rather a poor opinion of him.

"Come!" said the stranger, "I'll help you. You don't deserve help, but I'll help you. Look at that paper you hold in your hand. What is it?"

"What is it?" repeated Mr. Wopsle, eyeing it much at a loss.

"Is it," pursued the stranger in his most sarcastic and suspicious manner, "the printed paper you have just been reading from?"

"Undoubtedly."

"Undoubtedly. Now, turn to that paper, and tell me whether it distinctly states that the prisoner expressly said that his legal advisers instructed him altogether to reserve his defense?"[6]

---

6. **reserve his defense.** Not to say anything in his own defense until later in the trial

Words
For
Everyday
Use

in • ter • rog • a • tive (in′tə räg′ ə tiv) *adj.*, questioning

"I read that just now," Mr. Wopsle pleaded.

"Never mind what you read just now, sir; I don't ask you what you read just now. You may read the Lord's Prayer backwards, if you like—and, perhaps, have done it before today. Turn to the paper. No, no, no my friend; not to the top of the column; you know better than that; to the bottom, to the bottom." (We all began to think Mr. Wopsle full of <u>subterfuge</u>.) "Well? Have you found it?"

"Here it is," said Mr. Wopsle.

"Now, follow that passage with your eye, and tell me whether it distinctly states that the prisoner expressly said that he was instructed by his legal advisers wholly to reserve his defense? Come! Do you make that of it?"

Mr. Wopsle answered, "Those are not the exact words."

"Not the exact words!" repeated the gentleman bitterly. "Is that the exact substance?"

"Yes," said Mr. Wopsle.

► What does the stranger ask the group to consider?

"Yes," repeated the stranger, looking round at the rest of the company with his right hand extended towards the witness, Wopsle. "And now I ask you what you say to the conscience of that man who, with that passage before his eyes, can lay his head upon his pillow after having pronounced a fellow creature guilty, unheard?"

We all began to suspect that Mr. Wopsle was not the man we had thought him, and that he was beginning to be found out.

"And that same man, remember," pursued the gentleman, throwing his finger at Mr. Wopsle heavily, "that same man might be summoned as a juryman upon this very trial, and having thus deeply committed himself, might return to the bosom of his family and lay his head upon his pillow, after deliberately swearing that he would well and truly try the issue joined between Our Sovereign Lord the King and the prisoner at the bar, and would a true verdict give according to the evidence, so help him God!"

► How does the group feel about Wopsle once the stranger has made his argument?

We were all deeply persuaded that the unfortunate Wopsle had gone too far, and had better stop in his reckless career while there was yet time.

The strange gentleman, with an air of authority not to be disputed, and with a manner expressive of knowing something secret about every one of us that would effectually do for each individual if he chose to disclose it, left the back of

Words For Everyday Use	**sub • ter • fuge** (sub´tər fyōōj´) *n.*, plan used to hide one's true intentions

the settle, and came into the space between the two settles, in front of the fire, where he remained standing—his left hand in his pocket, and he biting the forefinger of his right.

"From information I have received," said he, looking round at us as we all quailed before him, "I have reason to believe there is a blacksmith among you, by name Joseph—or Joe—Gargery. Which is the man?"

◀ For whom is the stranger looking? From where does Pip recognize the stranger?

"Here is the man," said Joe.

The strange gentleman beckoned him out of his place, and Joe went.

"You have an apprentice," pursued the stranger, "commonly known as Pip? Is he here?"

"I am here!" I cried.

The stranger did not recognize me, but I recognized him as the gentleman I had met on the stairs on the occasion of my second visit to Miss Havisham. I had known him the moment I saw him looking over the settle, and now that I stood confronting him with his hand upon my shoulder, I checked off again in detail, his large head, his dark complexion, his deep-set eyes, his bushy black eyebrows, his large watch-chain, his strong black dots of beard and whisker, and even the smell of scented soap on his great hand.

"I wish to have a private conference with you two," said he, when he had <u>surveyed</u> me at his leisure. "It will take a little time. Perhaps we had better go to your place of residence. I prefer not to anticipate my communication[7] here; you will impart as much or as little of it as you please to your friends afterwards; I have nothing to do with that."

◀ What does the stranger request?

Amidst a wondering silence, we three walked out of the Jolly Bargemen, and in a wondering silence walked home. While going along, the strange gentleman occasionally looked at me, and occasionally bit the side of his finger. As we neared home, Joe vaguely acknowledging the occasion as an impressive and ceremonious one, went on ahead to open the front door. Our conference was held in the state parlor, which was feebly lighted by one candle.

It began with the strange gentleman's sitting down at the table, drawing the candle to him, and looking over some entries in his pocket book.[8] He then put up the pocket book

---

7. **anticipate my communication.** Disclose beforehand what I am going to say
8. **pocket book.** Book small enough to be carried in one's pocket

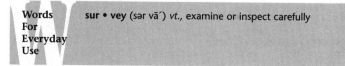

Words For Everyday Use

sur • vey (sər vā´) *vt.*, examine or inspect carefully

and set the candle a little aside, after peering round it into the darkness at Joe and me to ascertain which was which.

► Who is the stranger? Where is he from? What is his mission?

"My name," he said, "is Jaggers, and I am a lawyer in London. I am pretty well known. I have unusual business to transact with you, and I <u>commence</u> by explaining that it is not of my originating. If my advice had been asked, I should not have been here. It was not asked, and you see me here. What I have to do as the confidential agent of another, I do. No less, no more."

Finding that he could not see us very well from where he sat, he got up, and threw one leg over the back of a chair and leaned upon it; thus having one foot on the seat of the chair, and one foot on the ground.

► What does Jaggers try to ascertain from Joe?

"Now, Joseph Gargery, I am the bearer of an offer to relieve you of this young fellow, your apprentice. You would not object to cancel his indentures at his request and for his good? You would want nothing for so doing?"

"Lord forbid that I should want anything for not standing in Pip's way," said Joe, staring.

"Lord forbidding is <u>pious</u>, but not to the purpose," returned Mr. Jaggers. "The question is, would you want anything? Do you want anything?"

"The answer is," returned Joe sternly, "No."

I thought Mr. Jaggers glanced at Joe as if he considered him a fool for his disinterestedness.[9] But I was too much bewildered between breathless curiosity and surprise to be sure of it.

"Very well," said Mr. Jaggers. "Recollect the admission you have made, and don't try to go from it presently."

"Who's a-going to try?" retorted Joe.

"I don't say anybody is. Do you keep a dog?"

"Yes, I do keep a dog."

"Bear in mind then, that Brag is a good dog, but that Holdfast is a better.[10] Bear that in mind, will you?" repeated Mr. Jaggers, shutting his eyes and nodding his head at Joe, as if he were forgiving him something. "Now, I return to this young fellow. And the communication I have got to make is that he has great expectations."

Joe and I gasped, and looked at one another.

---

9. **disinterestedness.** Lack of desire for selfish gain
10. **Brag . . . better.** Proverbial saying; here, Jaggers is warning Joe not to brag about his lack of desire for compensation but to hold fast to his word that he desires no compensation.

Words For Everyday Use

com • mence (kə mens´) vi., begin
pi • ous (pī´əs) adj., coming from actual or pretended religious devotion

"I am instructed to communicate to him," said Mr. Jaggers, throwing his finger at me sideways, "that he will come into a handsome property. Further, that it is the desire of the present possessor of that property that he be immediately removed from his present sphere of life and from this place, and be brought up as a gentleman—in a word, as a young fellow of great expectations."

My dream was out; my wild fancy was surpassed by sober reality; Miss Havisham was going to make my fortune on a grand scale.

"Now, Mr. Pip," pursued the lawyer, "I address the rest of what I have to say to you. You are to understand, first, that it is the request of the person from whom I take my instructions that you always bear the name of Pip. You will have no objection, I dare say, to your great expectations being <u>encumbered</u> with that easy condition. But if you have any objection, this is the time to mention it."

My heart was beating so fast, and there was such a singing in my ears, that I could scarcely stammer I had no objection.

"I should think not! Now you are to understand, secondly, Mr. Pip, that the name of the person who is your liberal benefactor remains a profound secret, until the person chooses to reveal it. I am empowered to mention that it is the intention of the person to reveal it at first hand by word of mouth to yourself. When or where that intention may be carried out, I cannot say; no one can say. It may be years hence. Now, you are distinctly to understand that you are most positively prohibited from making any inquiry on this head, or any allusion or reference, however distant, to any individual whomsoever as *the* individual, in all the communications you may have with me. If you have a suspicion in your own breast, keep that suspicion in your own breast. It is not the least to the purpose what the reasons of this prohibition are; they may be the strongest and gravest reasons, or they may be a mere whim. This is not for you to inquire into. The condition is laid down. Your acceptance of it, and your observance of it as binding, is the only remaining condition that I am charged with by the person from whom I take my instructions, and for whom I am not otherwise responsible. That person is the person from whom you derive your expectations, and the secret is solely held by that person and by

◄ *What is Jaggers's surprising news? Whom does Pip assume is the "present possessor of that property"?*

◄ *What are the conditions of Pip's "great expectations"?*

◄ *Who knows the benefactor's name?*

Words For Everyday Use

en • cum • ber (en kum′ bər) *vt.,* load or weigh down

me. Again, not a very difficult condition with which to encumber such a rise in fortune; but if you have any objection to it, this is the time to mention it. Speak out."

Once more, I stammered with difficulty that I had no objection.

"I should think not! Now, Mr. Pip, I have done with stipulations." Though he called me Mr. Pip, and began rather to make up to me, he still could not get rid of a certain air of bullying suspicion; and even now he occasionally shut his eyes and threw his finger at me while he spoke, as much as to express that he knew all kinds of things to my <u>disparagement</u>, if he only chose to mention them. "We come next to mere details of arrangement. You must know that although I use the term 'expectations' more than once, you are not endowed with expectations only. There is already lodged in my hands a sum of money amply sufficient for your suitable education and maintenance. You will please consider me your guardian. Oh!" for I was going to thank him, "I tell you at once, I am paid for my services, or I shouldn't render them. It is considered that you must be better educated, in accordance with your altered position, and that you will be alive to the importance and necessity of at once entering on that advantage."

I said I had always longed for it.

"Never mind what you have always longed for, Mr. Pip," he retorted; "keep to the record. If you long for it now, that's enough. Am I answered that you are ready to be placed at once under some proper tutor? Is that it?"

I stammered yes, that was it.

"Good. Now, your inclinations are to be consulted. I don't think that wise, mind, but it's my trust. Have you ever heard of any tutor whom you would prefer to another?"

I had never heard of any tutor but Biddy, and Mr. Wopsle's great-aunt, so I replied in the negative.

"There is a certain tutor, of whom I have some knowledge, who I think might suit the purpose," said Mr. Jaggers. "I don't recommend him, observe; because I never recommend anybody. The gentleman I speak of is one Mr. Matthew Pocket."

Ah! I caught at the name directly. Miss Havisham's relation. The Matthew whom Mr. and Mrs. Camilla had spoken of. The Matthew whose place was to be at Miss Havisham's head, when she lay dead, in her bride's dress on the bride's table.

▶ Along with "great expectations," with what else is Pip endowed? What does he need to do?

▶ What tutor does Jaggers suggest? How does Pip recognize the name?

| Words For Everyday Use | **dis • par • age • ment** (di spar´ ij mənt) n., anything that discredits or lowers in esteem |

"You know the name?" said Mr. Jaggers, looking shrewdly at me, and then shutting up his eyes while he waited for my answer.

My answer was that I had heard of the name.

"Oh!" said he. "You have heard of the name. But the question is, what do you say of it?"

I said, or tried to say, that I was much obliged to him for his recommendation—

"No, my young friend!" he interrupted, shaking his great head very slowly. "Recollect yourself!"[11]

Not recollecting myself, I began again that I was much obliged to him for his recommendation—

"No, my young friend," he interrupted, shaking his head and frowning and smiling both at once; "no, no, no; it's very well done, but it won't do; you are too young to fix me with it. Recommendation is not the word, Mr. Pip. Try another."

Correcting myself, I said that I was much obliged to him for his mention of Mr. Matthew Pocket—

"That's more like it!" cried Mr. Jaggers.

—And (I added), I would gladly try that gentleman.

"Good. You had better try him in his own house. The way shall be prepared for you, and you can see his son first, who is in London. When will you come to London?"

◄ What is Jaggers's suggestion?

I said (glancing at Joe, who stood looking on, motionless), that I supposed I could come directly.

"First," said Mr. Jaggers, "you should have some new clothes to come in, and they should not be working clothes. Say this day week. You'll want some money. Shall I leave you twenty guineas?"

He produced a long purse, with the greatest coolness, and counted them out on the table and pushed them over to me. This was the first time he had taken his leg from the chair. He sat astride of the chair when he had pushed the money over, and sat swinging his purse and eyeing Joe.

"Well, Joseph Gargery? You look dumbfoundered!"[12]

"I *am!*" said Joe, in a very decided manner.

"It was understood that you wanted nothing for yourself, remember?"

"It were understood," said Joe. "And it are understood. And it ever will be similar according."

"But what," said Mr. Jaggers, swinging his purse, "what if it was in my instructions to make you a present, as compensation?"

◄ What does Jaggers offer Joe? How does Joe respond to this offer?

"As compensation what for?" Joe demanded.

"For the loss of his services."

11. **Recollect yourself.** Catch or save yourself from a slip or mistake
12. **dumbfoundered.** Dumfounded, made speechless by shock

Joe laid his hand upon my shoulder with the touch of a woman. I have often thought him since, like the steam-hammer that can crush a man or pat an egg-shell, in his combination of strength with gentleness. "Pip is that hearty welcome," said Joe, "to go free with his services, to honor and fortun', as no words can tell him. But if you think as money can make compensation to me for the loss of the little child—what come to the forge—and ever the best of friends!—"

Oh, dear good Joe, whom I was so ready to leave and so unthankful to, I see you again, with your muscular blacksmith's arm before your eyes, and your broad chest heaving, and your voice dying away. Oh, dear good faithful tender Joe, I feel the loving tremble of your hand upon my arm, as solemnly this day as if it had been the rustle of an angel's wing!

But I encouraged Joe at the time. I was lost in the mazes of my future fortunes, and could not retrace the bypaths we had trodden together. I begged Joe to be comforted, for (as he said) we had ever been the best of friends, and (as I said) we ever would be so. Joe scooped his eyes with his disengaged[13] wrist, as if he were bent on gouging himself, but said not another word.

Mr. Jaggers had looked on at this as one who recognized in Joe the village idiot, and in me his keeper. When it was over, he said, weighing in his hand the purse he had ceased to swing:

"Now, Joseph Gargery, I warn you this is your last chance. No half-measures with me. If you mean to take a present that I have it in charge to make you, speak out, and you shall have it. If on the contrary you mean to say—" Here, to his great amazement, he was stopped by Joe's suddenly working round him with every demonstration of a fell[14] <u>pugilistic</u> purpose.

▶ What does Joe do when the offer is made again?

"Which I meantersay," cried Joe, "that if you come into my place bull-baiting and badgering[15] me, come out! Which I meantersay as sech if you're a man, come on! Which I meantersay that what I say, I meantersay and stand or fall by!"

I drew Joe away, and he immediately became <u>placable</u>, merely stating to me, in an obliging manner and as a polite <u>expostulatory</u> notice to anyone whom it might happen to

---

13. **disengaged.** Free; the wrist of the hand not on Pip's shoulder
14. **fell.** Terrible
15. **bull-baiting and badgering.** *Bull-baiting*—harassing, refers to an old English pastime of setting dogs upon a chained bull; *badgering*—torment as if by baiting a badger

concern, that he were not a-going to be bull-baited and badgered in his own place. Mr. Jaggers had risen when Joe demonstrated, and had backed near the door. Without <u>evincing</u> any inclination to come in again, he there delivered his <u>valedictory</u> remarks. They were these:

"Well, Mr. Pip, I think the sooner you leave here—as you are to be a gentleman—the better. Let it stand for this day week, and you shall receive my printed address in the meantime. You can take a hackney-coach[16] at the stage-coach office in London, and come straight to me. Understand that I express no opinion, one way or other, on the trust I undertake. I am paid for undertaking it, and I do so. Now, understand that finally. Understand that!"

◀ What does Jaggers try to make clear about his role?

He was throwing his finger at both of us, and I think would have gone on, but for his seeming to think Joe dangerous, and going off.

Something came into my head which induced me to run after him as he was going down to the Jolly Bargemen, where he had left a hired carriage.

"I beg your pardon, Mr. Jaggers."

"Halloa!" said he, facing round, "what's the matter?"

"I wish to be quite right, Mr. Jaggers, and to keep to your directions, so I thought I had better ask. Would there be any objection to my taking leave of anyone I know, about here, before I go away?"

"No," said he, looking as if he hardly understood me.

"I don't mean in the village only, but uptown?"

"No," said he. "No objection."

I thanked him and ran home again, and there I found that Joe had already locked the front door and vacated the state parlor, and was seated by the kitchen fire with a hand on each knee, gazing intently at the burning coals. I too sat down before the fire and gazed at the coals, and nothing was said for a long time.

My sister was in her cushioned chair in her corner, and Biddy sat at her needlework before the fire, and Joe sat next Biddy, and I sat next Joe in the corner opposite my sister. The more I looked into the glowing coals, the more incapable I became of looking at Joe; the longer the silence lasted, the more unable I felt to speak.

---

16. **hackney-coach.** Carriage drawn by horses for hire

Words For Everyday Use

e • vince (ē vins´) *vt.*, show plainly; indicate

val • e • dic • to • ry (val´ə dik´tər ē) *adj.*, said or done at parting

► Who tells Biddy
the news? What does
Pip notice about Joe
and Biddy's reaction?

At length I got out, "Joe, have you told Biddy?"

"No, Pip," returned Joe, still looking at the fire, and holding his knees tight, as if he had private information that they intended to make off somewhere, "which I left it to yourself, Pip."

"I would rather you told, Joe."

"Pip's a gentleman of fortun' then," said Joe, "and God bless him in it!"

Biddy dropped her work, and looked at me. Joe held his knees and looked at me. I looked at both of them. After a pause they both heartily congratulated me; but there was a certain touch of sadness in their congratulations that I rather resented.

I took it upon myself to impress Biddy (and through Biddy, Joe) with the grave obligation I considered my friends under, to know nothing and say nothing about the maker of my fortune. It would all come out in good time, I observed, and in the meanwhile nothing was to be said, save that I had come into great expectations from a mysterious patron. Biddy nodded her head thoughtfully at the fire as she took up her work again, and said she would be very particular; and Joe, still detaining his knees, said, "Aye, aye, I'll be ekervally partickler,[17] Pip;" and then they congratulated me again, and went on to express so much wonder at the notion of my being a gentleman that I didn't half like it.

► Is Mrs. Joe able
to understand the
news? What is her
state of mind?

Infinite pains were then taken by Biddy to convey to my sister some idea of what had happened. To the best of my belief, those efforts entirely failed. She laughed and nodded her head a great many times, and even repeated after Biddy, the words "Pip" and "property." But I doubt if they had more meaning in them than an election cry, and I cannot suggest a darker picture of her state of mind.

► How does Pip feel
soon after learning of
his expectations?
Why?

I never could have believed it without experience, but as Joe and Biddy became more at their cheerful ease again, I became quite gloomy. Dissatisfied with my fortune, of course I could not be; but it is possible that I may have been, without quite knowing it, dissatisfied with myself.

Anyhow, I sat with my elbow on my knee and my face upon my hand, looking into the fire, as those two talked about my going away, and about what they should do without me, and all that. And whenever I caught one of them looking at me, though never so pleasantly (and they often looked at me—particularly Biddy), I felt offended; as if they were expressing some mistrust of me. Though Heaven knows they never did by word or sign.

---

17. **ekervally partickler.** Joe means that he, too, will be especially particular.

At those times I would get up and look out at the door—for our kitchen door opened at once upon the night, and stood open on summer evenings to air the room. The very stars to which I then raised my eyes, I am afraid I took to be but poor and humble stars for glittering on the rustic objects among which I had passed my life.

"Saturday night," said I, when we sat at our supper of bread-and-cheese and beer. "Five more days, and then the day before *the* day! They'll soon go."

"Yes, Pip," observed Joe, whose voice sounded hollow in his beer mug. "They'll soon go."

"Soon, soon go," said Biddy.

"I have been thinking, Joe, that when I go downtown on Monday, and order my new clothes, I shall tell the tailor that I'll come and put them on there, or that I'll have them sent to Mr. Pumblechook's. It would be very disagreeable to be stared at by all the people here."

◄ Why does Pip decide to have his new clothes sent to Pumblechook's?

"Mr. and Mrs. Hubble might like to see you in your new genteel figure too, Pip," said Joe, <u>industriously</u> cutting his bread with his cheese on it, in the palm of his left hand, and glancing at my untasted supper as if he thought of the time when we used to compare slices. "So might Wopsle. And the Jolly Bargemen might take it as a compliment."

"That's just what I don't want, Joe. They would make such a business of it—such a coarse and common business—that I couldn't bear myself."

◄ How would you describe Pip's attitude toward the villagers, Biddy, and Joe?

"Ah, that indeed, Pip!" said Joe. "If you couldn't a-bear yourself—"

Biddy asked me here, as she sat holding my sister's plate, "Have you thought about when you'll show yourself to Mr. Gargery, and your sister, and me? You will show yourself to us, won't you?"

"Biddy," I returned with some resentment, "you are so exceedingly quick that it's difficult to keep up with you."

("She always were quick," observed Joe.)

"If you had waited another moment, Biddy, you would have heard me say that I shall bring my clothes here in a bundle one evening—most likely on the evening before I go away."

Biddy said no more. Handsomely forgiving her, I soon exchanged an affectionate good night with her and Joe, and went up to bed. When I got into my little room, I sat down

Words For Everyday Use

in • dus • tri • ous • ly (in dus´trē əs lē) *adv.*, busily; with earnest, steady effort and took a long look at it, as a <u>mean</u> little room that I should soon be parted from and raised above, forever. It was furnished with fresh young remembrances too, and even at the same moment I fell into much the same confused division of mind between it and the better rooms to which I was going as I had been in so often between the forge and Miss Havisham's, and Biddy and Estella.

The sun had been shining brightly all day on the roof of my attic, and the room was warm. As I put the window open and stood looking out, I saw Joe come slowly forth at the dark door below, and take a turn or two in the air; and then I saw Biddy come, and bring him a pipe and light it for him. He never smoked so late, and it seemed to hint to me that he wanted comforting, for some reason or other.

He presently stood at the door immediately beneath me, smoking his pipe, and Biddy stood there too, quietly talking to him, and I knew that they talked of me, for I heard my name mentioned in an endearing tone by both of them more than once. I would not have listened for more, if I could have heard more; so I drew away from the window, and sat down in my one chair by the bedside, feeling it very sorrowful and strange that this first night of my bright fortunes should be the loneliest I had ever known.

Looking towards the open window, I saw light wreaths from Joe's pipe floating there, and I fancied it was like a blessing from Joe—not obtruded on me or paraded before me, but pervading the air we shared together. I put my light out, and crept into bed; and it was an uneasy bed now, and I never slept the old sound sleep in it anymore.

▶ What does Pip notice about Joe? Who goes to him? In what manner do the two discuss Pip?

▶ How does Pip feel on his first night of "bright fortunes"? What is Pip no longer able to do?

Words For Everyday Use

mean (mēn) *adj.,* low in quality, value, or importance

CHAPTER 19

Morning made a considerable difference in my general prospect of life, and brightened it so much that it scarcely seemed the same. What lay heaviest on my mind was the consideration that six days intervened between me and the day of departure, for I could not <u>divest</u> myself of a misgiving that something might happen to London in the meanwhile, and that, when I got there, it would be either greatly deteriorated or clean gone.

◄ What fear does Pip have?

Joe and Biddy were very sympathetic and pleasant when I spoke of our approaching separation, but they only referred to it when I did. After breakfast, Joe brought out my indentures from the press in the best parlor, and we put them in the fire, and I felt that I was free. With all the novelty of my <u>emancipation</u> on me, I went to church with Joe, and thought perhaps the clergyman wouldn't have read that about the rich man and the kingdom of Heaven,[1] if he had known all.

◄ What is the meaning of Joe's action?

After our early dinner, I strolled out alone, proposing to finish off the marshes[2] at once, and get them done with. As I passed the church, I felt (as I had felt during service in the morning) a <u>sublime</u> compassion for the poor creatures who were destined to go there, Sunday after Sunday, all their lives through, and to lie obscurely at last among the low green mounds. I promised myself that I would do something for them one of these days, and formed a plan in outline for bestowing a dinner of roast beef and plum pudding, a pint of ale, and a gallon of <u>condescension</u> upon everybody in the village.

◄ How does Pip feel toward the villagers? What does he hope to do?

If I had often thought before, with something allied to shame, of my companionship with the <u>fugitive</u> whom I had once seen limping among those graves, what were my thoughts on this Sunday, when the place recalled the wretch, ragged and shivering, with his felon iron and badge![3] My comfort was that it happened a long time ago, and that he had

---

1. **rich man . . . Heaven.** "Then Jesus said to His disciples, 'Assuredly, I say to you that it is hard for a rich man to enter the kingdom of heaven.'" (Matthew 19:23)
2. **finish . . . marshes.** Say goodbye to the marshes
3. **felon iron and badge.** Iron shackles or chains and mark of a criminal

---

Words For Everyday Use

di • vest (də vest´) vt., rid
e • man • ci • pa • tion (ē man´sə pā´shən) n., freedom from bondage
sub • lime (sə blīm´) adj., noble
con • de • scen • sion (kän di sen´shən) n., willingness to descend to the level of a social inferior and bestow kindness, often in a patronizing way
fu • gi • tive (fyoo´jə tiv) n., person fleeing from the law

doubtless been transported a long way off, and that he was dead to me, and might be <u>veritably</u> dead into the bargain.

No more low wet grounds, no more dikes and sluices, no more of these grazing cattle—though they seemed, in their dull manner, to wear a more respectful air now, and to face round, in order that they might stare as long as possible at the possessor of such great expectations—farewell, monotonous acquaintances of my childhood, henceforth I was for London and greatness—not for smith's work in general and for you! I made my <u>exultant</u> way to the old battery, and, lying down there to consider the question whether Miss Havisham intended me for Estella, fell asleep.

When I awoke, I was much surprised to find Joe sitting beside me, smoking his pipe. He greeted me with a cheerful smile on my opening my eyes, and said:

"As being the last time, Pip, I thought I'd foller."

"And Joe, I am very glad you did so."

"Thankee, Pip."

► What displeases Pip? Why does Pip feel this way?

"You may be sure, dear Joe," I went on, after we had shaken hands, "that I shall never forget you."

"No, no, Pip!" said Joe, in a comfortable tone, "I'm sure of that. Aye, aye, old chap! Bless you, it were only necessary to get it well round in a man's mind to be certain on it. But it took a bit of time to get it well round, the change come so oncommon plump;[4] didn't it?"

Somehow, I was not best pleased with Joe's being so mightily secure of me. I should have liked him to have betrayed emotion, or to have said, "It does you credit, Pip," or something of that sort. Therefore, I made no remark on Joe's first head, merely saying as to his second that the tidings had indeed come suddenly, but that I had always wanted to be a gentleman, and had often and often <u>speculated</u> on what I would do if I were one.

► What does Pip reveal to Joe? What is Joe's reaction?

"Have you though?" said Joe. "Astonishing!"

"It's a pity now, Joe," said I, "that you did not get on a little more, when we had our lessons here; isn't it?"

"Well, I don't know," returned Joe. "I'm so awful dull. I'm only master of my own trade. It were always a pity as I was

---

4. **oncommon plump.** Unusually abruptly

Words
For
Everyday
Use

ver • i • ta • bly (ver´i tə blē) *adv.*, truly
ex • ult • ant (eg zult´´nt) *adj.*, triumphant
spec • u • late (spek´yə lāt) *vi.*, make guesses

so awful dull; but it's no more of a pity now, than it was—this day twelvemonth[5]—don't you see?"

What I had meant was that when I came into my property and was able to do something for Joe, it would have been much more agreeable if he had been better qualified for a rise in station. He was so perfectly innocent of my meaning, however, that I thought I would mention it to Biddy in preference.

◄ Why does Pip want Joe to improve himself? What does Pip resolve to do?

So, when we had walked home and had had tea, I took Biddy into our little garden by the side of the lane, and, after throwing out in a general way for elevation of her spirits, that I should never forget her, said I had a favor to ask of her.

"And it is, Biddy," said I, "that you will not omit any opportunity of helping Joe on, a little."

"How helping him on?" asked Biddy, with a steady sort of glance.

"Well! Joe is a dear good fellow—in fact, I think he is the dearest fellow that ever lived—but he is rather backward in some things. For instance, Biddy, in his learning and his manners."

Although I was looking at Biddy as I spoke, and although she opened her eyes very wide when I had spoken, she did not look at me.

"Oh, his manners! won't his manners do, then?" asked Biddy, plucking a black-currant leaf.

◄ Why do Biddy and Pip argue?

"My dear Biddy, they do very well here—"

"Oh! they *do* very well here?" interrupted Biddy, looking closely at the leaf in her hand.

"Hear me out—but if I were to remove Joe into a higher sphere,[6] as I shall hope to remove him when I fully come into my property, they would hardly do him justice."

"And don't you think he knows that?" asked Biddy.

It was such a very <u>provoking</u> question (for it had never in the most distant manner occurred to me) that I said, snappishly, "Biddy, what do you mean?"

Biddy having rubbed the leaf to pieces between her hands—and the smell of a black-currant bush has ever since recalled to me that evening in the little garden by the side of the lane—said, "Have you never considered that he may be proud?"

◄ What is Biddy's defense of Joe? Of what does Pip accuse Biddy?

---

5. **twelvemonth.** A year ago
6. **sphere.** Here meaning "level of society"

Words For Everyday Use	**pro • vok • ing** (prə vō′kiŋ) *adj.,* irritating

"Proud?" I repeated, with disdainful emphasis.

"Oh! there are many kinds of pride," said Biddy, looking full at me and shaking her head; "pride is not all of one kind—"

"Well? What are you stopping for?" said I.

"Not all of one kind," resumed Biddy. "He may be too proud to let anyone take him out of a place that he is competent to fill, and fills well and with respect. To tell you the truth, I think he is—though it sounds bold in me to say so, for you must know him far better than I do."

"Now, Biddy," said I, "I am very sorry to see this in you. I did not expect to see this in you. You are envious, Biddy, and grudging. You are dissatisfied on account of my rise in fortune, and you can't help showing it."

"If you have the heart to think so," returned Biddy, "say so. Say so over and over again, if you have the heart to think so."

"If you have the heart to be so, you mean, Biddy," said I, in a virtuous and superior tone; "don't put it off upon me. I am very sorry to see it, and it's a—it's a bad side of human nature. I did intend to ask you to use any little opportunities you might have after I was gone of improving dear Joe. But after this, I ask you nothing. I am extremely sorry to see this in you, Biddy," I repeated. "It's a—it's a bad side of human nature."

► What does Biddy tell Pip? With what does she reproach him?

"Whether you scold me or approve of me," returned poor Biddy, "you may equally depend upon my trying to do all that lies in my power, here, at all times. And whatever opinion you take away of me shall make no difference in my remembrance of you. Yet a gentleman should not be unjust neither," said Biddy, turning away her head.

I again warmly repeated that it was a bad side of human nature (in which sentiment, waiving its application,[7] I have since seen reason to think I was right), and I walked down the little path away from Biddy, and Biddy went into the house, and I went out at the garden gate and took a dejected stroll until supper-time; again feeling it very sorrowful and strange that this, the second night of my bright fortunes, should be as lonely and unsatisfactory as the first.

But, morning once more brightened my view, and I extended my clemency to Biddy, and we dropped the subject.

---

7. **waiving its application.** Except for my applying this sentiment to Biddy by accusing her of jealousy

Words For Everyday Use

grudg • ing (gruj´iŋ) *adj.,* resentful
clem • en • cy (klem´ən sē) *n.,* forbearance or mercy, as toward an offender

Putting on the best clothes I had, I went into town as early as I could hope to find the shops open, and presented myself before Mr. Trabb, the tailor; who was having his breakfast in the parlor behind his shop, and who did not think it worth his while to come out to me, but called me in to him.

"Well!" said Mr. Trabb, in a hail-fellow-well-met kind of way. "How are you, and what can I do for you?"

Mr. Trabb had sliced his hot roll into three feather beds, and was slipping butter in between the blankets, and covering it up. He was a prosperous old bachelor, and his open window looked into a prosperous little garden and orchard, and there was a prosperous iron safe let into the wall at the side of his fireplace, and I did not doubt that heaps of his prosperity were put away in it in bags.

"Mr. Trabb," said I, "it's an unpleasant thing to have to mention, because it looks like boasting, but I have come into a handsome property."

A change passed over Mr. Trabb. He forgot the butter in bed, got up from the bedside, and wiped his fingers on the tablecloth, exclaiming, "Lord bless my soul!"

"I am going up to my guardian in London," said I, casually drawing some guineas out of my pocket and looking at them; "and I want a fashionable suit of clothes to go in. I wish to pay for them," I added—otherwise I thought he might only pretend to make them—"with ready money."[8]

Why does Pip go to Mr. Trabb? What does Pip tell him? In what manner does Trabb respond?

"My dear sir," said Mr. Trabb, as he respectfully bent his body, opened his arms, and took the liberty of touching me on the outside of each elbow, "don't hurt me by mentioning that. May I <u>venture</u> to congratulate you? Would you do me the favor of stepping into the shop?"

Mr. Trabb's boy was the most audacious boy in all that countryside. When I had entered he was sweeping the shop, and he had sweetened his labors by sweeping over me. He was still sweeping when I came out into the shop with Mr. Trabb, and he knocked the broom against all possible corners and obstacles to express (as I understood it) equality with any blacksmith, alive or dead.

"Hold that noise," said Mr. Trabb, with the greatest sternness, "or I'll knock your head off! Do me the favor to be

---

8. **ready money.** Cash

Words
For
Everyday
Use   ven • ture (ven´chər) vi., take a risk

seated, sir. Now, this," said Mr. Trabb, taking down a roll of cloth, and tiding it out in a flowing manner over the counter, preparatory to getting his hand under it to show the gloss, "is a very sweet article. I can recommend it for your purpose, sir, because it really is extra super. But you shall see some others. Give me number four, you!" (To the boy, and with a dreadfully severe stare, foreseeing the danger of that <u>miscreant's</u> brushing me with it, or making some other sign of familiarity.)

▶ How does Mr. Trabb treat Pip and the boy differently?

Mr. Trabb never removed his stern eye from the boy until he had deposited number four on the counter and was at a safe distance again. Then, he commanded him to bring number five, and number eight. "And let me have none of your tricks here," said Mr. Trabb, "or you shall repent it, you young scoundrel, the longest day you have to live."

Mr. Trabb then bent over number four, and in a sort of <u>deferential</u> confidence recommended it to me as a light article for summer wear, an article much in vogue among the nobility and gentry,[9] an article that it would ever be an honor to him to reflect upon a distinguished fellow-townsman's (if he might claim me for a fellow-townsman) having worn. "Are you bringing numbers five and eight, you vagabond," said Mr. Trabb to the boy after that, "or shall I kick you out of the shop and bring them myself?"

I selected the materials for a suit, with the assistance of Mr. Trabb's judgment, and re-entered the parlor to be measured. For, although Mr. Trabb had my measure already, and had previously been quite contented with it, he said apologetically that it "wouldn't do under existing circumstances, sir—wouldn't do at all." So, Mr. Trabb measured and calculated me in the parlor, as if I were an estate and he the finest species of surveyor,[10] and gave himself such a world of trouble that I felt that no suit of clothes could possibly <u>remunerate</u> him for his pains. When he had at last done and had appointed to send the articles to Mr. Pumblechook's on the Thursday evening, he said, with his hand upon the parlor lock, "I know, sir, that London gentlemen cannot

---

9. **gentry.** People of high social standing
10. **estate . . . surveyor.** Pip is comparing Trabb to a surveyor, or person who examines the location, form, and boundaries of a tract of land, and himself to the land.

Words For Everyday Use

mis • cre • ant (mis krē´ənt) *n.,* villain

def • er • en • tial (def´ə ren´shəl) *adj.,* showing courteous respect

re • mu • ner • ate (ri myo͞o´nə rāt) *vt.,* pay or reward for work be expected to patronize local work, as a rule; but if you would give me a turn now and then in the quality of a townsman, I should greatly <u>esteem</u> it. Good morning, sir, much obliged. Door!"

◀ What request does Trabb make?

The last word was flung at the boy, who had not the least notion what it meant. But I saw him collapse as his master rubbed me out with his hands, and my first <u>decided</u> experience of the stupendous power of money was that it had morally laid upon his back, Trabb's boy.

◀ Of what does Pip become aware?

After this memorable event, I went to the hatter's, and the bootmaker's, and the hosier's,[11] and felt rather like Mother Hubbard's dog[12] whose outfit required the services of so many trades. I also went to the coach-office and took my place for seven o'clock on Saturday morning. It was not necessary to explain everywhere that I had come into a handsome property; but whenever I said anything to that effect, it followed that the <u>officiating</u> tradesman ceased to have his attention diverted through the window by the High Street, and concentrated his mind upon me. When I had ordered everything I wanted, I directed my steps towards Pumblechook's, and, as I approached that gentleman's place of business, I saw him standing at his door.

◀ What happens as Pip visits each shop? What prompts this reaction?

He was waiting for me with great impatience. He had been out early with the chaise-cart, and had called at the forge and heard the news. He had prepared a collation[13] for me in the Barnwell parlor, and he too ordered his shopman to "come out of the gangway" as my sacred person passed.

"My dear friend," said Mr. Pumblechook, taking me by both hands, when he and I and the collation were alone, "I give you joy of your good fortune. Well deserved, well deserved!"

◀ For what does Pumblechook take credit? Why does he do so?

This was coming to the point, and I thought it a sensible way of expressing himself.

"To think," said Mr. Pumblechook, after snorting admiration at me for some moments, "that I should have been the humble instrument of leading up to this is a proud reward."

I begged Mr. Pumblechook to remember that nothing was to be ever said or hinted on that point.

---

11. **hosier's.** Shop of a person who makes and sells hosiery—stockings and socks
12. **Mother Hubbard's dog.** Dog in Sarah Catherine Martin's "The Comic Adventures of Old Mother Hubbard and Her Dog," which went to a hatter, boot maker, hosier, barber, and seamstress
13. **collation.** Light meal

Words For Everyday Use

es • teem (ə stēm´) vt., value

de • cid • ed (dē sīd´id) adj., definite; clear-cut

of • fi • ci • at • ing (ə fish´ē āt´iŋ) adj., performing the duties of an office

"My dear young friend," said Mr. Pumblechook, "if you will allow me to call you so—"

I murmured "Certainly," and Mr. Pumblechook took me by both hands again, and communicated a movement to his waistcoat, which had an emotional appearance, though it was rather low down, "My dear young friend, rely upon my doing my little all in your absence, by keeping the fact before the mind of Joseph. Joseph!" said Mr. Pumblechook, in the way of a compassionate adjuration. "Joseph!! Joseph!!!" Thereupon he shook his head and tapped it, expressing his sense of deficiency in Joseph.

► How does Pumblechook treat Pip? In what way is this different from how Pumblechook used to treat Pip?

"But my dear young friend," said Mr. Pumblechook, "you must be hungry, you must be exhausted. Be seated. Here is a chicken had round from the Boar,[14] here is a tongue had round from the Boar, here's one or two little things had round from the Boar that I hope you may not despise. But do I," said Mr. Pumblechook, getting up again the moment after he had sat down, "see afore me him as I ever sported with in his times of happy infancy? And may I—*may* I—?"

This "May I" meant might he shake hands? I consented, and he was fervent, and then sat down again.

"Here is wine," said Mr. Pumblechook. "Let us drink, thanks to fortune, and may she ever pick out her favorites with equal judgment! And yet I cannot," said Mr. Pumblechook, getting up again, "seeing afore me one—and likewise drink to one—without again expressing—may I—*may* I—?"

I said he might, and he shook hands with me again, and emptied his glass and turned it upside down. I did the same; and if I had turned myself upside down before drinking, the wine could not have gone more direct to my head.

Mr. Pumblechook helped me to the liver wing, and to the best slice of tongue (none of those out-of-the-way No Thoroughfares of pork[15] now), and took, comparatively speaking, no care of himself at all. "Ah! poultry, poultry! You little thought," said Mr. Pumblechook, apostrophizing[16] the fowl in the dish, "when you was a young fledgling, what was in store for you. You little thought you was to be refreshment

---

14. **had round from the Boar.** Sent from the Blue Boar, the town's inn
15. **No . . . pork.** Undesirable, almost inedible pieces of pork, such as were served to Pip as a child when Pumblechook came to holiday dinners
16. **apostrophizing.** Speaking in direct address to the roast chicken

ad • ju • ra • tion (aj´ oo rā´ shən) n., solemn command; earnest appeal

de • fi • cien • cy (di fish´ ən sē) n., defectiveness; lack of something essential

fer • vent (fur´ vənt) adj., showing great warmth of feeling beneath this humble roof for one as—call it a weakness, if you will," said Mr. Pumblechook, getting up again, "but may I? *may* I—?"

It began to be unnecessary to repeat the form of saying he might, so he did it at once. How he ever did it so often without wounding himself with my knife, I don't know.

"And your sister," he resumed, after a little steady eating, "which had the honor of bringing you up by hand! It's a sad picter, to reflect that she's no longer equal to fully understanding the honor. May—"

I saw he was about to come at me again, and I stopped him.

"We'll drink her health," said I.

"Ah!" cried Mr. Pumblechook, leaning back in his chair, quite <u>flaccid</u> with admiration, "that's the way you know 'em, sir!" (I don't know who sir was, but he certainly was not I, and there was no third person present.) "That's the way you know the nobleminded, sir! Ever forgiving and ever <u>affable</u>. It might," said the <u>servile</u> Pumblechook, putting down his untasted glass in a hurry and getting up again, "to a common person, have the appearance of repeating—but *may* I—?"

When he had done it, he resumed his seat and drank to my sister. "Let us never be blind," said Mr. Pumblechook, "to her faults of temper, but it is to be hoped she meant well."

◄ *What does Pumblechook admit about Mrs. Joe?*

At about this time, I began to observe that he was getting flushed in the face; as to myself, I felt all face, <u>steeped</u> in wine and smarting.

I mentioned to Mr. Pumblechook that I wished to have my new clothes sent to his house, and he was ecstatic on my so distinguishing him. I mentioned my reason for desiring to avoid observation in the village, and he <u>lauded</u> it to the skies. There was nobody but himself, he intimated, worthy of my confidence, and—in short, might he? Then he asked me tenderly if I remembered our boyish games at sums, and how we had gone together to have me bound apprentice, and, in effect, how he had ever been my favorite fancy and my chosen friend? If I had taken ten times as many glasses of wine as I had, I should have known that he never had stood in that relation towards me, and should in my heart of hearts have <u>repudiated</u> the idea. Yet for all that, I remember feeling convinced that I had been much mistaken in him, and that he was a sensible practical good-hearted prime fellow.

◄ *What does Pumblechook do to ingratiate himself? What does Pip think of Pumblechook now?*

Words For Everyday Use

flac • cid (flak´sid) *adj.,* weak; feeble

af • fa • ble (af´ə bəl) *adj.,* gentle and kindly

ser • vile (sur´vəl) *adj.,* too humble or submissive

steeped (stēpd) *adj.,* soaked; immersed

laud (lôd) *vt.,* praise

re • pu • di • ate (ri pyoo´dē āt´) *vt.,* refuse to accept

► What does Pumblechook want from Pip?

By degrees he fell to reposing such great confidence in me as to ask my advice in reference to his own affairs. He mentioned that there was an opportunity for a great amalgamation and monopoly[17] of the corn and seed trade on those premises, if enlarged, such as had never occurred before in that, or any other neighborhood. What alone was wanting to the realization of a vast fortune he considered to be More Capital.[18] Those were the two little words, More Capital. Now it appeared to him (Pumblechook) that if that capital were got into the business, through a sleeping partner,[19] sir— which sleeping partner would have nothing to do but walk in, by self or <u>deputy</u>, whenever he pleased, and examine the books—and walk in twice a year and take his profits away in his pocket, to the tune of fifty per cent—it appeared to him that that might be an opening for a young gentleman of spirit combined with property, which would be worthy of his attention. But what did I think? He had great confidence in my opinion, and what did I think? I gave it as my opinion, "Wait a bit!" The united vastness and distinctiveness of this view so struck him that he no longer asked me if he might shake hands with me, but said he really must—and did.

We drank all the wine, and Mr. Pumblechook pledged himself over and over again to keep Joseph up to the mark (I don't know what mark), and to render me efficient and constant service (I don't know what service). He also made known to me for the first time in my life, and certainly after having kept his secret wonderfully well, that he had always said of me, "That boy is no common boy, and mark me, his fortun' will be no common fortun'." He said with a tearful smile that it was a singular thing to think of now, and I said so too. Finally, I went out into the air, with a dim perception that there was something unwonted in the conduct of the sunshine, and found that I had slumberously[20] got to the turnpike without having taken any account of the road.

---

17. **amalgamation and monopoly.** Gathering all the sources of and thus being the only supplier of a product
18. **Capital.** Money
19. **sleeping partner.** Partner who shares in financing but not management
20. **slumberously.** Sleepily

Words For Everyday Use

dep • u • ty (dep′yə tē) *n.*, person appointed to substitute for another

There I was roused by Mr. Pumblechook's hailing me. He was a long way down the sunny street, and was making expressive gestures for me to stop. I stopped, and he came up breathless.

"No, my dear friend," said he, when he had recovered wind for speech. "Not if I can help it. This occasion shall not entirely pass without that affability on your part. May I, as an old friend and well-wisher? *May* I?"

We shook hands for the hundredth time at least, and he ordered a young carter[21] out of my way with the greatest indignation. Then, he blessed me, and stood waving his hand to me until I had passed the crook in the road; and then I turned into a field and had a long nap under a hedge before I pursued my way home.

I had scant luggage to take with me to London, for little of the little I possessed was adapted to my new station. But, I began packing that same afternoon, and wildly packed up things that I knew I should want next morning, in a <u>fiction</u> that there was not a moment to be lost.

So, Tuesday, Wednesday, and Thursday passed; and on Friday morning I went to Mr. Pumblechook's, to put on my new clothes and pay my visit to Miss Havisham. Mr. Pumblechook's own room was given up to me to dress in, and was decorated with clean towels expressly for the event. My clothes were rather a disappointment, of course. Probably every new and eagerly expected garment ever put on since clothes came in fell a trifle short of the wearer's expectation. But after I had had my new suit on some half an hour, and had gone through an immensity of posturing[22] with Mr. Pumblechook's very limited dressing glass,[23] in the futile endeavor to see my legs, it seemed to fit me better. It being market morning[24] at a neighboring town some ten miles off, Mr. Pumblechook was not at home. I had not told him exactly when I meant to leave, and was not likely to shake hands with him again before departing. This was all as it should be, and I went out in my new <u>array</u>, fearfully

◀ *Why does Pip return to Pumblechook's on Friday?*

◀ *Why does Pip travel the back way to Miss Havisham's?*

---

21. **carter.** Person who delivers goods
22. **immensity of posturing.** Assuming a great number of poses
23. **dressing glass.** Mirror
24. **market morning.** Morning when producers and sellers bring their goods to market

Words
For
Everyday
Use

fic • tion (fĭk´shən) *n.,* imaginary idea
ar • ray (ə rā´) *n.,* fine clothes

ashamed of having to pass the shopman, and suspicious after all that I was at a personal disadvantage, something like Joe's in his Sunday suit.

I went <u>circuitously</u> to Miss Havisham's by all the back ways, and rang at the bell <u>constrainedly</u>, on account of the stiff long fingers of my gloves. Sarah Pocket came to the gate, and positively <u>reeled</u> back when she saw me so changed; her walnut-shell countenance likewise, turned from brown to green and yellow.

"You?" said she. "You? Good gracious! What do you want?"

"I am going to London, Miss Pocket," said I, "and want to say good-bye to Miss Havisham."

I was not expected, for she left me locked in the yard, while she went to ask if I were to be admitted. After a very short delay, she returned and took me up, staring at me all the way.

Miss Havisham was taking exercise in the room with the long spread table, leaning on her crutch stick. The room was lighted as of yore,[25] and at the sound of our entrance, she stopped and turned. She was then just abreast of the rotted bride-cake.

"Don't go, Sarah," she said. "Well, Pip?"

▶ How does Miss Havisham receive Pip? What does he tell her?

"I start for London, Miss Havisham, tomorrow," I was exceedingly careful what I said, "and I thought you would kindly not mind my taking leave of you."

"This is a gay figure, Pip," said she, making her crutch stick play round me, as if she, the fairy godmother who had changed me, were bestowing the finishing gift.

"I have come into such good fortune since I saw you last, Miss Havisham," I murmured. "And I am so grateful for it, Miss Havisham!"

▶ What does Miss Havisham know of Pip's situation? Why does Miss Havisham enjoy questioning Pip in front of Sarah Pocket?

"Aye, aye!" said she, looking at the discomfited and envious Sarah with delight. "I have seen Mr. Jaggers. I have heard about it, Pip. So you go tomorrow?"

"Yes, Miss Havisham."

"And you are adopted by a rich person?"

"Yes, Miss Havisham."

"Not named?"

"No, Miss Havisham."

"And Mr. Jaggers is made your guardian?"

---

25. **of yore.** Formerly; in days long past

"Yes, Miss Havisham."

She quite gloated on these questions and answers, so keen was her enjoyment of Sarah Pocket's jealous dismay. "Well!" she went on; "you have a promising career before you. Be good—deserve it—and abide by Mr. Jaggers's instructions." She looked at me, and looked at Sarah, and Sarah's countenance wrung out of her watchful face a cruel smile. "Good-bye, Pip! You will always keep the name of Pip, you know."

"Yes, Miss Havisham."

"Good-bye, Pip!"

She stretched out her hand, and I went down on my knee and put it to my lips. I had not considered how I should take leave of her; it came naturally to me at the moment to do this. She looked at Sarah Pocket with triumph in her weird eyes, and so I left my fairy godmother, with both her hands on her crutch stick, standing in the midst of the dimly lighted room beside the rotten bride-cake that was hidden in cobwebs.

Sarah Pocket conducted me down, as if I were a ghost who must be seen out. She could not get over my appearance, and was in the last degree confounded. I said "Good-bye, Miss Pocket;" but she merely stared, and did not seem collected enough to know that I had spoken. Clear of the house, I made the best of my way back to Pumblechook's, took off my new clothes, made them into a bundle, and went back home in my older dress, carrying it—to speak the truth— much more at my ease, too, though I had the bundle to carry.

And now those six days which were to have run out so slowly had run out fast and were gone, and tomorrow looked me in the face more steadily than I could look at it. As the six evenings had dwindled away to five, to four, to three, to two, I had become more and more appreciative of the society of Joe and Biddy. On this last evening, I dressed myself out in my new clothes for their delight, and sat in my splendor until bedtime. We had a hot supper on the occasion, graced by the inevitable roast fowl, and we had some flip[26] to finish with. We were all very low, and none the higher for pretending to be in spirits.

◀ *What is Miss Pocket's reaction to Pip?*

---

26. **flip.** Mixed drink made with any of various alcoholic beverages, usually including beaten eggs

Words For Everyday Use

col • lect • ed (kə lek´tid) *adj.,* in control of oneself

► What does Pip deny about wanting to walk to town alone? Does he change his mind?

I was to leave our village at five in the morning, carrying my little hand-portmanteau,[27] and I had told Joe that I wished to walk away all alone. I am afraid—sore afraid—that this purpose originated in my sense of the contrast there would be between me and Joe, if we went to the coach together. I had pretended with myself that there was nothing of this <u>taint</u> in the arrangement; but when I went up to my little room on this last night, I felt compelled to admit that it might be so, and had an impulse upon me to go down again and <u>entreat</u> Joe to walk with me in the morning. I did not.

All night there were coaches in my broken sleep, going to wrong places instead of to London, and having in the traces[28] now dogs, now cats, now pigs, now men—never horses. Fantastic failures of journeys occupied me until the day dawned and the birds were singing. Then, I got up and partly dressed, and sat at the window to take a last look out, and in taking it fell asleep.

Biddy was astir so early to get my breakfast that, although I did not sleep at the window an hour, I smelt the smoke of the kitchen fire when I started up with a terrible idea that it must be late in the afternoon. But long after that, and long after I had heard the clinking of the teacups and was quite ready, I wanted the resolution to go downstairs. After all, I remained up there, repeatedly unlocking and unstrapping my small portmanteau and locking and strapping it up again, until Biddy called to me that I was late.

► What do Biddy and Joe do to send him off? How does Pip feel about this custom?

It was a hurried breakfast with no taste in it. I got up from the meal, saying with a sort of briskness, as if it had only just occurred to me, "Well! I suppose I must be off!" and then I kissed my sister, who was laughing, and nodding and shaking in her usual chair, and kissed Biddy, and threw my arms around Joe's neck. Then I took up my little portmanteau and walked out. The last I saw of them was when I presently heard a scuffle behind me, and looking back, saw Joe throwing an old shoe after me and Biddy throwing another old shoe. I stopped then, to wave my hat, and dear old Joe waved his strong right arm above his head, crying huskily, "Hooroar!" and Biddy put her apron to her face.

---

27. **portmanteau.** Traveling case or bag
28. **traces.** Straps connecting a draft animal's harness to the vehicle drawn

Words For Everyday Use

taint (tānt) *n.*, trace of something that spoils or corrupts
en • treat (in trēt´) *vt.*, ask earnestly

I walked away at a good pace, thinking it was easier to go than I had supposed it would be, and reflecting that it would never have done to have an old shoe thrown after the coach, in sight of all the High Street. I whistled and made nothing of going. But the village was very peaceful and quiet, and the light mists were solemnly rising, as if to show me the world, and I had been so innocent and little there, and all beyond was so unknown and great, that in a moment with a strong heave and sob I broke into tears. It was by the finger-post at the end of the village, and I laid my hand upon it, and said, "Good-bye, O my dear, dear friend!"

◄ What does Pip do when he gets to the village? Why?

Heaven knows we need never be ashamed of our tears, for they are rain upon the blinding dust of earth, overlying our hard hearts. I was better after I had cried than before—more sorry, more aware of my own ingratitude, more gentle. If I had cried before, I should have had Joe with me then.

◄ What does Pip regret?

So subdued I was by those tears, and by their breaking out again in the course of the quiet walk, that when I was on the coach, and it was clear of the town, I deliberated with an aching heart whether I would not get down when we changed horses and walk back, and have another evening at home, and a better parting. We changed, and I had not made up my mind, and still reflected for my comfort that it would be quite practicable[29] to get down and walk back, when we changed again. And while I was occupied with these deliberations, I would fancy an exact resemblance to Joe in some man coming along the road towards us, and my heart would beat high. As if he could possibly be there!

We changed again, and yet again, and it was now too late and too far to go back, and I went on. And the mists had all solemnly risen now, and the world lay spread before me.

THIS IS THE END OF THE FIRST STAGE
OF PIP'S EXPECTATIONS.

---

29. **practicable.** Possible, practical

Responding to the Selection

Imagine that you are in Pip's position—you suddenly learn that you stand to inherit a large amount of money and that your unknown benefactor wishes for you to move to a distant city to begin a new sort of life. How would you feel about leaving your friends and family behind? How would you feel about your "great expectations"? Explain whether you think your altered financial prospect would change your personality as well.

Reviewing the Selection

Recalling and Interpreting

1. **R:** What happens to Mrs. Joe? With what was she attacked? Whom does Pip suspect of the crime and why?

2. **I:** In what way does what happens to Mrs. Joe alter Pip's household? How is Mrs. Joe herself different? Explain your feelings about what has happened to Mrs. Joe. In what way do her past actions contribute to your feelings?

3. **R:** Describe the relationship between Pip and Biddy. What "confidence" does Pip share with her? What does Pip say he wishes he could do? What advice does Biddy have for Pip?

4. **I:** How do you think Biddy feels about Pip? How do you think she feels when he talks in the manner he does about a possible relationship between the two of them? about his dreams for the future? What do you think of Biddy as a character? What do Pip's interactions with Biddy reveal about the way Pip is changing as a character?

5. **R:** Who is Jaggers? What important information does he reveal? What does Jaggers offer Joe? How does Joe react to this character and to his offer?

6. **I:** Explain what Jaggers's major characteristics are. Why does Joe react to Jaggers and his offer in this way? What does Joe's reaction reveal about his values? In what way do Joe's values differ from Pip's?

7. **R:** When Pip goes shopping, how do people treat him once they learn that he has "great expectations"? What plans does Pip have for Joe? About what is he worried? What does Biddy tell Pip about his plans for Joe? Of what does Pip accuse Biddy? Why doesn't Pip want Joe to accompany him to town to meet his coach for London?

8. **I:** Explain which character is right about Joe, Pip or Biddy. What do you think of Pip's attitude toward and treatment of Joe and Biddy? In what way have Pip's "great expectations" altered him as a character? What might the author be indicating about the effect money has on people?

Synthesizing

9. Explain why Pip believes that Miss Havisham is his secret benefactor. What evidence does he have? Is his assumption reasonable given this evidence? What special hope helps to inspire his belief?

10. Explain how Pip's feelings toward leaving his old way of life behind change throughout chapters 18 and 19.

Understanding Literature (QUESTIONS FOR DISCUSSION)

1. Point of View and Narrator. Point of view is the vantage point from which a story is told. A **narrator** is one who tells a story. In stories told from a first-person point of view, the narrator uses words such as *I* and *we* and may be a participant or witness of the action. Pip is the narrator of this novel and is both a participant in and witness to its action. He also reveals his private thoughts and reactions to the reader. Explain whether Pip's voice is that of a youthful narrator who relates actions as they are happening or that of an older narrator who reflects upon past events critically and with more self-knowledge. How can you tell? What feelings about his youthful actions does Pip, the narrator, reveal? What does this indicate about the way in which Pip must have changed as he grew older?

2. Scene. A scene is a short section of a literary work that presents action that occurs in a single place or at a single time. In chapter 19, there is a revealing scene between Pip and Pumblechook. They meet and their interaction and conversation are very different from those in the past. The change is prompted by Pip's sudden fortune. Identify examples of the ways in which their relationship has changed.

3. Allusion and Imagery. An allusion is a rhetorical technique in which reference is made to a person, event, object, or work from history or literature. An **image** is a word or phrase that names something that can be seen, heard, touched, tasted, or smelled. The images in a literary work are referred to collectively as the work's **imagery**. In describing Orlick as a character, Dickens makes allusion to Cain and the Wandering Jew. In the Bible, Cain becomes an outcast for the crime of killing his brother. According to legend, the Wandering Jew was a Jew condemned to wander around the world until Jesus' second coming for the crime of taunting Jesus to go faster as he carried the cross. What do these allusions reveal about the way Dickens intends for the reader to view Orlick? What imagery contributes to this view of Orlick as a character akin to Cain and the Wandering Jew?

CHAPTER 20

The journey from our town to the <u>metropolis</u> was a journey of about five hours. It was a little past midday when the four-horse stagecoach by which I was a passenger got into the ravel[1] of traffic frayed out about the Cross Keys, Wood Street, Cheapside, London.

We Britons had at that time particularly settled that it was <u>treasonable</u> to doubt our having and our being the best of everything: otherwise, while I was scared by the immensity of London, I think I might have had some faint doubts whether it was not rather ugly, crooked, narrow, and dirty.

Mr. Jaggers had duly sent me his address; it was Little Britain, and he had written after it on his card, "just off of Smithfield, and close by the coach-office." Nevertheless, a hackney-coachman, who seemed to have as many capes to his greasy great-coat as he was years old, packed me up in his coach and hemmed me in with a folding and jingling barrier of steps, as if he were going to take me fifty miles. His getting on his box, which I remember to have been decorated with an old weather-stained pea-green hammercloth,[2] moth-eaten into rags, was quite a work of time. It was a wonderful equipage,[3] with six great coronets[4] outside, and ragged things behind for I don't know how many footmen[5] to hold on by, and a harrow[6] below them to prevent amateur footmen from yielding to the temptation.

I had scarcely had time to enjoy the coach and to think how like a straw yard it was, and yet how like a rag shop, and to wonder why the horses' nose-bags were kept inside, when I observed the coachman beginning to get down, as if we were going to stop presently. And stop we presently did, in a gloomy street, at certain offices with an open door, whereon was painted MR. JAGGERS.

► What is Pip's impression of London?

► What makes the ride interesting for Pip?

1. **ravel.** Tangle
2. **hammercloth.** Name taken from the tools kept in a box under the coachman's seat
3. **equipage.** Horse-drawn carriage
4. **coronets.** Ornamental bands of metal
5. **footmen.** Male servants who run on foot beside their master's horse or carriage
6. **harrow.** Frame with spikes affixed to the coach to prevent footmen and others from trying to jump on the coach to catch a free ride

Words For Everyday Use

me • trop • o • lis (mə träp´əl is) *n.*, main city, often a capital

trea • son • a • ble (trē´zən ə bəl) *adj.*, traitorous

"How much?" I asked the coachman.

The coachman answered, "A shilling—unless you wish to make it more."

I naturally said I had no wish to make it more.

"Then it must be a shilling," observed the coachman. "I don't want to get into trouble. I know *him!*" He darkly closed an eye at Mr. Jaggers's name, and shook his head.

◄ Why doesn't the coachman wish to overcharge Pip?

When he had got his shilling, and had in course of time completed the ascent to his box, and had got away (which appeared to relieve his mind), I went into the front office with my little portmanteau in my hand, and asked, was Mr. Jaggers at home?

"He is not," returned the clerk. "He is in court at present. Am I addressing Mr. Pip?"

I signified that he was addressing Mr. Pip.

"Mr. Jaggers left word would you wait in his room. He couldn't say how long he might be, having a case on. But it stands to reason, his time being valuable, that he won't be longer than he can help."

With those words, the clerk opened a door, and ushered me into an inner chamber at the back. Here we found a gentleman with one eye, in a velveteen[7] suit and knee breeches, who wiped his nose with his sleeve on being interrupted in the <u>perusal</u> of the newspaper.

"Go and wait outside, Mike," said the clerk.

I began to say that I hoped I was not interrupting—when the clerk shoved this gentleman out with as little ceremony as I ever saw used, and tossing his fur cap out after him, left me alone.

Mr. Jaggers's room was lighted by a skylight only, and was a most dismal place; the skylight, <u>eccentrically</u> patched like a broken head, and the distorted adjoining houses looking as if they had twisted themselves to peep down at me through it. There were not so many papers about as I should have expected to see; and there were some odd objects about that I should not have expected to see—such as an old rusty pistol, a sword in a scabbard,[8] several strange-looking boxes and packages, and two dreadful casts[9] on a shelf, of faces peculiarly

◄ What details in Jaggers's office does Pip find interesting?

---

7. **velveteen.** Cotton cloth with a short, thick pile, resembling velvet
8. **scabbard.** Sheath or case to hold the blade of a sword
9. **casts.** Bronze or plaster statues formed in a mold

Words For Everyday Use

per • u • sal (pə roo′zəl) *n.*, thorough or leisurely reading

ec • cen • tri • cal • ly (ik sen′trik lē) *adv.*, unevenly; oddly swollen, and twitchy about the nose. Mr. Jaggers's own high-backed chair was of deadly black horsehair, with rows of brass nails round it, like a coffin; and I fancied I could see how he leaned back in it, and bit his forefinger at the clients. The room was but small, and the clients seemed to have had a habit of backing up against the wall: the wall, especially opposite to Mr. Jaggers's chair, being greasy with shoulders. I recalled, too, that the one-eyed gentleman had shuffled forth against the wall when I was the innocent cause of his being turned out.

I sat down in the cliental chair placed over against Mr. Jaggers's chair, and became fascinated by the dismal atmosphere of the place. I called to mind that the clerk had the same air of knowing something to everybody else's disadvantage as his master had. I wondered how many other clerks there were upstairs, and whether they all claimed to have the same <u>detrimental</u> mastery of their fellow-creatures. I wondered what was the history of all the odd litter about the room, and how it came there. I wondered whether the two swollen faces were of Mr. Jaggers's family, and, if he were so unfortunate as to have had a pair of such ill-looking relations, why he stuck them on that dusty perch for the blacks and flies to settle on, instead of giving them a place at home. Of course I had no experience of a London summer day, and my spirits may have been oppressed by the hot exhausted air, and by the dust and grit that lay thick on everything. But I sat wondering and waiting in Mr. Jaggers's close room, until I really could not bear the two casts on the shelf above Mr. Jaggers's chair, and got up and went out.

▶ *Why does Pip leave the office?*

When I told the clerk that I would take a turn in the air while I waited, he advised me to go round the corner and I should come into Smithfield.[10] So, I came into Smithfield; and the shameful place, being all asmear with filth and fat and blood and foam, seemed to stick to me. So, I rubbed it off with all possible speed by turning into a street where I saw the great black dome of Saint Paul's[11] bulging at me from behind a grim stone building which a bystander said was Newgate Prison.[12] Following the wall of the jail, I found the

▶ *What does Pip find in the neighborhood?*

10. **Smithfield.** Open market where horses and cattle were sold
11. **St. Paul's.** Cathedral in London
12. **Newgate Prison.** Famous prison in London, demolished in 1902

Words For Everyday Use

det • ri • men • tal (deˊtrə menˊtʼl) *adj.,* harmful

roadway covered with straw to deaden the noise of passing vehicles; and from this, and from the quantity of people standing about smelling strongly of spirits and beer, I inferred that the trials were on.

While I looked about me here, an exceedingly dirty and partially drunk minister of justice asked me if I would like to step in and hear a trial or so, informing me that he could give me a front place for half-a-crown,[13] whence I should command a full view of the Lord Chief Justice in his wig and robes—mentioning that awful[14] <u>personage</u> like waxwork,[15] and presently offering him at the reduced price of eighteen-pence. As I declined the proposal on the plea of an appointment, he was so good as to take me into a yard and show me where the gallows[16] was kept, and also where people were publicly whipped, and then he showed me the debtors' door, out of which culprits came to be hanged, heightening the interest of that dreadful portal[17] by giving me to understand that "four on 'em" would come out at that door the day after tomorrow at eight in the morning to be killed in a row. This was horrible, and gave me a sickening idea of London, the more so as the Lord Chief Justice's proprietor[18] wore (from his hat down to his boots and up again to his pocket-hand-kerchief inclusive) mildewed clothes, which had evidently not belonged to him originally, and which, I took it into my head, he had bought cheap of the executioner. Under these circumstances I thought myself well rid of him for a shilling.

I dropped into the office to ask if Mr. Jaggers had come in yet, and I found he had not, and I strolled out again. This time I made the tour of Little Britain, and turned into Bartholomew Close;[19] and now I became aware that other people were waiting about for Mr. Jaggers, as well as I. There were two men of secret appearance lounging in Bartholomew Close, and thoughtfully fitting their feet into the cracks of

◀ What are many other people also doing?

---

13. **half-a-crown.** British coin equal to twenty-five pence
14. **awful.** Here means "highly impressive; causing fear or dread"
15. **waxwork.** Human figure made of wax, on exhibition
16. **gallows.** Frame with crossbar and rope for hanging condemned persons
17. **portal.** Doorway
18. **proprietor.** Manager, here referring humorously to the individual trying to sell Pip a place from which to view the Lord Chief Justice
19. **Close.** British term for an enclosed place beside a building or for a narrow street

---

Words For Everyday Use

per • son • age (pur´sən ij´) *adj.*, person of importance or distinction

► What opinion do people seem to hold of Jaggers?

the pavement as they talked together, one of whom said to the other when they first passed me that "Jaggers would do it if it was to be done." There was a knot of three men and two women standing at a corner, and one of the women was crying on her dirty shawl, and the other comforted her by saying, as she pulled her own shawl over her shoulders, "Jaggers is for him, 'Melia, and what more *could* you have?" There was a red-eyed little Jew who came into the close while I was loitering there, in company with a second little Jew whom he sent upon an errand; and while the messenger was gone, I remarked this Jew, who was of a highly excitable temperament, performing a jig of anxiety under a lamp-post, and accompanying himself, in a kind of frenzy, with the words, "Oh Jaggerth, Jaggerth, Jaggerth! All otherth ith Cag-Maggerth, give me Jaggerth!" These testimonies to the popularity of my guardian made a deep impression on me, and I admired and wondered more than ever.

► What is Pip's reaction to the words of those who wait for Jaggers?

At length, as I was looking out at the iron gate of Bartholomew Close into Little Britain, I saw Mr. Jaggers coming across the road towards me. All the others who were waiting saw him at the same time, and there was quite a rush at him. Mr. Jaggers, putting a hand on my shoulder and walking me on at his side without saying anything to me, addressed himself to his followers.

First, he took the two secret men.

► What is Jaggers's attitude toward the men?

"Now, I have nothing to say to *you*," said Mr. Jaggers, throwing his finger at them. "I want to know no more than I know. As to the result, it's a toss-up. I told you from the first it was toss-up. Have you paid Wemmick?"

"We made the money up this morning, sir," said one of the men submissively, while the other perused Mr. Jaggers's face.

"I don't ask you when you made it up, or where, or whether you made it up at all. Has Wemmick got it?"

"Yes, sir," said both the men together.

"Very well; then you may go. Now, I won't have it!" said Mr. Jaggers, waving his hand at them to put them behind him. "If you say a word to me, I'll throw up the case."[20]

"We thought, Mr. Jaggers—" one of the men began, pulling off his hat.

---

20. **throw up the case.** Give up or abandon the case

Words
For
Everyday
Use

sub • mis • sive • ly (səb mis´ iv lē) *adv.*, obediently

"That's what I told you not to do," said Mr. Jaggers. "*You* thought! I think for you; that's enough for you. If I want you, I know where to find you; I don't want you to find me. Now I won't have it. I won't hear a word."

The two men looked at one another as Mr. Jaggers waved them behind again, and humbly fell back and were heard no more.

"And now *you!*" said Mr. Jaggers, suddenly stopping and turning on the two women with the shawls, from whom the three men had meekly separated.—"Oh! Amelia, is it?"

"Yes, Mr. Jaggers."

"And do you remember," retorted Mr. Jaggers, "that but for me you wouldn't be here and couldn't be here?"

"Oh, yes, sir!" exclaimed both women together. "Lord bless you, sir, well we knows that!"

"Then why," said Mr. Jaggers, "do you come here?"

"My Bill, sir!" the crying woman pleaded.

"Now, I tell you what!" said Mr. Jaggers. "Once for all. If you don't know that your Bill's in good hands, I know it. And if you come here bothering about your Bill, I'll make an example of both your Bill and you, and let him slip through my fingers. Have you paid Wemmick?"

"Oh, yes, sir! Every farden."[21]

"Very well. Then you have done all you have got to do. Say another word—one single word—and Wemmick shall give you your money back."

This terrible threat caused the two women to fall off immediately. No one remained now but the excitable Jew, who had already raised the skirts of Mr. Jaggers's coat to his lips several times.

"I don't know this man!" said Mr. Jaggers, in the same devastating <u>strain</u>. "What does this fellow want?"

"Ma thear Mithter Jaggerth. Hown brother to Habraham Latharuth?"

"Who's he?" said Mr. Jaggers. "Let go of my coat."

The suitor, kissing the hem of the garment again before <u>relinquishing</u> it, replied, "Habraham Latharuth, on thuthpithion of plate."

"You're too late," said Mr. Jaggers. "I am over the way."

◄ What does Jaggers say he has done for the women? With what does he threaten them?

---

21. **farden.** Farthing, coin of small value worth one-fourth a penny

Words For Everyday Use

strain (strān) *n.*, style; tone
re • lin • quish (ri liṇ´kwish) *vt.*, let go of

► What does the man request of Jaggers? How does Jaggers respond?

"Holy father, Mithter Jaggerth!" cried my excitable acquaintance, turning white, "don't thay you're again[22] Habraham Latharuth!"

"I am," said Mr. Jaggers, "and there's an end of it. Get out of the way."

"Mithter Jaggerth! Half a moment! My hown cuthen'th gone to Mithter Wemmick at thith prethenth minute to hoffer him hany termth. Mithter Jaggerth! Half a quarter of a moment! If you'd have the condethenthun to be bought off from the t'other thide—at any thuperior prithe!—money no object!—Mithter Jaggerth—Mithter—!"

My guardian threw his <u>supplicant</u> off with supreme indifference, and left him dancing on the pavement as if it were red-hot. Without further interruption, we reached the front office, where we found the clerk and the man in velveteen with the fur cap.

"Here's Mike," said the clerk, getting down from his stool, and approaching Mr. Jaggers confidentially.

"Oh!" said Mr. Jaggers, turning to the man who was pulling a lock of hair in the middle of his forehead, like the Bull in Cock Robin pulling at the bell-rope.[23] "Your man comes on this afternoon. Well?"

"Well, Mas'r Jaggers," returned Mike, in the voice of a sufferer from a constitutional[24] cold; "arter a deal o' trouble, I've found one, sir, as might do."

"What is he prepared to swear?"

► Whom has Mike found for Jaggers? What is this person willing to do? About what does Jaggers warn Mike?

"Well, Mas'r Jaggers," said Mike, wiping his nose on his fur cap this time; "in a general way, anythink."

Mr. Jaggers suddenly became most <u>irate</u>. "Now, I warned you before," said he, throwing his forefinger at the terrified client, "that if you ever presumed to talk in that way here, I'd make an example of you. You infernal scoundrel, how dare you tell ME that?"

The client looked scared, but bewildered too, as if he were unconscious what he had done.

"Spooney!"[25] said the clerk, in a low voice, giving him a stir with his elbow. "Soft-head! Need you say it face to face?"

---

22. **again.** Against
23. **Bull . . . bell-rope.** Refers to a popular verse
24. **constitutional.** Contained in a person's basic nature
25. **Spooney.** Fool

Words For Everyday Use	**sup • pli • cant** (sup´lə kənt) *n.*, one who makes a humble request **i • rate** (ī´rāt) *adj.*, very angry

"Now, I ask you, you <u>blundering</u> booby," said my guardian very sternly, "once more and for the last time, what the man you have brought here is prepared to swear?"

Mike looked hard at my guardian, as if he were trying to learn a lesson from his face, and slowly replied, "Ayther to character, or to having been in his company and never left him all the night in question."

"Now, be careful. In what station of life is this man?"

Mike looked at his cap, and looked at the floor, and looked at the ceiling, and looked at the clerk, and even looked at me, before beginning to reply in a nervous manner, "We've dressed him up like—" when my guardian blustered[26] out:

"What? You WILL, will you?"

("Spooney!" added the clerk again, with another stir.)

After some helpless casting about, Mike brightened and began again:

"He is dressed like a 'spectable pieman. A sort of a pastry-cook."

"Is he here?" asked my guardian.

"I left him," said Mike, "a-setting on some doorsteps round the corner."

"Take him past that window, and let me see him."

The window indicated was the office window. We all three went to it, behind the wire blind, and presently saw the client go by in an accidental manner, with a murderous-looking tall individual, in a short suit of white linen and a paper cap. This <u>guileless</u> confectioner[27] was not by any means sober, and had a black eye in the green stage of recovery, which was painted over.

◀ Why is Jaggers disgusted by the "witness" Mike has found?

"Tell him to take his witness away directly," said my guardian to the clerk, in extreme disgust, "and ask him what he means by bringing such a fellow as that."

My guardian then took me into his own room, and while he lunched, standing, from a sandwich-box and a pocket flask of sherry (he seemed to bully his very sandwich as he ate it), informed me what arrangements he had made for me. I was to go to "Barnard's Inn," to young Mr. Pocket's rooms, where a bed had been sent in for my accommodation; I was

◀ What are Pip's instructions?

---

26. **blustered.** Said in a noisy, bullying way
27. **confectioner.** Maker of candy and other sweets

Words For Everyday Use

blun • der • ing (blunˊdər iŋ) *adj.*, clumsy; foolish

guile • less (gīlˊ lis) *adj.*, frank; without slyness and cunning to remain with young Mr. Pocket until Monday; on Monday I was to go with him to his father's house on a visit, that I might try how I liked it. Also, I was told what my allowance was to be—it was a very <u>liberal</u> one—and had handed to me from one of my guardian's drawers the cards of certain tradesmen with whom I was to deal for all kinds of clothes, and such other things as I could in reason want. "You will find your credit good, Mr. Pip," said my guardian, whose flask of sherry smelt like a whole cask-full, as he hastily refreshed himself, "but I shall by this means be able to check your bills, and to pull you up if I find you outrunning the constable.[28] Of course you'll go wrong somehow, but that's no fault of mine."

After I had <u>pondered</u> a little over this encouraging sentiment, I asked Mr. Jaggers if I could send for a coach. He said it was not worthwhile, I was so near my destination; Wemmick should walk round with me, if I pleased.

▶ *Who is Wemmick? In what way does he seem to be like his employer?*

I then found that Wemmick was the clerk in the next room. Another clerk was rung down from upstairs to take his place while he was out, and I accompanied him into the street, after shaking hands with my guardian. We found a new set of people lingering outside, but Wemmick made a way among them by saying coolly yet decisively, "I tell you it's no use; he won't have a word to say to one of you"; and we soon got clear of them, and went on side by side.

---

28. **constable.** Police officer

Words For Everyday Use

lib • er • al (lib′ər əl) *adj.,* generous
pon • der (pän′dər) *vt.,* consider carefully

CHAPTER 21

Casting my eyes on Mr. Wemmick as we went along, to see what he was like in the light of day, I found him to be a dry man, rather short in stature, with a square wooden face, whose expression seemed to have been imperfectly chipped out with a dull-edged chisel. There were some marks in it that might have been dimples, if the material had been softer and the instrument finer, but which, as it was, were only dints.[1] The chisel had made three or four of these attempts at <u>embellishment</u> over his nose, but had given them up without an effort to smooth them off. I judged him to be a bachelor from the <u>frayed</u> condition of his linen, and he appeared to have sustained a good many <u>bereavements</u>; for he wore at least four mourning rings,[2] besides a brooch[3] representing a lady and a weeping willow at a tomb with an urn[4] on it. I noticed, too, that several rings and seals hung at his watch chain, as if he were quite laden with remembrances of departed friends. He had glittering eyes—small, keen, and black—and thin wide <u>mottled</u> lips. He had had them, to the best of my belief, from forty to fifty years.

◄ *What are three interesting facts about Wemmick?*

"So you were never in London before?" said Mr. Wemmick to me.

"No," said I.

"I was new here once," said Mr. Wemmick. "Rum to think of now!"

"You are well acquainted with it now?"

"Why, yes," said Mr. Wemmick. "I know the moves of it."

"Is it a very wicked place?" I asked, more for the sake of saying something than for information.

◄ *What does Wemmick think of London?*

"You may get cheated, robbed, and murdered in London. But there are plenty of people anywhere who'll do that for you."

"If there is bad blood between you and them," said I, to soften it off a little.

---

1. **dints.** Dents
2. **mourning rings.** Rings worn to pay homage to those who have died. Many of these rings opened up, as a locket, to carry strands of the deceased's hair; others were formed as a cameo displaying a portrait of the deceased.
3. **brooch.** Large ornamental pin with a clasp
4. **urn.** Vase used to hold the ashes of a cremated body

Words For Everyday Use

em • bel • lish • ment (əm belʹish mənt) *n.*, ornamentation; something that serves to make fancier

frayed (frād) *adj.*, worn or ragged

be • reave • ment (bē rēvʹmənt) *n.*, loss, as by death

mot • tled (mätʹ ʹld) *adj.*, blotched

"Oh! I don't know about bad blood," returned Mr. Wemmick. "There's not much bad blood about. They'll do it, if there's anything to be got by it."

"That makes it worse."

"You think so?" returned Mr. Wemmick. "Much about the same, I should say."

He wore his hat on the back of his head, and looked straight before him, walking in a self-contained way as if there were nothing in the streets to claim his attention. His mouth was such a post office of a mouth that he had a mechanical appearance of smiling. We had got to the top of Holborn Hill before I knew that it was merely a mechanical appearance, and that he was not smiling at all.

▶ What does Pip notice about Wemmick's mouth? What does it take him a while to figure out?

"Do you know where Mr. Matthew Pocket lives?" I asked Mr. Wemmick.

"Yes," said he, nodding in the direction. "At Hammersmith, west of London."

"Is that far?"

"Well! Say five miles."

"Do you know him?"

"Why, you are a regular cross-examiner!" said Mr. Wemmick, looking at me with an approving air. "Yes, I know him. *I* know him!"

▶ What had Pip expected of Barnard's Inn? What does he find instead?

There was an air of toleration or <u>depreciation</u> about his utterance of these words that rather depressed me; and I was still looking sideways at his block of a face in search of any encouraging note to the text, when he said here we were at Barnard's Inn. My depression was not <u>alleviated</u> by the announcement, for I had supposed that establishment to be a hotel kept by Mr. Barnard, to which the Blue Boar in our town was a mere public house. Whereas I now found Barnard to be a disembodied spirit, or a fiction, and his inn the dingiest collection of shabby buildings ever squeezed together in a rank corner as a club for tomcats.

We entered this haven through a wicket-gate, and were <u>disgorged</u> by an introductory passage into a <u>melancholy</u> little square that looked to me like a flat burying-ground. I thought it had the most dismal trees in it, and the most dismal sparrows, and the most dismal cats, and the most dismal houses (in number half a dozen or so) that I had ever seen. I thought the windows of the sets of chambers into which

Words
For
Everyday
Use

de • pre • ci • a • tion (dē prē´shē ā´shən) *n.*, belittling; lowering of value

al • le • vi • ate (ə lē´vē āt) *vt.*, make more bearable

dis • gorge (dis gôrj´) *vt.*, throw out

mel • an • chol • y (mel´ən käl´ē) *adj.*, sad; gloomy

those houses were divided were in every stage of <u>dilapidated</u> blind and curtain, crippled flower-pot, cracked glass, dusty decay, and miserable makeshift; while To Let[5] To Let To Let glared at me from empty rooms, as if no new wretches ever came there, and the vengeance of the soul of Barnard were being slowly <u>appeased</u> by the gradual suicide of the present occupants and their unholy <u>interment</u> under the gravel. A frowzy mourning[6] of soot and smoke attired this <u>forlorn</u> creation of Barnard, and it had strewn ashes on its head, and was undergoing <u>penance</u> and humiliation as a mere dust-hole. Thus far my sense of sight; while dry rot and wet rot and all the silent rots that rot in neglected roof and cellar—rot of rat and mouse and bug and coaching-stables near at hand besides—addressed themselves faintly to my sense of smell, and moaned, "Try Barnard's Mixture."

◀ *What sights and smells make the place particularly dismal?*

So imperfect was this realization of the first of my great expectations that I looked in dismay at Mr. Wemmick. "Ah!" said he, mistaking me, "the retirement[7] reminds you of the country. So it does me."

He led me into a corner and conducted me up a flight of stairs—which appeared to me to be slowly collapsing into sawdust, so that one of those days the upper lodgers would look out at their doors and find themselves without the means of coming down—to a set of chambers on the top floor. MR. POCKET, JUN., was painted on the door, and there was a label on the letter box, "Return shortly."

"He hardly thought you'd come so soon," Mr. Wemmick explained. "You don't want me anymore?"

"No, thank you," said I.

"As I keep the cash," Mr. Wemmick observed, "we shall most likely meet pretty often. Good day."

◀ *Why will Pip and Wemmick see one another often?*

"Good day."

I put out my hand, and Mr. Wemmick at first looked at it as if he thought I wanted something. Then he looked at me, and said, correcting himself,

"To be sure! Yes. You're in the habit of shaking hands?"

I was rather confused, thinking it must be out of the London fashion, but said yes.

---

5. **To Let.** For rent
6. **frowzy mourning.** Shabby expression of grief
7. **retirement.** Retreat; place of seclusion

Words For Everyday Use

di • lap • i • dat • ed (də lap´ə dāt´id) *adj.*, shabby and neglected

ap • pease (ə pēz´) *vt.*, satisfy or relieve

in • ter • ment (in tur´mənt) *n.*, burial

for • lorn (fôr lôrn´) *adj.*, miserable; pitiful

pen • ance (pen´əns) *n.*, self-punishment done in repentance for wrongdoing

"I have got so out of it!" said Mr. Wemmick—"except at last. Very glad, I'm sure, to make your acquaintance. Good day!"

When we had shaken hands and he was gone, I opened the staircase window and had nearly beheaded myself, for the lines had rotted away, and it came down like the guillotine.[8] Happily it was so quick that I had not put my head out. After this escape, I was content to take a foggy view of the Inn through the window's encrusting dirt, and to stand <u>dolefully</u> looking out, saying to myself that London was decidedly overrated.

Mr. Pocket, Junior's, idea of shortly was not mine, for I had nearly maddened myself with looking out for half an hour, and had written my name with my finger several times in the dirt of every pane in the window, before I heard footsteps on the stairs. Gradually there arose before me the hat, head, neckcloth, waistcoat, trousers, boots, of a member of society of about my own standing. He had a paper bag under each arm and a pottle[9] of strawberries in one hand, and was out of breath.

"Mr. Pip?" said he.

"Mr. Pocket?" said I.

▶ Why is Pocket late?

"Dear me!" he exclaimed. "I am extremely sorry; but I knew there was a coach from your part of the country at midday, and I thought you would come by that one. The fact is, I have been out on your account—not that that is any excuse—for I thought, coming from the country, you might like a little fruit after dinner, and I went to Covent Garden Market to get it good."

For a reason that I had, I felt as if my eyes would start out of my head. I acknowledged his attention <u>incoherently</u>, and began to think this was a dream.

"Dear me!" said Mr. Pocket, Junior. "This door sticks so!"

As he was fast making jam of his fruit by wrestling with the door while the paper bags were under his arms, I begged him to allow me to hold them. He relinquished them with an agreeable smile, and <u>combated</u> with the door as if it were a wild beast. It yielded so suddenly at last that he staggered back upon me, and I staggered back upon the opposite door, and we both laughed. But still I felt as if my eyes must start out of my head, and as if this must be a dream.

---

8. **guillotine.** Instrument for beheading by dropping a heavy blade
9. **pottle.** Amount equal to a half gallon

Words For Everyday Use	
	dole • ful • ly (dōlʹfəl lē) *adv.*, mournfully; sadly
	in • co • her • ent • ly (inʹkō hirʹənt lē) *adv.*, illogically; irrationally
	com • bat (kəm batʹ) *vi.*, struggle

"Pray come in," said Mr. Pocket, Junior. "Allow me to lead the way. I am rather bare here, but I hope you'll be able to make out tolerably well till Monday. My father thought you would get on more agreeably through tomorrow with me than with him, and might like to take a walk about London. I am sure I shall be very happy to show London to you. As to our table, you won't find that bad, I hope, for it will be supplied from our coffeehouse here, and (it is only right I should add) at your expense, such being Mr. Jaggers's directions. As to our lodging, it's not by any means splendid, because I have my own bread to earn, and my father hasn't anything to give me, and I shouldn't be willing to take it, if he had. This is our sitting room—just such chairs and tables and carpet and so forth, you see, as they could spare from home. You mustn't give me credit for the tablecloth and spoons and castors,[10] because they come for you from the coffeehouse. This is my little bedroom; rather musty, but Barnard's *is* musty. This is your bedroom; the furniture's hired for the occasion, but I trust it will answer the purpose; if you should want anything, I'll go and fetch it. The chambers are retired, and we shall be alone together, but we sha'n't fight, I dare say. But, dear me, I beg your pardon, you're holding the fruit all this time. Pray let me take these bags from you. I am quite ashamed."

As I stood opposite to Mr. Pocket, Junior, delivering him the bags, one, two, I saw the starting appearance come into his own eyes that I knew to be in mine, and he said, falling back:

"Lord bless me, you're the prowling boy!"

"And you," said I, "are the pale young gentleman!"

◄ *What explanations does Pocket make about the rooms and their furnishings? Why does he live at the inn?*

◄ *From where do Pocket and Pip know each other?*

---

10. **castors.** Small container for serving vinegar, mustard, or salt

▶ In what way does the pale young gentleman's and Pip's past meeting affect their relationship?

The pale young gentleman and I stood <u>contemplating</u> one another in Barnard's Inn, until we both burst out laughing. "The idea of its being you!" said he. "The idea of its being *you!*" said I. And then we contemplated one another afresh, and laughed again. "Well!" said the pale young gentleman, reaching out his hand good-humoredly, "it's all over now, I hope, and it will be <u>magnanimous</u> in you if you'll forgive me for having knocked you about so."

I derived from this speech that Mr. Herbert Pocket (for Herbert was the pale young gentleman's name) still rather <u>confounded</u> his intention with his execution. But I made a modest reply, and we shook hands warmly.

"You hadn't come into your good fortune at that time?" said Herbert Pocket.

"No," said I.

"No," he acquiesced. "I heard it had happened very lately. *I* was rather on the look-out for good fortune then."

"Indeed?"

▶ Why had Miss Havisham invited Herbert to Satis House? Why was Herbert "on the lookout for good fortune"?

"Yes. Miss Havisham had sent for me, to see if she could take a fancy to me. But she couldn't—at all events, she didn't."

I thought it polite to remark that I was surprised to hear that.

"Bad taste," said Herbert, laughing, "but a fact. Yes, she had sent for me on a trial visit, and if I had come out of it successfully, I suppose I should have been provided for; perhaps I should have been what-you-may-called it to Estella."

"What's that?" I asked, with sudden gravity.

He was arranging his fruit in plates while we talked, which divided his attention, and was the cause of his having made this lapse of a word. "Affianced," he explained, still busy with the fruit. "Betrothed. Engaged. What's-his-named. Any word of that sort."

"How did you bear your disappointment?" I asked.

▶ What opinion does Herbert have of Estella?

"Pooh!" said he, "I didn't care much for it. *She's* a Tartar."[1]

"Miss Havisham?"

"I don't say no to that, but I meant Estella. That girl's hard and haughty and <u>capricious</u> to the last degree, and has been brought up by Miss Havisham to wreak revenge on all the male sex."

---

1. **Tartar.** Stubborn, unruly, and irritable person

Words For Everyday Use

con • tem • plate (kän′ təm plāt′) *vt.*, consider carefully

mag • nan • i • mous (mag nan′ ə məs) *adj.*, noble in mind

con • found (kən found′) *vt.*, confuse

ca • pri • cious (kə prish′əs) *adj.*, inconstant

"What relation is she to Miss Havisham?"

"None," said he. "Only adopted."

"Why should she wreak revenge on all the male sex? What revenge?"

"Lord, Mr. Pip!" said he. "Don't you know?"

"No," said I.

"Dear me! It's quite a story, and shall be saved till dinner time. And now let me take the liberty of asking you a question. How did you come there, that day?"

I told him, and he was attentive until I had finished, and then burst out laughing again, and asked me if I was sore afterwards? I didn't ask him if *he* was, for my conviction on that point was perfectly established.

"Mr. Jaggers is your guardian, I understand?" he went on.

"Yes."

"You know he is Miss Havisham's man of business and solicitor,[2] and has her confidence when nobody else has?"

This was bringing me (I felt) towards dangerous ground. I answered with a constraint I made no attempt to disguise, that I had seen Mr. Jaggers in Miss Havisham's house on the very day of our combat, but never at any other time, and that I believed he had no recollection of having ever seen me there.

"He was so obliging as to suggest my father for your tutor, and he called on my father to propose it. Of course he knew about my father from his connection with Miss Havisham. My father is Miss Havisham's cousin; not that that implies familiar intercourse between them, for he is a bad courtier[3] and will not <u>propitiate</u> her."

◀ How is Herbert related to Miss Havisham? What does Herbert's father refuse to do?

Herbert Pocket had a frank and easy way with him that was very taking. I had never seen anyone then, and I have never seen anyone since, who more strongly expressed to me, in every look and tone, a natural incapacity to do anything secret and mean. There was something wonderfully hopeful about his general air, and something that at the same time whispered to me he would never be very successful or rich. I don't know how this was. I became imbued with the notion on that first occasion before we sat down to dinner, but I cannot define by what means.

◀ What aspects of Herbert's personality does Pip find "taking"? What does he predict about Herbert?

---

2. **solicitor.** Member of the legal profession who advises clients on legal matters

3. **courtier.** Person who uses flattery to get something or to win favor

Words For Everyday Use

pro • pi • ti • ate (prō pish´ē āt´) *vt.*, cause to become favorably inclined

He was still a pale young gentleman, and had a certain conquered <u>languor</u> about him in the midst of his spirits and briskness, that did not seem <u>indicative</u> of natural strength. He had not a handsome face, but it was better than handsome, being extremely <u>amiable</u> and cheerful. His figure was a little ungainly, as in the days when my knuckles had taken such liberties with it, but it looked as if it would always be light and young. Whether Mr. Trabb's local work would have sat more gracefully on him than on me may be a question, but I am conscious that he carried off his rather old clothes much better than I carried off my new suit.

► What does Pip notice about Herbert's clothes? What does Pip think of his own new clothes?

As he was so communicative, I felt that reserve on my part would be a bad return unsuited to our years. I therefore told him my small story, and laid stress on my being forbidden to inquire who my benefactor was. I further mentioned that as I had been brought up a blacksmith in a country place, and knew very little of the ways of politeness, I would take it as a great kindness in him if he would give me a hint whenever he saw me at a loss or going wrong.

► What favor does Pip ask?

"With pleasure," said he, "though I venture to prophesy that you'll want very few hints. I dare say we shall be often together, and I should like to banish any needless restraint between us. Will you do me the favor to begin at once to call me by my Christian name, Herbert?"

I thanked him, and said I would. I informed him in exchange that my Christian name was Philip.

"I don't take to Philip," said he, smiling, "for it sounds like a moral boy out of the spelling-book, who was so lazy that he fell into a pond, or so fat that he couldn't see out of his eyes, or so <u>avaricious</u> that he locked up his cake till the mice ate it, or so determined to go a-bird's-nesting that he got himself eaten by bears who lived handy in the neighborhood. I tell you what I should like. We are so harmonious, and you have been a blacksmith—would you mind it?"

► Why doesn't Herbert like the name Philip? Why does he want to call Pip by the name Handel?

"I shouldn't mind anything that you propose," I answered, "but I don't understand you."

"Would you mind Handel[4] for a familiar name? There's a charming piece of music by Handel called 'The Harmonious Blacksmith.'"

"I should like it very much."

---

4. **Handel.** George Frederic Handel (1685–1759) was a famous German-born British composer.

Words For Everyday Use

lan • guor (laŋ´gər) n., lack of vigor or vitality

in • dic • a • tive (in dik´ə tive) adj., giving an indication or suggestion

a • mi • a • ble (ā´mē ə bəl) adj., good-natured; likable

av • a • ri • cious (av´ə rish´əs) adj., greedy

"Then, my dear Handel," said he, turning round as the door opened, "here is the dinner, and I must beg of you to take the top of the table, because the dinner is of your providing."

This I would not hear of, so he took the top, and I faced him. It was a nice little dinner—seemed to me then, a very Lord Mayor's Feast—and it acquired additional relish from being eaten under those independent circumstances, with no old people by, and with London all around us. This again was heightened by a certain gypsy character that set the banquet off; for, while the table was, as Mr. Pumblechook might have said, the lap of luxury—being entirely furnished forth from the coffee-house—the circumjacent[5] region of sitting room was of a comparatively pastureless and shifty character,[6] imposing on the waiter the wandering habits of putting the covers on the floor (where he fell over them), the melted butter in the armchair, the bread on the bookshelves, the cheese in the coalscuttle,[7] and the boiled fowl into my bed in the next room—where I found much of its parsley and butter in a state of <u>congelation</u> when I retired for the night. All this made the feast delightful, and when the waiter was not there to watch me, my pleasure was without <u>alloy</u>.

We had made some progress in the dinner when I reminded Herbert of his promise to tell me about Miss Havisham.

"True," he replied. "I'll redeem it at once. Let me introduce the topic, Handel, by mentioning that in London it is not the custom to put the knife in the mouth—for fear of accidents—and that while the fork is reserved for that use, it is not put further in than necessary. It is scarcely worth mentioning, only it's as well to do as other people do. Also, the spoon is not generally used overhand, but under. This has two advantages. You get at your mouth better (which after all is the object), and you save a good deal of the attitude of opening oysters on the part of the right elbow."[8]

He offered these friendly suggestions in such a lively way that we both laughed and I scarcely blushed.

"Now," he pursued, "concerning Miss Havisham. Miss Havisham, you must know, was a spoiled child. Her mother

◀ Why is this dinner special?

◀ What advice does Herbert offer Pip? In what manner does he give this advice?

---

5. **circumjacent.** Adjoining
6. **pastureless and shifty character.** Pip is describing the sitting room furniture as being inadequate and of a makeshift nature.
7. **coalscuttle.** Wide-lipped bucket used for pouring coal on a fire
8. **save . . . elbow.** Don't look as if you are opening oysters

Words
For
Everyday
Use

con • ge • la • tion (kän′ jə lā′shən) *n.,* solidifying or thickening by cooling or freezing
al • loy (al′oi) *n.,* anything added that lowers value or purity

► What is Miss
Havisham's family
background?

died when she was a baby, and her father denied her nothing. Her father was a country gentleman down in your part
of the world, and was a brewer. I don't know why it should
be a crack[9] thing to be a brewer, but it is indisputable that
while you cannot possibly be genteel and bake, you may be
as genteel as never was and brew. You see it every day."

"Yet a gentleman may not keep a public house, may he?"
said I.

"Not on any account," returned Herbert; "but a public
house may keep a gentleman. Well! Mr. Havisham was very
rich and very proud. So was his daughter."

"Miss Havisham was an only child?" I hazarded.

"Stop a moment, I am coming to that. No, she was not an
only child; she had a half-brother. Her father privately married again—his cook, I rather think."

"I thought he was proud," said I.

"My good Handel, so he was. He married his second wife
privately, because he was proud, and in course of time *she*
died. When she was dead, I <u>apprehend</u> he first told his
daughter what he had done, and then the son became a part
of the family, residing in the house you are acquainted with.

► What kind of
person is Miss
Havisham's half-
brother?

As the son grew a young man, he turned out riotous, <u>extrav-
agant</u>, undutiful—altogether bad. At last his father disinher-
ited him; but he softened when he was dying, and left him
well off, though not nearly so well off as Miss Havisham.
Take another glass of wine, and excuse my mentioning that
society as a body does not expect one to be so strictly <u>con-
scientious</u> in emptying one's glass, as to turn it bottom
upwards with the rim on one's nose."

I had been doing this, in an excess of attention to his
recital. I thanked, and apologized. He said, "Not at all,"
and resumed.

► Why might Miss
Havisham's half-
brother seek
revenge?

"Miss Havisham was now an heiress,[10] and you may suppose was looked after as a great match. Her half-brother had
now ample means again, but what with debts and what with
new madness, wasted them most fearfully again. There were
stronger differences between him and her than there had
been between him and his father, and it is suspected that he

---

9. **crack.** Superior; first-rate
10. **heiress.** Female who is legally entitled to inherit another's property upon
that person's death

Words
For
Everyday
Use

ap • pre • hend (ap´rē hend´) *vt.*, understand

ex • trav • a • gant (ek strav´ə gənt) *adj.*,
given to excessive spending

con • sci • en • tious (kän´shē en´shəs) *adj.*,
thorough; diligent; painstaking

cherished a deep and mortal grudge against her as having influenced the father's anger. Now, I come to the cruel part of the story—merely breaking off, my dear Handel, to remark that a dinner-napkin will not go into a tumbler."[11]

Why I was trying to pack mine into my tumbler, I am wholly unable to say. I only know that I found myself, with a <u>perseverance</u> worthy of a much better cause, making the most <u>strenuous</u> exertions to compress it within those limits. Again I thanked him and apologized, and again he said in the cheerfullest manner, "Not at all, I am sure!" and resumed.

"There appeared upon the scene—say at the races, or the public balls, or anywhere else you like—a certain man who made love to[12] Miss Havisham. I never saw him (for this happened five-and-twenty years ago, before you and I were, Handel), but I have heard my father mention that he was a showy man, and the kind of man for the purpose. But that he was not to be, without ignorance or prejudice, mistaken for a gentleman, my father most strongly <u>asseverates</u>; because it is a principle of his that no man who was not a true gentleman at heart, ever was, since the world began, a true gentleman in manner. He says, no varnish can hide the grain of the wood, and that the more varnish you put on, the more the grain will express itself. Well! This man pursued Miss Havisham closely, and professed to be devoted to her. I believe she had not shown much <u>susceptibility</u> up to that time, but all the susceptibility she possessed certainly came out then, and she passionately loved him. There is no doubt that she perfectly idolized him. He practiced on her affection in that systematic way that he got great sums of money from her, and he induced her to buy her brother out of a share in the brewery (which had been weakly left him by his father) at an immense price, on the plea that when he was her husband he must hold and manage it all. Your guardian was not at that time in Miss Havisham's councils, and she was too haughty and too much in love to be advised by anyone. Her relations were poor and scheming, with the exception of my father; he was poor enough, but not time-serving or jealous. The only independent one among them, he warned her that she was doing too much for this man, and was placing herself too

◄ Why does Herbert's father insist that the man who pursued Miss Havisham was not a gentleman? What does he believe about gentlemen?

◄ What did the suitor convince Miss Havisham to do?

◄ In what way does Mr. Pocket differ from Miss Havisham's other relations? Why does she become angry with him?

---

11. **tumbler.** Ordinary drinking glass
12. **made love to.** Professed to love

<u>unreservedly</u> in his power. She took the first opportunity of angrily ordering my father out of the house, in his presence, and my father has never seen her since."

I thought of her having said, "Matthew will come and see me at last when I am laid dead upon that table;" and I asked Herbert whether his father was so <u>inveterate</u> against her?

"It's not that," said he, "but she charged him, in the presence of her intended husband, with being disappointed in the hope of <u>fawning</u> upon her for his own advancement, and, if he were to go to her now, it would look true—even to him—and even to her. To return to the man and make an end of him. The marriage day was fixed, the wedding dresses were bought, the wedding tour was planned out, the wedding guests were invited. The day came, but not the bridegroom. He wrote her a letter—"

"Which she received," I struck in, "when she was dressing for her marriage? At twenty minutes to nine?"

"At the hour and minute," said Herbert, nodding, "at which she afterwards stopped all the clocks. What was in it, further than that it most heartlessly broke the marriage off, I can't tell you, because I don't know. When she recovered from a bad illness that she had, she laid the whole place waste, as you have seen it, and she has never since looked upon the light of day."

"Is that all the story?" I asked, after considering it.

"All I know of it; and indeed I only know so much, through piecing it out for myself; for my father always avoids it, and, even when Miss Havisham invited me to go there, told me no more of it than it was absolutely <u>requisite</u> I should understand. But I have forgotten one thing. It has been supposed that the man to whom she gave her misplaced confidence acted throughout in concert with her halfbrother; that it was a conspiracy between them; and that they shared the profits."

"I wonder he didn't marry her and get all the property," said I.

"He may have been married already, and her cruel <u>mortification</u> may have been a part of her half-brother's scheme," said Herbert. "Mind! I don't know that."

"What became of the two men?" I asked, after again considering the subject.

▶ Why does Pip know what time the letter arrived? What news arrived in the letter?

▶ What conspiracy do people suspect is behind Miss Havisham's humiliation?

Words For Everyday Use

un • re • serv • ed • ly (un´ri zɜr´ vid lē) adv., without limits; without holding back

in • vet • er • ate (in vet´ər it) adj., firmly established

fawn (fôn) vi., act servilely; cringe and flatter

req • ui • site (rek´wi zit) adj., essential

mor • ti • fi • ca • tion (môr´tə fi kā´shən) n., shame; humiliation

"They fell into deeper shame and degradation—if there can be deeper—and ruin."

"Are they alive now?"

"I don't know."

"You said just now that Estella was not related to Miss Havisham, but adopted. When adopted?"

Herbert shrugged his shoulders. "There has always been an Estella, since I have heard of a Miss Havisham. I know no more. And now, Handel," said he, finally throwing off the story as it were, "there is a perfectly open understanding between us. All I know about Miss Havisham, you know."

"And all I know," I retorted, "you know."

"I fully believe it. So there can be no competition or <u>per-plexity</u> between you and me. And as to the condition on which you hold your advancement in life—namely, that you are not to inquire or discuss to whom you owe it—you may be very sure that it will never be <u>encroached</u> upon, or even approached, by me, or by anyone belonging to me."

In truth, he said this with so much delicacy that I felt the subject done with, even though I should be under his father's roof for years and years to come. Yet he said it with so much meaning, too, that I felt he as perfectly understood Miss Havisham to be my benefactress as I understood the fact myself.

It had not occurred to me before that he had led up to the theme for the purpose of clearing it out of our way; but we were so much the lighter and easier for having broached it that I now perceived this to be the case. We were very gay and sociable, and I asked him, in the course of conversation, what he was? He replied, "A capitalist—an insurer of ships." I suppose he saw me glancing about the room in search of some tokens of shipping, or <u>capital</u>, for he added, "In the City."

I had grand ideas of the wealth and importance of insurers of ships in the City, and I began to think with awe, of having laid a young insurer on his back, blackened his enterprising eye, and cut his responsible head open. But, again, there came upon me, for my relief, that odd <u>impression</u> that Herbert Pocket would never be very successful or rich.

"I shall not rest satisfied with merely employing my capital in insuring ships. I shall buy up some good life assurance

◄ What happened to the two men?

◄ What does Pip assume Herbert knows?

◄ What are Herbert's goals?

Words For Everyday Use

per • plex • i • ty (pər pleks´ə tē) *n.*, bewilderment; confusion
en • croach (en krōch´) *vi.*, trespass or intrude
cap • i • tal (kap´ət'l) *n.*, wealth
im • pres • sion (im presh´ən) *n.*, idea

shares, and cut into the direction. I shall also do a little in the mining way.[13] None of these things will interfere with my <u>chartering</u> a few thousand tons on my own account. I think I shall trade," said he, leaning back in his chair, "to the East Indies, for silks, shawls, spices, dyes, drugs, and precious woods. It's an interesting trade."

"And the profits are large?" said I.

"Tremendous!" said he.

I <u>wavered</u> again, and began to think here were greater expectations than my own.

"I think I shall trade, also," said he, putting his thumbs in his waistcoat pockets, "to the West Indies, for sugar, tobacco, and rum. Also to Ceylon, especially for elephants' tusks."

"You will want a good many ships," said I.

"A perfect fleet," said he.

Quite overpowered by the magnificence of these transactions, I asked him where the ships he insured mostly traded to at present?

"I haven't begun insuring yet," he replied. "I am looking about me."

Somehow that pursuit seemed more in keeping with Barnard's Inn. I said (in a tone of conviction), "Ah-h!"

▶ What is Herbert's job? How much money is he earning?

"Yes. I am in a countinghouse,[14] and looking about me."

"Is a countinghouse profitable?" I asked.

"To—do you mean to the young fellow who's in it?" he asked, in reply.

"Yes; to you."

"Why, n-no; not to me." He said this with the air of one carefully <u>reckoning</u> up and striking a balance. "Not directly profitable. That is, it doesn't pay me anything, and I have to—keep myself."

This certainly had not a profitable appearance, and I shook my head as if I would imply that it would be difficult to lay by much <u>accumulative</u> capital from such a source of income.

▶ What does "look about you" mean?

"But the thing is," said Herbert Pocket, "that you look about you. *That's* the grand thing. You are in a countinghouse, you know, and you look about you."

---

13. **mining way.** Investing in the business of extracting coal or ore from a mine
14. **countinghouse.** Office in which a firm keeps records and handles correspondence

---

Words For Everyday Use

char • ter (chärt´ər) vt., authorize; commission

wa • ver (wā´vər) vi., show doubt or indecision

reck • on (rek´ən) vi., figure; calculate

ac • cu • mu • la • tive (ə kyo͞om´yo͞o lət iv) adj., collected; gathered together

It struck me as a singular implication that you couldn't be out of a countinghouse, you know, and look about you; but I silently <u>deferred</u> to his experience.

"Then the time comes," said Herbert, "when you see your opening. And you go in, and you swoop upon it and you make your capital, and then there you are! When you have once made your capital, you have nothing to do but employ it."

This was very like his way of conducting that encounter in the garden; very like. His manner of bearing his poverty, too, exactly corresponded to his manner of bearing that defeat. It seemed to me that he took all blows and buffets now with just the same air as he had taken mine then. It was evident that he had nothing around him but the simplest necessaries, for everything that I remarked upon turned out to have been sent in on my account from the coffee-house or somewhere else.

Yet, having already made his fortune in his own mind, he was so unassuming with it that I felt quite grateful to him for not being puffed up. It was a pleasant addition to his naturally pleasant ways, and we got on famously. In the evening we went out for a walk in the streets, and went half-price to the theater; and next day we went to church at Westminster Abbey, and in the afternoon we walked in the parks; and I wondered who shod all the horses there, and wished Joe did.

On a moderate computation, it was many months, that Sunday, since I had left Joe and Biddy. The space <u>interposed</u> between myself and them partook of that expansion, and our marshes were any distance off. That I could have been at our old church in my old church-going clothes, on the very last Sunday that ever was, seemed a combination of impossibilities, geographical and social, solar and lunar.[15] Yet in the London streets, so crowded with people and so brilliantly lighted in the dusk of evening, there were depressing hints of <u>reproaches</u> for that I had put the poor old kitchen at home so far away; and in the dead of night, the footsteps of some incapable <u>impostor</u> of a porter[16] mooning about Barnard's Inn, under <u>pretense</u> of watching it, fell hollow on my heart.

◀ How is Herbert's attitude toward life similar to the attitude he had while Pip was beating him up?

◀ What seems impossible? In what does Pip find reproaches for putting his former home to the back of his mind?

---

15. **solar and lunar.** Respectively of the sun and of the moon
16. **incapable . . . porter.** So-called watchman

Words For Everyday Use

de • fer (di fur´) *vi.,* submit to the opinion of another

in • ter • pose (in´tər pōz´) *vt.,* place between

re • proach (ri prōch´) *n.,* blame; rebuke

im • pos • tor (im päs´tər) *n.,* one who deceives others by pretending to be someone or something that he or she is not

pre • tense (prē´tens´) *n.,* false claim

► What is Pip's impression of the countinghouse?

On the Monday morning, at a quarter before nine, Herbert went to the countinghouse to report himself—to look about him, too, I suppose—and I bore him company. He was to come away in an hour or two to attend me to Hammersmith, and I was to wait about for him. It appeared to me that the eggs from which young insurers were hatched were incubated in dust and heat, like the eggs of ostriches, judging from the places to which those incipient giants repaired[17] on a Monday morning. Nor did the counting house where Herbert assisted show in my eyes as at all a good observatory, being a back second floor up a yard, of a grimy presence in all particulars, and with a look into another back second floor, rather than a look out.

► What opinion did Pip originally hold of the eating establishment they frequent? What does he think of it now? What does his change of opinion suggest about his worldliness?

I waited about until it was noon, and I went upon 'Change, and I saw fluey[18] men sitting there under the bills about shipping, whom I took to be great merchants, though I couldn't understand why they should all be out of spirits. When Herbert came, we went and had lunch at a celebrated house which I then quite venerated, but now believe to have been the most abject superstition in Europe, and where I could not help noticing, even then, that there was much more gravy on the tablecloths and knives and waiters' clothes than in the steaks. This collation disposed of at a moderate price (considering the grease, which was not charged for), we went back to Barnard's Inn and got my little portmanteau, and then took coach for Hammersmith. We arrived there at two or three o'clock in the afternoon, and had very little way to walk to Mr. Pocket's house. Lifting the latch of a gate, we passed direct into a little garden overlooking the river, where Mr. Pocket's children were playing about. And, unless I deceive myself on a point where my interests or prepossessions are certainly not concerned, I saw that Mr. and Mrs. Pocket's children were not growing up or being brought up, but were tumbling up.

► Whom does Pip meet at Hammersmith? Who else is there?

Mrs. Pocket was sitting on a garden chair under a tree, reading, with her legs upon another garden chair; and Mrs. Pocket's two nursemaids were looking about them while the children played. "Mamma," said Herbert, "this is young Mr. Pip." Upon which Mrs. Pocket received me with an appearance of amiable dignity.

---

17. **repaired.** Went
18. **fluey.** Covered with fluff, untidy

Words For Everyday Use	
in • cip • i • ent (in sip´ē ənt) *adj.*, in an early stage	
ven • er • ate (ven´ər āt´) *vt.*, look upon with deep feelings of respect; revere	
pre • pos • ses • sion (prē´pə zesh´ən) *n.*, preconception	

"Master Alick and Miss Jane," cried one of the nurses to two of the children, "if you go a-bouncing up against them bushes, you'll fall over into the river and be drownded, and what'll your pa say then?"

At the same time this nurse picked up Mrs. Pocket's handkerchief, and said, "If that don't make six times you've dropped it, mum!" Upon which Mrs. Pocket laughed and said, "Thank you, Flopson," and settling herself in one chair only, resumed her book. Her countenance immediately assumed a knitted and <u>intent</u> expression, as if she had been reading for a week, but before she could have read half a dozen lines, she fixed her eyes upon me, and said, "I hope your mamma is quite well?" This unexpected <u>inquiry</u> put me into such a difficulty that I began saying in the absurdest way that if there had been any such person I had no doubt she would have been quite well and would have been very much obliged and would have sent her compliments, when the nurse came to my rescue.

◄ Why is Pip disconcerted?

"Well!" she cried, picking up the pocket handkerchief, "if that don't make seven times! What ARE you a-doing of this afternoon, mum!" Mrs. Pocket received her property, at first with a look of unutterable surprise as if she had never seen it before, and then with a laugh of recognition, and said, "Thank you, Flopson," and forgot me, and went on reading.

I found, now I had <u>leisure</u> to count them, that there were no fewer than six little Pockets present, in various stages of tumbling up. I had scarcely arrived at the total when a seventh was heard, as in the region of air, wailing dolefully.

"If there ain't Baby!" said Flopson, appearing to think it most surprising. "Make haste up, Millers!"

Millers, who was the other nurse, retired into the house, and by degrees the child's wailing was hushed and stopped, as if it were a young ventriloquist[19] with something in its mouth. Mrs. Pocket read all the time, and I was curious to know what the book could be.

We were waiting, I supposed, for Mr. Pocket to come out to us; at any rate we waited there, and so I had an opportunity of observing the remarkable family <u>phenomenon</u> that whenever any of the children strayed near Mrs. Pocket in their

◄ What happens when the children come near Mrs. Pocket?

---

19. **ventriloquist.** Person who practices the art of speaking so that the voice seems to come from some source other than the speaker

Words For Everyday Use	
in • tent (in tent´) adj., firmly directed or fixed	**lei • sure** (lē´zhər) n., free or spare time
in • quir • y (in´kwə rē) n., question	**phe • nom • e • non** (fə näm´ ə nən´) n., unusual or extraordinary occurrence

play, they always tripped themselves up and tumbled over her—always very much to her momentary astonishment, and their own more enduring <u>lamentation</u>. I was at a loss to account for this surprising circumstance, and could not help giving my mind to speculations about it, until by-and-by Millers came down with the baby, which Baby was handed to Flopson, which Flopson was handing it to Mrs. Pocket, when she too went fairly head foremost over Mrs. Pocket, baby and all, and was caught by Herbert and myself.

"Gracious me, Flopson!" said Mrs. Pocket, looking off her book for a moment, "everybody's tumbling!"

"Gracious you, indeed, mum!" returned Flopson, very red in the face; "what have you got there?"

"*I* got here, Flopson?" asked Mrs. Pocket.

"Why, if it ain't your footstool!" cried Flopson. "And if you keep it under your skirts like that, who's to help tumbling? Here! Take the baby, mum, and give me your book."

Mrs. Pocket acted on the advice, and inexpertly danced the infant a little in her lap, while the other children played about it. This had lasted but a very short time, when Mrs. Pocket issued <u>summary</u> orders that they were all to be taken into the house for a nap. Thus I made the second discovery on that first occasion, that the <u>nurture</u> of the little Pockets consisted of <u>alternately</u> tumbling up and lying down.

Under these circumstances, when Flopson and Millers had got the children into the house, like a little flock of sheep, and Mr. Pocket came out of it to make my acquaintance, I was not much surprised to find that Mr. Pocket was a gentleman with a rather <u>perplexed</u> expression of face, and with his very gray hair disordered on his head, as if he didn't quite see his way to putting anything straight.

▶ What expression does Mr. Pocket wear?

Words For Everyday Use

lam • en • ta • tion (lam´ən tā´shən) *n.,* outward expression of grief, especially wailing or weeping
sum • ma • ry (sum´ə rē) *adj.,* concise

nur • ture (nʉr´chər) *n.,* upbringing
al • ter • nate • ly (ôl´tər nit´lē) *adv.,* by turns; following each other continuously
per • plexed (pər plekst´) *adj.,* confused

CHAPTER 23

Mr. Pocket said he was glad to see me, and he hoped I was not sorry to see him. "For, I really am not," he added, with his son's smile, "an alarming personage." He was a young-looking man, in spite of his perplexities and his very gray hair, and his manner seemed quite natural. I use the word natural in the sense of its being unaffected; there was something comic in his <u>distraught</u> way, as though it would have been downright <u>ludicrous</u> but for his own perception that it was very near being so. When he had talked with me a little, he said to Mrs. Pocket, with a rather anxious contraction of his eyebrows, which were black and handsome, "Belinda, I hope you have welcomed Mr. Pip?" And she looked up from her book, and said "Yes." She then smiled upon me in an absent state of mind, and asked me if I liked the taste of orange-flower water. As the question had no bearing, near or remote, on any foregone or subsequent transaction, I consider it to have been thrown out, like her previous approaches, in general conversational condescension.

I found out within a few hours, and may mention at once, that Mrs. Pocket was the only daughter of a certain quite accidental deceased knight, who had invented for himself a conviction that his deceased father would have been made a baronet[1] but for somebody's determined opposition arising out of entirely personal motives—I forget whose, if I ever knew—the Sovereign's, the Prime Minister's, the Lord Chancellor's, the Archbishop of Canterbury's, anybody's—and had tacked himself on to the nobles of the earth in right of this quite suppositious fact. I believe he had been knighted himself for storming[2] the English grammar at the point of the pen, in a desperate address engrossed on vellum,[3] on the occasion of the laying of the first stone of some building or other,[4] and for handing some royal personage either the

What type of person does Mr. Pocket seem to be?

Who were Mrs. Pocket's father and grandfather?

---

1. **baronet.** British hereditary title of honor, ranking below a baron but above a knight; a knight's title was not hereditary.
2. **storming.** Trying to capture by a sudden attack
3. **engrossed on vellum.** Written on fine parchment sheets prepared from skins
4. **I believe . . . other.** Pip is suggesting that Mrs. Pocket's father was knighted for writing something to please a royal person rather than for his valor in war.

Words For Everyday Use

dis • traught (di strôt´) *adj.*, extremely anxious; frantic

lu • di • crous (loō´di krəs) *adj.*, absurd; ridiculous

trowel or the mortar.[5] Be that as it may, he had directed Mrs.
Pocket to be brought up from her cradle as one who in the
nature of things must marry a title, and who was to be
guarded from the <u>acquisition</u> of <u>plebeian</u> domestic knowledge.

So successful a watch and <u>ward</u> had been established over
the young lady by this <u>judicious</u> parent that she had grown
up highly ornamental, but perfectly helpless and useless.
With her character thus happily formed, in the first bloom of
her youth she had encountered Mr. Pocket, who was also in
the first bloom of youth, and not quite decided whether to
mount to the Woolsack, or to roof himself in with a miter.[6]
As his doing the one or the other was a mere question of time,
he and Mrs. Pocket had taken time by the forelock (when, to
judge from its length, it would seem to have wanted cutting),[7] and had married without the knowledge of the judicious parent. The judicious parent, having nothing to bestow
or withhold but his blessing, had handsomely settled that
dower[8] upon them after a short struggle, and had informed
Mr. Pocket that his wife was "a treasure for a prince." Mr.
Pocket had invested the prince's treasure in the ways of the
world ever since, and it was supposed to have brought him
in but indifferent interest. Still, Mrs. Pocket was in general
the object of a queer sort of respectful pity because she had
not married a title; while Mr. Pocket was the object of a queer
sort of forgiving reproach because he had never got one.

Mr. Pocket took me into the house and showed me my
room; which was a pleasant one, and so furnished as that I
could use it with comfort for my own private sitting room.
He then knocked at the doors of two other similar rooms,
and introduced me to their occupants, by name Drummle
and Startop. Drummle, an old-looking young man of a heavy
order of architecture, was whistling. Startop, younger in
years and appearance, was reading and holding his head, as
if he thought himself in danger of exploding it with too
strong a charge of knowledge.

► Who also studies
and boards at the
Pockets'?

---

5. **trowel . . . mortar.** Respectively: tool with a thin, flat blade used for
smoothing plaster; cement mixture used to bind bricks or stones
6. **mount . . . miter.** Ascend to a high seat in the House of Lords, or wear the
headpiece of a high-ranking church official; i.e., enter government or the church
7. **taken time . . . cutting.** Rushed ahead
8. **dower.** Dowry; gift

Words
For
Everyday
Use

ac • qui • si • tion (ak´wə zish´ən) *n.*, acquiring; attainment
ple • be • ian (pli bē´ən) *adj.*, characteristic of common people
ward (wôrd) *n.*, guard
ju • di • cious (jōō dish´əs) *adj.*, wise

Both Mr. and Mrs. Pocket had such a noticeable air of being in somebody else's hands that I wondered who really was in possession of the house and let them live there, until I found this unknown power to be the servants. It was a smooth way of going on, perhaps, in respect of saving trouble; but it had the appearance of being expensive, for the servants felt it a duty they owed to themselves to be nice in their eating and drinking, and to keep a deal of company downstairs. They allowed a very liberal table to Mr. and Mrs. Pocket, yet it always appeared to me that by far the best part of the house to have boarded in would have been the kitchen—always supposing the boarder capable of self-defense, for, before I had been there a week, a neighboring lady with whom the family were personally unacquainted wrote in to say that she had seen Millers slapping the baby. This greatly distressed Mrs. Pocket, who burst into tears on receiving the note, and said that it was an extraordinary thing that the neighbors couldn't mind their own business.

◄ Who runs the Pocket household?

By degrees I learned, and chiefly from Herbert, that Mr. Pocket had been educated at Harrow and at Cambridge, where he had distinguished himself, but that when he had had the happiness of marrying Mrs. Pocket very early in life, he had <u>impaired</u> his <u>prospects</u> and taken up the calling of a grinder.[9] After grinding a number of dull blades—of whom it was remarkable that their fathers, when influential, were always going to help him to <u>preferment</u>, but always forgot to do it when the blades had left the grindstone—he had wearied of that poor work and had come to London. Here, after gradually failing in loftier hopes, he had "read" with divers[10] who had lacked opportunities or neglected them, and had <u>refurbished</u> divers others for special occasions, and had turned his acquirements to the account of literary compilation and correction, and on such means, added to some very moderate private resources, still maintained the house I saw.

◄ What is Mr. Pocket's background? Why has he turned to tutoring?

Mr. and Mrs. Pocket had a toady[11] neighbor—a widow lady of that highly sympathetic nature that she agreed with

---

9. **grinder.** Dickens uses the metaphor of a grinder, or knife sharpener, to describe Mr. Pocket as a teacher. The "dull blades" are his students.
10. **"read" with divers.** Tutored various students
11. **toady.** One who attempts to win favor by flattery

Words For Everyday Use

im • pair (im per´) vt., make worse

pros • pect (prä´spekt´) n., chance for success

pre • fer • ment (prē fur´mənt) n., promotion

re • fur • bish (ri fur´bish) vt., renovate; improve

everybody, blessed everybody, and shed smiles and tears on everybody, according to circumstances. This lady's name was Mrs. Coiler, and I had the honor of taking her down to dinner on the day of my installation. She gave me to understand on the stairs that it was a blow to dear Mrs. Pocket that dear Mr. Pocket should be under the necessity of receiving gentlemen to read with him. That did not extend to me, she told me in a gush of love and confidence (at that time, I had known her something less than five minutes); if they were all like me, it would be quite another thing.

"But dear Mrs. Pocket," said Mrs. Coiler, "after her early disappointment (not that dear Mr. Pocket was to blame in that), requires so much luxury and elegance—"

"Yes, ma'am," I said, to stop her, for I was afraid she was going to cry.

"And she is of so <u>aristocratic</u> a <u>disposition</u>—"

"Yes, ma'am," I said again, with the same object as before.

"—that it *is* hard," said Mrs. Coiler, "to have dear Mr. Pocket's time and attention diverted from dear Mrs. Pocket."

I could not help thinking that it might be harder if the butcher's time and attention were diverted from dear Mrs. Pocket, but I said nothing, and indeed had enough to do in keeping a bashful watch upon my company-manners.

► Why do Mrs. Pocket and Bentley Drummle get along?

It came to my knowledge, through what passed between Mrs. Pocket and Drummle, while I was attentive to my knife and fork, spoon, glasses, and other instruments of self-destruction, that Drummle, whose Christian name[12] was Bentley, was actually the next heir but one to a baronetcy.[13] It further appeared that the book I had seen Mrs. Pocket reading in the garden was all about titles, and that she knew the exact date at which her grandpapa would have come into the book, if he ever had come at all. Drummle didn't say much, but in his limited way (he struck me as a sulky kind of fellow) he spoke as one of the elect, and recognized Mrs. Pocket as a woman and a sister. No one but themselves and Mrs. Coiler the toady neighbor showed any interest in this part of the conversation, and it appeared to me that it was painful to Herbert; but it promised to last a long time, when the page came in with the announcement of a domestic

---

12. **Christian name.** First name
13. **baronetcy.** Title, rank, or status of a baronet

Words For Everyday Use	a • ris • to • crat • ic (ə ris′tə krat′ik) *adj.*, having the tastes, manners, and other characteristics of the upper class
	dis • po • si • tion (dis′pə zish′ən) *n.*, nature; temperament

affliction. It was, in effect, that the cook had mislaid the beef. To my unutterable amazement, I now, for the first time, saw Mr. Pocket relieve his mind by going through a performance that struck me as very extraordinary, but which made no impression on anybody else, and with which I soon became as familiar as the rest. He laid down the carving-knife and fork—being engaged in carving at the moment—put his two hands into his disturbed hair, and appeared to make an extraordinary effort to lift himself up by it. When he had done this, and had not lifted himself up at all, he quietly went on with what he was about.

◀ What does Mr. Pocket do to calm himself?

Mrs. Coiler then changed the subject and began to flatter me. I liked it for a few moments, but she flattered me so very grossly that the pleasure was soon over. She had a <u>serpentine</u> way of coming close at me when she pretended to be vitally interested in the friends and localities I had left, which was altogether snaky and fork-tongued; and when she made an occasional bounce upon Startop (who said very little to her), or upon Drummle (who said less), I rather envied them for being on the opposite side of the table.

After dinner the children were introduced, and Mrs. Coiler made admiring comments on their eyes, noses, and legs—a <u>sagacious</u> way of improving their minds. There were four little girls, and two little boys, besides the baby who might have been either, and the baby's next successor who was as yet neither. They were brought in by Flopson and Millers, much as though those two noncommissioned officers[14] had been <u>recruiting</u> somewhere for children and had enlisted these: while Mrs. Pocket looked at the young nobles that ought to have been as if she rather thought she had had the pleasure of inspecting them before, but didn't quite know what to make of them.

"Here! Give me your fork, mum, and take the baby," said Flopson. "Don't take it that way, or you'll get its head under the table."

◀ What happens that shows Mrs. Pocket to be an inept mother?

Thus advised, Mrs. Pocket took it the other way, and got its head upon the table; which was announced to all present by a <u>prodigious</u> <u>concussion</u>.

---

14. **noncommissioned officers.** Members of the armed forces with leadership over other enlisted personnel

Words For Everyday Use	
ser • pen • tine (sur´pən tēn´) *adj.,* snake-like; evilly cunning or subtle	**pro • di • gious** (prə dij´əs) *adj.,* of great size, power, or extent
sa • ga • cious (sə gā´shəs) *adj.,* shrewd	**con • cus • sion** (kən kush´ən) *n.,* blow; violent shock
re • cruit (ri kro͞ot) *vi.,* seek or enlist new members	

► Who does know how to take care of the baby? What makes this person an unusual caretaker?

"Dear, dear! Give it me back, mum," said Flopson; "and Miss Jane, come and dance to baby, do!"

One of the little girls, a mere <u>mite</u> who seemed to have prematurely taken upon herself some charge of the others, stepped out of her place by me, and danced to and from the baby until it left off crying, and laughed. Then all the children laughed, and Mr. Pocket (who in the meantime had twice <u>endeavored</u> to lift himself up by the hair) laughed, and we all laughed and were glad.

Flopson, by dint of doubling the baby at the joints like a Dutch doll, then got it safely into Mrs. Pocket's lap, and gave it the nutcrackers to play with: at the same time recommending Mrs. Pocket to take notice that the handles of that instrument were not likely to agree with its eyes, and sharply charging Miss Jane to look after the same. Then, the two nurses left the room, and had a lively scuffle on the staircase with a <u>dissipated</u> page who had waited at dinner, and who had clearly lost half his buttons at the gaming table.

► Why does Jane "interfere" with her mother and the baby?

I was made very uneasy in my mind by Mrs. Pocket's falling into a discussion with Drummle respecting two baronetcies while she ate a sliced orange steeped in sugar and wine, and forgetting all about the baby on her lap, who did most <u>appalling</u> things with the nutcrackers. At length little Jane perceived its young brains to be imperiled, softly left her place, and with many small <u>artifices</u> coaxed the dangerous weapon away. Mrs. Pocket finishing her orange at about the same time, and not approving of this, said to Jane:

"You naughty child, how dare you? Go and sit down this instant!"

"Mamma dear," lisped the little girl, "baby ood have put hith eyeth out."

► Why is Mrs. Pocket angry with Jane?

"How dare you tell me so!" retorted Mrs. Pocket. "Go and sit down in your chair this moment!"

Mrs. Pocket's dignity was so crushing that I felt quite <u>abashed</u>, as if I myself had done something to rouse it.

"Belinda," remonstrated Mr. Pocket from the other end of the table, "how can you be so unreasonable? Jane only interfered for the protection of baby."

"I will not allow anybody to interfere," said Mrs. Pocket. "I am surprised, Matthew, that you should expose me to the <u>affront</u> of interference."

Words For Everyday Use

mite (mīt) *n.*, very small creature
en • deav • or (en dev´ər) *vi.*, make an earnest attempt
dis • si • pat • ed (dis´ə pā´tid) *adj.*, unrestrained in the pursuit of pleasure
ap • pall • ing (ə pôl´iŋ) *adj.*, causing shock or dismay
ar • ti • fice (är´tə fis) *n.*, skillful trick
a • bashed (ə bashd´) *adj.*, embarrassed
af • front (ə frunt´) *n.*, insult

"Good God!" cried Mr. Pocket, in an outbreak of desolate desperation. "Are infants to be nutcrackered into their tombs, and is nobody to save them?"

"I will not be interfered with by Jane," said Mrs. Pocket, with a majestic glance at that innocent little offender. "I hope I know my poor grandpapa's position. Jane, indeed!"

Mr. Pocket got his hands in his hair again, and this time really did lift himself some inches out of his chair. "Hear this!" he helplessly exclaimed to the elements. "Babies are to be nutcrackered dead for people's poor grandpapa's positions!" Then he let himself down again, and became silent.

We all looked awkwardly at the tablecloth while this was going on. A pause succeeded, during which the honest and <u>irrepressible</u> baby made a series of leaps and crows at little Jane, who appeared to me to be the only member of the family (irrespective of[15] the servants) with whom it had any decided acquaintance.

"Mr. Drummle," said Mrs. Pocket, "will you ring for Flopson? Jane, you undutiful little thing, go and lie down. Now, baby darling, come with ma!"

The baby was the soul of honor, and protested with all its might. It doubled itself up the wrong way over Mrs. Pocket's arm, exhibited a pair of knitted shoes and dimpled ankles to the company in lieu of[16] its soft face, and was carried out in the highest state of <u>mutiny</u>. And it gained its point after all, for I saw it through the window within a few minutes, being nursed by little Jane.

It happened that the other five children were left behind at the dinner table, through Flopson's having some private engagement, and their not being anybody else's business. I thus became aware of the mutual relations between them and Mr. Pocket, which were exemplified in the following manner. Mr. Pocket, with the normal perplexity of his face heightened, and his hair rumpled, looked at them for some minutes, as if he couldn't make out how they came to be boarding and lodging in that establishment, and why they hadn't been billeted[17] by nature on somebody else. Then, in a distant, missionary way he asked them certain questions—

◄ Why is Mr. Pocket upset? What does he do?

◄ What type of father is Mr. Pocket?

---

15. **irrespective of.** Not including
16. **in lieu of.** Instead of
17. **billeted.** Assigned living quarters

as why little Joe had that hole in his frill: who said, Pa, Flopson was going to mend it when she had time—and how little Fanny came by that whitlow:[18] who said, Pa, Millers was going to poultice[19] it when she didn't forget. Then he melted into parental tenderness, and gave them a shilling apiece and told them to go and play; and then, as they went out, with one very strong effort to lift himself up by the hair, he dismissed the hopeless subject.

▶ In what does Pip wish to excel? What support does he obtain? What concerns him?

In the evening there was rowing on the river. As Drummle and Startop had each a boat, I resolved to set up mine, and to cut them both out. I was pretty good at most exercises in which country boys are <u>adepts</u>, but as I was conscious of wanting elegance of style for the Thames—not to say for other waters—I at once engaged to place myself under the tuition of the winner of a prize-wherry[20] who plied at our stairs, and to whom I was introduced by my new allies. This practical authority confused me very much by saying I had the arm of a blacksmith. If he could have known how nearly the compliment lost him his pupil, I doubt if he would have paid it.

There was a supper tray after we got home at night, and I think we should all have enjoyed ourselves but for a rather disagreeable <u>domestic</u> occurrence. Mr. Pocket was in good spirits, when a housemaid came in, and said, "If you please, sir, I should wish to speak to you."

"Speak to your master?" said Mrs. Pocket, whose dignity was <u>roused</u> again. "How can you think of such a thing? Go and speak to Flopson. Or speak to me—at some other time."

"Begging your pardon, ma'am," returned the housemaid, "I should wish to speak at once, and to speak to master."

Hereupon Mr. Pocket went out of the room, and we made the best of ourselves until he came back.

▶ How does this scene reinforce Pip's perception of the household?

"This is a pretty thing, Belinda!" said Mr. Pocket, returning with a countenance expressive of grief and despair. "Here's the cook lying insensibly drunk on the kitchen floor, with a large bundle of fresh butter made up in the cupboard ready to sell for grease!"

---

18. **whitlow.** Painful abscess around a fingernail or toenail
19. **poultice.** Apply a hot, moist mass (as of flour, herbs, or mustard) to a sore
20. **prize-wherry.** Light rowboat used on rivers, probably won as a prize in a boating race

Words For Everyday Use

a • dept (ə dept´) *n.,* expert
do • mes • tic (dō mes´tik) *adj.,* having to do with the home or housekeeping
rouse (rouz) *vt.,* stir up

Mrs. Pocket instantly showed much amiable emotion, and said, "This is that odious Sophia's doing!"

"What do you mean, Belinda?" demanded Mr. Pocket.

"Sophia has told you," said Mrs. Pocket. "Did I not see her, with my own eyes, and hear her with my own ears, come into the room just now and ask to speak to you?"

"But has she not taken me downstairs, Belinda," returned Mr. Pocket, "and shown me the woman, and the bundle too?"

"And do you defend her, Matthew," said Mrs. Pocket, "for making mischief?"

Mr. Pocket uttered a dismal groan.

"Am I, Grandpapa's granddaughter, to be nothing in the house?" said Mrs. Pocket. "Besides, the cook has always been a very nice respectful woman, and said in the most natural manner when she came to look after the situation that she felt I was born to be a duchess."

There was a sofa where Mr. Pocket stood, and he dropped upon it in the attitude of a dying gladiator. Still in that attitude he said, with a hollow voice, "Good night, Mr. Pip," when I deemed it advisable to go to bed and leave him.

Words For Everyday Use

glad • i • a • tor (glad´ē ā´tər) n., prizefighter; warrior

CHAPTER 24

► What is the purpose of Pip's tutoring?

After two or three days, when I had established myself in my room and had gone backwards and forwards to London several times, and had ordered all I wanted of my tradesmen, Mr. Pocket and I had a long talk together. He knew more of my intended career than I knew myself, for he referred to his having been told by Mr. Jaggers that I was not designed for any profession, and that I should be well enough educated for my destiny if I could "hold my own" with the average of young men in prosperous circumstances. I <u>acquiesced</u>, of course, knowing nothing to the contrary.

He advised my attending certain places in London for the acquisition of such mere <u>rudiments</u> as I wanted, and my investing him with the functions of explainer and director of all my studies. He hoped that with intelligent assistance I should meet with little to discourage me, and should soon be able to dispense with[1] any aid but his. Through his way of saying this, and much more to similar purpose, he placed himself on confidential terms with me in an admirable man-ner—and I may state at once that he was always so zealous and honorable in fulfilling his compact with me that he made me zealous and honorable in fulfilling mine with him.

► What is Pip's assessment of Pocket as a tutor?

If he had shown indifference as a master, I have no doubt I should have returned the compliment as a pupil; he gave me no such excuse, and each of us did the other justice. Nor did I ever regard him as having anything ludicrous about him— or anything but what was serious, honest, and good—in his tutor communication with me.

When these points were settled, and so far carried out as that I had begun to work in earnest, it occurred to me that if I could retain my bedroom in Barnard's Inn, my life would be agreeably varied, while my manners would be none the worse for Herbert's society. Mr. Pocket did not object to this arrangement, but urged that before any step could possibly be taken in it, it must be submitted to my guardian. I felt that his <u>delicacy</u> arose out of the consideration that the plan would save Herbert some expense, so I went off to Little Britain and imparted my wish to Mr. Jaggers.

1. **dispense with.** Do without; do away with

Words For Everyday Use

ac • qui • esce (ak´wē es´) *vi.*, consent
ru • di • ment (rōō´də mənt) *n.*, basic skill or need
del • i • ca • cy (del´i kə sē) *n.*, tact in handling an issue

"If I could buy the furniture now hired for me," said I, "and one or two other little things, I should be quite at home there."

"Go it!" said Mr. Jaggers, with a short laugh. "I told you you'd get on. Well! How much do you want?"

I said I didn't know how much.

"Come!" retorted Mr. Jaggers. "How much? Fifty pounds?"

"Oh, not nearly so much."

"Five pounds?" said Mr. Jaggers.

This was such a great fall that I said in <u>discomfiture</u>, "Oh! more than that."

"More than that, eh!" retorted Mr. Jaggers, lying in wait for me, with his hands in his pockets, his head on one side, and his eyes on the wall behind me; "how much more?"

"It is so difficult to fix a sum," said I, hesitating.

"Come!" said Mr. Jaggers. "Let's get at it. Twice five; will that do? Three times five; will that do? Four times five; will that do?"

I said I thought that would do handsomely.[2]

"Four times five will do handsomely, will it?" said Mr. Jaggers, knitting his brows. "Now, what do you make of four times five?"

"What do I make of it?"

"Ah!" said Mr. Jaggers; "how much?"

"I suppose you make it twenty pounds," said I, smiling.

"Never mind what *I* make it, my friend," observed Mr. Jaggers, with a knowing and contradictory toss of his head. "I want to know what *you* make it."

"Twenty pounds, of course."

"Wemmick!" said Mr. Jaggers, opening his office door. "Take Mr. Pip's written order, and pay him twenty pounds."

This strongly marked way of doing business made a strongly marked impression on me, and that not of an agreeable kind. Mr. Jaggers never laughed; but he wore great bright creaking boots; and, in <u>poising</u> himself on these boots, with his large head bent down and his eyebrows joined together, awaiting an answer, he sometimes caused the boots to creak, as if *they* laughed in a dry and suspicious way. As he happened to go out now, and as Wemmick was brisk and talkative, I said to Wemmick that I hardly knew what to make of Mr. Jaggers's manner.

◀ What is Jaggers' "strong way of doing business"? What does Pip think of it?

---

2. **handsomely.** Nicely

| Words For Everyday Use | **dis • com • fi • ture** (dis kum′fi chər) *n.*, frustration; confusion
poise (poiz) *vt.*, balance; keep steady |

► How does Wemmick assess Mr. Jaggers's manner?

► Is the business successful? How do you know?

"Tell him that, and he'll take it as a compliment," answered Wemmick; "he don't mean that you *should* know what to make of it. Oh!" for I looked surprised, "it's not personal; it's professional, only professional."

Wemmick was at his desk, lunching—and crunching—on a dry hard biscuit, pieces of which he threw from time to time into his slit of a mouth, as if he were posting[3] them.

"Always seems to me," said Wemmick, "as if he had set a man-trap and was watching it. Suddenly—click—you're caught!"

Without remarking that man-traps were not among the <u>amenities</u> of life, I said I supposed he was very skillful?

"Deep," said Wemmick, "as Australia." Pointing with his pen at the office floor to express that Australia was understood, for the purposes of the figure, to be symmetrically on the opposite spot of the globe. "If there was anything deeper," added Wemmick, bringing his pen to paper, "he'd be it."

Then, I said I supposed he had a fine business, and Wemmick said, "Ca-pi-tal!" Then I asked if there were many clerks, to which he replied:

"We don't run much into clerks, because there's only one Jaggers, and people won't have him at second hand. There are only four of us. Would you like to see 'em? You are one of us, as I may say."

I accepted the offer. When Mr. Wemmick had put all the biscuit into the post, and had paid me my money from a cash-box in a safe, the key of which safe he kept somewhere down his back, and produced from his coat-collar like an iron pigtail, we went upstairs. The house was dark and shabby, and the greasy shoulders that had left their mark in Mr. Jaggers's room seemed to have been shuffling up and down the staircase for years. In the front first floor, a clerk who looked something between a publican[4] and a rat-catcher—a large pale puffed swollen man—was attentively engaged with three or four people of shabby appearance whom he treated as <u>unceremoniously</u> as everybody seemed to be treated who contributed to Mr. Jaggers's <u>coffers</u>. "Getting evidence together," said Mr. Wemmick, as we came

---

3. **posting.** Mailing; putting into a mailbox slot
4. **publican.** Tax collector

Words For Everyday Use

a • men • i • ty (ə menˊə tē) *n.,* attractive or desirable feature

un • cer • e • mo • ni • ous • ly (un serˊə mōˊnē əs lē) *adv.,* impolitely

cof • fers (kôˊfərz) *pl.n.,* funds

out, "for the Bailey."[5] In the room over that, a little flabby terrier of a clerk with dangling hair (his cropping[6] seemed to have been forgotten when he was a puppy) was similarly engaged with a man with weak eyes, whom Mr. Wemmick presented to me as a smelter[7] who kept his pot always boiling, and who would melt me anything I pleased—and who was in an excessive white-perspiration, as if he had been trying his art on himself. In a back room, a high-shouldered man with a face-ache[8] tied up in dirty flannel, who was dressed in old black clothes that bore the appearance of having been waxed, was stooping over his work of making fair copies of the notes of the other two gentlemen, for Mr. Jaggers's own use.

This was all the establishment. When we went downstairs again, Wemmick led me into my guardian's room, and said, "This you've seen already."

"Pray," said I, as the two <u>odious</u> casts with the twitchy leer upon them caught my sight again, "whose likenesses are those?"

◄ Whose faces are represented by the casts in Mr. Jaggers's office? When were they taken?

"These?" said Wemmick, getting upon a chair, and blowing the dust off the horrible heads before bringing them down. "These are two celebrated ones. Famous clients of ours that got us a world of credit. This chap (why you must have come down in the night and been peeping into the inkstand to get this blot upon your eyebrow, you old rascal!) murdered his master, and, considering that he wasn't brought up to evidence, didn't plan it badly."

"Is it like him?" I asked, recoiling from the brute, as Wemmick spat upon his eyebrow, and gave it a rub with his sleeve.

"Like him? It's himself, you know. The cast was made in Newgate, directly after he was taken down. You had a particular fancy for me, hadn't you, Old Artful?" said Wemmick. He then explained this affectionate <u>apostrophe</u> by touching his brooch representing the lady and the weeping willow at the tomb with the urn upon it, and saying, "Had it made for me, express!"

"Is the lady anybody?" said I.

---

5. **Bailey.** Old Bailey, site of the main criminal court in London
6. **cropping.** Trimming of the hair
7. **smelter.** Person who separates impurities from pure metal; here refers to the clerk's discernment
8. **face-ache.** Pain in a nerve in the skull

Words For Everyday Use

o • di • ous (ō′dē əs) *adj.,* offensive; arousing hatred
a • pos • tro • phe (ə päs′trə fē) *n.,* words addressed to an absent or imaginary person

"No," returned Wemmick. "Only his game. (You liked your bit of game, didn't you?) No; deuce a bit of a lady in the case, Mr. Pip, except one—and she wasn't of this slender ladylike sort, and you wouldn't have caught *her* looking after this urn—unless there was something to drink in it." Wemmick's attention being thus directed to his brooch, he put down the cast, and polished the brooch with his pocket-handkerchief.

"Did that other creature come to the same end?" I asked. "He has the same look."

"You're right," said Wemmick; "it's the genuine look. Much as if one nostril was caught up with a horsehair and a little fishhook. Yes, he came to the same end; quite the natural end here, I assure you. He <u>forged</u> wills, this blade[9] did, if he didn't also put the supposed testators[10] to sleep too. You were a gentlemanly cove,[11] though" (Mr. Wemmick was again apostrophizing), "and you said you could write Greek. Yah, Bounceable![12] What a liar you were! I never met such a liar as you!" Before putting his late friend on his shelf again, Wemmick touched the largest of his mourning rings, and said, "Sent out to buy it for me, only the day before."

► How does Wemmick obtain his jewelry?

While he was putting up the other cast and coming down from the chair, the thought crossed my mind that all his personal jewelry was derived from like sources. As he had shown no <u>diffidence</u> on the subject, I ventured on the liberty of asking him the question when he stood before me, dusting his hands.

"Oh yes," he returned, "these are all gifts of that kind. One brings another, you see; that's the way of it. I always take 'em. They're curiosities. And they're property. They may not be worth much, but, after all, they're property and portable. It don't signify to you with your brilliant lookout,[13] but as to myself, my guiding-star always is, Get hold of portable property."

► What is Wemmick's philosophy? Does he follow it?

When I had rendered homage to this light,[14] he went on to say in a friendly manner:

---

9. **blade.** Dashing young man
10. **testators.** Those who have made wills
11. **cove.** Chap; fellow
12. **Bounceable.** Blustering; loud and boastful
13. **lookout.** Outlook; prospects for the future
14. **rendered . . . light.** Acknowledged this information

Words For Everyday Use

forge (fôrj) *vt.*, make a fake document
dif • fi • dence (dif´ə dəns) *n.*, shyness

"If at any odd time when you have nothing better to do, you wouldn't mind coming over to see me at Walworth, I could offer you a bed, and I should consider it an honor. I have not much to show you; but such two or three curiosities as I have got, you might like to look over; and I am fond of a bit of garden and a summer house."

I said I should be delighted to accept his hospitality.

"Thankee," said he; "then we'll consider that it's to come off, when convenient to you. Have you dined with Mr. Jaggers yet?"

"Not yet."

"Well," said Wemmick, "he'll give you wine, and good wine. I'll give you punch, and not bad punch. And now I'll tell you something. When you go to dine with Mr. Jaggers, look at his housekeeper."

◀ What will Pip see at Jaggers's house?

"Shall I see something very uncommon?"

"Well," said Wemmick, "you'll see a wild beast tamed. Not so very uncommon, you'll tell me. I reply, that depends on the original wildness of the beast, and the amount of taming. It won't lower your opinion of Mr. Jaggers's powers. Keep your eye on it."

I told him I would do so, with all the interest and curiosity that his preparation awakened. As I was taking my departure, he asked me if I would like to devote five minutes to seeing Mr. Jaggers "at it"?

◀ Where does Wemmick take Pip?

For several reasons, and not least because I didn't clearly know what Mr. Jaggers would be found to be "at," I replied in the affirmative. We dived into the City, and came up in a crowded police court, where a blood relation (in the murderous sense) of the deceased with the fanciful taste in brooches was standing at the bar, uncomfortably chewing something; while my guardian had a woman under examination or cross-examination—I don't know which—and was striking her, and the bench, and everybody with awe. If anybody, of whatsoever degree, said a word that he didn't approve of, he instantly required to have it "taken down." If anybody wouldn't make an admission, he said, "I'll have it out of you!" and if anybody made an admission, he said, "Now I have got you!" The magistrates shivered under a single bite of his finger. Thieves and thieftakers hung in dread

◀ How does Jaggers conduct himself? What do the others in the courtroom think of him?

Words For Everyday Use

af • firm • a • tive (ə fɜrm´ə tiv) n., answer showing agreement

mag • is • trate (maj´ is trāt´) n., civil officer empowered to administer the law rapture[15] on his words, and shrank when a hair of his eyebrows turned in their direction. Which side he was on, I couldn't make out, for he seemed to me to be grinding the whole place in a mill; I only know that when I stole out on tiptoe, he was not on the side of the bench, for he was making the legs of the old gentleman who presided quite <u>convulsive</u> under the table by his <u>denunciations</u> of his conduct as the representative of British law and justice in that chair that day.

---

15. **dread rapture.** Powerful feeling of fear

Bentley Drummle, who was so <u>sulky</u> a fellow that he even took up a book as if its writer had done him an injury, did not take up an acquaintance in a more agreeable spirit. Heavy in figure, movement, and comprehension—in the sluggish complexion of his face, and in the large awkward tongue that seemed to loll about in his mouth as he himself lolled about in a room—he was <u>idle</u>, proud, <u>niggardly</u>, reserved, and suspicious. He came of rich people down in Somersetshire, who had nursed[1] this combination of qualities until they made the discovery that it was just of age and a blockhead. Thus, Bentley Drummle had come to Mr. Pocket when he was a head taller than that gentleman, and half a dozen heads thicker than most gentlemen.

◀ What makes Drummle unpleasant?

Startop had been spoiled by a weak mother, and kept at home when he ought to have been at school, but he was devotedly attached to her, and admired her beyond measure. He had a woman's delicacy of feature, and was—"as you may see, though you never saw her," said Herbert to me—"exactly like his mother." It was but natural that I should take to him much more kindly than to Drummle, and that, even in the earliest evenings of our boating, he and I should pull homeward <u>abreast</u> of one another, conversing from boat to boat, while Bentley Drummle came up in our wake alone, under the overhanging banks and among the rushes. He would always creep in shore like some uncomfortable <u>amphibious</u> creature, even when the tide would have sent him fast upon his way; and I always think of him as coming after us in the dark or by the backwater, when our own two boats were breaking the sunset or the moonlight in midstream.

◀ What positive and negative things does Pip note about Startop?

Herbert was my intimate companion and friend. I presented him with a half-share in my boat, which was the occasion of his often coming down to Hammersmith; and my possession of a half-share in his chambers often took me up to London. We used to walk between the two places at all hours. I have an affection for the road yet (though it is not so pleasant a road as it was then), formed in the <u>impressibility</u> of untried youth and hope.

◀ Why do Herbert and Pip see one another often?

---

1. **nursed.** Fostered; cultivated

Words For Everyday Use

sul • ky (sul´kē) *adj.*, dismal; sullen
i • dle (īd´'l) *adj.*, not inclined to work
nig • gard • ly (nig´ərd lē) *adj.*, stingy
a • breast (ə brest´) *adv.*, side by side

am • phib • i • ous (am fib´ē əs) *adj.*, that can live both on land and in water
im • pres • si • bil • i • ty (im pres´ə bil´ə tē) *n.*, tendency to be impressed by things

► What causes Mr. and Mrs. Camilla to feel as they do about Pip? How do they act towards him?

When I had been in Mr. Pocket's family a month or two, Mr. and Mrs. Camilla turned up. Camilla was Mr. Pocket's sister. Georgiana, whom I had seen at Miss Havisham's on the same occasion, also turned up. She was a cousin—an indigestive[2] single woman, who called her rigidity religion, and her liver[3] love. These people hated me with the hatred of cupidity and disappointment. As a matter of course, they fawned upon me in my prosperity with the basest meanness. Towards Mr. Pocket, as a grown-up infant with no notion of his own interests, they showed the complacent forbearance I had heard them express. Mrs. Pocket they held in contempt; but they allowed the poor soul to have been heavily disappointed in life, because that shed a feeble reflected light upon themselves.

► How well is Pip managing his money?

These were the surroundings among which I settled down, and applied myself to my education. I soon contracted expensive habits, and began to spend an amount of money that within a few short months I should have thought almost fabulous; but through good and evil I stuck to my books. There was no other merit in this than my having sense enough to feel my deficiencies. Between Mr. Pocket and Herbert I got on fast; and, with one or the other always at my elbow to give me the start I wanted, and clear obstructions out of my road, I must have been as great a dolt as Drummle if I had done less.

I had not seen Mr. Wemmick for some weeks, when I thought I would write him a note and propose to go home with him on a certain evening. He replied that it would give him much pleasure, and that he would expect me at the office at six o'clock. Thither I went, and there I found him, putting the key of his safe down his back as the clock struck.

"Did you think of walking down to Walworth?" said he.

"Certainly," said I, "if you approve."

"Very much," was Wemmick's reply, "for I have had my legs under the desk all day, and shall be glad to stretch them. Now I'll tell you what I've got for supper, Mr. Pip. I have got a stewed steak—which is of home preparation—and a cold roast fowl—which is from the cook's shop. I think it's tender,

---

2. **indigestive.** Causing indigestion
3. **liver.** Disagreeable disposition

Words For Everyday Use

cu • pid • i • ty (kyoō pid´ə tē) n., greed

bas • est (bās´est) adj., most contemptible; most despicable

com • pla • cent (kəm plā´sənt) adj., self-satisfied

for • bear • ance (fôr ber´əns) n., patience

con • tract (kən trakt´) vt., acquire

because the master of the shop was a juryman in some cases of ours the other day, and we let him down easy. I reminded him of it when I bought the fowl, and I said, 'Pick us out a good one, old Briton, because if we had chosen to keep you in the box another day or two, we could have done it.' He said to that, 'Let me make you a present of the best fowl in the shop.' I let him, of course. As far as it goes, it's property and portable. You don't object to an aged parent, I hope?"

I really thought he was still speaking of the fowl, until he added, "Because I have got an aged parent at my place." I then said what politeness required.

"So you haven't dined with Mr. Jaggers yet?" he pursued, as we walked along.

"Not yet."

"He told me so this afternoon when he heard you were coming. I expect you'll have an invitation tomorrow. He's going to ask your pals, too. Three of 'em; ain't there?"

Although I was not in the habit of counting Drummle as one of my intimate associates, I answered, "Yes."

"Well, he's going to ask the whole gang"—I hardly felt complimented by the word—"and whatever he gives you, he'll give you good. Don't look forward to variety, but you'll have excellence. And there's another rum[4] thing in his house," proceeded Wemmick after a moment's pause, as if the remark followed on, the housekeeper understood; "he never lets a door or window be fastened at night."

"Is he never robbed?"

"That's it!" returned Wemmick. "He says, and gives it out publicly, 'I want to see the man who'll rob *me*.' Lord bless you, I have heard him a hundred times if I have heard him once say to regular cracksmen[5] in our front office, 'You know where I live; now no bolt is ever drawn there; why don't you do a stroke of business with me? Come, can't I tempt you?' Not a man of them, sir, would be bold enough to try it on, for love or money."

"They dread him so much?" said I.

"Dread him," said Wemmick. "I believe you they dread him. Not but what he's artful, even in his <u>defiance</u> of them. No silver, sir. Britannia metal, every spoon."

◄ Why are Pip and Wemmick able to get a good fowl? What makes the fowl attractive to Wemmick?

◄ What is Jaggers's boast?

---

4. **rum.** Odd; strange
5. **cracksmen.** Burglars; safecrackers

"So they wouldn't have much," I observed, "even if they—"

"Ah! But *he* would have much," said Wemmick, cutting me short, "and they know it. He'd have their lives, and the lives of scores of 'em. He'd have all he could get. And it's impossible to say what he couldn't get, if he gave his mind to it."

I was falling into <u>meditation</u> on my guardian's greatness, when Wemmick remarked:

"As to the absence of plate,[6] that's only his natural depth, you know. A river's its natural depth, and he's his natural depth. Look at his watch chain. That's real enough."

"It's very massive," said I.

► Why is Jaggers's boast justified?

"Massive?" repeated Wemmick. "I think so. And his watch is a gold repeater,[7] and worth a hundred pound if it's worth a penny. Mr. Pip, there are about seven hundred thieves in this town who know all about that watch; there's not a man, a woman, or a child, among them who wouldn't identify the smallest link in that chain, and drop it as if it was red-hot, if <u>inveigled</u> into touching it."

At first with such discourse, and afterwards with conversation of a more general nature, did Mr. Wemmick and I beguile the time and the road,[8] until he gave me to understand that we had arrived in the district of Walworth.

It appeared to be a collection of back lanes, ditches, and little gardens, and to present the aspect of a rather dull retirement. Wemmick's house was a little wooden cottage in the midst of plots of garden, and the top of it was cut out and painted like a battery mounted with guns.

► What makes Wemmick's house unusual?

"My own doing," said Wemmick. "Looks pretty, don't it?"

I highly commended it. I think it was the smallest house I ever saw, with the queerest Gothic[9] windows (by far the greater part of them sham[10]), and a Gothic door, almost too small to get in at.

"That's a real flagstaff,[11] you see," said Wemmick, "and on Sundays I run up a real flag. Then look here. After I

► What does Wemmick do each night?

---

6. **plate.** Utensils made of silver
7. **repeater.** Nineteenth-century watch that chimed the hour when a spring was pressed
8. **beguile . . . road.** Cause the time to pass quickly and the journey to seem short.
9. **Gothic.** Of an architectural style from the Middle Ages
10. **sham.** Fake
11. **flagstaff.** Flagpole

Words For Everyday Use

med • i • ta • tion (med´ə tā´shən) *n.*, solemn reflection
in • vei • gle (in vē´gəl) *vt.*, lure, deceive

have crossed this bridge, I <u>hoist</u> it up—so—and cut off the communication."

The bridge was a plank, and it crossed a <u>chasm</u> about four feet wide and two deep. But it was very pleasant to see the pride with which he hoisted it up, and made it fast; smiling as he did so, with a relish, and not merely mechanically.

"At nine o'clock every night, Greenwich time," said Wemmick, "the gun fires. There he is, you see! And when you hear him go, I think you'll say he's a stinger."

The piece of ordnance[12] referred to was mounted in a separate fortress, constructed of lattice-work.[13] It was protected from the weather by an <u>ingenious</u> little tarpaulin[14] <u>contrivance</u> in the nature of an umbrella.

"Then, at the back," said Wemmick, "out of sight, so as not to <u>impede</u> the idea of fortifications—for it's a principle with me, if you have an idea, carry it out and keep it up—I don't know whether that's your opinion—"

I said, decidedly.

"—At the back, there's a pig, and there are fowls and rabbits; then I knock together my own little frame, you see, and grow cucumbers; and you'll judge at supper what sort of a salad I can raise. So, sir," said Wemmick, smiling again, but seriously, too, as he shook his head, "if you can suppose the little place <u>besieged</u>, it would hold out a devil of a time in point of provisions."

Then he conducted me to a bower[15] about a dozen yards off, but which was approached by such ingenious twists of path that it took quite a long time to get at; and in this retreat our glasses were already set forth. Our punch was cooling in an ornamental lake on whose margin the bower was raised. This piece of water (with an island in the middle which might have been the salad for supper) was of a circular form, and he had constructed a fountain in it which, when you set a little mill going and took a cork out of a pipe, played to that powerful extent that it made the back of your hand quite wet.

---

12. **ordnance.** Cannon or artillery
13. **lattice-work.** Structure made of crisscrossed strips of wood or metal
14. **tarpaulin.** Waterproof material used to cover something to protect it from getting wet
15. **bower.** Shady garden shelter; arbor

Words For Everyday Use

hoist (hoist) *vt.*, pull up
chasm (kaz´əm) *n.*, deep crack or opening in the earth's surface
in • ge • ni • ous (in jēn´yəs) *adj.*, clever
con • triv • ance (kən trīv´əns) *n.*, clever invention
im • pede (im pēd´) *vt.*, hinder; block
be • siege (bē sēg´) *vt.*, surround with armed forces for a sustained attack

► Why does he enjoy his home?

► Who lives with Wemmick?

► How does Wemmick feel about his father? How do you know?

"I am my own engineer, and my own carpenter, and my own plumber, and my own gardener, and my own jack-of-all-trades,"[16] said Wemmick, in acknowledging my compliments. "Well, it's a good thing, you know. It brushes the Newgate cobwebs away, and pleases the Aged. You wouldn't mind being at once introduced to the Aged, would you? It wouldn't put you out?"

I expressed the readiness I felt, and we went into the castle. There we found, sitting by a fire, a very old man in a flannel coat—clean, cheerful, comfortable, and well cared for, but intensely deaf.

"Well, aged parent," said Wemmick, shaking hands with him in a <u>cordial</u> and <u>jocose</u> way, "how am you?"

"All right, John; all right!" replied the old man.

"Here's Mr. Pip, aged parent," said Wemmick, "and I wish you could hear his name. Nod away at him, Mr. Pip; that's what he likes. Nod away at him, if you please, like winking!"

"This is a fine place of my son's, sir," cried the old man, while I nodded as hard as I possibly could. "This is a pretty pleasure-ground, sir. This spot and these beautiful works upon it ought to be kept together by the nation, after my son's time, for the people's enjoyment."

"You're as proud of it as Punch;[17] ain't you, Aged?" said Wemmick, contemplating the old man, with his hard face really softened; "*There's* a nod for you"—giving him a tremendous one. "*There's* another for you"—giving him a still more tremendous one. "You like that, don't you? If you're not tired, Mr. Pip—though I know it's tiring to strangers—will you tip him one more? You can't think how it pleases him."

I tipped him several more, and he was in great spirits. We left him <u>bestirring</u> himself to feed the fowls, and we sat down to our punch in the arbor, where Wemmick told me as he smoked a pipe that it had taken him a good many years to bring the property up to its present pitch of perfection.

"Is it your own, Mr. Wemmick?"

"O yes," said Wemmick, "I have got hold of it a bit at a time. It's a freehold,[18] by George!"

---

16. **jack-of-all-trades.** Person who can do many different kinds of work
17. **proud . . . Punch.** Highly satisfied; from the quarrelsome, hook-nosed husband of Judy in the comic puppet show, *Punch and Judy*
18. **freehold.** Outright ownership of land

Words For Everyday Use	cor • dial (kôr´jəl) *adj.*, warm and friendly
	jo • cose (jō kōs´) *adj.*, witty; humorous
	be • stir (bē stʉr´) *vt.*, exert or busy (oneself)

"Is it, indeed? I hope Mr. Jaggers admires it?"

"Never seen it," said Wemmick. "Never heard of it. Never seen the Aged. Never heard of him. No; the office is one thing, and private life is another. When I go into the office, I leave the castle behind me, and when I come into the castle, I leave the office behind me. If it's not in any way disagreeable to you, you'll oblige me by doing the same. I don't wish it professionally spoken about."

◄ What is Wemmick's attitude about life at home and at work?

Of course I felt my good faith involved in the observance of his request. The punch being very nice, we sat there drinking it and talking, until it was almost nine o'clock. "Getting near gun-fire," said Wemmick then, as he laid down his pipe; "it's the Aged's treat."

Proceeding into the castle again, we found the Aged heating the poker, with expectant eyes, as a <u>preliminary</u> to the performance of this great nightly ceremony. Wemmick stood with his watch in his hand until the moment was come for him to take the red-hot poker[19] from the Aged, and repair to the battery. He took it, and went out, and presently the stinger went off with a bang that shook the crazy little box of a cottage as if it must fall to pieces, and made every glass and teacup in it ring. Upon this the Aged—who I believe would have been blown out of his armchair but for holding on by the elbows—cried out <u>exultingly</u>, "He's fired! I heerd him!" and I nodded at the old gentleman until it is no figure of speech to declare that I absolutely could not see him.

◄ What is the Aged's response to the firing of the gun?

The interval between that time and supper Wemmick devoted to showing me his collection of curiosities. They were mostly of a <u>felonious</u> character; comprising the pen with which a celebrated forgery had been committed, a distinguished razor or two, some locks of hair, and several manuscript confessions written under <u>condemnation</u>—upon which Mr. Wemmick set particular value as being, to use his own words, "every one of 'em lies, sir." These were agreeably dispersed among small specimens of china and glass, various neat trifles made by the proprietor of the museum, and some tobacco-stoppers[20] carved by the Aged. They were all displayed in that chamber of the castle into which I had been

---

19. **poker.** Metal rod used to stir a fire
20. **tobacco-stoppers.** Devices used to stuff tobacco into a pipe

---

Words For Everyday Use

pre • lim • i • nar • y (prē lim´ ə ner´ē) *n.*, event that precedes the main event

ex • ult • ing • ly (eg zult´ iŋ lē) *adv.*, jubilantly; joyfully

fe • lo • ni • ous (fə lō´nē əs) *adj.*, relating to crimes

con • dem • na • tion (kän´dem nā´shən) *n.*, pronouncement of guilt first <u>inducted</u>, and which served, not only as the general sitting room but as the kitchen, too, if I might judge from a saucepan on the hob,[21] and a brazen bijou[22] over the fireplace designed for the suspension of a roasting-jack.[23]

There was a neat little girl in attendance, who looked after the Aged in the day. When she had laid the supper-cloth, the bridge was lowered to give her means of <u>egress</u>, and she withdrew for the night. The supper was excellent; and though the castle was rather subject to dry rot,[24] insomuch that it tasted like a bad nut, and though the pig might have been farther off, I was heartily pleased with my whole entertainment. Nor was there any drawback on my little turret[25] bedroom, beyond there being such a very thin ceiling between me and the flagstaff that, when I lay down on my back in bed, it seemed as if I had to balance that pole on my forehead all night.

Wemmick was up early in the morning, and I am afraid I heard him cleaning my boots. After that, he fell to gardening, and I saw him from my Gothic window pretending to employ the Aged, and nodding at him in a most devoted manner. Our breakfast was as good as the supper, and at half-past eight precisely we started for Little Britain. By degrees, Wemmick got dryer and harder as we went along, and his mouth tightened into a post office again. At last, when we got to his place of business and he pulled out his key from his coat-collar, he looked as unconscious of his Walworth property as if the castle and the drawbridge and the arbor and the lake and the fountain and the Aged had all been blown into space together by the last <u>discharge</u> of the stinger.

► *What change overcomes Wemmick as he walks to Little Britain? How does Pip express the completeness of this change?*

---

21. **hob.** Projecting ledge at the back or side of a fireplace, used for keeping a pan warm
22. **brazen bijou.** Small, delicately made brass ornament
23. **roasting-jack.** Device that turns a spit for roasting meat
24. **dry rot.** A fungous disease of timber that causes it to crumble; deterioration
25. **turret.** Tower

Words For Everyday Use

in • duct (in dukt´) *vt.*, formally admit

e • gress (ē´gres´) *n.*, exit; way out

dis • charge (dis´chärj) *n.*, firing

Responding to the Selection

Pip makes many new acquaintances in chapters 20–25. If you were in his position, whom would you be most interested in getting to know better, and why—Herbert Pocket, Startop, Drummle, or Wemmick?

Reviewing the Selection

Recalling and Interpreting

1. **R:** What is revealed about Mr. Jaggers's personality, profession, and clients in chapters 20–25?

2. **I:** Why is it unusual that Miss Havisham and Pip's mysterious benefactor are also Jaggers's clients? In what way does Dickens seems to be characterizing the legal system and its professionals as a whole? Explain.

3. **R:** Which characteristics of Herbert Pocket make Pip eager to be his friend? What doesn't Pip like about Drummle? How does Pip feel about Startop? What does Herbert reveal about Miss Havisham? What relationship might Herbert have had with Estella? How does Herbert view Estella?

4. **I:** In what way do the expectations of Pip and Herbert differ? How does Herbert feel about his lot in life? What differences does this indicate between Herbert's and Pip's values? Explain whether Miss Havisham's great tragedy, as described by Herbert, is what you guessed it to be. Explain who has a more accurate view of Estella—Pip or Herbert.

5. **R:** With what is Mrs. Pocket obsessed? In what ways does her obsession affect her life and that of her family? In what way does her obsession affect the way she views others?

6. **I:** Compare and contrast Mrs. Pocket's behavior and overriding concerns to those of Pip. In what ways are they more similar than different?

7. **R:** Who is Wemmick? What is his relationship with Pip? What actions show that Wemmick seeks to befriend Pip? Where does Wemmick live? What is unusual about this place?

8. **I:** What does Wemmick have a unique ability to do? How does Wemmick's approach to both his home life and his professional life compare with Pip's response to his home life and to Satis House, Miss Havisham's home, where he once worked?

Synthesizing

9. Dickens was a great observer of people and created in his novels many of the most eccentric and memorable characters in literature. What memorable eccentrics does Dickens create in chapters 20–25? In what ways are these characters eccentric? Explain whether you believe these characters are too eccentric to be considered realistic or whether characters such as these exist in real life.

10. In chapters 20–25, Pip encounters for the first time life outside his own small village. What members of different social groups does he encounter? In what way does Dickens characterize the members of these different social groups?

Understanding Literature (QUESTIONS FOR DISCUSSION)

1. Dialogue. Dialogue is conversation involving two or more people or characters. Fictional works are made up of dialogue, narration, and description. The reader learns much about Jaggers through his dialogue with other characters in the novel. Select one such dialogue and discuss what it tells the reader about the personality or character of Jaggers.

2. One-Dimensional Character and Three-Dimensional Character. A **character** is a person (or sometimes an animal) who figures in the action of a literary work. A **one-dimensional character** is one who exhibits a single dominant quality, or character trait. A **three-dimensional character** is one who exhibits the complexity of traits associated with actual human beings. Explain whether you would define each of the following characters as one-dimensional or three-dimensional as they have been revealed thus far in the story: Mr. Jaggers, Mr. Pocket, Mrs. Pocket, Herbert Pocket, Startop, Drummle, Mrs. Coiler, and Mr. Wemmick?

3. Motif. A **motif** is any element that recurs in one or more works of literature or art. One motif that recurs throughout Dickens's work as a whole is his sympathy and love toward children. In what way does the author express such an attitude toward the Pocket children? How does Mrs. Pocket's parenting style differ from Mrs. Joe's? What attitude does Dickens express toward caretakers such as Mrs. Joe and Mrs. Pocket? Explain how relationships between parents and children have been portrayed thus far in the story. Have you seen any examples of what you would consider to be a good parent-child or guardian-child relationship?

4. Aphorism. An **aphorism** is a short saying or a pointed statement. In chapter 22, Herbert Pocket relates his father's aphorism about gentlemen: "no man who was not a true gentleman at heart, ever was, since the world began, a true gentleman in manner. . . . no varnish can hide the grain of the wood, and that the more varnish you put on, the more the grain will express itself." In what way might this aphorism be applied to Pip and his new-found position?

CHAPTER 26

It fell out, as Wemmick had told me it would, that I had an early opportunity of comparing my guardian's establishment with that of his cashier and clerk. My guardian was in his room, washing his hands with his scented soap, when I went into the office from Walworth; and he called me to him, and gave me the invitation for myself and friends which Wemmick had prepared me to receive. "No ceremony," he stipulated, "and no dinner dress, and say tomorrow." I asked him where we should come to (for I had no idea where he lived), and I believe it was in his general objection to make anything like an admission that he replied, "Come here, and I'll take you home with me." I embrace this opportunity of remarking that he washed his clients off, as if he were a surgeon or a dentist. He had a closet in his room fitted up for the purpose, which smelt of the scented soap like a perfumer's shop. It had an unusually large jack-towel on a roller inside the door, and he would wash his hands, and wipe them and dry them all over this towel, whenever he came in from a police court or dismissed a client from his room. When I and my friends repaired to him at six o'clock next day, he seemed to have been engaged on a case of a darker <u>complexion</u> than usual, for we found him with his head butted into this closet, not only washing his hands, but laving[1] his face and gargling his throat. And even when he had done all that, and had gone all round the jack-towel, he took out his penknife and scraped the case out of his nails before he put his coat on.

There were some people slinking about as usual when we passed out into the street, who were <u>evidently</u> anxious to speak with him; but there was something so <u>conclusive</u> in the halo of scented soap which encircled his presence that they gave it up for that day. As we walked along westward, he was recognized ever and again by some face in the crowd of the streets, and whenever that happened he talked louder to me; but he never otherwise recognized anybody, or took notice that anybody recognized him.

▶ What does Jaggers do after each encounter with a client?

▶ How do anxious clients respond to Jaggers when they see him? Why?

---

1. **laving.** Washing

Words For Everyday Use

com • plex • ion (kəm plek´shən) n., general character or tone

ev • i • dent • ly (ev´ə dənt´lē) adv., obviously; clearly

con • clu • sive (kən kloo´siv) adj., that settles a question; final

He conducted us to Gerrard Street, Soho, to a house on the south side of that street, rather a stately house of its kind, but dolefully in want of painting, and with dirty windows. He took out his key and opened the door, and we all went into a stone hall, bare, gloomy, and little used. So up a dark brown staircase into a series of three dark brown rooms on the first floor. There were carved <u>garlands</u> on the paneled walls, and as he stood among them giving us welcome, I know what kind of loops I thought they looked like.

◄ *Of what might the garland loops remind Pip, given Jaggers's profession?*

Dinner was laid in the best of these rooms; the second was his dressing room; the third, his bedroom. He told us that he held the whole house, but rarely used more of it than we saw. The table was comfortably laid—no silver in the service, of course—and at the side of his chair was a <u>capacious</u> dumbwaiter,[2] with a variety of bottles and <u>decanters</u> on it, and four dishes of fruit for dessert. I noticed throughout that he kept everything under his own hand, and distributed everything himself.

There was a bookcase in the room; I saw from the backs of the books that they were about evidence, criminal law, criminal biography, trials, acts of Parliament,[3] and such things. The furniture was all very solid and good, like his watch chain. It had an official look, however, and there was nothing merely ornamental to be seen. In a corner was a little table of papers with a shaded lamp; so that he seemed to bring the office home with him in that respect, too, and to wheel it out of an evening and fall to work.

As he had scarcely seen my three companions until now— for he and I had walked together—he stood on the hearth-rug,[4] after ringing the bell, and took a searching look at them. To my surprise, he seemed at once to be principally, if not solely, interested in Drummle.

◄ *Why is Pip surprised? What name does Jaggers give Drummle?*

"Pip," said he, putting his large hand on my shoulder and moving me to the window, "I don't know one from the other. Who's the spider?"

"The spider?" said I.

"The blotchy, sprawly, sulky fellow."

---

2. **dumbwaiter.** Small, portable stand for serving food, often with shelves
3. **Parliament.** National legislative body of Great Britain, composed of the House of Commons and the House of Lords
4. **hearth-rug.** Rug made to be placed on the brick floor in front of a fireplace

---

Words For Everyday Use

gar • land (gär´lənd) *n.*, decorative wreath or woven chain of flowers or leaves

ca • pa • cious (kə pā´shəs) *adj.*, roomy

de • cant • er (dē kant´ər) *n.*, decorative glass bottle

"That's Bentley Drummle," I replied; "the one with the delicate face is Startop."

Not making the least account of "the one with the delicate face," he returned, "Bentley Drummle is his name, is it? I like the look of that fellow."

He immediately began to talk to Drummle, not at all deterred by his replying in his heavy reticent way, but apparently led on by it to screw[5] discourse out of him. I was looking at the two, when there came between me and them, the housekeeper, with the first dish for the table.

She was a woman of about forty, I supposed—but I may have thought her younger than she was. Rather tall, of a lithe nimble figure, extremely pale, with large faded eyes, and a quantity of streaming hair. I cannot say whether any diseased affection of the heart caused her lips to be parted as if she were panting, and her face to bear a curious expression of suddenness and flutter, but I know that I had been to see *Macbeth* at the theater, a night or two before, and that her face looked to me as if it were all disturbed by fiery air, like the faces I had seen rise out of the witches' caldron.[6]

She set the dish on, touched my guardian quietly on the arm with a finger to notify that dinner was ready, and vanished. We took our seats at the round table, and my guardian kept Drummle on one side of him, while Startop sat on the other. It was a noble dish of fish that the housekeeper had put on the table, and we had a joint of equally choice mutton[7] afterwards, and then an equally choice bird. Sauces, wines, all the accessories we wanted, and all of the best, were given out by our host from his dumbwaiter; and when they had made the circuit of the table, he always put them back again. Similarly, he dealt us clean plates and knives and forks for each course, and dropped those just disused into two baskets on the ground by his chair. No other attendant than the housekeeper appeared. She set on every dish; and I always saw in her face a face rising out of the caldron. Years afterwards, I made a dreadful likeness of that woman by causing

▶ In what way does Drummle answer Jaggers's questions? What does this prompt Jaggers to do?

▶ What is unusual about the housekeeper?

---

5. **screw.** Use pressure to obtain
6. ***Macbeth . . . caldron.*** In a famous scene from Shakespeare's play *The Tragedy of Macbeth,* eerie apparitions appear as the witches stir their potion in a caldron.
7. **mutton.** Meat from sheep

Words For Everyday Use

de • ter (dē tʉr´) *vt.,* discourage from acting

ret • i • cent (ret´i sənt) *adj.,* reserved; uncommunicative

dis • course (dis´kôrs´) *n.,* speech; conversation

lithe (līth) *adj.,* limber; flexible

nim • ble (nim´bəl) *adj.,* quick; agile

a face that had no other natural resemblance to it than it derived from flowing hair to pass behind a bowl of flaming spirits in a dark room.

Induced to take particular notice of the housekeeper, both by her own striking appearance and by Wemmick's preparation, I observed that whenever she was in the room, she kept her eyes attentively on my guardian, and that she would remove her hands from any dish she put before him, hesitatingly, as if she dreaded his calling her back, and wanted him to speak when she was nigh, if he had anything to say. I fancied that I could detect in his manner a consciousness of this, and a purpose of always holding her in suspense.

◀ Why does Pip watch the house-keeper closely? How does Jaggers treat her?

Dinner went off gaily, and, although my guardian seemed to follow rather than originate subjects, I knew that he <u>wrenched</u> the weakest part of our dispositions out of us. For myself, I found that I was expressing my tendency to <u>lavish</u> expenditure,[8] and to patronize Herbert, and to boast of my great prospects before I quite knew that I had opened my lips. It was so with all of us, but with no one more than Drummle, the development of whose inclination to gird[9] in a grudging and suspicious way at the rest was screwed out of him before the fish was taken off.

◀ What does Jaggers draw out from the young men? What does Pip divulge?

It was not then, but when we had got to the cheese, that our conversation turned upon our rowing feats, and that Drummle was rallied[10] for coming up behind of a night in that slow amphibious way of his. Drummle, upon this, informed our host that he much preferred our room to our company, and that as to skill he was more than our master, and that as to strength he could scatter us like chaff. By some invisible agency, my guardian wound him up to a <u>pitch</u> little short of ferocity about this trifle,[11] and he fell to baring and spanning his arm[12] to show how muscular it was, and we all fell to baring and spanning our arms in a ridiculous manner.

◀ What does Drummle tell Jaggers?

Now the housekeeper was at that time clearing the table; my guardian, taking no heed of her, but with the side of his face turned from her, was leaning back in his chair, biting

---

8. **expenditure.** Spending
9. **gird.** Jeer; mock
10. **rallied.** Teased
11. **trifle.** Something of little importance
12. **baring . . . arm.** Rolling up his sleeve and flexing his muscles

Words For Everyday Use

wrench (rench) *vt.,* pull out with force
lav • ish (lav´ish) *adj.,* extravagant; excessive
pitch (pich) *n.,* point or degree

► Why do Pip, Herbert, Drummle, and Startop suddenly stop talking?

the side of his forefinger and showing an interest in Drummle that, to me, was quite <u>inexplicable</u>. Suddenly, he clapped his large hand on the housekeeper's, like a trap, as she stretched it across the table. So suddenly and smartly did he do this that we all stopped in our foolish contention.

"If you talk of strength," said Mr. Jaggers, "*I'll* show you a wrist. Molly, let them see your wrist."

Her entrapped hand was on the table, but she had already put her other hand behind her waist: "Master," she said, in a low voice, with her eyes attentively and <u>entreatingly</u> fixed upon him, "don't."

► What does Jaggers want Molly to do? In what way does she respond?

"*I'll* show you a wrist," repeated Mr. Jaggers, with an immovable determination to show it. "Molly, let them see your wrist."

"Master," she again murmured. "Please!"

"Molly," said Mr. Jaggers, not looking at her, but obstinately looking at the opposite side of the room, "let them see *both* your wrists. Show them. Come!"

He took his hand from hers, and turned that wrist up on the table. She brought her other hand from behind her, and held the two out side by side. The last wrist was much disfigured—deeply scarred and scarred across and across. When she held her hands out, she took her eyes from Mr. Jaggers, and turned them watchfully on every one of the rest of us in succession.

► What does Jaggers say Molly's wrists reveal?

"There's power here," said Mr. Jaggers, coolly tracing out the <u>sinews</u> with his forefinger. "Very few men have the power of wrist that this woman has. It's remarkable what mere force of grip there is in these hands. I have had occasion to notice many hands; but I never saw stronger in that respect, man's or woman's, than these."

While he said these words in a leisurely critical style, she continued to look at every one of us in regular succession as we sat. The moment he ceased, she looked at him again. "That'll do, Molly," said Mr. Jaggers, giving her a slight nod; "you have been admired, and can go." She withdrew her hands and went out of the room, and Mr. Jaggers, putting the decanters on from his dumbwaiter, filled his glass and passed round the wine.

"At half-past nine, gentlemen," said he, "we must break up. Pray make the best of your time. I am glad to see you all. Mr. Drummle, I drink to you."

Words For Everyday Use

in • ex • pli • ca • ble (in eks´pli kə bəl) *adj.,* that cannot be explained or understood

en• treat • ing • ly (en trēt´in lē) *adv.,* pleadingly; earnestly

sin • ew (sin´yo͞o) *n.,* tendon; muscular power

If his object in singling out Drummle were to bring him out still more, it perfectly succeeded. In a sulky triumph, Drummle showed his <u>morose</u> depreciation of the rest of us in a more and more offensive degree, until he became down-right intolerable. Through all his stages, Mr. Jaggers followed him with the same strange interest. He actually seemed to serve as a zest[13] to Mr. Jaggers's wine.

◄ What does Drummle do because of Jaggers's interest in him?

In our boyish want of <u>discretion</u> I dare say we took too much to drink, and I know we talked too much. We became particularly hot upon some <u>boorish</u> <u>sneer</u> of Drummle's to the effect that we were too free with our money. It led to my remarking, with more zeal than discretion, that it came with a bad grace from him, to whom Startop had lent money in my presence but a week or so before.

◄ Why does Pip bring up the borrowed money?

"Well," retorted Drummle, "he'll be paid."

"I don't mean to imply that he won't," said I, "but it might make you hold your tongue about us and our money, I should think."

"*You* should think!" retorted Drummle. "Oh, Lord!"

"I dare say," I went on, meaning to be very severe, "that you wouldn't lend money to any of us if we wanted it."

"You are right," said Drummle. "I wouldn't lend one of you a sixpence. I wouldn't lend anybody a sixpence."

"Rather mean to borrow under those circumstances, I should say."

"*You* should say," repeated Drummle. "Oh, Lord!"

This was so very aggravating—the more especially as I found myself making no way against his surly <u>obtuseness</u>—that I said, disregarding Herbert's efforts to check me:

"Come, Mr. Drummle, since we are on the subject, I'll tell you what passed between Herbert here and me, when you borrowed that money."

"*I* don't want to know what passed between Herbert there and you," growled Drummle. And I think he added in a lower growl that we might both go to the devil and shake ourselves.

"I'll tell you, however," said I, "whether you want to know or not. We said that as you put it in your pocket very glad to get it, you seemed to be immensely amused at his being so weak as to lend it."

◄ Why does Drummle dislike the others?

---

13. **zest.** Something that adds interest or flavor

| Words For Everyday Use | **mo • rose** (mə rōs´) *adj.*, gloomy; sullen
 dis • cre • tion (dis kresh´ən) *n.*, caution; good judgment
 boor • ish (boor´ish) *adj.*, ill-mannered | **sneer** (snir) *n.*, smile or expression that shows contempt
 ob • tuse • ness (äb tōōs´nəs) *n.*, stupidity; slowness to understand |

Drummle laughed outright, and sat laughing in our faces, with his hands in his pockets and his round shoulders raised, plainly signifying that it was quite true, and that he despised us as asses all.

Hereupon Startop took him in hand, though with a much better grace than I had shown, and <u>exhorted</u> him to be a little more agreeable. Startop, being a lively bright young fellow, and Drummle being the exact opposite, the latter was always disposed to resent him as a direct personal affront. He now retorted in a coarse lumpish[14] way, and Startop tried to turn the discussion aside with some small pleasantry[15] that made us all laugh. Resenting this little success more than anything, Drummle, without any threat or warning, pulled his hands out of his pockets, dropped his round shoulders, swore, took up a large glass, and would have flung it at his <u>adversary's</u> head, but for our entertainer's dexterously seizing it at the instant when it was raised for that purpose.

"Gentlemen," said Mr. Jaggers, deliberately putting down the glass, and hauling out his gold repeater by its massive chain, "I am exceedingly sorry to announce that it's half-past nine."

On this hint we all rose to depart. Before we got to the street door, Startop was cheerily calling Drummle "old boy," as if nothing had happened. But the old boy was so far from responding that he would not even walk to Hammersmith on the same side of the way, so Herbert and I, who remained in town, saw them going down the street on opposite sides; Startop leading, and Drummle lagging behind in the shadow of the houses, much as he was <u>wont</u> to follow in his boat.

As the door was not yet shut, I thought I would leave Herbert there for a moment, and run upstairs again to say a word to my guardian. I found him in his dressing room surrounded by his stock of boots, already hard at it, washing his hands of us.

I told him I had come up again to say how sorry I was that anything disagreeable should have occurred, and that I hoped he would not blame me much.

"Pooh!" said he, sluicing[16] his face, and speaking through the water-drops; "it's nothing, Pip. I like that spider, though."

---

14. **lumpish.** Stupid; dull
15. **pleasantry.** Humorous comment
16. **sluicing.** Splashing water on

▶ What further enrages Drummle? What does he almost do?

▶ What does Pip do to make amends? What does Jaggers say?

Words For Everyday Use	ex • hort (eg zôrt´) *vt.*, urge
	ad • ver • sar • y (ad´ vər ser´ē) *n.*, opponent; enemy
	wont (wônt) *adj.*, accustomed

He had turned towards me now, and was shaking his head, and blowing, and toweling himself.

"I am glad you like him, sir," said I, "but I don't."

◀ *What is Jaggers's warning?*

"No, no," my guardian assented; "don't have too much to do with him. Keep as clear of him as you can. But I like the fellow, Pip; he is one of the true sort. Why, if I was a fortune-teller—"

Looking out of the towel, he caught my eye.

"But I am not a fortune-teller," he said, letting his head drop into a festoon[17] of towel, and toweling away at his two ears. "You know what I am, don't you? Good night, Pip."

"Good night, sir."

In about a month after that, the spider's time with Mr. Pocket was up for good, and, to the great relief of all the house but Mrs. Pocket, he went home to the family hole.

◀ *What does "the spider" soon do?*

---

17. **festoon.** Loop

CHAPTER 27

▶ What news does
Pip receive?

MY DEAR MR. PIP,

I write this by request of Mr. Gargery, for to let you know that he is going to London in company with Mr. Wopsle and would be glad if agreeable to be allowed to see you. He would call at Barnard's Hotel Tuesday morning at nine o'clock, when if not agreeable please leave word. Your poor sister is much the same as when you left. We talk of you in the kitchen every night, and wonder what you are saying and doing. If now considered in the light of a liberty,[1] excuse it for the love of poor old days. No more, dear Mr. Pip, from

Your ever obliged, and affectionate servant,

BIDDY.

▶ What special
message does Joe ask
Biddy to add? What
sentence didn't Biddy
share with Joe?
Why might she have
kept this sentence
from him?

P. S. He wishes me most particular to write *what larks*. He says you will understand. I hope and do not doubt it will be agreeable to see him even though a gentleman, for you had ever a good heart, and he is a worthy worthy man. I have read him all excepting only the last little sentence, and he wishes me most particular to write again *what larks*.

I received this letter by post on Monday morning, and therefore its appointment was for next day. Let me confess exactly with what feelings I looked forward to Joe's coming.

Not with pleasure, though I was bound to him by so many ties; no; with considerable disturbance, some mortification, and a keen sense of <u>incongruity</u>. If I could have kept him away by paying money, I certainly would have paid money. My greatest reassurance was that he was coming to Barnard's Inn, not to Hammersmith, and consequently would not fall in Bentley Drummle's way. I had little objection to his being seen by Herbert or his father, for both of whom I had a respect, but I had the sharpest sensitiveness as to his being seen by Drummle, whom I held in contempt. So throughout life our worst weaknesses and meannesses are usually committed for the sake of the people whom we most despise.

▶ What would Pip
have done to avoid
a visit from Joe if he
could?

---

1. **in . . . liberty.** As an action that is too familiar given your status

Words For Everyday Use

in • con • gru • i • ty (in′ kän grōō′ ə tē) *n.,* lack of consistency with what is appropriate

I had begun to be always decorating the chambers in some quite unnecessary and inappropriate way or other, and very expensive those wrestles with Barnard proved to be. By this time, the rooms were vastly different from what I had found them, and I enjoyed the honor of occupying a few <u>prominent</u> pages in the books of a neighboring upholsterer.[2] I had got on so fast of late that I had even started a boy in boots—top boots[3]—in bondage and slavery to whom I might have been said to pass my days. For, after I had made this monster (out of the refuse of my washerwoman's family) and had clothed him with a blue coat, canary waistcoat, white cravat, creamy breeches,[4] and the boots already mentioned, I had to find him a little to do and a great deal to eat; and with both of these horrible requirements he haunted my existence.

◀ On what does Pip spend money?

This <u>Avenging</u> Phantom was ordered to be on duty at eight on Tuesday morning in the hall (it was two feet square, as charged for floor-cloth), and Herbert suggested certain things for breakfast that he thought Joe would like. While I felt sincerely obliged to him for being so interested and considerate, I had an odd half-provoked sense of suspicion upon me that if Joe had been coming to see *him,* he wouldn't have been quite so brisk about it.

However, I came into town on the Monday night to be ready for Joe, and I got up early in the morning, and caused the sitting room and breakfast table to assume their most splendid appearance. Unfortunately the morning was drizzly, and an angel could not have concealed the fact that Barnard was shedding sooty tears outside the window, like some weak giant of a sweep.[5]

◀ What does Pip do to prepare for Joe's arrival?

As the time approached I should have liked to run away, but the Avenger pursuant[6] to orders was in the hall, and presently I heard Joe on the staircase. I knew it was Joe by his clumsy manner of coming upstairs—his state boots being always too big for him—and by the time it took him to read the names

---

2. **pages . . . upholsterer.** Pip owes money to the upholsterer, or person who covers furniture with fabric and furnishes rooms with curtains and carpets.

3. **top boots.** High boots having the upper part trimmed with a contrasting color or texture of leather, often worn by gentlemen of that time

4. **cravat . . . breeches.** *Cravat*—neckerchief or scarf; *breeches*—tapered trousers reaching just below the knee

5. **Barnard . . . sweep.** See the description of Barnard's Inn on page 181.

6. **pursuant.** According

Words For Everyday Use

prom • i • nent (präm´ə nənt) *adj.,* noticeable; standing out
a • veng • ing (ə venj´ iŋ) *adj.,* retaliating; revengeful

► How can you tell that Joe feels hesitant and nervous about seeing Pip again?

on the other floors in the course of his ascent. When at last he stopped outside our door, I could hear his finger tracing over the painted letters of my name, and I afterwards <u>distinctly</u> heard him breathing in at the keyhole. Finally he gave a faint single rap, and Pepper—such was the compromising[7] name of the avenging boy—announced "Mr. Gargery!" I thought he never would have done wiping his feet, and that I must have gone out to lift him off the mat, but at last he came in.

"Joe, how are you, Joe?"

"Pip, how AIR you, Pip?"

With his good honest face all glowing and shining, and his hat put down on the floor between us, he caught both my hands and worked them straight up and down, as if I had been the last-patented pump.

"I am glad to see you, Joe. Give me your hat."

But Joe, taking it up carefully with both hands, like a bird's nest with eggs in it, wouldn't hear of parting with that piece of property, and persisted in standing talking over it in a most uncomfortable way.

"Which you have that growed," said Joe, "and that swelled and that gentle-folked"—Joe considered a little before he discovered this word—"as to be sure you are a honor to your king and country."

"And you, Joe, look wonderfully well."

"Thank God," said Joe, "I'm ekerval to[8] most. And your sister, she's no worse than she were. And Biddy, she's ever right and ready. And all friends is no backerder, if not no forarder. 'Ceptin' Wopsle; he's had a drop."

All this time (still with both hands taking great care of the bird's nest), Joe was rolling his eyes round and round the room, and round and round the flowered pattern of my dressing gown.

"Had a drop, Joe?"

► Why is Wopsle in London?

"Why, yes," said Joe, lowering his voice, "he's left the Church and went into the play-acting. Which the play-acting have likewise brought him to London along with me. And his wish were," said Joe, getting the bird's nest under his left arm for the moment, and groping in it for an egg with his right, "if no offense, as I would 'and you that."

---

7. **compromising.** Revealing
8. **ekerval to.** As well as

Words
For
Everyday
Use

dis • tinct • ly (di stiŋkt´lē) *adv.,* clearly

I took what Joe gave me, and found it to be the crumpled playbill[9] of a small <u>metropolitan</u> theater, announcing the first appearance, in that very week, of "the celebrated <u>provincial</u> amateur of Roscian renown,[10] whose unique performance in the highest tragic walk of our national bard[11] has lately occasioned so great a sensation in local dramatic circles."

"Were you at his performance, Joe?" I inquired.

"I *were*," said Joe, with emphasis and solemnity.

"Was there a great sensation?"

"Why," said Joe, "yes, there certainly were a peck of orange-peel. Partickler when he see the ghost.[12] Though I put it to yourself, sir, whether it were calc'lated to keep a man up to his work with a good hart, to be continiwally cutting in betwixt him and the ghost with 'Amen!' A man may have had a misfortun' and been in the Church," said Joe, lowering his voice to an argumentative and feeling tone, "but that is no reason why you should put him out at such a time. Which I meantersay, if the ghost of a man's own father cannot be allowed to claim his attention, what can, sir? Still more, when his mourning 'at is unfortunately made so small as that the weight of the black feathers brings it off,[13] try to keep it on how you may."

A ghost-seeing effect in Joe's own countenance informed me that Herbert had entered the room. So, I presented Joe to Herbert, who held out his hand; but Joe backed from it, and held on by the bird's nest.

◄ What confuses Joe?

"Your servant, sir," said Joe, "which I hope as you and Pip"—here his eye fell on the Avenger, who was putting some toast on table, and so plainly <u>denoted</u> an intention to make that young gentleman one of the family that I frowned it down and confused him more—"I meantersay, you two gentlemen—which I hope as you get your 'elths in this close spot? For the present may be a wery good inn, according to London opinions," said Joe confidentially, "and I believe its

---

9. **playbill.** Advertisement for a play or theater which often includes the cast list
10. **of Roscian renown.** Famous in respect to acting; from the famous Roman actor Quintus Roscius Gallus (died 62 BC)
11. **highest . . . bard.** Most outstanding tragedy by the national poet of England, i.e., *The Tragedy of Hamlet*, by William Shakespeare
12. **ghost.** In the play, Hamlet's dead father appears to him as a ghost.
13. **mourning . . . off.** During his performance, Wopsle wears a mourning hat that is too small and that keeps falling off.

Words For Everyday Use

met • ro • pol • i • tan (meˊtrō päl ˊi tən) *adj.*, of a major city

pro • vin • cial (prə vinˊshəl) *adj.*, from a rustic area of the country situated away from the capital or national cultural center

de • note (dē nōtˊ) *vt.*, indicate

▶ What does Joe think of Barnard's Inn?

▶ How does Joe feel about making his opinions known? How does he make them known despite his hesitancy?

character do stand it; but I wouldn't keep a pig in it myself—not in the case that I wished him to fatten wholesome and to eat with a meller[14] flavor on him."

Having borne[15] this flattering testimony to the merits of our dwelling-place, and having incidentally shown this tendency to call me "sir," Joe, being invited to sit down to table, looked all round the room for a suitable spot on which to deposit his hat—as if it were only on some very few rare substances in nature that it could find a resting-place—and ultimately stood it on an extreme corner of the chimney-piece,[16] from which it ever afterwards fell off at intervals.

"Do you take tea, or coffee, Mr. Gargery?" asked Herbert, who always <u>presided</u> of a morning.

"Thankee, sir," said Joe, stiff from head to foot, "I'll take whichever is most agreeable to yourself."

"What do you say to coffee?"

"Thankee, sir," returned Joe, evidently <u>dispirited</u> by the proposal, "since you *are* so kind as make chice of coffee, I will not run contrary to your own opinions. But don't you never find it a little 'eating?"

"Say tea, then," said Herbert, pouring it out.

Here Joe's hat tumbled off the mantelpiece, and he started out of his chair and picked it up, and fitted it to the same exact spot. As if it were an absolute point of good breeding that it should tumble off again soon.

"When did you come to town, Mr. Gargery?"

"Were it yesterday afternoon?" said Joe, after coughing behind his hand as if he had had time to catch the whooping-cough since he came. "No, it were not. Yes, it were. Yes. It were yesterday afternoon" (with an appearance of mingled wisdom, relief, and strict <u>impartiality</u>).

"Have you seen anything of London, yet?"

"Why, yes, sir," said Joe, "me and Wopsle went off straight to look at the Blacking Ware'us.[17] But we didn't find that it come up to its likeness in the red bills at the shop doors: which I meantersay," added Joe, in an explanatory manner, "as it is there drawd too architectooralooral."

---

14. **meller.** Mellow
15. **borne.** Offered; conveyed
16. **chimney-piece.** Mantel, projecting shelf over a fireplace
17. **Blacking Ware'us.** Blacking Warehouse; an allusion to the blacking factory where Dickens labeled bottles to support his family in his youth

Words For Everyday Use	
	pre • side (prē zīd´) *vi.,* exercise authority; take control
	dis • pir • i • ted (dis pir´it əd) *adj.,* disheartened; depressed
	im • par • ti • al • i • ty (im par´shē al´ə tē) *n.,* objectivity; judgment based on reason

I really believe Joe would have prolonged this word (mightily expressive to my mind of some architecture that I know) into a perfect chorus, but for his attention being <u>providentially</u> attracted by his hat, which was toppling. Indeed, it demanded from him a constant attention, and a quickness of eye and hand, very like that <u>exacted</u> by wicket-keeping.[18] He made extraordinary play with it, and showed the greatest skill; now, rushing at it and catching it neatly as it dropped; now, merely stopping it midway, beating it up, and humoring it[19] in various parts of the room and against a good deal of the pattern of the paper on the wall, before he felt it safe to close with it; finally splashing it into the slop-basin,[20] where I took the liberty of laying hands upon it.

As to his shirt-collar, and his coat-collar, they were perplexing to reflect upon—<u>insoluble</u> mysteries both. Why should a man scrape himself to that extent before he could consider himself fully dressed? Why should he suppose it necessary to be purified by suffering for his holiday clothes? Then he fell into such unaccountable fits of meditation, with his fork midway between his plate and his mouth; had his eyes attracted in such strange directions; was afflicted with such remarkable coughs; sat so far from the table and dropped so much more than he ate, and pretended that he hadn't dropped it; that I was heartily glad when Herbert left us for the City.

◄ *How does Pip seem to feel about Joe's presence?*

I had neither the good sense nor the good feeling to know that this was all my fault, and that if I had been easier with Joe, Joe would have been easier with me. I felt impatient of him and out of temper with him; in which condition he heaped coals of fire on my head.

◄ *What could Pip have done to make the situation easier and more comfortable?*

"Us two being now alone, sir,"—began Joe.

"Joe," I interrupted, <u>pettishly</u>, "how can you call me sir?"

Joe looked at me for a single instant with something faintly like reproach. Utterly preposterous as his cravat was, and as his collars were, I was conscious of a sort of dignity in the look.

◄ *What complaint does Pip make once the two are alone? How does Joe respond? Why do you think he responds in this way?*

---

18. **wicket-keeping.** In the game of cricket (similar to American baseball), a position requiring attention and alertness. The wicket-keeper tries to stop the ball and get the batter out.
19. **humoring it.** Going along with its whims
20. **slop-basin.** Bowl into which the dregs from tea cups are emptied at table

Words For Everyday Use

prov • i • den • tial • ly (präv´ə den´shəl lē) *adv.,* fortunately

ex • act (eg zakt´) *vt.,* require

in • sol • u • ble (in säl´yōō bəl) *adj.,* that cannot be solved

pet • tish • ly (pet´ish lē) *adv.,* with irritation; peevishly

"Us two being now alone," resumed Joe, "and me having the intentions and abilities to stay not many minutes more, I will now conclude—leastways begin—to mention what have led to my having had the present honor. For was it not," said Joe, with his old air of <u>lucid</u> <u>exposition</u>, "that my only wish were to be useful to you, I should not have had the honor of breaking wittles in the company and abode of gentlemen."

I was so unwilling to see the look again that I made no remonstrance against this tone.

"Well, sir," pursued Joe, "this is how it were. I were at the Bargemen t'other night, Pip"—whenever he subsided into affection, he called me Pip, and whenever he <u>relapsed</u> into politeness he called me sir—"when there come up in his shay-cart[21] Pumblechook. Which that same identical," said Joe, going down a new track, "do comb my 'air the wrong way[22] sometimes, awful, by giving out up and down town as it were him which ever had your infant companionation and were looked upon as a playfellow by yourself."

"Nonsense. It was you, Joe."

"Which I fully believed it were, Pip," said Joe, slightly tossing his head, "though it signify little now, sir. Well, Pip, this same identical, which his manners is given to <u>blusterous</u>, come to me at the Bargemen (wot a pipe and a pint of beer do give refreshment to the working-man, sir, and do not over-stimulate), and his word were, 'Joseph, Miss Havisham she wish to speak to you.'"

"Miss Havisham, Joe?"

"'She wished,' were Pumblechook's word, 'to speak to you.'" Joe sat and rolled his eyes at the ceiling.

"Yes, Joe? Go on, please."

"Next day, sir," said Joe, looking at me as if I were a long way off, "having cleaned myself, I go and I see Miss A."

"Miss A., Joe? Miss Havisham?"

"Which I say, sir," replied Joe, with an air of legal formality, as if he were making his will, "Miss A., or otherways Havisham. Her expression air then as follering: 'Mr. Gargery. You air in correspondence with Mr. Pip?' Having had a letter from you, I were able to say 'I am.' (When I married your sister, sir, I said 'I will;' and when I answered your friend, Pip, I said 'I

▶ What rumor is Pumblechook spreading?

▶ What news from Pip's hometown does Joe bring?

---

21. **shay-cart.** Chaise-cart
22. **comb . . . way.** Rub me the wrong way

am.') 'Would you tell him, then,' said she, 'that which Estella has come home, and would be glad to see him.'"

I felt my face fire up as I looked at Joe. I hope one remote cause of its firing may have been my consciousness that if I had known his errand, I should have given him more encouragement.

"Biddy," pursued Joe, "when I got home and asked her fur to write the message to you, a little hung back. Biddy says, 'I know he will be very glad to have it by word of mouth, it is holiday-time, you want to see him, go!' I have now concluded, sir," said Joe, rising from his chair, "and, Pip, I wish you ever well and ever prospering to a greater and greater height."

"But you are not going now, Joe?"

"Yes, I am," said Joe.

"But you are coming back to dinner, Joe?"

"No, I am not," said Joe.

Our eyes met, and all the "sir" melted out of that manly heart as he gave me his hand.

"Pip, dear old chap, life is made of ever so many partings <u>welded</u> together, as I may say, and one man's a blacksmith, and one's a whitesmith and one's a goldsmith, and one's a coppersmith.[23] Diwisions among such must come, and must be met as they come. If there's been any fault at all today, it's mine. You and me is not two figures to be together in London; nor yet anywheres else but what is private, and beknown, and understood among friends. It ain't that I am proud, but that I want to be right, as you shall never see me no more in these clothes. I'm wrong in these clothes. I'm wrong out of the forge, the kitchen, or off th' meshes. You won't find half so much fault in me if you think of me in my forge dress, with my hammer in my hand, or even my pipe. You won't find half so much fault in me if, supposing as you should ever wish to see me, you come and put your head in at the forge window and see Joe the blacksmith there at the old anwil, in the old burnt apron, sticking to the old work. I'm awful dull, but I hope I've beat out something nigh the rights of this at last. And so GOD bless you, dear old Pip, old chap, GOD bless you!"

◀ What does Joe insist upon?

◀ What does the phrase "all the 'sir' melted out of that manly heart" reveal about Joe's feelings for Pip?

◀ How does Joe perceive himself and his relationship to Pip? What does he say about the way their relationship has changed?

---

23. **blacksmith . . . coppersmith.** *Blacksmith*—smith who works in iron, including the making and fitting of horseshoes; *whitesmith*—worker in iron who does finishing, polishing, or galvanizing; *goldsmith*—artisan who makes and repairs articles of gold; *coppersmith*—person whose work is making items out of copper

Words For Everyday Use

weld • ed (weld´əd) *adj.*, united; fused

▶ How does Joe's final speech affect Pip?

I had not been mistaken in my fancy that there was a simple dignity in him. The fashion of his dress could no more come in its way when he spoke these words than it could come in its way in Heaven. He touched me gently on the forehead, and went out. As soon as I could recover myself sufficiently, I hurried out after him and looked for him in the neighboring streets, but he was gone.

CHAPTER 28

It was clear that I must repair to our town next day, and in the first flow of my <u>repentance</u> it was equally clear that I must stay at Joe's. But when I had secured my box-place by tomorrow's coach, and had been down to Mr. Pocket's and back, I was not by any means convinced on the last point, and began to invent reasons and make excuses for putting up at the Blue Boar. I should be an inconvenience at Joe's; I was not expected, and my bed would not be ready; I should be too far from Miss Havisham's, and she was exacting and mightn't like it. All other <u>swindlers</u> upon earth are nothing to the self-swindlers, and with such pretenses did I cheat myself. Surely a curious thing. That I should innocently take a bad half-crown of somebody else's manufacture is reasonable enough; but that I should knowingly reckon the <u>spurious</u> coin of my own make as good money! An obliging stranger, under pretense of compactly folding up my banknotes for security's sake, abstracts[1] the notes and gives me nutshells; but what is his sleight of hand[2] to mine, when I fold up my own nutshells and pass them on myself as notes!

Having settled that I must go to the Blue Boar, my mind was much disturbed by indecision whether or no to take the Avenger. It was tempting to think of that expensive mercenary[3] publicly airing his boots in the archway of the Blue Boar's posting-yard;[4] it was almost solemn to imagine him casually produced in the tailor's shop and confounding the disrespectful senses of Trabb's boy. On the other hand, Trabb's boy might worm himself into his intimacy and tell him things; or, reckless and desperate wretch as I knew he could be, might hoot him in the High Street. My patroness, too, might hear of him, and not approve. On the whole, I resolved to leave the Avenger behind.

It was the afternoon coach by which I had taken my place, and, as winter had now come round, I should not arrive at

◄ *Where does Pip decide to stay? What excuses does he come up with to come to this decision? Does he think he is doing the right thing?*

---

1. **abstracts.** Takes away; steals
2. **sleight of hand.** Trick performed so quickly that its manner of execution cannot be observed; cunning deception
3. **mercenary.** Person who will do anything for money; hireling
4. **posting-yard.** Yard where carriages traveling long distances changed horses

Words For Everyday Use

re • pent • ance (ri pen´təns) *n.,* feeling of sorrow for wrongdoing

swin • dler (swind´lər) *n.,* person who cheats or defrauds

spu • ri • ous (spyʊr´ē əs) *adj.,* counterfeit; fake

my destination until two or three hours after dark. Our time of starting from the Cross Keys was two o'clock. I arrived on the ground with a quarter of an hour to spare, attended by the Avenger—if I may connect that expression with one who never attended on me if he could possibly help it.

At that time it was customary to carry convicts down to the dockyards by stagecoach. As I had often heard of them in the capacity of outside passengers, and had more than once seen them on the high road dangling their ironed legs over the coach roof, I had no cause to be surprised when Herbert, meeting me in the yard, came up and told me there were two convicts going down with me. But I had a reason that was an old reason now for <u>constitutionally</u> faltering whenever I heard the word convict.

► Who will also ride in the coach? Why is Pip upset?

"You don't mind them, Handel?" said Herbert.

"Oh, no!"

"I thought you seemed as if you didn't like them."

"I can't pretend that I do like them, and I suppose you don't particularly. But I don't mind them."

"See! There they are," said Herbert, "coming out of the tap.[5] What a degraded and <u>vile</u> sight it is!"

They had been treating their guard, I suppose, for they had a jailer with them, and all three came out wiping their mouths on their hands. The two convicts were handcuffed together, and had irons on their legs—irons of a pattern that I knew well. They wore the dress that I likewise knew well. Their keeper had a brace[6] of pistols, and carried a thick-knobbed bludgeon[7] under his arm; but he was on terms of good understanding with them, and stood, with them beside him, looking on at the putting-to of the horses, rather with an air as if the convicts were an interesting exhibition not formally open at the moment, and he the curator.[8] One was a taller and stouter man than the other, and appeared, as a matter of course, according to the mysterious ways of the world both convict and free, to have had allotted to him the smaller suit of clothes. His arms and legs were like great pincushions of those shapes, and his attire disguised him

► Who does Pip recognize?

---

5. **tap.** Taproom, barroom, or tavern
6. **brace.** Pair of like things
7. **bludgeon.** Short club with a thick, heavy end
8. **curator.** Director of a museum or similar institution

Words For Everyday Use

con • sti • tu • tion • al • ly (kän′stə tōō´shən əl ē) *adv.,* by nature or temperament

vile (vīl) *adj.,* repulsive; low; most inferior

absurdly; but I knew his half-closed eye at one glance. There stood the man whom I had seen on the settle at the Three Jolly Bargemen on a Saturday night, and who had brought me down with his invisible gun!

It was easy to make sure that as yet he knew me no more than if he had never seen me in his life. He looked across at me, and his eye <u>appraised</u> my watch chain, and then he incidentally spat and said something to the other convict, and they laughed and slued[9] themselves round with a clink of their coupling[10] manacle, and looked at something else. The great numbers on their backs, as if they were street doors; their coarse <u>mangy</u> <u>ungainly</u> outer surface, as if they were lower animals; their ironed legs, apologetically garlanded with pocket-handkerchiefs; and the way in which all present looked at them and kept from them; made them (as Herbert had said) a most disagreeable and degraded spectacle.

◀ What about the men's appearance makes them "disagreeable"?

But this was not the worst of it. It came out that the whole of the back of the coach had been taken by a family removing from London, and that there were no places for the two prisoners but on the seat in front, behind the coachman. Hereupon, a <u>choleric</u> gentleman who had taken the fourth place on that seat flew into a most violent passion, and said that it was a breach[11] of contract to mix him up with such villainous company, and that it was poisonous and <u>pernicious</u> and infamous and shameful, and I don't know what else. At this time the coach was ready and the coachman impatient, and we were all preparing to get up, and the prisoners had come over with their keeper—bringing with them that curious flavor of bread-poultice, baize,[12] rope-yarn, and hearthstone which attends the convict presence.

◀ What problem arises on the coach?

"Don't take it so much amiss, sir," pleaded the keeper to the angry passenger; "I'll sit next you myself. I'll put 'em on the outside of the row. They won't interfere with you, sir. You needn't know they're there."

"And don't blame *me*," growled the convict I had recognized. "*I* don't want to go. *I* am quite ready to stay behind. As fur as I am concerned, anyone's welcome to *my* place."

◀ What do the convicts point out about the situation?

---

9. **slued.** Turned sideways
10. **coupling.** Linking
11. **breach.** Violation
12. **baize.** Thick woolen cloth made to resemble felt and often dyed green

Words For Everyday Use

ap • praise (ə prāz´) vt., decide the value of
man • gy (mān´jē) adj., shabby and filthy
un • gain • ly (un gān´lē) adj., without grace; clumsy

chol • er • ic (käl´ər ik) adj., bad-tempered; irritable
per • ni • cious (pər nish´əs) adj., causing great injury, destruction, or ruin

"Or mine," said the other gruffly. "*I* wouldn't have incommoded[13] none of you, if I'd a-had *my* way." Then, they both laughed, and began cracking nuts, and spitting the shells about. As I really think I should have liked to do myself, if I had been in their place and so despised.

At length, it was voted that there was no help for the angry gentleman, and that he must either go in his chance company or remain behind. So, he got into his place, still making complaints, and the keeper got into the place next him, and the convicts hauled themselves up as well as they could, and the convict I had recognized sat behind me with his breath on the hair of my head.

► Why is Pip relieved that Herbert addresses him as Handel?

"Goodbye, Handel!" Herbert called out as we started. I thought what a blessed fortune it was that he had found another name for me than Pip.

It is impossible to express with what <u>acuteness</u> I felt the convict's breathing, not only on the back of my head, but all along my spine. The sensation was like being touched in the marrow[14] with some <u>pungent</u> and searching acid; it set my very teeth on edge. He seemed to have more breathing business to do than another man, and to make more noise in doing it; and I was conscious of growing high-shouldered on one side, in my shrinking endeavors to fend him off.

The weather was miserably raw, and the two cursed the cold. It made us all <u>lethargic</u> before we had gone far, and when we had left the Halfway House behind, we habitually dozed and shivered and were silent. I dozed off, myself, in considering the question whether I ought to restore a couple of pounds sterling to this creature before losing sight of him, and how it could best be done. In the act of dipping forward, as if I were going to bathe among the horses, I woke in a fright and took the question up again.

But I must have lost it longer than I had thought, since although I could recognize nothing in the darkness and the fitful lights and shadows of our lamps, I traced marsh country in the cold damp wind that blew at us. Cowering forward for warmth and to make me a screen against the wind, the convicts were closer to me than before. The very first words

---

13. **incommoded.** Inconvenienced
14. **marrow.** Soft tissue that fills bone cavities; i.e., the inmost part

---

Words For Everyday Use

a • cute • ness (ə kyo͞ot´nəs) *n.*, sharpness; intensity

pun • gent (pun´jənt) *adj.*, producing a sharp sensation

le • thar • gic (li thär´jik) *adj.*, sluggish; drowsy

I heard them interchange as I became conscious were the words of my own thought, "Two one-pound notes."

"How did he get 'em?" said the convict I had never seen.

"How should I know?" returned the other. "He had 'em stowed away somehows. Giv him by friends, I expect."

"I wish," said the other, with a bitter curse upon the cold, "that I had 'em here."

"Two one-pound notes, or friends?"

"Two one-pound notes. I'd sell all the friends I ever had, for one, and think it a blessed good bargain. Well? So he says—?"

"So he says," resumed the convict I had recognized, "—it was all said and done in half a minute, behind a pile of timber in the dockyard—'You're a-going to be discharged?' Yes, I was. Would I find out that boy that had fed him and kep' his secret, and give him them two one-pound notes? Yes, I would. And I did."

"More fool you," growled the other. "I'd have spent 'em on a man, in wittles and drink. He must have been a green one. Mean to say he knowed nothing of you?"

"Not a ha'porth.[15] Different gangs and different ships. He was tried again for prison breaking, and got made a lifer."

"And was that—Honor!—the only time you worked out, in this part of the country?"

"The only time."

"What might have been your opinion of the place?"

"A most beastly place. Mudbank, mist, swamp, and work: work, swamp, mist, and mudbank."

They both execrated the place in very strong language, and gradually growled themselves out, and had nothing left to say.

After overhearing this dialogue, I should assuredly have got down and been left in the solitude and darkness of the highway, but for feeling certain that the man had no suspicion of my identity. Indeed, I was not only so changed in the course of nature, but so differently dressed and so differently circumstanced, that it was not at all likely he could have known me without accidental help. Still, the coincidence of our being together on the coach was sufficiently strange to fill me with a dread that some other coincidence might

◄ What are the two convicts discussing when Pip awakes?

◄ What does Pip overhear? Why is the convict a "lifer"? About whom are the convicts speaking?

◄ Why does Pip leave the coach quickly?

---

15. **ha'porth.** Half-penny worth

at any moment connect me, in his hearing, with my name. For this reason, I resolved to alight as soon as we touched the town, and put myself out of his hearing. This device I <u>executed</u> successfully. My little portmanteau was in the boot under my feet; I had but to turn a hinge to get it out; I threw it down before me, got down after it, and was left at the first lamp on the first stones of the town pavement. As to the convicts, they went their way with the coach, and I knew at what point they would be spirited off to the river. In my fancy, I saw the boat with its convict crew waiting for them at the slime-washed stairs; again heard the gruff "Give way, you!" like an order to dogs; again saw the wicked Noah's Ark lying out on the black water.

► What does Pip fear and dread?

I could not have said what I was afraid of, for my fear was altogether undefined and vague, but there was great fear upon me. As I walked on to the hotel, I felt that a dread, much exceeding the mere <u>apprehension</u> of a painful or disagreeable recognition, made me tremble. I am confident that it took no distinctness of shape, and that it was the revival for a few minutes of the terror of childhood.

The coffee room at the Blue Boar was empty, and I had not only ordered my dinner there, but had sat down to it, before the waiter knew me. As soon as he had apologized for the <u>remissness</u> of his memory, he asked me if he should send Boots for Mr. Pumblechook.

► Why does the waiter ask Pip if he should send for Pumblechook? Why does he show Pip the newspaper article?

"No," said I, "certainly not."

The waiter (it was he who had brought up the Great Remonstrance from the commercials[16] on the day when I was bound) appeared surprised, and took the earliest opportunity of putting a dirty old copy of a local newspaper so directly in my way that I took it up and read this paragraph:

> Our readers will learn, not altogether without interest, in reference to the recent romantic rise in fortune of a young artificer in iron of this neighborhood (what a theme, by the way, for the magic pen of our as yet not universally acknowledged townsman, TOOBY, the poet of

---

16. **Great . . . commercials.** The narrator is referring humorously to those townspeople outside Town Hall who urged him to reform the day Pumblechook led him there to be indentured; he is also alluding to a document listing complaints against Charles I that was presented in the House of Commons.

Words For Everyday Use

ex • e • cute (ek´si kyo͞ot´) vt., carry out; perform

ap • pre • hen • sion (ap´rē hen´shən) n., anxious feeling of foreboding

re • miss • ness (ri mis´nəs) n., carelessness; negligence

our columns!) that the youth's earliest patron, companion, and friend was a highly-respected individual not entirely unconnected with the corn and seed trade, and whose <u>eminently</u> convenient and <u>commodious</u> business premises are situated within a hundred miles of the High Street. It is not wholly irrespective of our personal feelings that we record HIM as the Mentor of our young Telemachus,[17] for it is good to know that our town produced the founder of the latter's fortunes. Does the thought-contracted brow of the local sage or the <u>lustrous</u> eye of local beauty inquire whose fortunes? We believe that Quintin Matsys was the BLACKSMITH of Antwerp.[18] VERB. SAP.[19]

I entertain a conviction, based upon large experience, that if in the days of my prosperity I had gone to the North Pole, I should have met somebody there, wandering Eskimo or civilized man, who would have told me that Pumblechook was my earliest patron and the founder of my fortunes.

◄ *What is Pip's reaction to the article?*

---

17. **Mentor . . . Telemachus.** In the *Odyssey*, Telemachus is the son of the hero Odysseus, and Mentor is his adviser; from Mentor's name we have acquired our English word *mentor*.
18. **Quintin . . . Antwerp.** Quintin Matsys (1466–1530) was a Flemish painter who lived in Antwerp and was supposed to have once worked as a blacksmith.
19. VERB. SAP. Abbreviation for *verbum sapienti satis est*, a Latin phrase meaning "A word to the wise is sufficient."

Words For Everyday Use

em • i • nent • ly (em´ə nənt lē) *adv.*, remarkably
com • mo • di • ous (kə mō´dē əs) *adj.*, spacious
lus • trous (lus´trəs) *adj.*, bright

▶ Why doesn't Pip visit Joe? What does he imagine Miss Havisham wishes him to be?

Betimes[1] in the morning I was up and out. It was too early yet to go to Miss Havisham's, so I <u>loitered</u> into the country on Miss Havisham's side of town—which was not Joe's side; I could go there tomorrow—thinking about my patroness, and painting brilliant pictures of her plans for me.

She had adopted Estella, she had as good as adopted me, and it could not fail to be her intention to bring us together. She reserved it for me to restore the desolate house, admit the sunshine into the dark rooms, set the clocks a-going and the cold hearths a-blazing, tear down the cobwebs, destroy the vermin[2]—in short, do all the shining deeds of the young knight of romance, and marry the princess. I had stopped to look at the house as I passed; and its <u>seared</u> red-brick walls, blocked windows, and strong green ivy clasping even the stacks of chimneys with its twigs and tendons, as if with <u>sinewy</u> old arms, had made up a rich attractive mystery, of which I was the hero. Estella was the inspiration of it, and the heart of it, of course. But though she had taken such strong possession of me, though my fancy and my hope were so set upon her, though her influence on my boyish life and character had been all-powerful, I did not, even that romantic morning, invest her with any attributes save those she possessed. I mention this in this place, of a fixed purpose, because it is the clue by which I am to be followed into my poor labyrinth.[3] According to my experience, the <u>conventional</u> notion of a lover cannot be always true. The unqualified truth is that, when I loved Estella with the love of a man, I loved her simply because I found her irresistible. Once for all; I knew to my sorrow, often and often, if not always, that

▶ Against what obstacles does Pip proclaim his love for Estella?

I loved her against reason, against promise, against peace, against hope, against happiness, against all discouragement that could be. Once for all; I loved her none the less because I knew it, and it had no more influence in restraining me than if I had devoutly believed her to be human perfection.

---

1. **Betimes.** Early or early enough
2. **vermin.** Animal or insect pests
3. **labyrinth.** Structure containing a network of winding passages, maze; here Pip refers to the tangle of his thoughts.

Words For Everyday Use

loi • ter (loit´ər) vi., spend time idly
seared (sird´) adj., burned
sin • ew • y (sin´yoō ē) adj., tough; strong

con • ven • tion • al (kən ven´shə nəl) adj., conforming to accepted standards

I so shaped out my walk as to arrive at the gate at my old time. When I had rung at the bell with an unsteady hand, I turned my back upon the gate, while I tried to get my breath and keep the beating of my heart moderately quiet. I heard the side door open, and steps come across the courtyard; but I pretended not to hear, even when the gate swung on its rusty hinges.

Being at last touched on the shoulder, I started and turned. I started much more naturally then, to find myself confronted by a man in a <u>sober</u> gray dress. The last man I should have expected to see in that place of porter at Miss Havisham's door.

◀ Who opens the gate for Pip?

"Orlick!"

"Ah, young master, there's more changes than yours. But come in, come in. It's opposed to my orders to hold the gate open."

I entered and he swung it, and locked it, and took the key out. "Yes!" said he, facing round, after <u>doggedly</u> preceding me a few steps towards the house. "Here I am!"

"How did you come here?"

"I come here," he retorted, "on my legs. I had my box brought alongside me in a barrow."

"Are you here for good?"

"I ain't here for harm, young master, I suppose."

I was not so sure of that. I had leisure to entertain the retort in my mind, while he slowly lifted his heavy glance from the pavement, up my legs and arms to my face.

"Then you have left the forge?" I said.

"Do this look like a forge?" replied Orlick, sending his glance all round him with an air of injury. "Now, do it look like it?"

I asked him how long he had left Gargery's forge.

"One day is so like another here," he replied, "that I don't know without casting⁴ it up. However, I come here some time since you left."

◀ How do Pip and Orlick treat each other?

"I could have told you that, Orlick."

"Ah!" said he, drily. "But then you've got to be a scholar."

By this time we had come to the house, where I found his room to be one just within the side door, with a little window in it looking on the courtyard. In its small proportions,

---

4. **casting.** Adding; calculating

Words
For
Everyday
Use

so • ber (sō´bər) *adj.,* not bright or flashy; plain
dog • ged • ly (dôg´id lē) *adv.,* stubbornly

it was not unlike the kind of place usually assigned to a gate-porter in Paris. Certain keys were hanging on the wall, to which he now added the gatekey; and his patchwork-covered bed was in a little inner division or recess. The whole had a <u>slovenly</u>, confined, and sleepy look, like a cage for a human dormouse[5]—while he, <u>looming</u> dark and heavy in the shadow of a corner by the window, looked like the human dormouse for whom it was fitted up—as indeed he was.

"I never saw this room before," I remarked; "but there used to be no porter here."

"No," said he, "not till it got about that there was no protection on the premises, and it come to be considered dangerous, with convicts and tag and rag and bobtail[6] going up and down. And then I was recommended to the place as a man who could give another man as good as he brought, and I took it. It's easier than bellowsing and hammering. That's loaded, that is."

My eye had been caught by a gun with a brass-bound stock over the chimney-piece, and his eye had followed mine.

"Well," said I, not desirous of more conversation, "shall I go up to Miss Havisham?"

"Burn me, if I know!" he retorted, first stretching himself and then shaking himself; "my orders ends here, young master. I give this here bell a rap with this here hammer, and you go on along the passage till you meet somebody."

"I am expected, I believe?"

"Burn me twice over if I can say!" said he.

Upon that I turned down the long passage which I had first trodden in my thick boots, and he made his bell sound. At the end of the passage, while the bell was still <u>reverberating</u>, I found Sarah Pocket, who appeared to have now become constitutionally green and yellow by reason of me.

"Oh!" said she. "You, is it, Mr. Pip?"

"It is, Miss Pocket. I am glad to tell you that Mr. Pocket and family are all well."

"Are they any wiser?" said Sarah with a dismal shake of the head; "they had better be wiser than well. Ah, Matthew, Matthew! You know your way, sir?"

▶ Why is Orlick working at Satis House? What does Pip notice?

▶ Why is Sarah Pocket envious of Pip? What is her response to him?

---

5. **dormouse.** Any of a family of small, furry-tailed rodents
6. **tag and rag and bobtail.** Contemptuous term for a crowd of miscellaneous lower class persons

Words For Everyday Use

slov • en • ly (sluv´ən lē) *adj.,* careless in appearance or manner; untidy

loom (lo͞om) *vi.,* appear; take shape indistinctly as through a mist

re • ver • ber • ate (ri vʉr´ bər āt´) *vt.,* reecho

Tolerably, for I had gone up the staircase in the dark, many a time. I ascended it now, in lighter boots than of yore, and tapped in my old way at the door of Miss Havisham's room. "Pip's rap," I heard her say immediately; "come in, Pip."

She was in her chair near the old table, in the old dress, with her two hands crossed on her stick, her chin resting on them, and her eyes on the fire. Sitting near her, with the white shoe that had never been worn in her hand, and her head bent as she looked at it, was an elegant lady whom I had never seen.

"Come in, Pip," Miss Havisham continued to mutter, without looking round or up; "come in, Pip; how do you do, Pip? So you kiss my hand as if I were a queen, eh? Well?"

She looked up at me suddenly, only moving her eyes, and repeated in a grimly playful manner:

"Well?"

"I heard, Miss Havisham," said I, rather at a loss, "that you were so kind as to wish me to come and see you, and I came directly."

"Well?"

The lady whom I had never seen before lifted up her eyes and looked <u>archly</u> at me, and then I saw that the eyes were Estella's eyes. But she was so much changed, was so much more beautiful, so much more womanly, in all things winning admiration had made such wonderful advance, that I seemed to have made none. I fancied, as I looked at her, that I slipped hopelessly back into the coarse and common boy again. Oh, the sense of distance and <u>disparity</u> that came upon me, and the <u>inaccessibility</u> that came about her!

She gave me her hand. I stammered something about the pleasure I felt in seeing her again, and about my having looked forward to it for a long, long time.

"Do you find her much changed, Pip?" asked Miss Havisham, with her greedy look, and striking her stick upon a chair that stood between them, as a sign to me to sit down there.

"When I came in, Miss Havisham, I thought there was nothing of Estella in the face or figure; but now it all settles down so curiously into the old—"

"What? You are not going to say into the old Estella?" Miss Havisham interrupted. "She was proud and insulting, and you wanted to go away from her. Don't you remember?"

◀ *Who is the young woman? How has she changed? How does Pip react?*

Words
For
Everyday
Use

arch • ly (ärch´lē) *adv.,* mischievously

dis • par • i • ty (di spar´ə tē) *n.,* inequality or difference

in • ac • ces • si • bil • i • ty (in´ək ses´ə bil´ə tē) *n.,* state of being unreachable or unattainable

▶ How does Estella treat Pip?

I said confusedly that that was long ago, and that I knew no better then, and the like. Estella smiled with perfect <u>composure</u>, and said she had no doubt of my having been quite right, and of her having been very disagreeable.

"Is *he* changed?" Miss Havisham asked her.

"Very much," said Estella, looking at me.

"Less coarse and common?" said Miss Havisham, playing with Estella's hair.

Estella laughed, and looked at the shoe in her hand, and laughed again, and looked at me, and put the shoe down. She treated me as a boy still, but she lured me on.

We sat in the dreamy room among the old strange influences which had so wrought[7] upon me, and I learned that she had but just come home from France, and that she was going to London. Proud and willful as of old, she had brought those qualities into such subjection to her beauty that it was impossible and out of nature—or I thought so—to separate them from her beauty. Truly it was impossible to dissociate her presence from all those wretched <u>hankerings</u> after money and gentility that had disturbed my boyhood—from all those ill-regulated <u>aspirations</u> that had first made me ashamed of home and Joe—from all those visions that had raised her face in the glowing fire, struck it out of the iron on the anvil, extracted it from the darkness of night to look in at the wooden window of the forge and flit away. In a word, it was impossible for me to separate her, in the past or in the present from the innermost life of my life.

▶ What is impossible for Pip?

It was settled that I should stay there all the rest of the day, and return to the hotel at night, and to London tomorrow. When we had conversed for a while, Miss Havisham sent us two out to walk in the neglected garden: on our coming in by-and-by, she said I should wheel her about a little, as in times of yore.

So Estella and I went out into the garden by the gate through which I had strayed to my encounter with the pale young gentleman, now Herbert; I, trembling in spirit and worshipping the very hem of her dress; she, quite composed and most decidedly not worshipping the hem of mine. As we drew near to the place of encounter, she stopped and said:

---

7. **wrought.** Past tense of *work,* meaning "have an effect"

Words For Everyday Use

com • po • sure (kəm pō´zhər) *n.,* calmness of mind or manner

han • ker • ing (haŋ´kər iŋ) *n.,* craving; yearning

as • pi • ra • tion (as´pə rā´shən) *n.,* strong desire or ambition

"I must have been a singular little creature to hide and see that fight that day—but I did, and I enjoyed it very much."

"You rewarded me very much."

"Did I?" she replied, in an incidental and forgetful way. "I remember I entertained a great objection to your adversary, because I took it ill that he should be brought here to pester me with his company."

◄ What are Estella's feelings about Herbert?

"He and I are great friends now."

"Are you? I think I recollect though, that you read with his father?"

"Yes."

I made the admission with reluctance, for it seemed to have a boyish look, and she already treated me more than enough like a boy.

"Since your change of fortune and prospects, you have changed your companions," said Estella.

"Naturally," said I.

"And necessarily," she added, in a haughty tone; "what was fit company for you once would be quite unfit company for you now."

◄ What makes Pip finally dismiss any thoughts of Joe?

In my conscience, I doubt very much whether I had any lingering intention left of going to see Joe; but if I had, this observation put it to flight.

"You had no idea of your <u>impending</u> good fortune in those times?" said Estella, with a slight wave of her hand, signifying the fighting times.

"Not the least."

The air of completeness and superiority with which she walked at my side, and the air of youthfulness and submission with which I walked at hers, made a contrast that I strongly felt. It would have <u>rankled</u> in me more than it did, if I had not regarded myself as eliciting it by being so set apart for her and assigned to her.

The garden was too overgrown and rank for walking in with ease, and after we had made the round of it twice or thrice, we came out again into the brewery yard.[8] I showed her to a nicety[9] where I had seen her walking on the casks that first old day, and she said with a cold and careless look

---

8. **brewery yard.** Place where beer or ale is brewed
9. **to a nicety.** With great precision; exactly

Words For Everyday Use

im • pend • ing (im pend´iŋ) *adj.,* due to happen soon
ran • kle (raŋ´kəl) *vi.,* cause resentment

► *What do they talk about?*

in that direction, "Did I?" I reminded her where she had come out of the house and given me my meat and drink, and she said, "I don't remember." "Not remember that you made me cry?" said I. "No," said she, and shook her head and looked about her. I verily[10] believe that her not remembering and not minding in the least, made me cry again, inwardly—and that is the sharpest crying of all.

"You must know," said Estella, condescending to me as a brilliant and beautiful woman might, "that I have no heart—if that has anything to do with my memory."

I got through some jargon[11] to the effect that I took the liberty of doubting that. That I knew better. That there could be no such beauty without it.

► *What does Estella admit?*

"Oh! I have a heart to be stabbed in or shot in, I have no doubt," said Estella; "and, of course, if it ceased to beat, I should cease to be. But you know what I mean. I have no softness there, no—sympathy—sentiment—nonsense."

► *What is troubling Pip?*

What *was* it that was borne in upon my mind when she stood still and looked attentively at me? Anything that I had seen in Miss Havisham? No. In some of her looks and gestures there was that <u>tinge</u> of resemblance to Miss Havisham, which may often be noticed to have been acquired by children from grown persons with whom they have been much associated and secluded, and which, when childhood is passed, will produce a remarkable occasional likeness of expression between faces that are otherwise quite different. And yet I could not trace this to Miss Havisham. I looked again, and though she was still looking at me, the suggestion was gone.

What *was* it?

"I am serious," said Estella, not so much with a frown (for her brow was smooth) as with a darkening of her face; "if we are to be thrown much together, you had better believe it at once. No!" <u>imperiously</u> stopping me as I opened my lips. "I have not bestowed my tenderness anywhere. I have never had any such thing."

In another moment we were in the brewery so long disused, and she pointed to the high gallery where I had seen her going out on that same first day, and told me she remembered to

---

10. **verily.** Truly
11. **jargon.** Incoherent or gibberish speech

Words For Everyday Use	
	tinge (tinj) *n.,* slight trace
	im • per • i • ous • ly (im pir´ ē əs lē) *adv.,* arrogantly

have been up there, and to have seen me standing scared below. As my eyes followed her white hand, again the same dim suggestion that I could not possibly grasp crossed me. My involuntary start occasioned her to lay her hand upon my arm. Instantly the ghost passed once more and was gone.

What *was* it?

"What is the matter?" asked Estella. "Are you scared again?"

"I should be if I believed what you said just now," I replied, to turn it off.

"Then you don't? Very well. It is said, at any rate. Miss Havisham will soon be expecting you at your old post, though I think that might be laid aside now, with other old belongings. Let us make one more round of the garden, and then go in. Come! You shall not shed tears for my cruelty today; you shall be my page,[12] and give me your shoulder."

◄ How do they spend their time together?

Her handsome dress had trailed upon the ground. She held it in one hand now and with the other lightly touched my shoulder as we walked. We walked round the ruined garden twice or thrice more, and it was all in bloom for me. If the green and yellow growth of weed in the chinks[13] of the old wall had been the most precious flowers that ever blew, it could not have been more cherished in my remembrance.

There was no <u>discrepancy</u> of years between us to remove her far from me—we were of nearly the same age, though of course the age told for more in her case than in mine—but the air of inaccessibility which her beauty and her manner gave her tormented me in the midst of my delight, and at the height of the assurance I felt that our patroness had chosen us for one another. Wretched boy!

At last we went back into the house, and there I heard, with surprise, that my guardian had come down to see Miss Havisham on business, and would come back to dinner. The old wintry branches of chandeliers in the room where the <u>moldering</u> table was spread had been lighted while we were out, and Miss Havisham was in her chair and waiting for me.

◄ Who is coming to dinner?

It was like pushing the chair itself back into the past, when we began the old slow circuit round about the ashes of the bridal feast. But, in the <u>funereal</u> room, with that figure of the

---

12. **page.** Boy employed to run errands or act as a guide
13. **chinks.** Cracks

Words For Everyday Use	**dis • crep • an • cy** (di skrep´ən sē) *n.,* difference; lack of agreement
	mold • er • ing (mōl´dər iŋ) *adj.,* decaying
	fu • ne • re • al (fyo͞o nir´ē əl) *adj.,* sad and solemn; gloomy

grave fallen back in the chair fixing its eyes upon her, Estella looked more bright and beautiful than before, and I was under stronger enchantment.

The time so melted away that our early dinner-hour drew close at hand, and Estella left us to prepare herself. We had stopped near the center of the long table, and Miss Havisham, with one of her withered arms stretched out of the chair, rested that clenched hand upon the yellow cloth. As Estella looked back over her shoulder before going out at the door, Miss Havisham kissed that hand to her, with a <u>ravenous</u> intensity that was of its kind quite dreadful.

Then, Estella being gone and we two left alone, she turned to me and said in a whisper:

► What does Miss Havisham urge Pip to do?

"Is she beautiful, graceful, well grown? Do you admire her?"

"Everybody must who sees her, Miss Havisham."

She drew an arm round my neck, and drew my head close down to hers as she sat in the chair. "Love her, love her, love her! How does she use you?"

Before I could answer (if I could have answered so difficult a question at all), she repeated, "Love her, love her, love her! If she favors you, love her. If she wounds you, love her. If she tears your heart to pieces—and as it gets older and stronger it will tear deeper—love her, love her, love her!"

Never had I seen such passionate eagerness as was joined to her utterance of these words. I could feel the muscles of the thin arm round my neck swell with the <u>vehemence</u> that possessed her.

"Hear me, Pip! I adopted her to be loved. I bred her and educated her to be loved. I developed her into what she is, that she might be loved. Love her!"

► To what does Pip compare her admonition?

She said the word often enough, and there could be no doubt that she meant to say it, but if the often repeated word had been hate instead of love—despair—revenge—dire death—it could not have sounded from her lips more like a curse.

► What is real love to Miss Havisham? To what does she admit?

"I'll tell you," said she, in the same hurried passionate whisper, "what real love is. It is blind devotion, unquestioning self-humiliation, utter submission, trust and belief against yourself and against the whole world, giving up your whole heart and soul to the smiter[14]—as I did!"

---

14. **smiter.** One who strikes and wounds

| Words For Everyday Use | rav • e • nous (rav′ə nəs) *adj.*, extremely eager for gratification |
| | ve • he • mence (vē′ə məns) *n.*, intensity of emotion, passion, or conviction |

When she came to that, and to a wild cry that followed that, I caught her round the waist. For she rose up in the chair, in her shroud of a dress, and struck at the air as if she would as soon have struck herself against the wall and fallen dead.

All this passed in a few seconds. As I drew her down into her chair, I was conscious of a scent that I knew, and turning, saw my guardian in the room.

He always carried (I have not yet mentioned it, I think) a pocket-handkerchief of rich silk and of <u>imposing</u> proportions which was of great value to him in his profession. I have seen him so terrify a client or a witness by ceremoniously unfolding this pocket-handkerchief as if he were immediately going to blow his nose, and then pausing, as if he knew he should not have time to do it before such client or witness <u>committed</u> himself, that the self-committal has followed directly, quite as a matter of course. When I saw him in the room, he had this expressive pocket handkerchief in both hands, and was looking at us. On meeting my eye, he said plainly, by a momentary and silent pause in that attitude, "Indeed? Singular!" and then put the handkerchief to its right use with wonderful effect.

Miss Havisham had seen him as soon as I, and was (like everybody else) afraid of him. She made a strong attempt to compose herself, and stammered that he was as <u>punctual</u> as ever.

◀ How does she react to Jaggers?

"As punctual as ever," he repeated, coming up to us. "(How do you do, Pip? Shall I give you ride, Miss Havisham? Once round?) And so you are here, Pip?"

I told him when I had arrived, and how Miss Havisham wished me to come and see Estella. To which he replied, "Ah! Very fine young lady!" Then he pushed Miss Havisham in her chair before him, with one of his large hands, and put the other in his trouser-pocket as if the pocket were full of secrets.

"Well, Pip! How often have you seen Miss Estella before?" said he, when he came to a stop.

"How often?"

"Ah! How many times? Ten thousand times?"

"Oh! Certainly not so many."

"Twice?"

"Jaggers," interposed Miss Havisham, much to my relief, "leave my Pip alone, and go with him to your dinner."

Words For Everyday Use	im • pos • ing (im pō´ziŋ) *adj.,* impressive
	com • mit (kə mit´) *vt.,* make known the opinions or views of
	punc • tu • al (puŋk´chōō əl) *adj.,* appointed time; prompt

He <u>complied</u>, and we <u>groped</u> our way down the dark stairs together. While we were still on our way to those detached apartments across the paved yard at the back, he asked me how often I had seen Miss Havisham eat and drink, offering me a <u>breadth</u> of choice, as usual, between a hundred times and once.

I considered, and said, "Never."

"And never will, Pip," he retorted, with a frowning smile. "She has never allowed herself to be seen doing either, since she lived this present life of hers. She wanders about in the night, and then lays hands on such food as she takes."

"Pray, sir," said I, "may I ask you a question?"

"You may," said he, "and I may decline to answer it. Put your question."

"Estella's name, is it Havisham or—?" I had nothing to add.

"Or what?" said he.

"Is it Havisham?"

"It is Havisham."

This brought us to the dinner table, where she and Sarah Pocket awaited us. Mr. Jaggers presided, Estella sat opposite to him, I faced my green and yellow friend. We dined very well, and were waited on by a maid-servant whom I had never seen in all my comings and goings, but who, for anything I know, had been in that mysterious house the whole time. After dinner a bottle of choice old port was placed before my guardian (he was evidently well acquainted with the vintage[15]), and the two ladies left us.

Anything to equal the determined reticence of Mr. Jaggers under that roof I never saw elsewhere, even in him. He kept his very looks to himself, and scarcely directed his eyes to Estella's face once during dinner. When she spoke to him, he listened, and in due course, answered, but never looked at her that I could see. On the other hand, she often looked at him with interest and curiosity, if not distrust, but his face never showed the least consciousness. Throughout dinner, he took a dry delight in making Sarah Pocket greener and yellower by often referring in conversation with me to my expectations; but here, again, he showed no consciousness,

▶ *What will Pip never see?*

▶ *What is Estella's last name?*

▶ *What is different about Jaggers's behavior?*

▶ *What does Jaggers do to irritate Sarah Pocket?*

---

15. **vintage.** Crop of a particular vineyard or grape-growing region in a single season, with reference to either the grapes or the wine made from them

---

Words For Everyday Use

com • ply (kəm plī´) *vi.*, act in accordance with a command or request

grope (grōp) *vi.*, seek or find (one's way) by feeling or searching about blindly

breadth (bredth) *n.*, range; broadness

and even made it appear that he <u>extorted</u>—and even did extort, though I don't know how—those references out of my innocent self.

And when he and I were left alone together, he sat with an air upon him of general lying by[16] in consequence of information he possessed that really was too much for me. He <u>cross-examined</u> his very wine when he had nothing else in hand. He held it between himself and the candle, tasted the port, rolled it in his mouth, swallowed it, looked at his glass again, smelt the port, tried it, drank it, filled again, and cross-examined the glass again, until I was as nervous as if I had known the wine to be telling him something to my disadvantage. Three or four times I feebly thought I would start conversation, but whenever he saw me going to ask him anything, he looked at me with his glass in his hand, and rolling his wine about in his mouth, as if requesting me to take notice that it was of no use, for he couldn't answer.

◀ What does Jaggers prevent Pip from doing?

I think Miss Pocket was conscious that the sight of me involved her in the danger of being <u>goaded</u> to madness, and perhaps tearing off her cap—which was a very hideous one, in the nature of a muslin mop[17]—and strewing the ground with her hair—which assuredly had never grown on *her* head. She did not appear when we afterwards went up to Miss Havisham's room, and we four played at whist.[18] In the interval, Miss Havisham, in a fantastic way, had put some of the most beautiful jewels from her dressing table into Estella's hair, and about her bosom and arms; and I saw even my guardian look at her from under his thick eyebrows, and raise them a little when her loveliness was before him, with those rich flushes of glitter and color in it.

◀ How does Jaggers behave toward Estella?

Of the manner and extent to which he took our trumps into custody,[19] and came out with mean little cards at the ends of hands, before which the glory of our kings and queens was utterly <u>abased</u>,[20] I say nothing; nor of the feeling that I had respecting his looking upon us personally in the

---

16. **lying by.** Keeping quiet
17. **muslin mop.** Mop made from strong cotton cloth of plain weave
18. **whist.** Card game similar to bridge, of which it is the forerunner
19. **took . . . custody.** Captured our high-ranking cards in the game of whist
20. **the glory . . . abased.** Our high cards were practically useless, capturing only very low cards.

Words For Everyday Use

ex • tort (eks tôrt´) *vt.*, get money or goods from someone by violence, threats, or misuse of authority

cross- • ex • am • ine (krôs´ ig zam´ in) *vt.*, question closely

goad (gōd) *vt.*, drive; urge on

a • based (ə bāsd´) *adj.*, degraded; lowered in value

► What upsets Pip?

light of three very obvious and poor riddles that he had found out long ago. What I suffered from was the <u>incompatibility</u> between his cold presence and my feelings towards Estella. It was not that I knew I could never bear to speak to him about her, that I knew I could never bear to hear him creak his boots at her, that I knew I could never bear to see him wash his hands of her; it was that my admiration should be within a foot or two of him—it was that my feelings should be in the same place with him—*that* was the <u>agonizing</u> circumstance.

► What are the plans?

We played until nine o'clock, and then it was arranged that when Estella came to London I should be forewarned of her coming and should meet her at the coach; and then I took leave of her, and touched her, and left her.

My guardian lay at the Boar in the next room to mine. Far into the night, Miss Havisham's words, "Love her, love her, love her!" sounded in my ears. I adapted them for my own repetition, and said to my pillow, "I love her, I love her, I love her!" hundreds of times. Then a burst of gratitude came upon me that she should be destined for me, once the blacksmith's boy. Then I thought if she were, as I feared, by no means <u>rapturously</u> grateful for that destiny yet, when would she begin to be interested in me? When should I awaken the heart within her that was <u>mute</u> and sleeping now?

► What is Pip's internal conflict?

Ah me! I thought those were high and great emotions. But I never thought there was anything low and small in my keeping away from Joe, because I knew she would be contemptuous of him. It was but a day gone, and Joe had brought the tears into my eyes; they had soon dried—God forgive me!—soon dried.

Words For Everyday Use

in • com • pat • i • bil • i • ty (in´kəm pat´ə bil´ə tē) *n.*, condition of not being able to exist in harmony; conflict

ag • o • niz • ing (ag´ə nīz´iŋ) *adj.*, distressing; tormenting

rap • tur • ous • ly (rap´chər əs´lē) *adv.*, with great joy, pleasure, contentment

mute (myo͞ot) *adj.*, silent

After well considering the matter while I was dressing at the Blue Boar in the morning, I resolved to tell my guardian that I doubted Orlick's being the right sort of man to fill a <u>post</u> of trust at Miss Havisham's. "Why, of course he is not the right sort of man, Pip," said my guardian, comfortably satisfied beforehand on the general head, "because the man who fills the post of trust never is the right sort of man." It seemed quite to put him in spirits to find that this particular post was not exceptionally held by the right sort of man, and he listened in a satisfied manner while I told him what knowledge I had of Orlick. "Very good, Pip," he observed, when I had concluded, "I'll go round presently, and pay our friend off." Rather alarmed by this summary action, I was for a little delay, and even hinted that our friend himself might be difficult to deal with. "Oh, no, he won't," said my guardian, making his pocket-handkerchief point, with perfect confidence; "I should like to see him argue the question with *me*."

◀ What does Pip tell Jaggers? What is Jaggers's plan?

As we were going back together to London by the midday coach, and as I breakfasted under such terrors of Pumblechook that I could scarcely hold my cup, this gave me an opportunity of saying that I wanted a walk, and that I would go on along the London road while Mr. Jaggers was occupied, if he would let the coachman know that I would get into my place when overtaken. I was thus enabled to fly from the Blue Boar immediately after breakfast. By then making a loop of about a couple of miles into the open country at the back of Pumblechook's premises,[1] I got round into the High Street again, a little beyond that pitfall, and felt myself in comparative security.

◀ Why is Pip afraid? What does he do?

It was interesting to be in the quiet old town once more, and it was not disagreeable to be here and there suddenly recognized and stared after. One or two of the tradespeople even darted out of their shops, and went a little way down the street before me, that they might turn, as if they had forgotten something, and pass me face to face—on which occasions I don't know whether they or I made the worse <u>pretense</u>; they

◀ How do Pip and the tradesmen treat one another?

---

1. **premises.** One's property, land, or real estate

Words For Everyday Use

post (pōst) *n.*, position; job

pre • tence (prē´tens´) *n.*, false appearance or action intended to deceive of not doing it, or I of not seeing it. Still, my position was a distinguished one, and I was not at all dissatisfied with it, until Fate threw me in the way of that unlimited miscreant, Trabb's boy.

▶ Whom does Pip see on the street? What happens?

Casting my eyes along the street at a certain point of my progress, I beheld Trabb's boy approaching, lashing himself with an empty blue bag. Deeming that a <u>serene</u> and unconscious contemplation of him would best beseem[2] me, and would be most likely to <u>quell</u> his evil mind, I advanced with that expression of countenance, and was rather congratulating myself on my success, when suddenly the knees of Trabb's boy smote[3] together, his hair uprose, his cap fell off, he trembled violently in every limb, staggered out into the road, and crying to the populace,[4] "Hold me! I'm so frightened!" <u>feigned</u> to be in a <u>paroxysm</u> of terror and <u>contrition</u>, occasioned by the dignity of my appearance. As I passed him, his teeth loudly chattered in his head, and with every mark of extreme humiliation, he <u>prostrated</u> himself in the dust.

This was a hard thing to bear, but this was nothing. I had not advanced another two hundred yards, when, to my inexpressible terror, amazement, and <u>indignation</u>, I again beheld Trabb's boy approaching. He was coming round a narrow corner. His blue bag was slung over his shoulder, honest industry[5] beamed in his eyes, a determination to proceed to Trabb's with cheerful briskness was indicated in his gait.[6] With a shock he became aware of me, and was severely visited as before; but this time his motion was rotatory,[7] and he staggered round and round me with knees more afflicted, and with uplifted hands as if beseeching for mercy. His sufferings were hailed with the greatest joy by a knot of spectators, and I felt utterly confounded.

▶ What does Trabb's boy do the second time he approaches?

I had not got as much further down the street as the post office, when I again beheld Trabb's boy shooting round by a back way. This time, he was entirely changed. He wore the blue bag in the manner of my greatcoat, and was strutting

---

2. **beseem.** Be suitable or appropriate to
3. **smote.** Past tense of *smite,* to strike or knock
4. **populace.** Common people; masses
5. **industry.** Diligence
6. **gait.** Manner of walking
7. **rotatory.** Characterized by rotation; turning around

Words For Everyday Use

se • rene (sə rēn´) *adj.,* calm; unruffled
quell (kwel) *vt.,* bring under control
feign (fān) *vt.,* pretend
par • ox • ysm (par´əks iz´əm) *n.,* sudden attack; spasm

con • tri • tion (kən tri´shən) *n.,* remorse for having done wrong
pros • trate (präs´trāt´) *vt.,* make (oneself) lie flat on the ground
in • dig • na • tion (in´dig nā´shən) *n.,* anger

along the pavement towards me on the opposite side of the street, attended by a company of delighted young friends to whom he from time to time exclaimed, with a wave of his hand, "Don't know yah!" Words cannot state the amount of aggravation and injury wreaked upon me by Trabb's boy, when, passing abreast of me, he pulled up his shirt-collar, twined his side-hair, stuck an arm akimbo,[8] and smirked extravagantly by, wriggling his elbows and body, and <u>drawling</u> to his attendants, "Don't know yah, don't know yah, 'pon my soul, don't know yah!" The disgrace attendant on his immediately afterwards taking to crowing[9] and pursuing me across the bridge with crows, as from an exceedingly dejected fowl who had known me when I was a blacksmith, <u>culminated</u> the disgrace with which I left the town, and was, so to speak, <u>ejected</u> by it into the open country.

◀ *In what condition does Pip leave the village?*

But unless I had taken the life of Trabb's boy on that occasion, I really do not even now see what I could have done save endure. To have struggled with him in the street, or to have exacted any lower recompense from him than his heart's best blood, would have been futile and degrading. Moreover, he was a boy whom no man could hurt; an invulnerable and dodging serpent who, when chased into a corner, flew out again between his captor's legs, scornfully yelping. I wrote, however, to Mr. Trabb by next day's post to say that Mr. Pip must decline to deal further with one who could so far forget what he owed to the best interests of society as to employ a boy who excited loathing in every respectable mind.

◀ *What does Pip send Trabb? Why? What does he send Joe? Why?*

The coach, with Mr. Jaggers inside, came up in due time, and I took my box-seat again, and arrived in London safe— but not sound, for my heart was gone. As soon as I arrived, I sent a penitential codfish and barrel of oysters to Joe (as <u>reparation</u> for not having gone myself), and then went on to Barnard's Inn.

I found Herbert dining on cold meat, and delighted to welcome me back. Having dispatched the Avenger to the coffeehouse for an addition to the dinner, I felt that I must open my breast that very evening to my friend and chum. As confidence was out of the question with the Avenger in the hall,

---

8. **arm akimbo.** With his hand on his hip and his elbow bent
9. **crowing.** Boasting, especially over the misfortune of another

Words For Everyday Use	**drawl** (drôl) *vi.,* speak in a slow and lazy manner	**e • ject • ed** (ē jek´tid) *adj.,* thrown out
	cul • mi • nate (kul´mə nāt´) *vt.,* bring to the highest point	**rep • a • ra • tion** (rep´ə rā´shən) *n.,* something done or paid to make amends

► How does Pip describe his relationship with his servant? Why is this description ironic?

which could merely be regarded in the light of an ante-chamber[10] to the keyhole, I sent him to the play. A better proof of the <u>severity</u> of my bondage to that taskmaster could scarcely be afforded than the degrading shifts to which I was constantly driven to find him employment. So mean is <u>extremity</u> that I sometimes sent him to Hyde Park corner to see what o'clock it was.

Dinner done and we sitting with our feet upon the fender,[11] I said to Herbert, "My dear Herbert, I have something very particular to tell you."

"My dear Handel," he returned, "I shall esteem and respect your confidence."

"It concerns myself, Herbert," said I, "and one other person."

Herbert crossed his feet, looked at the fire with his head on one side, and having looked at it in vain for some time, looked at me because I didn't go on.

► To what does Pip confess?

► Why is Herbert not surprised at what Pip tells him?

"Herbert," said I, laying my hand upon his knee, "I love— I adore—Estella."

Instead of being <u>transfixed</u>, Herbert replied in an easy matter-of-course way, "Exactly. Well?"

"Well, Herbert. Is that all you say? Well?"

"What next, I mean?" said Herbert. "Of course I know *that*."

"How do you know it?" said I.

"How do I know it, Handel? Why, from you."

"I never told you."

"Told me! You have never told me when you have got your hair cut, but I have had senses to perceive it. You have always adored her, ever since I have known you. You brought your adoration and your portmanteau here together. Told me! Why, you have always told me all day long. When you told me your own story, you told me plainly that you began adoring her the first time you saw her, when you were very young indeed."

"Very well, then," said I, to whom this was a new and not unwelcome light, "I have never left off adoring her. And she has come back, a most beautiful and most elegant creature. And I saw her yesterday. And if I adored her before, I now doubly adore her."

---

10. **antechamber.** Smaller room leading into a larger or main room
11. **fender.** Metal grate placed in front of a fireplace to keep hot coals and debris from falling out

Words For Everyday Use	
se • ver • i • ty (sə ver´ə tē) *n.*, strictness; harshness
ex • trem • i • ty (ek strem´ə tē) *n.*, extreme measure; severe or strong action
trans • fixed (trans fiksd´) *adj.*, made motionless with awe

"Lucky for you then, Handel," said Herbert, "that you are picked out for her and allotted to her. Without <u>encroaching</u> on forbidden ground, we may venture to say that there can be no doubt between ourselves of that fact. Have you any idea yet of Estella's views on the adoration question?"

I shook my head gloomily. "Oh! She is thousands of miles away from me," said I.

"Patience, my dear Handel—time enough, time enough. But you have something more to say?"

"I am ashamed to say it," I returned, "and yet it's no worse to say it than to think it. You call me a lucky fellow. Of course I am. I was a blacksmith's boy but yesterday; I am—what shall I say I am today?"

"Say, a good fellow, if you want a phrase," returned Herbert, smiling, and clapping his hand on the back of mine, "a good fellow, with <u>impetuosity</u> and hesitation, boldness and <u>diffidence</u>, action and dreaming curiously mixed in him."

I stopped for a moment to consider whether there really was this mixture in my character. On the whole, I by no means recognized the analysis, but thought it not worth disputing.

"When I ask what I am to call myself today, Herbert," I went on, "I suggest what I have in my thoughts. You say I am lucky. I know I have done nothing to raise myself in life, and that fortune alone has raised me; that is being very lucky. And yet, when I think of Estella—"

("And when don't you, you know." Herbert threw in, with his eyes on the fire, which I thought kind and sympathetic of him.)

"—Then, my dear Herbert, I cannot tell you how dependent and uncertain I feel, and how exposed to hundreds of chances. Avoiding forbidden ground, as you did just now, I may still say that on the constancy of one person (naming no person) all my expectations depend. And at the best, how indefinite and unsatisfactory only to know so vaguely what they are!" In saying this, I relieved my mind of what had always been there, more or less, though no doubt most since yesterday.

"Now, Handel," Herbert replied, in his gay hopeful way, "it seems to me that in the <u>despondency</u> of the tender passion, we are looking into our gift-horse's mouth[12] with a magnifying-

◀ How does Pip describe Estella's feelings for him?

◀ How does Herbert evaluate Pip's character?

◀ Of what is Pip unsure?

---

12. **looking . . . mouth.** Finding fault with a gift or a lucky chance

glass. Likewise, it seems to me that, concentrating our attention on the examination, we altogether overlook one of the best points of the animal. Didn't you tell me that your guardian, Mr. Jaggers, told you in the beginning that you were not <u>endowed</u> with expectations only? And even if he had not told you so—though that is a very large if, I grant—could you believe that of all men in London, Mr. Jaggers is the man to hold his present relations towards you unless he was sure of his ground?"

I said I could not deny that this was a strong point. I said it (people often do so in such cases) like a rather reluctant <u>concession</u> to truth and justice—as if I wanted to deny it!

"I should think it *was* a strong point," said Herbert, "and I should think you would be puzzled to imagine a stronger; as to the rest, you must bide your guardian's time,[13] and he must bide his client's time. You'll be one-and-twenty before you know where you are, and then perhaps you'll get some further enlightenment. At all events, you'll be nearer getting it for it must come at last."

"What a hopeful disposition you have!" said I, gratefully admiring his cheery ways.

"I ought to have," said Herbert, "for I have not much else. I must acknowledge, by-the-bye,[14] that the good sense of what I have just said is not my own, but my father's. The only remark I ever heard him make on your story, was the final one: 'The thing is settled and done, or Mr. Jaggers would not be in it.' And now, before I say anything more about my father, or my father's son, and repay confidence with confidence, I want to make myself seriously disagreeable to you for a moment—positively repulsive."

"You won't succeed," said I.

"Oh, yes, I shall!" said he. "One, two, three, and now I am in for it. Handel, my good fellow"—though he spoke in this light tone, he was very much in earnest—"I have been thinking since we have been talking with our feet on this fender that Estella cannot surely be a condition of your inheritance, if she was never referred to by your guardian. Am I right in so understanding what you have told me, as that he never

▶ *What is Herbert's advice?*

▶ *What kind of message is Herbert going to give to Pip?*

---

13. **bide . . . time.** Wait for the right time
14. **by-the-bye.** Incidentally; by the way

Words For Everyday Use	en • dowed (en doud´) *adj.,* provided with income or specified qualities con • ces • sion (kən sesh´ən) *n.,* act of acknowledging as true

referred to her, directly or indirectly, in any way? Never even hinted, for instance, that your patron might have views as to your marriage ultimately?"

"Never."

"Now, Handel, I am quite free from the flavor of sour grapes,[15] upon my soul and honor! Not being bound to her, can you not detach yourself from her? I told you I should be disagreeable."

◄ *What does Herbert recommend?*

I turned my head aside, for, with a rush and a sweep, like the old marsh winds coming up from the sea, a feeling like that which had subdued me on the morning when I left the forge, when the mists were solemnly rising, and when I laid my hand upon the village finger-post,[16] smote upon my heart again. There was silence between us for a little while.

◄ *How does Pip feel about Herbert's advice?*

"Yes; but my dear Handel," Herbert went on, as if we had been talking instead of silent, "its having been so strongly rooted in the breast of a boy whom nature and circumstances made so romantic renders it very serious. Think of her bringing-up, and think of Miss Havisham. Think of what she is herself (now I am repulsive and you <u>abominate</u> me). This may lead to miserable things."

"I know it, Herbert," said I, with my head still turned away, "but I can't help it."

◄ *What is Pip's response to Herbert's advice?*

"You can't detach yourself?"

"No. Impossible!"

"You can't try, Handel?"

"No. Impossible!"

"Well!" said Herbert, getting up with a lively shake as if he had been asleep, and stirring the fire; "now I'll endeavor to make myself agreeable again!"

So, he went round the room and shook the curtains out, put the chairs in their places, tidied the books and so forth that were lying about, looked into the hall, peeped into the letter box, shut the door, and came back to his chair by the fire, when he sat down, nursing his left leg in both arms.

---

15. **sour grapes.** Disparaging attitude toward something that one secretly wants but cannot attain (from Aesop's fable of the fox that is unable to reach the grapes it wants and so decides they must be sour anyway)

16. **finger-post.** Post with a sign, often shaped like a pointing finger or hand, indicating the way to a particular place

Words For Everyday Use

a • bom • i • nate (ə bäm´ə nāt´) *vt.*, feel hatred and disgust for; loathe

"I was going to say a word or two, Handel, concerning my father and my father's son. I am afraid it is scarcely necessary for my father's son to remark that my father's establishment is not particularly brilliant in its housekeeping."

"There is always plenty, Herbert," said I, to say something encouraging.

"Oh, yes! And so the dustman[17] says, I believe, with the strongest approval, and so does the marine-store shop in the back street. Gravely, Handel, for the subject is grave enough, you know how it is as well as I do. I suppose there was a time once when my father had not given matters up; but if ever there was, the time is gone. May I ask you if you have ever had an opportunity of remarking, down in your part of the country, that the children of not exactly suitable marriages are always most particularly anxious to be married?"

▶ What does Herbert observe about the children of unsuitable marriages?

This was such a singular question that I asked him, in return, "Is it so?"

"I don't know," said Herbert; "that's what I want to know. Because it is decidedly the case with us. My poor sister Charlotte who was next me and died before she was fourteen, was a striking example. Little Jane is the same. In her desire to be matrimonially established,[18] you might suppose her to have passed her short existence in the <u>perpetual</u> contemplation of domestic <u>bliss</u>. Little Alick in a frock has already made arrangements for his union with a suitable young person at Kew. And, indeed, I think we are all engaged, except the baby."

▶ What is Herbert's secret?

"Then you are?" said I.

"I am," said Herbert; "but it's a secret."

I assured him of my keeping the secret, and begged to be favored with further particulars. He had spoken so sensibly and feelingly of my weakness that I wanted to know something about his strength.

"May I ask the name?" I said.

"Name of Clara," said Herbert.

"Live in London?"

"Yes. Perhaps I ought to mention," said Herbert, who had become curiously <u>crestfallen</u> and meek, since we entered on the interesting theme, "that she is rather below my mother's nonsensical family notions. Her father had to do

---

17. **dustman.** Trash collector
18. **matrimonially established.** Married

Words For Everyday Use	
per • pet • u • al (pər pech′ ō͞o əl) *adj.*, continual	
bliss (blis) *n.*, great joy or happiness	
crest • fall • en (krest′ fôl′ ən) *adj.*, disappointed	

with the victualing[19] of passenger-ships. I think he was a species of purser."[20]

"What is he now?" said I.

"He's an invalid now," replied Herbert.

"Living on—?"

"On the first floor," said Herbert. Which was not at all what I meant, for I had intended my question to apply to his means. "I have never seen him, for he has always kept his room overhead, since I have known Clara. But I have heard him constantly. He makes tremendous rows—roars, and pegs at the floor with some frightful instrument." In looking at me and then laughing heartily, Herbert for the time recovered his usual lively manner.

"Don't you expect to see him?" said I.

"Oh, yes, I constantly expect to see him," returned Herbert, "because I never hear him without expecting him to come tumbling through the ceiling. But I don't know how long the <u>rafters</u> may hold."

When he had once more laughed heartily, he became meek again, and told me that the moment he began to realize capital, it was his intention to marry this young lady. He added as a self-evident <u>proposition</u>, <u>engendering</u> low spirits, "But you *can't* marry, you know, while you're looking about you."

◄ *Why is Herbert hesitant to marry?*

As we contemplated the fire, and as I thought what a difficult vision to realize this same capital sometimes was, I put my hands in my pockets. A folded piece of paper in one of them attracting my attention, I opened it and found it to be the playbill I had received from Joe, relative to the celebrated provincial amateur of Roscian renown. "And bless my heart," I involuntarily added aloud, "it's tonight!"

This changed the subject in an instant, and made us hurriedly resolve to go to the play. So, when I had pledged myself to comfort and <u>abet</u> Herbert in the affair of his heart by all practicable and impracticable means, and when Herbert had told me that his affianced already knew me by reputation, and that I should be presented to her, and when we had warmly shaken hands upon our mutual confidence, we blew out our candles, made up our fire, locked our door, and issued forth in quest of Mr. Wopsle and Denmark.

◄ *What do Herbert and Pip promise one another?*

19. **victualing.** Supplying with provisions
20. **purser.** Officer in charge of money matters and welfare of passengers on a ship

---

Words For Everyday Use

raf • ter (raf´tər) *n.*, board that supports the roof
pro • po • si • tion (präp´ə zish´ən) *n.*, proposal
en • gen • der (en jen´dər) *vt.*, produce
a • bet (ə bet´) *vt.*, encourage and assist

On our arrival in Denmark,[1] we found the king and queen of that country elevated in two armchairs on a kitchen table, holding a court. The whole of the Danish nobility were in attendance, consisting of a noble boy in the wash-leather boots of a gigantic ancestor, a <u>venerable</u> peer with a dirty face who seemed to have risen from the people late in life, and the Danish chivalry,[2] with a comb in its hair and a pair of white silk legs, and presenting on the whole a feminine appearance. My gifted townsman[3] stood gloomily apart, with folded arms, and I could have wished that his curls and forehead had been more probable.

▶ What does the ghost do while on stage?

Several curious little circumstances <u>transpired</u> as the action proceeded. The late king of the country not only appeared to have been troubled with a cough at the time of his decease, but to have taken it with him to the tomb, and to have brought it back. The royal phantom[4] also carried a ghostly manuscript round its truncheon,[5] to which it had the appearance of occasionally referring, and that, too, with an air of anxiety and a tendency to lose the place of reference which were suggestive of a state of mortality. It was this, I conceive, which led to the shade's[6] being advised by the gallery[7] to "turn over!"—a recommendation which it took extremely ill.

▶ How does the audience react to the ghost's performance?

It was likewise to be noted of this majestic spirit that whereas it always appeared with an air of having been out a long time and walked an immense distance, it perceptibly came from a closely <u>contiguous</u> wall. This occasioned its terrors to be received <u>derisively</u>. The Queen of Denmark, a very buxom lady, though no doubt historically brazen, was considered by the public to have too much brass about her, her chin being

---

1. **Denmark.** Pip and Herbert are attending a performance of Shakespeare's play *The Tragedy of Hamlet,* which takes place in Denmark.
2. **chivalry.** Knight
3. **gifted townsman.** i.e., Mr. Wopsle
4. **royal phantom.** The late king of Denmark, Hamlet's father, was murdered by his brother, who then married the queen. The ghost of the king now appears to urge Hamlet to take revenge.
5. **truncheon.** Staff or baton used as a symbol of authority
6. **shade's.** Ghost's
7. **gallery.** Audience

Words For Everyday Use

ven • er • a • ble (ven´ər ə bəl) *adj.,* worthy of respect or reverence by reason of age, dignity, character, or position

tran • spire (tran spīr´) *vi.,* happen

con • tig • u • ous (kən tig´yo͞o əs) *adj,* adjacent; near

de • ri • sive • ly (də rī´siv lē) *adv.,* with scorn

attached to her diadem[8] by a broad band of that metal (as if she had a gorgeous toothache), her waist being encircled by another, and each of her arms by another, so that she was openly mentioned as "the kettledrum." The noble boy in the ancestral boots was inconsistent, representing himself, as it were in one breath, as an able seaman, a strolling actor, a gravedigger, a clergyman, and a person of the utmost importance at a court fencing-match,[9] on the authority of whose practiced eye and nice discrimination the finest strokes were judged. This gradually led to a want of toleration for him, and even—on his being detected in holy orders,[10] and declining to perform the funeral service—to the general <u>indignation</u> taking the form of nuts.[11] Lastly, Ophelia[12] was a prey to such slow musical madness that when, in course of time, she had taken off her white muslin scarf, folded it up, and buried it, a sulky man who had been long cooling his impatient nose against an iron bar in the front row of the gallery growled, "Now the baby's put to bed, let's have supper!" Which, to say the least of it, was out of keeping.

Upon my unfortunate townsman all these incidents accumulated with playful effect. Whenever that undecided prince[13] had to ask a question or state a doubt, the public helped him out with it. As for example; on the question whether 'twas <u>nobler</u> in the mind to suffer, some roared yes, and some no, and some inclining to both opinions, said "toss up for it;" and quite a debating society arose. When he asked what should such fellows as he do crawling between earth and heaven, he was encouraged with loud cries of "Hear, hear!" When he appeared with his stocking disordered (its disorder

◄ *What roles are played by the boy in the boots?*

◄ *How does the audience respond when the prince voices his doubt about whether it is nobler to suffer?*

---

8. **diadem.** Crown
9. **fencing match.** Tournament in which two opponents fight using swords that have buffers on the points to prevent injuries
10. **in holy orders.** With the rank of an ordained minister
11. **taking . . . nuts.** The audience expresses its disapproval by throwing nuts at the actors.
12. **Ophelia.** Daughter of Polonius, the king's advisor, who is killed by Hamlet. Ophelia is in love with Hamlet, and when she learns that he has killed her father, she goes insane and drowns herself.
13. **undecided prince.** Hamlet is tormented by indecision regarding his response to his father's murder, and in several soliloquies he verbalizes the conflicts raging in his mind. For example, he asks himself, "To be, or not to be, that is the question:/Whether 'tis nobler in the mind to suffer / The slings and arrows of outrageous fortune, / Or to take arms against a sea of troubles . . ."

Words For Everyday Use

in • dig • na • tion (in´dig nā´shən) n., anger
no • bler (nō´blŭr) adj., loftier; grander

expressed, according to usage, by one very neat fold in the top, which I suppose to be always got up with a flat iron), a conversation took place in the gallery respecting the paleness of his leg, and whether it was occasioned by the turn the ghost had given him. On his taking the recorders—very like a little black flute that had just been played in the orchestra and handed out at the door—he was called upon <u>unanimously</u> for "Rule Britannia." When he recommended the player not to saw the air thus, the sulky man said, "And don't *you* do it, neither; you're a deal worse than *him*!" And I grieve to add that peals of laughter greeted Mr. Wopsle on every one of these occasions.

But his greatest trials were in the churchyard,[14] which had the appearance of a primeval[15] forest, with a kind of small ecclesiastical[16] wash-house on one side, and a turnpike[17] gate on the other. Mr. Wopsle, in a <u>comprehensive</u> black cloak, being <u>descried</u> entering at the turnpike, the gravedigger was <u>admonished</u> in a friendly way, "Look out! Here's the undertaker a-coming to see how you're a getting on with your work!" I believe it is well known in a constitutional country that Mr. Wopsle could not possibly have returned the skull,[18] after moralizing over it, without dusting his fingers on a white napkin taken from his breast; but even that innocent and indispensable action did not pass without the comment "Wai-ter!" The arrival of the body for interment[19] (in an empty black box with the lid tumbling open), was the signal for a general joy which was much enhanced by the discovery, among the bearers, of an individual obnoxious to identification. The joy attended Mr. Wopsle through his struggle with Laertes[20] on the brink of the orchestra and the grave, and slackened no more until he had tumbled the king off the kitchen table, and had died by inches from the ankles upward.

► *What is the mood of the audience during the burial scene?*

---

14. **churchyard.** In one scene of the play, gravediggers are preparing a grave for Ophelia as Hamlet looks on.
15. **primeval.** Of the earliest times or ages
16. **ecclesiastical.** Of the church or the clergy
17. **turnpike.** Turnstile
18. **skull.** Seeing the skull of Yorick, the late king's jester, causes Hamlet to ponder the meaninglessness of life.
19. **interment.** Burial
20. **Laertes.** Brother of Ophelia. In his grief he throws himself into his sister's grave. Hamlet leaps in after him and the two grapple there.

Words For Everyday Use

u • nan • i • mous • ly (yoo nan´ə məs lē) *adv*, in complete agreement

com • pre • hen • sive (käm´pre hen´siv) *adj.*, large; extensive

de • scry (di skrī´) *vt.*, detect; see

ad • mon • ish (ad män´ish) *vt.*, advise

We had made some pale efforts in the beginning to applaud Mr. Wopsle, but they were too hopeless to be persisted in. Therefore we had sat, feeling keenly for him, but laughing, nevertheless, from ear to ear. I laughed in spite of myself all the time, the whole thing was so <u>droll</u>; and yet I had a <u>latent</u> impression that there was something decidedly fine in Mr. Wopsle's <u>elocution</u>—not for old associations' sake, I am afraid, but because it was very slow, very dreary, very uphill and downhill, and very unlike any way in which any man in any natural circumstances of life or death ever expressed himself about anything. When the tragedy was over, and he had been called for and hooted, I said to Herbert, "Let us go at once, or perhaps we shall meet him."

◀ What do Herbert and Pip do in spite of themselves? What does Pip think of Wopsle's performance?

We made all the haste we could downstairs, but we were not quick enough either. Standing at the door was a Jewish man with an unnatural heavy smear of eyebrow, who caught my eyes as we advanced, and said, when we came up with him:

"Mr. Pip and friend?"

Identity of Mr. Pip and friend confessed.

"Mr. Waldengarver," said the man, "would be glad to have the honor."

"Waldengarver?" I repeated—when Herbert murmured in my ear, "Probably Wopsle."

"Oh!" said I. "Yes. Shall we follow you?"

"A few steps, please." When we were in a side alley, he turned and asked, "How did you think he looked? *I* dressed him."

◀ What does the man talk about?

I don't know what he had looked like, except a funeral; with the addition of a large Danish sun or star hanging round his neck by a blue ribbon that had given him the appearance of being insured in some extraordinary fire office. But I said he had looked very nice.

"When he come to the grave," said our conductor, "he showed his cloak beautiful. But, judging from the wing, it looked to me that when he see the ghost in the queen's apartment, he might have made more of his stockings."

I <u>modestly</u> <u>assented</u>, and we all fell through a little dirty swing door, into a sort of hot packing-case[21] immediately behind it. Here Mr. Wopsle was <u>divesting</u> himself of his Danish garments, and here there was just room for us to look

---

21. **packing-case.** Storage compartment

Words For Everyday Use

droll (drōl) *adj.,* amusingly odd
la • tent (lāt´ nt) *adj.,* lying hidden or undeveloped within a person or thing
el • o • cu • tion (el´ə kyōō´ shən) *n.,* style of speaking or reading in public
mod • est • ly (mäd´ist lē) *adv.,* shyly
as • sent (ə sent´) *vi.,* consent; agree
di • vest (də vest´) *vt.,* rid; dispossess

at him over one another's shoulders, by keeping the packing-case door, or lid, wide open.

"Gentlemen," said Mr. Wopsle, "I am proud to see you. I hope, Mr. Pip, you will excuse my sending round. I had the happiness to know you in former times, and the drama has ever had a claim which has ever been acknowledged on the noble and the <u>affluent</u>."

► What process proves very difficult for "Mr. Waldengarver"?

Meanwhile, Mr. Waldengarver, in a frightful perspiration, was trying to get himself out of his princely sables.[22]

"Skin the stockings off, Mr. Waldengarver," said the owner of that property, "or you'll bust 'em. Bust 'em, and you'll bust five-and-thirty shillings. Shakespeare never was complimented with a finer pair. Keep quiet in your chair now, and leave 'em to me."

With that, he went upon his knees, and began to <u>flay</u> his victim; who, on the first stocking coming off, would certainly have fallen over backward with his chair, but for there being no room to fall anyhow.

I had been afraid until then to say a word about the play. But then Mr. Waldengarver looked up at us <u>complacently</u>, and said:

► What does Wopsle want to know? How do the young men answer?

"Gentlemen, how did it seem to you, to go, in front?"

Herbert said from behind (at the same time poking me), "Capitally." So I said, "Capitally."

"How did you like my reading of the character, gentlemen?" said Mr. Waldengarver, almost, if not quite, with patronage.

Herbert said from behind (again poking me), "Massive and concrete." So I said boldly, as if I had originated it, and must beg to insist upon it, "Massive and concrete."

"I am glad to have your <u>approbation</u>, gentlemen," said Mr. Waldengarver, with an air of dignity, in spite of his being ground against the wall at the time, and holding on by the seat of the chair.

"But I'll tell you one thing, Mr. Waldengarver," said the man who was on his knees, "in which you're out in your reading. Now mind! I don't care who says contrary; I tell you so. You're out in your reading of Hamlet when you get your legs in profile. The last Hamlet as I dressed made the same

---

22. **sables.** Black mourning clothes

Words For Everyday Use

af • flu • ent (af´ lōō ənt) *adj.,* rich; prosperous
flay (flā) *vt.,* strip off (the skin of)
com • pla • cent • ly (kəm plā´sənt lē) *adv.,* with self-satisfaction; smugly
ap • pro • ba • tion (ap´rə bā´shən) *n.,* official approval, sanction, or commendation

mistakes in his reading at rehearsal, till I got him to put a large red wafer on each of his shins, and then at that rehearsal (which was the last), I went in front, sir, to the back of the pit, and whenever his reading brought him into profile, I called out 'I don't see no wafers!' And at night his reading was lovely."

Mr. Waldengarver smiled at me, as much as to say "a faithful dependent—I overlook his folly;" and then said aloud, "My view is a little classic and thoughtful for them here; but they will improve, they will improve."

Herbert and I said together, Oh, no doubt they would improve.

"Did you observe, gentlemen," said Mr. Waldengarver, "that there was a man in the gallery who endeavored to cast <u>derision</u> on the service—I mean the representation?"

We <u>basely</u> replied that we rather thought we had noticed such a man. I added, "He was drunk no doubt."

"Oh, dear, no, sir," said Mr. Wopsle, "not drunk. His employer would see to that, sir. His employer would not allow him to be drunk."

"You know his employer?" said I.

Mr. Wopsle shut his eyes and opened them again; performing both ceremonies very slowly. "You must have observed, gentlemen," said he, "an ignorant and a <u>blatant</u> ass, with a rasping throat and a countenance expressive of low <u>malignity</u>, who went through—I will not say sustained—the role (if I may use a French expression) of Claudius[23] King of Denmark. That is his employer, gentlemen. Such is the profession!"

Without distinctly knowing whether I should have been more sorry for Mr. Wopsle if he had been in despair, I was so sorry for him as it was, that I took the opportunity of his turning round to have his braces[24] put on—which <u>jostled</u> us out at the doorway—to ask Herbert what he thought of having him home to supper? Herbert said he thought it would be kind to do so; therefore I invited him, and he went to Barnard's with us, wrapped up to the eyes, and we did our best for him, and he sat until two o'clock in the morning,

◄ How does Pip feel toward Mr. Wopsle? What does Pip do for him?

---

23. **Claudius.** Hamlet's uncle, who killed the rightful king and usurped his throne
24. **braces.** Suspenders

Words For Everyday Use	de • ri • sion (di rizh´ən) n., contempt or ridicule base • ly (bās´ lē) adv., rudely bla • tant (blāt´ 'nt) adj., disagreeably loud	or boisterous ma • lig • ni • ty (mə lig´nə tē) n., quality of being harmful; ill will jos • tle (jäs´əl) vt., bump; shove

reviewing his success and developing his plans. I forget in detail what they were, but I have a general recollection that he was to begin with <u>reviving</u> the drama, and to end with crushing it; inasmuch as his <u>decease</u> would leave it utterly <u>bereft</u> and without a chance or hope.

Miserably I went to bed after all, and miserably thought of Estella, and miserably dreamed that my expectations were all cancelled, and that I had to give my hand in marriage to Herbert's Clara, or play Hamlet to Miss Havisham's Ghost, before twenty thousand people, without knowing twenty words of it.

► *What is Pip's nightmare?*

Words For Everyday Use	re • vive (rē vīv´) *vt.*, bring back to a healthy, vigorous, or flourishing condition
	de • cease (di sēs´) *n.*, death
	be • reft (bi reft´) *adj.*, deprived; lacking something needed

Responding to the Selection

Imagine that you are Joe and that you have just returned from London and your visit with Pip. What are your thoughts and feelings about your experiences in the city? Consider your perceptions of Pip's surroundings, his friends, your reactions to Pip's behavior, your opinion about his anticipated visit to Miss Havisham, and your prospects for a continued relationship with him.

Reviewing the Selection

Recalling and Interpreting

1. **R:** What does Jaggers always do after dealing with his clients all day? What happens among Pip and his friends when they dine with Jaggers? In whom is Jaggers especially interested? What advice does Jaggers give Pip about this person?

2. **I:** What does Jaggers's habit reveal about his clients? about the legal profession? Jaggers seems to instigate much of the boys' behavior. Why might Jaggers be interested in instigating such behavior? Why does Jaggers show so much interest in this one character and claim that he "likes" him? What does his interest and his advice to Pip reveal about this particular character? What might Jaggers "see" in this character's future?

3. **R:** Of what does Biddy's letter inform Pip? What phrase did Joe particularly wish for Biddy to write? How does Pip feel about this news? What goes wrong with the visit? What does Joe do to reveal "simple dignity" at the visit's end? What news draws Pip back to his hometown? Whom does he see, and whom does he avoid while there?

4. **I:** How would you characterize the tone of Biddy's letter? What does she seem to be trying to indicate to Pip about his behavior? Why might Joe have wished for Biddy to write this phrase? How does Pip feel about Joe at the beginning of the visit? at its end? How does this scene make you feel about Joe? about Pip? Although the visit changes Pip's attitude toward Joe temporarily, it does not alter Pip's behavior. Why?

5. **R:** Besides Joe and Biddy, other characters from Pip's past reappear in these chapters. Who are they?

6. **I:** Explain why you think these characters have been reintroduced.

7. **R:** What "secret" does Pip finally reveal to Herbert? Why isn't this really a secret? What does Herbert urge Pip to try to do? What secret does Herbert reveal to Pip?

8. **I:** How does Herbert's relationship with Clara compare and contrast to that between Pip and Estella? Why do you think Herbert tries to urge Pip to do this? Why is Pip unwilling and unable to follow Herbert's advice? Based on Estella's behavior, explain whether it is possible for her to reciprocate Pip's feelings.

Synthesizing

9. Pip is moving forward in his new life as a gentleman in London. Identify at least two examples of Pip's false pride in his new status. He still, however, harbors the same conflicts and guilt he felt as a young boy. About what does he still agonize?

10. In chapter 29, Miss Havisham tells Pip to love Estella and that she bred and educated Estella to be loved. In what way does Pip interpret Miss Havisham? What do you think she really means? Why does Pip misread her despite so many clues, and in what way is his false interpretation likely to affect his future? What is Miss Havisham's definition of love? In what way does Pip's love for Estella meet this definition? Explain your thoughts about Miss Havisham's definition of love. Is what she describes love, or is it something else altogether?

Understanding Literature (QUESTIONS FOR DISCUSSION)

1. **Comic Relief.** Writers sometimes insert into a serious work of fiction or drama a humorous scene that is said to provide **comic relief,** because it relieves the seriousness or emotional intensity felt by the audience. Paradoxically, a scene introduced for comic relief can sometimes, because of the contrast provided, increase the perceived intensity or seriousness of the action around it. Why might the scene in which Trabb's boy mocks Pip be considered an example of comic relief? With what serious issues is Pip wrapped up? At what does Trabb's boy poke fun? What serious issues does this comic scene raise about Pip and his behavior? Dickens had an inordinate fondness for amateur theater. In what way is Mr. Wopsle's performance and the amateur production of Shakespeare's *The Tragedy of Hamlet, Prince of Denmark* an example of comic relief? Why is this scene comic?

2. **Foreshadowing. Foreshadowing** is the act of presenting materials that hint at events to occur later in a story. Predict what Jaggers's warning about Drummle might foreshadow. What might Pip's meeting a convict again foreshadow? What other elements of foreshadowing might be present in chapters 26–31?

CHAPTER 32

One day when I was busy with my books and Mr. Pocket, I received a note by the post, the mere outside of which threw me into a great flutter; for though I had never seen the handwriting in which it was addressed, I <u>divined</u> whose hand it was. It had no set beginning, as Dear Mr. Pip, or Dear Pip, or Dear Sir, or Dear Anything, but ran thus:

I am to come to London the day after tomorrow by the mid-day coach. I believe it was settled you should meet me? At all events Miss Havisham has that impression, and I write in obedience to it. She sends you her regard.

—Yours, ESTELLA.

If there had been time, I should probably have ordered several suits of clothes for this occasion; but as there was not, I was fain to be content with those I had. My appetite vanished instantly, and I knew no peace or rest until the day arrived. Not that its arrival brought me either, for then I was worse than ever, and began haunting the coach-office in Wood Street, Cheapside, before the coach had left the Blue Boar in our town. For all that I knew this perfectly well, I still felt as if it were not safe to let the coach-office be out of my sight longer than five minutes at a time; and in this condition of unreason I had performed the first half-hour of a watch of four or five hours, when Wemmick ran against me.

"Halloa, Mr. Pip," said he, "how do you do? I should hardly have thought this was *your* beat."

I explained that I was waiting to meet somebody who was coming up by coach, and I inquired after the castle and the Aged.

"Both flourishing, thankye," said Wemmick, "and particularly the Aged. He's in wonderful feather.[1] He'll be eighty-two next birthday. I have a notion of firing eighty-two times, if the neighborhood shouldn't complain, and that cannon of mine should prove equal to the pressure. However, this is not London talk. Where do you think I am going to?"

◀ *What is unusual about the letter? Who is it from?*

◀ *What details describe Pip's anxiety about Estella's arrival?*

---

1. **wonderful feather.** Wonderful humor; excellent physical and emotional condition for his age

Words For Everyday Use

di • vine (də vīn′) *vt.,* guess

"To the office," said I, for he was tending in that direction.

"Next thing to it," returned Wemmick, "I am going to New-gate. We are in a banker's-parcel case[2] just at present, and I have been down the road taking a squint at the scene of action, and thereupon must have a word or two with our client."

"Did your client commit the robbery?" I asked

"Bless your soul and body, no," answered Wemmick very drily. "But he is accused of it. So might you or I be. Either of us might be accused of it, you know."

"Only neither of us is," I remarked.

► Where does Wemmick invite Pip?

"Yah!" said Wemmick, touching me on the breast with his forefinger; "you're a deep one, Mr. Pip! Would you like to have a look at Newgate? Have you time to spare?"

I had so much time to spare that the proposal came as a relief, notwithstanding its irreconcilability with my latent desire to keep my eye on the coach-office. Muttering that I would make the inquiry whether I had time to walk with him, I went into the office, and ascertained from the clerk with the nicest precision and much to the trying of his temper, the earliest moment at which the coach could be expected—which I knew beforehand quite as well as he. I then rejoined Mr. Wemmick, and affecting to consult my watch and to be surprised by the information I had received, accepted his offer.

► What does Pip do before he joins Wemmick?

We were at Newgate in a few minutes, and we passed through the lodge where some fetters were hanging up on the bare walls among the prison rules, into the interior of the jail. At that time, jails were much neglected, and the period of exaggerated reaction consequent on all public wrong-doing—and which is always its heaviest and longest punishment—was still far off. So felons were not lodged and fed better than soldiers (to say nothing of paupers), and seldom set fire to their prisons with the excusable object of improving the flavor of their soup.[3] It was visiting time when Wemmick took me in; and a potman was going his rounds with beer, and the prisoners, behind bars in yards, were buying beer and talking to friends; and a frowzy, ugly, disorderly, depressing scene it was.

► In what condition are the prisons?

---

2. **banker's-parcel case.** Legal case involving a bank robbery

3. **the period . . . soup.** At this time prisoners were not likely to protest the poor quality of their food and lodgings. Prison reform was not a priority at this time.

Words For Everyday Use

ir • rec • on • cil • a • bil • i • ty (ir rek´ən sīl ə bil´ə tē) n., incompatibility; inability to be agreed upon

la • tent (lā´tənt) adj., hidden

as • cer • tain (as´ər tān´) vt., learn

pre • ci • sion (prē sizh´ən) n., quality of being precise, exact, or accurate

frow • zy (frou´zē) adj., untidy; sloppy

It struck me that Wemmick walked among the prisoners much as a gardener might walk among his plants. This was first put into my head by his seeing a shoot[4] that had come up in the night, and saying, "What, Captain Tom? Are *you* there? Ah, indeed?" and also, "Is that Black Bill behind the cistern?[5] Why I didn't look for you these two months; how do you find yourself?" Equally in his stopping at the bars and attending to anxious whisperers—always singly—Wemmick, with his post office in an immovable state, looked at them while in conference, as if he were taking particular notice of the advance they had made, since last observed, towards coming out in full blow[6] at their trial.

He was highly popular, and I found that he took the familiar department of Mr. Jaggers's business, though something of the state of Mr. Jaggers hung about him too, forbidding approach beyond certain limits. His personal recognition of each successive client was <u>comprised</u> in a nod, and in his settling his hat a little easier on his head with both hands, and then tightening the post office, and putting his hands in his pockets. In one or two instances, there was a difficulty respecting the raising of fees, and then Mr. Wemmick, backing as far as possible from the insufficient money produced, said, "It's no use, my boy. I am only a subordinate.[7] I can't take it. Don't go on in that way with a subordinate. If you are unable to make up your quantum,[8] my boy, you had better address yourself to a principal;[9] there are plenty of principals in the profession, you know, and what is not worth the while of one, may be worth the while of another; that's my recommendation to you, speaking as a subordinate. Don't try on useless measures. Why should you? Now, who's next?"

Thus, we walked through Wemmick's greenhouse, until he turned to me and said, "Notice the man I shall shake hands with." I should have done so without the preparation, as he had shaken hands with no one yet.

◄ *What is Wemmick's status among the prisoners?*

◄ *What does Wemmick do to collect the fees for Jaggers?*

---

4. **shoot.** New growing part; here, a newly-arrived prisoner
5. **cistern.** Large tank for storing water
6. **in full blow.** Fully prepared to stand trial
7. **subordinate.** Person in lower-ranking position, subject to the authority of another
8. **quantum.** Quantity; amount
9. **principal.** One who holds a position of highest rank or importance

Words For Everyday Use   **com • prise** (kəm prīz´) *vt.*, consist of; include

Almost as soon as he had spoken, a <u>portly</u> upright man (whom I can see now, as I write) in a well-worn olive-colored frock coat, with a peculiar <u>pallor</u> overspreading the red in his complexion, and eyes that went wandering about when he tried to fix them, came up to a corner of the bars, and put his hand to his hat—which had a greasy and fatty surface like cold broth—with a half-serious and half-<u>jocose</u> military salute.

"Colonel, to you!" said Wemmick; "how are you, Colonel?"

"All right, Mr. Wemmick."

"Everything was done that could be done, but the evidence was too strong for us, Colonel."

"Yes, it was too strong, sir—but *I* don't care."

"No, no," said Wemmick, coolly, "*you* don't care." Then, turning to me, "Served his Majesty, this man. Was a soldier in the line and bought his discharge."

I said, "Indeed?" and the man's eyes looked at me, and then looked over my head, and then looked all round me, and then he drew his hand across his lips and laughed.

"I think I shall be out of this on Monday, sir," he said to Wemmick.

"Perhaps," returned my friend, "but there's no knowing."

"I am glad to have the chance of bidding you goodbye, Mr. Wemmick," said the man, stretching out his hand between two bars.

"Thankye," said Wemmick, shaking hands with him. "Same to you, Colonel."

"If what I had upon me when taken had been real, Mr. Wemmick," said the man, unwilling to let his hand go, "I should have asked the favor of your wearing another ring—in acknowledgment of your attentions."

"I'll accept the will for the deed,"[10] said Wemmick. "By-the-bye; you were quite a pigeon-fancier." The man looked up at the sky. "I am told you had a remarkable breed of tumblers.[11] *Could* you commission any friend of yours to bring me a pair, if you've no further use for 'em?"

"It shall be done, sir."

"All right," said Wemmick, "they shall be taken care of. Good afternoon, Colonel. Goodbye!" They shook hands again, and

---

10. **the will . . . deed.** The intention to do it is as good as the act itself.
11. **tumblers.** Types of pigeons that do somersaults in flight

Words For Everyday Use	port • ly (pôrt´ lē) *adj.*, large and heavy in a dignified and stately way
	pal • lor (pal´ər) *n.*, lack of color
	jo • cose (jō kōs´) *adj.*, playful; humorous

as we walked away Wemmick said to me, "A coiner,[12] a very good workman. The recorder's report is made today, and he is sure to be executed on Monday. Still you see, as far as it goes, a pair of pigeons are portable property, all the same." With that he looked back, and nodded at his dead plant, and then cast his eyes about him in walking out of the yard, as if he were considering what other pot would go best in its place.

◄ What does Wemmick accept? Why?

As we came out of the prison through the lodge, I found that the great importance of my guardian was appreciated by the turnkeys[13] no less than by those whom they held in charge. "Well, Mr. Wemmick," said the turnkey, who kept us between the two studded and spiked lodge gates, and who carefully locked one before he unlocked the other, "What's Mr. Jaggers going to do with that Waterside murder? Is he going to make it manslaughter, or what is he going to make of it?"

"Why don't you ask him?" returned Wemmick.

"Oh, yes, I dare say!" said the turnkey.

"Now, that's the way with them here, Mr. Pip," remarked Wemmick, turning to me with his post office elongated. "They don't mind what they ask of me, the subordinate; but you'll never catch 'em asking any questions of my principal."

◄ How do the wardens at Newgate treat Wemmick? How do they treat Jaggers?

"Is this young gentleman one of the 'prentices or articled ones of your office?" asked the turnkey, with a grin at Mr. Wemmick's humor.

"There he goes again, you see!" cried Wemmick, "I told you so! Asks another question of the subordinate before the first is dry! Well, supposing Mr. Pip is one of them?"

"Why, then," said the turnkey, grinning again, "he knows what Mr. Jaggers is."

"Yah!" cried Wemmick, suddenly hitting out at the turnkey in a <u>facetious</u> way, "you're as dumb as one of your own keys when you have to do with my principal, you know you are. Let us out, you old fox, or I'll get him to bring an action against you for false imprisonment."

The turnkey laughed, and gave us good day, and stood laughing at us over the spikes of the wicket when we descended the steps into the street.

---

12. **coiner.** Maker of (counterfeit) coins
13. **turnkeys.** Jail wardens

Words For Everyday Use

fa • ce • tious (fə sē´shəs) *adj.,* witty

► What is Mr. Jaggers's strategy? How does this strategy help him?

"Mind you, Mr. Pip," said Wemmick gravely in my ear, as he took my arm to be more confidential; "I don't know that Mr. Jaggers does a better thing than the way in which he keeps himself so high. He's always so high. His constant height is of a piece with his immense abilities. That colonel durst no more take leave of *him* than that turnkey durst ask him his intentions respecting a case. Then, between his height and them, he slips in his subordinate—don't you see?—and so he has 'em, soul and body."

I was very much impressed, and not for the first time, by my guardian's subtlety. To confess the truth, I very heartily wished, and not for the first time, that I had had some other guardian of minor abilities.

Mr. Wemmick and I parted at the office in Little Britain, where suppliants for Mr. Jaggers's notice were lingering about as usual, and I returned to my watch in the street of the coach-office, with some three hours on hand. I con-

► What connection does Pip make to this visit?

sumed the whole time in thinking how strange it was that I should be encompassed by all this <u>taint</u> of prison and crime; that, in my childhood out on our lonely marshes on a winter evening, I should have first encountered it; that it should have reappeared on two occasions, starting out like a stain that was faded but not gone; that it should in this new way pervade my fortune and advancement. While my mind was thus engaged, I thought of the beautiful young Estella, proud and refined, coming towards me, and I thought with absolute <u>abhorrence</u> of the contrast between the jail and her.

► What does Pip try to do? Why?

I wished that Wemmick had not met me, or that I had not yielded to him and gone with him, so that, of all days in the year on this day, I might not have had Newgate in my breath and on my clothes. I beat the prison dust off my feet as I sauntered to and fro, and I shook it out of my dress, and I exhaled its air from my lungs. So <u>contaminated</u> did I feel, remembering who was coming, that the coach came quickly after all, and I was not yet free from the soiling consciousness of Mr. Wemmick's conservatory,[14] when I saw her face at the coach window and her hand waving to me.

What *was* the nameless shadow which again in that one instant had passed?

---

14. **conservatory.** Place where plants are grown; here, a reference to the prison

Words For Everyday Use	**taint** (tānt) *n.*, trace of corruption
	ab • hor • rence (ab hôr´əns) *n.*, loathing; detestation
	con • tam • i • nated (kən tam´ə nāt´ 'd) *adj.*, infected; impure; corrupted

CHAPTER 33

In her furred traveling dress, Estella seemed more delicately beautiful than she had ever seemed yet, even in my eyes. Her manner was more winning than she had cared to let it be to me before, and I thought I saw Miss Havisham's influence in the change.

We stood in the inn yard while she pointed out her luggage to me, and when it was all collected I remembered—having forgotten everything but herself in the meanwhile—that I knew nothing of her destination.

"I am going to Richmond," she told me. "Our lesson is that there are two Richmonds, one in Surrey and one in Yorkshire, and that mine is the Surrey Richmond. The distance is ten miles. I am to have a carriage, and you are to take me. This is my purse, and you are to pay my charges out of it. Oh, you must take the purse! We have no choice, you and I, but to obey our instructions. We are not free to follow our own devices, you and I."

As she looked at me in giving me the purse, I hoped there was an inner meaning in her words. She said them slightingly, but not with displeasure.

"A carriage will have to be sent for, Estella. Will you rest here a little?"

"Yes, I am to rest here a little, and I am to drink some tea, and you are to take care of me the while."

She drew her arm through mine, as if it must be done, and I requested a waiter who had been staring at the coach like a man who had never seen such a thing in his life to show us a private sitting room. Upon that, he pulled out a napkin, as if it were a magic clue without which he couldn't find the way upstairs, and led us to the black hole of the establishment: fitted up with a <u>diminishing</u> mirror (quite a <u>superfluous</u> article considering the hole's proportions), an anchovy sauce-cruet,[1] and somebody's pattens.[2] On my objecting to this retreat, he took us into another room with a dinner table for thirty, and in the grate a scorched leaf of a copy-book

◄ *What does Pip say about Estella's appearance and manner?*

◄ *What does Estella tell Pip? What does this imply?*

---

1. **anchovy sauce-cruet.** Small glass bottle for holding a salty fish paste; often the paste is used as a relish or seasoning
2. **pattens.** Thick, wooden sandals or clogs worn for walking over wet ground

Words For Everyday Use

di • min • ish • ing (də min′ish iŋ) *adj.*, reducing; making smaller

su • per • flu • ous (sə pʉr′flo͞o əs) *adj.*, extra; unnecessary under a bushel of coal dust. Having looked at this extinct <u>conflagration</u> and shaken his head, he took my order—which, proving to be merely "Some tea for the lady," sent him out of the room in a very low state of mind.

I was, and I am, sensible that the air of this chamber, in its strong combination of stable with soup-stock, might have led one to infer that the coaching department was not doing well, and that the enterprising proprietor was boiling down the horses for the refreshment department. Yet the room was all in all to me, Estella being in it. I thought that with her I could have been happy there for life. (I was not at all happy there at the time, observe, and I knew it well.)

"Where are you going to at Richmond?" I asked Estella.

"I am going to live," said she, "at a great expense, with a lady there, who has the power—or says she has—of taking me about, and introducing me, and showing people to me and showing me to people."

"I suppose you will be glad of variety and admiration?"

"Yes, I suppose so."

She answered so carelessly that I said, "You speak of yourself as if you were someone else."

"Where did you learn how I speak of others? Come, come," said Estella, smiling delightfully, "you must not expect me to go to school to *you*; I must talk in my own way. How do you thrive with Mr. Pocket?"

"I live quite pleasantly there; at least—" It appeared to me that I was losing a chance.

"At least?" repeated Estella.

"As pleasantly as I could anywhere, away from you."

"You silly boy," said Estella quite <u>composedly</u>, "how can you talk such nonsense? Your friend Mr. Matthew, I believe, is superior to the rest of his family?"

"Very superior indeed. He is nobody's enemy—"

"Don't add but his own," interposed Estella, "for I hate that class of man. But he really is disinterested, and above small jealousy and spite, I have heard?"

"I am sure I have every reason to say so."

"You have not every reason to say so of the rest of his people," said Estella, nodding at me with an expression of face that was at once grave and <u>rallying</u>, "for they beset Miss Havisham with reports and <u>insinuations</u> to your disadvantage.

► What makes the dismal surroundings acceptable?

► What does Estella say that reflects her attitude about Pip?

Words For Everyday Use

con • fla • gra • tion (kän´flə grā´shən) *n.*, big, destructive fire

com • po • sed • ly (kəm pō´zəd lē) *adv.*, calmly; tranquilly

ral • ly • ing (ral´ē iŋ) *adj.*, stirring

in • sin • u • a • tion (in sin´yoo ā´shən) *n.*, slight hint or suggestion

They watch you, misrepresent you, write letters about you (anonymous sometimes), and you are the torment and occupation of their lives. You can scarcely realize to yourself the hatred those people feel for you."

"They do me no harm, I hope?"

Instead of answering, Estella burst out laughing. This was very singular to me, and I looked at her in considerable perplexity. When she left off—and she had not laughed languidly, but with real enjoyment—I said, in my diffident way with her:

"I hope I may suppose that you would not be amused if they did me any harm?"

"No, no, you may be sure of that," said Estella. "You may be certain that I laugh because they fail. Oh, those people with Miss Havisham, and the tortures they undergo!" She laughed again, and even now, when she had told me why, her laughter was very singular to me, for I could not doubt its being genuine, and yet it seemed too much for the occasion. I thought there must really be something more here than I knew; she saw the thought in my mind and answered it.

"It is not easy for even you," said Estella, "to know what satisfaction it gives me to see those people thwarted, or what an enjoyable sense of the ridiculous I have when they are made ridiculous. For you were not brought up in that strange house from a mere baby—I was. You had not your little wits sharpened by their intriguing against you, suppressed and defenseless, under the mask of sympathy and pity and what not that is soft and soothing—I had. You did not gradually open your round childish eyes wider and wider to the discovery of that impostor of a woman who calculates her stores of peace of mind for when she wakes up in the night—I did."

It was no laughing matter with Estella now, nor was she summoning these remembrances from any shallow place. I would not have been the cause of that look of hers for all my expectations in a heap.

"Two things I can tell you," said Estella. "First, notwithstanding the <u>proverb</u> that constant dropping will wear away a stone, you may set your mind at rest that these people never will—never would in a hundred years—<u>impair</u> your ground with Miss Havisham, in any particular, great or small. Second, I am beholden to you as the cause of their being so busy and so mean in vain, and there is my hand upon it."

◄ *What effect does Pip have on the Pocket family?*

◄ *How does Estella describe her relationship with the Pockets?*

◄ *What does Estella say to reassure Pip?*

Words For Everyday Use

pro • verb (präv´ərb) *n.*, short, traditional saying that expresses some obvious truth or familiar experience

im • pair (im per´) *vt.*, make worse, less, or weaker

As she gave it me playfully—for her darker mood had been but momentary—I held it and put it to my lips. "You ridiculous boy," said Estella, "will you never take warning? Or do you kiss my hand in the same spirit in which I once let you kiss my cheek?"

"What spirit was that?" said I.

"I must think a moment. A spirit of contempt for the fawners[3] and plotters."

► How does Estella respond to Pip's kiss?

"If I say yes, may I kiss the cheek again?"

"You should have asked before you touched the hand. But, yes, if you like."

I leaned down, and her calm face was like a statue's. "Now," said Estella, gliding away the instant I touched her cheek, "you are to take care that I have some tea, and you are to take me to Richmond."

► What troubles Pip?

Her <u>reverting</u> to this tone, as if our association were forced upon us and we were mere puppets, gave me pain; but everything in our intercourse did give me pain. Whatever her tone with me happened to be, I could put no trust in it, and build no hope on it; and yet I went on against trust and against hope. Why repeat it a thousand times? So it always was.

I rang for the tea, and the waiter, reappearing with his magic clue, brought in by degrees some fifty <u>adjuncts</u> to that refreshment, but of tea not a glimpse. A teaboard, cups and saucers, plates, knives and forks (including carvers), spoons (various), salt-cellars,[4] a meek little muffin confined with the utmost precaution under a strong iron cover, Moses in the bulrushes typified by a soft bit of butter in a quantity of parsley,[5] a pale loaf with a powdered head, two proof impressions of the bars of the kitchen fireplace on triangular bits of bread, and ultimately a fat family urn, which the waiter staggered in with, expressing in his countenance burden and suffering. After a prolonged absence at this stage of the entertainment, he at length came back with a casket of precious appearance containing twigs. These I steeped in hot water, and so from the whole of these appliances <u>extracted</u> one cup of I don't know what for Estella.

---

3. **fawners.** Those who seek favor or attention by flattery or servile behavior
4. **salt-cellars.** Saltshakers
5. **Moses . . . parsley.** The butter in the bed of parsley reminds Pip of the Hebrew infant Moses, who was placed in the Nile River in a basket made of bulrushes (Exodus 2).

Words For Everyday Use

re • vert • ing (ri vʉrt´iŋ) n., going back in action, thought, or speech

ad • junct (a´jʌŋkt) n., thing added to something else, but secondary or not essential to it

ex • tract (eks trakt´) vt., draw out by effort

The bill paid, and the waiter remembered, and the ostler[6] not forgotten, and the chambermaid taken into consideration—in a word, the whole house bribed into a state of contempt and <u>animosity</u>, and Estella's purse much lightened—we got into our post-coach and drove away. Turning into Cheapside and rattling up Newgate Street, we were soon under the walls of which I was so ashamed.

"What place is that?" Estella asked me.

◀ What is Estella's reaction upon seeing the prison? Pip's?

I made a foolish pretense of not at first recognizing it, and then told her. As she looked at it, and drew in her head again, murmuring "Wretches!" I would not have confessed to my visit for any consideration.

"Mr. Jaggers," said I, by way of putting it neatly on somebody else, "has the reputation of being more in the secrets of that dismal place than any man in London."

"He is more in the secrets of every place, I think," said Estella, in a low voice.

"You have been accustomed to see him often, I suppose?"

◀ What does Estella know of Jaggers?

"I have been accustomed to see him at uncertain intervals, ever since I can remember. But I know him no better now than I did before I could speak plainly. What is your own experience of him? Do you advance with him?"

"Once habituated[7] to his distrustful manner," said I, "I have done very well."

"Are you intimate?"

"I have dined with him at his private house."

"I fancy," said Estella, shrinking, "that must be a curious place."

"It is a curious place."

I should have been chary[8] of discussing my guardian too freely even with her, but I should have gone on with the subject so far as to describe the dinner in Gerrard Street, if we had not then come into a sudden glare of gas.[9] It seemed, while it lasted, to be all alight and alive with that inexplicable feeling I had had before; and when we were out of it, I was as much <u>dazed</u> for a few moments as if I had been in lightning.

So we fell into other talk, and it was principally about the way by which we were traveling, and about what parts of

◀ What do they talk about? To what question does Estella answer, "God forbid!"?

---

6. **ostler.** Innkeeper
7. **habituated.** Accustomed
8. **chary.** Careful, wary
9. **glare of gas.** Glare of lights

Words For Everyday Use	an • i • mos • i • ty (an′ə mäs′ ə tē) *n.,* feeling of strong dislike or hatred
	dazed (dāzd) *adj.,* bewildered

London lay on this side of it, and what on that. The great city was almost new to her, she told me, for she had never left Miss Havisham's neighborhood until she had gone to France, and she had merely passed through London then in going and returning. I asked her if my guardian had any charge of her while she remained here. To that she <u>emphatically</u> said, "God forbid!" and no more.

▶ *Does Estella's behavior convince Pip that she cares about him? Explain.*

It was impossible for me to avoid seeing that she cared to attract me; that she made herself winning; and would have won me even if the task had needed pains. Yet this made me none the happier, for even if she had not taken that tone of our being disposed of by others, I should have felt that she held my heart in her hand because she wilfully chose to do it, and not because it would have wrung any tenderness in her to crush it and throw it away.

When we passed through Hammersmith, I showed her where Mr. Matthew Pocket lived, and said it was no great way from Richmond, and that I hoped I should see her sometimes.

▶ *What news should make Pip feel better?*

"Oh yes, you are to see me; you are to come when you think proper; you are to be mentioned to the family; indeed, you are already mentioned."

I inquired, was it a large household she was going to be a member of?

"No, there are only two; mother and daughter. The mother is a lady of some station, though not <u>averse</u> to increasing her income."

"I wonder Miss Havisham could part with you again so soon."

"It is a part of Miss Havisham's plans for me, Pip," said Estella, with a sigh, as if she were tired; "I am to write to her constantly and see her regularly and report how I go on—I and the jewels—for they are nearly all mine now."

It was the first time she had ever called me by my name. Of course she did so purposely, and knew that I should treasure it up.

We came to Richmond all too soon, and our destination there was a house by the green—a <u>staid</u> old house, where hoops and powder and patches,[10] embroidered coats, rolled

---

10. **hoops . . . patches.** *Hoops*—Hoop skirts, long, full skirts belled out with a series of hoops; *powder*—white cosmetic powder applied to the face, hair, or wigs; *patches*—small pieces of silk worn on the face to hide blemishes or to show off the complexion

---

Words For Everyday Use	
em • phat • i • cal • ly (em fat´ik lē) *adv.,* with emphasis
a • verse (ə vʉrs´) *adj.,* reluctant; opposed
staid (stād) *adj.,* resisting change; fixed; serious

stockings, ruffles, and swords had had their court days many a time. Some ancient trees before the house were still cut into fashions as formal and unnatural as the hoops and wigs and stiff skirts, but their own <u>allotted</u> places in the great procession of the dead were not far off, and they would soon drop into them and go the silent way of the rest.

A bell with an old voice—which I dare say in its time had often said to the house, Here is the green farthingale,[11] Here is the diamond-hilted sword, Here are the shoes with red heels and the blue solitaire—sounded gravely in the moonlight, and two cherry-colored maids came fluttering out to receive Estella. The doorway soon absorbed her boxes, and she gave me her hand and a smile, and said good night, and was absorbed likewise. And still I stood looking at the house, thinking how happy I should be if I lived there with her, and knowing that I never was happy with her, but always miserable.

◀ *What happens at Richmond? What does Pip realize?*

I got into the carriage to be taken back to Hammersmith, and I got in with a bad heartache, and I got out with a worse heartache. At our own door I found little Jane Pocket coming home from a little party, escorted by her little lover; and I envied her little lover, in spite of his being subject to Flopson.

Mr. Pocket was out lecturing; for he was a most delightful lecturer on domestic economy, and his <u>treatises</u> on the management of children and servants were considered the very best textbooks on those themes. But Mrs. Pocket was at home, and was in a little difficulty, on account of the baby's having been accommodated with a needle-case to keep him quiet during the unaccountable absence (with a relative in the footguards[12]) of Millers. And more needles were missing than it could be regarded as quite wholesome for a patient of such tender years either to apply externally or to take as a tonic.

◀ *Where is Mr. Pocket? What was the "little difficulty"?*

Mr. Pocket being justly celebrated for giving most excellent practical advice, and for having a clear and sound perception of things and a highly judicious mind, I had some notion in my heartache of begging him to accept my confidence. But happening to look up at Mrs. Pocket as she sat reading her book of dignities after prescribing bed as a <u>sovereign</u> remedy for baby, I thought—Well, no, I wouldn't.

◀ *What does Pip decide not to do?*

---

11. **farthingale.** Hoop skirt
12. **footguards.** A body of foot-soldiers chosen for special service as a guard

Words For Everyday Use	**al • lot • ed** (ə lät´ ʼd) *adj.,* given or assigned **trea • tise** (trēt´is) *n.,* formal, systematic article or book on some subject	**sov • er • eign** (säv´rən) *adj.,* very effectual as a cure or remedy

As I had grown accustomed to my expectations, I had insensibly begun to notice their effect upon myself and those around me. Their influence on my own character I disguised from my recognition as much as possible, but I knew very well that it was not all good. I lived in a state of <u>chronic</u> uneasiness respecting my behavior to Joe. My conscience was not by any means comfortable about Biddy. When I woke up in the night—like Camilla—I used to think, with a weariness of my spirits, that I should have been happier and better if I had never seen Miss Havisham's face, and had risen to manhood content to be partners with Joe in the honest old forge. Many a time of an evening, when I sat alone looking at the fire, I thought, after all, there was no fire like the forge fire and the kitchen fire at home.

Yet Estella was so inseparable from all my restlessness and <u>disquiet</u> of mind that I really fell into confusion as to the limits of my own part in its production. That is to say, supposing I had had no expectations, and yet had had Estella to think of, I could not make out to my satisfaction that I should have done much better. Now, concerning the influence of my position on others, I was in no such difficulty, and so I perceived—though dimly enough perhaps—that it was not beneficial to anybody, and, above all, that it was not beneficial to Herbert. My lavish habits led his easy nature into expenses that he could not afford, corrupted the simplicity of his life, and disturbed his peace with anxieties and regrets. I was not at all remorseful for having unwittingly set those other branches of the Pocket family to the poor arts they practiced: because such littlenesses were their natural bent, and would have been <u>evoked</u> by anybody else, if I had left them <u>slumbering</u>. But Herbert's was a very different case, and it often caused me a twinge to think that I had done him evil service in crowding his sparely-furnished chambers with <u>incongruous</u> upholstery work, and placing the canary-breasted Avenger at his disposal.

So now, as an <u>infallible</u> way of making little ease great ease, I began to contract a quantity of debt. I could hardly begin but Herbert must begin, too, so he soon followed. At Startop's

► What does Pip begin to realize?

► What does Pip feel guilty about?

Words For Everyday Use

chron • ic (krän´ik) *adj.,* habitual
dis • qui • et (dis kwī´ət) *n.,* uneasiness
e • voke (ē vōk´) *vt.,* call forth or summon
slum • ber (slum´bər) *vi.,* sleep

in • con • gru • ous (in kän´grōō əs) *adj.,* not in harmony with the surroundings
in • fal • li • ble (in fal´ə bəl) *adj.,* incapable of error; never wrong

suggestion, we put ourselves down for election into a club called the Finches of the Grove—the object of which institution I have never divined, if it were not that the members should dine expensively once a fortnight, to quarrel among themselves as much as possible after dinner, and to cause six waiters to get drunk on the stairs. I know that these gratifying social ends were so invariably accomplished that Herbert and I understood nothing else to be referred to in the first standing toast of the society, which ran, "Gentlemen, may the present promotion of good feeling ever <u>reign</u> <u>predominant</u> among the Finches of the Grove."

◄ What is the club Pip wants to join? What do they do?

The Finches spent their money foolishly (the hotel we dined at was in Covent Garden), and the first Finch I saw when I had the honor of joining the Grove was Bentley Drummle, at that time <u>floundering</u> about town in a cab of his own, and doing a great deal of damage to the posts at the street corners. Occasionally, he shot himself out of his equipage head-foremost over the apron,[1] and I saw him on one occasion deliver himself at the door of the Grove in this unintentional way—like coals. But here I anticipate a little, for I was not a Finch, and could not be, according to the sacred laws of the society, until I came of age.

◄ Who is a member? How does he behave?

In my confidence in my own resources, I would willingly have taken Herbert's expenses on myself; but Herbert was proud, and I could make no such proposal to him. So, he got into difficulties in every direction, and continued to look about him. When we gradually fell into keeping late hours and late company, I noticed that he looked about him with a desponding eye at breakfast-time; that he began to look about him more hopefully about midday; that he drooped when he came into dinner; that he seemed to descry capital in the distance rather clearly, after dinner; that he all but realized capital towards midnight; and that at about two o'clock in the morning, he became so deeply despondent again as to talk of buying a rifle and going to America, with a general purpose of compelling buffaloes to make his fortune.

I was usually at Hammersmith about half the week, and when I was at Hammersmith I haunted Richmond—whereof separately by-and-by. Herbert would often come to

◄ Where does Pip spend his time?

---

1. **apron.** Leather covering for the legs in an open carriage

Words For Everyday Use	**reign** (rān) *vi.*, rule
	pre • dom • i • nant (prē dämʹə nənt) *adj.*, superior; dominant
	floun • der (flounʹdər) *vi.*, struggle awkwardly to move

Hammersmith when I was there, and I think at those seasons his father would occasionally have some passing <u>perception</u> that the opening he was looking for had not appeared yet. But in the general tumbling up of the family, his tumbling out in life somewhere was a thing to <u>transact</u> itself somehow. In the meantime Mr. Pocket grew grayer, and tried oftener to lift himself out of his perplexities by the hair. While Mrs. Pocket tripped up the family with her footstool, read her book of dignities, lost her pocket-handkerchief, told us about her grandpapa, and taught the young idea how to shoot by shooting it into bed whenever it attracted her notice.

As I am now generalizing a period of my life with the object of clearing my way before me, I can scarcely do so better than by at once completing the description of our usual manners and customs at Barnard's Inn.

▶ What does Pip's money bring him? Of what does Pip try to convince himself?

We spent as much money as we could, and got as little for it as people could make up their minds to give us. We were always more or less miserable, and most of our acquaintance were in the same condition. There was a gay fiction among us that we were constantly enjoying ourselves, and a skeleton truth that we never did. To the best of my belief, our case was in the last aspect a rather common one.

Every morning, with an air ever new, Herbert went into the city to look about him. I often paid him a visit in the dark backroom in which he <u>consorted</u> with an ink-jar, a hat-peg,[2] a coal-box, a string-box, an <u>almanac</u>, a desk and stool, and a ruler; and I do not remember that I ever saw him do anything else but look about him. If we all did what we undertake to do as faithfully as Herbert did, we might live in a Republic of the Virtues. He had nothing else to do, poor fellow, except at a certain hour of every afternoon to "go to Lloyd's"—in observance of a ceremony of seeing his principal, I think. He never did anything else in connection with Lloyd's that I could find out, except come back again. When he felt his case unusually serious, and that he positively must find an opening, he would go on 'Change at a busy time, and walk in and out, in a kind of gloomy country dance figure, among the assembled magnates.[3] "For," says Herbert to me,

---

2. **hat-peg.** Hat rack
3. **magnates.** Very important or influential persons, especially in a large business

---

Words For Everyday Use

per • cep • tion (pər sep´shən) *n.,* insight or intuition

trans • act (tran zakt´) *vt.,* carry on; conduct, as in business

con • sort (kən sôrt´) *vi.,* keep company

al • ma • nac (ôl´mə nak´) *n.,* book that contains information, usually statistical, on many subjects coming home to dinner on one of those special occasions, "I find the truth to be, Handel, that an opening won't come to one, but one must go to it—so I have been."

◄ What does Herbert admit?

If we had been less attached to one another, I think we must have hated one another regularly every morning. I detested the chambers beyond expression at that period of repentance, and could not endure the sight of the Avenger's livery,[4] which had a more expensive and a less <u>remunerative</u> appearance then than at any other time in the four-and-twenty hours. As we got more and more into debt, breakfast became a hollower and hollower form, and being on one occasion at breakfast-time threatened (by letter) with legal proceedings, "not unwholly unconnected," as my local paper might put it, "with jewelry," I went so far as to seize the Avenger by his blue collar and shake him off his feet—so that he was actually in the air, like a booted Cupid—for <u>presuming</u> to suppose that we wanted a roll.

At certain times—meaning at uncertain times, for they depended on our humor—I would say to Herbert, as if it were a remarkable discovery:

◄ What do Pip and Herbert attempt to do?

"My dear Herbert, we are getting on badly."

"My dear Handel," Herbert would say to me, in all sincerity, "if you will believe me, those very words were on my lips, by a strange coincidence."

"Then, Herbert," I would respond, "let us look into our affairs."

We always derived profound satisfaction from making an appointment for this purpose. I always thought this was business, this was the way to confront the thing, this was the way to take the foe by the throat. And I know Herbert thought so, too.

We ordered something rather special for dinner, with a bottle of something similarly out of the common way, in order that our minds might be <u>fortified</u> for the occasion, and we might come well up to the mark. Dinner over, we produced a bundle of pens, a <u>copious</u> supply of ink, and a goodly show of writing and blotting paper. For there was something very comfortable in having plenty of stationery.

◄ What steps do Pip and Herbert take? Is their strategy effective?

---

4. **livery.** Uniform

Words For Everyday Use

re • mu • ner • a • tive (ri myōō´ nə rāt´ iv) adj., profitable

pre • sume (prē zōōm´) vi., accept as true; take for granted

for • ti • fied (fôrt´ə fīd) adj., strengthened

co • pi • ous (kō´ pē əs) adj., plentiful

I would then take a sheet of paper, and write across the top of it, in a neat hand, the heading, "Memorandum of Pip's debts;" with Barnard's Inn and the date very carefully added. Herbert would also take a sheet of paper, and write across it with similar <u>formalities</u>, "Memorandum of Herbert's debts."

Each of us would then refer to a confused heap of papers at his side, which had been thrown into drawers, worn into holes in pockets, half-burnt in lighting candles, stuck for weeks into the looking glass, and otherwise damaged. The sound of our pens going refreshed us exceedingly, insomuch that I sometimes found it difficult to distinguish between this <u>edifying</u> business proceeding and actually paying the money. In point of meritorious character, the two things seemed about equal.

When we had written a little while, I would ask Herbert how he got on. Herbert probably would have been scratching his head in a most rueful manner at the sight of his <u>accumulating</u> figures.

"They are mounting up, Handel," Herbert would say; "upon my life, they are mounting up."

"Be firm, Herbert," I would retort, plying my own pen with great assiduity. "Look the thing in the face. Look into your affairs. Stare them out of countenance."

"So I would, Handel, only they are staring *me* out of countenance."

However, my determined manner would have its effect, and Herbert would fall to work again. After a time he would give up once more, on the plea that he had not got Cobbs's bill, or Lobbs's, or Nobbs's, as the case might be.

"Then, Herbert, estimate; estimate it in round numbers, and put it down."

"What a fellow of resource you are!" my friend would reply, with <u>admiration</u>. "Really, your business powers are very remarkable."

I thought so, too. I established with myself, on these occasions, the reputation of a first-rate man of business—prompt, decisive, energetic, clear, cool-headed. When I had got all my responsibilities down upon my list, I compared each with the bill, and ticked it off. My self-approval when I ticked an entry was quite a <u>luxurious</u> sensation. When I had no more ticks to make, I folded all my bills up uniformly, docketed

▶ *What does Pip think of his business sense? Why is this ironic?*

each on the back, and tied the whole into a symmetrical bundle. Then I did the same for Herbert (who modestly said he had not my administrative genius), and felt that I had brought his affairs into a focus for him.

My business habits had one other bright feature, which I called "leaving a margin." For example, supposing Herbert's debts to be one hundred and sixty-four pounds four-and-twopence, I would say, "Leave a margin, and put them down at two hundred." Or, supposing my own to be four times as much, I would leave a margin, and put them down at seven hundred. I had the highest opinion of the wisdom of this same margin, but I am bound to acknowledge that on looking back, I deem it to have been an expensive device. For we always ran into new debt immediately, to the full extent of the margin, and sometimes, in the sense of freedom and <u>solvency</u> it imparted, got pretty far on into another margin.

◀ What effect does leaving a generous margin in their budgets have?

But there was a calm, a rest, a <u>virtuous</u> hush consequent on these examinations of our affairs that gave me, for the time, an admirable opinion of myself. Soothed by my exertions, my method, and Herbert's compliments, I would sit with his symmetrical bundle and my own on the table before me among the stationery, and feel like a bank of some sort, rather than a private individual.

We shut our outer door on these solemn occasions in order that we might not be interrupted. I had fallen into my <u>serene</u> state one evening, when we heard a letter dropped through the slit in the said door, and fall on the ground. "It's for you, Handel," said Herbert, going out and coming back with it, "and I hope there is nothing the matter." This was in allusion to its heavy black seal and border.

The letter was signed TRABB & CO., and its contents were simply that I was an honored sir, and that they begged to inform me that Mrs. J. Gargery had departed this life on Monday last at twenty minutes past six in the evening, and that my attendance was requested at the interment on Monday next at three o'clock in the afternoon.

◀ What news does Pip receive?

Words For Everyday Use	
sol • ven • cy (säl′vən sē) *n.*, ability to meet financial obligations
vir • tu • ous (vʉr′cho͞o əs) *adj.*, characterized by moral excellence, right action and thinking, or goodness
se • rene (sə rēn′) *adj.*, calm, peaceful, tranquil

CHAPTER 35

▶ What is Pip unable to believe? What is his image of Mrs. Joe?

It was the first time that a grave had opened in my road of life, and the gap it made in the smooth ground was wonderful. The figure of my sister in her chair by the kitchen fire haunted me night and day. That the place could possibly be without her was something my mind seemed unable to <u>compass</u>, and whereas she had seldom or never been in my thoughts of late, I had now the strangest idea that she was coming towards me in the street, or that she would presently knock at the door. In my rooms, too, with which she had never been at all associated, there was at once the blankness of death and a perpetual suggestion of the sound of her voice or the turn of her face or figure, as if she were still alive and had been often there.

▶ What are Pip's feelings about his sister?

Whatever my fortunes might have been, I could scarcely have recalled my sister with much tenderness. But I suppose there is a shock of regret which may exist without much tenderness. Under its influence (and perhaps to make up for the want of the softer feeling), I was seized with a violent indignation against the <u>assailant</u> from whom she had suffered so much; and I felt that on sufficient proof I could have revengefully pursued Orlick, or anyone else, to the last extremity.

Having written to Joe to offer <u>consolation</u>, and to assure him that I would come to the funeral, I passed the <u>intermediate</u> days in the curious state of mind I have glanced at. I went down early in the morning, and alighted at the Blue Boar in good time to walk over to the forge.

It was fine summer weather again, and, as I walked along, the times when I was a little helpless creature, and my sister did not spare me, vividly returned. But they returned with a gentle tone upon them that softened even the edge of Tickler. For now the very breath of the beans and clover whispered to my heart that the day must come when it would be well for my memory that others walking in the sunshine should be softened as they thought of me.

▶ What does Trabb do?

At last I came within sight of the house, and saw that Trabb and Co. had put in a funereal execution and taken possession. Two dismally absurd persons, each <u>ostentatiously</u> exhibiting a crutch done up in a black bandage—as if that instrument

---

Words For Everyday Use

com • pass (kum′pəs) *vt.,* comprehend
as • sail • ant (ə sāl′ənt) *n.,* one who attacks or assaults
con • so • la • tion (kän′sə lā′shən) *n.,* comfort

in • ter • me • di • ate (in′tər mē′dē it) *adj.,* between two things, places, or stages
os • ten • ta • tious • ly (äs′tən tā′shəs lē) *adv.,* pretentiously; in a flashy or showy manner, as to display one's knowledge

could possibly communicate any comfort to anybody—were posted at the front door; and in one of them I recognized a postboy <u>discharged</u> from the Boar for turning a young couple into a sawpit[1] on their bridal morning, in consequence of intoxication[2] rendering it necessary for him to ride his horse clasped round the neck with both arms. All the children of the village, and most of the women, were admiring these sable warders[3] and the closed windows of the house and forge; and as I came up, one of the two warders (the postboy) knocked at the door—implying that I was far too much exhausted by grief to have strength remaining to knock for myself.

Another sable warder (a carpenter, who had once eaten two geese for a wager) opened the door, and showed me into the best parlor. Here, Mr. Trabb had taken unto himself the best table, and had got all the leaves up, and was holding a kind of black bazaar, with the aid of a quantity of black pins. At the moment of my arrival, he had just finished putting somebody's hat into black long-clothes, like an African baby; so he held out his hand for mine. But I, misled by the action, and confused by the occasion, shook hands with him with every testimony of warm affection.

Poor dear Joe, entangled in a little black cloak tied in a large bow under his chin, was seated apart at the upper end of the room; where, as chief mourner, he had evidently been stationed by Trabb. When I bent down and said to him, "Dear Joe, how are you?" he said, "Pip, old chap, you know'd her when she were a fine figure of a—" and clasped my hand and said no more.

◀ *In what emotional state is Joe?*

Biddy, looking very neat and modest in her black dress, went quietly here and there, and was very helpful. When I had spoken to Biddy, as I thought it not a time for talking, I went and sat down near Joe, and there began to wonder in what part of the house it—she—my sister—was. The air of the parlor being <u>faint</u> with the smell of sweet cake, I looked about for the table of refreshments; it was scarcely visible until one had got accustomed to the gloom, but there was a cut-up plum-cake upon it, and there were cut-up oranges, and sandwiches, and

---

1. **sawpit.** Hole in the ground, over the mouth of which timber is placed to be sawn by two people. One person stands in the pit and the other above.
2. **intoxication.** Drunkenness
3. **sable warders.** Funeral attendants

Words For Everyday Use

dis • charged (dis chärjd´) *adj.*, released
faint (fānt) *adj.*, weak; barely perceptible

biscuits, and two decanters that I knew very well as ornaments, but had never seen used in all my life—one full of port,[4] and one of sherry.[5] Standing at this table, I became conscious of the servile Pumblechook in a black cloak and several yards of hatband, who was alternately stuffing himself, and making <u>obsequious</u> movements to catch my attention. The moment he succeeded, he came over to me (breathing sherry and crumbs), and said in a subdued voice, "May I, dear sir?" and did. I then descried Mr. and Mrs. Hubble, the last-named in a decent speechless paroxysm in a corner. We were all going to "follow," and were all in course of being tied up separately (by Trabb) into ridiculous bundles.

▶ What kind of funeral does Joe want for his wife?

"Which I meantersay, Pip," Joe whispered me, as we were being what Mr. Trabb called "formed" in the parlor, two and two—and it was dreadfully like a preparation for some grim kind of dance; "which I meantersay, sir, as I would in preference have carried her to the church myself, along with three or four friendly ones wot come to it with willing harts and arms, but it were considered wot the neighbors would look down on such and would be of opinions as it were wanting in respect."

"Pocket-handkerchiefs out, all!" cried Mr. Trabb at this point, in a depressed business-like voice. "Pocket-handkerchiefs out! We are ready!"

▶ Who is in the procession? What do the bearers look like in their costumes?

So, we all put our pocket-handkerchiefs to our faces, as if our noses were bleeding, and filed out two and two; Joe and I; Biddy and Pumblechook; Mr. and Mrs. Hubble. The remains of my poor sister had been brought round by the kitchen door, and, it being a point of undertaking ceremony that the six bearers must be <u>stifled</u> and blinded under a horrible black velvet housing with a white border, the whole looked like a blind monster with twelve human legs, shuffling and blundering along under the guidance of two keepers—the postboy and his comrade.

▶ What is the response in the village?

The neighborhood, however, highly approved of these arrangements, and we were much admired as we went through the village; the more youthful and <u>vigorous</u> part of the community making dashes now and then to cut us off, and lying in wait to intercept us at points of vantage. At such

---

4. **port.** Sweet, dark red wine made in Portugal
5. **sherry.** Sweet to dry golden wine made in Spain

Words For Everyday Use

ob • se • qui • ous (əb sēˊkwē əs) *adj.*, showing too great a willingness to obey; fawning

sti • fle (stīˊfəl) *vt.*, smother

vig • or • ous (vigˊər əs) *adj.*, strong; robust

times the more <u>exuberant</u> among them called out in an excited manner on our emergence round some corner of expectancy, *"Here* they come!" *"Here* they are!" and we were all but cheered. In this progress I was much annoyed by the abject Pumblechook, who, being behind me, persisted all the way, as a delicate attention in arranging my streaming hatband, and smoothing my cloak. My thoughts were further distracted by the excessive pride of Mr. and Mrs. Hubble, who were surpassingly conceited and <u>vainglorious</u> in being members of so distinguished a procession.

And now the range of marshes lay clear before us, with the sails of the ships on the river growing out of it; and we went into the churchyard, close to the graves of my unknown parents, Philip Pirrip, Late of this Parish, and Also Georgiana, Wife of the Above. And there my sister was laid quietly in the earth while the larks sang high above it, and the light wind strewed it with beautiful shadows of clouds and trees.

◄ *Where is Mrs. Joe buried?*

Of the conduct of the worldly-minded Pumblechook while this was doing, I desire to say no more than it was all addressed to me; and that even when those noble passages were read which remind humanity how it brought nothing into the world and can take nothing out, and how it fleeth like a shadow and never continueth long in one stay, I heard him cough a reservation of the case of a young gentleman who came unexpectedly into large property. When we got back, he had the hardihood to tell me that he wished my sister could have known I had done her so much honor, and to hint that she would have considered it reasonably purchased at the price of her death. After that, he drank all the rest of the sherry, and Mr. Hubble drank the port, and the two talked (which I have since observed to be customary in such cases) as if they were of quite another race from the deceased, and were notoriously immortal. Finally, he went away with Mr. and Mrs. Hubble—to make an evening of it, I felt sure, and to tell the Jolly Bargemen that he was the founder of my fortunes and my earliest benefactor.

When they were all gone, and when Trabb and his men—but not his boy: I looked for him—had crammed their mummery[6] into bags, and were gone, too, the house felt wholesomer.

---

6. **mummery.** Articles used in a ridiculous or hypocritical ceremony

Words For Everyday Use

ex • u • ber • ant (eg zoo´ bər ənt) *adj.,* full of life

vain • glo • ri • ous (vān´ glôr´ ē əs) *adj.,* boastfully vain

► How do they spend the evening? What does Joe try to do?

Soon afterwards, Biddy, Joe, and I had a cold dinner together; but we dined in the best parlor, not in the old kitchen, and Joe was so exceedingly particular what he did with his knife and fork and the saltcellar and what not that there was great restraint upon us. But after dinner, when I made him take his pipe, and when I had <u>loitered</u> with him about the forge, and when we sat down together on the great block of stone outside it, we got on better. I noticed that after the funeral Joe changed his clothes so far as to make a compromise between his Sunday dress and working dress: in which the dear fellow looked natural, and like the man he was.

He was very much pleased by my asking if I might sleep in my own little room, and I was pleased, too, for, I felt that I had done rather a great thing in making the request. When the shadows of evening were closing in, I took an opportunity of getting into the garden with Biddy for a little talk.

► About what do Biddy and Pip disagree?

"Biddy," said I, "I think you might have written to me about these sad matters."

"Do you, Mr. Pip?" said Biddy. "I should have written if I had thought that."

"Don't suppose that I mean to be unkind, Biddy, when I say I consider that you ought to have thought that."

"Do you, Mr. Pip?"

She was so quiet, and had such an orderly, good, and pretty way with her that I did not like the thought of making her cry again. After looking a little at her downcast eyes as she walked beside me, I gave up that point.

► Where will Biddy go? Why?

"I suppose it will be difficult for you to remain here now, Biddy, dear?"

"Oh! I can't do so, Mr. Pip," said Biddy, in a tone of regret, but still of quiet conviction. "I have been speaking to Mrs. Hubble, and I am going to her tomorrow. I hope we shall be able to take some care of Mr. Gargery, together, until he settles down."

"How are you going to live, Biddy? If you want any mo—"

► What are Biddy's plans?

"How am I going to live?" repeated Biddy, striking in, with a momentary flush upon her face. "I'll tell you, Mr. Pip. I am going to try to get the place of mistress in the new school nearly finished here. I can be well recommended by all the neighbors, and I hope I can be industrious and patient, and teach myself while I teach others. You know, Mr. Pip," pursued

Words For Everyday Use

loi • ter (loit´ər) *vi.*, linger in an aimless way

Biddy, with a smile, as she raised her eyes to my face, "the new schools are not like the old, but I learnt a good deal from you after that time, and have had time since then to improve."

"I think you would always improve, Biddy, under any circumstances."

"Ah! Except in my bad side of human nature," murmured Biddy.

It was not so much a reproach, as an irresistible thinking aloud. Well! I thought I would give up that point, too. So I walked a little further with Biddy, looking silently at her downcast eyes.

"I have not heard the particulars of my sister's death, Biddy."

"They are very slight, poor thing. She had been in one of her bad states—though they had got better of late, rather than worse—for four days, when she came out of it in the evening, just at teatime, and said quite plainly, 'Joe.' As she had never said any word for a long while, I ran and fetched in Mr. Gargery from the forge. She made signs to me that she wanted him to sit down close to her, and wanted me to put her arms round his neck. So I put them round his neck, and she laid her head down on his shoulder quite content and satisfied. And so she presently said 'Joe' again, and once 'Pardon,' and once 'Pip.' And so she never lifted her head up any more, and it was just an hour later when we laid it down on her own bed, because we found she was gone."

◀ What does Mrs. Joe say on her deathbed?

Biddy cried; the darkening garden, and the lane, and the stars that were coming out were blurred in my own sight.

"Nothing was ever discovered, Biddy?"

"Nothing."

"Do you know what is become of Orlick?"

"I should think from the color of his clothes that he is working in the quarries."[7]

"Of course you have seen him then? Why are you looking at that dark tree in the lane?"

◀ What does Orlick do that bothers Biddy? What will Pip do if necessary?

"I saw him there, on the night she died."

"That was not the last time either, Biddy?"

"No, I have seen him there since we have been walking here. It is of no use," said Biddy, laying her hand upon my arm, as I was for running out, "you know I would not deceive you; he was not there a minute, and he is gone."

It revived my utmost indignation to find that she was still pursued by this fellow, and I felt inveterate[8] against him. I told her so, and told her that I would spend any money or

---

7. **quarries.** Places where building stone, marble, or slate is excavated by cutting or blasting
8. **inveterate.** Firmly established (in my indignation)

take any pains to drive him out of that country. By degrees she led me into more <u>temperate</u> talk, and she told me how Joe loved me, and how Joe never complained of anything—she didn't say of me; she had no need; I knew what she meant—but ever did his duty in his way of life, with a strong hand, quiet tongue, and a gentle heart.

"Indeed, it would be hard to say too much for him," said I; "and Biddy, we must often speak of these things, for of course I shall be often down here now. I am not going to leave poor Joe alone."

Biddy said never a single word.

"Biddy, don't you hear me?"

"Yes, Mr. Pip."

"Not to mention your calling me Mr. Pip—which appears to me to be in bad taste, Biddy—what do you mean?"

"What do I mean?" asked Biddy, timidly.

"Biddy," said I, in a virtuously self-asserting manner, "I must request to know what you mean by this?"

"By this?" said Biddy.

"Now, don't echo," I retorted. "You used not to echo, Biddy."

"Used not!" said Biddy. "Oh, Mr. Pip! Used!"

Well! I rather thought I would give up that point too. After another silent turn in the garden, I fell back on the main position.

"Biddy," said I, "I made a remark respecting my coming down here often, to see Joe, which you received with a marked silence. Have the goodness, Biddy, to tell me why."

"Are you quite sure, then, that you WILL come to see him often?" asked Biddy, stopping in the narrow garden walk, and looking at me under the stars with a clear and honest eye.

"Oh, dear me!" said I, as if I found myself compelled to give up Biddy in despair. "This really is a very bad side of human nature! Don't say any more, if you please, Biddy. This shocks me very much."

For which <u>cogent</u> reason I kept Biddy at a distance during supper, and when I went up to my own old little room, took as stately a leave of her as I could, in my murmuring soul, deem <u>reconcilable</u> with the churchyard and the event of the day. As often as I was restless in the night, and that was every quarter of an hour, I reflected what an unkindness, what an

► What does Pip promise? How does Biddy respond?

► What does Biddy ask Pip? How does he respond to her question?

Words For Everyday Use

tem • per • ate (tem´pər it) *adj.*, self-restrained; moderate in actions

co • gent (kō´jənt) *adj.*, valid

rec • on • cil • a • ble (rek´ən sīl´ ə bəl) *adj.*, that which can be settled or brought to harmony injury, what an injustice Biddy had done me.

Early in the morning, I was to go. Early in the morning, I was out, and looking in, unseen, at one of the wooden windows of the forge. There I stood for minutes, looking at Joe, already at work with a glow of health and strength upon his face that made it show as if the bright sun of the life in store for him were shining on it.

"Good-bye, dear Joe! No, don't wipe it off—for God's sake, give me your blackened hand! I shall be down soon and often."

"Never too soon, sir," said Joe, "and never too often, Pip!"

Biddy was waiting for me at the kitchen door, with a mug of new milk and a crust of bread. "Biddy," said I, when I gave her my hand at parting, "I am not angry, but I am hurt."

"No, don't be hurt," she pleaded quite pathetically; "let only me be hurt, if I have been ungenerous."

Once more, the mists were rising as I walked away. If they <u>disclosed</u> to me, as I suspect they did, that I should *not* come back, and that Biddy was quite right, all I can say is—they were quite right, too.

◄ *To what does Pip admit?*

Words For Everyday Use

dis • close (dis klōz´) *vt.,* reveal

CHAPTER 36

▶ In what state are
the young men's
financial affairs?

▶ How does Pip's
birthday compare
with Herbert's?

Herbert and I went on from bad to worse, in the way of increasing our debts, looking into our affairs, leaving margins,[1] and the like <u>exemplary</u> <u>transactions</u>; and time went on, whether or no, as he has a way of doing; and I came of age—in fulfillment of Herbert's prediction, that I should do so before I knew where I was.

Herbert himself had come of age eight months before me. As he had nothing else than his majority to come into, the event did not make a profound sensation in Barnard's Inn. But we had looked forward to my one-and-twentieth birthday, with a crowd of <u>speculations</u> and anticipations, for we had both considered that my guardian could hardly help saying something definite on that occasion.

I had taken care to have it well understood in Little Britain when my birthday was. On the day before it, I received an official note from Wemmick, informing me that Mr. Jaggers would be glad if I would call upon him at five in the afternoon of the <u>auspicious</u> day. This convinced us that something great was to happen, and threw me into an unusual flutter when I repaired to my guardian's office, a model of punctuality.

In the outer office Wemmick offered me his congratulations, and incidentally rubbed the side of his nose with a folded piece of tissue paper that I liked the look of. But he said nothing respecting it, and motioned me with a nod into my guardian's room. It was November, and my guardian was standing before his fire leaning his back against the chimney piece, with his hands under his coattails.

"Well, Pip," said he, "I must call you Mr. Pip today. Congratulations, Mr. Pip."

We shook hands—he was always a remarkably short shaker—and I thanked him.

"Take a chair, Mr. Pip," said my guardian.

As I sat down, and he preserved his attitude and bent his brows at his boots, I felt at a disadvantage, which reminded

---

1. **leaving margins.** Setting aside money to provide security against a possible loss

---

ex • em • pla • ry (eg zem´plə rē) *adj.*, serving as a model or example

trans • ac • tion (tran zak´shən) *n.*, business agreement

spec • u • la • tion (spek´yo͞o lā´shən) *adj.*, guess; opinion or conclusion based on incomplete evidence

aus • pi • cious (ôs´pish´əs) *adj.*, favorable

me of that old time when I had been put upon a tombstone. The two ghastly casts on the shelf were not far from him, and their expression was as if they were making a stupid apoplectic attempt[2] to attend to the conversation.

"Now, my young friend," my guardian began, as if I were a witness in the box, "I am going to have a word or two with you."

"If you please, sir."

"What do you suppose," said Mr. Jaggers, bending forward to look at the ground, and then throwing his head back to look at the ceiling, "what do you suppose you are living at the rate of?"

"At the rate of, sir?"

◀ What does Jaggers ask Pip about his finances?

"At," repeated Mr. Jaggers, still looking at the ceiling, "the—rate—of?" And then looked all round the room, and paused with his pocket-handkerchief in his hand, halfway to his nose.

I had looked into my affairs so often that I had thoroughly destroyed any slight notion I might ever have had of their <u>bearings</u>. Reluctantly, I confessed myself quite unable to answer the question. This reply seemed agreeable to Mr. Jaggers, who said, "I thought so!" and blew his nose with an air of satisfaction.

"Now, I have asked *you* a question, my friend," said Mr. Jaggers. "Have you anything to ask *me?*"

◀ What does Pip try to learn?

"Of course it would be a great relief to me to ask you several questions, sir; but I remember your <u>prohibition</u>."

"Ask one," said Mr. Jaggers.

"Is my benefactor to be made known to me today?"

"No. Ask another."

"Is that confidence to be imparted to me soon?"

"<u>Waive</u> that, a moment," said Mr. Jaggers, "and ask another."

I looked about me, but there appeared to be now no possible escape from the inquiry, "Have—I—anything to receive, sir?" On that, Mr. Jaggers said triumphantly, "I thought we should come to it!" and called to Wemmick to give him that piece of paper. Wemmick appeared, handed it in, and disappeared.

---

2. **apoplectic attempt.** *Apoplectic* means so excited as to be likely to cause an apoplexy or stroke. Pip describes the casts as trying wildly or excitedly to listen to the conversations.

Words For Everyday Use

bear • ings (ber´iŋz) *n.*, position or situation relative to the circumstances

pro • hi • bi • tion (prō´i bish´ən) *n.*, something that is forbidden

waive (wāv) *vt.*, set aside temporarily

"Now, Mr. Pip," said Mr. Jaggers, "attend if you please. You have been drawing pretty freely here; your name occurs pretty often in Wemmick's cashbook: but you are in debt, of course?"

"I am afraid I must say yes, sir."

"You know you must say yes, don't you?" said Mr. Jaggers.

"Yes, sir."

"I don't ask you what you owe, because you don't know; and if you did know, you wouldn't tell me; you would say less. Yes, yes, my friend," cried Mr. Jaggers, waving his forefinger to stop me, as I made a show of protesting, "it's likely enough that you think you wouldn't, but you would. You'll excuse me, but I know better than you. Now, take this piece of paper in your hand. You have got it? Very good. Now, unfold it and tell me what it is."

▶ What does Pip receive?

"This is a bank note," said I, "for five hundred pounds."

"That is a bank note," repeated Mr. Jaggers, "for five hundred pounds. And a very handsome sum of money, too, I think. You consider it so?"

"How could I do otherwise!"

"Ah! But answer the question," said Mr. Jaggers.

"Undoubtedly."

▶ What are the conditions that go with the money?

"You consider it, undoubtedly, a handsome sum of money. Now, that handsome sum of money, Pip, is your own. It is a present to you on this day, in earnest[3] of your expectations. And at the rate of that handsome sum of money per annum,[4] and at no higher rate, you are to live until the donor of the whole appears. That is to say, you will now take your money affairs entirely into your own hands, and you will draw from Wemmick one hundred and twenty-five pounds per quarter, until you are in communication with the fountainhead,[5] and no longer with the mere agent. As I have told you before, I am the mere agent. I execute my instructions, and I am paid for doing so. I think them injudicious, but I am not paid for giving any opinion on their merits."

I was beginning to express my gratitude to my benefactor for the great liberality with which I was treated, when Mr. Jaggers stopped me. "I am not paid, Pip," said he, coolly, "to carry your words to anyone;" and then gathered up his coat-tails,

3. **earnest.** Money paid in advance as part of an agreed-upon payment
4. **per annum.** Per year
5. **fountainhead.** Main source

Words For Everyday Use

lib • er • al • i • ty (lib´ər al´ i tē) *n.*, willingness to give freely as he had gathered up the subject, and stood frowning at his boots as if he suspected them of designs against him.

After a pause, I hinted:

"There was a question just now, Mr. Jaggers, which you desired me to waive for a moment. I hope I am doing nothing wrong in asking it again?"

◄ What does Pip want to know? What is the answer Jaggers gives him?

"What is it?" said he.

I might have known that he would never help me out, but it took me aback to have to shape the question afresh, as if it were quite new. "Is it likely," I said, after hesitating, "that my patron, the fountainhead you have spoken of, Mr. Jaggers, will soon—" there I delicately stopped.

"Will soon what?" asked Mr. Jaggers. "That's no question as it stands, you know."

"Will soon come to London," said I, after casting about for a precise form of words, "or summon me anywhere else?"

"Now here," replied Mr. Jaggers, fixing me for the first time with his dark deep-set eyes, "we must revert to the evening when we first encountered one another in your village. What did I tell you then, Pip?"

"You told me, Mr. Jaggers, that it might be years hence when that person appeared."

"Just so," said Mr. Jaggers; "that's my answer."

As we looked full at one another, I felt my breath come quicker in my strong desire to get something out of him. And as I felt that it came quicker, and as I felt that he saw that it came quicker, I felt that I had less chance than ever of getting anything out of him.

"Do you suppose it will still be years hence, Mr. Jaggers?"

Mr. Jaggers shook his head—not in negativing the question, but in altogether negativing the notion that he could anyhow be got to answer it—and the two horrible casts of the twitched faces looked, when my eyes strayed up to them, as if they had come to a crisis in their <u>suspended</u> attention, and were going to sneeze.

"Come!" said Mr. Jaggers, warming the backs of his legs with the backs of his warmed hands, "I'll be plain with you, my friend Pip. That's a question I must not be asked. You'll understand that better when I tell you it's a question that might compromise *me*. Come! I'll go a little further with you; I'll say something more."

Words For Everyday Use

sus • pend • ed (sə spen´did) *adj.*, halted

► *What will happen when Pip's benefactor appears?*

► *What is Pip thinking?*

He bent down so low to frown at his boots, that he was able to rub the calves of his legs in the pause he made.

"When that person discloses," said Mr. Jaggers, straightening himself, "you and that person will settle your own affairs. When that person discloses, my part in this business will <u>cease</u> and determine. When that person discloses, it will not be necessary for me to know anything about it. And that's all I have got to say."

We looked at one another until I withdrew my eyes, and looked thoughtfully at the floor. From this last speech I derived the notion that Miss Havisham, for some reason or no reason, had not taken him into her confidence as to her designing me for[6] Estella; that he resented this, and felt a jealousy about it; or that he really did object to that scheme, and would have nothing to do with it. When I raised my eyes again, I found that he had been shrewdly looking at me all the time, and was doing so still.

"If that is all you have to say, sir," I remarked, "there can be nothing left for me to say."

He nodded assent, and pulled out his thief-dreaded watch, and asked me where I was going to dine. I replied at my own chambers, with Herbert. As a necessary sequence,[7] I asked him if he would favor us with his company, and he promptly accepted the invitation. But he insisted on walking home with me, in order that I might make no extra preparation for him, and first he had a letter or two to write, and (of course) had his hands to wash. So, I said I would go into the outer office and talk to Wemmick.

The fact was that when the five hundred pounds had come into my pocket, a thought had come into my head which had been often there before; and it appeared to me that Wemmick was a good person to advise with, concerning such thought.

He had already locked up his safe, and made preparations for going home. He had left his desk, brought out his two greasy office candlesticks and stood them in line with the snuffers[8] on a slab near the door, ready to be extinguished;

---

6. **designing me for.** Intending or planning for me to marry
7. **sequence.** Related event in a series
8. **snuffers.** Cone-shaped devices used to extinguish candles by placing the cone over the flame

Words
For
Everyday
Use

cease (sēs) *vi.,* come to an end

he had raked his fire low, put his hat and greatcoat[9] ready, and was beating himself all over the chest with his safe-key, as an athletic exercise after business.

"Mr. Wemmick," said I, "I want to ask your opinion. I am very desirous to serve a friend."

◄ What does Pip want to do?

Wemmick tightened his post office and shook his head, as if his opinion were dead against any fatal weakness of that sort.

"This friend," I pursued, "is trying to get on in commercial life, but has no money, and finds it difficult and disheartening to make a beginning. Now, I want somehow to help him to a beginning."

"With money down?" said Wemmick, in a tone drier than any sawdust.

"With *some* money down," I replied, for an uneasy remembrance shot across me of that <u>symmetrical</u> bundle of papers at home; "with *some* money down, and perhaps some anticipation of my expectations."

"Mr. Pip," said Wemmick, "I should like just to run over with you on my fingers, if you please, the names of the various bridges up as high as Chelsea Reach. Let's see; there's London, one; Southwark, two; Blackfriars, three; Waterloo, four; Westminster, five; Vauxhall, six." He had checked off each bridge in its turn, with the handle of his safe-key on the palm of his hand. "There's as many as six, you see, to choose from."

"I don't understand you," said I.

"Choose your bridge, Mr. Pip," returned Wemmick, "and take a walk upon your bridge, and pitch your money into the Thames[10] over the center arch of your bridge, and you know the end of it. Serve a friend with it, and you may know the end of it too—but it's a less pleasant and profitable end."

◄ What is Wemmick's advice?

I could have posted a newspaper in his mouth, he made it so wide after saying this.

"This is very discouraging," said I.

"Meant to be so," said Wemmick.

"Then is it your opinion," I inquired, with some little indignation, "that a man should never—"

"—Invest portable property[11] in a friend?" said Wemmick. "Certainly he should not. Unless he wants to get rid of the

◄ What does Wemmick tell Pip?

---

9. **greatcoat.** Heavy overcoat
10. **Thames.** River in England which flows through London
11. **portable property.** Movable possessions, such as money, as opposed to land

Words For Everyday Use

sym • met • ri • cal (si met´ri kəl) *adj.,* well-balanced; orderly friend—and then it becomes a question how much portable property it may be worth to get rid of him."

"And that," said I, "is your deliberate opinion, Mr. Wemmick?"

"That," he returned, "is my deliberate opinion in this office."

"Ah!" said I, pressing him, for I thought I saw him near a loophole here. "But would that be your opinion at Walworth?"

"Mr. Pip," he replied with gravity, "Walworth is one place, and this office is another. Much as the Aged is one person, and Mr. Jaggers is another. They must not be confounded together. My Walworth sentiments must be taken at Walworth; none but my official sentiments can be taken in this office."

"Very well," said I, much relieved, "then I shall look you up at Walworth, you may depend upon it."

"Mr. Pip," he returned, "you will be welcome there, in a private and personal capacity."

We had held this conversation in a low voice, well knowing my guardian's ears to be the sharpest of the sharp. As he now appeared in his doorway, toweling his hands, Wemmick got on his greatcoat and stood by to snuff out the candles. We all three went into the street together, and from the doorstep Wemmick turned his way, and Mr. Jaggers and I turned ours.

▶ With whom does Pip spend his birthday? With whom would he have preferred to spend it?

I could not help wishing more than once that evening, that Mr. Jaggers had had an Aged in Gerrard Street, or a stinger, or a something, or a somebody, to unbend his brows a little. It was an uncomfortable consideration, on a twenty-first birthday, that coming of age at all seemed hardly worthwhile in such a guarded and suspicious world as he made of it. He was a thousand times better informed and cleverer than Wemmick, and yet I would a thousand times rather have had Wemmick to dinner. And Mr. Jaggers made not me alone intensely melancholy, because, after he was gone, Herbert said of himself, with his eyes fixed on the fire, that he thought he must have committed a felony and forgotten the details of it, he felt so dejected and guilty.

CHAPTER 37

<u>Deeming</u> Sunday the best day for taking Mr. Wemmick's Walworth sentiments, I devoted the next ensuing Sunday afternoon to a pilgrimage[1] to the castle. On arriving before the battlements, I found the Union Jack[2] flying and the drawbridge up, but <u>undeterred</u> by this show of defiance and resistance, I rang at the gate, and was admitted in a most pacific manner by the Aged.

"My son, sir," said the old man, after securing the drawbridge, "rather had it in his mind that you might happen to drop in, and he left word that he would soon be home from his afternoon's walk. He is very regular in his walks, is my son. Very regular in everything, is my son."

I nodded at the old gentleman as Wemmick himself might have nodded, and we went in and sat down by the fireside.

"You made acquaintance with my son, sir," said the old man, in his chirping way, while he warmed his hands at the blaze, "at his office, I expect?" I nodded. "Hah! I have heerd that my son is a wonderful hand at his business, sir?" I nodded hard. "Yes, so they tell me. His business is the law?" I nodded harder. "Which makes it more surprising in my son," said the old man, "for he was not brought up to the law, but to the wine-coopering."[3]

Curious to know how the old gentleman stood informed concerning the reputation of Mr. Jaggers, I roared that name at him. He threw me into the greatest confusion by laughing heartily and replying in a very sprightly[4] manner, "No, to be sure; you're right." And to this hour I have not the faintest notion what he meant, or what joke he thought I had made.

As I could not sit there nodding at him perpetually without making some other attempt to interest him, I shouted at inquiry whether his own calling in life had been "the wine-coopering." By dint of straining that term out of myself several times and tapping the old gentleman on the chest to

◀ *Why is it difficult to communicate with the Aged?*

---

1. **pilgrimage.** Long journey made to a place of religious or historic interest
2. **Union Jack.** Flag of the United Kingdom (England, Scotland, Wales, and Northern Ireland)
3. **wine-coopering.** Engaging in the trade of sampling, bottling, or selling wine
4. **sprightly.** Full of energy and spirit

Words For Everyday Use

deem (dēm) *vt.*, judge

un • de • terred (un dē tɜrd´) *adj.*, not discouraged from doing something associate it with him, I at last succeeded in making my meaning understood.

"No," said the old gentleman; "the warehousing, the warehousing. First, over yonder"—he appeared to mean up the chimney, but I believe he intended to refer me to Liverpool—"and then in the City of London here. However, having an infirmity—for I am hard of hearing, sir—"

I expressed in pantomime the greatest astonishment.

"—Yes, hard of hearing; having that infirmity coming upon me, my son he went into the law, and he took charge of me, and he by little and little made out this elegant and beautiful property. But returning to what you said, you know," pursued the old man, again laughing heartily,[5] "what I say is, No, to be sure; you're right."

I was modestly wondering whether my utmost <u>ingenuity</u> would have enabled me to say anything that would have amused him half as much as this imaginary pleasantry, when I was startled by a sudden click in the wall on one side of the chimney, and the ghostly tumbling open of a little wooden flap with "JOHN" upon it. The old man, following my eyes, cried with great triumph, "My son's come home!" and we both went out to the drawbridge.

It was worth any money to see Wemmick waving a salute to me from the other side of the moat, when we might have shaken hands across it with the greatest ease. The Aged was so delighted to work the drawbridge that I made no offer to assist him, but stood quiet until Wemmick had come across, and had presented me to Miss Skiffins; a lady by whom he was accompanied.

Miss Skiffins was of a wooden appearance, and was, like her escort, in the post-office branch of the service. She might have been some two or three years younger than Wemmick, and I judged her to stand possessed of portable property. The cut of her dress from the waist upward, both before and behind, made her figure very like a boy's kite; and I might have pronounced her gown a little too decidedly orange, and her gloves a little too intensely green. But she seemed to be a good sort of fellow, and showed a high regard for the Aged. I was not long in discovering that she was a frequent visitor at the castle; for, on our going in, and my complimenting Wemmick

---

5. **heartily.** With enthusiasm and vigor

▶ Why does Wemmick take up law?

▶ What is the gadget? What does it do?

▶ Who is with Wemmick? What does she look like?

▶ What tells Pip that this woman is a frequent visitor?

Words For Everyday Use

in • ge • nu • i • ty (in′ jə noo′ə tē) *n.,* quality of cleverness; skill on his ingenious <u>contrivance</u> for announcing himself to the Aged, he begged me to give my attention for a moment to the other side of the chimney, and disappeared. Presently another click came, and another little door tumbled open with "Miss Skiffins" on it; then Miss Skiffins shut up and John tumbled open; then Miss Skiffins and John both tumbled open together, and finally shut up together. On Wemmick's return from working these mechanical appliances, I expressed the great admiration with which I regarded them, and he said, "Well, you know, they're both pleasant and useful to the Aged. And by George, sir, it's a thing worth mentioning, that of all the people who come to this gate, the secret of those pulls is only known to the Aged, Miss Skiffins, and me!"

"And Mr. Wemmick made them," added Miss Skiffins, "with his own hands out of his own head."

While Miss Skiffins was taking off her bonnet (she retained her green gloves during the evening as an outward and visible sign that there was company), Wemmick invited me to take a walk with him round the property, and see how the island looked in wintertime. Thinking that he did this to give me an opportunity of taking his Walworth sentiments, I seized the opportunity as soon as we were out of the castle.

Having thought of the matter with care, I approached my subject as if I had never hinted at it before. I informed Wemmick that I was anxious in behalf of Herbert Pocket, and I told him how we had first met, and how we had fought. I glanced at Herbert's home, and at his character, and at his having no means[6] but such as he was dependent on his father for— those, uncertain and unpunctual. I alluded to the advantages I had derived in my first rawness and ignorance from his society, and I confessed that I feared I had but ill repaid them, and that he might have done better without me and my expectations. Keeping Miss Havisham in the background at a great distance, I still hinted at the possibility of my having competed with him in his prospects, and at the certainty of his possessing a generous soul, and being far above any mean distrusts, <u>retaliations</u>, or designs. For all these reasons (I told Wemmick), and because he was my young companion and friend, and I had a great affection for him, I wished my own good fortune to reflect some rays upon him, and therefore I sought advice

◄ Why does Pip want to help Herbert?

6. **means.** Resources, i.e., money

from Wemmick's experience and knowledge of men and affairs, how I could best try with my resources to help Herbert to some present income—say of a hundred a year, to keep him in good hope and heart—and gradually to buy him on to some small partnership. I begged Wemmick, in conclusion, to understand that my help must always be <u>rendered</u> without Herbert's knowledge or suspicion, and that there was no one else in the world with whom I could advise. I wound up by laying my hand upon his shoulder, and saying, "I can't help confiding in you, though I know it must be troublesome to you; but that is your fault, in having ever brought me here."

▶ What does Wemmick agree to do for Pip? Why?

Wemmick was silent for a little while, and then said with a kind of start, "Well, you know, Mr. Pip, I must tell you one thing. This is devilish good of you."

"Say you'll help me to be good then," said I.

"Ecod," replied Wemmick, shaking his head, "that's not my trade."

"Nor is this your trading place," said I.

"You are right," he returned. "You hit the nail on the head. Mr. Pip, I'll put on my considering cap, and I think all you want to do, may be done by degrees. Skiffins (that's her brother) is an accountant and agent. I'll look him up and go to work for you."

"I thank you ten thousand times."

"On the contrary," said he, "I thank you, for though we are strictly in our private and personal <u>capacity</u>, still it may be mentioned that there *are* Newgate cobwebs about, and it brushes them away."

After a little further conversation to the same effect, we returned into the castle, where we found Miss Skiffins preparing tea. The responsible duty of making the toast was <u>delegated</u> to the Aged, and that excellent old gentleman was so intent upon it that he seemed to me in some danger of melting his eyes. It was no <u>nominal</u> meal that we were going to make, but a vigorous reality. The Aged prepared such a haystack of buttered toast, that I could scarcely see him over it as it simmered on an iron stand hooked on to the top-bar; while Miss Skiffins brewed such a jorum[7] of tea that the pig in the back premises became strongly excited, and repeatedly expressed his desire to participate in the entertainment.

---

7. **jorum.** Large drinking bowl

ren • der (ren´dər) *vt.*, give; present

ca • pac • i • ty (kə pas´i tē) *n.*, position in which one functions; role

del • e • gate (del´ə gāt) *vt.*, appoint

nom • i • nal (näm´ə nəl) *adj.*, very small

The flag had been struck, and the gun had been fired, at the right moment of time, and I felt as snugly cut off from the rest of Walworth as if the moat[8] were thirty feet wide by as many deep. Nothing disturbed the tranquility of the castle, but the occasional tumbling open of John and Miss Skiffins; which little doors were a prey to some <u>spasmodic</u> infirmity that made me sympathetically uncomfortable until I got used to it. I inferred from the methodical nature of Miss Skiffins's arrangements that she made tea there every Sunday night, and I rather suspected that a classic brooch[9] she wore, representing the profile of an undesirable female with a very straight nose and a very new moon, was a piece of portable property that had been given her by Wemmick.

We ate the whole of the toast, and drank tea in proportion, and it was delightful to see how warm and greasy we all got after it. The Aged especially might have passed for some clean old chief of a savage tribe, just oiled. After a short pause of repose, Miss Skiffins—in the absence of the little servant who, it seemed, retired to the bosom of her family on Sunday afternoons—washed up the tea-things, in a <u>trifling</u> ladylike amateur manner that compromised[10] none of us. Then she put on her gloves again, and we drew round the fire, and Wemmick said, "Now, Aged Parent, tip us the paper."

Wemmick explained to me while the Aged got his spectacles[11] out that this was according to custom, and that it gave the old gentleman infinite satisfaction to read the news aloud. "I won't offer an apology," said Wemmick, "for he isn't capable of many pleasures—are you, Aged P.?"

"All right, John, all right," returned the old man, seeing himself spoken to.

"Only tip him a nod every now and then when he looks off his paper," said Wemmick, "and he'll be as happy as a king. We are all attention, Aged One."

"All right, John, all right!" returned the cheerful old man, so busy and so pleased, that it really was quite charming.

The Aged's reading reminded me of the classes at Mr. Wopsle's great-aunt's, with the pleasanter peculiarity that it

◄ *Why does Pip enjoy being at the castle?*

◄ *What does Wemmick do that shows his love for the Aged?*

◄ *Why does the Aged need close watching? Of what does the evening remind Pip?*

---

8. **moat.** Deep, broad ditch dug around a castle
9. **brooch.** Large ornamental pin
10. **compromised.** Made to look bad
11. **spectacles.** Glasses

Words For Everyday Use

spas • mod • ic (spaz mäd´ik) *adj.,* having the nature of sudden emotional or physical fits

tri • fling (trī´fliŋ) *adj.,* frivolous; shallow

seemed to come through a keyhole. As he wanted the candles close to him, and as he was always on the verge of putting either his head or the newspaper into them, he required as much watching as a powder-mill.[12] But Wemmick was equally untiring and gentle in his <u>vigilance</u>, and the Aged read on, quite unconscious of his many rescues. Whenever he looked at us, we all expressed the greatest interest and amazement, and nodded until he resumed again.

► *What does Wemmick try to do? What happens next?*

As Wemmick and Miss Skiffins sat side by side, and as I sat in a shadowy corner, I observed a slow and gradual elongation of Mr. Wemmick's mouth, powerfully suggestive of his slowly and gradually stealing his arm round Miss Skiffins's waist. In course of time I saw his hand appear on the other side of Miss Skiffins, but at that moment Miss Skiffins neatly stopped him with the green glove; unwound his arm again as if it were an article of dress, and with the greatest deliberation laid it on the table before her. Miss Skiffins's composure while she did this was one of the most remarkable sights I have ever seen, and if I could have thought the act consistent with abstraction of mind, I should have deemed that Miss Skiffins performed it mechanically.

By-and-by, I noticed Wemmick's arm beginning to disappear again, and gradually fading out of view. Shortly afterwards, his mouth began to widen again. After an interval of suspense on my part that was quite <u>enthralling</u> and almost painful, I saw his hand appear on the other side of Miss Skiffins. Instantly, Miss Skiffins stopped it with the neatness of a placid boxer, took off that girdle or cestus[13] as before, and laid it on the table. Taking the table to represent the path of virtue, I am justified in stating that during the whole time of the Aged's reading, Wemmick's arm was straying from the path of virtue and being recalled to it by Miss Skiffins.

At last the Aged read himself into a light slumber. This was the time for Wemmick to produce a little kettle, a tray of glasses, and a black bottle with a porcelain-topped cork, representing some clerical dignitary of a rubicund and social aspect.[14] With the aid of these appliances we all had something

---

12. **powder-mill.** Place where gunpowder is produced. Gunpowder is very volatile
13. **cestus.** Elasticized undergarment worn by women to shape the waist and hips; here refers to Wemmick's arm, encircling her waist
14. **clerical . . . aspect.** A metaphor comparing a bottle of wine to a particularly jolly minister dressed in black robes and white collar

Words For Everyday Use
vig • i • lance (vij´ə ləns) *n.*, watchfulness
en • thrall • ing (en thrôl´iŋ) *adj.*, captivating; fascinating

warm to drink, including the Aged, who was soon awake again. Miss Skiffins mixed, and I observed that she and Wemmick drank out of one glass. Of course I knew better than to offer to see Miss Skiffins home, and under the circumstances I thought I had best go first—which I did, taking a <u>cordial</u> leave of the Aged, and having passed a pleasant evening.

Before a week was out, I received a note from Wemmick, dated Walworth, stating that he hoped he had made some advance in that matter appertaining[15] to our private and personal capacities, and that he would be glad if I could come and see him again upon it. So, I went out to Walworth again, and yet again, and yet again, and I saw him by appointment in the City several times, but never held any communication with him on the subject in or near Little Britain. The upshot was that we found a worthy young merchant or shipping-broker, not long established in business, who wanted intelligent help, and who wanted capital, and who in due course of time and receipt would want a partner. Between him and me, secret articles were signed of which Herbert was the subject, and I paid him half of my five hundred pounds down, and engaged for <u>sundry</u> other payments: some, to fall due at certain dates out of my income; some <u>contingent</u> on my coming into my property. Miss Skiffins's brother conducted the negotiation. Wemmick pervaded it throughout, but never appeared in it.

> ◀ What does Pip do for Herbert?

The whole business was so cleverly managed that Herbert had not the least suspicion of my hand being in it. I never shall forget the radiant face with which he came home one afternoon, and told me as a mighty piece of news, of his having fallen in with one Clarriker (the young merchant's name), and of Clarriker's having shown an extraordinary <u>inclination</u> towards him, and of his belief that the opening had come at last. Day by day as his hopes grew stronger and his face brighter, he must have thought me a more and more affectionate friend, for I had the greatest difficulty in restraining my tears of triumph when I saw him so happy.

> ◀ What is Herbert's reaction? Why doesn't he know that Pip is involved?

At length, the thing being done, and he having that day entered Clarriker's House, and he having talked to me for a whole evening in a flush of pleasure and success, I did really

---

15. **appertaining.** Belonging or pertaining

cry in good earnest when I went to bed, to think that my expectations had done some good to somebody.

A great event in my life, the turning point of my life, now opens on my view. But before I proceed to narrate it, and before I pass on to all the changes it involved, I must give one chapter to Estella. It is not much to give to the theme that so long filled my heart.

Responding to the Selection

At the end of chapter 37, Pip at last obtains some happiness from his wealth. Discuss how Pip has used his money up to this point and the effect this use has had on him. For what reasons does Pip want to help Herbert? What do these reasons reveal about his character? Predict whether Herbert will be successful or not, giving evidence to support your opinion.

Reviewing the Selection

Recalling and Interpreting

1. **R:** What is Newgate? Describe the conditions there. Of what does the visit to Newgate remind Pip? How does Pip feel after visiting Newgate?

2. **I:** Dickens devotes much of chapter 32 to describe Pip's experience at Newgate. What significance do you think this place has? Why does Dickens juxtapose the scene at Newgate with that of Estella's arrival?

3. **R:** Why does Miss Havisham send Estella to London? What does Estella say about her plans or "instructions" when Pip picks her up at the coach office? What tone does she use when saying this? How does she behave toward Pip?

4. **I:** What does Estella's comment reveal about her personality? What does her tone reveal about her emotions? Does Estella's behavior convince Pip that she cares about him?

5. **R:** What does Pip do that gets him into debt?

6. **I:** In what ways do these actions show Pip's immaturity?

7. **R:** What continues to trouble Pip after his sister's funeral? What does Pip say he will do? What does Biddy say that hurts Pip?

8. **I:** What are some possible reasons for Pip's turmoil? Why might Biddy have questioned Pip as she did?

Synthesizing

9. During this time, as Pip comes into his majority, several important things happen to him. Identify two events and describe how his response reflects his developing maturity as a young man.

10. Select what you think is the most important event in these chapters. Explain why you think it is important and how it may affect Pip in the future.

Understanding Literature (QUESTIONS FOR DISCUSSION)

1. Three-dimensional Character. A **character** is a person (or sometimes an animal) who figures in the action of a literary work. A **three-dimensional, full, or rounded character** is one who exhibits the complexity of traits associated with actual human beings. The reader learns more about Wemmick as an individual in this section—through his relationship with the Aged and Miss Skiffins, his role as Jaggers's representative, and the way in which he helps Pip. Cite a quotation from, or an action by, Wemmick and discuss what it reveals about his character.

2. Simile and Extended Metaphor. A **simile** is a comparison using *like* or *as.* A simile is a type of *metaphor,* and like any other metaphor, can be divided into two parts, the *tenor* (or subject being described), and the *vehicle* (or object being used in the description). For example, in the simile "her locks are as white as the snow," the tenor is locks of hair and the vehicle is snow. An **extended metaphor** is a point-by-point presentation of one thing as though it were another. The description is meant as an implied comparison, inviting the reader to associate the thing being described with something that is quite different from it. Identify the tenor and vehicle in the following simile: "Wemmick walked among the prisoners, much as a gardener might walk among his plants." Explain how Wemmick's actions are like a gardener's. Then identify and explain the significance of other points in the extended gardening metaphor.

CHAPTER 38

If that staid old house near the green at Richmond should ever come to be haunted when I am dead, it will be haunted, surely, by my ghost. Oh, the many, many nights and days through which the unquiet spirit within me haunted that house when Estella lived there! Let my body be where it would, my spirit was always wandering, wandering, wandering about that house.

The lady with whom Estella was placed, Mrs. Brandley by name, was a widow, with one daughter several years older than Estella. The mother looked young and the daughter looked old; the mother's complexion was pink, and the daughter's was yellow; the mother set up for <u>frivolity</u>, and the daughter for <u>theology</u>. They were in what is called a good position, and visited, and were visited by, numbers of people. Little, if any, community of feeling subsisted[1] between them and Estella, but the understanding was established that they were necessary to her, and that she was necessary to them. Mrs. Brandley had been a friend of Miss Havisham's before the time of her seclusion.

◄ What is the relationship between the Brandleys and Estella?

In Mrs. Brandley's house and out of Mrs. Brandley's house, I suffered every kind and degree of torture that Estella could cause me. The nature of my relations with her, which placed me on terms of familiarity without placing me on terms of favor, <u>conduced</u> to my distraction. She made use of me to tease other admirers, and she turned the very familiarity between herself and me to the account of putting a constant slight on my devotion to her. If I had been her secretary, steward,[2] half-brother, poor relation—if I had been a younger brother of her appointed husband—I could not have seemed to myself further from my hopes when I was nearest to her. The privilege of calling her by her name and hearing her call me by mine became under the circumstances an aggravation of my trials, and while I think it likely that it almost maddened her other lovers, I knew too certainly that it also maddened me.

◄ Why doesn't Pip feel hopeful?

---

1. **subsisted.** Managed to exist
2. **steward.** Person in charge of a large house or estate

Words For Everyday Use

fri • vol • i • ty (fri väl´ə tē) *n.*, quality of silliness; amusement
the • ol • o • gy (thē äl´ə jē) *n.*, study of religion
con • duce (kən do͞os´) *vi.*, contribute; lead

She had admirers without end. No doubt my jealousy made an admirer of everyone who went near her, but there were more than enough of them without that.

I saw her often at Richmond, I heard of her often in town, and I used often to take her and the Brandleys on the water; there were picnics, fête[3] days, plays, operas, concerts, parties, all sorts of pleasures, through which I pursued her—and they were all miseries to me. I never had one hour's happiness in her society, and yet my mind all round the four-and-twenty hours was <u>harping</u> on the happiness of having her with me unto death.

Throughout this part of our intercourse—and it lasted, as will presently be seen, for what I then thought a long time—she habitually reverted to that tone which expressed that our association was forced upon us. There were other times when she would come to a sudden check in this tone and in all her many tones, and would seem to pity me.

"Pip, Pip," she said one evening, coming to such a check, when we sat apart at a darkening window of the house in Richmond; "will you never take warning?"

"Of what?"

"Of me."

"Warning not to be attracted by you, do you mean, Estella?"

"Do I mean! If you don't know what I mean, you are blind."

I should have replied that love was commonly <u>reputed</u> blind, but for the reason that I always was restrained—and this was not the least of my miseries—by a feeling that it was ungenerous to press myself upon her, when she knew that she could not choose but obey Miss Havisham. My dread always was that this knowledge on her part laid me under a heavy disadvantage with her pride, and made me the subject of a rebellious struggle in her bosom.

"At any rate," said I, "I have no warning given me just now, for you wrote to me to come to you, this time."

"That's true," said Estella, with a cold careless smile that always chilled me.

After looking at the twilight without for a little while, she went on to say:

"The time has come round when Miss Havisham wishes to have me for a day at Satis. You are to take me there, and bring

---

3. **fête.** Outdoor festival, gala entertainment

> ▶ *What do Estella and Pip do together? Does it make Pip happy? What does he want?*

> ▶ *What warning should Pip take?*

Words For Everyday Use

harp (härp) *vi.,* persist in talking or thinking continuously on one subject

re • pute (ri pyo͞ot´) *vt.,* regard; consider

me back, if you will. She would rather I did not travel alone, and objects to receiving my maid, for she has a sensitive horror of being talked of by such people. Can you take me?"

"Can I take you, Estella!"

"You can then? The day after tomorrow, if you please. You are to pay all charges out of my purse. You hear the condition of your going?"

"And must obey," said I.

This was all the preparation I received for that visit, or for others like it: Miss Havisham never wrote to me, nor had I ever so much as seen her handwriting. We went down on the next day but one, and we found her in the room where I had first beheld her, and it is needless to add that there was no change in Satis House.

She was even more dreadfully fond of Estella than she had been when I last saw them together; I repeat the word advisedly, for there was something positively dreadful in the energy of her looks and embraces. She hung upon Estella's beauty, hung upon her words, hung upon her gestures, and sat mumbling her own trembling fingers while she looked at her, as though she were devouring the beautiful creature she had <u>reared</u>.

◀ What is Miss Havisham's behavior toward Estella?

From Estella she looked at me, with a searching glance that seemed to pry into my heart and probe its wounds. "How does she use you, Pip, how does she use you?" she asked me again, with her witch-like eagerness, even in Estella's hearing. But, when we sat by her flickering fire at night, she was most weird; for then, keeping Estella's hand drawn through her arm and clutched in her own hand, she extorted from her by dint of referring back to what Estella had told her in her regular letters, the names and conditions of the men whom she had fascinated; and as Miss Havisham dwelt upon this roll[4] with the intensity of a mind mortally hurt and diseased, she sat with her other hand on her crutch stick, and her chin on that, and her <u>wan</u> bright eyes glaring at me, a very specter.[5]

◀ Why does Estella retell her activities?

I saw in this, wretched though it made me, and bitter the sense of dependence, even of degradation, that it awakened—I saw in this that Estella was set to wreak Miss Havisham's

◀ What does Pip understand?

---

4. **roll.** List of names
5. **specter.** Ghost or apparition

Words
For
Everyday
Use

rear (rir) *vt.*, raise; nurture; train
wan (wän) *adj.*, sickly; pallid

revenge on men, and that she was not to be given to me until she had gratified it for a term. I saw in this a reason for her being beforehand assigned to me. Sending her out to attract and torment and do mischief, Miss Havisham sent her with the malicious assurance that she was beyond the reach of all admirers, and that all who staked upon that cast[6] were secured to lose. I saw in this, that I, too, was tormented by a perversion of ingenuity, even while the prize was reserved for me. I saw in this the reason for my being staved off[7] so long, and the reason for my late guardian's declining to commit himself to the formal knowledge of such a scheme. In a word, I saw in this Miss Havisham as I had her then and there before my eyes; and always had had her before my eyes; and I saw in this the distinct shadow of the darkened and unhealthy house in which her life was hidden from the sun.

The candles that lighted that room of hers were placed in sconces[8] on the wall. They were high from the ground, and they burnt with the steady dullness of artificial light in air that is seldom renewed. As I looked round at them, and at the pale gloom they made, and at the stopped clock, and at the withered articles of bridal dress upon the table and the ground, and at her own awful figure with its ghostly reflection thrown large by the fire upon the ceiling and the wall, I saw in everything the construction that my mind had come to, repeated and thrown back to me. My thoughts passed into the great room across the landing where the table was spread, and I saw it written, as it were, in the falls of the cobwebs from the centerpiece, in the crawlings of the spiders on the cloth, in the tracks of the mice as they betook their little quickened hearts behind the panels, and in the gropings and pausings of the beetles on the floor.

▶ What surprises Pip?

It happened on the occasion of this visit that some sharp words arose between Estella and Miss Havisham. It was the first time I had ever seen them opposed.

▶ About what do they argue?

We were seated by the fire, as just now described, and Miss Havisham still had Estella's arm drawn through her own, and still clutched Estella's hand in hers, when Estella gradually began to detach herself. She had shown a proud impatience more than once before, and had rather endured that fierce affection than accepted or returned it.

"What!" said Miss Havisham, flashing her eyes upon her, "are you tired of me?"

---

6. **staked . . . cast.** Appeared on that list
7. **staved off.** Warded off; prevented
8. **sconces.** Decorative wall brackets for candles

"Only a little tired of myself," replied Estella, disengaging her arm, and moving to the great chimney-piece, where she stood looking down at the fire.

"Speak the truth, you <u>ingrate</u>!" cried Miss Havisham passionately striking her stick upon the floor; "you are tired of me."

Estella looked at her with perfect composure, and again looked down at the fire. Her graceful figure and her beautiful face expressed a self-possessed indifference to the wild heat of the other that was almost cruel.

"You stock and stone!" exclaimed Miss Havisham. "You cold, cold heart!"

"What!" said Estella, preserving her attitude of indifference as she leaned against the great chimney-piece and only moving her eyes; "do you reproach me for being cold? You?"

"Are you not?" was the fierce retort.

"You should know," said Estella. "I am what you have made me. Take all the praise, take all the blame; take all the success, take all the failure; in short, take me."

"Oh, look at her, look at her!" cried Miss Havisham bitterly, "Look at her, so hard and thankless, on the hearth where she was reared! Where I took her into this wretched breast when it was first bleeding from its stabs, and where I have lavished years of tenderness upon her!"

◄ *What does Miss Havisham want?*

"At least I was no party to the compact,"[9] said Estella, "for if I could walk and speak, when it was made, it was as much as I could do. But what would you have? You have been very good to me, and I owe everything to you. What would you have?"

"Love," replied the other.

"You have it."

"I have not," said Miss Havisham.

"Mother by adoption," retorted Estella, never departing from the easy grace of her attitude, never raising her voice as the other did, never yielding either to anger or tenderness. "Mother by adoption, I have said that I owe everything to you. All I possess is freely yours. All that you have given me is at your command to have again. Beyond that, I have nothing. And if you ask me to give you what you never gave me, my gratitude and duty cannot do impossibilities."

---

9. **compact.** Agreement

"Did I never give her love!" cried Miss Havisham, turning wildly to me. "Did I never give her a burning love, inseparable from jealousy at all times, and from sharp pain, while she speaks thus to me! Let her call me mad, let her call me mad!"

"Why should I call you mad," returned Estella, "I, of all people? Does anyone live who knows what set purposes you have half as well as I do? Does anyone live who knows what a steady memory you have half as well as I do? I who have sat on this same hearth on the little stool that is even now beside you there, learning your lessons and looking up into your face, when your face was strange and frightened me!"

▶ Why is Estella indignant?

"Soon forgotten!" moaned Miss Havisham. "Times soon forgotten!"

"No, not forgotten," retorted Estella. "Not forgotten, but treasured up in my memory. When have you found me false to your teaching? When have you found me unmindful of your lessons? When have you found me giving <u>admission</u> here," she touched her bosom with her hand, "to anything that you excluded? Be just to me."

"So proud, so proud!" moaned Miss Havisham, pushing away her gray hair with both her hands.

"Who taught me to be proud?" returned Estella. "Who praised me when I learnt my lesson?"

"So hard, so hard!" moaned Miss Havisham, with her former action.

▶ What upsets Miss Havisham?

"Who taught me to be hard?" returned Estella. "Who praised me when I learnt my lesson?"

"But to be proud and hard to *me!*" Miss Havisham quite shrieked, as she stretched out her arms. "Estella, Estella, Estella, to be proud and hard to *me!*"

Estella looked at her for a moment with a kind of calm wonder, but was not otherwise disturbed; when the moment was past, she looked down at the fire again.

"I cannot think," said Estella, raising her eyes after a silence, "why you should be so unreasonable when I come to see you after a separation. I have never forgotten your wrongs and their causes. I have never been unfaithful to you or your schooling. I have never shown any weakness that I can charge myself with."

"Would it be weakness to return my love?" exclaimed Miss Havisham. "But yes, yes, she would call it so!"

Words
For
Everyday
Use

ad • mis • sion (ad mish´ən) *n.*, giving as a right; entrance

"I begin to think," said Estella, in a musing way, after another moment of calm wonder, "that I almost understand how this comes about. If you had brought up your adopted daughter wholly in the dark <u>confinement</u> of these rooms, and had never let her know that there was such a thing as the daylight by which she has never once seen your face—if you had done that, and then, for a purpose, had wanted her to understand the daylight and know all about it, you would have been disappointed and angry?"

Miss Havisham, with her head in her hands, sat making a low moaning, and swaying herself on her chair, but gave no answer.

"Or," said Estella, "—which is a nearer case—if you had taught her, from the dawn of her intelligence, with your utmost energy and might, that there was such a thing as daylight, but that it was made to be her enemy and destroyer, and she must always turn against it, for it had <u>blighted</u> you and would else blight her—if you had done this, and then, for a purpose, had wanted her to take naturally to the daylight and she could not do it, you would have been disappointed and angry?"

Miss Havisham sat listening (or it seemed so, for I could not see her face), but still made no answer.

"So," said Estella, "I must be taken as I have been made. The success is not mine, the failure is not mine, but the two together make me."

Miss Havisham had settled down, I hardly knew how, upon the floor, among the faded bridal relics[10] with which it was strewn. I took advantage of the moment—I had sought one from the first—to leave the room, after beseeching Estella's attention to her with a movement of my hand. When I left, Estella was yet standing by the great chimney-piece, just as she had stood throughout. Miss Havisham's gray hair was all adrift upon the ground, among the other bridal wrecks, and was a miserable sight to see.

It was with a depressed heart that I walked in the starlight for an hour and more, about the courtyard, and about the brewery, and about the ruined garden. When I at last took courage to return to the room, I found Estella sitting at Miss

◄ What has Miss Havisham done to make Estella who she is? What metaphor does Estella use to communicate her point?

---

10. **relics.** Objects kept as souvenirs of the past

Words For Everyday Use

con • fine • ment (kən fīn′mənt) n., restriction; restraint
blight (blīt) vt., disappoint; frustrate; wither the hopes of

Havisham's knee, taking up some stitches in one of those old articles of dress that were dropping to pieces, and of which I have often been reminded since by the faded tatters of old banners that I have seen hanging up in cathedrals. Afterwards, Estella and I played at cards, as of yore—only we were skillful now, and played French games—and so the evening wore away, and I went to bed.

I lay in that separate building across the courtyard. It was the first time I had ever lain down to rest in Satis House, and sleep refused to come near me. A thousand Miss Havishams haunted me. She was on this side of my pillow, on that, at the head of the bed, at the foot, behind the half-opened door of the dressing room, in the dressing room, in the room overhead, in the room beneath—everywhere. At last, when the night was slow to creep on towards two o'clock, I felt that I absolutely could no longer bear the place as a place to lie down in, and that I must get up. I therefore got up and put on my clothes, and went out across the yard into the long stone passage, designing to gain the outer courtyard and walk there for the relief of my mind. But, I was no sooner in the passage than I extinguished my candle, for I saw Miss Havisham going along in a ghostly manner, making a low cry. I followed her at a distance, and saw her go up the staircase. She carried a bare candle in her hand, which she had probably taken from one of the sconces in her own room, and was a most unearthly object by its light. Standing at the bottom of the staircase, I felt the mildewed air of the feast-chamber, without seeing her open the door, and I heard her walking there, and so across into her own room, and so across again into that, never ceasing the low cry. After a time, I tried in the dark both to get out and to go back, but I could do neither until some streaks of day strayed in and showed me where to lay my hands. During the whole interval, whenever I went to the bottom of the staircase, I heard her footstep, saw her light pass above, and heard her ceaseless low cry.

Before we left next day, there was no revival of the difference between her and Estella, nor was it ever revived on any similar occasion; and there were four similar occasions, to the best of my remembrance. Nor did Miss Havisham's manner towards Estella in anywise change, except that I believed it to have something like fear <u>infused</u> among its former characteristics.

▶ *What does Pip see and hear?*

▶ *What changes between the women?*

Words For Everyday Use	**in • fuse** (in fyōoz´) *vt.,* fill with a quality or feeling

It is impossible to turn this leaf of my life without putting Bentley Drummle's name upon it; or I would, very gladly.

On a certain occasion when the Finches were assembled in force, and when good feeling was being promoted in the usual manner by nobody's agreeing with anybody else, the presiding Finch called the Grove to order, forasmuch as Mr. Drummle had not yet toasted a lady; which, according to the solemn constitution of the society, it was the brute's turn to do that day. I thought I saw him <u>leer</u> in an ugly way at me while the decanters were going round, but as there was no love lost between us, that might easily be. What was my indignant surprise when he called upon the company to pledge him to "Estella!"

◄ Whom does Drummle toast? What does Pip do?

"Estella who?" said I.

"Never you mind," retorted Drummle.

"Estella of where?" said I. "You are bound to say of where." Which he was, as a Finch.

"Of Richmond, gentlemen," said Drummle, putting me out of the question, "and a peerless beauty."

Much he knew about peerless beauties, a mean miserable idiot! I whispered Herbert.

"I know that lady," said Herbert, across the table, when the toast had been honored.

"*Do* you?" said Drummle.

"And so do I," I added with a scarlet face.

"*Do* you?" said Drummle. "*Oh,* Lord!"

This was the only retort—except glass or crockery—that the heavy creature was capable of making; but, I became as highly <u>incensed</u> by it as if it had been barbed with wit, and I immediately rose in my place and said that I could not but regard it as being like the honorable Finch's impudence to come down to that Grove—we always talked about coming down to that Grove, as a neat Parliamentary turn of expression—down to that Grove, proposing a lady of whom he knew nothing. Mr. Drummle upon this, starting up, demanded what I meant by that. Whereupon I made him the extreme reply that I believed he knew where I was to be found.

Whether it was possible in a Christian country to get on without blood, after this, was a question on which the Finches were divided. The debate upon it grew so lively, indeed, that at least six more honorable members told six

| Words For Everyday Use | **leer** (lir) *vi.*, look at in a sly, lewd way |
| | **in • censed** (in sensd´) *adj.*, very angry |

more, during the discussion, that they believed *they* knew where *they* were to be found. However, it was decided at last (the Grove being a court of honor) that if Mr. Drummle would bring never so slight a certificate from the lady, <u>importing</u> that he had the honor of her acquaintance, Mr. Pip must express his regret, as a gentleman and a Finch, for "having been betrayed into a warmth which." Next day was appointed for the production (lest our honor should take cold from delay), and next day Drummle appeared with a polite little <u>avowal</u> in Estella's hand that she had had the honor of dancing with him several times. This left me no course but to regret that I had been "betrayed into a warmth which," and on the whole to repudiate, as <u>untenable</u>, the idea that I was to be found anywhere. Drummle and I then sat snorting at one another for an hour, while the Grove engaged in <u>indiscriminate</u> contradiction, and finally the promotion of good feeling was declared to have gone ahead at an amazing rate.

▶ *Why is Pip angry?*

I tell this lightly, but it was no light thing to me. For I cannot adequately express what pain it gave me to think that Estella should show any favor to a contemptible, clumsy, sulky booby, so very far below the average. To the present moment, I believe it to have been referable to some pure fire of generosity and disinterestedness in my love for her that I could not endure the thought of her stooping to that hound. No doubt I should have been miserable whomsoever she had favored, but a worthier object would have caused me a different kind and degree of distress.

It was easy for me to find out, and I did soon find out, that Drummle had begun to follow her closely, and that she allowed him to do it. A little while, and he was always in pursuit of her, and he and I crossed one another every day. He held on, in a dull persistent way, and Estella held him on; now with encouragement, now with discouragement, now almost flattering him, now openly despising him, now knowing him very well, now scarcely remembering who he was.

The Spider, as Mr. Jaggers had called him, was used to lying in wait, however, and had the patience of his tribe. Added to that, he had a blockhead confidence in his money and in his family greatness, which sometimes did him good service— almost taking the place of concentration and determined

---

Words For Everyday Use

im • port (im pôrt´) *vt.*, mean; signify an important action

a • vow • al (ə vou´əl) *n.*, acknowledgment

un • ten • a • ble (un ten´ə bəl) *adj.*, not defendable

in • dis • crim • i • nate (in´dis krim´ə nit) *adj.*, random; haphazard; confused purpose. So, the Spider, <u>doggedly</u> watching Estella, out-watched many brighter insects, and would often uncoil himself and drop at the right nick of time.

At a certain Assembly Ball[11] at Richmond (there used to be Assembly Balls at most places then), where Estella had outshone all other beauties, this blundering Drummle so hung about her, and with so much toleration on her part, that I resolved to speak to her concerning him. I took the next opportunity, which was when she was waiting for Mrs. Brandley to take her home, and was sitting apart among some flowers, ready to go. I was with her, for I almost always accompanied them to and from such places.

"Are you tired, Estella?"

"Rather, Pip."

"You should be."

"Say, rather, I should not be, for I have my letter to Satis House to write before I go to sleep."

"Recounting tonight's triumph?" said I. "Surely a very poor one, Estella."

"What do you mean? I didn't know there had been any."

"Estella," said I, "do look at that fellow in the corner yonder who is looking over here at us."

"Why should I look at him?" returned Estella, with her eyes on me instead. "What is there in that fellow in the corner yonder—to use your words—that I need look at?"

"Indeed, that is the very question I want to ask you," said I. "For he has been hovering about you all night."

◀ What is Estella's plan for her suitors?

"Moths, and all sorts of ugly creatures," replied Estella, with a glance towards him, "hover about a lighted candle. Can the candle help it?"

"No," I returned: "but cannot the Estella help it?"

"Well!" said she, laughing after a moment, "perhaps. Yes. Anything you like."

"But, Estella, do hear me speak. It makes me wretched that you should encourage a man so generally despised as Drummle. You know he is despised."

"Well?" said she.

"You know he is as ungainly within as without. A <u>deficient</u>, ill-tempered, lowering, stupid fellow."

---

11. **Assembly Ball.** Formal gathering for social dancing

Words For Everyday Use

dog • ged • ly (dôg´id lē) *adv.*, persistently
de • fi • cient (dē fish´ənt) *adj.*, lacking; incomplete; defective

"Well?" said she.

"You know he has nothing to recommend him but money, and a ridiculous roll of addle-headed predecessors;[12] now, don't you?"

"Well?" said she again; and each time she said it, she opened her lovely eyes the wider.

To overcome the difficulty of getting past that monosyllable, I took it from her, and said, repeating it with emphasis, "Well! Then, that is why it makes me wretched."

Now, if I could have believed that she favored Drummle with any idea of making me—me—wretched, I should have been in better heart about it; but in that habitual way of hers, she put me so entirely out of the question that I could believe nothing of the kind.

"Pip," said Estella, casting her glance over the room, "don't be foolish about its effect on you. It may have its effect on others, and may be meant to have. It's not worth discussing."

"Yes it is," said I, "because I cannot bear that people should say, 'She throws away her graces and attractions on a mere boor, the lowest in the crowd.'"

"I can bear it," said Estella.

"Oh! don't be so proud, Estella, and so inflexible."

"Calls me proud and inflexible in this breath!" said Estella, opening her hands. "And in his last breath reproached me for stooping to a boor!"

▶ What does Pip ask Estella? What is her answer?

"There is no doubt you do," said I something hurriedly, "for I have seen you give him looks and smiles this very night, such as you never give to—me."

"Do you want me then," said Estella, turning suddenly with a fixed and serious, if not angry, look "to deceive and entrap you?"

"Do you deceive and entrap him, Estella?"

"Yes, and many others—all of them but you. Here is Mrs. Brandley. I'll say no more."

And now that I have given the one chapter to the theme that so filled my heart, and so often made it ache and ache again, I pass on, unhindered, to the event that had <u>impended</u> over me longer yet; the event that had begun to be prepared

---

12. **roll . . . predecessors.** Line of silly, useless ancestors

Words
For
Everyday
Use

im • **pend** (im pend´) *vi.*, hang; be about to take place for, before I knew that the world held Estella, and in the days when her baby intelligence was receiving its first <u>distortions</u> from Miss Havisham's wasting hands.

In the Eastern story,[13] the heavy slab[14] that was to fall on the bed of state[15] in the flush[16] of conquest was slowly wrought out of the quarry, the tunnel for the rope to hold it in its place was slowly carried through the leagues[17] of rock, the slab was slowly raised and fitted in the roof, the rope was rove[18] to it and slowly taken through the miles of hollow to the great iron ring. All being made ready with much labor, and the hour come, the sultan[19] was aroused in the dead of the night, and the sharpened axe that was to <u>sever</u> the rope from the great iron ring was put into his hand, and he struck with it, and the rope parted and rushed away, and the ceiling fell. So, in my case; all the work, near and afar, that tended to the end had been accomplished, and in an instant the blow was struck, and the roof of my stronghold dropped upon me.

---

13. **Eastern story.** A Persian story from *Tales of the Genii*
14. **slab.** Broad, thick piece of rock
15. **bed of state.** Bed of the ruler
16. **flush.** Exhilaration
17. **leagues.** Units of distance equal to three miles
18. **rove.** Fastened
19. **sultan.** Muslim ruler

Words For Everyday Use

dis • tor • tion (di stôr´shən) *n.,* misrepresentation; twisted information

sev • er (sev´ər) *vt.,* separate by cutting

CHAPTER 39

▶ *What are the details of Pip's life?*

I was three-and-twenty years of age. Not another word had I heard to enlighten me on the subject of my expectations, and my twenty-third birthday was a week gone. We had left Barnard's Inn more than a year, and lived in the Temple.[1] Our chambers were in Garden Court, down by the river.

Mr. Pocket and I had for some time parted company as to our original relations, though we continued on the best terms. Notwithstanding my inability to settle to anything—which I hope arose out of the restless and incomplete <u>tenure</u> on which I held my means—I had a taste for reading, and read regularly so many hours a day. That matter of Herbert's was still progressing, and everything with me was as I have brought it down to the close of the last preceding chapter.

Business had taken Herbert on a journey to Marseilles.[2] I was alone, and had a dull sense of being alone. Dispirited and anxious, long hoping that tomorrow or next week would clear my way, and long disappointed, I sadly missed the cheerful face and ready response of my friend.

It was wretched weather; stormy and wet, stormy and wet; mud, mud, mud, deep in all the streets. Day after day, a vast heavy veil had been driving over London from the east, and it drove still, as if in the east there were an eternity of cloud and wind. So furious had been the gusts that high buildings in town had had the lead stripped off their roofs; and in the country, trees had been torn up, and sails of windmills carried away; and gloomy accounts had come in from the coast of shipwreck and death. Violent blasts of rain had accompanied these rages of wind, and the day just closed as I sat down to read had been the worst of all.

Alterations have been made in that part of the Temple since that time, and it has not now so lonely a character as it had then, nor is it so exposed to the river. We lived at the top of the last house, and the wind rushing up the river shook the house that night, like discharges of cannon, or

---

1. **Temple.** A building between Fleet Street and the Thames River, named for the Knights Templar, thirteenth-century owners of the site
2. **Marseilles.** Principal seaport of France

Words For Everyday Use

ten • ure (ten´yər) *n.*, right of holding property

breakings of a sea. When the rain came with it and dashed against the windows, I thought, raising my eyes to them as they rocked, that I might have fancied myself in a storm-beaten lighthouse. Occasionally, the smoke came rolling down the chimney as though it could not bear to go out into such a night; and when I set the doors open and looked down the staircase, the staircase lamps were blown out; and when I shaded my face with my hands and looked through the black windows (opening them ever so little was out of the question in the teeth of such wind and rain), I saw that the lamps in the court were blown out, and that the lamps on the bridges and the shore were shuddering, and that the coal fires in barges³ on the river were being carried away before the wind like red-hot splashes in the rain.

I read with my watch upon the table, purposing to close my book at eleven o'clock. As I shut it, Saint Paul's, and all the many church-clocks in the City—some leading, some accompanying, some following—struck that hour. The sound was curiously <u>flawed</u> by the wind; and I was listening, and thinking how the wind assailed and tore it, when I heard a footstep on the stair.

◀ What does Pip hear? What does he do? Who is there?

What nervous <u>folly</u> made me start, and awfully connect it with the footstep of my dead sister, matters not. It was past in a moment, and I listened again, and heard the footstep stumble in coming on. Remembering, then, that the stair-case lights were blown out, I took up my reading lamp and went out to the stair-head. Whoever was below had stopped on seeing my lamp, for all was quiet.

"There is someone down there, is there not?" I called out, looking down.

"Yes," said a voice from the darkness beneath.

"What floor do you want?"

"The top. Mr. Pip."

"That is my name. There is nothing the matter?"

"Nothing the matter," returned the voice. And the man came on.

I stood with my lamp held out over the stair-rail, and he came slowly within its light. It was a shaded lamp, to shine upon a book, and its circle of light was very <u>contracted</u>; so

---

3. **barges.** Large flat-bottomed boats used for carrying freight

Words For Everyday Use

flaw (flô) *vt.,* spoil

fol • ly (fäl´ē) *n.,* foolishness

con • tract (kən trakt´) *vt.,* reduce in size; limit

that he was in it for a mere instant, and then out of it. In the instant I had seen a face that was strange to me, looking up with an incomprehensible air of being touched and pleased by the sight of me.

► What does the man look like? What surprises Pip?

Moving the lamp as the man moved, I made out that he was <u>substantially</u> dressed, but roughly, like a voyager by sea. That he had long iron-gray hair. That his age was about sixty. That he was a muscular man, strong on his legs, and that he was browned and hardened by exposure to weather. As he ascended the last stair or two, and the light of my lamp included us both, I saw, with a stupid kind of amazement, that he was holding out both his hands to me.

"Pray what is your business?" I asked him.

"My business?" he repeated, pausing. "Ah! Yes. I will explain my business, by your leave."

"Do you wish to come in?"

"Yes," he replied; "I wish to come in, master."

► Why does Pip resent the man's behavior?

I had asked him the question inhospitably enough, for I resented the sort of bright and gratified recognition that still shone in his face. I resented it because it seemed to imply that he expected me to respond to it. But I took him into the room I had just left, and, having set the lamp on the table, asked him as civilly as I could to explain himself.

He looked about him with the strangest air—an air of wondering pleasure, as if he had some part in the things he admired—and he pulled off a rough outer coat, and his hat. Then, I saw that his head was <u>furrowed</u> and bald, and that the long iron-gray hair grew only on its sides. But I saw nothing that in the least explained him. On the contrary, I saw him next moment once more holding out both his hands to me.

"What do you mean?" said I, half-suspecting him to be mad.

He stopped in his looking at me, and slowly rubbed his right hand over his head. "It's disappointing to a man," he said, in a coarse broken voice, "arter having looked for'ard so distant, and come so fur; but you're not to blame for that—neither on us is to blame for that. I'll speak in half a minute. Give me half a minute, please."

He sat down on a chair that stood before the fire, and covered his forehead with his large brown veinous hands. I looked at him attentively then, and <u>recoiled</u> a little from him; but I did not know him.

Words For Everyday Use

sub • stan • tial • ly (səb stan´shə lē) *adv.*, amply; plentifully

fur • rowed (fur´ōd) *adj.*, deeply wrinkled

re • coil (ri koil´) *vi.*, shrink back, as in fear or repugnance

"There's no one nigh," said he, looking over his shoulder, "is there?"

"Why do you, a stranger coming into my rooms at this time of the night, ask that question?" said I.

"You're a game one," he returned, shaking his head at me with a deliberate affection, at once most unintelligible and most <u>exasperating</u>; "I'm glad you've grow'd up a game[4] one! But don't catch hold of me. You'd be sorry arterwards to have done it."

◀ Why is the man proud? Who does Pip recognize him to be?

I <u>relinquished</u> the intention he had detected, for I knew him! Even yet I could not recall a single feature, but I knew him! If the wind and the rain had driven away the intervening years, had scattered all the intervening objects, had swept us to the churchyard where we first stood face to face on such different levels, I could not have known my convict more distinctly than I knew him now, as he sat in the chair before the fire. No need to take a file from his pocket and show it to me; no need to take the handkerchief from his neck and twist it round his head; no need to hug himself with both his arms, and take a shivering turn across the room, looking back at me for recognition. I knew him before he gave me one of those aids, though, a moment before, I had not been conscious of <u>remotely</u> suspecting his identity.

He came back to where I stood, and again held out both his hands. Not knowing what to do—for, in my astonishment I had lost my self-possession—I reluctantly gave him my hands. He grasped them heartily, raised them to his lips, kissed them, and still held them.

◀ What does the convict tell Pip? What is his response?

"You acted noble, my boy," said he. "Noble Pip! And I have never forgot it!"

At a change in his manner as if he were even going to embrace me, I laid a hand upon his breast and put him away.

"Stay!" said I. "Keep off! If you are grateful to me for what I did when I was a little child, I hope you have shown your gratitude by mending your way of life. If you have come here to thank me, it was not necessary. Still, however, you have found me out, there must be something good in the feeling that has brought you here, and I will not repulse you; but surely you must understand that—I—"

---

4. **game.** Plucky, spirited, and resourceful

Words For Everyday Use	**ex • as • per • at • ing** (eg zas′pər āt′iŋ) *adj.*, irritating; frustrating
	re • lin • quish (ri liŋ′kwish) *vt.*, give up; abandon; set aside
	re • mote • ly (ri mōt′lē) *adv.*, distantly; faintly

My attention was so attracted by the singularity of his fixed look at me that the words died away on my tongue.

"You was a-saying," he observed, when we had confronted one another in silence, "that surely I must understand. What, surely must I understand?"

► What does Pip say he cannot do? Why?

"That I cannot wish to renew that chance intercourse with you of long ago, under these different circumstances. I am glad to believe you have repented and recovered yourself. I am glad to tell you so. I am glad that, thinking I deserve to be thanked, you have come to thank me. But our ways are different ways, none the less. You are wet, and you look weary. Will you drink something before you go?"

He had replaced his neckerchief loosely, and had stood, keenly observant of me, biting a long end of it. "I think," he answered, still with the end at his mouth and still observant of me, "that I *will* drink (I thank you) afore I go."

There was a tray ready on a side-table. I brought it to the table near the fire, and asked him what he would have. He touched one of the bottles without looking at it or speaking, and I made him some hot rum-and-water. I tried to keep my hand steady while I did so, but his look at me as he leaned back in his chair with the long draggled[5] end of his neckerchief between his teeth—evidently forgotten—made my hand very difficult to master. When at last I put the glass to him, I saw with amazement that his eyes were full of tears.

► What is the convict's response to Pip's coldness?

Up to this time I had remained standing, not to disguise that I wished him gone. But I was softened by the softened aspect[6] of the man, and felt a touch of reproach. "I hope," said I, hurriedly putting something into a glass for myself, and drawing a chair to the table, "that you will not think I spoke harshly to you just now. I had no intention of doing it, and I am sorry for it if I did. I wish you well, and happy!"

As I put my glass to my lips, he glanced with surprise at the end of his neckerchief, dropping from his mouth when he opened it, and stretched out his hand. I gave him mine, and then he drank, and drew his sleeve across his eyes and forehead.

"How are you living?" I asked him.

► For what is the convict famous?

"I've been a sheep-farmer, stock-breeder,[7] other trades besides, away in the New World,"[8] said he, "many a thousand mile of stormy water off from this."

"I hope you have done well."

5. **draggled.** Wet and dirty
6. **aspect.** Appearance
7. **stock-breeder.** Person who raises livestock
8. **New World.** Usually refers to the countries of the Western Hemisphere, but here he means Australia.

"I've done wonderful well. There's others went out alonger[9] me as has done well, too, but no man has done nigh as well as me. I'm famous for it."

"I am glad to hear it."

"I hope to hear you say so, my dear boy."

Without stopping to try to understand those words or the tone in which they were spoken, I turned off to a point that had just come into my mind.

"Have you ever seen a messenger you once sent to me," I inquired, "since he undertook that trust?"

"Never set eyes upon him. I warn't likely to it."

"He came faithfully, and he brought me the two one-pound notes.[10] I was a poor boy then, as you know, and to a poor boy they were a little fortune. But, like you, I have done well since, and you must let me pay them back. You can put them to some other poor boy's use." I took out my purse.

He watched me as I laid my purse upon the table and opened it, and he watched me as I separated two one-pound notes from its contents. They were clean and new, and I spread them out and handed them over to him. Still watching me, he laid them one upon the other, folded them longwise, gave them a twist, set fire to them at the lamp, and dropped the ashes into the tray.

◄ Of what does Pip reassure the convict? What does he do?

"May I make so bold," he said then, with a smile that was like a frown, and with a frown that was like a smile, "as ask you *how* you have done well, since you and me was out on them lone shivering marshes?"

"How?"

"Ah!"

◄ What does the convict want to know?

He emptied his glass, got up, and stood at the side of the fire, with his heavy brown hand on the mantelshelf. He put a foot up to the bars, to dry and warm it, and the wet boot began to steam; but he neither looked at it, nor at the fire, but steadily looked at me. It was only now that I began to tremble.

When my lips had parted, and had shaped some words that were without sound, I forced myself to tell him (though I could not do it distinctly), that I had been chosen to succeed to[11] some property.

"Might a mere warmint[12] ask what property?" said he.

I faltered, "I don't know."

"Might a mere warmint ask whose property?" said he.

I faltered again, "I don't know."

---

9. **alonger.** Along with
10. **notes.** Bills; cash money
11. **succeed to.** Come into ownership of
12. **warmint.** Varmint; undesirable, obnoxious, or troublesome person

▶ What does Pip come to realize?

"Could I make a guess, I wonder," said the convict, "at your income since you come of age! As to the first figure, now. Five?"

With my heart beating like a heavy hammer of disordered action, I rose out of my chair, and stood with my hand upon the back of it, looking wildly at him.

"Concerning a guardian," he went on. "There ought to have been some guardian or such-like, whiles you was a minor. Some lawyer, maybe. As to the first letter of that lawyer's name, now. Would it be J?"

All the truth of my position came flashing on me, and its disappointments, dangers, disgraces, consequences of all kinds rushed in in such a multitude that I was borne down by them and had to struggle for every breath I drew. "Put it," he resumed, "as the employer of that lawyer whose name begun with a J, and might be Jaggers—put it as he had come over sea to Portsmouth, and had landed there, and had wanted to come on to you. 'However, you have found me out,' you says just now. Well, however, did I find you out? Why, I wrote from Portsmouth to a person in London for particulars of your address. That person's name? Why, Wemmick."

▶ What is Pip's reaction to this unexpected news?

I could not have spoken one word, though it had been to save my life. I stood, with a hand on the chair-back and a hand on my breast, where I seemed to be suffocating—I stood so, looking wildly at him, until I grasped at the chair, when the room began to <u>surge</u> and turn. He caught me, drew me to the sofa, put me up against the cushions, and bent on one knee before me, bringing the face that I now well remembered, and that I shuddered at, very near to mine.

▶ What was the convict's pledge?

"Yes, Pip, dear boy, I've made a gentleman on you! It's me wot has done it! I swore that time, sure as ever I earned a guinea, that guinea should go to you. I swore arterwards, sure as ever I spec'lated[13] and got rich, you should get rich. I lived rough, that you should live smooth; I worked hard that you should be above work. What odds, dear boy? Do I tell it fur you to feel a <u>obligation</u>? Not a bit. I tell it fur you to know as that there hunted dunghill dog wot you kep life in got his head so high that he could make a gentleman—and, Pip, you're him!"

---

13. **spec'lated.** Speculated; engaged in buying and selling with an element of risk in hopes of large profit

Words For Everyday Use

surge (sʉrj) *vi.*, move in a swelling motion

ob • li • ga • tion (äb´lə gā´shən) *n.*, responsibility

The abhorrence in which I held the man, the dread I had of him, the <u>repugnance</u> with which I shrank from him could not have been exceeded if he had been some terrible beast.

◄ How does Pip view the convict? How does the convict view him?

"Look'ee here, Pip. I'm your second father. You're my son—more to me nor any son. I've put away money, only for you to spend. When I was a hired-out shepherd in a solitary hut, not seeing no faces but faces of sheep till I half-forgot wot men's and women's faces wos like, I see yourn. I drops my knife many a time in that hut when I was a-eating my dinner or my supper, and I says, 'Here's the boy again, a-looking at me whiles I eats and drinks!' I see you there a many times as plain as ever I see you on them misty marshes. 'Lord strike me dead!' I says each time—and I goes out in the open air to say it under the open heavens—'but wot, if I gets liberty and money, I'll make that boy a gentleman!' And I done it. Why, look at you, dear boy! Look at these here lodgings of yourn, fit for a lord! A lord? Ah! You shall show money with lords for wagers, and beat 'em!"

In his heat and triumph, and in his knowledge that I had been nearly fainting, he did not remark on[14] my reception of all this. It was the one grain of relief I had.

◄ What does the convict not notice? To what does he pay attention?

"Look'ee here!" he went on, taking my watch out of my pocket, and turning towards him a ring on my finger, while I recoiled from his touch as if he had been a snake, "a gold 'un and a beauty—*that's* a gentleman's, I hope! A diamond all set round with rubies—*that's* a gentleman's, I hope! Look at your linen—fine and beautiful! Look at your clothes—better ain't to be got! And your books, too," turning his eyes round the room, "mounting up, on their shelves, by hundreds! And you read 'em, don't you? I see you'd been a-reading of 'em when I come in. Ha, ha, ha! You shall read 'em to me, dear boy! And if they're in foreign languages wot I don't understand, I shall be just as proud as if I did."

Again he took both my hands and put them to his lips, while my blood ran cold within me.

"Don't you mind talking, Pip," said he, after again drawing his sleeve over his eyes and forehead, as the click came in his throat which I well remembered—and he was all the more horrible to me that he was so much in earnest;[15] "you can't do

◄ Does the convict expect Pip to know that he was the secret benefactor?

---

14. **remark on.** Notice
15. **in earnest.** In a serious or determined manner

Words For Everyday Use	**re • pug • nance** (ri pug´nəns) *n.,* aversion; distaste

better nor keep quiet, dear boy. You ain't looked slowly forward to this as I have; you wosn't prepared for this, as I wos. But didn't you never think it might be me?"

"Oh, no, no, no," I returned, "Never, never!"

"Well, you see it *wos* me, and single-handed. Never a soul in it but my own self and Mr. Jaggers."

"Was there no one else?" I asked.

"No," said he, with a glance of surprise. "Who else should there be? And, dear boy, how good-looking you have growed! There's bright eyes somewheres—eh? Isn't there bright eyes somewheres, wot you love the thoughts on?"

O Estella, Estella!

"They shall be yourn, dear boy, if money can buy 'em. Not that a gentleman like you, so well set up as you, can't win 'em off of his own game; but money shall back you! Let me finish wot I was a-telling you, dear boy. From that there hut and that there hiring-out, I got money left me by my master (which died, and had been the same as me), and got my liberty and went for myself. In every single thing I went for, I went for you. 'Lord strike a blight upon it,' I says, wotever it was I went for, 'if it ain't for him!' It all prospered wonderful. As I giv' you to understand just now, I'm famous for it. It was the money left me, and the gains of the first few year, wot I sent home to Mr. Jaggers—all for you—when he first come arter you, agreeable to my letter."

O that he had never come! That he had left me at the forge—far from contented, yet, by comparison, happy!

"And then, dear boy, it was a <u>recompense</u> to me, look'ee here, to know in secret that I was making a gentleman. The blood horses of them colonists might fling up the dust over me as I was walking; what do I say? I says to myself, 'I'm making a better gentleman nor ever *you'll* be!' When one of 'em says to another, 'He was a convict, a few year ago, and is a ignorant common fellow now, for all he's lucky,' what do I say? I says to myself, 'If I ain't a gentleman, nor yet ain't got no learning, I'm the owner of such. All on you owns stock and land; which on you owns a brought-up London gentleman?' This way I kep myself a-going. And this way I held steady afore my mind that I would for certain come one day and see my boy, and make myself known to him, on his own ground."

How did the convict get his start?

What motivates the convict? What is his dream?

Words For Everyday Use

rec • om • pense (rek´əm pens´) *n.*, repayment; reward

He laid his hand on my shoulder. I <u>shuddered</u> at the thought that for anything I knew, his hand might be stained with blood.

"It warn't easy, Pip, for me to leave them parts, nor yet it warn't safe. But I held to it, and the harder it was, the stronger I held, for I was determined, and my mind firm made up. At last I done it. Dear boy, I done it!"

I tried to collect my thoughts, but I was stunned. Throughout, I had seemed to myself to attend more to the wind and the rain than to him; even now I could not separate his voice from those voices, though those were loud and his was silent.

"Where will you put me?" he asked presently. "I must be put somewheres, dear boy."

"To sleep?" said I.

"Yes. And to sleep long and sound," he answered, "for I've been sea-tossed and sea-washed, months and months."

"My friend and companion," said I, rising from the sofa, "is absent; you must have his room."

"He won't come back tomorrow, will he?"

"No," said I, answering almost mechanically, in spite of my utmost efforts, "not tomorrow."

"Because, look'ee here, dear boy," he said, dropping his voice, and laying a long finger on my breast in an impressive manner, "caution is necessary."

◄ *What danger does the convict face?*

"How do you mean, caution?"

"By G—, it's death!"

"What's death?"

"I was sent for life. It's death to come back. There's been overmuch coming back of late years, and I should of certainty be hanged if took."

Nothing was needed but this; the wretched man, after loading me with his wretched gold and silver chains for years, had risked his life to come to me, and I held it there in my keeping! If I had loved him instead of abhorring him, if I had been attracted to him by the strongest admiration and affection, instead of shrinking from him with the strongest repugnance, it could have been no worse. On the contrary, it would have been better, for his preservation would then have naturally and tenderly addressed my heart.

◄ *What does Pip realize?*

My first care was to close the shutters, so that no light might be seen from without, and then to close and make fast

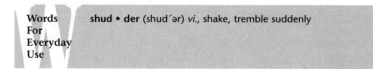

Words For Everyday Use

shud • der (shud´ər) *vi.,* shake, tremble suddenly

the doors. While I did so, he stood at the table drinking rum and eating biscuit; and when I saw him thus engaged, I saw my convict on the marshes at his meal again. It almost seemed to me as if he must stoop down presently, to file at his leg.

When I had gone into Herbert's room, and had shut off any other communication between it and the staircase than through the room in which our conversation had been held, I asked him if he would go to bed. He said yes, but asked me for some of my "gentleman's linen" to put on in the morning. I brought it out, and laid it ready for him, and my blood again ran cold when he again took me by both hands to give me good night.

I got away from him, without knowing how I did it, and mended the fire in the room where we had been together, and sat down by it, afraid to go to bed. For an hour or more, I remained too stunned to think; and it was not until I began to think that I began fully to know how wrecked I was, and how the ship in which I had sailed was gone to pieces.

▶ What painful realization does Pip come to? What troubles him even more?

Miss Havisham's intentions towards me, all a mere dream; Estella not designed for me; I only suffered in Satis House as a convenience, a sting for the greedy relations, a model with a mechanical heart to practice on when no other practice was at hand; those were the first smarts[16] I had. But, sharpest and deepest pain of all—it was for the convict, guilty of I knew not what crimes, and liable to be taken out of those rooms where I sat thinking, and hanged at the Old Bailey door, that I had deserted Joe.

I would not have gone back to Joe now, I would not have gone back to Biddy now, for any consideration—simply, I suppose, because my sense of my own worthless conduct to them was greater than every consideration. No wisdom on earth could have given me the comfort that I should have derived from their simplicity and <u>fidelity</u>; but I could never, never, never undo what I had done.

▶ Why is Pip frightened?

In every rage of wind and rush of rain, I heard pursuers. Twice I could have sworn there was a knocking and whispering at the outer door. With these fears upon me, I began either to imagine or recall that I had had mysterious warnings of this man's approach. That for weeks gone by I had passed

---

16. **smarts.** Stings; blows

Words For Everyday Use	**fi • del • i • ty** (fə del´ə tē) *n.*, faithfulness; trustworthiness

faces in the streets which I had thought like his. That these likenesses had grown more numerous, as he, coming over the sea, had drawn nearer. That his wicked spirit had somehow sent these messengers to mine, and that now on this stormy night he was as good as his word, and with me.

Crowding up with these reflections came the reflection that I had seen him with my childish eyes to be a desperately violent man; that I had heard that other convict <u>reiterate</u> that he had tried to murder him; that I had seen him down in the ditch, tearing and fighting like a wild beast. Out of such remembrances I brought into the light of the fire, a half-formed terror that it might not be safe to be shut up there with him in the dead of the wild solitary night. This <u>dilated</u> until it filled the room, and impelled me to take a candle and go in and look at my dreadful burden.

He had rolled a handkerchief round his head, and his face was set and lowering in his sleep. But he was asleep, and quietly, too, though he had a pistol lying on the pillow. Assured of this, I softly removed the key to the outside of his door, and turned it on him before I again sat down by the fire. Gradually I slipped from the chair and lay on the floor. When I awoke without having parted in my sleep with the perception of my wretchedness, the clocks of the eastward churches were striking five, the candles were wasted out, the fire was dead, and the wind and rain intensified the thick black darkness.

THIS IS THE END OF THE SECOND STAGE OF
PIP'S EXPECTATIONS

Words For Everyday Use

re • it • er • ate (rē it´ə rāt) vt., repeat
di • late (dī´ lāt) vt., expand

It was fortunate for me that I had to take precautions to insure (so far as I could) the safety of my dreaded visitor, for this thought pressing on me when I awoke held other thoughts in a confused concourse[1] at a distance.

► What is Pip's problem? What does he decide to do about it?

The impossibility of keeping him concealed in the chambers was self-evident. It could not be done, and the attempt to do it would inevitably <u>engender</u> suspicion. True, I had no Avenger in my service now, but I was looked after by an inflammatory[2] old female, assisted by an <u>animated</u> rag-bag whom she called her niece, and to keep a room secret from them would be to invite curiosity and exaggeration. They both had weak eyes, which I had long attributed to their chronically looking in at keyholes, and they were always at hand when not wanted; indeed, that was their only reliable quality besides larceny. Not to get up a mystery with these people, I resolved to announce in the morning that my uncle had unexpectedly come from the country.

► Why does Pip go downstairs? What does he find?

This course I decided on while I was yet groping about in the darkness for the means of getting a light. Not stumbling on the means after all, I was fain[3] to go out to the adjacent lodge and get the watchman there to come with his lantern. Now, in groping my way down the black staircase, I fell over something, and that something was a man crouching in a corner.

As the man made no answer when I asked him what he did there, but eluded my touch in silence, I ran to the lodge and urged the watchman to come quickly, telling him of the incident on the way back. The wind being as fierce as ever, we did not care to endanger the light in the lantern by <u>rekindling</u> the extinguished lamps on the staircase, but we examined the staircase from the bottom to the top and found no one there. It then occurred to me as possible that the man might have slipped into my rooms; so, lighting my candle at the watchman's, and leaving him standing at the door, I

---

1. **concourse.** Flowing together
2. **inflammatory.** Characterized by strong emotion, especially anger or aggression
3. **fain.** Obliged

Words For Everyday Use	**en • gen • der** (en jen´dər) *vt.*, bring about; cause
	an • i • ma • ted (an´ə mā´təd) *adj.*, lively
	re • kin • dle (rē kin´dəl) *vt.*, relight

examined them carefully, including the room in which my dreaded guest lay asleep. All was quiet, and assuredly no other man was in those chambers.

It troubled me that there should have been a lurker on the stairs, on that night of all nights in the year, and I asked the watchman, on the chance of <u>eliciting</u> some hopeful explanation as I handed him a dram[4] at the door, whether he had admitted at his gate any gentleman who had <u>perceptibly</u> been dining out? Yes, he said; at different times of the night, three. One lived in Fountain Court, and the other two lived in the Lane, and he had seen them all go home. Again, the only other man who dwelt in the house of which my chambers formed a part had been in the country for some weeks; and he certainly had not returned in the night, because we had seen his door with his seal on it as we came upstairs.

◄ Why is Pip troubled? What does he ask the watchman?

"The night being so bad, sir," said the watchman, as he gave me back my glass, "uncommon few have come in at my gate. Besides them three gentlemen that I have named, I don't call to mind another since about eleven o'clock, when a stranger asked for you."

"My uncle," I muttered. "Yes."

"You saw him, sir?"

"Yes. Oh, yes."

"Likewise the person with him?"

"Person with him!" I repeated.

◄ What is Pip told? How does the watchman describe the second man?

"I judged the person to be with him," returned the watchman. "The person stopped, when he stopped to make inquiry of me, and the person took this way when he took this way."

"What sort of person?"

The watchman had not particularly noticed; he should say a working person; to the best of his belief, he had a dust-colored kind of clothes on, under a dark coat. The watchman made more light of the matter than I did, and naturally, not having my reason for attaching weight to it.

When I had got rid of him, which I thought it well to do without prolonging explanations, my mind was much troubled by these two circumstances taken together. Whereas they were easy of innocent solution apart—as, for instance, some diner-out or diner-at-home who had not gone near this

---

4. **dram.** Small drink of liquor

Words For Everyday Use

e • lic • it (ē lis´it) *vt.,* draw forth; evoke

per • cep • ti • bly (pər sep´tə blē) *adv.,* noticeably

watchman's gate might have strayed to my staircase and dropped asleep there—and my nameless visitor might have brought someone with him to show him the way—still, joined, they had an ugly look to one as prone to distrust and fear as the changes of a few hours had made me.

I lighted my fire, which burnt with a raw pale flare at that time of the morning, and fell into a doze before it. I seemed to have been dozing a whole night when the clocks struck six. As there was full an hour and a half between me and daylight, I dozed again; now waking up uneasily, with prolix[5] conversations about nothing, in my ears; now making thunder of the wind in the chimney; at length falling off into a profound sleep from which the daylight woke me with a start.

► What does Pip find it impossible to do?

All this time I had never been able to consider my own situation, nor could I do so yet. I had not the power to attend to it. I was greatly dejected and distressed, but in an incoherent wholesale sort of way. As to forming any plan for the future, I could as soon have formed an elephant. When I opened the shutters and looked out at the wet wild morning, all of a leaden hue; when I walked from room to room; when I sat down again shivering, before the fire, waiting for my laundress[6] to appear; I thought how miserable I was, but hardly knew why, or how long I had been so, or on what day of the week I made the reflection, or even who I was that made it.

At last, the old woman and the niece came in—the latter with a head not easily distinguishable from her dusty broom—and testified surprise at sight of me and the fire. To whom I imparted how my uncle had come in the night and was then asleep, and how the breakfast preparations were to be modified accordingly. Then I washed and dressed while they knocked the furniture about and made a dust; and so, in a sort of dream or sleep-waking, I found myself sitting by the fire again, waiting for—him—to come to breakfast.

By-and-by, his door opened and he came out. I could not bring myself to bear the sight of him, and I thought he had a worse look by daylight.

"I do not even know," said I, speaking low as he took his seat at the table, "by what name to call you. I have given out that you are my uncle."

---

5. **prolix.** Wordy; long-winded
6. **laundress.** Woman whose work is washing and ironing clothes

| Words For Everyday Use | pro • found (prō found´) *adj.,* very deep |
| | mod • i • fy (mäd´ə fī´) *vt.,* change or alter |

"That's it, dear boy! Call me uncle."

"You <u>assumed</u> some name, I suppose, on board ship?"

"Yes, dear boy. I took the name of Provis."[7]

"Do you mean to keep that name?"

"Why, yes, dear boy, it's as good as another—unless you'd like another."

"What is your real name?" I asked him in a whisper.

"Magwitch," he answered, in the same tone; "chrisen'd Abel."

"What were you brought up to be?"

"A warmint, dear boy."

He answered quite seriously, and used the word as if it <u>denoted</u> some profession.

"When you came into the Temple last night—" said I, pausing to wonder whether that could really have been last night, which seemed so long ago.

"Yes, dear boy?"

"When you came in at the gate and asked the watchman the way here, had you anyone with you?"

"With me? No, dear boy."

"But there was someone there?"

"I didn't take particular notice," he said <u>dubiously</u>, "not knowing the ways of the place. But I think there *was* a person, too, come in alonger me."

"Are you known in London?"

"I hope not!" said he, giving his neck a jerk with his forefinger that made me turn hot and sick.

"Were you known in London, once?"

"Not over and above, dear boy. I was in the provinces[8] mostly."

"Were you—tried—in London?"

"Which time?" said he, with a sharp look.

"The last time."

He nodded. "First knowed Mr. Jaggers that way. Jaggers was for me."

It was on my lips to ask him what he was tried for, but he took up a knife, gave it a flourish, and with the words, "And what I done is worked out and paid for!" fell to[9] at his breakfast.

◀ What is the convict's assumed name? His real name?

◀ What does Pip learn about Provis's experiences in London?

---

7. **Provis.** Derived from a Latin word meaning "to provide"
8. **provinces.** Part of a country away from populated cultural centers
9. **fell to.** Began (an activity) energetically

Words
For
Everyday
Use

as • sume (ə so͞om´) *vt.*, adopt; pretend to have
de • note (dē nōt´) *vt.*, stand for
du • bi • ous • ly (do͞o´ bē əs lē) *adv.*, doubtfully; with hesitation

► What makes Provis's table manners so disagreeable?

He ate in a ravenous way that was very disagreeable, and all his actions were <u>uncouth</u>, noisy, and greedy. Some of his teeth had failed him since I saw him eat on the marshes, and as he turned his food in his mouth, and turned his head sideways to bring his strongest fangs to bear upon it, he looked terribly like a hungry old dog.

If I had begun with any appetite, he would have taken it away, and I should have sat much as I did—repelled from him by an <u>insurmountable</u> aversion, and gloomily looking at the cloth.

► What two activities does Provis enjoy most?

"I'm a heavy grubber,[10] dear boy," he said, as a polite kind of apology when he had made an end of his meal, "but I always was. If it had been in my constitution to be a lighter grubber, I might ha' got into lighter trouble. Similarly, I must have my smoke. When I was first hired out as shepherd t'other side the world, it's my belief I should ha' turned into a molloncolly-mad[11] sheep myself, if I hadn't a-had my smoke."

As he said so he got up from table, and putting his hand into the breast of the pea-coat he wore, brought out a short black pipe, and a handful of loose tobacco of the kind that is called Negro-head. Having filled his pipe, he put the surplus tobacco back again, as if his pocket were a drawer. Then he took a live coal from the fire with the tongs, and lighted his pipe at it, and then turned round on the hearth-rug with his back to the fire, and went through his favorite action of holding out both his hands for mine.

"And this," said he, <u>dandling</u> my hands up and down in his, as he puffed at his pipe, "and this is the gentleman what I made! The real genuine one! It does me good fur to look at you, Pip. All I stip'late[12] is to stand by and look at you, dear boy!"

I released my hands as soon as I could, and found that I was beginning slowly to settle down to the contemplation of my condition. What I was chained to, and how heavily, became intelligible to me, as I heard his hoarse voice, and sat looking up at his furrowed bald head with its iron gray hair at the sides.

---

10. **heavy grubber.** Heavy eater
11. **molloncolly-mad.** Melancholy; depressed; suffering from a mental disorder
12. **stip'late.** Stipulate; require

Words For Everyday Use

un • couth (un kōōth´) *adj.*, uncultured; crude

in • sur • mount • a • ble (in´sər mount´ə bəl) *adj.*, that cannot be overcome

dan • dle (dan´dəl) *vt.*, play with

"I mustn't see my gentleman a-footing it in the mire of the streets; there mustn't be no mud on *his* boots. My gentleman must have horses, Pip! Horses to ride, and horses to drive, and horses for his servant to ride and drive as well. Shall colonists have their horses (and blood-'uns, if you please, good Lord!) and not my London gentleman? No, no. We'll show 'em another pair of shoes than that, Pip, won't us?"

He took out of his pocket a great thick pocket-book, bursting with papers, and tossed it on the table.

◀ What does Provis show Pip? Why is he proud? What is he trying to prove?

"There's something worth spending in that there book, dear boy. It's yourn. All I've got ain't mine; it's yourn. Don't you be afeerd on it. There's more where that come from. I've come to the old country fur to see my gentleman spend his money *like* a gentleman. That'll be *my* pleasure. *My* pleasure 'ull be fur to see him do it. And blast you all!" he wound up, looking round the room and snapping his fingers once with a loud snap. "Blast you every one, from the judge in his wig to the colonist a-stirring up the dust, I'll show a better gentleman than the whole kit on you put together!"

"Stop!" said I, almost in a frenzy of fear and dislike, "I want to speak to you. I want to know what is to be done. I want to know how you are to be kept out of danger, how long you are going to stay, what projects you have."

"Look'ee here, Pip," said he, laying his hand on my arm in a suddenly altered and subdued manner; "first of all, look'ee here. I forgot myself half a minute ago. What I said was low; that's what it was; low. Look'ee here, Pip. Look over it. I ain't a-going to be low."

"First," I resumed, half-groaning, "what precautions can be taken against your being recognized and <u>seized</u>?"

"No, dear boy," he said, in the same tone as before, "that don't go first. Lowness goes first. I ain't took so many year to make a gentleman, not without knowing what's due to him. Look'ee here, Pip. I was low; that's what I was; low. Look over it, dear boy.

Some sense of the grimly <u>ludicrous</u> moved me to a fretful laugh, as I replied, "I *have* looked over it. In Heaven's name, don't harp upon it!"

"Yes, but look'ee here," he persisted. "Dear boy, I ain't come so fur, not fur to be low. Now, go on, dear boy. You was a-saying—"

| Words For Everyday Use | seize (sēz) *vt.*, take; capture |
| | lu • di • crous (lōō´di krəs) *adj.*, absurd |

► Who knows about Provis? What is the danger? Why isn't this danger enough to keep him away?

"How are you to be guarded from the danger you have incurred?"

"Well, dear boy, the danger ain't so great. Without I was informed agen, the danger ain't so much to signify. There's Jaggers, and there's Wemmick, and there's you. Who else is there to inform?"

"Is there no chance person who might identify you in the street?" said I.

"Well," he returned, "there ain't many. Nor yet I don't intend to advertise myself in the newspapers by the name of A. M. come back from Botany Bay;[13] and years have rolled away, and who's to gain by it? Still, look'ee here, Pip. If the danger had been fifty times as great, I should ha' come to see you, mind you, just the same."

"And how long do you remain?"

"How long?" said he, taking his black pipe from his mouth, and dropping his jaw as he stared at me. "I'm not a-going back. I've come for good."

"Where are you to live?" said I. "What is to be done with you? Where will you be safe?"

"Dear boy," he returned, "there's disguising wigs can be bought for money, and there's hair powder, and spectacles, and black clothes—shorts and what not. Others has done it safe afore, and what others has done afore, others can do agen. As to the where and how of living, dear boy, give me your own opinions on it."

"You take it smoothly now," said I, "but you were very serious last night, when you swore it was death."

► What does Provis not fear?

"And so I swear it is death," said he, putting his pipe back in his mouth, "and death by the rope, in the open street not fur from this, and it's serious that you should fully understand it to be so. What then, when that's once done? Here I am. To go back now 'ud be as bad as to stand ground—worse. Besides, Pip, I'm here, because I've meant it by you, years and years. As to what I dare, I'm a old bird now, as has dared all manner of traps since first he was fledged,[14] and I'm not afeerd to perch upon a scarecrow. If there's death hid inside of it, there is, and let him come out, and I'll face him, and

---

13. **Botany Bay.** Bay on the southeast coast of Australia, used as a convict settlement
14. **fledged.** Ready to fly

Words
For
Everyday
Use
    in • cur (in kʉr´) *vt.,* bring upon oneself

then I'll believe in him and not afore. And now let me have a look at my gentleman agen."

Once more he took me by both hands and surveyed me with an air of admiring proprietorship,[15] smoking with great <u>complacency</u> all the while.

It appeared to me that I could do no better than secure him some quiet lodging hard by, of which he might take possession when Herbert returned—whom I expected in two or three days. That the secret must be confided to Herbert as a matter of unavoidable necessity, even if I could have put the immense relief I should derive from sharing it with him out of the question, was plain to me. But it was by no means so plain to Mr. Provis (I resolved to call him by that name), who reserved his consent to Herbert's participation until he should have seen him and formed a favorable judgment of his physiognomy.[16] "And even then, dear boy," said he, pulling a greasy little clasped black Testament[17] out of his pocket, "we'll have him on his oath."

◄ What is the plan? Why does Pip want to tell Herbert? What does Provis want to do?

To state that my terrible patron carried this little black book about the world solely to swear people on in cases of emergency would be to state what I never quite established—but this I can say, that I never knew him put it to any other use. The book itself had the appearance of having been stolen from some court of justice, and perhaps his knowledge of its <u>antecedents</u>, combined with his own experience in that wise, gave him a reliance on its powers as a sort of legal spell or charm. On this first occasion of his producing it, I recalled how he had made me swear fidelity in the churchyard long ago, and how he had described himself last night as always swearing to his resolutions in his solitude.

As he was at present dressed in a seafaring slop suit, in which he looked as if he had some parrots and cigars to dispose of, I next discussed with him what dress he should wear. He cherished an extraordinary belief in the virtues of "shorts" as a disguise, and had in his own mind sketched a dress for himself that would have made him something between a dean and a dentist. It was with considerable difficulty that I won him over to the assumption of a dress more like a prosperous

◄ How is Provis dressed? How does Pip disguise him?

---

15. **proprietorship.** Ownership
16. **physiognomy.** Judgment of character by observations of facial features
17. **Testament.** New Testament; second part of the Bible

Words For Everyday Use

com • pla • cen • cy (kəm plā´sən sē) *n.*, contentment; quiet satisfaction

an • te • ced • ent (an´tə sēd´ 'nt) *n.*, previous happenings farmer's; and we arranged that he should cut his hair close, and wear a little powder. Lastly, as he had not yet been seen by the laundress or her niece, he was to keep himself out of their view until his change of dress was made.

It would seem a simple matter to decide on these precautions; but in my dazed, not to say distracted, state, it took so long that I did not get out to further them until two or three in the afternoon. He was to remain shut up in the chambers while I was gone, and was on no account to open the door.

There being to my knowledge a respectable lodging house in Essex Street, the back of which looked into the Temple, and was almost within hail[18] of my windows, I first of all repaired to that house, and was so fortunate as to secure the second floor for my uncle, Mr. Provis. I then went from shop to shop, making such purchases as were necessary to the change in his appearance. This business transacted, I turned my face, on my own account, to Little Britain. Mr. Jaggers was at his desk, but, seeing me enter, got up immediately and stood before his fire.

"Now, Pip," said he, "be careful."

"I will, sir," I returned. For coming along I had thought well of what I was going to say.

▶ What is Jaggers's warning?

"Don't commit yourself," said Mr. Jaggers, "and don't commit anyone. You understand—anyone. Don't tell me anything; I don't want to know anything; I am not curious."

Of course I saw that he knew the man was come.

"I merely want, Mr. Jaggers," said I, "to assure myself what I have been told is true. I have no hope of its being untrue, but at least I may verify it."

Mr. Jaggers nodded. "But did you say 'told' or 'informed'?" he asked me, with his head on one side, and not looking at me, but looking in a listening way at the floor. "Told would seem to <u>imply</u> verbal communication. You can't have verbal communication with a man in New South Wales,[19] you know."

"I will say informed, Mr. Jaggers."

"Good."

▶ What does Jaggers confirm?

"I have been informed by a person named Abel Magwitch that he is the benefactor so long unknown to me."

---

18. **within hail.** Within yelling distance
19. **New South Wales.** State of southeast Australia

Words For Everyday Use

im • ply (im plī´) vt., indicate; suggest

"That is the man," said Mr. Jaggers, "—in New South Wales."

"And only he?" said I.

"And only he," said Mr. Jaggers.

"I am not so unreasonable, sir, as to think you at all responsible for my mistakes and wrong conclusions, but I always supposed it was Miss Havisham."

"As you say, Pip," returned Mr. Jaggers, turning his eyes upon me coolly, and taking a bite at his forefinger, "I am not at all responsible for that."

"And yet it looked so like it, sir," I pleaded with a downcast heart.

"Not a particle of evidence, Pip," said Mr. Jaggers, shaking his head and gathering up his skirts. "Take nothing on its looks; take everything on evidence. There's no better rule."

"I have no more to say," said I, with a sigh, after standing silent for a little while. "I have verified my information, and there's an end."

"And Magwitch—in New South Wales—having at last disclosed himself," said Mr. Jaggers, "you will comprehend, Pip, how rigidly throughout my communication with you I have always <u>adhered</u> to the strict line of fact. There has never been the least departure from the strict line of fact. You are quite aware of that?"

◀ What does Jaggers make clear? Why?

"Quite, sir."

"I communicated to Magwitch—in New South Wales— when he first wrote to me—from New South Wales—the caution that he must not expect me ever to <u>deviate</u> from the strict line of fact. I also communicated to him another caution. He appeared to me to have obscurely hinted in his letter at some distant idea of seeing you in England here. I cautioned him that I must hear no more of that; that he was not at all likely to obtain a pardon; that he was <u>expatriated</u> for the term of his natural life; and that his presenting himself in this country would be an act of felony, rendering him <u>liable</u> to the extreme penalty of the law. I gave Magwitch that caution," said Mr. Jaggers, looking hard at me; "I wrote it to New South Wales. He guided himself by it, no doubt."

◀ What advice did Jaggers give Magwitch (Provis)?

"No doubt," said I.

"I have been informed by Wemmick," pursued Mr. Jaggers, still looking hard at me, "that he has received a letter, under date Portsmouth, from a colonist of the name of Purvis, or—"

Words For Everyday Use

ad • here (ad hir´) vi., stick; stay firm

de • vi • ate (dē´vē āt´) vi., turn aside

ex • pa • tri • ate (eks pā´trē āt´) vt., drive from one's native land

li • a • ble (lī´ə bəl) adj., legally bound; subject

"Or Provis," I suggested.

"Or Provis—thank you, Pip. Perhaps it *is* Provis? Perhaps you know it's Provis?"

"Yes," said I.

"You know it's Provis. A letter, under date Portsmouth, from a colonist of the name of Provis, asking for the particulars of your address, on behalf of Magwitch. Wemmick sent him the particulars, I understand, by return of post. Probably it is through Provis that you have received the explanation of Magwitch—in New South Wales?"

"It came through Provis," I replied.

► What will Pip receive?

"Good day, Pip," said Mr. Jaggers, offering his hand; "glad to have seen you. In writing by post to Magwitch—in New South Wales—or in communicating with him through Provis, have the goodness to mention that the particulars and <u>vouchers</u> of our long account shall be sent to you, together with the balance; for there is still a balance remaining. Good day, Pip!"

We shook hands, and he looked hard at me as long as he could see me. I turned at the door, and he was still looking hard at me, while the two vile casts on the shelf seemed to be trying to get their eyelids open, and to force out of their swollen throats, "Oh, what a man he is!"

Wemmick was out, and though he had been at his desk he could have done nothing for me. I went straight back to the Temple, where I found the terrible Provis drinking rum-and-water, and smoking Negro-head, in safety.

Next day the clothes I had ordered all came home, and he put them on. Whatever he put on became him less (it dismally seemed to me) than what he had worn before. To my thinking there was something in him that made it hopeless to attempt to disguise him. The more I dressed him, and the better I dressed him, the more he looked like the slouching fugitive on the marshes. This effect on my anxious fancy was partly referable, no doubt, to his old face and manner growing more familiar to me; but I believed, too, that he dragged one of his legs as if there were still a weight of iron on it, and that from head to foot there was convict in the very grain of the man.

► What about Provis cannot be disguised?

The influences of his solitary hut-life were upon him besides, and gave him a savage air that no dress could tame; added to these were the influences of his <u>subsequent</u>

Words For Everyday Use	**vouch • er** (vouˊchər) *n.*, statement of expense **sub • se • quent** (subˊsi kwənt) *adj.*, following in time, place, or order

branded life among men, and, crowning all, his conscious-ness that he was dodging and hiding now. In all his ways of sitting and standing, and eating and drinking—of <u>brooding</u> about, in a high-shouldered reluctant style—of taking out his great horn-handled jackknife and wiping it on his legs and cutting his food—of lifting light glasses and cups to his lips as if they were clumsy pannikins[20]—of chopping a wedge off his bread, and soaking up with it the last fragments of gravy round and round his plate, as if to make the most of an allowance, and then drying his fingers on it, and then swal-lowing it—in these ways and a thousand other small nameless instances arising every minute in the day, there was prisoner, felon, bondsman, plain as plain could be.

It had been his own idea to wear that touch of powder, and I conceded the powder after overcoming the shorts. But I can compare the effect of it, when on, to nothing but the proba-ble effect of rouge[21] upon the dead, so awful was the manner in which everything in him that it was most desirable to <u>repress</u> started through that thin layer of pretense, and seemed to come blazing out at the crown of his head. It was aban-doned as soon as tried, and he wore his grizzled hair cut short.

Words cannot tell what a sense I had, at the same time, of the dreadful mystery that he was to me. When he fell asleep of an evening, with his knotted hands clenching the sides of the easy chair, and his bald head tattooed with deep wrinkles falling forward on his breast, I would sit and look at him, won-dering what he had done, and loading him with all the crimes in the calendar, until the impulse was powerful on me to start up and fly from him. Every hour so increased my abhorrence of him that I even think I might have yielded to this impulse in the first agonies of being so haunted, notwithstanding all he had done for me and the risk he ran, but for the knowledge that Herbert must soon come back. Once, I actually did start out of bed in the night, and begin to dress myself in my worst clothes, hurriedly intending to leave him there with every-thing else I possessed, and enlist for India, as a private soldier.

I doubt if a ghost could have been more terrible to me, up in those lonely rooms in the long evenings and long nights, with the wind and the rain always rushing by. A ghost could

◄ *What urge seizes Pip? Why doesn't he follow through on it?*

---

20. **pannikins.** Metal cups
21. **rouge.** Reddish makeup for coloring the face

Words For Everyday Use

brood (bro͞od) *vi.,* ponder in a troubled way
re • press (ri pres´) *vt.,* keep down; hold back

not have been taken and hanged on my account, and the consideration that he could be, and the dread that he would be, were no small addition to my horrors. When he was not asleep, or playing a complicated kind of Patience with a ragged pack of cards of his own—a game that I never saw before or since, and in which he recorded his winnings by sticking his jackknife into the table—when he was not engaged in either of these pursuits, he would ask me to read to him—"Foreign language, dear boy!" While I complied, he, not comprehending a single word, would stand before the fire surveying me with the air of an exhibitor, and I would see him, between the fingers of the hand with which I shaded my face, appealing in dumb show to the furniture to take notice of my <u>proficiency</u>. The imaginary student pursued by the misshapen creature he had <u>impiously</u> made was not more wretched than I, pursued by the creature who had made me, and recoiling from him with a stronger repulsion the more he admired me and the fonder he was of me.

This is written of, I am sensible, as if it had lasted a year. It lasted about five days. Expecting Herbert all the time, I dared not go out, except when I took Provis for an airing after dark. At length, one evening when dinner was over and I had dropped into a slumber quite worn out—for my nights had been <u>agitated</u> and my rest broken by fearful dreams—I was roused by the welcome footstep on the staircase. Provis, who had been asleep, too, staggered up at the noise I made, and in an instant I saw his jackknife shining in his hand.

"Quiet! It's Herbert!" I said, and Herbert came bursting in, with the airy freshness of six hundred miles of France upon him.

"Handel, my dear fellow, how are you, and again how are you, and again how are you? I seem to have been gone a twelvemonth! Why, so I must have been, for you have grown quite thin and pale! Handel, my—Halloa! I beg your pardon."

He was stopped in his running on and in his shaking hands with me, by seeing Provis. Provis, regarding him with a fixed attention, was slowly putting up his jackknife, and groping in another pocket for something else.

"Herbert, my dear friend," said I, shutting the double doors, while Herbert stood staring and wondering, "something very strange has happened. This is—a visitor of mine."

▶ When does Herbert arrive? How does Pip respond? Provis?

Words For Everyday Use

pro • fi • cien • cy (prō fish´ən sē) *n.*, skill; competency

im • pi • ous • ly (im´pē əs lē) *adv.*, without due respect

ag • i • tate (aj´ i tāt´) *vt.*, excite; disturb

"It's all right, dear boy!" said Provis, coming forward, with his little clasped black book, and then addressing himself to Herbert. "Take it in your right hand. Lord strike you dead on the spot, if ever you split in any way sumever! Kiss it!"

"Do so, as he wishes it," I said to Herbert. So Herbert, looking at me with a friendly uneasiness and amazement, complied, and Provis immediately shaking hands with him, said, "Now, you're on your oath, you know. And never believe me on mine, if Pip sha'n't make a gentleman on you!"

◀ *What does Provis make Herbert do? Why?*

CHAPTER 41

► How does Pip know that Herbert feels the same way he does about Provis?

In vain should I attempt to describe the astonishment and disquiet of Herbert when he and I and Provis sat down before the fire, and I recounted the whole of the secret. Enough that I saw my own feelings reflected in Herbert's face, and, not least among them, my repugnance towards the man who had done so much for me.

What would alone have set a division between that man and us, if there had been no other dividing circumstance, was his triumph in my story. Saving his troublesome sense of having been "low" on one occasion since his return—on which point he began to hold forth to Herbert, the moment my <u>revelation</u> was finished—he had no perception of the possibility of my finding any fault with my good fortune. His boast that he had made me a gentleman, and that he had come to see me support the character[1] on his ample resources, was made for me quite as much as for himself. And that it was a highly agreeable boast to both of us, and that we must both be very proud of it, was a conclusion quite established in his own mind.

► What is Provis proud of? Does Pip share his feelings?

"Though, look'ee here, Pip's comrade," he said to Herbert, after having <u>discoursed</u> for some time, "I know very well that once since I come back—for half a minute—I've been low. I said to Pip I knowed as how I had been low. But don't you fret yourself on that score. I ain't made Pip a gentleman, and Pip ain't a-goin to make you a gentleman, not fur me not to know what's due to ye both. Dear boy, and Pip's comrade, you two may count upon me always having a genteel muzzle[2] on. Muzzled I have been since that half a minute when I was betrayed into lowness, muzzled I am at the present time, muzzled I ever will be."

► Why is Pip relieved?

Herbert said, "Certainly," but looked as if there were no specific consolation in this, and remained perplexed and dismayed. We were anxious for the time when he would go to his lodging, and leave us together, but he was evidently jealous of leaving us together, and sat late. It was midnight

---

1. **support the character.** Play the role (of gentleman)
2. **muzzle.** Device fastened over the mouth to prevent speaking

---

Words For Everyday Use

rev • e • la • tion (rev′ə lā′shən) *n.*, revealing or disclosure of something

dis • course (dis kôrs′) *vi.*, carry on conversation

before I took him round to Essex Street, and saw him safely in at his own dark door. When it closed upon him, I experienced the first moment of relief I had known since the night of his arrival.

Never quite free from an uneasy remembrance of the man on the stairs, I had always looked about me in taking my guest out after dark, and in bringing him back; and I looked about me now. Difficult as it is in a large city to avoid the suspicion of being watched when the mind is conscious of danger in that regard, I could not persuade myself that any of the people within sight cared about my movements. The few who were passing passed on their several ways, and the street was empty when I turned back into the Temple. Nobody had come out at the gate with us, nobody went in at the gate with me. As I crossed by the fountain, I saw his lighted back windows looking bright and quiet, and, when I stood for a few moments in the doorway of the building where I lived, before going up the stairs, Garden Court was as still and lifeless as the staircase was when I ascended it.

Herbert received me with open arms, and I had never felt before so blessedly what it is to have a friend. When he had spoken some sound words of sympathy and encouragement, we sat down to consider the question, What was to be done?

The chair that Provis had occupied still remaining where it had stood—for he had a barrack way[3] with him of hanging about one spot, in one unsettled manner, and going through one round of observances with his pipe and his Negro-head and his jackknife and his pack of cards, and what not, as if it were all put down for him on a slate—I say, his chair remaining where it had stood, Herbert unconsciously took it, but next moment started out of it, pushed it away, and took another. He had no occasion to say, after that, that he had conceived an aversion for my patron, neither had I occasion to confess my own. We interchanged that confidence without shaping a syllable.

◄ Upon what do they silently agree?

"What," said I to Herbert, when he was safe in another chair, "what is to be done?"

"My poor dear Handel," he replied, holding his head, "I am too stunned to think."

"So was I, Herbert, when the blow first fell. Still, something must be done. He is intent upon various new expenses[4]— horses, and carriages, and lavish appearances of all kinds. He must be stopped somehow."

"You mean that you can't accept—"

---

3. **barrack way.** Like the ways of the army; regimented; uniform
4. **intent . . . expenses.** Determined to buy more things

"How can I?" I interposed, as Herbert paused. "Think of him! Look at him!"

An involuntary shudder passed over both of us.

▶ What facts make it difficult for Pip to get free of Provis?

"Yet I am afraid the dreadful truth is, Herbert, that he is attached to me, strongly attached to me. Was there ever such a fate!"

"My poor dear Handel," Herbert repeated.

"Then," said I, "after all, stopping short here, never taking another penny from him, think what I owe him already! Then again, I am heavily in debt—very heavily for me, who have now no expectations—and I have been bred to no calling, and I am fit for nothing."

"Well, well, well!" Herbert remonstrated. "Don't say fit for nothing."

"What am I fit for? I know only one thing that I am fit for, and that is to go for a soldier. And I might have gone, my dear Herbert, but for the prospect of taking counsel with your friendship and affection."

Of course I broke down there, and of course Herbert, beyond seizing a warm grip of my hand, pretended not to know it.

"Anyhow, my dear Handel," said he presently; "soldiering won't do. If you were to <u>renounce</u> this patronage and these favors, I suppose you would do so with some faint hope of one day repaying what you have already had. Not very strong, that hope, if you went soldiering. Besides, it's absurd. You would be infinitely better in Clarriker's house, small as it is. I am working up towards a partnership, you know."

Poor fellow! He little suspected with whose money.

▶ Against what does Herbert warn Pip? What does he think Provis might do?

"But there is another question," said Herbert. "This is an ignorant determined man who has long had one fixed idea. More than that, he seems to me (I may misjudge him) to be a man of a desperate and fierce character."

"I know he is," I returned. "Let me tell you what evidence I have seen of it." And I told him what I had not mentioned in my narrative, of that encounter with the other convict.

"See, then," said Herbert; "think of this! He comes here at the <u>peril</u> of his life for the realization of his fixed idea. In the moment of realization, after all his toil and waiting, you cut the ground from under his feet, destroy his idea, and make his gains worthless to him. Do you see nothing that he might do under the disappointment?"

Words For Everyday Use

re • nounce (ri nouns´) vt., formally give up

per • il (per´əl) n., exposure to harm or danger

"I have seen it, Herbert, and dreamed of it ever since the fatal night of his arrival. Nothing has been in my thoughts so distinctly as his putting himself in the way of being taken."

"Then you may rely upon it," said Herbert, "that there would be great danger of his doing it. That is his power over you as long as he remains in England, and that would be his reckless course if you forsook him."

I was so struck by the horror of this idea, which had weighed upon me from the first, and the working out of which would make me regard myself, in some sort, as his murderer, that I could not rest in my chair, but began pacing to and fro. I said to Herbert, meanwhile, that even if Provis were recognized and taken, in spite of himself, I should be wretched as the cause, however innocently. Yes; even though I was so wretched in having him at large[5] and near me, and even though I would far rather have worked at the forge all the days of my life than I would ever have come to this!

◄ How would Pip feel if Provis were caught? Why?

But there was no staving off[6] the question, What was to be done?

"The first and the main thing to be done," said Herbert, "is to get him out of England. You will have to go with him, and then he may be induced to go."

"But get him where I will, could I prevent his coming back?"

"My good Handel, is it not obvious that, with Newgate in the next street, there must be far greater hazard in your breaking your mind to him and making him reckless here than elsewhere. If a pretext to get him away could be made out of that other convict, or out of anything else in his life, now."

"There again!" said I, stopping before Herbert, with my open hands held out, as if they contained the desperation of the case. "I know nothing of his life. It has almost made me mad to sit here of a night and see him before me, so bound up with my fortunes and misfortunes, and yet so unknown to me, except as the miserable wretch who terrified me two days in my childhood!"

Herbert got up, and linked his arm in mine, and we slowly walked to and fro together, studying the carpet.

---

5. **at large.** Roaming free
6. **staving off.** Warding off; putting off

Words For Everyday Use

pre • text (prē´tekst´) *n.*, excuse; false reason

► *What does Pip decide to do about his relationship with Provis?*

"Handel," said Herbert, stopping, "you feel convinced that you can take no further benefits from him, do you?"

"Fully. Surely you would, too, if you were in my place?"

"And you feel convinced that you must break with him?"

"Herbert, can you ask me?"

"And you have, and are bound to have, that tenderness for the life he has risked on your account, that you must save him, if possible, from throwing it away. Then you must get him out of England before you stir a finger to <u>extricate</u> yourself. That done, extricate yourself, in Heaven's name, and we'll see it out together, dear old boy."

It was a comfort to shake hands upon it, and walk up and down again, with only that done.

"Now Herbert," said I, "with reference to gaining some knowledge of his history. There is but one way that I know of. I must ask him point-blank."

"Yes. Ask him," said Herbert, "when we sit at breakfast in the morning." For, he had said, on taking leave of Herbert, that he would come to breakfast with us.

With this project formed, we went to bed. I had the wildest dreams concerning him, and woke unrefreshed; I woke, too, to recover the fear which I had lost in the night of his being found out as a returned transport.[7] Waking, I never lost that fear.

He came round at the appointed time, took out his jack-knife, and sat down to his meal. He was full of plans "for his gentleman's coming out strong, and like a gentleman," and urged me to begin speedily upon the pocket-book, which he had left in my possession. He considered the chambers and his own lodging as temporary residences, and advised me to look out at once for a "fashionable crib"[8] near Hyde Park, in which he could have "a shake-down."[9] When he had made an end of his breakfast, and was wiping his knife on his leg, I said to him, without a word of preface:[10]

"After you were gone last night, I told my friend of the struggle that the soldiers found you engaged in on the marshes, when we came up. You remember?"

"Remember!" said he. "I think so!"

---

7. **transport.** Criminal banished to a convict settlement
8. **crib.** Small house
9. **shake-down.** Makeshift bed
10. **preface.** Introductory remarks

Words For Everyday Use

ex • tri • cate (eks′tri kāt) *vt.*, set free; release

"We want to know something about that man—and about you. It is strange to know no more about either, and particularly you, than I was able to tell last night. Is not this as good a time as another for our knowing more?"

"Well!" he said, after consideration. "You're on your oath,[11] you know, Pip's comrade?"

"Assuredly," replied Herbert.

"As to anything I say, you know," he insisted. "The oath applies to all."

"I understand it to do so."

"And look'ee here! Wotever I done is worked out and paid for," he insisted again.

"So be it."

He took out his black pipe and was going to fill it with Negro-head, when, looking at the tangle of tobacco in his hand, he seemed to think it might perplex the thread of his narrative. He put it back again, stuck his pipe in a button-hole of his coat, spread a hand on each knee, and, after turning an angry eye on the fire for a few silent moments, looked around at us and said what follows.

---

11. **on your oath.** On your honor; bound by your honesty

CHAPTER 42

► Where has Provis spent most of his life?

"Dear boy and Pip's comrade. I am not a-going fur to tell you my life, like a song or a storybook. But to give it you short and handy, I'll put it at once into a mouthful of English. In jail and out of jail, in jail and out of jail, in jail and out of jail. There, you've got it. That's *my* life pretty much, down to such times as I got shipped off, arter Pip stood my friend.

"I've been done everything to, pretty well—except hanged. I've been locked up as much as silver tea-kittle. I've been carted here and carted there, and put out of this town and put out of that town, and stuck in the stocks, and whipped and worried and drove. I've no more notion where I was born than you have—if so much. I first become aware of myself down in Essex, a-thieving turnips for my living. Summun had run away from me—a man—a tinker—and he'd took the fire with him, and left me wery cold.

"I know'd my name to be Magwitch, chrisen'd Abel. How did I know it? Much as I know'd the birds' names in the hedges to be chaffinch, sparrer, thrush. I might have thought it was all lies together, only as the birds' names come out true, I supposed mine did.

"So fur as I could find, there warn't a soul that see young Abel Magwitch, with as little on him as in him, but wot caught fright at him, and either drove him off, or took him up. I was took up, took up, took up to that <u>extent</u> that I reg'larly grow'd up took up.

► Why did Provis steal? Why weren't the prison officials effective in helping him to reform?

"This is the way it was, that when I was a ragged little creetur as much to be pitied as ever I see (not that I looked in the glass, for there warn't many insides of furnished houses known to me), I got the name of being hardened. 'This is a terrible hardened one,' they says to prison visitors, picking out me. 'May be said to live in jails, this boy.' Then they looked at me, and I looked at them, and they measured my head, some on 'em—they had better a-measured my stomach—and others on 'em giv me tracts[1] what I couldn't read, and made me speeches what I couldn't unnerstand. They always went on agen me about the devil. But what the devil was I to do? I

---

1. **tracts.** Pamphlets about religion

Words For Everyday Use **ex • tent** (ek stent´) *n.,* range or limits

must put something into my stomach, mustn't I?—
Howsomever, I'm a-getting low, and I know what's due. Dear
boy and Pip's comrade, don't you be afeerd of me being low.

"Tramping, begging, thieving, working sometimes when I
could—though that warn't as often as you may think, till you
put the question whether you would ha' been over-ready to
give me work yourselves—a bit of a poacher,[2] a bit of a laborer,
a bit of a wagoner, a bit of a haymaker, a bit of a hawker,[3] a
bit of most things that don't pay and lead to trouble, I got to
be a man. A deserting soldier in a traveler's rest, what lay hid
up to the chin under a lot of taturs, learnt me to read; and a
traveling giant what signed his name at a penny a time
learnt me to write. I warn't locked up as often now as formerly, but I wore out my good share of key-metal still.

"At Epsom races, a matter of over twenty year ago, I got
acquainted wi' a man whose skull I'd crack wi' this poker,
like the claw of a lobster, if I'd got it on this hob. His right
name was Compeyson; and that's the man, dear boy, what
you see me a-pounding in the ditch, according to what you
truly told your comrade arter I was gone last night.

"He set up fur a gentleman, this Compeyson, and he'd
been to a public boarding school and had learning. He was a
smooth one to talk, and was a dab at the ways of gentlefolks.
He was good-looking, too. It was the night afore the great
race, when I found him on the heath, in a booth that I
know'd on. Him and some more was a-sitting among the
tables when I went in, and the landlord (which had a knowledge of me, and was a sporting one) called him out, and said,
'I think this is a man that might suit you'—meaning I was.

"Compeyson, he looks at me very noticing, and I look at
him. He has a watch and a chain and a ring and a breast-pin
and a handsome suit of clothes.

"'To judge from appearances, you're out of luck,' says
Compeyson to me.

"'Yes, master, and I've never been in it much.' (I had come
out of Kingston Jail last on a vagrancy committal.[4] Not but
what it might have been for something else, but it warn't.)

"'Luck changes,' says Compeyson; 'perhaps yours is going
to change.'

"I says, 'I hope it may be so. There's room.'

"'What can you do?' says Compeyson.

"'Eat and drink,' I says, 'if you'll find the materials.'

◄ Whom did Provis
meet? When? How
does Pip know him?

---

2. **poacher.** Person who hunts illegally
3. **hawker.** Aggressive, haggling salesperson who sells goods on the street
4. **vagrancy committal.** Shiftless or idle wandering without money or work, as
of tramps or beggars; often a statutory offense chargeable as a misdemeanor crime

"Compeyson laughed, looked at me again very noticing, giv me five shillings, and appointed me for next night. Same place.

"I went to Compeyson next night, same place, and Compeyson took me on to be his man and pardner. And what was Compeyson's business in which we was to go pardners? Compeyson's business was the swindling, handwriting forging, stolen bank-note passing, and such-like. All sorts of traps as Compeyson could set with his head, and keep his own legs out of and get the profits from and let another man in for, was Compeyson's business. He'd no more heart than a iron file, he was as cold as death, and he had the head of the devil afore mentioned.

▶ Who else was in
business with
Compeyson? What
did the two of
them do?

"There was another in with Compeyson, as was called Arthur—not as being so chrisen'd, but as a <u>surname</u>. He was in a decline, and was a shadow to look at. Him and Compeyson had been in a bad thing with a rich lady some years afore, and they'd made a pot of money by it; but Compeyson betted and gamed, and he'd have run through the king's taxes. So Arthur was a-dying and a-dying poor and with the horrors on him, and Compeyson's wife (which Compeyson kicked mostly) was a-having pity on him when she could, and Compeyson was a-having pity on nothing and nobody.

"I mighta took warning by Arthur, but I didn't; and I won't pretend I was partick'ler—for where 'ud be the good on it, dear boy and comrade? So I begun wi' Compeyson, and a poor tool I was in his hands. Arthur lived at the top of Compeyson's house (over nigh Brentford, it was), and Compeyson kept a careful account agen him for board and lodging, in case he should ever get better to work it out. But Arthur soon settled the account. The second or third time as

ever I see him, he come a-tearing down into Compeyson's parlor late at night, in only a flannel gown, with his hair all in a sweat, and he says to Compeyson's wife, 'Sally, she really is upstairs alonger me, now, and I can't get rid of her. She's all in white,' he says, 'wi' white flowers in her hair, and she's awful mad, and she's got a shroud hanging over her arm, and she says she'll put it on me at five in the morning.'

"Says Compeyson: 'Why, you fool, don't you know, she's got a living body? And how should she be up there, without coming through the door, or in at the window, and up the stairs?'

**Words
For
Everyday
Use**   **sur • name** (sʉr´nām´) *n.,* family name or last name

"'I don't know how she's there,' says Arthur, shivering dreadful with the horrors, 'but she's standing in the corner at the foot of the bed, awful mad. And over where her heart's broke—*you* broke it!—there's drops of blood.'

"Compeyson spoke hardy, but he was always a coward. 'Go up alonger this <u>driveling</u> sick man,' he says to his wife, 'and Magwitch, lend her a hand, will you?' But he never come nigh himself.

"Compeyson's wife and me took him up to bed agen, and he raved most dreadful. 'Why look at her!' he cries out. 'She's a-shaking the shroud at me! Don't you see her? Look at her eyes! Ain't it awful to see her so mad?' Next, he cries, 'She'll put it on me, and then I'm done for! Take it away from her, take it away!' And then he catched hold of us, and kep on a-talking to her, and answering of her, till I half-believed I see her myself.

"Compeyson's wife, being used to him, give him some liquor to get the horrors off, and by-and-by he quieted. 'Oh, she's gone! Has her keeper been for her?' he says. 'Yes,' says Compeyson's wife. 'Did you tell him to lock and bar her in?' 'Yes.' 'And to take that ugly thing away from her?' 'Yes, yes, all right.' 'You're a good creetur,' he says, 'don't leave me, whatever you do, and thank you!'

"He rested pretty quiet till it might want a few minutes of five, and then he starts up with a scream, and screams out, 'Here she is! She's got the shroud again. She's unfolding it. She's coming out of the corner. She's coming to the bed. Hold me, both on you—one of each side—don't let her touch me with it. Hah! She missed me that time. Don't let her throw it over my shoulders. Don't let her lift me up to get it round me. She's lifting me up. Keep me down!' Then he lifted himself up hard, and was dead.

◀ How did Arthur die?

"Compeyson took it easy as a good riddance[5] for both sides. Him and me was soon busy, and first he swore me (being ever artful) on my own book—this here little black book, dear boy, what I swore your comrade on.

"Not to go into the things that Compeyson planned, and I done—which 'ud take a week—I'll simply say to you, dear boy, and Pip's comrade, that that man got me into such nets

◀ Why did Compeyson have a hold over Provis? Whom else does Provis mention?

---

5. **good riddance.** Welcome relief at getting rid of someone or something

Words For Everyday Use

driv • el • ing (driv´əl iŋ) *adj.*, slobbering

as made me his black slave. I was always in debt to him, always under his thumb, always a-working, always a-getting into danger. He was younger than me, but he'd got craft,[6] and he'd got learning, and he overmatched me five hundred times told and no mercy. My missis as I had the hard time wi'—Stop though! I ain't brought *her* in—"

He looked about him in a confused way, as if he had lost his place in the book of his remembrance; and he turned his face to the fire, and spread his hands broader on his knees, and lifted them off and put them on again.

"There ain't no need to go into it," he said, looking round once more. "The time wi' Compeyson was a'most as hard a time as ever I had; that said, all's said. Did I tell you as I was tried, alone, for misdemeanor,[7] while with Compeyson?"

I answered, No.

▶ What crime was Provis convicted of?

"Well!" he said, "I *was,* and got convicted. As to took up on suspicion, that was twice or three times in the four or five year that it lasted; but evidence was wanting. At last, me and Compeyson was both committed for felony[8]—on a charge of putting stolen notes in circulation[9]—and there was other charges behind. Compeyson says to me, 'Separate defenses, no communication,' and that was all. And I was so miserable poor that I sold all the clothes I had, except what hung on my back, afore I could get Jaggers.

"When we was put in the dock, I noticed first of all what a gentleman Compeyson looked, wi' his curly hair and his black clothes and his white pocket-handkercher, and what a common sort of a wretch I looked. When the <u>prosecution</u> opened and the evidence was put short, aforehand, I noticed how heavy it all bore on me, and how light on him. When the evidence was giv in the box, I noticed how it was always me that had come for'ard, and could be swore to, how it was always me that the money had been paid to, how it was always me that had seemed to work the thing and get the profit. But, when the defense come on, then I see the plan plainer; for, says the counselor for Compeyson, 'My lord and gentlemen, here you has afore you, side by side, two persons

---

6. **craft.** Skill in deception; cunning
7. **misdemeanor.** An offense less serious than a felony; punishment is likely to be a fine or a brief imprisonment.
8. **felony.** A serious crime, punishable by a severe sentence
9. **stolen notes in circulation.** Spending stolen money

Words
For
Everyday
Use

pros • e • cu • tion (präs´i kyo͞o´shən) *n.,* the state as the party that carries on legal proceedings against criminals as your eyes can separate wide; one, the younger, well brought up, who will be spoke to as such; one, the elder, ill brought up, who will be spoke to as such; one, the younger, <u>seldom</u> if ever seen in these here transactions, and only suspected; t'other, the elder, always seen in 'em and always wi' his guilt brought home. Can you doubt, if there is but one in it, which is the one, and if there is two in it, which is much the worst one?' And such-like. And when it come to character, warn't it Compeyson as had been to school, and warn't it his schoolfellows as was in this position and in that, and warn't it him as had been know'd by witnesses in such clubs and societies, and nowt to his disadvantage? And warn't it me as had been tried afore, and as had been know'd up hill and down dale in Bridewells and Lock-ups? And when it come to speech-making, warn't it Compeyson as could speak to 'em wi' his face dropping every now and then into his white pocket-handkercher—ah! and wi' verses in his speech, too—and warn't it me as could only say, 'Gentlemen, this man at my side is a most precious[10] rascal'? And when the verdict come, warn't it Compeyson as was recommended to mercy on account of good character and bad company, and giving up all the information he could agen me, and warn't it me as got never a word but guilty? And when I says to Compeyson, 'Once out of this court, I'll smash that face of yourn!' ain't it Compeyson as prays the judge to be protected, and gets two turnkeys stood betwixt us? And when we're sentenced, ain't it him as gets seven year, and me fourteen, and ain't it him as the judge is sorry for, because he mighta done so well, and ain't it me as the judge perceives to be a old offender of violent passion, likely to come to worse?"

◄ Why did Compeyson get a lighter sentence than Provis?

He had worked himself into a state of great excitement, but he checked it, took two or three short breaths, swallowed as often, and stretching out his hand towards me, said, in a reassuring manner, "I ain't a-going to be low, dear boy!"

He had so heated himself that he took out his handkerchief and wiped his face and head and neck and hands, before he could go on.

"I had said to Compeyson that I'd smash that face of his, and I swore Lord smash mine! to do it. We was in the same prison-ship, but I couldn't get at him for long, though I tried.

◄ What did Provis pledge? What happened when he succeeded? How did he escape? Whom did he see in the marshes?

10. **precious.** Notorious

Words For Everyday Use

sel • dom (sel'dəm) *adv.,* rarely

At last I come behind him and hit him on the cheek to turn him round and get a smashing one at him, when I was seen and seized. The blackhole[11] of that ship warn't a strong one, to a judge of blackholes that could swim and dive. I escaped to the shore, and I was a-hiding among the graves there, envying them as was in 'em and all over, when I first see my boy!"

He regarded me with a look of affection that made him almost <u>abhorrent</u> to me again, though I had felt great pity for him.

"By my boy, I was giv to understand as Compeyson was out on them marshes, too. Upon my soul, I half-believe he escaped in his terror, to get quit of me, not knowing it was me as had got ashore. I hunted him down. I smashed his face. 'And now,' says I, 'as the worst thing I can do, caring nothing for myself, I'll drag you back.' And I'd have swum off, towing him by the hair, if it had come to that, and I'd a-got him aboard without the soldiers.

"Of course he'd much the best of it to the last—his character was so good. He had escaped when he was made half-wild by me and my murderous intentions; and his punishment was light. I was put in irons, brought to trial again, and sent for life. I didn't stop for life, dear boy and Pip's comrade, being here."

He wiped himself again, as he had done before, and then slowly took his tangle of tobacco from his pocket, and plucked his pipe from his buttonhole, and slowly filled it, and began to smoke.

"Is he dead?" I asked after a silence.

"Is who dead, dear boy?"

"Compeyson."

"He hopes *I* am, if he's alive, you may be sure," with a fierce look. "I never heard no more of him."

▶ *Whom does Herbert identify Compeyson to be? Whom does he identify Arthur to be?*

Herbert had been writing with his pencil in the cover of a book. He softly pushed the book over to me, as Provis stood smoking with his eyes on the fire, and I read in it:

Young Havisham's name was Arthur. Compeyson is the man who <u>professed</u> to be Miss Havisham's lover.

I shut the book and nodded slightly to Herbert, and put the book by; but we neither of us said anything, and both looked at Provis as he stood smoking by the fire.

11. **blackhole.** Ship's prison; brig

Words
For
Everyday
Use

ab • hor • rent (əb hôr´ənt) *adj.*, causing disgust and hatred
pro • fess (prə fes´) *vt.*, affirm, declare; claim

Why should I pause to ask how much of my shrinking from Provis might be traced to Estella? Why should I loiter on my road to compare the state of mind in which I had tried to rid myself of the stain of the prison before meeting her at the coach-office, with the state of mind in which I now reflected on the <u>abyss</u> between Estella in her pride and beauty, and the returned transport whom I <u>harbored</u>? The road would be none the smoother for it, the end would be none the better for it, he would not be helped, nor I extenuated.[1]

A new fear had been engendered in my mind by his narrative; or rather, his narrative had given form and purpose to the fear that was already there. If Compeyson were alive and should discover his return, I could hardly doubt the consequence. That Compeyson stood in mortal fear of him, neither of the two could know much better than I; and that any such man as that man had been described to be would hesitate to release himself for good from a dreaded enemy by the safe means of becoming an informer, was scarcely to be imagined.

Never had I breathed, and never would I breathe—or so I resolved—a word of Estella to Provis. But I said to Herbert that before I could go abroad, I must see both Estella and Miss Havisham. This was when we were left alone on the night of the day when Provis told us his story. I resolved to go out to Richmond next day, and I went.

◄ *Whom does Pip want to visit? What surprises him?*

On my presenting myself at Mrs. Brandley's, Estella's maid was called to tell me that Estella had gone into the country. Where? To Satis House, as usual. Not as usual, I said, for she had never yet gone there without me; when was she coming back? There was an air of reservation in the answer which increased my perplexity, and the answer was that her maid believed she was only coming back at all for a little while. I could make nothing of this, except that it was meant that I should make nothing of it, and I went home again in complete discomfiture.

Another night consultation with Herbert after Provis was gone home (I always took him home, and always looked well about me), led us to the conclusion that nothing

---

1. **nor I extenuated.** The magnitude of my guilt and pain would not be lessened.

Words For Everyday Use

a • byss (ə bis´) *n.,* yawning gulf; huge gape
har • bor (här´ bər) *vt.,* shelter

► Why is Pip certain that Provis will agree with his plan to go abroad?

should be said about going abroad until I came back from Miss Havisham's. In the meantime Herbert and I were to consider separately what it would be best to say; whether we should <u>devise</u> any pretense of being afraid that he was under suspicious observation; or whether I, who had never yet been abroad,[2] should propose an expedition. We both knew that I had but to propose anything, and he would consent. We agreed that his remaining many days in his present hazard was not to be thought of.

Next day, I had the meanness to feign that I was under a binding promise to go down to Joe; but I was capable of almost any meanness towards Joe or his name. Provis was to be strictly careful while I was gone, and Herbert was to take the charge of him that I had taken. I was to be absent only one night, and, on my return, the <u>gratification</u> of his impatience for my starting as a gentleman on a greater scale was to be begun. It occurred to me then, and as I afterwards found to Herbert also, that he might be best got away across the water, on that pretense—as to make purchases, or the like.

Having thus cleared the way for my expedition to Miss Havisham's, I set off by the early morning coach before it was yet light, and was out in the open country road when the day came creeping on, halting and whimpering and shivering, and wrapped in patches of clouds and rags of mist, like a beggar. When we drove up to the Blue Boar after a drizzly ride, whom should I see come out under the gateway, toothpick in hand, to look at the coach, but Bentley Drummle!

► Whom does Pip meet?

As he pretended not to see me, I pretended not to see him. It was a very lame pretense on both sides; the lamer because we both went into the coffee-room, where he had just finished his breakfast, and where I ordered mine. It was poisonous to me to see him in the town, for I very well knew why he had come there.

Pretending to read a smeary newspaper long out of date, which had nothing half so <u>legible</u> in its local news as the foreign matter of coffee, pickles, fish-sauces, gravy, melted butter, and wine with which it was sprinkled all over, as if it had taken the measles in a highly irregular form, I sat at my table while he stood before the fire. By degrees it became an enormous

---

2. **abroad.** Outside one's own country

Words For Everyday Use

de • vise (di vīz´) *vt.,* plan; contrive

grat • i • fi • ca • tion (grat´ə fi kā´shən) *n.,* satisfaction

leg • i • ble (lej´ə bəl) *adj.,* readable

injury to me that he stood before the fire. And I got up, determined to have my share of it. I had to put my hands behind his legs for the poker when I went up to the fireplace to stir the fire, but still pretended not to know him. "Is this a cut?" said Mr. Drummle.

"Oh?" said I, poker in hand; "it's you, is it? How do you do? I was wondering who it was, who kept the fire off."

With that I poked tremendously, and having done so, planted myself side by side with Mr. Drummle, my shoulders squared, and my back to the fire.

"You have just come down?" said Mr. Drummle, edging me a little away with his shoulder.

"Yes," said I, edging *him* a little away with *my* shoulder.

◄ *What does Drummle think of the area?*

"Beastly place," said Drummle. "Your part of the country, I think?"

"Yes," I assented. "I am told it's very like your Shropshire."[3]

"Not in the least like it," said Drummle.

Here Mr. Drummle looked at his boots and I looked at mine, and then Mr. Drummle looked at my boots and I looked at his.

"Have you been here long?" I asked, determined not to yield an inch of the fire.

"Long enough to be tired of it," returned Drummle, pretending to yawn, but equally determined.

"Do you stay here long?"

"Can't say," answered Mr. Drummle. "Do you?"

"Can't say," said I.

I felt here, through a tingling in my blood, that if Mr. Drummle's shoulder had claimed another hair's <u>breadth</u> of room, I should have jerked him into the window; equally, that if my shoulder had urged a similar claim, Mr. Drummle would have jerked me into the nearest box. He whistled a little. So did I.

"Large tract of marshes about here, I believe?" said Drummle.

"Yes. What of that?" said I.

Mr. Drummle looked at me, and then at my boots, and then said, "Oh!" and laughed.

"Are you amused, Mr. Drummle?"

"No," said he, "not particularly. I am going out for a ride in the saddle. I mean to explore those marshes for amusement.

---

3. **Shropshire.** County of western England, on the Welsh border

Words For Everyday Use

breadth (bredth) *n.,* width

► How does
Drummle insult Pip?
What does he say his
plans are?

Out-of-the-way villages there, they tell me. Curious little public houses—and smithies[4]—and that. Waiter!"

"Yes, sir."

"Is that horse of mine ready?"

"Brought round to the door, sir."

"I say. Look here, you sir. The lady won't ride today; the weather won't do."

"Very good, sir."

"And I don't dine, because I am going to dine at the lady's."

"Very good, sir."

Then Drummle glanced at me, with an insolent triumph on his great-jowled[5] face that cut me to the heart, dull as he was, and so exasperated me that I felt inclined to take him in my arms (as the robber in the storybook is said to have taken the old lady) and seat him on the fire.

One thing was manifest to both of us, and that was that until relief came, neither of us could relinquish the fire. There we stood, well squared up before it, shoulder to shoulder and foot to foot, with our hands behind us, not budging an inch. The horse was visible outside in the drizzle at the door, my breakfast was put on table, Drummle's was cleared away, the waiter invited me to begin, I nodded, we both stood our ground.

► What makes Pip
angry?

"Have you been to the Grove since?" said Drummle.

"No," said I, "I had quite enough of the Finches the last time I was there."

"Was that when we had a difference of opinion?"

"Yes," I replied very shortly.

"Come, come! They let you off easily enough," sneered Drummle. "You shouldn't have lost your temper."

"Mr. Drummle," said I, "you are not <u>competent</u> to give advice on that subject. When I lose my temper (not that I admit having done so on that occasion), I don't throw glasses."

"I do," said Drummle.

Again glancing at him once or twice, in an increased state of <u>smoldering</u> <u>ferocity</u>, I said:

"Mr. Drummle, I did not seek this conversation, and I don't think it's an agreeable one."

---

4. **smithies.** Blacksmiths
5. **great-jowled.** With heavy flesh around the cheeks and jawline

Words
For
Everyday
Use

com • pe • tent (käm′pə tənt) *adj.*, qualified; capable

smol • der • ing (smōl′dər iŋ) *adj.*, with feelings of suppressed anger or hate

fe • roc • i • ty (fə räs′ə tē) *n.*, state or quality of being fierce or savage

"I am sure it's not," said he superciliously over his shoulder, "I don't think anything about it."

"And therefore," I went on, "with your leave, I will suggest that we hold no kind of communication in future."

"Quite my opinion," said Drummle, "and what I should have suggested myself, or done—more likely—without suggesting. But don't lose your temper. Haven't you lost enough without that?"

"What do you mean, sir?"

"Waiter," said Drummle, by way of answering me.

The waiter reappeared.

"Look here, you sir. You quite understand that the young lady don't ride today, and that I dine at the young lady's?"

"Quite so, sir!"

When the waiter had felt my fast cooling teapot with the palm of his hand, and had looked imploringly at me, and had gone out, Drummle, careful not to move the shoulder next me, took a cigar from his pocket and bit the end off, but showed no sign of stirring. Choking and boiling as I was, I felt that we could not go a word further without introducing Estella's name, which I could not endure to hear him utter; and therefore I looked stonily at the opposite wall, as if there were no one present, and forced myself to silence. How long we might have remained in this ridiculous position it is impossible to say, but for the <u>incursion</u> of three thriving farmers—laid on by the waiter, I think—who came into the coffee-room unbuttoning their greatcoats and rubbing their hands, and before whom, as they charged at the fire, we were obliged to give way.

I saw him through the window, seizing his horse's mane, and mounting in his blundering brutal manner, and <u>sidling</u> and backing away. I thought he was gone, when he came back, calling for a light for the cigar in his mouth, which he had forgotten. A man in a dust-colored dress appeared with what was wanted—I could not have said from where, whether from the inn yard, or the street, or where not—and as Drummle leaned down from the saddle and lighted his cigar and laughed with a jerk of his head towards the coffee-room windows, the slouching shoulders, and ragged hair of this man, whose back was towards me, reminded me of Orlick.

| Words For Everyday Use | in • cur • sion (in kʉr´zhen) n., coming in when undesired, as an invasion |
| | si • dle (sī´dəl) vi., move sideways; edge along, especially in a nervous manner |

▶ *Where is Pip going? What does he regret?*

Too heavily out of sorts to care much at the time whether it were he or no, or after all to touch the breakfast, I washed the weather and the journey from my face and hands, and went out to the memorable old house that it would have been so much the better for me never to have entered, never to have seen.

Responding to the Selection

Discuss your reactions to Magwitch—what you admire or dislike about him and whether you sympathize with him, considering the life he has led. What are your thoughts on Pip's reaction to Magwitch? Would you react in the same way if you were in Pip's position? Why, or why not?

Reviewing the Selection

Recalling and Interpreting

1. **R:** When Pip and Estella return to Satis House in chapter 38, about what do Estella and Miss Havisham argue? What does Miss Havisham want from Estella?

2. **I:** What does the reader learn about Estella from her argument with Miss Havisham? Why can't Estella give Miss Havisham what she wants?

3. Who arrives at Pip's house late in the evening on a dark and stormy night? Where and when did Pip first meet this person? What surprising news does this person deliver? What does Pip finally resolve to do about this person in chapters 38–43?

4. **I:** What might the weather indicate about the effect of this person's arrival on Pip's life? How does Pip feel about this person's arrival? Why does Pip feel this way? What motivated this person to act toward Pip as he has? What does Pip's behavior toward and plans for this person tell you about Pip—his values, his personality, his growth as a person?

5. **R:** In chapter 42, what does Magwitch reveal about his past? With whom has he been associated, and what other crime central to this story have these people committed? What does he say happened to Miss Havisham's long-lost half brother?

6. **I:** Describe how the story of Magwitch's past makes you feel about him as a character. Even after Magwitch tells the sad story of his life, Pip still feels abhorrence toward him. Explain whether, in your view, Magwitch deserves this abhorrence. Also, explain whether Miss Havisham finally got her revenge upon her half brother, or whether her half brother's own guilty conscience finally caught up with him.

7. **R:** In chapter 38, what does Bentley Drummle do to anger Pip? When Pip confronts Estella, what does she say about the way she treats Pip in comparison with the way she treats most men? What does Drummle do to try to hurt Pip in chapter 43?

8. **I:** Why does Drummle's fixation on Estella especially anger Pip? Explain whether you think Estella's words are true. Judging from her conversation with Pip in chapter 38, how does Estella seem to feel about Drummle? By the end of chapter 43, what relationship do you think exists between them? Explain whether you think Estella's feelings toward Drummle have changed. If not, why do you think Estella's relationship with Drummle has changed?

Synthesizing

9. In chapters 38–43, in what ways do characters view other characters as objects rather than people? What examples can you find of Pip speaking of Estella as if she were an object rather than a person? How do both Pip and Drummle seem to view Estella? How does Estella describe and seem to feel about herself? Why might she feel this way? In what way does Magwitch refer to Pip as an object? What might the author be pointing out about the dangers of viewing people as objects rather than as people with thoughts, feelings, and motivations of their own?

10. In what ways have different characters in *Great Expectations* focused on appearances or outer qualities rather than true substance or inner qualities? In what way does the encounter with Magwitch force Pip to examine the falseness of his beliefs and dreams? On what were these dreams based rather than substance or evidence? Who points out the mistake Pip has made? Is Pip's love for Estella based on her outward appearance or her inner qualities? In what way is Pip's reaction to Magwitch another example of a character focusing on appearances rather than on truth or substance?

Understanding Literature (QUESTIONS FOR DISCUSSION)

1. **Irony and Irony of Situation. Irony** is a difference between appearance and reality. In **irony of situation,** an event occurs that violates the expectations of the characters, the reader, or the audience. Explain why the fact that Miss Havisham seeks love from Estella is ironic.

2. **Analogy.** An **analogy** is a comparison of two things that are alike in some respects but different in others. What analogy does Estella use when she tries to explain why Miss Havisham's resentment is unreasonable? In what way are these two situations similar? In what ways are they different? Explain whether you believe that the analogy Estella has chosen to describe her situation is an apt one.

3. **Allusion.** An **allusion** is a rhetorical technique in which reference is made to a person, event, object, or work from history or literature. On page 360, Pip describes the situation with Magwitch in the following words: "The imaginary student pursued by the misshapen creature he had impiously made was not more wretched than I, pursued by the creature who had made me, and recoiling from him with a stronger repulsion the more he admired me and the fonder he was of me." This passage is an allusion to Mary Shelley's *Frankenstein,* in which Frankenstein, a university student, tries to uncover the secrets of life itself, creating a misshapen monster from the limbs of the dead, and later recoiling from his creation. In what sense is Pip Magwitch's creation? What is the narrator (or author) implying about Magwitch's actions by comparing him to Frankenstein? In what way is Pip like Frankenstein's creation, the monster?

CHAPTER 44

In the room where the dressing table stood, and where the wax candles burnt on the wall, I found Miss Havisham and Estella; Miss Havisham seated on a settee near the fire, and Estella on a cushion at her feet. Estella was knitting, and Miss Havisham was looking on. They both raised their eyes as I went in, and both saw an alteration in me. I derived that from the look they interchanged.

"And what wind," said Miss Havisham, "blows you here, Pip?"

Though she looked steadily at me, I saw that she was rather confused. Estella, pausing a moment in her knitting with her eyes upon me, and then going on, I fancied that I read in the action of her fingers, as plainly as if she had told me in the dumb alphabet,[1] that she perceived I had discovered my real benefactor.

"Miss Havisham," said I, "I went to Richmond yesterday, to speak to Estella; and finding that some wind had blown *her* here, I followed."

Miss Havisham motioning to me for the third or fourth time to sit down, I took the chair by the dressing table, which I had often seen her occupy. With all that ruin at my feet and about me, it seemed a natural place for me that day.

"What I had to say to Estella, Miss Havisham, I will say before you, presently—in a few moments. It will not surprise you, it will not displease you. I am as unhappy as you can ever have meant me to be."

Miss Havisham continued to look steadily at me. I could see in the action of Estella's fingers as they worked that she attended to what I said—but she did not look up.

"I have found out who my patron is. It is not a fortunate discovery, and is not likely ever to enrich me in reputation, station,[2] fortune, anything. There are reasons why I must say no more of that. It is not my secret, but another's."

As I was silent for a while, looking at Estella and considering how to go on, Miss Havisham repeated, "It is not your secret, but another's. Well?"

"When you first caused me to be brought here, Miss Havisham; when I belonged to the village over yonder, that I wish I had never left; I suppose I did really come here, as any other chance boy might have come—as a kind of servant, to gratify a want or a whim, and to be paid for it?"

◄ How is Pip received? What does he assume about Estella?

◄ What does Pip tell Miss Havisham?

---

1. **dumb alphabet.** Sign language for the deaf
2. **station.** Social position; status

"Aye, Pip," replied Miss Havisham, steadily nodding her head; "you did."

"And that Mr. Jaggers—"

"Mr. Jaggers," said Miss Havisham, taking me up in a firm tone, "had nothing to do with it, and knew nothing of it. His being my lawyer, and his being the lawyer of your patron, is a coincidence. He holds the same relation towards numbers of people, and it might easily arise. Be that as it may, it did arise, and was not brought about by anyone."

Anyone might have seen in her <u>haggard</u> face that there was no suppression or <u>evasion</u> so far.

"But when I fell into the mistake I have so long remained in, at least you led me on?" said I.

"Yes," she returned, again nodding steadily, "I let you go on."

"Was that kind?"

"Who am I," cried Miss Havisham, striking her stick upon the floor, and flashing into <u>wrath</u> so suddenly that Estella glanced up at her in surprise, "who am I, for God's sake, that I should be kind?"

It was a weak complaint to have made, and I had not meant to make it. I told her so, as she sat brooding over this outburst.

"Well, well, well!" she said. "What else?"

"I was liberally paid for my old attendance here," I said, to soothe her, "in being apprenticed, and I have asked these questions only for my own information. What follows has another (and I hope more disinterested) purpose. In humoring my mistake, Miss Havisham, you punished—practiced on—perhaps you will supply whatever term expresses your intention, without offense—your self-seeking relations?"

"I did. Why, they would have it so! So would you. What has been my history that I should be at the pains of entreating either them or you not to have it so! You made your own <u>snares.</u> I never made them."

Waiting until she was quiet again—for this, too, flashed out of her in a wild and sudden way—I went on.

"I have been thrown among one family of your relations, Miss Havisham, and have been constantly among them since I went to London. I know them to have been as honestly under my delusion as I myself. And I should be false and base if I did not tell you, whether it is acceptable to you or no, and

► To what does Miss Havisham admit? What is her defense?

► How did Miss Havisham use Pip?

► Of what is Pip trying to convince Miss Havisham?

Words For Everyday Use

hag • gard (hag´ərd) *adj.*, worn out; drawn

e • va • sion (ē vā´zhən) *n.*, avoiding or escaping by cleverness or deceit

wrath (rath) *n.*, anger

snare (snar) *n.*, trap for small animals

whether you are inclined to give <u>credence</u> to it or no, that you deeply wrong both Mr. Matthew Pocket and his son Herbert, if you suppose them to be otherwise than generous, upright, open, and incapable of anything <u>designing</u> or mean."

"They are your friends," said Miss Havisham.

"They made themselves my friends," said I, "when they supposed me to have <u>superseded</u> them; and when Sarah Pocket, Miss Georgiana, and Mistress Camilla were not my friends, I think."

This contrasting of them with the rest seemed, I was glad to see, to do them good with her. She looked at me keenly for a little while, and then said quietly:

"What do you want for them?"

"Only," said I, "that you would not confound them with the others. They may be of the same blood, but, believe me, they are not of the same nature."

Still looking at me keenly, Miss Havisham repeated:

"What do you want for them?"

"I am not so cunning, you see," I said in answer, conscious that I reddened a little, "as that I could hide from you, even if I desired, that I do want something. Miss Havisham, if you could spare the money to do my friend Herbert a lasting service in life, but which from the nature of the case must be done without his knowledge, I could show you how."

◄ For whom does Pip ask a favor? What favor does he ask? Why?

"Why must it be done without his knowledge?" she asked, settling her hands upon her stick, that she might regard me the more attentively.

"Because," said I, "I began the service myself, more than two years ago, without his knowledge, and I don't want to be betrayed. Why I fail in my ability to finish it, I cannot explain. It is a part of the secret which is another person's and not mine."

She gradually withdrew her eyes from me, and turned them on the fire. After watching it for what appeared in the silence and by the light of the slowly wasting candles to be a long time, she was roused by the collapse of some of the red coals, and looked towards me again—at first, <u>vacantly</u>—then, with a gradually concentrating attention. All this time, Estella knitted on. When Miss Havisham had fixed her attention on me, she said, speaking as if there had been no lapse in our dialogue:

"What else?"

Words
For
Everyday
Use

cre • dence (krē´dəns) *n.,* belief in a report of another

de • sign • ing (di zī´niŋ) *adj.,* conniving; crafty

su • per • sede (soō´pər sēd´) *vt.,* replace; cause to be set aside

va • cant • ly (vā´kənt lē) *adv.,* blankly; without expression

"Estella," said I turning to her now, and trying to command my trembling voice, "you know I love you. You know that I have loved you long and dearly."

She raised her eyes to my face on being thus addressed, and her fingers <u>plied</u> their work, and she looked at me with an unmoved countenance. I saw that Miss Havisham glanced from me to her and from her to me.

"I should have said this sooner, but for my long mistake. It induced me to hope that Miss Havisham meant us for one another. While I thought you could not help yourself, as it were, I refrained from saying it. But I must say it now."

Preserving her unmoved[3] countenance, and with her fingers still going, Estella shook her head.

"I know," said I, in answer to that action; "I know. I have no hope that I shall ever call you mine, Estella. I am ignorant what may become of me very soon, how poor I may be, or where I may go. Still, I love you. I have loved you ever since I first saw you in this house."

Looking at me perfectly unmoved and with her fingers busy, she shook her head again.

"It would have been cruel in Miss Havisham, horribly cruel, to practice on the <u>susceptibility</u> of a poor boy, and to torture me through all these years with a vain hope and an <u>idle</u> pursuit, if she had reflected on the gravity of what she did. But I think she did not. I think that in the endurance of her own trial, she forgot mine, Estella."

► How does Miss Havisham respond to Pip's declaration? How does Estella respond?

I saw Miss Havisham put her hand to her heart and hold it there, as she sat looking by turns at Estella and at me.

"It seems," said Estella very calmly, "that there are sentiments, fancies[4]—I don't know how to call them—which I am not able to comprehend. When you say you love me, I know what you mean as a form of words, but nothing more. You address nothing in my breast,[5] you touch nothing there. I don't care for what you say at all. I have tried to warn you of this, now, have I not?"

I said, in a miserable manner, "Yes."

"Yes. But you would not be warned, for you thought I did not mean it. Now, did you not think so?"

---

3 unmoved. Expressing no feeling
4. fancies. Whims; fantasies
5. breast. Seat of affection and emotion

Words For Everyday Use	ply (plī) *vt.*, engage in diligently
	sus • cep • ti • bil • i • ty (sə sep´tə bil´ə tē) *n.*, state of being easily affected emotionally; sensitive nature
	i • dle (ī´dəl) *adj.*, vain; pointless

"I thought and hoped you could not mean it. You, so young, untried, and beautiful, Estella! Surely it is not in nature."

"It is in *my* nature," she returned. And then she added, with a stress upon the words, "It is in the nature formed within me. I make a great difference between you and all other people when I say so much. I can do no more."

"Is it not true," said I, "that Bentley Drummle is in town here, and pursuing you?"

"It is quite true," she replied, referring to him with the indifference of utter contempt.

"That you encourage him, and ride out with him, and that he dines with you this very day?"

She seemed a little surprised that I should know it, but again replied, "Quite true."

"You cannot love him, Estella?"

Her fingers stopped for the first time, as she <u>retorted</u> rather angrily, "What have I told you? Do you still think, in spite of it, that I do not mean what I say?"

"You would never marry him, Estella?"

She looked towards Miss Havisham, and considered for a moment with her work in her hands. Then she said, "Why not tell you the truth? I am going to be married to him."

I dropped my face into my hands, but was able to control myself better than I could have expected, considering what agony it gave me to hear her say those words. When I raised my face again, there was such a ghastly look upon Miss Havisham's, that it impressed me, even in my passionate hurry and grief.

"Estella, dearest, dearest Estella, do not let Miss Havisham lead you into this fatal step. Put me aside forever—you have done so, I well know—but bestow yourself on[6] some worthier person than Drummle. Miss Havisham gives you to him as the greatest slight and injury that could be done to the many far better men who admire you, and to the few who truly love you. Among those few, there may be one who loves you even as dearly, though he has not loved you as long as I. Take him, and I can bear it better for your sake!"

My earnestness awoke a wonder in her that seemed as if it would have been touched with compassion, if she could have <u>rendered</u> me at all intelligible to her own mind.

◀ What does Estella say about her nature? In what way does she favor Pip?

◀ Whom will Estella marry?

◀ What is Pip's reaction when he hears the news? Miss Havisham's?

---

6. **bestow yourself on.** Give yourself in marriage to

Words For Everyday Use

re • tort (ri tôrt´) *vi.*, answer (an argument) in kind
ren • der (ren´dər) *vt.*, cause to be or become

"I am going," she said again, in a gentler voice, "to be married to him. The preparations for my marriage are making, and I shall be married soon. Why do you injuriously introduce the name of my mother by adoption? It is my own act."

"Your own act, Estella, to fling yourself away upon a <u>brute</u>?"

"On whom should I fling myself away?" she retorted, with a smile. "Should I fling myself away upon the man who would the soonest feel (if people do feel such things) that I took nothing to him? There! It is done. I shall do well enough, and so will my husband. As to leading me into what you call this fatal step, Miss Havisham would have had me wait, and not marry yet; but I am tired of the life I have led, which has very few charms for me, and I am willing enough to change it. Say no more. We shall never understand each other."

"Such a mean brute, such a stupid brute!" I urged in despair.

"Don't be afraid of my being a blessing to him," said Estella; "I shall not be that. Come! Here is my hand. Do we part on this, you <u>visionary</u> boy—or man?"

"Oh, Estella!" I answered, as my bitter tears fell fast on her hand, do what I would to restrain them; "even if I remained in England and could hold my head up with the rest, how could I see you Drummle's wife?"

"Nonsense," she returned, "nonsense. This will pass in no time."

"Never, Estella!"

"You will get me out of your thoughts in a week."

"Out of my thoughts! You are part of my existence, part of myself. You have been in every line I have ever read, since I first came here, the rough common boy whose poor heart you wounded even then. You have been in every prospect I have ever seen since—on the river, on the sails of the ships, on the marshes, in the clouds, in the light, in the darkness, in the wind, in the woods, in the sea, in the streets. You have been the <u>embodiment</u> of every graceful fancy that my mind has ever become acquainted with. The stones of which the strongest London buildings are made are not more real, or more impossible to be displaced by your hands, than your presence and influence have been to me, there and everywhere, and will be. Estella, to the last hour of my life, you cannot choose but remain part of my character, part of the

▶ *What are Estella's reasons for marrying? Why is she marrying Drummle?*

▶ *How will Pip remember Estella?*

little good in me, part of the evil. But, in this separation I associate you only with the good, and I will faithfully hold you to that always, for you must have done me far more good than harm, let me feel now what sharp distress I may. O God bless you, God forgive you!"

In what ecstasy of unhappiness I got these broken words out of myself, I don't know. The rhapsody welled up[7] within me, like blood from an inward wound, and gushed out. I held her hand to my lips some lingering moments, and so I left her. But ever afterwards, I remembered—and soon afterwards with stronger reason—that while Estella looked at me merely with <u>incredulous</u> wonder, the <u>spectral</u> figure of Miss Havisham, her hand still covering her heart, seemed all resolved[8] into a ghastly stare of pity and remorse.

◀ In what state is Miss Havisham as Pip leaves?

All done, all gone! So much was done and gone that when I went out at the gate, the light of the day seemed of a darker color than when I went in. For a while, I hid myself among some lanes and bypaths, and then struck off to walk all the way to London. For I had by that time come to myself so far as to consider that I could not go back to the inn and see Drummle there; that I could not bear to sit upon the coach and be spoken to; that I could do nothing half so good for myself as tire myself out.

It was past midnight when I crossed London Bridge. Pursuing the narrow <u>intricacies</u> of the streets which at that time tended westward near the Middlesex shore of the river, my readiest access to the Temple was close by the riverside, through Whitefriars. I was not expected till tomorrow, but I had my keys, and, if Herbert were gone to bed, could get to bed myself without disturbing him.

As it seldom happened that I came in at that Whitefriars gate after the Temple was closed, and as I was very muddy and weary, I did not take it ill that the night-porter examined me with much attention as he held the gate a little way open for me to pass in. To help his memory I mentioned my name.

"I was not quite sure, sir, but I thought so. Here's a note, sir. The messenger that brought it said, Would you be so good as to read it by my lantern?"

◀ What does the night-porter give to Pip? What is the message?

---

7. **rhapsody welled up.** Impassioned music flowed through me and overcame me with emotion
8. **resolved.** Changed; converted

Words For Everyday Use	in • cred • u • lous (in krej′o͞o ləs) *adj.*, unwilling to believe; doubting
	spec • tral (spek′trəl) *adj.*, like a phantom or ghost
	in • tri • ca • cy (in′tri kə sē) *n.*, quality of being complex

Much surprised by the request, I took the note. It was directed to Philip Pip, Esquire,[9] and on the top of the superscription[10] were the words, "PLEASE READ THIS HERE." I opened it, the watchman holding up his light, and read inside, in Wemmick's writing:

"DON'T GO HOME."

---

9. **Esquire.** Used as a title of courtesy after a man's name
10. **superscription.** Address on a letter

CHAPTER 45

Turning from the Temple gate as soon as I had read the warning, I made the best of my way to Fleet Street, and there got a late hackney chariot[1] and drove to the Hummums in Covent Garden. In those times a bed was always to be got there at any hour of the night, and the chamberlain,[2] letting me in at his ready wicket,[3] lighted the candle next in order on his shelf, and showed me straight into the bedroom next in order on his list. It was a sort of vault on the ground floor at the back, with a <u>despotic</u> monster of a four-post bedstead in it, straddling over the whole place, putting one of his arbitrary[4] legs into the fireplace, and another into the doorway, and squeezing the wretched little washing-stand in quite a divinely righteous manner.

◄ Where does Pip spend the night? Why?

As I had asked for a night light, the chamberlain had brought me in, before he left me, the good old constitutional rushlight[5] of those virtuous days—an object like the ghost of a walking cane, which instantly broke its back if it were touched, which nothing could ever be lighted at, and which was placed in solitary confinement at the bottom of a high tin tower, <u>perforated</u> with round holes that made a staringly wide-awake pattern on the walls. When I had got into bed, and lay there, footsore, weary, and wretched, I found that I could no more close my own eyes than I could close the eyes of this foolish Argus.[6] And thus, in the gloom and death of the night, we stared at one another.

What a doleful night! How anxious, how dismal, how long! There was an inhospitable smell in the room of cold soot and hot dust; and, as I looked up into the corners of the tester[7] over my head, I thought what a number of blue-bottle flies from the butcher's, and earwigs[8] from the market, and grubs from the country, must be holding on up there,

◄ What makes the room unpleasant?

---

1. **hackney chariot.** Carriage for hire
2. **chamberlain.** Bedchamber attendant
3. **wicket.** Small door or gate
4. **arbitrary.** Marked by the tyrannical use of power
5. **constitutional rushlight.** Candle that was part of the establishment
6. **Argus.** A mythological giant with a hundred eyes
7. **tester.** Canopy over a bed
8. **earwigs.** Biting insects

Words For Everyday Use

des • pot • ic (des pät´ik) *adj.*, like a dictator; tyrannical

per • for • ate (pʉr´fə rāt´) *vt.*, pierce or punch holes in lying by for next summer. This led me to speculate whether any of them ever tumbled down, and then I fancied that I felt light falls on my face—a disagreeable turn of thought, suggesting other and more objectionable approaches up my back. When I had lain awake a little while, those extraordinary voices with which silence <u>teems</u>, began to make themselves <u>audible</u>. The closet whispered, the fireplace sighed, the little washing-stand ticked, and one guitar-string played occasionally in the chest of drawers. At about the same time, the eyes on the wall acquired a new expression, and in every one of those staring rounds I saw written, DON'T GO HOME.

Whatever night-fancies and night-noises crowded on me, they never warded off this DON'T GO HOME. It plaited[9] itself into whatever I thought of, as a bodily pain would have done. Not long before, I had read in the newspapers how a gentleman unknown had come to the Hummums in the night, and had gone to bed, and had destroyed himself, and had been found in the morning weltering[10] in blood. It came into my head that he must have occupied this very vault of mine, and I got out of bed to assure myself that there were no red marks about; then opened the door to look out into the passages, and cheer myself with the companionship of a distant light, near which I knew the chamberlain to be dozing. But all this time, why I was not to go home, and what had happened at home, and when I should go home, and whether Provis was safe at home, were questions occupying my mind so busily that one might have supposed there could be no more room in it for any other theme. Even when I thought of Estella, and how we had parted that day forever, and when I recalled all the circumstances of our parting, and all her looks and tones, and the action of her fingers while she knitted—even then I was pursuing, here and there and everywhere, the caution DON'T GO HOME. When at last I dozed, in sheer exhaustion of mind and body it became a vast shadowy verb which I had to conjugate, imperative mood, present tense:[11] Do not thou go home, let him not go home, let us not go home, do not ye or you go home, let not them go home. Then, potentially: I may not and I cannot go

▶ *What frightens Pip?*

▶ *What are Pip's worries?*

---

9. **plaited.** Wove
10. **weltering.** Soaked, stained
11. **verb . . . tense.** As in a grammar drill, Pip is restlessly turning over in his mind the different forms of the verb in the command "Don't go home."

| Words For Everyday Use | **teem** (tēm) *vi.,* swarm; be abundant |
| | **au • di • ble** (ô´də bəl) *adj.,* able to be heard |

home; and I might not, could not, would not, and should not go home; until I felt that I was going distracted,[12] and rolled over on the pillow, and looked at the staring rounds upon the wall again.

I had left directions that I was to be called at seven, for it was plain that I must see Wemmick before seeing anyone else, and equally plain that this was a case in which his Walworth sentiments only could be taken. It was a relief to get out of the room where the night had been so miserable, and I needed no second knocking at the door to startle me from my uneasy bed.

◄ Whom will Pip visit?

The castle battlements arose upon my view at eight o'clock. The little servant happening to be entering the fortress with two hot rolls, I passed through the postern[13] and crossed the drawbridge in her company, and so came without announcement into the presence of Wemmick as he was making tea for himself and the Aged. An open door afforded a perspective view of the Aged in bed.

"Halloa, Mr. Pip!" said Wemmick. "You did come home, then?"

"Yes," I returned; "but I didn't go home."

"That's all right," said he, rubbing his hands. "I left a note for you at each of the Temple gates, on the chance. Which gate did you come to?"

I told him.

"I'll go round to the others in the course of the day and destroy the notes," said Wemmick; "it's a good rule never to leave documentary[14] evidence if you can help it, because you don't know when it may be put in. I'm going to take a liberty with you—*Would* you mind toasting this sausage for the Aged P.?"

◄ Why will Wemmick destroy the notes?

I said I should be delighted to do it.

"Then you can go about your work, Mary Anne," said Wemmick to the little servant, "which leaves us to ourselves, don't you see, Mr. Pip?" he added, winking, as she disappeared.

I thanked him for his friendship and caution, and our discourse proceeded in a low tone, while I toasted the Aged's sausage and he buttered the crumb of the Aged's roll.

"Now, Mr. Pip, you know," said Wemmick, "you and I understand one another. We are in our private and personal capacities, and we have been engaged in a confidential transaction before today. Official sentiments are one thing. We are extra official."[15]

---

12. **distracted.** Crazy
13. **postern.** Back door or gate
14. **documentary.** Consisting of documents; i.e., written
15. **extra official.** Outside the scope of what is official

I cordially assented. I was so very nervous that I had already lighted the Aged's sausage like a torch, and been obliged to blow it out.

"I accidentally heard, yesterday morning," said Wemmick, "being in a certain place where I once took you—even between you and me, it's as well not to mention names when avoidable—"

"Much better not," said I. "I understand you."

"I heard there by chance, yesterday morning," said Wemmick, "that a certain person not altogether of uncolonial pursuits, and not unpossessed of portable property[16]—I don't know who it may really be—we won't name this person—"

"Not necessary," said I.

"—had made some little stir in a certain part of the world where a good many people go, not always in gratification of their own inclinations, and not quite irrespective of the government expense—"[17]

In watching his face, I made quite a firework of the Aged's sausage, and greatly discomposed both my own attention and Wemmick's; for which I apologized.

"—by disappearing from such place, and being no more heard of thereabouts. From which," said Wemmick, "conjectures had been raised and theories formed. I also heard that you at your chambers in Garden Court, Temple, had been watched, and might be watched again."

"By whom?" said I.

"I wouldn't go into that," said Wemmick evasively; "it might clash with official responsibilities. I heard it, as I have in my time heard other curious things in the same place. I don't tell it to you on information received. I heard it."

He took the toasting-fork and sausage from me as he spoke, and set forth the Aged's breakfast neatly on a little tray. Previous to placing it before him, he went into the Aged's room with a clean white cloth, and tied the same under the old gentleman's chin, and propped him up, and put his nightcap on one side, and gave him quite a rakish air. Then, he placed his breakfast before him with great care, and

► What does Wemmick tell Pip? Where does he get this information? Why does he speak in a code?

---

16. **not altogether . . . property.** Who has spent time in the colonies and owns material possessions

17. **not always . . . expense.** Not by their own choice; at the expense of the government

---

Words For Everyday Use

rak • ish (rāk´ish) *adj.,* dashing; elegant

said, "All right, ain't you, Aged P.?" To which the cheerful Aged replied, "All right, John, my boy, all right!" As there seemed to be a <u>tacit</u> understanding that the Aged was not in a presentable state, and was therefore to be considered invisible, I made a pretense of being in complete ignorance of these proceedings.

"This watching of me at my chambers (which I have once had reason to suspect)," I said to Wemmick when he came back, "is inseparable from the person to whom you have adverted,[18] is it?"

Wemmick looked very serious. "I couldn't undertake to say that, of my own knowledge. I mean, I couldn't undertake to say it was at first. But it either is, or it will be, or it's in great danger of being."

As I saw that he was restrained by fealty[19] to Little Britain from saying as much as he could, and as I knew with thankfulness to him how far out of his way he went to say what he did, I could not press him. But I told him, after a little meditation over the fire, that I would like to ask him a question, subject to his answering or not answering, as he deemed right, and sure that his course would be right. He paused in his breakfast, and crossing his arms, and pinching his shirtsleeves (his notion of indoor comfort was to sit without any coat), he nodded to me once, to put my question.

"You have heard of a man of bad character whose true name is Compeyson?"

He answered with one other nod.

"Is he living?"

One other nod.

"Is he in London?"

He gave me one other nod, compressed the post office exceedingly, gave me one last nod, and went on with his breakfast.

"Now," said Wemmick, "questioning being over"—which he emphasized and repeated for my guidance—"I come to what I did, after hearing what I heard. I went to Garden Court to find you; not finding you, I went to Clarriker's to find Mr. Herbert."

"And him you found?" said I, with great anxiety.

◀ What does Pip learn about Compeyson?

18. **adverted.** Called attention; alluded
19. **fealty.** Allegiance; oath of loyalty

Words For Everyday Use

tac • it (tas´it) *adj.*, unspoken; silent

"And him I found. Without mentioning any names or going into any details, I gave him to understand that if he was aware of anybody—Tom, Jack, or Richard—being about the chambers, or about the immediate neighborhood, he had better get Tom, Jack, or Richard out of the way while you were out of the way."

"He would be greatly puzzled what to do?"

▶ What is Wemmick's advice?

"He *was* puzzled what to do; not the less, because I gave him my opinion that it was not safe to try to get Tom, Jack, or Richard too far out of the way at present. Mr. Pip, I'll tell you something. Under existing circumstances there is no place like a great city when you are once in it. Don't break cover too soon. Lie close. Wait till things slacken[19] before you try the open, even for foreign air."

I thanked him for his valuable advice, and asked him what Herbert had done?

"Mr. Herbert," said Wemmick, "after being all of a heap for half an hour, struck out a plan. He mentioned to me as a secret that he is courting a young lady who has, as no doubt you are aware, a bedridden[21] pa. Which pa, having been in the purser[22] line of life, lies a-bed in a bow-window where he can see the ships sail up and down the river. You are acquainted with the young lady, most probably?"

"Not personally," said I.

▶ How does Clara feel about Pip? Why haven't the two met?

The truth was that she had objected to me as an expensive companion who did Herbert no good, and that, when Herbert had first proposed to present me to her, she had received the proposal with such very moderate warmth that Herbert had felt himself obliged to confide the state of the case to me, with a view to the lapse of a little time before I made her acquaintance. When I had begun to advance Herbert's prospects by stealth, I had been able to bear this with cheerful philosophy; he and his affianced, for their part, had naturally not been very anxious to introduce a third person into their interviews; and thus, although I was assured that I had risen in Clara's <u>esteem</u>, and although the young lady and I had long regularly interchanged messages and remembrances by Herbert, I had never seen her. However, I did not trouble Wemmick with these particulars.

---

20. **slacken.** Settle down
21. **bedridden.** Too ill to be out of bed
22. **purser.** A ship official in charge of accounts

Words For Everyday Use

es • teem (e stēm´) *n.*, respect; regard

"The house with the bow-window," said Wemmick, "being by the riverside, down the Pool there between Limehouse and Greenwich, and being kept, it seems, by a very respectable widow, who has a furnished upper floor to let, Mr. Herbert put it to me, what did I think of that as a temporary tenement[23] for Tom, Jack, or Richard. Now, I thought very well of it, for three reasons I'll give you. That is to say, firstly, it's altogether out of all your beats, and is well away from the usual heap of streets great and small. Secondly, without going near it yourself, you could always hear of the safety of Tom, Jack, or Richard through Mr. Herbert. Thirdly, after a while, and when it might be prudent, if you should want to slip Tom, Jack, or Richard, on board a foreign packet-boat,[24] there he is—ready."

◄ Why is Clara's home a good place for Provis to stay?

Much comforted by these considerations, I thanked Wemmick again and again, and begged him to proceed.

"Well, sir! Mr. Herbert threw himself into the business with a will, and by nine o'clock last night he housed Tom, Jack, or Richard—whichever it may be—you and I don't want to know—quite successfully. At the old lodgings it was understood that he was summoned to Dover, and in fact he was taken down the Dover road and cornered out of it. Now, another great advantage of all this is that it was done without you, and when, if anyone was concerning himself about your movements, you must be known to be ever so many miles off, and quite otherwise engaged. This <u>diverts</u> suspicion and confuses it, and for the same reason I recommended that even if you came back last night, you should not go home. It brings in more confusion, and you want confusion."

Wemmick, having finished his breakfast, here looked at his watch, and began to get his coat on.

"And now, Mr. Pip," said he, with his hands still in the sleeves, "I have probably done the most I can do; but if I can ever do more—from a Walworth point of view, and in a strictly private and personal capacity—I shall be glad to do it. Here's the address. There can be no harm in your going here tonight and seeing for yourself that all is well with Tom, Jack, or Richard before you go home—which is another reason for

---

23. **tenement.** Apartment; flat
24. **packet-boat.** Boat that travels a regular route carrying passengers, freight, and mail

Words
For
Everyday
Use

di • vert (də vʉrt´) vt., distract attention

your not going home last night. But after you have gone home, don't go back here. You are very welcome, I am sure, Mr. Pip"—his hands were now out of his sleeves, and I was shaking them—"and let me finally impress one important point upon you." He laid his hands upon my shoulders, and added in a solemn whisper: "<u>Avail</u> yourself of this evening to lay hold of his portable property. You don't know what may happen to him. Don't let anything happen to the portable property."

Quite <u>despairing</u> of making my mind clear to Wemmick on this point, I forbore[25] to try.

"Time's up," said Wemmick, "and I must be off. If you had nothing more pressing to do than to keep here till dark, that's what I should advise. You look very much worried, and it would do you good to have a perfectly quiet day with the Aged—he'll be up presently—and a little bit of—you remember the pig?"

"Of course," said I.

"Well, and a little bit of *him*. That sausage you toasted was his, and he was in all respects a first-rater. Do try him, if it is only for old acquaintance sake. Good-bye, Aged Parent!" in a cheery shout.

"All right, John; all right, my boy!" piped the old man from within.

I soon fell asleep before Wemmick's fire, and the Aged and I enjoyed one another's society by falling asleep before it more or less all day. We had loin of pork for dinner, and greens grown on the estate, and I nodded at the Aged with a good intention whenever I failed to do it drowsily. When it was quite dark, I left the Aged preparing the fire for toast; and I inferred from the number of teacups, as well as from his glances at the two little doors in the wall, that Miss Skiffins was expected.

---

25. **forbore.** Refrained or abstained

Words For Everyday Use	a • **vail** (ə vāl´) *vt.*, take advantage; make use
	de • **spair** (di sper´) *vi.*, feel or show hopelessness

Eight o'clock had struck before I got into the air that was scented, not disagreeably, by the chips and shavings of the long-shore boatbuilders, and mast oar,[1] and block makers. All that waterside region of the upper and lower Pool below Bridge, was unknown ground to me, and when I struck down by the river, I found that the spot I wanted was not where I had supposed it to be, and was anything but easy to find. It was called Mill Pond Bank, Chinks's Basin, and I had no other guide to Chinks's Basin than the Old Green Copper Rope-Walk.[2]

It matters not what stranded ships repairing in dry docks I lost myself among, what old hulls[3] of ships in course of being knocked to pieces, what ooze and slime and other dregs of tide, what yards of ship-builders and ship-breakers, what rusty anchors blindly biting into the ground though for years off duty, what mountainous country of accumulated casks and timber, how many rope-walks that were not the Old Green Copper. After several times falling short of my destination and as often over-shooting it, I came unexpectedly round a corner, upon Mill Pond Bank. It was a fresh kind of place, all circumstances considered, where the wind from the river had room to turn itself round; and there were two or three trees in it, and there was the stump of a ruined windmill, and there was the Old Green Copper Rope-Walk— whose long and narrow vista I could trace in the moonlight, along a series of wooden frames set in the ground, that looked like <u>superannuated</u> haymaking-rakes which had grown old and lost most of their teeth.

Selecting from the few queer houses upon Mill Pond Bank, a house with a wooden front and three stories of bow-window (not bay-window, which is another thing), I looked at the plate upon the door, and read there, Mrs. Whimple. That being the name I wanted, I knocked, and an elderly woman of a pleasant and thriving appearance responded. She was immediately <u>deposed</u>, however, by Herbert, who silently led

◄ *Why does Pip have difficulty finding the address?*

◄ *What does he find?*

---

1. **mast oar.** Oar made of metal, usually hollow
2. **Rope-Walk.** Long path or alley where ropes are made
3. **hulls.** Frames or bodies of ships

Words For Everyday Use	**su • per • an • nu • at • ed** (so͞o′pər an′yo͞o ā′təd) *adj.,* too old or worn for further work **de • pose** (di pōz′) *vt.,* remove from office or a position of power

me into the parlor and shut the door. It was an odd sensation to see his very familiar face established quite at home in that very unfamiliar room and region; and I found myself looking at him, much as I looked at the corner cupboard with the glass and china, the shells upon the chimney piece, and the colored engravings on the wall, representing the death of Captain Cook,[4] a ship-launch, and his Majesty King George the Third[5] in a state-coachman's wig, leather breeches, and top boots, on the terrace at Windsor.[6]

▶ *Whom will Pip meet?*

"All is well, Handel," said Herbert, "and he is quite satisfied, though eager to see you. My dear girl is with her father; and if you'll wait till she comes down, I'll make you known to her, and then we'll go upstairs. *That's* her father."

I had become aware of an alarming growling overhead, and had probably expressed the fact in my countenance.

"I am afraid he is a sad old rascal," said Herbert, smiling, "but I have never seen him. Don't you smell rum? He is always at it."

"At rum?" said I.

"Yes," returned Herbert, "and you may suppose how mild it makes his gout.[7] He persists, too, in keeping all the provisions upstairs in his room, and serving them out. He keeps them on shelves over his head, and *will* weigh them all. His room must be like a chandler's shop."[8]

While he thus spoke, the growling noise became a prolonged roar, and then died away.

"What else can be the consequence," said Herbert, in explanation, "if he *will* cut the cheese? A man with the gout in his right hand—and everywhere else—can't expect to get through a Double Gloucester[9] without hurting himself."

He seemed to have hurt himself very much, for he gave another furious roar.

▶ *Why is it good for Provis to be there?*

"To have Provis for an upper lodger is quite a <u>godsend</u> to Mrs. Whimple," said Herbert, "for of course people in general won't stand that noise. A curious place, Handel, isn't it?"

---

4. **Captain Cook.** James Cook, eighteenth-century British explorer and navigator who reached New Zealand, Australia, the South Pacific, and the Antarctic Circle
5. **Majesty . . . Third.** King of Great Britain during the American Revolution
6. **Windsor.** Windsor Castle, a residence for the British royal family
7. **gout.** Joint disease causing pain and deformity
8. **chandler's shop.** Store of a dealer in specified goods
9. **Double Gloucester.** Kind of cheese made in the English county of Gloucester

Words For Everyday Use

god • send (gäd send´) *n.*, anything unexpected or needed that comes at an opportune moment, as if sent by God

It was a curious place, indeed, but remarkably well kept and clean.

"Mrs. Whimple," said Herbert, when I told him so, "is the best of housewives, and I really do not know what my Clara would do without her motherly help. For Clara has no mother of her own, Handel, and no relation in the world but old Gruffandgrim."

"Surely that's not his name, Herbert?"

"No, no," said Herbert, "that's my name for him. His name is Mr. Barley. But what a blessing it is for the son of my father and mother, to love a girl who has no relations, and who can never bother herself, or anybody else, about her family!"

Herbert had told me on former occasions, and now reminded me, that he first knew Miss Clara Barley when she was completing her education at an establishment at Hammersmith, and that on her being recalled home to nurse her father, he and she had confided their affection to the motherly Mrs. Whimple, by whom it had been <u>fostered</u> and regulated with equal kindness and <u>discretion</u> ever since. It was understood that nothing of a tender nature could possibly be confided to old Barley, by reason of his being totally unequal to the consideration of any subject more psychological than gout, rum, and purser's stores.

◄ How does Mrs. Whimple help Herbert and Clara? Why doesn't Mr. Barley know of their relationship?

As we were thus conversing in a low tone while Old Barley's sustained growl vibrated in the beam that crossed the ceiling, the room door opened, and a very pretty, slight, dark-eyed girl of twenty or so came in with a basket in her hand: whom Herbert tenderly relieved of the basket, and presented blushing, as "Clara." She really was a most charming girl, and might have passed for a captive fairy whom that <u>truculent</u> ogre, Old Barley, had pressed into his service.

"Look here," said Herbert, showing me the basket, with a compassionate and tender smile after we had talked a little; "here's poor Clara's supper, served out every night. Here's her allowance of bread, and here's her slice of cheese, and here's her rum—which I drink. This is Mr. Barley's breakfast for tomorrow, served out to be cooked. Two mutton chops, three potatoes, some split peas, a little flour, two ounces of butter, a pinch of salt, and all this black pepper. It's stewed up together, and taken hot, and it's a nice thing for the gout, I should think!"

Words For Everyday Use

fos • ter (fôs´tər) *vt.,* promote the development of; cultivate
dis • cre • tion (di skresh´ən) *n.,* quality of being careful of what one does or says
truc • u • lent (truk´yo͞o lənt) *adj.,* fierce; cruel

► Why does Pip feel
so tenderly about
Herbert and Clara?

There was something so natural and winning in Clara's resigned way of looking at these stores in detail, as Herbert pointed them out—and something so confiding, loving, and innocent, in her modest manner of yielding herself to Herbert's embracing arm—and something so gentle in her, so much needing protection on Mill Pond Bank, by Chinks's Basin, and the Old Green Copper Rope-Walk, with Old Barley growing in the beam—that I would not have undone the engagement between her and Herbert for all the money in the pocketbook I had never opened.

I was looking at her with pleasure and admiration when suddenly the growl swelled into a roar again, and a frightful bumping noise was heard above, as if a giant with a wooden leg were trying to bore it through the ceiling to come to us. Upon this Clara said to Herbert, "Papa wants me, darling!" and ran away.

"There is an <u>unconscionable</u> old shark for you!" said Herbert. "What do you suppose he wants now, Handel?"

"I don't know," said I. "Something to drink?"

"That's it!" cried Herbert, as if I had made a guess of extraordinary merit. "He keeps his grog[10] ready-mixed in a little tub on the table. Wait a moment, and you'll hear Clara lift him up to take some. There he goes!" Another roar, with a prolonged shake at the end. "Now," said Herbert, as it was succeeded by silence, "he's drinking. Now," said Herbert, as the growl resounded in the beam once more, "he's down again on his back!"

Clara returned soon afterwards, and Herbert accompanied me upstairs to see our charge. As we passed Mr. Barley's door, he was heard hoarsely muttering within, in a strain that rose and fell like wind, the following <u>refrain</u>; in which I substitute good wishes for something quite the reverse.

"Ahoy! Bless your eyes, here's old Bill Barley. Here's old Bill Barley, bless your eyes. Here's old Bill Barley on the flat of his back, by the Lord. Lying on the flat of his back, like a drifting old dead flounder,[11] here's your old Bill Barley, bless your eyes. Ahoy! Bless you."

In this strain of consolation, Herbert informed me the invisible Barley would <u>commune</u> with himself by the day

---

10. **grog.** Alcoholic drink, especially rum mixed with water
11. **flounder.** Flat fish like a halibut or grouper

Words
For
Everyday
Use

un • con • scion • a • ble (un kän′shən ə bəl) *adj.*, unreasonable; without conscience

re • frain (ri frān′) *n.*, verse repeated at intervals throughout a song or poem

com • mune (kə myo͞on′) *vi.*, have close rapport or communication and night together, often while it was light, having at the same time one eye at a telescope which was fitted on his bed for the convenience of sweeping the river.

In his two cabin rooms at the top of the house, which were fresh and airy, and in which Mr. Barley was less audible than below, I found Provis comfortably settled. He expressed no alarm, and seemed to feel none that was worth mentioning, but it struck me that he was softened—indefinably, for I could have said how, and could never afterwards recall how when I tried; but certainly.

The opportunity that the day's rest had given me for reflection had resulted in my fully determining to say nothing to him respecting Compeyson. For anything I knew, his <u>animosity</u> towards the man might otherwise lead to his seeking him out and rushing on his own destruction. Therefore, when Herbert and I sat down with him by his fire, I asked him first of all whether he relied on Wemmick's judgment and sources of information.

"Aye, aye, dear boy!" he answered, with a grave nod, "Jaggers knows."

"Then, I have talked with Wemmick," said I, "and have come to tell you what caution he gave me and what advice."

This I did accurately, with the reservation just mentioned, and I told him how Wemmick had heard, in Newgate prison (whether from officers or prisoners I could not say), that he was under some suspicion, and that my chambers had been watched; how Wemmick had recommended his keeping close for a time, and my keeping away from him; and what Wemmick had said about getting him abroad. I added that, of course, when the time came, I should go with him, or should follow close upon him, as might be safest in Wemmick's judgment. What was to follow that, I did not touch upon; neither, indeed, was I at all clear or comfortable about it in my own mind, now that I saw him in that softer condition, and in declared peril for my sake. As to altering my way of living by enlarging my expenses I put it to him whether in our present unsettled and difficult circumstances it would not be simply ridiculous, if it were no worse.

◄ *What are Pip's plans?*

He could not deny this, and indeed was very reasonable throughout. His coming back was a <u>venture</u>, he said, and he had always known it to be a venture. He would do nothing

◄ *How does Provis feel about the plans?*

Words For Everyday Use

an • i • mos • i • ty (an´ə mäs´ə tē) *n.*, ill will; hostility

ven • ture (ven´chər) *n.*, risky or dangerous undertaking to make it a desperate venture, and he had very little fear of his safety with such good help.

Herbert, who had been looking at the fire and pondering, here said that something had come into his thoughts arising out of Wemmick's suggestion, which it might be worthwhile to pursue. "We are both good watermen, Handel, and could take him down the river ourselves when the right time comes. No boat would then be hired for the purpose, and no boatmen; that would save at least a chance of suspicion, and any chance is worth saving. Never mind the season; don't you think it might be a good thing if you began at once to keep a boat at the Temple stairs, and were in the habit of rowing up and down the river? You fall into that habit, and then who notices or minds? Do it twenty or fifty times, and there is nothing special in your doing it the twenty-first or fifty-first."

▶ *What does Herbert suggest?*

I liked this scheme, and Provis was quite elated by it. We agreed that it should be carried into execution, and that Provis should never recognize us if we came below Bridge and rowed past Mill Pond Bank. But we further agreed that he should pull down the blind[12] in that part of his window which gave upon the east, whenever he saw us and all was right.

▶ *What signal do they establish?*

Our conference being now ended, and everything arranged, I rose to go, remarking to Herbert that he and I had better not go home together, and that I would take half an hour's start of him. "I don't like to leave you here," I said to Provis, "though I cannot doubt your being safer here than near me. Goodbye!"

"Dear boy," he answered, clasping my hands, "I don't know when we may meet again, and I don't like goodbye. Say good night!"

"Good night! Herbert will go regularly between us, and when the time comes you may be certain I shall be ready. Good night, good night!"

We thought it best that he should stay in his own rooms, and we left him on the landing outside his door, holding a light over the stair-rail to light us downstairs. Looking back at him, I thought of the first night of his return when our positions were reversed, and when I little supposed my heart could ever be as heavy and anxious at parting from him as it was now.

Old Barley was growling and swearing when we repassed his door, with no appearance of having ceased or of meaning to cease. When we got to the foot of the stairs, I asked Herbert whether he had preserved the name of Provis. He

---

12. **blind.** Shade; window covering

replied, certainly not, and that the lodger was Mr. Campbell. He also explained that the utmost known of Mr. Campbell there, was, that he (Herbert) had Mr. Campbell <u>consigned</u> to him, and felt a strong personal interest in his being well cared for, and living a secluded life. So, when we went into the parlor where Mrs. Whimple and Clara were seated at work, I said nothing of my own interest in Mr. Campbell, but kept it to myself.

◀ What is Provis's new alias? Under what guise is he staying at Clara's home?

When I had taken leave of the pretty, gentle, dark-eyed girl, and of the motherly woman who had not outlived her honest sympathy with a little affair of true love, I felt as if the Old Green Copper Rope-Walk had grown quite a different place. Old Barley might be as old as the hills and might swear like a whole field of troopers, but there were <u>redeeming</u> youth and trust and hope enough in Chinks's Basin to fill it to overflowing. And then I thought of Estella, and of our parting, and went home very sadly.

◀ How does Pip feel about Clara's home? What saddens him?

All things were as quiet in the Temple as ever I had seen them. The windows of the rooms of that side lately occupied by Provis were dark and still, and there was no lounger in Garden Court. I walked past the fountain twice or thrice before I descended the steps that were between me and my rooms, but I was quite alone. Herbert coming to my bedside when he came in—for I went straight to bed, dispirited and fatigued—made the same report. Opening one of the windows after that, he looked out into the moonlight, and told me that the pavement was as solemnly empty as the pavement of any cathedral at that same hour.

Next day, I set myself to get the boat. It was soon done, and the boat was brought round to the Temple stairs, and lay where I could reach her within a minute or two. Then, I began to go out as for training and practice—sometimes alone, sometimes with Herbert. I was often out in cold, rain, and sleet, but nobody took much note of me after I had been out a few times. At first, I kept above Blackfriars Bridge; but as the hours of the tides changed, I took towards London Bridge. It was Old London Bridge in those days, and at certain states of the tide there was a race and fall of water there which gave it a bad reputation. But I knew well enough how to "shoot" the bridge after seeing it done, and so began to row about among the shipping in the Pool, and down to

◀ What next step does Pip take?

Words For Everyday Use	**con • sign** (kən sīn′) vt., place in the care of another
	re • deem • ing (ri dēm′iŋ) adj., compensating

Erith. The first time I passed Mill Pond Bank, Herbert and I were pulling a pair of oars; and, both in going and returning, we saw the blind towards the east come down. Herbert was rarely there less frequently than three times in a week, and he never brought me a single word of intelligence that was at all alarming. Still, I knew that there was cause for alarm, and I could not get rid of the notion of being watched. Once received, it is a haunting idea; how many undesigning[13] persons I suspected of watching me it would be hard to calculate.

In short, I was always full of fears for the rash man who was in hiding. Herbert had sometimes said to me that he found it pleasant to stand at one of our windows after dark, when the tide was running down, and to think that it was flowing, with everything it bore, towards Clara. But I thought with dread that it was flowing towards Magwitch, and that any black mark on its surface might be his pursuers, going swiftly, silently, and surely, to take him.

► *Of what or whom is Pip afraid?*

___

13. **undesigning.** Innocent

Some weeks passed without bringing any change. We waited for Wemmick, and he made no sign. If I had never known him out of Little Britain, and had never enjoyed the privilege of being on a familiar footing at the castle, I might have doubted him; not so for a moment, knowing him as I did.

My worldly affairs began to wear a gloomy appearance, and I was pressed for money by more than one creditor.[1] Even I myself began to know the want of money (I mean of ready money in my own pocket), and to relieve it by <u>converting</u> some easily spared articles of jewelry into cash. But I had quite determined that it would be a heartless <u>fraud</u> to take more money from my patron in the existing state of my uncertain thoughts and plans. Therefore, I had sent him the unopened pocketbook by Herbert, to hold in his own keeping, and I felt a kind of satisfaction—whether it was a false kind or a true, I hardly know—in not having profited by his generosity since his revelation of himself.

◄ *In what state are Pip's finances? Why?*

As the time wore on, an impression settled heavily upon me that Estella was married. Fearful of having it confirmed, though it was all but a conviction, I avoided the newspapers, and begged Herbert (to whom I had confided the circumstances of our last interview) never to speak of her to me. Why I hoarded up this last wretched little rag of the robe of hope that was rent and given to the winds, how do I know? Why did you who read this commit that not dissimilar inconsistency of your own, last year, last month, last week?

◄ *What does Pip avoid?*

It was an unhappy life that I lived, and its one dominant anxiety, towering over all its other anxieties like a high mountain above a range of mountains, never disappeared from my view. Still, no new cause for fear arose. Let me start from my bed as I would, with the terror fresh upon me that he was discovered; let me sit listening as I would, with dread for Herbert's returning step at night, lest it should be fleeter[2] than ordinary, and winged with evil news; for all that, and much more to like purpose, the round of things went on.

---

1. **creditor.** Person to whom one owes money
2. **fleeter.** Faster

Words For Everyday Use	con • vert (kən vʉrt´) *vt.,* transform; change fraud (frôd) *n.,* deception

► *What does Pip do to pass the time?*

Condemned to inaction and a state of constant restlessness and suspense, I rowed about in my boat, and waited, waited, waited, as I best could.

There were states of the tide when, having been down the river, I could not get back through the eddy-chafed[3] arches and starlings[4] of old London Bridge; then I left my boat at a wharf near the Custom House, to be brought up afterwards to the Temple stairs. I was not averse to doing this, as it served to make me and my boat a commoner incident among the waterside people there. From this slight occasion sprang two meetings that I have now to tell of.

One afternoon, late in the month of February, I came ashore at the wharf at dusk. I had pulled down as far as Greenwich with the ebb tide, and had turned with the tide. It had been a fine bright day, but had become foggy as the sun dropped, and I had had to feel my way back among the shipping pretty carefully. Both in going and returning, I had seen the signal in his window, All well.

► *What will Pip do this evening?*

As it was a raw evening and I was cold, I thought I would comfort myself with dinner at once; and as I had hours of dejection and solitude before me if I went home to the Temple, I thought I would afterwards go to the play. The theater where Mr. Wopsle had achieved his questionable triumph was in that waterside neighborhood (it is nowhere now), and to that theater I resolved to go. I was aware that Mr. Wopsle had not succeeded in reviving the drama, but, on the contrary, had rather partaken of its decline. He had been <u>ominously</u> heard of, through the playbills, as a faithful black, in connection with a little girl of noble birth, and a monkey. And Herbert had seen him as a <u>predatory</u> Tartar[5] of comic <u>propensities</u>, with a face like a red brick, and an outrageous hat all over bells.

I dined at what Herbert and I used to call a geographical chophouse[6]—where there were maps of the world in porterpot[7] rims on every half-yard of the table-cloths, and charts of gravy on every one of the knives—to this day there is scarcely

---

3. **eddy-chafed.** Worn away by swirling water
4. **starlings.** Protective structures surrounding a bridge
5. **Tartar.** Person of Turkish origin, often portrayed by Western Europeans as irritable and violent
6. **chophouse.** Restaurant specializing in chops and steaks
7. **porterpot.** Pot used to hold dark-brown beer made from browned malt (grain)

Words For Everyday Use

om • i • nous • ly (äm´ə nəs lē) *adv.*, threateningly, as of a bad omen

pred • a • tor • y (pred´ə tôr´ē) *adj.*, living by plundering or exploiting

pro • pen • si • ty (prə pen´sə tē) *n.*, natural inclination or tendency a single chophouse within the Lord Mayor's <u>dominions</u> which is not geographical—and wore out the time in dozing over crumbs, staring at gas, and baking in a hot blast of dinners. By-and-by, I roused myself and went to the play.

There I found a virtuous boatswain[8] in his Majesty's service—a most excellent man, though I could have wished his trousers not quite so tight in some places and not quite so loose in others—who knocked all the little men's hats over their eyes, though he was very generous and brave, and who wouldn't hear of anybody's paying taxes, though he was very patriotic. He had a bag of money in his pocket, like a pudding in the cloth, and on that property married a young person in bed-furniture, with great rejoicings; the whole population of Portsmouth (nine in number at the last census) turning out on the beach, to rub their own hands and shake everybody else's, and sing "Fill, fill!" A certain dark-complexioned swab,[9] however, who wouldn't fill, or do anything else that was proposed to him, and whose heart was openly stated (by the boatswain) to be as black as his figure-head,[10] proposed to two other swabs to get all mankind into difficulties; which was so effectually done (the swab family having considerable political influence) that it took half the evening to set things right, and then it was only brought about through an honest little grocer with a white hat, black gaiters,[11] and red nose, getting into a clock, with a gridiron, and listening, and coming out, and knocking everybody down from behind with the gridiron whom he couldn't confute[12] with what he had overheard. This led to Mr. Wopsle's (who had never been heard of before) coming in with a star and garter[13] on, as a <u>plenipotentiary</u> of great power direct from the Admiralty, to say that the swabs were all to go to prison on the spot, and that he had brought the boatswain down the Union Jack, as a slight acknowledgment of his public services. The boatswain, unmanned for the first time, respectfully dried his eyes on the Jack, and then cheering up and addressing Mr. Wopsle as Your

◄ Who is in the play?

---

8. **boatswain.** Ship's petty officer in charge of crew, rigging, anchors, and boats
9. **swab.** Sailor who mops the deck of a ship
10. **figure-head.** Face, a reference to the carved figure on the prow of a ship
11. **gaiters.** High overshoes with cloth upper
12. **confute.** Prove to be wrong
13. **garter.** Arm band

Words For Everyday Use

do • min • ion (də min´yən) *n.*, governed territory or country

plen • i • po • ten • ti • ar • y (plen´i pō ten´shē er´ē) *n.*, diplomat working as a representative of government

Honor, <u>solicited</u> permission to take him by the fin.[14] Mr. Wopsle <u>conceding</u> his fin with a gracious dignity, was immediately shoved into a dusty corner while everybody danced a hornpipe; and from that corner, surveying the public with a discontented eye, became aware of me.

The second piece was the last new grand comic Christmas <u>pantomime</u>, in the first scene of which it pained me to suspect that I detected Mr. Wopsle with red worsted[15] legs under a highly magnified phosphoric countenance[16] and a shock of red curtain-fringe for his hair, engaged in the manufacture of thunderbolts in a mine, and displaying great cowardice when his gigantic master came home (very hoarse) to dinner. But he presently presented himself under worthier circumstances; for, the Genius of Youthful Love being in want of assistance—on account of the parental brutality of an ignorant farmer who opposed the choice of his daughter's heart, by purposely falling upon the object in a flour sack, out of the first-floor window—summoned a sententious[17] enchanter; and he, coming up from the antipodes[18] rather unsteadily, after an apparently violent journey, proved to be Mr. Wopsle in a high-crowned hat, with a necromantic work[19] in one volume under his arm. The business of this enchanter on earth being principally to be talked at, sung at, butted at, danced at, and flashed at with fires of various colors, he had a good deal of time on his hands. And I observed with great surprise that he devoted it to staring in my direction as if he were lost in amazement.

> ► What does Wopsle do during the play? After?

There was something so remarkable in the increasing glare of Mr. Wopsle's eye, and he seemed to be turning so many things over in his mind and to grow so confused that I could not make it out. I sat thinking of it long after he had ascended to the clouds in a large watchcase, and still I could not make it out. I was still thinking of it when I came out of the theater an hour afterwards, and found him waiting for me near the door.

---

14. **fin.** Slang term for hand or arm
15. **worsted.** Wool
16. **phosphoric countenance.** Pale white face
17. **sententious.** Fond of using maxims and proverbs as moralizing statements
18. **antipodes.** Opposite side of the world; here, the actor probably emerges from the floor of the stage.
19. **necromantic work.** Book of sorcery, black magic

Words For Everyday Use

so • lic • it (sə lis´it) *vt.*, ask or seek earnestly

con • cede (kən sēd´) *vt.*, grant as a right or privilege

pan • to • mime (pan´ tə mīm´) *n.*, dramatic presentation played without words

"How do you do?" said I, shaking hands with him as we turned down the street together. "I saw that you saw me."

◄ What does Wopsle tell Pip?

"Saw you, Mr. Pip!" he returned. "Yes, of course I saw you. But who else was there?"

"Who else?"

"It is the strangest thing," said Mr. Wopsle, drifting into his lost look again, "and yet I could swear to him."

Becoming alarmed, I entreated Mr. Wopsle to explain his meaning.

"Whether I should have noticed him at first but for your being there," said Mr. Wopsle, going on in the same lost way, "I can't be positive; yet I think I should."

Involuntarily I looked round me, as I was accustomed to look round me when I went home, for these mysterious words gave me a chill.

"Oh! He can't be in sight," said Mr. Wopsle. "He went out, before I went off. I saw him go."

Having the reason that I had for being suspicious, I even suspected this poor actor. I mistrusted a design to entrap me into some admission. Therefore, I glanced at him as we walked on together, but said nothing.

"I had a ridiculous fancy that he must be with you, Mr. Pip, till I saw that you were quite unconscious of him, sitting behind you there, like a ghost."

My former chill crept over me again, but I was resolved not to speak yet, for it was quite consistent with his words that he might be set on to induce me to connect these references with Provis. Of course, I was perfectly sure and safe that Provis had not been there.

"I dare say you wonder at me, Mr. Pip; indeed, I see you do. But it is so very strange! You'll hardly believe what I am going to tell you. I could hardly believe it myself, if you told me."

"Indeed?" said I.

"No, indeed. Mr. Pip, you remember in old times a certain Christmas Day, when you were quite a child, and I dined at Gargery's, and some soldiers came to the door to get a pair of handcuffs <u>mended</u>?"

◄ Whom has Wopsle recognized in the audience?

"I remember it very well."

"And you remember that there was a chase after two convicts, and that we joined in it, and that Gargery took you on

Words
For
Everyday
Use

mend (mend) *vt.*, repair

his back, and that I took the lead and you kept up with me as well as you could?"

"I remember it all very well." Better than he thought—except the last clause.

"And you remember that we came up with the two in a ditch, and that there was a <u>scuffle</u> between them, and that one of them had been severely handled and much <u>mauled</u> about the face by the other?"

"I see it all before me."

"And that the soldiers lighted torches, and put the two in the center, and that we went on to see the last of them, over the black marshes, with the torchlight shining on their faces—I am particular about that—with the torchlight shining on their faces, when there was an outer ring of dark night all about us?"

"Yes," said I. "I remember all that."

"Then, Mr. Pip, one of those two prisoners sat behind you tonight. I saw him over your shoulder."

"Steady!" I thought. I asked him then, "Which of the two do you suppose you saw?"

"The one who had been mauled," he answered readily, "and I'll swear I saw him! The more I think of him, the more certain I am of him."

"This is very curious!" said I, with the best assumption I could put on of its being nothing more to me. "Very curious indeed!"

▶ How does Pip feel when he learns who sat behind him? What does he find ironic?

I cannot exaggerate the enhanced disquiet into which this conversation threw me, or the special and peculiar terror I felt at Compeyson's having been behind me "like a ghost." For if he had ever been out of my thoughts for a few moments together since the hiding had begun, it was in those very moments when he was closest to me; and to think that I should be so unconscious and off my guard after all my care was as if I had shut an avenue of a hundred doors to keep him out, and then had found him at my elbow. I could not doubt either that he was there, because I was there, and that however slight an appearance of danger there might be about us, danger was always near and active.

I put such questions to Mr. Wopsle as, When did the man come in? He could not tell me that; he saw me, and over my shoulder he saw the man. It was not until he had seen him

Words For Everyday Use	scuf • fle (skufˊəl) n., rough fight
	maul (môl) vt., injure by beating

for some time that he began to identify him; but he had from the first vaguely associated him with me, and known him as somehow belonging to me in the old village time. How was he dressed? Prosperously, but not noticeably otherwise; he thought, in black. Was his face at all disfigured? No, he believed not. I believed not, too, for although in my brooding state I had taken no especial notice of the people behind me, I thought it likely that a face at all disfigured would have attracted my attention.

When Mr. Wopsle had <u>imparted</u> to me all that he could recall or I extract, and when I had treated him to a little appropriate refreshment after the fatigues of the evening, we parted. It was between twelve and one o'clock when I reached the Temple, and the gates were shut. No one was near me when I went in and went home.

Herbert had come in, and we held a very serious council by the fire. But there was nothing to be done, saving to communicate to Wemmick what I had that night found out, and to remind him that we waited for his hint. As I thought that I might compromise him if I went too often to the castle, I made this communication by letter. I wrote it before I went to bed and went out and posted it; and again no one was near me. Herbert and I agreed that we could do nothing else but be very cautious. And we were very cautious, indeed— more cautious than before, if that were possible—and I for my part never went near Chinks's Basin, except when I rowed by, and then I only looked at Mill Pond Bank as I looked at anything else.

◄ *What do Herbert and Pip decide to do?*

CHAPTER 48

The second of the two meetings referred to in the last chapter occurred about a week after the first. I had again left my boat at the wharf below Bridge; the time was an hour earlier in the afternoon; and, undecided where to dine, I had strolled up into Cheapside, and was strolling along it, surely the most unsettled person in all the busy <u>concourse</u>, when a large hand was laid upon my shoulder by someone overtaking me. It was Mr. Jaggers's hand, and he passed it through my arm.

"As we are going in the same direction, Pip, we may walk together. Where are you bound for?"

"For the Temple, I think," said I.

"Don't you know?" said Mr. Jaggers.

"Well," I returned, glad for once to get the better of him in cross-examination, "I do *not* know, for I have not made up my mind."

"You are going to dine?" said Mr. Jaggers. "You don't mind admitting that, I suppose?"

"No," I returned, "I don't mind admitting that."

"And are not engaged?"

"I don't mind admitting also that I am not engaged."

"Then," said Mr. Jaggers, "come and dine with me."

I was going to excuse myself, when he added, "Wemmick's coming." So, I changed my excuse into an acceptance—the few words I had uttered serving for the beginning of either—and we went along Cheapside and slanted off to Little Britain, while the lights were springing up brilliantly in the shop windows, and the street lamplighters, scarcely finding ground enough to plant their ladders on in the midst of the afternoon's bustle, were skipping up and down and running in and out, opening more red eyes in the gathering fog than my rushlight tower at the Hummums had opened white eyes in the ghostly wall.

At the office in Little Britain there was the usual letter-writing, hand-washing, candle-snuffing, and safe-locking, that closed the business of the day. As I stood idle by Mr. Jaggers's fire, its rising and falling flame made the two casts on the shelf look as if they were playing a <u>diabolical</u> game at

> ► *Whom does Pip meet?*

> ► *Why does Pip join him?*

Words For Everyday Use

con • course (kän′ kôrs′) *n.*, open area where crowds gather

di • a • bol • i • cal (dī′ ə bäl′ i kəl) *adj.*, wicked or cruel bo-peep with me; while the pair of coarse, fat office candles that dimly lighted Mr. Jaggers as he wrote in a corner were decorated with dirty winding-sheets, as if in remembrance of a host of hanged clients.

We went to Gerrard Street, all three together, in a hackney-coach, and as soon as we got there, dinner was served. Although I should not have thought of making, in that place, the most distant reference by so much as a look to Wemmick's Walworth sentiments, yet I should have had no objection to catching his eye now and then in a friendly way. But it was not to be done. He turned his eyes on Mr. Jaggers whenever he raised them from the table, and was as dry and distant to me as if there were twin Wemmicks and this was the wrong one.

◄ How does Wemmick behave at dinner?

"Did you send that note of Miss Havisham's to Mr. Pip, Wemmick?" Mr. Jaggers asked, soon after we began dinner.

"No, sir," returned Wemmick; "it was going by post, when you brought Mr. Pip into the office. Here it is." He handed it to his principal, instead of to me.

"It's a note of two lines, Pip," said Mr. Jaggers, handing it on, "sent up to me by Miss Havisham, on account of her not being sure of your address. She tells me that she wants to see you on a little matter of business you mentioned to her. You'll go down?"

◄ Who sends a letter? About what?

"Yes," said I, casting my eyes over the note, which was exactly in those terms.

"When do you think of going down?"

"I have an impending engagement," said I, glancing at Wemmick, who was putting fish into the post office, "that renders me rather uncertain of my time. At once, I think."

"If Mr. Pip has the intention of going at once," said Wemmick to Mr. Jaggers, "he needn't write an answer, you know."

Receiving this as an <u>intimation</u> that it was best not to delay, I settled that I would go tomorrow, and said so. Wemmick drank a glass of wine and looked with a grimly satisfied air at Mr. Jaggers, but not at me.

"So, Pip! Our friend the Spider," said Mr. Jaggers, "has played his cards. He has won the pool."

It was as much as I could do to assent.

"Hah! He is a promising fellow—in his way—but he may not have it all his own way. The stronger will win in the end,

Words For Everyday Use

in • ti • ma • tion (in′tə mā′shən) *n.,* hint

► What does
Jaggers think
Drummle and
Estella's relationship
will be like? Does Pip
agree?

but the stronger has to be found out first. If he should turn to, and beat her—"

"Surely," I interrupted, with a burning face and heart, "you do not seriously think that he is scoundrel enough for that, Mr. Jaggers?"

"I didn't say so, Pip. I am putting a case. If he should turn to and beat her, he may possibly get the strength on his side; if it should be a question of intellect, he certainly will not. It would be chance work to give an opinion how a fellow of that sort will turn out in such circumstances, because it's a toss-up between two results."

"May I ask what they are?"

"A fellow like our friend the Spider," answered Mr. Jaggers, "either beats, or <u>cringes</u>. He may cringe and growl, or cringe and not growl; but he either beats or cringes. Ask Wemmick *his* opinion."

"Either beats or cringes," said Wemmick, not at all addressing himself to me.

"So, here's to Mrs. Bentley Drummle," said Mr. Jaggers, taking a decanter of choicer wine from his dumbwaiter, and filling for each of us and for himself, "and may the question of supremacy be settled to the lady's satisfaction! To the satisfaction of the lady *and* the gentleman, it never will be. Now, Molly, Molly, Molly, Molly, how slow you are today!"

She was at his elbow when he addressed her, putting a dish upon the table. As she withdrew her hands from it, she fell back a step or two, nervously muttering some excuse. And a certain action of her fingers as she spoke arrested my attention.

"What's the matter?" said Mr. Jaggers.

"Nothing. Only the subject we were speaking of," said I, "was rather painful to me."

The action of her fingers was like the action of knitting. She stood looking at her master, not understanding whether she was free to go, or whether he had more to say to her and would call her back if she did go. Her look was very intent. Surely, I had seen exactly such eyes and such hands on a memorable occasion very lately!

► To whom does Pip
connect Molly?

He dismissed her, and she glided out of the room. But she remained before me, as plainly as if she were still there. I looked at those hands, I looked at those eyes, I looked at that flowing hair, and I compared them with other hands, other

---

Words
For
Everyday
Use

cringe (krinj) *vi.,* shrink back with fear; act like a slave

---

eyes, other hair, that I knew of, and with what those might be after twenty years of a brutal husband and a stormy life. I looked again at those hands and eyes of the housekeeper, and thought of the inexplicable feeling that had come over me when I last walked—not alone—in the ruined garden, and through the deserted brewery. I thought how the same feeling had come back when I saw a face looking at me, and a hand waving to me, from a stagecoach window; and how it had come back again and had flashed about me like lightning, when I had passed in a carriage—not alone—through a sudden glare of light in a dark street. I thought how one link of association had helped that identification in the theater, and how such a link, wanting before, had been <u>riveted</u> for me now, when I had passed by a chance swift from Estella's name to the fingers with their knitting action, and the attentive eyes. And I felt absolutely certain that this woman was Estella's mother.

Mr. Jaggers had seen me with Estella, and was not likely to have missed the sentiments I had been at no pains to conceal. He nodded when I said the subject was painful to me, clapped me on the back, put round the wine again, and went on with his dinner.

Only twice more did the housekeeper reappear, and then her stay in the room was very short, and Mr. Jaggers was sharp with her. But her hands were Estella's hands, and her eyes were Estella's eyes, and if she had reappeared a hundred times I could have been neither more sure nor less sure that my conviction was the truth.

It was a dull evening, for Wemmick drew his wine when it came round, quite as a matter of business—just as he might have drawn his salary when that came round—and with his eyes on his chief, sat in a state of perpetual readiness for cross-examination. As to the quantity of wine, his post office was as indifferent and ready as any other post office for its quantity of letters. From my point of view, he was the wrong twin all the time, and only externally like the Wemmick of Walworth.

We took our leave early, and left together. Even when we were groping among Mr. Jaggers's stock of boots for our hats, I felt that the right twin was on his way back; and we had not gone half a dozen yards down Gerrard Street in the Walworth

Words
For
Everyday
Use

riv • et (riv´it) *vt.,* secure firmly

direction before I found that I was walking arm-in-arm with the right twin, and that the wrong twin had evaporated into the evening air.

"Well!" said Wemmick, "that's over! He's a wonderful man, without his living likeness, but I feel that I have to screw myself up when I dine with him—and I dine more comfortably unscrewed."

I felt that this was a good statement of the case, and told him so.

"Wouldn't say it to anybody but yourself," he answered. "I know that what is said between you and me, goes no further."

▶ What does Pip ask Wemmick?

I asked him if he had ever seen Miss Havisham's adopted daughter, Mrs. Bentley Drummle? He said no. To avoid being too abrupt, I then spoke of the Aged, and of Miss Skiffins. He looked rather sly when I mentioned Miss Skiffins, and stopped in the street to blow his nose, with a roll of the head and a <u>flourish</u> not quite free from latent boastfulness.

"Wemmick," said I, "do you remember telling me, before I first went to Mr. Jaggers's private house, to notice that housekeeper?"

"Did I?" he replied. "Ah, I dare say I did. Deuce take me," he added suddenly, "I know I did. I find I am not quite unscrewed yet."

"A wild beast tamed, you called her?"

"And what do *you* call her?"

"The same. How did Mr. Jaggers tame her, Wemmick?"

"That's his secret. She has been with him many a long year."

"I wish you would tell me her story. I feel a particular interest in being acquainted with it. You know that what is said between you and me goes no further."

"Well!" Wemmick replied, "I don't know her story—that is, I don't know all of it. But what I do know, I'll tell you. We are in our private and personal capacities, of course."

"Of course."

▶ How did Jaggers and Molly meet? What binds them together?

"A score[1] or so of years ago, that woman was tried at the Old Bailey for murder and was <u>acquitted</u>. She was a very handsome young woman, and I believe had some gypsy[2] blood in her. Anyhow, it was hot enough when it was up, as you may suppose."

---

1. **score.** Twenty
2. **gypsy.** Member of a nomadic race of Hindu origin

Words For Everyday Use	**flour • ish** (flʉr´ish) *n.*, any motion done in a showy way **ac • quit** (ə kwit´) *vt.*, clear from a criminal charge

"But she was acquitted."

"Mr. Jaggers was for her," pursued Wemmick, with a look full of meaning, "and worked the case in a way quite astonishing. It was a desperate case, and it was comparatively early days with him then, and he worked it to general admiration; in fact, it may almost be said to have made him. He worked it himself at the police office, day after day for many days, <u>contending</u> against even a committal; and at the trial, where he couldn't work it himself, sat under counsel, and—every one knew—put in all the salt and pepper. The murdered person was a woman; a woman, a good ten years older, very much larger, and very much stronger. It was a case of jealousy. They both led tramping lives, and this woman in Gerrard Street here had been married very young, over the broomstick³ (as we say), to a tramping man, and was a perfect fury in point of jealousy. The murdered woman—more a match for the man, certainly, in point of years—was found dead in a barn near Hounslow Heath. There had been a violent struggle, perhaps a fight. She was bruised and scratched and torn, and had been held by the throat at last and choked. Now, there was no reasonable evidence to <u>implicate</u> any person but this woman, and, on the improbabilities of her having been able to do it, Mr. Jaggers principally rested his case. You may be sure," said Wemmick, touching me on the sleeve, "that he never dwelt upon the strength of her hands then, though he sometimes does now."

◀ *What were the circumstances of Molly's crime?*

I had told Wemmick of his showing us her wrists, that day of the dinner party.

"Well, sir!" Wemmick went on; "it happened—happened, don't you see?—that this woman was so very artfully dressed from the time of her apprehension that she looked much slighter than she really was; in particular, her sleeves are always remembered to have been so skillfully contrived that her arms had quite a delicate look. She had only a bruise or two about her—nothing for a tramp—but the backs of her hands were <u>lacerated</u>, and the question was, was it with fingernails? Now, Mr. Jaggers showed that she had struggled through a great lot of <u>brambles</u> which were not as high as her face; but which she could not have got through and kept her

---

3. **over the broomstick.** In a phony wedding ceremony

hands out of; and bits of those brambles were actually found in her skin and put in evidence, as well as the fact that the brambles in question were found on examination to have been broken through, and to have little shreds of her dress and little spots of blood upon them here and there. But the boldest point he made was this. It was attempted to be set up in proof of her jealousy that she was under strong suspicion of having, at about the time of the murder, frantically destroyed her child by this man—some three years old—to revenge herself upon him. Mr. Jaggers worked that in this way: 'We say these are not marks of fingernails, but marks of brambles, and we show you the brambles. You say they are marks of fingernails, and you set up the <u>hypothesis</u> that she destroyed her child. You must accept all consequences of that hypothesis. For anything we know, she may have destroyed her child, and the child in clinging to her may have scratched her hands. What then? You are not trying her for the murder of her child; why don't you? As to this case, if you *will* have scratches, we say that, for anything we know, you may have accounted for them, assuming for the sake of argument that you have not invented them.' To sum up, sir," said Wemmick, "Mr. Jaggers was altogether too many for the jury, and they gave in."

"Has she been in his service ever since?"

"Yes; but not only that," said Wemmick. "She went into his service immediately after her acquittal, tamed as she is now. She has since been taught one thing and another in the way of her duties, but she was tamed from the beginning."

"Do you remember the sex of the child?"

"Said to have been a girl."

"You have nothing more to say to me tonight?"

"Nothing. I got your letter and destroyed it. Nothing."

We exchanged a cordial good night, and I went home, with new matter for my thoughts, though with no relief from the old.

► *What argument did Jaggers give in Molly's defense?*

► *What else does Pip learn about Molly?*

Words For Everyday Use

hy • poth • e • sis (hī päth´ə sis) *n.,* theory

CHAPTER 49

Putting Miss Havisham's note in my pocket, that it might serve as my <u>credentials</u> for so soon reappearing at Satis House, in case her <u>waywardness</u> should lead her to express any surprise at seeing me, I went down again by the coach next day. But I alighted at the Halfway House, and breakfasted there, and walked the rest of the distance, for I sought to get into the town quietly by the unfrequented ways, and to leave it in the same manner.

The best light of the day was gone when I passed along the quiet echoing courts behind the High Street. The <u>nooks</u> of ruin where the old monks had once had their refectories[1] and gardens, and where the strong walls were now pressed into the service of humble sheds and stables, were almost as silent as the old monks in their graves. The cathedral chimes had at once a sadder and a more remote sound to me, as I hurried on avoiding observation, than they had ever had before; so, the swell of the old organ was borne to my ears like funeral music; and the rooks, as they hovered about the gray tower and swung in the bare high trees of the priory-garden,[2] seemed to call to me that the place was changed, and that Estella was gone out of it forever.

An elderly woman whom I had seen before as one of the servants who lived in the supplementary house across the back courtyard opened the gate. The lighted candle stood in the dark passage within, as of old, and I took it up and ascended the staircase alone. Miss Havisham was not in her own room, but was in the larger room across the landing. Looking in at the door, after knocking in vain, I saw her sitting on the hearth in a ragged chair, close before, and lost in the contemplation of, the ashy fire.

Doing as I had often done, I went in, and stood, touching the old chimneypiece, where she could see me when she raised her eyes. There was an air of utter loneliness upon her that would have moved me to pity though she had willfully done me a deeper injury than I could charge her with. As I

◄ Why does Pip bring the note? What does he do to avoid being seen?

◄ How does Miss Havisham appear? What is Pip's reaction to seeing her this way?

---

1. **refectories.** Dining halls of monasteries
2. **priory-garden.** Monastery or convent garden, or open area

---

Words For Everyday Use

cre • den • tial (krĭ dĕn´shəl) *n.*, written evidence of qualification

way • ward • ness (wā´wərd nəs) *n.*, quality of being unpredictable or erratic

nook (nʊ͝ok) *n.*, small recess or secluded spot

stood compassionating[3] her, and thinking how in the progress of time I too had come to be a part of the wrecked fortunes of that house, her eyes rested on me. She stared, and said in a low voice, "Is it real?"

"It is I, Pip. Mr. Jaggers gave me your note yesterday, and I have lost no time."

"Thank you. Thank you."

As I brought another of the ragged chairs to the hearth and sat down, I remarked a new expression on her face, as if she were afraid of me.

► Why has Miss Havisham summoned Pip?

"I want," she said, "to pursue that subject you mentioned to me when you were last here, and to show you that I am not all stone. But perhaps you can never believe, now, that there is anything human in my heart?"

When I said some reassuring words, she stretched out her <u>tremulous</u> right hand, as though she was going to touch me, but she recalled it again before I understood the action, or knew how to receive it.

"You said, speaking for your friend, that you could tell me how to do something useful and good. Something that you would like done, is it not?"

"Something that I would like done very very much."

"What is it?"

I began explaining to her that secret history of the partnership. I had not got far into it when I judged from her looks that she was thinking in a discursive[4] way of me, rather than of what I said. It seemed to be so, for when I stopped speaking, many moments passed before she showed that she was conscious of the fact.

► What does Miss Havisham ask Pip? Why? What is his answer?

"Do you break off," she asked then, with her former air of being afraid of me, "because you hate me too much to bear to speak to me?"

"No, no," I answered, "how can you think so, Miss Havisham! I stopped because I thought you were not following what I said."

"Perhaps I was not," she answered, putting a hand to her head. "Begin again, and let me look at something else. Stay! Now tell me."

---

3. **compassionating.** Feeling pity
4. **discursive.** Wandering from one topic to another

Words For Everyday Use

trem • u • lous (trem´yo͞o ləs) *adj.,* trembling; quivering

She set her hand upon her stick in the resolute way that sometimes was <u>habitual</u> to her, and looked at the fire with a strong expression of forcing herself to attend. I went on with my explanation, and told her how I had hoped to complete the transaction out of my means, but how in this I was disappointed. That part of the subject (I reminded her) involved matters which could form no part of my explanation, for they were the weighty secrets of another.

"So!" said she, assenting with her head, but not looking at me. "And how much money is wanting to complete the purchase?"

I was rather afraid of stating it, for it sounded a large sum. "Nine hundred pounds."

"If I give you the money for this purpose, will you keep my secret as you have kept your own?"

"Quite as faithfully."

"And your mind will be more at rest?"

"Much more at rest."

"Are you very unhappy now?"

◄ What is Pip's request? Does Miss Havisham agree to fulfill it? On what condition?

She asked this question, still without looking at me, but in an unwonted tone of sympathy. I could not reply at the moment, for my voice failed me. She put her left arm across the head of her stick, and softly laid her forehead on it.

"I am far from happy, Miss Havisham, but I have other causes of disquiet than any you know of. They are the secrets I have mentioned."

After a little while, she raised her head and looked at the fire again.

"It is noble in you to tell me that you have other causes of unhappiness. Is it true?"

"Too true."

"Can I only serve you, Pip, by serving your friend? Regarding that as done, is there nothing I can do for you yourself?"

◄ What does Pip refuse?

"Nothing. I thank you for the question. I thank you even more for the tone of the question. But there is nothing."

She presently rose from her seat, and looked about the <u>blighted</u> room for the means of writing. There were none there, and she took from her pocket a yellow set of ivory tablets, mounted in tarnished gold, and wrote upon them with a pencil in a case of tarnished gold that hung from her neck.

Words For Everyday Use

ha • bit • u • al (hə bich´ o͞o əl) *adj.,* usual; customary; as a habit

blight • ed (blīt´id) *adj.,* destroyed; with no growth or life

"You are still on friendly terms with Mr. Jaggers?"

"Quite. I dined with him yesterday."

"This is an authority to him to pay you that money, to lay out at your irresponsible <u>discretion</u> for your friend. I keep no money here; but if you would rather Mr. Jaggers knew nothing of the matter, I will send it to you."

"Thank you, Miss Havisham; I have not the least objection to receiving it from him."

She read me what she had written, and it was direct and clear, and evidently intended to <u>absolve</u> me from any suspicion of profiting by the receipt of the money. I took the tablets from her hand, and it trembled again, and it trembled more as she took off the chain to which the pencil was attached, and put it in mine. All this she did without looking at me.

► What does she ask of Pip?

"My name is on the first leaf. If you can ever write under my name, 'I forgive her,' though ever so long after my broken heart is dust, pray do it!"

"Oh, Miss Havisham," said I, "I can do it now. There have been sore mistakes; and my life has been a blind and thankless one; and I want forgiveness and direction far too much to be bitter with you."

► What does Miss Havisham do? What shocks Pip? Why does he let her cry?

She turned her face to me for the first time since she had averted it, and to my amazement, I may even add to my terror, dropped on her knees at my feet, with her folded hands raised to me in the manner in which, when her poor heart was young and fresh and whole, they must often have been raised to Heaven from her mother's side.

To see her, with her white hair and her worn face, kneeling at my feet, gave me a shock through all my frame. I entreated her to rise, and got my arms about her to help her up, but she only pressed that hand of mine which was nearest to her grasp, and hung her head over it, and wept. I had never seen her shed a tear before, and, in the hope that the relief might do her good, I bent over her without speaking. She was not kneeling now, but was down upon the ground.

"Oh!" she cried, despairingly. "What have I done! What have I done!"

"If you mean, Miss Havisham, what have you done to injure me, let me answer. Very little. I should have loved her under any circumstances. Is she married?"

| Words For Everyday Use | **dis • cre • tion** (di skresh´ən) *n.*, freedom to act on one's own |
| | **ab • solve** (əb zälv´) *vt.*, pronounce free of blame or guilt |

"Yes."

It was a needless question, for a new desolation in the desolate house had told me so.

"What have I done! What have I done!" She wrung her hands, and crushed her white hair, and returned to this cry over and over again. "What have I done!"

◀ What does Pip realize about Miss Havisham?

I knew not how to answer, or how to comfort her. That she had done a grievous thing in taking an impressionable child to mold into the form that her wild resentment, spurned affection, and wounded pride found vengeance in, I knew full well. But that, in shutting out the light of day, she had shut out infinitely more; that, in seclusion, she had secluded herself from a thousand natural and healing influences; that, her mind, brooding solitary, had grown diseased, as all minds do and must and will that reverse the appointed order of their Maker; I knew equally well. And could I look upon her without compassion, seeing her punishment in the ruin she was, in her profound unfitness for this earth on which she was placed, in the <u>vanity</u> of sorrow which had become a master <u>mania</u>, like the vanity of penitence, the vanity of remorse, the vanity of unworthiness, and other monstrous vanities that have been curses in this world?

"Until you spoke to her the other day, and until I saw in you a looking glass that showed me what I once felt myself, I did not know what I had done. What have I done! What have I done!" And so again, twenty, fifty times over, What had she done!

"Miss Havisham," I said, when her cry had died away, "you may dismiss me from your mind and conscience. But Estella is a different case, and if you can ever undo any scrap of what you have done <u>amiss</u> in keeping a part of her right nature away from her, it will be better to do that than to <u>bemoan</u> the past through a hundred years."

"Yes, yes, I know it. But, Pip—my dear!" There was an earnest womanly compassion for me in her new affection. "My Dear! Believe this: when she first came to me, I meant to save her from misery like my own. At first I meant no more."

◀ What does Miss Havisham admit?

"Well, well!" said I. "I hope so."

"But as she grew, and promised to be very beautiful, I gradually did worse, and with my praises, and with my jewels, and with my teachings, and with this figure of myself always

Words For Everyday Use	**van • i • ty** (van´ə tē) *n.,* futility; worthlessness
	ma • ni • a (mā´nē ə) *n.,* abnormally intense desire
	a • miss (ə mis´) *adj.,* wrong; faulty; improper
	be • moan (bi mōn´) *vt.,* mourn over; express grief for

before her, a warning to back and point my lessons, I stole her heart away and put ice in its place."

"Better," I could not help saying, "to have left her a natural heart, even to be bruised or broken."

With that, Miss Havisham looked distractedly at me for a while, and then burst out again, What had she done!

"If you knew all my story," she pleaded, "you would have some compassion for me, and a better understanding of me."

"Miss Havisham," I answered, as delicately as I could, "I believe I may say that I do know your story, and have known it ever since I first left this neighborhood. It has inspired me with great <u>commiseration,</u> and I hope I understand it and its influences. Does what has passed between us give me any excuse for asking you a question relative to Estella? Not as she is, but as she was when she first came here?"

She was seated on the ground, with her arms on the ragged chair, and her head leaning on them. She looked full at me when I said this, and replied, "Go on."

"Whose child was Estella?"

She shook her head.

"You don't know?"

She shook her head again.

"But Mr. Jaggers brought her here, or sent her here?"

"Brought her here."

"Will you tell me how that came about?"

She answered in a low whisper and with caution: "I had been shut up in these rooms a long time (I don't know how long; you know what time the clocks keep here), when I told him that I wanted a little girl to rear and love, and save from my fate. I had first seen him when I sent for him to lay this place waste for me, having read of him in the newspapers before I and the world parted. He told me that he would look about him for such an orphan child. One night he brought her here asleep, and I called her Estella."

"Might I ask her age then?"

"Two or three. She herself knows nothing, but that she was left an orphan and I adopted her."

So convinced I was of that woman's being her mother that I wanted no evidence to establish the fact in my mind. But to any mind, I thought, the connection here was clear and straight.

▶ *How did Estella come to live there?*

Words For Everyday Use

com • mis • er • a • tion (kə miz´ər ā´shən) *n.*, feeling of sympathy for the distress of another

What more could I hope to do by prolonging the interview? I had succeeded on behalf of Herbert, Miss Havisham had told me all she knew of Estella, I had said and done what I could to ease her mind. No matter with what other words we parted; we parted.

◀ What causes Pip to feel nostalgic?

Twilight was closing in when I went downstairs into the natural air. I called to the woman who had opened the gate when I entered that I would not trouble her just yet, but would walk round the place before leaving. For I had a presentiment that I should never be there again, and I felt that the dying light was suited to my last view of it.

By the wilderness of casks that I had walked on long ago, and on which the rain of years had fallen since, rotting them in many places, and leaving miniature swamps and pools of water upon those that stood on end, I made my way to the ruined garden. I went all round it; round by the corner where Herbert and I had fought our battle; round by the paths where Estella and I had walked. So cold, so lonely, so dreary all!

Taking the brewery on my way back, I raised the rusty latch of a little door at the garden end of it, and walked through. I was going out at the opposite door—not easy to open now, for the damp wood had started and swelled, and the hinges were yielding, and the threshold was encumbered with a growth of fungus—when I turned my head to look back. A childish association revived with wonderful force in the moment of the slight action, and I fancied that I saw Miss Havisham hanging to the beam. So strong was the impression that I stood under the beam shuddering from head to foot before I knew it was a fancy—though to be sure I was there in an instant.

◀ Why does Pip not leave the house yet?

The mournfulness of the place and time, and the great terror of this illusion, though it was but momentary, caused me to feel an indescribable awe as I came out between the open wooden gates where I had once wrung my hair after Estella had wrung my heart. Passing on into the front courtyard, I hesitated whether to call the woman to let me out at the locked gate, of which she had the key, or first to go upstairs and assure myself that Miss Havisham was as safe and well as I had left her. I took the latter course and went up.

I looked into the room where I had left her, and I saw her seated in the ragged chair upon the hearth close to the fire, with her back towards me. In the moment when I was withdrawing my head to go quietly away, I saw a great flaming light spring up. In the same moment, I saw her running at me, shrieking, with a whirl of fire blazing all about her, and soaring at least as many feet above her head as she was high.

◀ What begins to happen?

I had a double-caped great-coat on, and over my arm another thick coat. That I got them off, closed with her, threw her down, and got them over her; that I dragged the great cloth from the table for the same purpose, and with it dragged down the heap of rottenness in the midst, and all the ugly things that sheltered there; that we were on the ground struggling like desperate enemies, and that the closer I covered her, the more wildly she shrieked and tried to free herself; that this occurred I knew through the result, but not through anything I felt, or thought, or knew I did. I knew nothing until I knew that we were on the floor by the great table, and that patches of <u>tinder</u> yet alight were floating in the smoky air, which a moment ago, had been her faded bridal dress.

▶ How does Pip save Miss Havisham?

Then I looked round and saw the disturbed beetles and spiders running away over the floor, and the servants coming in with breathless cries at the door. I still held her forcibly down with all my strength, like a prisoner who might escape, and I doubt if I even knew who she was, or why we had struggled, or that she had been in flames, or that the flames were out, until I saw the patches of tinder that had been her garments, no longer alight but falling in a black shower around us.

She was insensible, and I was afraid to have her moved, or even touched. Assistance was sent for, and I held her until it came, as if I unreasonably fancied (I think I did) that if I let her go, the fire would break out again and consume her. When I got up, on the surgeon's coming to her with other aid, I was astonished to see that both my hands were burnt, for I had no knowledge of it through the sense of feeling.

On examination it was pronounced that she had received serious hurts, but that they of themselves were far from hopeless; the danger lay mainly in the nervous shock. By the surgeon's directions, her bed was carried into that room and laid upon the great table, which happened to be well suited to the dressing of her injuries. When I saw her again, an hour afterwards, she lay indeed where I had seen her strike her stick, and had heard her say that she would lie one day.

Though every <u>vestige</u> of her dress was burnt, as they told me, she still had something of her old ghastly bridal appearance, for they had covered her to the throat with white cotton wool, and as she lay with a white sheet loosely overlying

---

Words For Everyday Use

tin • der (tin´dər) *n.,* dry, easily flammable material
ves • tige (ves´tij) *n.,* trace; bit

that, the phantom air of something that had been and was changed was still upon her.

I found, on questioning the servants, that Estella was in Paris, and I got a promise from the surgeon that he would write by the next post. Miss Havisham's family I took upon myself, intending to communicate with Matthew Pocket only, and leave him to do as he liked about informing the rest. This I did next day, through Herbert, as soon as I returned to town.

There was a stage, that evening, when she spoke collectedly of what had happened, though with a certain terrible <u>vivacity</u>. Towards midnight she began to wander in her speech, and after that it gradually set in that she said innumerable times in a low solemn voice, "What have I done!" And then, "When she first came, I meant to save her from misery like mine." And then, "Take the pencil and write under my name, 'I forgive her!'" She never changed the order of these three sentences, but she sometimes left out a word in one or other of them, never putting in another word, but always leaving a blank and going on to the next word.

As I could do no service there, and as I had, nearer home, that pressing reason for anxiety and fear which even her wanderings could not drive out of my mind, I decided in the course of the night that I would return by the early morning coach, walking on a mile or so, and being taken up clear of the town. At about six o'clock of the morning, therefore, I leaned over her and touched her lips with mine, just as they said, not stopping for being touched, "Take the pencil and write under my name, 'I forgive her.'"

◄ What does Miss Havisham worry about in her illness? For what does she want to be forgiven?

Words For Everyday Use

vi • vac • i • ty (vī vas´ə tē) *n.*, liveliness of spirit

Responding to the Selection

Wemmick plays an important role in helping Pip to solve his problems. Pretend that you are Pip and explain why you appreciate Wemmick as a friend. Use specific examples from the novel to illustrate how and why Wemmick has shown himself to be a good friend. You may discuss your responses to these questions, or you may write your responses as a note to Wemmick.

Reviewing the Selection

Recalling and Interpreting

1. **R:** During his visit with Miss Havisham and Estella, what favor does Pip ask of Miss Havisham? What does he say to Estella, and how does she respond? What reasons does Estella give for agreeing to marry Drummle?

2. **I:** Why does Pip ask for Miss Havisham's help? Why can't Estella return Pip's love? What does Estella's engagement to Drummle reveal about her character?

3. **R:** What message does Pip receive when he returns home from Miss Havisham's? What have Wemmick and Herbert done while Pip was away? Why does Pip begin to row on the river?

4. **I:** Why is Pip so cautious? What aspects of the plan contribute to the sense of secrecy and urgency?

5. **R:** What event does Wopsle ask Pip to remember? Whom does Wopsle say he saw at the play?

6. **I:** What does the presence of this person contribute to the plot?

7. **R:** What questions does Pip ask Miss Havisham about Estella? What is her answer to his questions? What does Miss Havisham agree to do for Pip? What does she ask Pip to do? What three phrases does she repeat after Pip saves her from the fire?

8. **I:** Why does Pip question Miss Havisham about Estella? What do the three things Miss Havisham repeats reveal about her?

Synthesizing

9. Compare and contrast Herbert's relationship with Clara with Pip's relationship with Estella.

10. In these chapters, many of the complications that have been set into the plot are made clear. Identify two of these difficulties and the information that is given to clarify them. Discuss what you think will happen next, based on this new information.

Understanding Literature (QUESTIONS FOR DISCUSSION)

1. **Tone. Tone** is the emotional attitude toward the reader or toward the subject implied by a literary work. Examples of different tones that a work may have include familiar, ironic, playful, sarcastic, serious, and sincere. In chapter 46 Pip has the opportunity to meet Clara and see her and Herbert together. Describe the tone of their first meeting, using words and phrases to support your analysis.

2. **Personification. Personification** is a figure of speech in which an idea, animal, or thing is described as if it were a person. In the beginning of chapter 45, Pip spends a restless night at Hummums. His inner fears and confusion are described in terms of the furniture. Identify two examples of personification in this scene, and explain what human qualities are being ascribed to objects.

3. **Dynamic Character and Characterization.** A **dynamic character** is one who changes during the course of the action of a story. **Characterization** is the use of literary techniques to create a character. Examine the scene in chapter 49 in which Pip again sees Miss Havisham. What aspects of his character are revealed? What elements of his behavior show that he has changed? In what way has he changed?

CHAPTER 50

My hands had been dressed twice or <u>thrice</u> in the night, and again in the morning. My left arm was a good deal burned to the elbow, and, less severely, as high as the shoulder; it was very painful, but the flames had set in that direction, and I felt thankful it was no worse. My right hand was not so badly burnt but that I could move the fingers. It was bandaged, of course, but much less inconveniently than my left hand and arm; those I carried in a sling; and I could only wear my coat like a cloak, loose over my shoulders and fastened at the neck. My hair had been caught by the fire, but not my head or face.

▶ *What shows Herbert to be a good friend?*

When Herbert had been down to Hammersmith and had seen his father, he came back to me at our chambers, and devoted the day to attending on me. He was the kindest of nurses, and at stated times took off the bandages, and steeped them in the cooling liquid that was kept ready, and put them on again, with a patient tenderness that I was deeply grateful for.

At first, as I lay quiet on the sofa, I found it painfully difficult, I might say impossible, to get rid of the impression of the glare of the flames, their hurry and noise, and the fierce burning smell. If I dozed for a minute, I was awakened by Miss Havisham's cries, and by her running at me with all that height of fire above her head. This pain of the mind was much harder to strive against than any bodily pain I suffered, and Herbert, seeing that, did his utmost to hold my attention engaged.

▶ *What unspoken agreement do Herbert and Pip come to? Why is it important?*

Neither of us spoke of the boat, but we both thought of it. That was made apparent by our avoidance of the subject, and by our agreeing—without agreement—to make my recovery of the use of my hands a question of so many hours, not of so many weeks.

My first question when I saw Herbert had been, of course, whether all was well down the river. As he replied in the affirmative, with perfect confidence and cheerfulness, we did not resume the subject until the day was wearing away. But then, as Herbert changed the bandages, more by the light of the fire than by the outer light, he went back to it <u>spontaneously</u>.

Words For Everyday Use

thrice (thrīs) *adv.*, three times

spon • ta • ne • ous • ly (spän tā´nē əs lē) *adv.*, having no apparent external cause

"I sat with Provis last night, Handel, two good hours."

"Where was Clara?"

"Dear little thing!" said Herbert. "She was up and down with Gruffandgrim all the evening. He was perpetually pegging[1] at the floor, the moment she left his sight. I doubt if he can hold out long, though. What with rum and pepper—and pepper and rum—I should think his pegging must be nearly over."

"And then you will be married, Herbert?"

"How can I take care of the dear child otherwise? Lay your arm out upon the back of the sofa, my dear boy, and I'll sit down here, and get the bandage off so gradually that you shall not know when it comes. I was speaking of Provis. Do you know, Handel, he improves?"

"I said to you I thought he was softened when I last saw him."

"So you did. And so he is. He was very communicative last night, and told me more of his life. You remember his breaking off here about some woman that he had had great trouble with. Did I hurt you?"

◄ What did Provis tell Herbert?

I had started, but not under his touch. His words had given me a start.

"I had forgotten that, Herbert, but I remember it now you speak of it."

"Well! He went into that part of his life, and a dark wild part it is. Shall I tell you? Or would it worry you just now?"

"Tell me by all means. Every word."

Herbert bent forward to look at me more nearly, as if my reply had been rather more hurried or more eager than he could quite account for. "Your head is cool?" he said, touching it.

"Quite," said I. "Tell me what Provis said, my dear Herbert."

"It seems," said Herbert, "—there's a bandage off most charmingly, and now comes the cool one—makes you shrink at first, my poor dear fellow, don't it? But it will be comfortable presently—it seems that the woman was a young woman, and a jealous woman, and a revengeful woman; revengeful, Handel, to the last degree."

"To what last degree?"

"Murder—does it strike too cold on that sensitive place?"

"I don't feel it. How did she murder? Whom did she murder?"

"Why, the deed may not have merited quite so terrible a name," said Herbert, "but she was tried for it, and Mr. Jaggers defended her, and the reputation of that defense first made his name known to Provis. It was another and a strong woman who was the victim, and there had been a struggle—

◄ What story is repeated?

---

1. **pegging.** Striking

in a barn. Who began it, or how fair it was, or how unfair, may be doubtful; but how it ended is certainly not doubtful, for the victim was found throttled."[2]

"Was the woman brought in guilty?"

"No, she was acquitted. My poor Handel, I hurt you!"

"It is impossible to be gentler, Herbert. Yes? What else?"

"This acquitted young woman and Provis had a little child, a little child of whom Provis was exceedingly fond. On the evening of the very night when the object of her jealousy was strangled as I tell you, the young woman presented herself before Provis for one moment, and swore that she would destroy the child (which was in her possession), and he should never see it again; then she vanished. . . There's the worst arm comfortably in the sling once more, and now there remains but the right hand, which is a far easier job. I can do it better by this light than by a stronger, for my hand is steadiest when I don't see the poor blistered patches too distinctly. You don't think your breathing is affected, my dear boy? You seem to breathe quickly."

"Perhaps I do, Herbert. Did the woman keep her oath?"

"There comes the darkest part of Provis's life. She did."

"That is, he says she did."

"Why, of course, my dear boy," returned Herbert, in a tone of surprise, and again bending forward to get a nearer look at me. "He says it all. I have no other information."

"No, to be sure."

▶ What did Provis do to help the woman? Why?

"Now, whether," pursued Herbert, "he had used the child's mother ill, or whether he had used the child's mother well, Provis doesn't say; but she had shared some four or five years of the wretched life he described to us at this fireside, and he seems to have felt pity for her, and <u>forbearance</u> towards her. Therefore, fearing he should be called upon to <u>depose</u> about this destroyed child, and so be the cause of her death, he hid himself (much as he grieved for the child), kept himself dark, as he says, out of the way and out of the trial, and was only vaguely talked of as a certain man called Abel, out of whom the jealousy arose. After the acquittal she disappeared, and thus he lost the child and the child's mother."

"I want to ask—"

---

2. **throttled.** Choked

Words For Everyday Use

for • bear • ance (fôr ber´əns) *n.*, self-control; patient restraint

de • pose (dē pōz´) *vt.*, state or testify under oath, but out of court

"A moment, my dear boy, and I have done. That evil genius, Compeyson, the worst of scoundrels among many scoundrels, knowing of his keeping out of the way at that time, and of his reasons for doing so, of course afterwards held the knowledge over his head as a means of keeping him poorer, and working him harder. It was clear last night that this barbed the point of Provis's <u>animosity</u>."

"I want to know," said I, "and particularly, Herbert, whether he told you when this happened."

◄ Why does Provis hate Compeyson?

"Particularly? Let me remember, then, what he said as to that. His expression was, 'a round score o' year ago, and a'most directly after I took up wi' Compeyson.' How old were you when you came upon him in the little churchyard?"

"I think in my seventh year."

"Aye. It had happened some three or four years, then, he said, and you brought into his mind the little girl so tragically lost, who would have been about your age."

"Herbert," said I, after a short silence, in a hurried way, "can you see me best by the light of the window, or the light of the fire?"

"By the firelight," answered Herbert, coming close again.

"Look at me."

"I do look at you, my dear boy."

"Touch me."

"I do touch you, my dear boy."

"You are not afraid that I am in any fever, or that my head is much disordered by the accident of last night?"

"N-no, my dear boy," said Herbert, after taking time to examine me. "You are rather excited, but you are quite yourself."

"I know I am quite myself. And the man we have in hiding down the river is Estella's father."

◄ Of what is Pip now certain?

Words For Everyday Use

an • i • mos • i • ty (an´ə mäs´ə tē) *n.,* strong dislike; hatred

CHAPTER 51

What purpose I had in view when I was hot on tracing out and proving Estella's parentage, I cannot say. It will presently be seen that the question was not before me in a distinct shape until it was put before me by a wiser head than my own.

▶ *Why does Pip go to see Jaggers?*

But, when Herbert and I had held our momentous conversation, I was seized with a feverish conviction that I ought to hunt the matter down—that I ought not to let it rest, but that I ought to see Mr. Jaggers, and come at the bare truth. I really do not know whether I felt that I did this for Estella's sake, or whether I was glad to transfer to the man in whose preservation I was so much concerned some rays of the romantic interest that had so long surrounded her. Perhaps the latter possibility may be the nearer to the truth.

Anyway, I could scarcely be withheld from going out to Gerrard Street that night. Herbert's representations that if I did, I should probably be laid up and stricken useless, when our fugitive's safety would depend upon me, alone restrained my impatience. On the understanding, again and again <u>reiterated</u>, that come what would, I was to go to Mr. Jaggers tomorrow, I at length submitted to keep quiet, and to have my hurts looked after, and to stay at home. Early next morning we went out together, and at the corner of Giltspur Street by Smithfield, I left Herbert to go his way into the City, and took my way to Little Britain.

There were periodical occasions when Mr. Jaggers and Mr. Wemmick went over the office accounts, and checked off the vouchers, and put all things straight. On these occasions Wemmick took his books and papers into Mr. Jaggers's room, and one of the upstairs clerks came down into the outer office. Finding such clerk on Wemmick's post that morning, I knew what was going on but I was not sorry to have Mr. Jaggers and Wemmick together, as Wemmick would then hear for himself that I said nothing to compromise him.

My appearance, with my arm bandaged and my coat loose over my shoulders, favored my object. Although I had sent Mr. Jaggers a brief account of the accident as soon as I had arrived in town, yet I had to give him all the details now; and the specialty of the occasion caused our talk to be less dry and hard,

Words For Everyday Use

re • it • er • ate (rē it´ə rāt) *vt.,* say again repeatedly and less strictly regulated by the rules of evidence, than it had been before. While I described the disaster, Mr. Jaggers stood, according to his wont,[1] before the fire. Wemmick leaned back in his chair, staring at me, with his hands in the pockets of his trousers, and his pen put horizontally into the post. The two brutal casts, always inseparable in my mind from the official proceedings, seemed to be congestively[2] considering whether they didn't smell fire at the present moment.

My narrative finished, and their questions exhausted, I then produced Miss Havisham's authority to receive the nine hundred pounds for Herbert. Mr. Jaggers's eyes retired a little deeper into his head when I handed him the tablets, but he presently handed them over to Wemmick, with instructions to draw the check for his signature. While that was in course of being done, I looked on at Wemmick as he wrote, and Mr. Jaggers, <u>poising</u> and swaying himself on his well-polished boots, looked on at me. "I am sorry, Pip," said he, as I put the check in my pocket, when he had signed it, "that we do nothing for *you.*"

◄ What do Jaggers and Wemmick think Pip should have done?

"Miss Havisham was good enough to ask me," I returned, "whether she could do nothing for me, and I told her no."

"Everybody should know his own business," said Mr. Jaggers. And I saw Wemmick's lips form the words "portable property."

"I should *not* have told her no, if I had been you," said Mr. Jaggers, "but every man ought to know his own business best."

"Every man's business," said Wemmick, rather reproachfully towards me, "is 'portable property.'"

As I thought the time was now come for pursuing the theme I had at heart, I said, turning on Mr. Jaggers:

"I did ask something of Miss Havisham, however, sir. I asked her to give me some information relative to her adopted daughter, and she gave me all she possessed."

"Did she?" said Mr. Jaggers, bending forward to look at his boots and then straightening himself. "Hah! I don't think I should have done so, if I had been Miss Havisham. But *she* ought to know her own business best."

"I know more of the history of Miss Havisham's adopted child than Miss Havisham herself does, sir. I know her mother."

---

1. **wont.** Usual habit or practice
2. **congestively.** Together

Words For Everyday Use

poise (poiz) *vi.*, balance

Mr. Jaggers looked at me inquiringly, and repeated "Mother?"

"I have seen her mother within these three days."

"Yes?" said Mr. Jaggers.

"And so have you, sir. And you have seen her still more recently."

"Yes?" said Mr. Jaggers.

"Perhaps I know more of Estella's history than even you do," said I. "I know her father, too."

A certain stop that Mr. Jaggers came to in his manner—he was too self-possessed to change his manner, but he could not help its being brought to an indefinably attentive stop—assured me that he did not know who her father was. This I had strongly suspected from Provis's account (as Herbert had repeated it) of his having kept himself dark; which I pieced on to the fact that he himself was not Mr. Jaggers's client until some four years later, and when he could have no reason for claiming his identity. But, I could not be sure of this unconsciousness on Mr. Jaggers's part before, though I was quite sure of it now.

"So! You know the young lady's father, Pip?" said Mr. Jaggers.

"Yes," I replied, "and his name is Provis—from New South Wales."

Even Mr. Jaggers started when I said those words. It was the slightest start that could escape a man, the most carefully <u>repressed</u> and the soonest checked, but he did start, though he made it a part of the action of taking out his pocket-handkerchief. How Wemmick received the announcement I am unable to say, for I was afraid to look at him just then, lest Mr. Jaggers's sharpness should detect that there had been some communication unknown to him between us.

> ► *What does Pip do to protect Wemmick?*

"And on what evidence, Pip," asked Mr. Jaggers, very coolly, as he paused with his handkerchief halfway to his nose, "does Provis make this claim?"

"He does not make it," said I, "and has never made it, and has no knowledge or belief that his daughter is in existence."

For once, the powerful pocket-handkerchief failed. My reply was so unexpected that Mr. Jaggers put the handkerchief back into his pocket without completing the usual performance, folded his arms, and looked with stern attention at me, though with an immovable face.

Words
For
Everyday
Use

re • pressed (ri presd´) *adj.,* held back; stifled; controlled

Then I told him all I knew, and how I knew it, with the one reservation that I left him to infer that I knew from Miss Havisham what I in fact knew from Wemmick. I was very careful indeed as to that. Nor did I look towards Wemmick until I had finished all I had to tell, and had been for some time silently meeting Mr. Jaggers's look. When I did at last turn my eyes in Wemmick's direction, I found that he had unposted his pen, and was intent upon the table before him.

"Hah!" said Mr. Jaggers at last, as he moved towards the papers on the table, "—What item was it you were at, Wemmick, when Mr. Pip came in?"

But I could not submit to be thrown off in that way, and I made a passionate, almost an indignant appeal to him to be more frank and manly with me. I reminded him of the false hopes into which I had lapsed, the length of time they had lasted, and the discovery I had made, and I hinted at the danger that weighed upon my spirits. I represented myself as being surely worthy of some little confidence from him, in return for the confidence I had just now imparted. I said that I did not blame him, or suspect him, or mistrust him, but I wanted assurance of the truth from him. And if he asked me why I wanted it and why I thought I had any right to it, I would tell him, little as he cared for such poor dreams, that I had loved Estella dearly and long, and that, although I had lost her and must live a bereaved life, whatever concerned her was still nearer and dearer to me than anything else in the world. And seeing that Mr. Jaggers stood quite still and silent, and apparently quite <u>obdurate</u>, under this appeal, I turned to Wemmick, and said, "Wemmick, I know you to be a man with a gentle heart. I have seen your pleasant home, and your old father, and all the innocent cheerful playful ways with which you refresh your business life. And I entreat you to say a word for me to Mr. Jaggers, and to represent to him that, all circumstances considered, he ought to be more open with me!"

I have never seen two men look more oddly at one another than Mr. Jaggers and Wemmick did after this apostrophe.[3] At first, a misgiving crossed me that Wemmick would be instantly dismissed from his employment, but, it melted as I

◄ *What is Pip's plea?*

---

3. **apostrophe.** Device in which a speaker breaks off speaking to one person and addresses another

saw Mr. Jaggers relax into something like a smile, and Wemmick become bolder.

"What's all this?" said Mr. Jaggers. "You with an old father, and you with pleasant and playful ways?"

"Well!" returned Wemmick. "If I don't bring 'em here, what does it matter?"

▶ What surprises Jaggers? What is Wemmick's defense?

"Pip," said Mr. Jaggers, laying his hand upon my arm, and smiling openly, "this man must be the most cunning impostor in all London."

"Not a bit of it," returned Wemmick, growing bolder and bolder. "I think you're another."

Again they exchanged their former odd looks, each apparently still distrustful that the other was taking him in.

"*You* with a pleasant home?" said Mr. Jaggers.

"Since it don't interfere with business," returned Wemmick, "let it be so. Now, I look at you, sir, I shouldn't wonder if *you* might be planning and contriving to have a pleasant home of your own, one of these days, when you're tired of all this work."

Mr. Jaggers nodded his head <u>retrospectively</u> two or three times, and actually drew a sigh. "Pip," said he, "we won't talk about 'poor dreams'; you know more about such things than I, having much fresher experience of that kind. But now, about this other matter. I'll put a case to you. Mind! I admit nothing."

He waited for me to declare that I quite understood that he expressly said that he admitted nothing.

"Now, Pip," said Mr. Jaggers, "put this case. Put the case that a woman, under such circumstances as you have mentioned, held her child concealed, and was obliged to communicate the fact to her legal adviser, on his representing to her that he must know, with an eye to the latitude[4] of his defense, how the fact stood about that child. Put the case that at the same time he held a trust to find a child for an <u>eccentric</u> rich lady to adopt and bring up."

"I follow you, sir."

▶ What are Jaggers's reasons for wanting to save the child?

"Put the case that he lived in an atmosphere of evil, and that all he saw of children was their being <u>generated</u> in great numbers for certain destruction. Put the case that he often

---

4. **latitude.** Width; scope

Words For Everyday Use	ret • ro • spec • tive • ly (ret´rə spek´tiv lē) *adv.*, in a way that looks back on the past
	ec • cen • tric (ek sen´trik) *adj.*, odd or unconventional
	gen • er • ate (jen´ə rāt) *vt.*, bring into existence

saw children solemnly tried at a criminal bar, where they were held up to be seen; put the case that he habitually knew of their being imprisoned, whipped, transported, neglected, cast out, qualified in all ways for the hangman, and growing up to be hanged. Put the case that pretty nigh all the children he saw in his daily business life, he had reason to look upon as so much spawn,[5] to develop into the fish that were to come to his net—to be prosecuted, defended, forsworn,[6] made orphans, bedeviled somehow."

"I follow you, sir."

"Put the case, Pip, that here was one pretty little child out of the heap who could be saved; whom the father believed dead, and dared make no stir about; as to whom, over the mother, the legal adviser had this power: 'I know what you did, and how you did it. You came so and so, this was your manner of attack and this the manner of resistance, you went so and so, you did such and such things to divert suspicion. I have tracked you through it all, and I tell it you all. Part with the child, unless it should be necessary to produce it to clear you, and then it shall be produced. Give the child into my hands, and I will do my best to bring you off. If you are saved, your child will be saved, too; if you are lost, your child is still saved.' Put the case that this was done, and that the woman was cleared."

"I understand you perfectly."

"But that I make no admissions?"

"That you make no admissions." And Wemmick repeated, "No admissions."

"Put the case, Pip, that passion and the terror of death had a little shaken the woman's intellects, and that when she was set at liberty, she was scared out of the ways of the world and went to him to be sheltered. Put the case that he took her in, and that he kept down the old wild violent nature, whenever he saw an inkling of its breaking out, by asserting his power over her in the old way. Do you comprehend the imaginary case?"

"Quite."

"Put the case that the child grew up, and was married for money. That the mother was still living. That the father was still living. That the mother and father, unknown to one another, were dwelling within so many miles, furlongs,[7] yards if you like, of one another. That the secret was still a secret, except that you had got wind of it. Put that last case to yourself very carefully."

◄ What does Jaggers ask Pip to consider? Would there be value in telling the secret?

---

5. **spawn.** Fish eggs; offspring emerging in large numbers
6. **forsworn.** Forsaken; disowned
7. **furlongs.** Units of distance equal to about one-eighth mile or 220 yards

"I do."

"I ask Wemmick to put it to *him*self very carefully."

And Wemmick said, "I do."

"For whose sake would you reveal the secret? For the father's? I think he would not be much the better for the mother. For the mother's? I think if she had done such a deed, she would be safer where she was. For the daughter's? I think it would hardly serve her to establish her parentage for the information of her husband, and to drag her back to disgrace, after an escape of twenty years, pretty secure to last for life. But, add the case that you had loved her, Pip, and had made her the subject of those 'poor dreams' which have, at one time or another, been in the heads of more men than you think likely, then I tell you that you had better—and would much sooner when you had thought well of it—chop off that bandaged left hand of yours with your bandaged right hand, and then pass the chopper on to Wemmick there, to cut *that* off, too."

I looked at Wemmick, whose face was very grave. He gravely touched his lips with his forefinger. I did the same. Mr. Jaggers did the same. "Now, Wemmick," said the latter then, <u>resuming</u> his usual manner, "what item was it you were at when Mr. Pip came in?"

▶ Why did the relationship of Jaggers and Wemmick change?

Standing by for a little, while they were at work, I observed that the odd looks they had cast at one another were repeated several times—with this difference, now, that each of them seemed suspicious, not to say conscious, of having shown himself in a weak and unprofessional light to the other. For this reason, I suppose, they were now inflexible with one another, Mr. Jaggers being highly dictatorial, and Wemmick obstinately justifying himself whenever there was the smallest point in <u>abeyance</u> for a moment. I had never seen them on such ill terms, for generally they got on very well indeed together.

But they were both happily relieved by the opportune appearance of Mike, the client with the fur cap, and the habit of wiping his nose on his sleeve, whom I had seen on the very first day of my appearance within those walls. This individual, who, either in his own person or in that of some member of his family, seemed to be always in trouble (which in that place meant Newgate), called to announce that his

| Words For Everyday Use | **re • sume** (ri zo͞om´) *vt.,* take on again; continue after interruption |
| | **a • bey • ance** (ə bā´əns) *n.,* temporary suspension of activity |

eldest daughter was taken up on suspicion of shoplifting. As he imparted this melancholy circumstance to Wemmick, Mr. Jaggers standing <u>magisterially</u> before the fire and taking no share in the proceedings, Mike's eye happened to twinkle with a tear.

"What are you about?" demanded Wemmick, with the utmost indignation. "What do you come <u>sniveling</u> here for?"

"I didn't go to do it, Mr. Wemmick."

"You did," said Wemmick. "How dare you? You're not in a fit state to come here, if you can't come here without spluttering like a bad pen. What do you mean by it?"

"A man can't help his feelings, Mr. Wemmick," pleaded Mike.

"His what?" demanded Wemmick, quite savagely. "Say that again!"

"Now look here, my man," said Mr. Jaggers, advancing a step, and pointing to the door. "Get out of this office. I'll have no feelings here. Get out."

"It serves you right," said Wemmick, "Get out."

So the unfortunate Mike very humbly withdrew, and Mr. Jaggers and Wemmick appeared to have re-established their good understanding, and went to work again with an air of refreshment upon them as if they had just had lunch.

<table>
<tr><td rowspan="4">**Words For Everyday Use**</td><td>**mag • is • te • ri • al • ly** (majˊis tirˊē ə lē) *adv.*,
authoritatively</td></tr>
<tr><td>**sniv • el** (snivˊəl) *vi.*, make a whining, tearful display of
false grief</td></tr>
</table>

CHAPTER 52

▶ What brings Pip satisfaction?

From Little Britain, I went, with my check in my pocket, to Miss Skiffins's brother, the accountant; and Miss Skiffins's brother, the accountant, going straight to Clarriker's and bringing Clarriker to me, I had the great satisfaction of concluding that arrangement. It was the only good thing I had done, and the only completed thing I had done, since I was first <u>apprised</u> of my great expectations.

Clarriker informing me on that occasion that the affairs of the house were steadily progressing, that he would now be able to establish a small branch-house in the East which was much wanted for the extension of the business, and that Herbert in his new partnership capacity would go out and take charge of it, I found that I must have prepared for a separation from my friend, even though my own affairs had been more settled. And now indeed I felt as if my last anchor were loosening its hold, and I should soon be driving with the winds and waves.

But there was recompense in the joy with which Herbert would come home of a night and tell me of these changes, little imagining that he told me no news, and would sketch airy pictures of himself conducting Clara Barley to the land of the Arabian Nights,[1] and of me going out to join them (with a caravan of camels, I believe), and of our all going up the Nile and seeing wonders. Without being sanguine as to my own part in those bright plans, I felt that Herbert's way was clearing fast, and that old Bill Barley had but to stick to his pepper and rum, and his daughter would soon be happily provided for.

▶ What is Pip's physical condition?

We had now got into the month of March. My left arm, though it presented no bad symptoms, took in the natural course so long to heal that I was still unable to get a coat on. My right arm was tolerably restored—disfigured, but fairly serviceable.

On a Monday morning, when Herbert and I were at breakfast, I received the following letter from Wemmick by the post.

▶ What message does Wemmick send?

"Walworth. Burn this as soon as read. Early in the week, or say Wednesday, you might do what you know of, if you felt disposed to try it. Now, burn."

---

1. **land . . . Nights.** Middle East

Words For Everyday Use

ap • prise (ə prīz´) *vt.*, inform; make aware

When I had shown this to Herbert and had put it in the fire—but not before we had both got it by heart—we considered what to do. For, of course, my being disabled could now be no longer kept out of view.

"I have thought it over, again and again," said Herbert, "and I think I know a better course than taking a Thames waterman. Take Startop. A good fellow, a skilled hand, fond of us, and enthusiastic and honorable."

I had thought of him more than once.

"But how much would you tell him, Herbert?"

◄ What changes in the plan to move Provis? Why?

"It is necessary to tell him very little. Let him suppose it a mere freak, but a secret one, until the morning comes—then let him know that there is urgent reason for your getting Provis aboard and away. You go with him?"

"No doubt."

"Where?"

It had seemed to me, in the many anxious considerations I had given the point, almost indifferent what port we made for—Hamburg, Rotterdam, Antwerp[2]—the place signified little, so that he was out of England. Any foreign steamer that fell in our way and would take us up would do. I had always proposed to myself to get him well down the river in the boat; certainly well beyond Gravesend, which was a critical place for search or inquiry if suspicion were afoot. As foreign steamers would leave London at about the time of high-water, our plan would be to get down the river by a previous ebb-tide, and lie by in some quiet spot until we could pull off to one. The time when one would be due where we lay, wherever that might be, could be calculated pretty nearly, if we made inquiries beforehand.

Herbert assented to all this, and we went out immediately after breakfast to pursue our investigations. We found that a steamer for Hamburg was likely to suit our purpose best, and we directed our thoughts chiefly to that vessel. But we noted down what other foreign steamers would leave London with the same tide, and we satisfied ourselves that we knew the build and color of each. We then separated for a few hours, I to get at once such passports as were necessary, Herbert to see Startop at his lodgings. We both did what we had to do without any <u>hindrance</u>, and when we met again at one

---

2. **Hamburg, Rotterdam, Antwerp.** Cities in Germany, the Netherlands, and Belgium, respectively

Words For Everyday Use

hin • drance (hin′drəns) *n.,* obstacle

o'clock reported it done. I, for my part, was prepared with passports; Herbert had seen Startop, and he was more than ready to join.

▶ What is the plan?

Those two would pull a pair of oars, we settled, and I would steer: our charge would be sitter, and keep quiet; as speed was not our object, we should make way enough. We arranged that Herbert should not come home to dinner before going to Mill Pond Bank that evening; that he should not go there at all tomorrow evening, Tuesday; that he should prepare Provis to come down to some stairs hard by the house, on Wednesday, when he saw us approach, and not sooner; that all the arrangements with him should be concluded that Monday night; and that he should be communicated with no more in any way, until we took him on board.

These precautions well understood by both of us, I went home.

On opening the outer door of our chambers with my key, I found a letter in the box, directed to me; a very dirty letter, though not ill-written. It had been delivered by hand (of course since I left home), and its contents were these:

▶ What message does Pip receive? What must he decide?

"If you are not afraid to come to the old marshes tonight or tomorrow night at nine, and to come to the little sluice-house by the limekiln,[3] you had better come. If you want information regarding *your uncle Provis,* you had much better come and tell no one and lose no time. *You must come alone.* Bring this with you."

▶ What does Pip decide to do? Why?

I had had load enough upon my mind before the receipt of this strange letter. What to do now, I could not tell. And the worse was that I must decide quickly, or I should miss the afternoon coach, which would take me down in time for tonight. Tomorrow night I could not think of going, for it would be too close upon the time of the flight. And again, for anything I knew, the <u>proffered</u> information might have some important bearing on the flight itself.

If I had had ample time for consideration, I believe I should still have gone. Having hardly any time for consideration—my watch showing me that the coach started within half an hour—I resolved to go. I should certainly not have

---

3. **limekiln.** Furnace used to produce lime, a soft white powder used in making cement, etc.

Words For Everyday Use

prof • fered (präf´ərd) *adj.,* offered; presented

gone but for the reference to my Uncle Provis. That, coming on Wemmick's letter and the morning's busy preparation, turned the scale.

It is so difficult to become clearly possessed of the contents of almost any letter in a violent hurry that I had to read this mysterious epistle again, twice, before its <u>injunction</u> to me to be secret got mechanically into my mind. Yielding to it in the same mechanical kind of way, I left a note in pencil for Herbert, telling him that as I should be so soon going away, I knew not for how long, I had decided to hurry down and back to ascertain for myself how Miss Havisham was faring.[4] I had then barely time to get my greatcoat, lock up the chambers, and make for the coach-office by the short by-ways. If I had taken a hackney-chariot and gone by the streets, I should have missed my aim; going as I did, I caught the coach just as it came out of the yard. I was the only inside passenger, jolting away knee-deep in straw, when I came to myself.

For I really had not been myself since the receipt of the letter; it had so bewildered me, ensuing[5] on the hurry of the morning. The morning hurry and flutter had been great, for, long and anxiously as I had waited for Wemmick, his hint had come like a surprise at last. And now I began to wonder at myself for being in the coach, and to doubt whether I had sufficient reason for being there, and to consider whether I should get out presently and go back, and to argue against ever heeding an anonymous communication, and, in short, to pass through all those phases of contradiction and indecision to which I suppose very few hurried people are strangers. Still, the reference to Provis by name mastered everything. I reasoned as I had reasoned already without knowing it—if that be reasoning—in case any harm should befall him through my not going, how could I ever forgive myself?

It was dark before we got down, and the journey seemed long and dreary to me who could see little of it inside, and who could not go outside in my disabled state. Avoiding the Blue Boar, I put up at an inn of minor reputation down the town, and ordered some dinner. While it was preparing, I went to Satis House and inquired for Miss Havisham; she was still very ill, though considered something better.

---

4. **faring.** Doing
5. **ensuing.** Following immediately

Words For Everyday Use

in • junc • tion (in juŋk′shən) *n.*, command

► *What is the story that the innkeeper tells Pip? Why is it amusing?*

My inn had once been a part of an ancient ecclesiastical house, and I dined in a little <u>octagonal</u> common room, like a font.[6] As I was not able to cut my dinner, the old landlord with a shining bald head did it for me. This bringing us into conversation, he was so good as to entertain me with my own story—of course with the popular feature that Pumblechook was my earliest benefactor and the founder of my fortunes.

"Do you know the young man?" said I.

"Know him?" repeated the landlord. "Ever since he was— no height at all."

"Does he ever come back to this neighborhood?"

"Aye, he comes back," said the landlord, "to his great friends, now and again, and gives the cold shoulder[7] to the man that made him."

"What man is that?"

"Him that I speak of," said the landlord. "Mr. Pumblechook."

"Is he ungrateful to no one else?"

"No doubt he would be, if he could," returned the landlord, "but he can't. And why? Because Pumblechook done everything for him."

"Does Pumblechook say so?"

"Say so!" replied the landlord. "He han't no call to say so."

"But does he say so?"

"It would turn a man's blood to white wine winegar to hear him tell of it, sir," said the landlord.

I thought, "Yet Joe, dear Joe, *you* never tell of it. Long suffering[8] and loving Joe, *you* never complain. Nor you, sweet-tempered Biddy!"

"Your appetite's been touched like, by your accident," said the landlord, glancing at the bandaged arm under my coat. "Try a tenderer bit."

"No, thank you," I replied, turning from the table to brood over the fire. "I can eat no more. Please take it away."

► *What does Pip come to realize at last?*

I had never been struck at so keenly, for my thanklessness to Joe, as through the brazen impostor Pumblechook. The falser he, the truer Joe; the meaner he, the nobler Joe.

---

6. **font.** Large basin
7. **cold shoulder.** Deliberately unkind or unfriendly treatment; snub
8. **Long suffering.** Patiently enduring wrongs or difficulties

Words For Everyday Use	**oc • tag • o • nal** (äk tag′ə nəl) *adj.,* eight-sided

My heart was deeply and most deservedly humbled as I mused over the fire for an hour or more. The striking of the clock aroused me, but not from my dejection or remorse, and I got up and had my coat fastened round my neck, and went out. I had previously sought in my pockets for the letter, that I might refer to it again, but I could not find it, and was uneasy to think that it must have been dropped in the straw of the coach. I knew very well, however, that the appointed place was the little sluice-house by the limekiln on the marshes, and the hour nine. Towards the marshes I now went straight, having no time to spare.

◄ *What does Pip misplace?*

CHAPTER 53

It was a dark night, though the full moon rose as I left the enclosed lands, and passed out upon the marshes. Beyond their dark line there was a ribbon of clear sky, hardly broad enough to hold the red large moon. In a few minutes she had ascended out of that clear field, in among the piled mountains of cloud.

▶ *What is the mood on the marshes?*

There was a melancholy wind, and the marshes were very dismal. A stranger would have found them insupportable, and even to me they were so oppressive that I hesitated, half-inclined to go back. But, I knew them well, and could have found my way on a far darker night, and had no excuse for returning, being there. So, having come there against my inclination, I went on against it.

The direction that I took was not that in which my old home lay, nor that in which we had pursued the convicts. My back was turned towards the distant Hulks as I walked on, and, though I could see the old lights away on the spits of sand, I saw them over my shoulder. I knew the limekiln as well as I knew the old battery, but they were miles apart, so that if a light had been burning at each point that night, there would have been a long strip of the blank horizon between the two bright specks.

At first, I had to shut some gates after me, and now and then to stand still while the cattle that were lying in the banked-up pathway arose and blundered down among the grass and reeds. But after a little while, I seemed to have the whole flats to myself.

It was another half-hour before I drew near to the kiln. The lime was burning with a sluggish stifling smell, but the fires were made up and left, and no workmen were visible. Hard by was a small stone quarry. It lay directly in my way, and had been worked that day, as I saw by the tools and barrows that were lying about.

Coming up again to the marsh level out of this excavation—for the rude path lay through it—I saw a light in the old sluice-house. I quickened my pace, and knocked at the door with my hand. Waiting for some reply, I looked about me, noticing how the sluice was abandoned and broken, and how the house—of wood with a tiled roof—would not be proof against the weather much longer, if it were so even now, and how the mud and ooze were coated with lime, and how the choking vapor of the kiln crept in a ghostly way towards me. Still there was no answer, and I knocked again. No answer still, and I tried the latch.

It rose under my hand, and the door yielded. Looking in, I saw a lighted candle on a table, a bench, and a mattress on a truckle[1] bedstead. As there was a loft above, I called, "Is there anyone here?" but no voice answered. Then, I looked at my watch, and, finding that it was past nine, called again, "Is there anyone here?" There being still no answer, I went out at the door, <u>irresolute</u> what to do.

It was beginning to rain fast. Seeing nothing save what I had seen already, I turned back into the house, and stood just within the shelter of the doorway, looking out into the night. While I was considering that someone must have been there lately and must soon be coming back, or the candle would not be burning, it came into my head to look if the wick were long. I turned round to do so, and had taken up the candle in my hand, when it was extinguished by some violent shock, and the next thing I comprehended was that I had been caught in a strong running noose, thrown over my head from behind.

◄ What is the violent shock Pip receives?

"Now," said a suppressed voice with an oath, "I've got you!"

"What is this?" I cried, struggling. "Who is it? Help, help, help!"

Not only were my arms pulled close to my sides, but the pressure on my bad arm caused me <u>exquisite</u> pain. Sometimes a strong man's hand, sometimes a strong man's breast, was set against my mouth to deaden my cries, and with a hot breath always close to me, I struggled ineffectually in the dark, while I was fastened tight to the wall. "And now," said the suppressed voice with another oath, "call out again, and I'll make short work of you!"

Faint and sick with the pain of my injured arm, bewildered by the surprise, and yet conscious how easily this threat could be put in execution, I <u>desisted</u>, and tried to ease my arm were it ever so little. But it was bound too tight for that. I felt as if, having been burnt before, it were now being boiled.

The sudden exclusion of the night and the substitution of black darkness in its place warned me that the man had closed a shutter. After groping about for a little, he found the flint[2] and steel he wanted, and began to strike a light. I

---

1. **truckle.** Trundle bed that fits underneath a larger bed
2. **flint.** Very hard quartz that sparks when struck with steel; used to light a fire

---

Words For Everyday Use

ir • res • o • lute (ir rez´ə lo͞ot) *adj.*, indecisive

ex • qui • site (ek skwi´zit) *adj.*, intense; acute

de • sist (di zist´) *vi.*, stop

strained my sight upon the sparks that fell among the tinder, and upon which he breathed and breathed, match in hand, but I could only see his lips, and the blue point of the match, even those but fitfully. The tinder was damp—no wonder there—and one after another the sparks died out.

► Who is the man?

The man was in no hurry, and struck again with the flint and steel. As the sparks fell thick and bright about him, I could see his hands and touches of his face, and could make out that he was seated and bending over the table, but nothing more. Presently I saw his blue lips again, breathing on the tinder, and then a flare of light flashed up, and showed me Orlick.

Whom I had looked for, I don't know. I had not looked for him. Seeing him, I felt that I was in a dangerous strait[3] indeed, and I kept my eyes upon him.

He lighted the candle from the flaring match with great deliberation, and dropped the match, and trod it out. Then, he put the candle away from him on the table, so that he could see me, and sat with his arms folded on the table and looked at me. I made out that I was fastened to a stout perpendicular ladder a few inches from the wall—a fixture there—the means of ascent to the loft above.

► Why has Orlick kidnapped Pip?

"Now," said he, when we had surveyed one another for some time, "I've got you."

"Unbind me. Let me go!"

"Ah!" he returned, *"I'll* let you go. I'll let you go to the moon, I'll let you go to the stars. All in good time."

"Why have you lured me here?"

"Don't you know?" said he, with a deadly look.

"Why have you set upon me in the dark?"

"Because I mean to do it all myself. One keeps a secret better than two. Oh, you enemy, you enemy!"

His enjoyment of the spectacle I furnished, as he sat with his arms folded on the table, shaking his head at me and hugging himself, had a <u>malignity</u> in it that made me tremble. As I watched him in silence, he put his hand into the corner at his side, and took up a gun with a brass-bound stock.

"Do you know this?" said he, making as if he would take aim at me. "Do you know where you saw it afore? Speak, wolf!"

---

3. **strait.** Position of difficulty, distress, or need

Words For Everyday Use	**ma • lig • ni • ty** (mə lig′nə tē) *n.,* quality of being very harmful

"Yes," I answered.

"You cost me that place. You did. Speak!"

"What else could I do?"

"You did that, and that would be enough, without more. How dared you come betwixt me and a young woman I liked?"

"When did I?"

"When didn't you? It was you as always give Old Orlick a bad name to her."

"You gave it to yourself; you gained it for yourself. I could have done you no harm, if you had done yourself none."

"You're a liar. And you'll take any pains, and spend any money, to drive me out of this country, will you?" said he, repeating my words to Biddy in the last interview I had with her. "Now, I'll tell you a piece of information. It was never so well worth your while to get me out of this country as it is tonight. Ah! If it was all your money twenty times told, to the last brass farden!" As he shook his heavy hand at me, with his mouth snarling like a tiger's, I felt that it was true.

"What are you going to do to me?"

"I'm a-going," said he, bringing his first down upon the table with a heavy blow, and rising as the blow fell, to give it greater force, "I'm a-going to have your life!"

He leaned forward, staring at me, slowly unclenched his hand, and drew it across his mouth as if his mouth watered for me, and sat down again.

"You was always in Old Orlick's way since ever you was a child. You goes out of his way this present night. He'll have no more on you. You're dead."

I felt that I had come to the brink of my grave. For a moment I looked wildly round my trap for any chance of escape, but there was none.

"More than that," said he, folding his arms on the table again, "I won't have a rag of you, I won't have a bone of you, left on earth. I'll put your body in the kiln—I'd carry two such to it, on my shoulders—and, let people suppose what they may of you, they shall never know nothing."

My mind, with inconceivable rapidity, followed out all the consequences of such a death. Estella's father would believe I had deserted him, would be taken, would die accusing me; even Herbert would doubt me, when he compared the letter I had left for him with the fact that I had called at Miss Havisham's gate for only a moment; Joe and Biddy would never know how sorry I had been that night, none would ever know what I had suffered, how true I had meant to be, what an agony I had passed through. The death close before me was terrible, but far more terrible than death was the dread

◄ Of what does Orlick accuse Pip?

◄ What does Orlick plan to do?

◄ What are Pip's fears and regrets?

of being misremembered after death. And so quick were my thoughts that I saw myself despised by unborn generations—Estella's children, and their children—while the wretch's words were yet on his lips.

"Now, wolf," said he, "afore I kill you like any other beast—which is wot I mean to do and wot I have tied you up for—I'll have a good look at you and a good goad at you. Oh, you enemy!"

It had passed through my thoughts to cry out for help again, though few could know better than I the solitary nature of the spot, and the hopelessness of aid. But as he sat gloating over me, I was supported by a scornful detestation of him that sealed my lips. Above all things, I resolved that I would not entreat him, and that I would die making some last poor resistance to him. Softened as my thoughts of all the rest of men were in that dire extremity; humbly beseeching pardon, as I did, of Heaven; melted at heart, as I was, by the thought that I had taken no farewell, and never now could take farewell, of those who were dear to me, or could explain myself to them, or ask for their compassion on my miserable errors; still, if I could have killed him, even in dying, I would have done it.

He had been drinking, and his eyes were red and bloodshot. Around his neck was slung a tin bottle, as I had often seen his meat and drink slung about him in other days. He brought the bottle to his lips, and took a fiery drink from it, and I smelt the strong spirits that I saw flash into his face.

"Wolf!" said he, folding his arms again, "Old Orlick's a-going to tell you somethink. It was you as did for your shrew[4] sister."

Again my mind, with its former inconceivable rapidity, had exhausted the whole subject of the attack upon my sister, her illness, and her death before his slow and hesitating speech had formed these words.

"It was you, villain," said I.

"I tell you it was your doing—I tell you it was done through you," he retorted, catching up the gun, and making a blow with the stock at the vacant air between us. "I come upon her from behind, as I come upon you tonight. I giv' it her! I left her for dead, and if there had been a limekiln as nigh her as there is now nigh you, she shouldn't have come to life again. But it warn't Old Orlick as did it; it was you. You was favored, and he was bullied and beat. Old Orlick bullied and beat, eh? Now you pays for it. You done it; now you pays for it."

---

4. **shrew.** Woman with a violent or nagging temperament

▶ What does Pip resolve?

▶ What effect does the alcohol have on Orlick?

▶ To what crime does Orlick confess? Why does he blame Pip for the crime?

He drank again, and became more ferocious. I saw by his tilting of the bottle that there was no great quantity left in it. I distinctly understood that he was working himself up with its contents to make an end of me. I knew that every drop it held was a drop of my life. I knew that when I was changed into a part of the vapor that had crept towards me but a little while before, like my own warning ghost, he would do as he had done in my sister's case—make all haste to the town, and be seen slouching about there, drinking at the ale-houses. My rapid mind pursued him to the town, made a picture of the street with him in it, and contrasted its lights and life with the lonely marsh and the white vapor creeping over it, into which I should have dissolved.

◀ Why do you think Orlick has followed Pip all these years?

It was not only that I could have summed up years and years and years while he said a dozen words, but that what he did say presented pictures to me, and not mere words. In the excited and exalted state of my brain, I could not think of a place without seeing it, or of persons without seeing them. It is impossible to overstate the vividness of these images, and yet I was so intent, all the time, upon him himself—who would not be intent on the tiger crouching to spring!—that I knew of the slightest action of his fingers.

When he had drunk this second time, he rose from the bench on which he sat, and pushed the table aside. Then he took up the candle, and shading it with his murderous hand so as to throw its light on me, stood before me, looking at me and enjoying the sight.

"Wolf, I'll tell you something more. It was Old Orlick as you tumbled over on your stairs that night."

I saw the staircase with its extinguished lamps. I saw the shadows of the heavy stair-rails, thrown by the watchman's lantern on the wall. I saw the rooms that I was never to see again, here a door half-open, there a door closed, all the articles of furniture around.

"And why was Old Orlick there? I'll tell you something more, wolf. You and her *have* pretty well hunted me out of this country, so far as getting a easy living in it goes, and I've took up with new companions, and new masters. Some of 'em writes my letters when I wants 'em wrote—do you mind?— writes my letters, wolf! They writes fifty hands; they're not like sneaking you, as writes but one. I've had a firm mind and a firm will to have your life, since you was down here at your sister's burying. I han't seen a way to get you safe, and I've looked arter you to know your ins and outs. For, says Old Orlick to himself, 'Somehow or another I'll have him!' What! When I looks for you, I finds your Uncle Provis, eh?"

Mill Pond Bank, and Chinks's Basin, and the Old Green Copper Rope-Walk, all so clear and plain! Provis in his rooms, the signal whose use was over, pretty Clara, the good motherly woman, old Bill Barley on his back, all drifting by, as on the swift stream of my life fast running out to sea!

"*You* with a uncle, too! Why, I knowed you at Gargery's when you were so small a wolf that I could have took your weazen[5] betwixt this finger and thumb and chucked you away dead (as I'd thoughts o' doing, odd times, when I saw you a-loitering among the pollards[6] on a Sunday), and you hadn't found no uncles then. No, not you! But when Old Orlick come for to hear that your Uncle Provis had mostlike wore the leg-iron wot Old Orlick had picked up, filed asunder, on these meshes ever so many year ago, and wot he kep by him till he dropped your sister with it, like a bullock, as he means to drop you—hey?—when he come for to hear that—hey?—"

▶ Whose identity does Orlick know? What does he know about him?

In his savage taunting, he flared the candle so close at me that I turned my face aside to save it from the flame.

"Ah!" he cried, laughing, after doing it again, "the burnt child dreads the fire! Old Orlick knowed you was burnt, Old Orlick knowed you was a-smuggling your Uncle Provis away, Old Orlick's a match for you and know'd you'd come tonight! Now I'll tell you something more, wolf, and this ends it. There's them that's as good a match for your Uncle Provis as Old Orlick has been for you. Let him 'ware[7] them when he's lost his nevvy![8] Let him 'ware them, when no man can't find a rag of his dear relation's clothes, nor yet a bone of his body. There's them that can't and that won't have Magwitch—yes, *I* know the name!—alive in the same land with them, and that's had such sure information of him when he was alive in another land, as that he couldn't and shouldn't leave it unbeknown and put them in danger. P'raps it's them that writes fifty hands, and that's not like sneaking you as writes but one. 'Ware Compeyson, Magwitch, and the gallows!"

▶ Whom is Orlick working with?

He flared the candle at me again, smoking my face and hair, and for an instant blinding me, and turned his powerful back as he replaced the light on the table. I had thought a prayer, and had been with Joe and Biddy and Herbert, before he turned towards me again.

There was a clear space of a few feet between the table and the opposite wall. Within this space, he now slouched backwards and forwards. His great strength seemed to sit stronger

---

5. **weazen.** Throat
6. **pollards.** Trees with their branches cut back to promote dense growth
7. **'ware.** Beware
8. **nevvy.** Nerve

upon him than ever before, as he did this with his hands hanging loose and heavy at his sides, and with his eyes scowling at me. I had no grain of hope left. Wild as my inward hurry was, and wonderful the force of the pictures that rushed by me instead of thoughts, I could yet clearly understand that unless he had resolved that I was within a few moments of surely perishing out of all human knowledge, he would never have told me what he had told.

Of a sudden, he stopped, took the cork out of his bottle, and tossed it away. Light as it was, I heard it fall like a plummet.[9] He swallowed slowly, tilting up the bottle by little and little, and now he looked at me no more. The last few drops of liquor he poured into the palm of his hand, and licked up. Then with a sudden hurry of violence and swearing horribly, he threw the bottle from him, and stooped; and I saw in his hand a stone-hammer with a long heavy handle.

The resolution I had made did not desert me, for, without uttering one vain word of appeal to him, I shouted out with all my might, and struggled with all my might. It was only my head and my legs that I could move, but to that extent I struggled with all the force, until then unknown, that was within me. In the same instant I heard responsive shouts, saw figures and a gleam of light dash in at the door, heard voices and tumult, and saw Orlick emerge from a struggle of men, as if it were tumbling water, clear the table at a leap, and fly out into the night!

▼ Why does Pip cry out and fight? What happens?

After a blank, I found that I was lying unbound, on the floor, in the same place, with my head on someone's knee. My eyes were fixed on the ladder against the wall, when I came to myself—had opened on it before my mind saw it—and thus as I recovered consciousness, I knew that I was in the place where I had lost it.

Too indifferent at first even to look round and ascertain who supported me, I was lying looking at the ladder when there came between me and it, a face. The face of Trabb's boy!

◄ Who saves Pip?

"I think he's all right!" said Trabb's boy, in a sober voice, "but ain't he just pale though!"

At these words, the face of him who supported me looked over into mine, and I saw my supporter to be—

"Herbert! Great Heaven!"

"Softly," said Herbert. "Gently, Handel. Don't be too eager."

"And our old comrade, Startop!" I cried, as he too bent over me.

"Remember what he is going to assist us in," said Herbert, "and be calm."

---

9. **plummet.** Lead weight attached to a line to measure depth or verticality

The <u>allusion</u> made me spring up, though I dropped again from the pain in my arm. "The time has not gone by, Herbert, has it? What night is tonight? How long have I been here?" For, I had a strange and strong <u>misgiving</u> that I had been lying there a long time—a day and a night—two days and nights—more.

"The time has not gone by. It is still Monday night."

"Thank God!"

"And you have all tomorrow, Tuesday, to rest in," said Herbert. "But you can't help groaning, my dear Handel. What hurt have you got? Can you stand?"

"Yes, yes," said I, "I can walk. I have no hurt but in this throbbing arm."

► What happened to Pip's arms?

They laid it bare, and did what they could. It was violently swollen and inflamed, and I could scarcely endure to have it touched. But they tore up their handkerchiefs to make fresh bandages, and carefully replaced it in the sling, until we could get to the town and obtain some cooling lotion to put upon it. In a little while we had shut the door of the dark and empty sluice-house, and were passing through the quarry on our way back. Trabb's boy—Trabb's overgrown young man now—went before us with a lantern, which was the light I had seen come in at the door. But the moon was a good two hours higher than when I had last seen the sky, and the night though rainy was much lighter. The white vapor of the kiln was passing from us as we went by, and, as I had thought a prayer before, I thought a thanksgiving now.

► Why did Herbert come?

Entreating Herbert to tell me how he had come to my rescue—which at first he had flatly refused to do, but had insisted on my remaining quiet—I learned that I had in my hurry dropped the letter, open, in our chambers, where he, coming home to bring with him Startop, whom he had met in the street on his way to me, found it very soon after I was gone. Its tone made him uneasy, and the more so because of the inconsistency between it and the hasty letter I had left for him. His uneasiness increasing instead of subsiding after a quarter of an hour's consideration, he set off for the coach-office with Startop, who volunteered his company, to make inquiry when the next coach went down. Finding that the afternoon coach was gone, and finding that his uneasiness grew into positive alarm, as obstacles came in his way, he

Words For Everyday Use	al • lu • sion (ə lo͞o´zhən) n., casual reference
	mis • giv • ing (mis giv´iŋ) n., feeling of uncertainty or apprehension

resolved to follow in a post-chaise. So he and Startop arrived at the Blue Boar, fully expecting there to find me, or tidings of me but finding neither, went on to Miss Havisham's, where they lost me. Hereupon they went back to the hotel (doubtless at about the time when I was hearing the popular local version of my own story), to refresh themselves and to get someone to guide them out upon the marshes. Among the loungers under the Boar's archway happened to be Trabb's boy—true to his ancient habit of happening to be everywhere where he had no business—and Trabb's boy had seen me passing from Miss Havisham's in the direction of my dining place. Thus, Trabb's boy became their guide, and with him they went out to the sluice-house: though by the town way to the marshes, which I had avoided. Now, as they went along, Herbert reflected that I might, after all, have been brought there on some genuine and serviceable errand tending to Provis's safety, and bethinking himself that in that case interruption might be mischievous,[10] left his guide and Startop on the edge of the quarry, and went on by himself, and stole round the house two or three times, endeavoring to ascertain whether all was right within. As he could hear nothing but indistinct sounds of one deep rough voice (this was while my mind was so busy), he even at last began to doubt whether I was there, when suddenly I cried out loudly, and he answered the cries, and rushed in, closely followed by the other two.

When I told Herbert what had passed within the house, he was for our immediately going before a magistrate in the town, late at night as it was, and getting out a warrant. But I had already considered that such a course, by detaining us there, or binding us to come back, might be fatal to Provis. There was no gainsaying[11] this difficulty, and we relinquished all thoughts of pursuing Orlick at that time. For the present, under the circumstances, we deemed it prudent to make rather light of the matter to Trabb's boy, who I am convinced would have been much affected by disappointment, if he had known that his intervention saved me from the limekiln. Not that Trabb's boy was of a malignant nature, but that he had too much spare vivacity, and that it was in his constitution to want variety and excitement at anybody's expense. When we parted, I presented him with two guineas (which seemed to meet his views), and told him that I was sorry ever to have had an ill opinion of him (which made no impression on him at all).

◄ *What do Pip and Herbert decide? Why?*

---

10. **mischievous.** Causing harm
11. **gainsaying.** Denying

Wednesday being so close upon us, we determined to go back to London that night, three in the post-chaise; the rather, as we should then be clear away, before the night's adventure began to be talked of. Herbert got a large bottle of stuff for my arm, and by dint of having this stuff dropped over it all the night through, I was just able to bear its pain on the journey. It was daylight when we reached the Temple, and I went at once to bed, and lay in bed all day.

My terror, as I lay there, of falling ill and being unfitted for tomorrow, was so besetting that I wonder it did not disable me of itself. It would have done so, pretty surely, in <u>con-junction</u> with the mental wear and tear I had suffered, but for the unnatural strain upon me that tomorrow was. So anxiously looked forward to, charged with such consequences, its results so impenetrably hidden though so near.

No precaution could have been more obvious than our refraining from communication with him that day, yet this again increased my restlessness. I started at every footstep and every sound, believing that he was discovered and taken, and this was the messenger to tell me so. I persuaded myself that I knew he was taken; that there was something more upon my mind than a fear or a presentiment; that the fact had occurred, and I had a mysterious knowledge of it. As the day wore on and no ill news came, as the day closed in and darkness fell, my overshadowing dread of being disabled by illness before tomorrow morning altogether mastered me. My burning arm throbbed, and my burning head throbbed, and I fancied I was beginning to wander. I counted up to high numbers to make sure of myself, and repeated passages that I knew in prose and verse. It happened sometimes that in the mere escape of a fatigued mind, I dozed for some moments or forgot; then I would say to myself with a start, "Now it has come, and I am turning <u>delirious</u>!"

▶ *What keeps Pip from resting?*

They kept me very quiet all day, and kept my arm constantly dressed, and gave me cooling drinks. Whenever I fell asleep, I awoke with the notion I had had in the sluice-house, that a long time had elapsed and the opportunity to save him was gone. About midnight I got out of bed and went to Herbert, with the conviction that I had been asleep for four-and-twenty hours, and that Wednesday was past. It was the last self-exhausting effort of my fretfulness, for after that I slept soundly.

Words For Everyday Use

con • junc • tion (kən juŋk´shən) *n.*, combination; being joined

de • lir • i • ous (di lir´ē əs) *adj.*, raving wildly

Wednesday morning was dawning when I looked out of window. The winking lights upon the bridges were already pale, the coming sun was like a marsh of fire on the horizon. The river, still dark and mysterious, was spanned by bridges that were turning coldly gray, with here and there at top a warm touch from the burning in the sky. As I looked along the clustered roofs, with church towers and spires shooting into the unusually clear air, the sun rose up, and a veil seemed to be drawn from the river, and millions of sparkles burst out upon its waters. From me, too, a veil seemed to be drawn, and I felt strong and well.

Herbert lay asleep in his bed, and our old fellow student lay asleep on the sofa. I could not dress myself without help, but I made up the fire which was still burning, and got some coffee ready for them. In good time they too started up strong and well, and we admitted the sharp morning air at the windows, and looked at the tide that was still flowing towards us.

"When it turns at nine o'clock," said Herbert cheerfully, "look out for us, and stand ready, you over there at Mill Pond Bank!"

CHAPTER 54

It was one of those March days when the sun shines hot and the wind blows cold—when it is summer in the light, and winter in the shade. We had our peacoats[1] with us, and I took a bag. Of all my worldly possessions I took no more than the few necessaries that filled the bag. Where I might go, what I might do, or when I might return were questions utterly unknown to me; nor did I vex my mind with them, for it was wholly set on Provis's safety. I only wondered for the passing moment, as I stopped at the door and looked back, under what altered circumstances I should next see those rooms, if ever.

▶ What are Pip's prospects? What is Pip's goal?

We loitered down to the Temple stairs, and stood loitering there, as if we were not quite decided to go upon the water at all. Of course I had taken care that the boat should be ready, and everything in order. After a little show of indecision, which there were none to see but the two or three <u>amphibious</u> creatures belonging to our Temple stairs, we went on board and cast off—Herbert in the bow, I steering. It was then about high-water—half-past eight.

Our plan was this. The tide beginning to run down at nine, and being with us until three, we intended still to creep on after it had turned, and row against it until dark. We should then be well in those long reaches below Gravesend, between Kent and Essex, where the river is broad and solitary, where the waterside inhabitants are very few, and where lone public houses are scattered here and there, of which we could choose one for a resting place. There we meant to lie by all night. The steamer for Hamburg, and the steamer for Rotterdam, would start from London at about nine on Thursday morning. We should know at what time to expect them, according to where we were, and would hail the first, so that if by any accident we were not taken aboard, we should have another chance. We knew the distinguishing marks of each vessel.

The relief of being at last engaged in the <u>execution</u> of the purpose was so great to me that I felt it difficult to realize the

---

1. **peacoats.** Heavy wool coats worn by sailors

Words For Everyday Use

am • phib • i • ous (am fib′ē əs) *adj.,* that can live both on land and in water

ex • e • cu • tion (ek′si kyo͞o′shən) *n.,* act of carrying out condition in which I had been a few hours before. The crisp air, the sunlight, the movement on the river, and the moving river itself—the road that ran with us, seeming to sympathize with us, animate us, and encourage us on—freshened me with new hope. I felt <u>mortified</u> to be of so little use in the boat, but there were few better oarsmen than my two friends, and they rowed with a steady stroke that was to last all day.

At that time, the steam traffic on the Thames was far below its present extent, and watermen's boats were far more numerous. Of barges, sailing colliers,[2] and coasting traders, there were perhaps as many as now, but of steamships, great and small, not a tithe[3] or a twentieth part so many. Early as it was, there were plenty of scullers[4] going here and there that morning, and plenty of barges dropping down with the tide; the navigation of the river between bridges in an open boat was a much easier and commoner matter in those days than it is in these; and we went ahead among many skiffs and wherries briskly.

◄ What is the scene on the river?

Old London Bridge was soon passed, and old Billingsgate market with its oyster-boats and Dutchmen, and the White Tower and Traitor's Gate, and we were in among the tiers of shipping. Here were the Leith, Aberdeen, and Glasgow[5] steamers, loading and unloading goods, and looking immensely high out of the water as we passed alongside; here were colliers by the score and score, with the coal-whippers[6] plunging off stages on deck, as counterweights to measures of coal swinging up, which were then rattled over the side into barges; here, at her moorings, was tomorrow's steamer for Rotterdam, of which we took good notice; and here tomorrow's for Hamburg, under whose bowsprit we crossed. And now I, sitting in the stern, could see with a faster beating heart Mill Pond Bank and Mill Pond stairs.

"Is he there?" said Herbert.

"Not yet."

"Right! He was not to come down till he saw us. Can you see his signal?"

---

2. **colliers.** Coal ships
3. **tithe.** One-tenth
4. **scullers.** Oarsmen in small, light boats
5. **Leith . . . Glasgow.** Cities in Scotland
6. **coal-whippers.** Those who raise coal out of a ship's hold by means of a pulley

Words For Everyday Use
mor • ti • fied (môr′tə fīd) *adj.,* humiliated

"Not well from here; but I think I see it. Now I see him! Pull both. Easy, Herbert. Oars!"

We touched the stairs lightly for a single moment, and he was on board and we were off again. He had a boat-cloak with him, and a black canvas bag, and he looked as like a river pilot as my heart could have wished.

▶ Who comes on board? In what disguise?

"Dear boy!" he said, putting his arm on my shoulder, as he took his seat. "Faithful dear boy, well done. Thankye, thankye!"

Again among the tiers of shipping, in and out, avoiding rusty chain-cables, frayed hempen hawsers,[7] and bobbing buoys, sinking for the moment floating broken baskets, scattering floating chips of wood and shaving, cleaving floating scum of coal, in and out, under the figurehead of the John of Sunderland making a speech to the winds (as is done by many Johns), and the Betsy of Yarmouth with a firm formality of bosom and her nobby eyes starting two inches out of her head; in and out, hammers going in shipbuilders' yards, saws going at timber, clashing engines going at things unknown, pumps going in leaky ships, capstans[8] going, ships going out to sea, and unintelligible sea creatures roaring curses over the bulwarks[9] at respondent lightermen;[10] in and out—out at last upon the clearer river, where the ships' boys might take their fenders in, no longer fishing in troubled waters with them over the side, and where the festooned[11] sails might fly out to the wind.

At the stairs where we had taken him aboard, and ever since, I had looked warily for any token of our being suspected. I had seen none. We certainly had not been, and at that time as certainly we were not, either attended or followed by any boat. If we had been waited on by any boat, I should have run in to shore, and have obliged her to go on, or to make her purpose evident. But we held our own, without any appearance of molestation.

▶ Are they noticed?

He had his boat-cloak on him, and looked, as I have said, a natural part of the scene. It was remarkable (but perhaps the wretched life he had led accounted for it), that he was the least anxious of any of us. He was not indifferent, for he told me that he hoped to live to see his gentleman one of the best of gentlemen in a foreign country; he was not disposed to be passive or resigned, as I understood it; but he had no notion of meeting danger halfway. When it came upon him he confronted it, but it must come before he troubled himself.

▶ What is Magwitch's reaction to what is happening?

7. **hempen hawsers.** Hemp ropes used to tow ships
8. **capstans.** Apparatus on ships used to coil the hawsers
9. **bulwarks.** Parts of ship's sides that extend like walls above the deck
10. **lightermen.** Men who work on boats used to unload large ships
11. **festooned.** Decorated with hanging decorations

"If you knowed, dear boy," he said to me, "what it is to sit here alonger my dear boy and have my smoke, arter having been day by day betwixt four walls, you'd envy me. But you don't know what it is."

"I think I know the delights of freedom," I answered.

"Ah," said he, shaking his head gravely. "But you don't know it equal to me. You must have been under lock and key, dear boy, to know it equal to me—but I ain't a-going to be low."

It occurred to me as inconsistent that, for any mastering idea, he should have endangered his freedom and even his life. But I reflected that perhaps freedom without danger was too much apart from all the habit of his existence to be to him what it would be to another man. I was not far out, since he said, after smoking a little:

"You see, dear boy, when I was over yonder, t'other side the world, I was always a-looking to this side; and it come flat to be there, for all I was a-growing rich. Everybody knowed Magwitch, and Magwitch could come, and Magwitch could go, and nobody's head would be troubled about him. They ain't so easy concerning me here, dear boy—wouldn't be, leastwise, if they knowed where I was."

◄ How does Magwitch's life in England differ from his life back in Australia?

"If all goes well," said I, "you will be perfectly free and safe again, within a few hours."

"Well," he returned, drawing a long breath, "I hope so."

"And think so?"

He dipped his hand in the water over the boat's gunwale,[12] and said, smiling with that softened air upon him which was not new to me:

"Aye, I s'pose I think so, dear boy. We'd be puzzled to be more quiet and easygoing than we are at present. But—it's a-flowing so soft and pleasant through the water, p'raps, as makes me think it—I was a-thinking through my smoke just then that we can no more see to the bottom of the next few hours than we can see to the bottom of this river what I catches hold of. Nor yet we can't no more hold their tide than I can hold this. And it's run through my fingers and gone, you see!" holding up his dripping hand.

◄ What is Magwitch's philosophy?

"But for your face, I should think you were a little <u>despondent</u>," said I.

---

12. **gunwale.** Upper edge of a ship's side

Words
For
Everyday
Use

de • spond • ent (di spän′dənt) *adj.,* feeling hopeless

"Not a bit on it, dear boy! It comes of flowing on so quiet, and of that there rippling at the boat's head making a sort of a Sunday tune. Maybe I'm a-growing a trifle old besides."

He put his pipe back in his mouth with an undisturbed expression of face, and sat as composed and contented as if we were already out of England. Yet he was as submissive to a word of advice as if he had been in constant terror, for, when we ran ashore to get some bottles of beer into the boat, and he was stepping out, I hinted that I thought he would be safest where he was, and he said, "Do you, dear boy?" and quietly sat down again.

The air felt cold upon the river, but it was a bright day, and the sunshine was very cheering. The tide ran strong. I took care to lose none of it, and our steady stroke carried us on thoroughly well. By <u>imperceptible</u> degrees, as the tide ran out, we lost more and more of the nearer woods and hills, and dropped lower and lower between the muddy banks, but the tide was yet with us when we were off Gravesend. As our charge was wrapped in his cloak, I purposely passed within a boat or two's length of the floating custom house,[13] and so out to catch the stream, alongside of two emigrant ships,[14] and under the bows of a large transport with troops on the forecastle[15] looking down at us. And soon the tide began to slacken, and the craft lying at anchor to swing, and presently they had all swung round, and the ships that were taking advantage of the new tide to get up to the Pool began to crowd upon us in a fleet, and we kept under the shore, as much out of the strength of the tide now as we could, standing carefully off from low shallows and mudbanks.

Our oarsmen were so fresh, by dint of having occasionally let her drive with the tide for a minute or two, that a quarter of an hour's rest proved full as much as they wanted. We got ashore among some slippery stones while we ate and drank what we had with us, and looked about. It was like my own marsh country, flat and monotonous, and with a dim horizon; while the winding river turned and turned, and the great floating buoys upon it turned and turned, and everything else seemed stranded and still. For now the last of the fleet of ships was

---

13. **custom house.** Government building where ships are cleared for entering or leaving the country and taxes on imported goods are collected
14. **emigrant ships.** Ships carrying those who leave their native region
15. **forecastle.** Section of the upper deck of a ship located at the bow

Words For Everyday Use

im • per • cep • ti • ble (im′pər sep′ tə bəl) *adj.*, barely noticeable round the last low point we had headed; and the last green barge, straw-laden, with a brown sail, had followed; and some ballast-lighters, shaped like a child's first rude imitation of a boat, lay low in the mud; and a little squat shoal-lighthouse[16] on open piles stood crippled in the mud on stilts and crutches; and slimy stakes stuck out of the mud, and slimy stones stuck out of the mud, and red landmarks and tidemarks stuck out of the mud, and an old landing-stage and an old roofless building slipped into the mud, and all about us was stagnation and mud.

We pushed off again, and made what way we could. It was much harder work now, but Herbert and Startop persevered, and rowed, and rowed, and rowed, until the sun went down. By that time the river had lifted us a little, so that we could see above the bank. There was the red sun, on the low level of the shore, in a purple haze, fast deepening into black; and there was the solitary flat marsh; and far away there were the rising grounds, between which and us there seemed to be no life, save here and there in the foreground a melancholy gull.

As the night was fast falling, and as the moon, being past the full, would not rise early, we held a little council—a short one, for clearly our course was to lie by at the first lonely tavern we could find. So they plied their oars once more, and I looked out for anything like a house. Thus we held on, speaking little, for four or five dull miles. It was very cold, and a collier coming by us, with her galley-fire smoking and flaring, looked like a comfortable home. The night was as dark by this time as it would be until morning; what light we had seemed to come more from the river than the sky, as the oars in their dipping struck at a few reflected stars.

At this dismal time we were evidently all possessed by the idea that we were followed. As the tide made, it flapped heavily at irregular intervals against the shore; and whenever such a sound came, one or other of us was sure to start and look in that direction. Here and there, the set of the current had worn down the bank into a little creek, and we were all suspicious of such places, and eyed them nervously. Sometimes, "What was that ripple?" one of us would say in a low voice. Or another, "Is that a boat yonder?" And afterwards we would fall into a dead silence, and I would sit impatiently thinking with what an unusual amount of noise the oars worked in the thowels.[17]

At length we descried a light and a roof, and presently afterwards ran alongside a little causeway made of stones that had been picked up hard by. Leaving the rest in the boat, I stepped ashore, and found the light to be in the window of a public

◀ *What do Pip, Herbert, Startop, and Magwitch worry about?*

◀ *Where does the group spend the night?*

---

16. **shoal-lighthouse.** Lighthouse located in a shallow area
17. **thowels.** Oarlocks; metal plates that hold the oars in place

house. It was a dirty place enough, and I dare say not unknown to smuggling adventurers, but there was a good fire in the kitchen, and there were eggs and bacon to eat, and various liquors to drink. Also, there were two double-bedded rooms—"such as they were," the landlord said. No other company was in the house than the landlord, his wife, and a grizzled male creature, the "Jack"[18] of the little causeway, who was as slimy and smeary as if he had been low-water mark, too.

With this assistant, I went down to the boat again, and we all came ashore, and brought out the oars, and rudder, and boat-hook, and all else, and hauled her up for the night. We made a very good meal by the kitchen fire, and then apportioned[19] the bedrooms: Herbert and Startop were to occupy one; I and our charge the other. We found the air as carefully excluded from both as if air were fatal to life, and there were more dirty clothes and bandboxes[20] under the beds than I should have thought the family possessed. But we considered ourselves well off, notwithstanding, for a more solitary place we could not have found.

While we were comforting ourselves by the fire after our meal, the Jack—who was sitting in a corner, and who had a bloated pair of shoes on, which he had exhibited while we were eating our eggs and bacon, as interesting relics that he had taken a few days ago from the feet of a drowned seaman washed ashore—asked me if we had seen a four-oared galley[21] going up with the tide. When I told him no, he said she must have gone down then, and yet she "took up too," when she left there.

▶ What does the Jack see?

"They must ha' thought better on't for some reason or another," said the Jack, "and gone down."

"A four-oared galley did you say?" said I.

"A four," said the Jack, "and two sitters."

"Did they come ashore here?"

"They put in with a stone two-gallon jar, for some beer. I'd ha' been glad to pison the beer myself," said the Jack, "or put some rattling physic[22] in it."

"Why?"

"*I* know why," said the Jack. He spoke in a slushy voice, as if much mud had washed into his throat.

"He thinks," said the landlord, a weakly meditative man with a pale eye, who seemed to rely greatly on his Jack, "he thinks they was what they wasn't."

---

18. **Jack.** Fellow; one who does odd jobs
19. **apportioned.** Divided up; assigned
20. **bandboxes.** Lightweight boxes used to hold small articles of clothing
21. **galley.** Large rowboat
22. **rattling physic.** Laxative

"*I* knows what I thinks," observed the Jack.

"*You* thinks custom 'us,[23] Jack?" said the landlord.

"I do," said the Jack.

"Then you're wrong, Jack."

"*Am* I!"

In the infinite meaning of his reply and his boundless confidence in his views, the Jack took one of his bloated shoes off, looked into it, knocked a few stones out of it on the kitchen floor, and put it on again. He did this with the air of a Jack who was so right that he could afford to do anything.

"Why, what do you make out that they done with their buttons[24] then, Jack?" asked the landlord, <u>vacillating</u> weakly.

"Done with their buttons?" returned the Jack. "Chucked 'em overboard. Swallered 'em. Sowed 'em, to come up small salad. Done with their buttons!"

"Don't be cheeky, Jack," remonstrated the landlord, in a melancholy and pathetic way.

"A custom 'us officer knows what to do with his buttons," said the Jack, repeating the obnoxious word with the greatest contempt, "when they comes betwixt him and his own light. A four and two sitters don't go hanging and hovering, up with one tide and down with another, and both with and against another, without there being custom 'us at the bottom of it." Saying which he went out in disdain; and the landlord, having no one to reply upon, found it impracticable to pursue the subject.

This dialogue made us all uneasy, and me very uneasy. The dismal wind was muttering round the house, the tide was flapping at the shore, and I had a feeling that we were caged and threatened. A four-oared galley hovering about in so unusual a way as to attract this notice was an ugly circumstance that I could not get rid of. When I had induced Provis to go up to bed, I went outside with my two companions (Startop by this time knew the state of the case), and held another council. Whether we should remain at the house until near the steamer's time, which would be about one in the afternoon, or whether we should put off early in the morning, was the question we discussed. On the whole, we

◄ Who does the Jack believe the men in the boat to be?

◄ What does the Jack think of the officials of the "custom 'us?"

◄ Why does Pip feel trapped?

---

23. **custom 'us.** Custom house
24. **buttons.** Badges

Words For Everyday Use

vac • il • late (vas´ə lāt´) *vi.*, waver in mind; show indecision deemed it the better course to lie where we were, until within an hour or so of the steamer's time, and then to get out in her track, and drift easily with the tide. Having settled to do this, we returned into the house and went to bed.

I lay down with the greater part of my clothes on, and slept well for a few hours. When I awoke, the wind had risen, and the sign of the house (the Ship) was creaking and banging about, with noises that startled me. Rising softly, for my charge lay fast asleep, I looked out of the window. It commanded the causeway where we had hauled up our boat, and, as my eyes adapted themselves to the light of the clouded moon, I saw two men looking into her. They passed by under the window, looking at nothing else, and they did not go down to the landing-place which I could discern to be empty, but struck across the marsh in the direction of the Nore.

► Why doesn't Pip wake up Herbert?

My first impulse was to call up Herbert, and show him the two men going away. But, reflecting before I got into his room, which was at the back of the house and adjoined mine, that he and Startop had had a harder day than I, and were fatigued, I forbore. Going back to my window, I could see the two men moving over the marsh. In that light, however, I soon lost them, and feeling very cold, lay down to think of the matter, and fell asleep again.

We were up early. As we walked to and fro, all four together, before breakfast, I deemed it right to recount what I had seen. Again our charge was the least anxious of the party. It was very likely that the men belonged to the custom house, he said quietly, and that they had no thought of us. I tried to persuade myself that it was so—as, indeed, it might easily be. However, I proposed that he and I should walk away together to a distant point we could see, and that the boat should take us aboard there, or as near there as might prove <u>feasible</u>, at about noon. This being considered a good precaution, soon after breakfast he and I set forth, without saying anything at the tavern.

► Who does Pip think the men are? What does Magwitch point out about the men?

He smoked his pipe as we went along, and sometimes stopped to clap me on the shoulder. One would have supposed that it was I who was in danger, not he, and that he was reassuring me. We spoke very little. As we approached the point, I begged him to remain in a sheltered place, while I went on to <u>reconnoiter</u>; for it was towards it that the men had passed in the night. He complied, and I went on alone.

| Words For Everyday Use | fea • si • ble (fē´zə bəl) *adj.*, likely; possible |
| | rec • on • noi • ter (rek´ə noit´ər) *vi.*, make a survey or exploration |

There was no boat off the point, nor any boat drawn up any-where near it, nor were there any signs of the men having embarked there. But, to be sure, the tide was high, and there might have been some footprints underwater.

When he looked out from his shelter in the distance, and saw that I waved my hat to him to come up, he rejoined me, and there we waited—sometimes lying on the bank wrapped in our coats, and sometimes moving about to warm our-selves—until we saw our boat coming round. We got aboard easily, and rowed out into the track of the steamer. By that time it wanted but ten minutes of one o'clock, and we began to look out for her smoke.

But it was half-past one before we saw her smoke, and soon after we saw behind it the smoke of another steamer. As they were coming on at full speed, we got the two bags ready, and took that opportunity of saying good-bye to Herbert and Startop. We had all shaken hands cordially, and neither Herbert's eyes nor mine were quite dry, when I saw a four-oared galley shoot out from under the bank but a little way ahead of us, and row out into the same track.

◄ *Where does the new boat come from?*

A stretch of shore had been as yet between us and the steamer's smoke, by reason of the bend and wind of the river; but now she was visible coming head on. I called to Herbert and Startop to keep before the tide, that she might see us lying by for her, and I <u>adjured</u> Provis to sit quite still, wrapped in his cloak. He answered cheerily, "Trust to me, dear boy," and sat like a statue. Meantime the galley, which was very skillfully handled, had crossed us, let us come up with her, and fallen alongside. Leaving just room enough for the play of the oars, she kept alongside, drifting when we drifted, and pulling a stroke or two when we pulled. Of the two sitters, one held the rudder lines, and looked at us attentively—as did all the row-ers; the other sitter was wrapped up, much as Provis was, and seemed to shrink, and whisper some instruction to the steerer as he looked at us. Not a word was spoken in either boat.

Startop could make out, after a few minutes, which steamer was first, and gave me the word "Hamburg," in a low voice as we sat face to face. She was nearing us very fast, and the beating of her paddles grew louder and louder. I felt as if her shadow were absolutely upon us, when the galley hailed us. I answered.

◄ *What are Pip and Startop waiting for?*

Words
For
Everyday
Use

ad • jure (ə joor´) *vt.*, appeal to earnestly

"You have a returned transport there," said the man who held the lines. "That's the man, wrapped in the cloak. His name is Abel Magwitch, otherwise Provis. I apprehend that man, and call upon him to surrender, and you to assist."

At the same moment, without giving any audible direction to his crew, he ran the galley aboard of us. They had pulled one sudden stroke ahead, had got their oars in, had run athwart[24] us, and were holding on to our gunwale, before we knew what they were doing. This caused great confusion on board the steamer, and I heard them calling to us, and heard the order given to stop the paddles, and heard them stop, but felt her driving down upon us irresistibly. In the same moment, I saw the steersman of the galley lay his hand on his prisoner's shoulder, and saw that both boats were swinging round with the force of the tide, and saw that all hands on board the steamer were running forward quite frantically. Still in the same moment, I saw the prisoner start up, lean across his captor, and pull the cloak from the neck of the shrinking sitter in the galley. Still in the same moment, I saw that the face disclosed was the face of the other convict of long ago. Still in the same moment, I saw the face tilt backward with a white terror on it that I shall never forget, and heard a great cry on board the steamer and a loud splash in the water, and felt the boat sink from under me.

▶ Who is the man in the cloak? How does he react when Magwitch pulls off his cloak?

It was but for an instant that I seemed to struggle with a thousand mill-weirs[25] and a thousand flashes of light; that instant passed, I was taken on board the galley. Herbert was there, and Startop was there, but our boat was gone, and the two convicts were gone.

What with the cries aboard the steamer, and the furious blowing off of her steam, and her driving on, and our driving on, I could not at first distinguish sky from water or shore from shore; but the crew of the galley righted her with great speed, and, pulling certain swift strong strokes ahead, lay upon their oars, every man looking silently and eagerly at the water astern. Presently a dark object was seen in it, bearing towards us on the tide. No man spoke, but the steersman held up his hand, and all softly backed water, and kept the boat straight and true before it. As it came nearer, I saw it to be Magwitch, swimming, but not swimming freely. He was taken on board, and instantly manacled at the wrists and ankles.

▶ Who is found swimming?

The galley was kept steady, and the silent eager lookout at the water was resumed. But the Rotterdam steamer now came up, and apparently not understanding what had happened,

---

24. **athwart.** Aside
25. **mill-weirs.** Dams placed across a river or canal to raise the water in order to drive a millwheel

came on at speed. By the time she had been hailed and stopped, both steamers were drifting away from us, and we were rising and falling in a troubled wake of water. The lookout was kept, long after all was still again and the two steamers were gone, but everybody knew that it was hopeless now.

◄ Why do they miss the steamer?

At length we gave it up, and pulled under the shore towards the tavern we had lately left, where we were received with no little surprise. Here I was able to get some comforts for Magwitch—Provis no longer—who had received some very severe injury in the chest and a deep cut in the head.

◄ In what condition is Magwitch?

He told me that he believed himself to have gone under the keel[26] of the steamer, and to have been struck on the head in rising. The injury to his chest (which rendered his breathing extremely painful) he thought he had received against the side of the galley. He added that he did not pretend to say what he might or might not have done to Compeyson, but, that in the moment of his laying his hand on his cloak to identify him, that villain had staggered up and staggered back, and they had both gone overboard together; when the sudden wrenching of him (Magwitch) out of our boat, and the endeavor of his captor to keep him in it, had <u>capsized</u> us. He told me in a whisper that they had gone down, fiercely locked in each other's arms, and that there had been a struggle under water, and that he had <u>disengaged</u> himself, struck out, and swum away.

◄ What happened to Compeyson?

I never had any reason to doubt the exact truth of what he thus told me. The officer who steered the galley gave the same account of their going overboard.

When I asked this officer's permission to change the prisoner's wet clothes by purchasing any spare garments I could get at the public house, he gave it readily, merely observing that he must take charge of everything his prisoner had about him. So the pocket book which had once been in my hands passed into the officer's. He further gave me leave to accompany the prisoner to London, but declined to <u>accord</u> that grace to my two friends.

◄ What happened to Magwitch's money?

The Jack at the Ship was instructed where the drowned man had gone down, and undertook to search for the body in the places where it was likeliest to come ashore. His interest in its recovery seemed to me to be much heightened when he

---

26. **keel.** Backbone of a ship, running along the center line from bow to stern

---

Words For Everyday Use

cap • size (kap´sīz) *vt.,* overturn

dis • en • gage (dis´in gāj´) *vt.,* release from something that holds or entangles

ac • cord (ə kôrd´) *vt.,* give; grant; bestow

► Why is the Jack interested in the stockings of the drowned man?

heard that it had stockings on. Probably it took about a dozen drowned men to fit him out completely and that may have been the reason why the different articles of his dress were in various stages of decay.

We remained at the public house until the tide turned, and then Magwitch was carried down to the galley and put on board. Herbert and Startop were to get to London by land, as soon as they could. We had a doleful parting, and when I took my place by Magwitch's side, I felt that that was my place henceforth while he lived.

► How do Pip's feelings change towards Magwitch?

For now my <u>repugnance</u> to him had all melted away, and in the hunted wounded shackled creature who held my hand in his, I only saw a man who had meant to be my benefactor, and who had felt affectionately, gratefully, and generously towards me with great constancy through a series of years. I only saw in him a much better man than I had been to Joe.

His breathing became more difficult and painful as the night drew on, and often he could not repress a groan. I tried to rest him on the arm I could use, in any easy position, but it was dreadful to think that I could not be sorry at heart for his being badly hurt, since it was unquestionably best that he should die. That there were, still living, people enough who were able and willing to identify him, I could not doubt. That he would be <u>leniently</u> treated, I could not hope. He who had been presented in the worst light at his trial, who had since broken prison and been tried again, who had returned from transportation[27] under a life sentence, and who had occasioned the death of the man who was the cause of his arrest.

As we returned towards the setting sun we had yesterday left behind us, and as the stream of our hopes seemed all running back, I told him how grieved I was to think that he had come home for my sake.

► What does Magwitch say about his capture? What does Pip realize?

"Dear boy," he answered, "I'm quite content to take my chance. I've seen my boy, and he can be a gentleman without me."

No. I had thought about that while we had been there side by side. No. Apart from any inclinations of my own, I understood Wemmick's hint now. I foresaw that, being convicted, his possessions would be forfeited to the Crown.

---

27. **transportation.** Expulsion of a convict from a country

Words For Everyday Use	**re • pug • nance** (ri pug´nəns) *n.*, extreme dislike
	le • ni • ent • ly (lēn´yənt lē) *adv.*, not harshly or severely

"Lookee here, dear boy," said he. "It's best as a gentleman should not be knowed to belong to me now. Only come to see me as if you come by chance alonger Wemmick. Sit where I can see you when I am swore to, for the last o' many times, and I don't ask no more."

"I will never stir from your side," said I, "when I am suffered to be near you. Please God, I will be as true to you as you have been to me!"

◄ What does Pip vow?

I felt his hand tremble as it held mine, and he turned his face away as he lay in the bottom of the boat, and I heard that old sound in his throat—softened now, like all the rest of him. It was a good thing that he had touched this point, for it put into my mind what I might not otherwise have thought of until too late: that he need never know how his hopes of enriching me had perished.

CHAPTER 55

► Why is the trial delayed?

He was taken to the police court next day, and would have been immediately committed for trial, but that it was necessary to send down for an old officer of the prison-ship from which he had once escaped, to speak to his identity. Nobody doubted it; but Compeyson, who had meant to <u>depose</u> to it, was tumbling on the tides, dead, and it happened that there was not at that time any prison officer in London who could give the required evidence. I had gone direct to Mr. Jaggers at his private house, on my arrival over night, to retain his assistance, and Mr. Jaggers on the prisoner's behalf would admit nothing. It was the sole resource, for he told me that the case must be over in five minutes when the witness was there, and that no power on earth could prevent its going against us.

► Why is Jaggers angry with Pip?

I imparted to Mr. Jaggers my design of keeping him in ignorance of the fate of his wealth. Mr. Jaggers was <u>querulous</u> and angry with me for having "let it slip through my fingers," and said we must memorialize[1] by-and-by, and try at all events for some of it. But he did not conceal from me that although there might be many cases in which the forfeiture[2] would not be <u>exacted</u>, there were no circumstances in this case to make it one of them. I understood that very well. I was not related to the outlaw, or connected with him by any recognizable tie; he had put his hand to no writing or settlement in my favor before his apprehension, and to do so now would be idle. I had no claim, and I finally resolved, and ever afterwards abided by the resolution, that my heart should never be sickened with the hopeless task of attempting to establish one.

► What was Compeyson's apparent motive?

There appeared to be reason for supposing that the drowned informer had hoped for a reward out of this forfeiture, and had obtained some accurate knowledge of Magwitch's affairs. When his body was found, many miles from the scene of his death, and so horribly disfigured that he was only recognizable by the contents of his pockets, notes were still legible, folded in a case he carried. Among these were the name of a banking-house in New South Wales

1. **memorialize.** Review the events that have happened
2. **forfeiture.** Loss of money and goods as a result of having committed a crime

Words For Everyday Use

de • pose (dē pōz´) *vi.*, bear witness
quer • u • lous (kwer´yōō ləs) *adj.*, full of complaint
ex • act (ig zakt´) *vt.*, demand; require

where a sum of money was, and the designation of certain lands of considerable value. Both these heads of information were in a list that Magwitch, while in prison, gave to Mr. Jaggers, of the possessions he supposed I should inherit. His ignorance, poor fellow, at last served him; he never mistrusted but that my inheritance was quite safe, with Mr. Jaggers's aid.

◄ What does Magwitch want Pip to inherit?

After three days' delay, during which the crown prosecution stood over for the production of the witness from the prison-ship, the witness came, and completed the easy case. He was committed to take his trial at the next sessions which would come on in a month.

It was at this dark time of my life that Herbert returned home one evening, a good deal cast down, and said:

◄ Where is Herbert going? Why?

"My dear Handel, I fear I shall soon have to leave you."

His partner having prepared me for that, I was less surprised than he thought.

"We shall lose a fine opportunity if I put off going to Cairo, and I am very much afraid I must go, Handel, when you most need me."

"Herbert, I shall always need you, because I shall always love you, but my need is no greater now than at another time."

"You will be so lonely."

"I have not leisure to think of that," said I. "You know that I am always with him to the full extent of the time allowed, and that I should be with him all day long, if I could. And when I come away from him, you know that my thoughts are with him."

The dreadful condition to which he was brought was so appalling to both of us that we could not refer to it in plainer words.

"My dear fellow," said Herbert, "let the near prospect of our separation—for it is very near—be my justification for troubling you about yourself. Have you thought of your future?"

"No, for I have been afraid to think of any future."

"But yours cannot be dismissed; indeed, my dear, dear Handel, it must not be dismissed. I wish you would enter on it now, as far as a few friendly words go, with me."

"I will," said I.

"In this branch-house of ours, Handel, we must have a—"

◄ What does Herbert propose to Pip?

I saw that his delicacy was avoiding the right word, so I said, "A clerk."

"A clerk. And I hope it is not at all unlikely that he may expand (as a clerk of your acquaintance has expanded) into a partner. Now, Handel—in short, my dear boy, will you come to me?"

There was something charmingly cordial and <u>engaging</u> in the manner in which, after saying, "Now, Handel," as if it were the grave beginning of a <u>portentous</u> business <u>exordium</u>, he had suddenly given up that tone, stretched out his honest hand, and spoken like a schoolboy.

► What do Clara and Herbert invite Pip to do?

"Clara and I have talked about it again and again," Herbert pursued, "and the dear little thing begged me only this evening, with tears in her eyes, to say to you that if you will live with us when we come together, she will do her best to make you happy, and to convince her husband's friend that he is her friend, too. We should get on so well, Handel!"

I thanked her heartily, and I thanked him heartily, but said I could not yet make sure of joining him as he so kindly offered. Firstly, my mind was too preoccupied to be able to take in the subject clearly. Secondly—Yes! Secondly, there was a vague something lingering in my thoughts that will come out very near the end of this slight narrative.

"But if you thought, Herbert, that you could, without doing any injury to your business, leave the question open for a little while—"

"For any while," cried Herbert. "Six months, a year!"

"Not so long as that," said I. "Two or three months at most."

Herbert was highly delighted when we shook hands on this arrangement, and said he could now take courage to tell me that he believed he must go away at the end of the week.

"And Clara?" said I.

► Why isn't Clara going to Cairo?

"The dear little thing," returned Herbert, "holds dutifully to her father as long as he lasts; but he won't last long. Mrs. Whimple confides to me that he is certainly going."

"Not to say an unfeeling thing," said I, "he cannot do better than go."

"I am afraid that must be admitted," said Herbert; "and then I shall come back for the dear little thing, and the dear little thing and I will walk quietly into the nearest church. Remember! The blessed darling comes of no family, my dear Handel, and never looked into the red book,[3] and hasn't a notion about her grandpapa. What a fortune for the son of my mother!"

On the Saturday in that same week, I took my leave of Herbert—full of bright hope, but sad and sorry to leave me—

---

3. **red book.** Register listing members of the nobility

Words For Everyday Use	**en • gag • ing** (en gā′jiŋ) *adj.,* charming
	por • ten • tous (pôr ten′təs) *adj.,* ominous
	ex • or • di • um (eg zôr′dē əm) *n.,* opening part of an oration or speech

as he sat on one of the seaport mail-coaches. I went into a coffee-house to write a little note to Clara, telling her he had gone off, sending his love to her over and over again, and then went to my lonely home—if it deserved the name, for it was now no home to me, and I had no home anywhere.

On the stairs I encountered Wemmick, who was coming down, after an unsuccessful application of his knuckles to my door. I had not seen him alone since the disastrous issue of the attempted flight, and he had come, in his private and personal capacity, to say a few words of explanation in reference to that failure.

"The late Compeyson," said Wemmick, "had by little and little got at the bottom of half of the regular business now transacted, and it was from the talk of some of his people in trouble (some of his people being always in trouble) that I heard what I did. I kept my ears open, seeming to have them shut, until I heard that he was absent, and I thought that would be the best time for making the attempt. I can only suppose now that it was a part of his policy, as a very clever man, habitually to deceive his own instruments. You don't blame me, I hope, Mr. Pip? I'm sure I tried to serve you, with all my heart."

◀ What has Wemmick learned about Compeyson?

"I am as sure of that, Wemmick, as you can be, and I thank you most earnestly for all your interest and friendship."

"Thank you, thank you very much. It's a bad job," said Wemmick, scratching his head, "and I assure you I haven't been so cut up for a long time. What I look at is the sacrifice of so much portable property. Dear me!"

"What *I* think of, Wemmick, is the poor owner of the property."

"Yes, to be sure," said Wemmick. "Of course there can be no objection to your being sorry for him, and I'd put down a five-pound note myself to get him out of it. But what I look at is this. The late Compeyson having been beforehand with him in intelligence of his return, and being so determined to bring him to book, I do not think he could have been saved. Whereas the portable property certainly could have been saved. That's the difference between the property and the owner, don't you see?"

◀ Who could not have been saved? Why? What could have been saved?

I invited Wemmick to come upstairs, and refresh himself with a glass of grog before walking to Walworth. He accepted the invitation. While he was drinking his moderate allowance, he said, with nothing to lead up to it, and after having appeared rather fidgety:

"What do you think of my meaning to take a holiday on Monday, Mr. Pip?"

► What does
Wemmick invite Pip
to do?

"Why, I suppose you have not done such a thing these twelve months."

"These twelve years, more likely," said Wemmick. "Yes. I'm going to take a holiday. More than that; I'm going to take a walk. More than that; I'm going to ask you to take a walk with me."

I was about to excuse myself, as being but a bad companion just then, when Wemmick anticipated me.

"I know your engagements," said he, "and I know you are out of sorts, Mr. Pip. But if you *could* oblige me, I should take it as a kindness. It ain't a long walk, and it's an early one. Say it might occupy you (including breakfast on the walk) from eight to twelve. Couldn't you stretch a point and manage it?"

He had done so much for me at various times that this was very little to do for him. I said I could manage it—would manage it—and he was so very much pleased by my <u>acquiescence</u> that I was pleased, too. At his particular request, I appointed to call for him at the castle at half-past eight on Monday morning, and so we parted for the time.

Punctual to my appointment, I rang at the castle gate on the Monday morning, and was received by Wemmick himself, who struck me as looking tighter than usual, and having a sleeker hat on. Within, there were two glasses of rum-and-milk prepared, and two biscuits. The Aged must have been stirring with the lark, for, glancing into the perspective of his bedroom, I observed that his bed was empty.

When we had fortified ourselves with the rum-and-milk and biscuits, and were going out for the walk with that training preparation on us, I was considerably surprised to see Wemmick take up a fishing rod, and put it over his shoulder. "Why, we are not going fishing!" said I. "No," returned Wemmick, "but I like to walk with one."

I thought this odd; however, I said nothing, and we set off. We went towards Camberwell Green, and when we were thereabouts, Wemmick said suddenly:

"Halloa! Here's a church!"

There was nothing very surprising in that; but again, I was rather surprised, when he said, as if he were animated by a brilliant idea:

"Let's go in!"

Words For Everyday Use

ac • qui • es • cence (ak´ wē es´ əns) *n.*, agreement without protest

We went in, Wemmick leaving his fishing rod in the porch, and looked all round. In the mean time, Wemmick was diving into his his coat pockets, and getting something out of paper there.

"Halloa!" said he. "Here's a couple of pair of gloves! Let's put 'em on!"

As the gloves were white kid gloves, and as the post office was widened to its utmost extent, I now began to have my strong suspicions. They were strengthened into certainty when I beheld the Aged enter at a side door, escorting a lady.

"Halloa!" said Wemmick. "Here's Miss Skiffins! Let's have a wedding."

◄ Who is at the church? What is going to take place there?

That discreet damsel was attired as usual, except that she was now engaged in substituting for her green kid gloves a pair of white. The Aged was likewise occupied in preparing a similar sacrifice for the altar of Hymen.[4] The old gentleman, however, experienced so much difficulty in getting his gloves on that Wemmick found it necessary to put him with his back against a pillar, and then to get behind the pillar himself and pull away at them, while I for my part held the old gentleman round the waist, that he might present an equal and safe resistance. By dint of this ingenious scheme, his gloves were got on to perfection.

The clerk and clergyman then appearing, we were ranged in order at those fatal rails.[5] True to his notion of seeming to do it all without preparation, I heard Wemmick say to himself as he took something out of his waistcoat pocket before the service began, "Halloa! Here's a ring!"

I acted in the capacity of backer or best man to the bridegroom, while a little limp pew opener in a soft bonnet like a baby's made a feint[6] of being the bosom friend of Miss Skiffins. The responsibility of giving the lady away <u>devolved</u> upon the Aged, which led to the clergyman's being unintentionally scandalized, and it happened thus. When he said, "Who giveth this woman to be married to this man?" the old gentleman, not in the least knowing what point of the ceremony we had arrived at, stood most amiably beaming at the ten commandments. Upon which, the clergyman said again,

◄ What is Pip's role in the wedding? The Aged's?

---

4. **altar of Hymen.** Altar of the god of marriage
5. **rails.** Railings in front of an altar
6. **feint.** False show

Words For Everyday Use

de • volve (di välv´) *vi.,* be passed on or delegated

"WHO giveth this woman to be married to this man?" The old gentleman being still in a state of most estimable unconsciousness, the bridegroom cried out in his accustomed voice, "Now Aged P. you know; who giveth?" To which the Aged replied with great briskness, before saying that *he* gave, "All right John, all right, my boy!" And the clergyman came to so gloomy a pause upon it that I had doubts for the moment whether we should get completely married that day.

It was completely done, however, and when we were going out of church, Wemmick took the cover off the font,[7] and put his white gloves in it, and put the cover on again. Mrs. Wemmick, more heedful of the future, put her white gloves in her pocket and assumed her green. *"Now,* Mr. Pip," said Wemmick, triumphantly shouldering the fishing rod as we came out, "let me ask you whether anybody would suppose this to be a wedding party!"

► *Why is it now appropriate for Wemmick to hug Miss Skiffins?*

Breakfast had been ordered at a pleasant little tavern a mile or so away upon the rising ground beyond the green, and there was a bagatelle[8] board in the room, in case we should desire to unbend our minds after the solemnity. It was pleasant to observe that Mrs. Wemmick no longer unwound Wemmick's arm when it adapted itself to her figure, but sat in a high-backed chair against the wall, like a violoncello in its case, and submitted to be embraced as that melodious instrument might have done.

We had an excellent breakfast, and when anyone declined anything on table, Wemmick said, "Provided by contract, you know; don't be afraid of it!" I drank to the new couple, drank to the Aged, drank to the castle, saluted the bride at parting, and made myself as agreeable as I could.

Wemmick came down to the door with me, and I again shook hands with him, and wished him joy.

► *Why does Wemmick wish to keep his marriage a secret?*

"Thankee!" said Wemmick, rubbing his hands. "She's such a manager of fowls, you have no idea. You shall have some eggs and judge for yourself. I say, Mr. Pip!" calling me back and speaking low. "This is altogether a Walworth sentiment, please."

"I understand. Not to be mentioned in Little Britain," said I.

Wemmick nodded. "After what you let out the other day, Mr. Jaggers may as well not know of it. He might think my brain was softening, or something of the kind."

---

7. **font.** Baptismal font; a receptacle filled with blessed water and used in the sacrament of baptism

8. **bagatelle.** Game similar to billiards

Responding to the Selection

At the end of chapter 54, Pip decides that Magwitch "need never know how his hopes of enriching [him have] perished." Pip seems to feel that Magwitch's plan of making him a better, more worthy person have failed. Do you agree? In what ways has Magwitch's plan failed? In what ways has Magwitch succeeded in "enriching" Pip? Explain.

Reviewing the Selection

Recalling and Interpreting

1. **R:** What does the reader learn about Estella's parents? What does Jaggers advise Pip on the subject?

2. **I:** Why does Dickens reveal this information at this point in the novel? Do you think Jaggers's advice is sound? Explain why or why not.

3. **R:** What does Pip realize when he is confronted with death at Orlick's hand?

4. **I:** What role has Orlick played in Pip's life? What does Pip's realization reveal about his priorities and the way Pip is changing?

5. **R:** When does the reader meet Compeyson again? What does Compeyson attempt to do?

6. **I:** What links does Compeyson create among the characters in the novel? Discuss how he affects each character.

7. **R:** What is Magwitch's behavior and frame of mind through all the tense moments of his escape?

8. **I:** What does Magwitch mean when he tells Pip, "I'm quite content to take my chance. I've seen my boy, and he can be a gentleman without me"? (See page 474.) What does this statement reveal about his character?

Synthesizing

9. Now that you know the history and relationships among all the major characters, what problems or issues do you think Pip will confront and perhaps solve in the remaining chapters of the book?

10. There has been a shift in Pip's feelings about Magwitch in this section. Describe this shift and give examples of the words and actions of Pip that reflect this change.

Understanding Literature (QUESTIONS FOR DISCUSSION)

1. Falling action. The **falling action** is all of the events that follow the climax. Identify the events in chapters 50–55 that follow the climax—Magwitch's revelation that he is Pip's secret benefactor.

2. Motivation. A **motivation** is a force that moves a character to think, feel, or behave in a certain way. Orlick makes clear his motives for wanting Pip dead. Identify and discuss what drives him to such violence.

3. *Bildungsroman*. A *Bildungsroman* is a novel that tells the story of the growth of a character from youth to adulthood. *Great Expectations* is commonly considered to be an example of a *Bildungsroman*, because it chronicles the growing and maturing of Pip. What evidence in chapters 50–55 shows that Pip has matured in his attitudes? Give examples of his behavior or words.

CHAPTER 56

He lay in prison very ill, during the whole interval between his committal for trial, and the coming round of the sessions. He had broken two ribs, they had wounded one of his lungs, and he breathed with great pain and difficulty which increased daily. It was a consequence of his hurt that he spoke so low as to be scarcely audible; therefore he spoke very little. But he was ever ready to listen to me, and it became the first duty of my life to say to him, and read to him, what I knew he ought to hear.

◄ What is Magwitch's condition? What does Pip do?

Being far too ill to remain in the common prison, he was removed, after the first day or so, into the infirmary. This gave me opportunities of being with him that I could not otherwise have had. And but for his illness he would have been put in irons, for he was regarded as a determined prison-breaker, and I know not what else.

Although I saw him every day, it was for only a short time; hence, the regularly recurring spaces of our separation were long enough to record on his face any slight changes that occurred in his physical state. I do not recollect that I once saw any change in it for the better; he wasted, and became slowly weaker and worse, day by day from the day when the prison door closed upon him.

The kind of submission or resignation that he showed was that of a man who was tired out. I sometimes derived an impression, from his manner or from a whispered word or two which escaped him, that he pondered over the question whether he might have been a better man under better circumstances. But he never justified himself by a hint tending that way, or tried to bend the past out of its eternal shape.

◄ What might have been? Does Magwitch make excuses for his behavior?

It happened on two or three occasions in my presence that his desperate reputation was alluded to by one or other of the people in attendance on him. A smile crossed his face then, and he turned his eyes on me with a trustful look, as if he were confident that I had seen some small redeeming touch in him, even so long ago as when I was a little child. As to all the rest, he was humble and <u>contrite</u>, and I never knew him complain.

Words For Everyday Use

con • trite (kən trīt´) *adj.,* showing remorse or sorrow

When the sessions came round, Mr. Jaggers caused an application to be made for the postponement of his trial until the following sessions. It was obviously made with the assurance that he could not live so long, and was refused. The trial came on at once, and when he was put to the bar, he was seated in a chair. No objection was made to my getting close to the dock, on the outside of it, and holding the hand that he stretched forth to me.

► What is said on Magwitch's behalf?

The trial was very short and very clear. Such things as could be said for him were said—how he had taken to industrious habits, and had thriven[1] lawfully and reputably. But nothing could unsay the fact that he had returned, and was there in presence of the judge and jury. It was impossible to try him for that, and do otherwise than find him guilty.

At that time it was the custom (as I learned from my terrible experience of that session) to devote a concluding day to the passing of sentences, and to make a finishing effect with the sentence of death. But for the <u>indelible</u> picture that my remembrance now holds before me, I could scarcely believe, even as I write these words, that I saw two-and-thirty men and women put before the judge to receive that sentence together. Foremost among the two-and-thirty was he; seated, that he might get breath enough to keep life in him.

► How many other people were sentenced?

The whole scene starts out again in the vivid colors of the moment, down to the drops of April rain on the windows of the court, glittering in the rays of April sun. Penned in the dock, as I again stood outside it at the corner with his hand in mine, were the two-and-thirty men and women—some defiant, some stricken with terror, some sobbing and weeping, some covering their faces, some staring gloomily about. There had been shrieks from among the women convicts, but they had been stilled; a hush had succeeded. The sheriffs with their great chains and nosegays,[2] other civic gewgaws[3] and monsters, criers, ushers, a great gallery full of people—a large theatrical audience—looked on, as the two-and-thirty and the judge were solemnly confronted. Then the judge addressed them. Among the wretched creatures before him whom he must single out for special address was one who

---

1. **thriven.** Steadily improved
2. **nosegays.** Small bunches of flowers
3. **gewgaws.** Showy but useless things

Words For Everyday Use	in • del • i • ble (in del´ə bəl) adj., that cannot be erased; permanent

almost from his infancy had been an offender against the laws; who, after repeated imprisonments and punishments, had been at length sentenced to exile for a term of years; and who, under circumstances of great violence and daring, had made his escape and been resentenced to exile for life. That miserable man would seem for a time to have become convinced of his errors, when far removed from the scenes of his old offenses, and to have lived a peaceable and honest life. But in a fatal moment, yielding to those <u>propensities</u> and passions, the indulgence of which had so long rendered him a scourge to society, he had quitted his haven of rest and repentance, and had come back to the country where he was <u>proscribed</u>. Being here presently denounced, he had for a time succeeded in evading the officers of justice, but being at length seized while in the act of flight, he had resisted them, and had—he best knew whether by express design, or in the blindness of his hardihood—caused the death of his denouncer, to whom his whole career was known. The appointed punishment for his return to the land that had cast him out being death, and his case being this aggravated case, he must prepare himself to die.

◄ What sentence is Magwitch given?

The sun was striking in at the great windows of the court, through the glittering drops of rain upon the glass, and it made a broad shaft of light between the two-and-thirty and the judge, linking both together, and perhaps reminding some among the audience how both were passing on, with absolute equality, to the greater Judgment that knoweth all things and cannot err. Rising for a moment, a distinct speck of face in this way of light, the prisoner said, "My Lord, I have received my sentence of death from the Almighty, but I bow to yours," and sat down again. There was some hushing, and the judge went on with what he had to say to the rest. Then they were all formally doomed, and some of them were supported out, and some of them sauntered out with a haggard look of bravery, and a few nodded to the gallery, and two or three shook hands, and others went out chewing the fragments of herb they had taken from the sweet herbs lying about. He went last of all, because of having to be helped from his chair and to go very slowly, and he held my hand while all the others were removed, and while the audience got up (putting their dresses right, as they might at church

◄ How do the prisoners respond to their sentence?

Words For Everyday Use

pro • pen • si • ty (prə pen´sə tē) *n.*, natural tendency or inclination

pro • scribe (prō skrīb´) *vt.*, banish; exile

or elsewhere) and pointed down at this criminal or at that, and most of all at him and me.

I earnestly hoped and prayed that he might die before the recorder's report was made, but, in the dread of his lingering on, I began that night to write out a petition to the Home Secretary of State, setting forth my knowledge of him, and how it was that he had come back for my sake. I wrote it as fervently and pathetically as I could, and when I had finished it and sent it in, I wrote out other petitions to such men in authority as I hoped were the most merciful, and drew up one to the Crown itself. For several days and nights after he was sentenced I took no rest, except when I fell asleep in my chair, but was wholly absorbed in these appeals. And after I had sent them in, I could not keep away from the places where they were, but felt as if they were more hopeful and less desperate when I was near them. In this unreasonable restlessness and pain of mind, I would roam the streets of an evening, wandering by those offices and houses where I had left the petitions. To the present hour, the weary western streets of London on a cold dusty spring night, with their ranges of stern shut-up mansions and their long rows of lamps, are melancholy to me from this association.

The daily visits I could make him were shortened now, and he was more strictly kept. Seeing, or fancying, that I was suspected of an intention of carrying poison to him, I asked to be searched before I sat down at his bedside, and told the officer who was always there that I was willing to do anything that would assure him of the singleness of my designs. Nobody was hard with him or with me. There was duty to be done, and it was done, but not harshly. The officer always gave me the assurance that he was worse, and some other sick prisoners in the room, and some other prisoners who attended on them as sick nurses (malefactors,[4] but not incapable of kindness, GOD be thanked!), always joined in the same report.

As the days went on, I noticed more and more that he would lie <u>placidly</u> looking at the white ceiling, with an absence of light in his face, until some word of mine brightened it for an instant, and then it would subside again. Sometimes he was

What does Pip do to try to help Magwitch?

Why is Pip searched before the visit?

---

4. **malefactors.** Criminals

| Words For Everyday Use | plac • id • ly (plas´id lē) *adv.,* calmly; quietly |

almost, or quite, unable to speak; then, he would answer me with slight pressures on my hand, and I grew to understand his meaning very well.

The number of the days had risen to ten, when I saw a greater change in him than I had seen yet. His eyes were turned towards the door, and lighted up as I entered.

"Dear boy," he said, as I sat down by his bed; "I thought you was late. But I knowed you couldn't be that."

"It is just the time," said I. "I waited for it at the gate."

"You always waits at the gate, don't you, dear boy?"

"Yes. Not to lose a moment of the time."

"Thank'ee, dear boy, thank'ee. God bless you! You've never deserted me, dear boy."

◄ For what does Magwitch thank Pip? How does Pip feel when he hears this?

I pressed his hand in silence, for I could not forget that I had once meant to desert him.

"And what's the best of all," he said, "you've been more comfortable alonger me since I was under a dark cloud, than when the sun shone. That's best of all."

He lay on his back, breathing with great difficulty. Do what he would, and love me though he did, the light left his face ever and again, and a film came over the placid look at the white ceiling.

"Are you in much pain today?"

"I don't complain of none, dear boy."

"You never do complain."

He had spoken his last words. He smiled, and I understood his touch to mean that he wished to lift my hand, and lay it on his breast. I laid it there, and he smiled again, and put both his hands upon it.

The allotted time ran out, while we were thus; but, looking round, I found the governor of the prison standing near me, and he whispered, "You needn't go yet." I thanked him gratefully, and asked, "Might I speak to him, if he can hear me?"

The governor stepped aside, and beckoned the officer away. The change, though it was made without noise, drew back the film from the placid look at the white ceiling, and he looked most affectionately at me.

"Dear Magwitch, I must tell you, now at last. You understand what I say?"

◄ What does Pip finally tell Magwitch?

A gentle pressure on my hand.

"You had a child once, whom you loved and lost."

A stronger pressure on my hand.

"She lived and found powerful friends. She is living now. She is a lady and very beautiful. And I love her!"

With a last faint effort, which would have been powerless but for my yielding to it, and assisting it, he raised my hand to his lips. Then he gently let it sink upon his breast again, with his own hands lying on it. The placid look at the white ceiling came back, and passed away, and his head dropped quietly on his breast.

► What is Pip's prayer?

Mindful, then, of what we had read together, I thought of the two men who went up into the Temple to pray, and I knew there were no better words that I could say beside his bed than "O Lord, be merciful to him, a sinner!"

CHAPTER 57

Now that I was left wholly to myself, I gave notice of my intention to quit the chambers in the Temple as soon as my tenancy could legally determine, and in the meanwhile to underlet[1] them. At once I put bills up in the windows, for I was in debt, and had scarcely any money, and began to be seriously alarmed by the state of my affairs. I ought rather to write that I should have been alarmed if I had energy and concentration enough to help me to the clear perception of any truth beyond the fact that I was falling very ill. The late stress upon me had enabled me to put off illness, but not to put it away; I knew that it was coming on me now, and I knew very little else, and was even careless as to that.

◀ How is Pip feeling?

For a day or two, I lay on the sofa, or on the floor—anywhere, according as I happened to sink down—with a heavy head and aching limbs, and no purpose, and no power. Then there came one night which appeared of great duration, and which teemed with anxiety and horror; and when in the morning I tried to sit up in my bed and think of it, I found I could not do so.

Whether I really had been down in Garden Court in the dead of the night, groping about for the boat that I supposed to be there; whether I had two or three times come to myself on the staircase with great terror, not knowing how I had got out of bed; whether I had found myself lighting the lamp, possessed by the idea that he was coming up the stairs, and that the lights were blown out; whether I had been inexpressibly harassed by the distracted talking, laughing, and groaning of someone, and had half-suspected those sounds to be of my own making; whether there had been a closed iron furnace in a dark corner of the room, and a voice had called out over and over again that Miss Havisham was consuming within it; these were things that I tried to settle with myself and get into some order, as I lay that morning on my bed. But the vapor of a limekiln would come between me and them, disordering them all, and it was through the vapor at last that I saw two men looking at me.

"What do you want?" I asked, starting; "I don't know you."

◀ Why is Pip arrested?

"Well, sir," returned one of them, bending down and touching me on the shoulder, "this is a matter that you'll soon arrange, I dare say, but you're arrested."

"What is the debt?"

"Hundred and twenty-three pound, fifteen, six. Jeweler's account, I think."

---

1. **underlet.** Sublet; rent out at less than the proper value

"What is to be done?"

"You had better come to my house," said the man. "I keep a very nice house."

I made some attempt to get up and dress myself. When I next attended to them, they were standing a little off from the bed, looking at me. I still lay there.

"You see my state," said I. "I would come with you if I could; but indeed I am quite unable. If you take me from here, I think I shall die by the way."

Perhaps they replied, or argued the point, or tried to encourage me to believe that I was better than I thought. Forasmuch as they hang in my memory by only this one slender thread, I don't know what they did, except that they forbore to remove[2] me.

That I had a fever and was avoided, that I suffered greatly, that I often lost my reason, that the time seemed <u>interminable</u>, that I confounded impossible existences with my own identity; that I was a brick in the house wall, and yet entreating to be released from the giddy[3] place where the builders had set me; that I was a steel beam of a vast engine, clashing and whirling over a gulf, and yet that I implored in my own person to have the engine stopped, and my part in it hammered off; that I passed through these phases of disease, I know of my own remembrance, and did in some sort know at the time. That I sometimes struggled with real people, in the belief that they were murderers, and that I would all at once comprehend that they meant to do me good, and would then sink exhausted in their arms, and suffer them to lay me down, I also knew at the time. But, above all, I knew that there was constant tendency in all these people—who, when I was very ill, would present all kinds of extraordinary transformations of the human face, and would be much dilated in size—above all, I say, I knew that there was an extraordinary tendency in all these people, sooner or later, to settle down into the likeness of Joe.

After I had turned the worst point of my illness, I began to notice that while all its other features changed, this one consistent feature did not change. Whoever came about me, still settled down into Joe. I opened my eyes in the night, and I saw in the great chair at the bedside, Joe. I opened my eyes

► What happens to Pip in his fever? Whom does he see?

---

2. **forbore to remove.** Did not remove
3. **giddy.** Causing dizziness

Words For Everyday Use

in • ter • min • a • ble (in tʉr´mə nə bəl) *adj.,* endless in the day, and, sitting on the window seat, smoking his pipe in the shaded open window, still I saw Joe. I asked for cooling drink, and the dear hand that gave it me was Joe's. I sank back on my pillow after drinking, and the face that looked so hopefully and tenderly upon me was the face of Joe.

◀ Who nurses Pip back to health?

At last, one day, I took courage, and said, *"Is it Joe?"*

And the dear old home-voice answered, "Which it air, old chap."

"Oh, Joe, you break my heart! Look angry at me, Joe. Strike me, Joe. Tell me of my ingratitude. Don't be so good to me!"

For Joe had actually laid his head down on the pillow at my side and put his arm round my neck, in his joy that I knew him.

"Which dear old Pip, old chap," said Joe, "you and me was ever friends. And when you're well enough to go out for a ride—what larks!"

After which, Joe withdrew to the window, and stood with his back towards me, wiping his eyes. And as my extreme weakness prevented me from getting up and going to him, I lay there, penitently whispering, "O God bless him! O God bless this gentle Christian man!"

◀ Why is Joe teary-eyed?

Joe's eyes were red when I next found him beside me, but I was holding his hand and we both felt happy.

"How long, dear Joe?"

"Which you meantersay, Pip, how long have your illness lasted, dear old chap?"

"Yes, Joe."

"It's the end of May, Pip. Tomorrow is the first of June."

"And have you been here all the time, dear Joe?"

"Pretty nigh, old chap. For, as I says to Biddy when the news of your being ill were brought by letter, which it were brought by the post, and being formerly single he is now married though underpaid for a great deal of walking and shoe-leather, but wealth were not a object on his part, and marriage were the great wish of his hart—"

"It is so delightful to hear you, Joe! But I interrupt you in what you said to Biddy."

"Which it were," said Joe, "that how you might be amongst strangers, and that how you and me having been ever friends, a wisit at such a moment might not prove unacceptabobble. And Biddy, her word were, 'Go to him, without loss of time.' That," said Joe, summing up with his judicial air, "were the word of Biddy. 'Go to him,' Biddy say, 'without loss of time.' In short, I shouldn't greatly deceive you," Joe added, after a little grave reflection, "if I represented to you that the word of that young woman were, 'without a minute's loss of time.'"

◀ Who urged Joe to help Pip?

There Joe cut himself short, and informed me that I was to be talked to in great moderation, and that I was to take a little nourishment at stated frequent times, whether I felt inclined for it or not, and that I was to submit myself to all his orders. So I kissed his hand, and lay quiet, while he proceeded to indite[3] a note to Biddy, with my love in it.

Evidently, Biddy had taught Joe to write. As I lay in bed looking at him, it made me, in my weak state, cry again with pleasure to see the pride with which he set about his letter. My bedstead, divested of its curtains, had been removed, with me upon it, into the sitting room, as the airiest and largest, and the carpet had been taken away, and the room kept always fresh and wholesome night and day. At my own writing table, pushed into a corner and cumbered with little bottles, Joe now sat down to his great work, first choosing a pen from the pen-tray as if it were a chest of large tools, and tucking up his sleeves as if he were going to wield a crowbar or sledgehammer. It was necessary for Joe to hold on heavily to the table with his left elbow, and to get his right leg well out behind him, before he could begin, and when he did begin, he made every down-stroke so slowly that it might have been six feet long, while at every up-stroke I could hear his pen spluttering extensively. He had a curious idea that the inkstand was on the side of him where it was not, and constantly dipped his pen into space, and seemed quite satisfied with the result. Occasionally, he was tripped up by some orthographical stumbling-block,[4] but on the whole he got on very well indeed, and when he had signed his name and had removed a finishing blot from the paper to the crown of his head with his two forefingers, he got up and hovered about the table, trying the effect of his performance from various points of view as it lay there, with unbounded satisfaction.

▶ *What happened to Miss Havisham?*

Not to make Joe uneasy by talking too much, even if I had been able to talk much, I deferred asking him about Miss Havisham until next day. He shook his head when I then asked him if she had recovered.

"Is she dead, Joe?"

"Why, you see, old chap," said Joe, in a tone of remonstrance, and by way of getting at it by degrees, "I wouldn't go so far as to say that, for that's a deal to say; but she ain't—"

"Living, Joe?"

"That's nigher where it is," said Joe; "she ain't living."

"Did she linger long, Joe?"

---

3. **indite.** Put in writing
4. **orthographical stumbling-block.** Difficult word to spell

"Arter you was took ill, pretty much about what you might call (if you was put to it) a week," said Joe; still determined, on my account, to come at everything by degrees.

"Dear Joe, have you heard what becomes of her property?"

"Well, old chap," said Joe, "it do appear that she had settled the most of it, which I meantersay tied it up, on Miss Estella. But she had wrote out a little coddleshell[5] in her own hand a day or two afore the accident, leaving a cool four thousand to Mr. Matthew Pocket. And why, do you suppose, above all things, Pip, she left that cool four thousand unto him? 'Because of Pip's account of him the said Matthew.' I am told by Biddy that air the writing," said Joe, repeating the legal turn as if it did him infinite good, "'account of him the said Matthew.' And a cool four thousand, Pip!"

I never discovered from whom Joe derived the conventional temperature of the four thousand pounds, but it appeared to make the sum of money more to him, and he had a manifest relish in insisting on its being cool.

This account gave me great joy, as it perfected the only good thing I had done. I asked Joe whether he had heard if any of the other relations had any <u>legacies</u>.

"Miss Sarah," said Joe, "she have twenty-five pound per-annium fur to buy pills, on account of being bilious.[6] Miss Georgiana, she have twenty pound down. Mrs.—— what's the name of them wild beasts with humps, old chap?"

"Camels?" said I, wondering why he could possibly want to know.

Joe nodded. "Mrs. Camels," by which I presently understood he meant Camilla, "she have five pound fur to buy rushlights to put her in spirits when she wake up in the night."

The accuracy of these recitals was sufficiently obvious to me to give me great confidence in Joe's information. "And now," said Joe, "you ain't that strong yet, old chap, that you can take in more nor one additional shovelful today. Old Orlick he's been a bustin' open a dwelling-'ouse."

"Whose?" said I.

"Not, I grant you, but what his manners is given to blusterous," said Joe apologetically; "still, a Englishman's 'ouse is

◄ Who did Miss Havisham leave money to?

◄ Who else benefited from the will? What reasons does Joe give for their inclusion?

◄ What has Orlick done?

---

5. **coddleshell.** Mispronunciation of "codicil," a supplement or revision to a last will and testament

6. **bilious.** Having an ailment of the bile or liver

Words For Everyday Use

leg • a • cy (leg´ə sē) *n.,* money or property handed down to someone by a will his castle, and castles must not be busted 'cept when done in wartime. And wotsome'er the failings on his part, he were a corn and seedsman in his hart."

"Is it Pumblechook's house that has been broken into, then?"

"That's it, Pip," said Joe; "and they took his till, and they took his cashbox, and they drinked his wine, and they partook of his wittles, and they slapped his face, and they pulled his nose, and they tied him up to his bedpust, and they giv' him a dozen, and they stuffed his mouth full of flowering annuals to perwent his crying out. But he knowed Orlick, and Orlick's in the country jail."

By these approaches we arrived at unrestricted conversation. I was slow to gain strength, but I did slowly and surely become less weak, and Joe stayed with me, and I fancied I was little Pip again.

▶ How does Joe care for Pip?

For, the tenderness of Joe was so beautifully proportioned to my need, that I was like a child in his hands. He would sit and talk to me in the old confidence, and with the old simplicity, and in the old unassertive protecting way, so that I would half believe that all my life since the days of the old kitchen was one of the mental troubles of the fever that was gone. He did everything for me except the household work, for which he had engaged a very decent woman, after paying off the laundress on his first arrival. "Which I do assure you, Pip," he would often say, in explanation of that liberty; "I found her a-tapping the spare bed, like a cask of beer, and drawing off the feathers in a bucket, for sale. Which she would have tapped yourn next, and draw'd it off with you a-laying on it, and was then a carrying away the coals gradiwally in the soup tureen[7] and wegetable-dishes, and the wine and spirits in your Wellington boots."[8]

We looked forward to the day when I should go out for a ride, as we had once looked forward to the day of my apprenticeship. And when the day came, and an open carriage was got into the lane, Joe wrapped me up, took me in his arms, carried me down to it, and put me in, as if I were still the small helpless creature to whom he had so abundantly given of the wealth of his great nature.

And Joe got in beside me, and we drove away together into the country, where the rich summer growth was already on the trees and on the grass, and sweet summer scents filled all the air. The day happened to be Sunday, and when I looked on the loveliness around me, and thought how it had grown and changed, and how the little wild flowers had been forming, and the voices of the birds had been strengthening, by

7. **tureen.** Broad, deep dish with a lid
8. **Wellington boots.** Calf- or knee-length waterproof boots

day and by night, under the sun and under the stars, while poor I lay burning and tossing on my bed, the mere remembrance of having burned and tossed there came like a check upon my peace. But when I heard the Sunday bells, and looked around a little more upon the outspread beauty, I felt that I was not nearly thankful enough—that I was too weak yet, to be even that—and I laid my head on Joe's shoulder, as I had laid it long ago when he had taken me to the fair or where not, and it was too much for my young senses.

More composure came to me after a while, and we talked as we used to talk, lying on the grass at the old battery. There was no change whatever in Joe. Exactly what he had been in my eyes then, he was in my eyes still; just as simply faithful, just as simply right.

When we got back again and he lifted me out, and carried me—so easily!—across the court and up the stairs, I thought of that eventful Christmas Day when he had carried me over the marshes. We had not yet made any allusion to my change of fortune, nor did I know how much of my late history he was acquainted with. I was so doubtful of myself now, and put so much trust in him, that I could not satisfy myself whether I ought to refer to it when he did not.

"Have you heard, Joe," I asked him that evening, upon further consideration, as he smoked his pipe at the window, "who my patron was?"

◄ What does Joe know about Pip's benefactor?

"I heerd," returned Joe, "as it were not Miss Havisham, old chap."

"Did you hear who it was, Joe?"

"Well! I heerd as it were a person what sent the person what giv' you the bank notes at the Jolly Bargemen, Pip."

"So it was."

"Astonishing!" said Joe, in the placidest way.

"Did you hear that he was dead, Joe?" I presently asked, with increasing diffidence.

"Which? Him as sent the bank notes, Pip?"

"Yes."

"I think," said Joe, after meditating a long time, and looking rather <u>evasively</u> at the window seat, "as I *did* hear tell that how he were something or another in a general way in that direction."

"Did you hear anything of his circumstances, Joe?"

Words For Everyday Use

e • va • sive • ly (ē vā´siv lē) *adv.*, in a manner characterized by avoiding

▶ What does Joe say about the story?

"Not partickler, Pip."

"If you would like to hear, Joe—" I was beginning, when Joe got up and came to my sofa.

"Look'ee here, old chap," said Joe, bending over me. "Ever the best of friends; ain't us, Pip?"

I was ashamed to answer him.

"Werry good, then," said Joe, as if I *had* answered; "that's all right, that's agreed upon. Then why go into subjects, old chap, which as betwixt two sech must be forever onnecessary ones. There's subjects enough as betwixt two sech, without onnecessary ones. Lord! To think of your poor sister and her rampages! And don't you remember Tickler?"

"I do indeed, Joe."

"Look'ee here, old chap," said Joe. "I done what I could to keep you and Tickler in sunders,[9] but my power were not always fully equal to my inclinations. For when your poor sister had a mind to drop into you, it were not so much," said Joe, in his favorite argumentative way, "that she dropped into me, too, if I put myself in opposition to her, but that she dropped into you always heavier for it. I noticed that. It ain't a grab at a man's whisker, not yet a shake or two of a man (to which your sister was quite welcome), that 'ud put a man off from getting a little child out of punishment. But when that little child is dropped into heavier[10] for that grab of whisker or shaking, then that man naterally up and says to himself, 'Where is the good as you are a-doing? I grant you I see the 'arm,' says the man, 'but I don't see the good. I call upon you, sir, theerfore, to pint out the good.'"

"The man says?" I observed, as Joe waited for me to speak.

"The man says," Joe assented. "Is he right, that man?"

"Dear Joe, he is always right."

▶ Why does Joe tell Pip that he doesn't need to know the story?

"Well, old chap," said Joe, "then abide by your words. If he's always right (which in general he's more likely wrong), he's right when he says this:—Supposing ever you kep any little matter to yourself, when you was a little child, you kep it mostly because you know'd as J. Gargery's power to part you and Tickler in sunders were not fully equal to his inclinations. Theerfore, think no more of it as betwixt two sech, and do not let us pass remarks upon onnecessary subjects. Biddy giv' herself a deal o' trouble with me afore I left (for I am almost awful dull), as I should view it in this light, and, viewing it in this light, as I should so put it. Both of which," said Joe, quite charmed with his logical arrangement, "being done, now this to you a true friend, say. Namely. You mustn't go a-overdoing

---

9. **in sunders.** Apart
10. **is dropped into heavier.** Receives harsher punishment

on it, but you must have your supper and your wine-and-water, and you must be put betwixt the sheets."

The delicacy with which Joe dismissed this theme, and the sweet tact and kindness with which Biddy—who with her woman's wit had found me out so soon—had prepared him for it, made a deep impression on my mind. But whether Joe knew how poor I was, and how my great expectations had all dissolved, like our own marsh mists before the sun, I could not understand.

Another thing in Joe that I could not understand when it first began to develop itself, but which I soon arrived at a sorrowful comprehension of, was this: as I became stronger and better, Joe became a little less easy with me. In my weakness and entire dependence on him, the dear fellow had fallen into the old tone, and called me by the old names, the dear "old Pip, old chap," that now were music in my ears. I, too, had fallen into the old ways, only happy and thankful that he let me. But, imperceptibly, though I held by them fast, Joe's hold upon them began to slacken; and whereas I wondered at this, at first, I soon began to understand that the cause of it was in me, and that the fault of it was all mine.

Ah! Had I given Joe no reason to doubt my constancy, and to think that in prosperity I should grow cold to him and cast him off? Had I given Joe's innocent heart no cause to feel instinctively that, as I got stronger, his hold upon me would be weaker, and that he had better loosen it in time and let me go, before I plucked myself away?

It was on the third or fourth occasion of my going out walking in the Temple gardens, leaning on Joe's arm, that I saw this change in him very plainly. We had been sitting in the bright warm sunlight, looking at the river, and I chanced to say as we got up:

"See, Joe! I can walk quite strongly. Now, you shall see me walk back by myself."

"Which do not overdo it, Pip," said Joe; "but I shall be happy fur to see you able, sir."

The last word grated on me, but how could I remonstrate! I walked no further than the gate of the gardens, and then pretended to be weaker than I was, and asked Joe for his arm. Joe gave it me, but was thoughtful.

I, for my part, was thoughtful too, for how best to check this growing change in Joe was a great perplexity to my remorseful thoughts. That I was ashamed to tell him exactly how I was placed, and what I had come down to, I do not seek to conceal; but, I hope my reluctance was not quite an unworthy one. He would want to help me out of his little

◄ What does Pip realize about Joe? How has Pip caused this problem?

savings, I knew, and I knew that he ought not to help me, and that I must not suffer him to do it.

It was a thoughtful evening with both of us. But before we went to bed, I had resolved that I would wait over tomorrow, tomorrow being Sunday, and would begin my new course with the new week. On Monday morning I would speak to Joe about this change, I would lay aside this last vestige of reserve, I would tell him what I had in my thoughts (that secondly, not yet arrived at), and why I had not decided to go out to Herbert, and then the change would be conquered forever. As I cleared, Joe cleared, and it seemed as though he had sympathetically arrived at a resolution too.

We had a quiet day on the Sunday, and we rode out into the country, and then walked in the fields.

"I feel thankful that I have been ill, Joe," I said.

"Dear old Pip, old chap, you're a'most come round, sir."

"It has been a memorable time for me, Joe."

"Likeways for myself, sir," Joe returned.

"We have had a time together, Joe, that I can never forget. There were days once, I know, that I did for a while forget; but I never shall forget these."

"Pip," said Joe, appearing a little hurried and troubled, "there has been larks. And, dear sir, what have been betwixt us—have been."

At night, when I had gone to bed, Joe came into my room, as he had done all through my recovery. He asked me if I felt sure that I was as well as in the morning.

"Yes, dear Joe, quite."

"And are always a-getting stronger, old chap?"

"Yes, dear Joe, steadily."

Joe patted the coverlet on my shoulder with his great good hand, and said, in what I thought a husky voice, "Good night!"

▶ Why does Joe leave? What has he done for Pip?

When I got up in the morning, refreshed and stronger yet, I was full of my resolution to tell Joe all, without delay. I would tell him before breakfast. I would dress at once and go to his room and surprise him, for it was the first day I had been up early. I went to his room, and he was not there. Not only was he not there, but his box was gone.

I hurried then to the breakfast table, and on it found a letter. These were its brief contents.

Not wishful to intrude I have departured fur you are well again dear Pip and will do better without——Jo. P.S. Ever the best of friends.

Enclosed in the letter was a receipt for the debt and costs on which I had been arrested. Down to that moment I had vainly supposed that my creditor had withdrawn or suspended proceedings until I should be quite recovered. I had never dreamed of Joe's having paid the money; but Joe had paid it, and the receipt was in his name.

What remained for me now, but to follow him to the dear old forge, and there to have out my disclosure to him, and my penitent remonstrance with him, and there to relieve my mind and heart of that reserved secondly, which had begun as a vague something lingering in my thoughts, and had formed into a settled purpose?

◄ What does Pip decide to do?

The purpose was that I would go to Biddy, that I would show her how humbled and repentant I came back, that I would tell her how I had lost all I once hoped for, that I would remind her of our old confidences in my first unhappy time. Then, I would say to her, "Biddy, I think you once liked me very well, when my <u>errant</u> heart, even while it strayed away from you, was quieter and better with you than it ever has been since. If you can like me only half as well once more, if you can take me with all my faults and disappointments on my head, if you can receive me like a forgiven child (and indeed I am as sorry, Biddy, and have as much need of a hushing voice and a soothing hand), I hope I am a little worthier of you that I was—not much, but a little. And, Biddy, it shall rest with you to say whether I shall work at the forge with Joe, or whether I shall try for any different occupation down in this country, or whether we shall go away to a distant place where an opportunity awaits me which I set aside when it was offered, until I knew your answer. And now, dear Biddy, if you can tell me that you will go through the world with me, you will surely make it a better world for me, and me a better man for it, and I will try hard to make it a better world for you."

Such was my purpose. After three days more of recovery, I went down to the old place, to put it in execution. And how I sped in it is all I have left to tell.

Words For Everyday Use

er • rant (er´ənt) *adj.*, roving; wandering

The tidings of my high fortunes having had a heavy fall, had got down to my native place and its neighborhood before I got there. I found the Blue Boar in possession of the intelligence, and I found that it made a great change in the Boar's demeanor. Whereas the Boar had cultivated my good opinion with warm <u>assiduity</u> when I was coming into property, the Boar was exceedingly cool on the subject now that I was going out of property.

▶ Why is Pip treated differently at the Blue Boar than he was formerly?

It was evening when I arrived, much fatigued by the journey I had so often made so easily. The Boar could not put me into my usual bedroom, which was engaged (probably by someone who had expectations), and could only assign me a very indifferent chamber among the pigeons and post-chaises up the yard. But I had as sound a sleep in that lodging as in the most superior accommodation the Boar could have given me, and the quality of my dreams was about the same as in the best bedroom.

▶ Why is the property of Miss Havisham being auctioned off?

Early in the morning while my breakfast was getting ready, I strolled round by Satis House. There were printed bills on the gate and on bits of carpet hanging out of the windows, announcing a sale by auction of the household furniture and effects, next week. The house itself was to be sold as old building materials and pulled down. Lot 1 was marked in whitewashed knock-knee letters on the brewhouse; Lot 2 on that part of the main building which had been so long shut up. Other lots were marked off on other parts of the structure, and the ivy had been torn down to make room for the inscriptions, and much of it trailed low in the dust and was withered already. Stepping in for a moment at the open gate and looking around me with the uncomfortable air of a stranger who had no business there, I saw the auctioneer's clerk walking on the casks and telling them off for the information of a catalogue compiler, pen in hand, who made a temporary desk of the wheeled chair I had so often pushed along to the tune of Old Clem.

When I got back to my breakfast in the Boar's coffee-room, I found Mr. Pumblechook conversing with the landlord. Mr. Pumblechook (not improved in appearance by his

Words For Everyday Use	**as • si • du • i • ty** (as′ə dyo͞o′ə tē) *n.*, diligence; constant attention

late nocturnal adventure) was waiting for me, and addressed me in the following terms.

"Young man, I am sorry to see you brought low. But what else could be expected! What else could be expected!"

As he extended his hand with a magnificently forgiving air, and as I was broken by illness and unfit to quarrel, I took it.

"William," said Mr. Pumblechook to the waiter, "put a muffin on table. And has it come to this! Has it come to this!"

I frowningly sat down to my breakfast. Mr. Pumblechook stood over me and poured out my tea—before I could touch the teapot—with the air of a benefactor who was resolved to be true to the last.

◄ How does Pumblechook treat Pip now?

"William," said Mr. Pumblechook mournfully, "put the salt on. In happier times," addressing me, "I think you took sugar. And did you take milk? You did. Sugar and milk. William, bring a watercress."[1]

"Thank you," said I, shortly, "but I don't eat watercresses."

"You don't eat 'em," returned Mr. Pumblechook, sighing and nodding his head several times, as if he might have expected that, and as if abstinence from watercresses were consistent with my downfall. "True. The simple fruits of the earth. No. You needn't bring any, William."

I went on with my breakfast, and Mr. Pumblechook continued to stand over me, staring fishily and breathing noisily, as he always did.

"Little more than skin and bone!" mused Mr. Pumblechook, aloud. "And yet when he went from here (I may say with my blessing), and I spread afore him my humble store, like the bee, he was as plump as a peach!"

This reminded me of the wonderful difference between the servile manner in which he had offered his hand in my new prosperity, saying, "May I?" and the ostentatious clemency with which he had just now exhibited the same fat five fingers.

"Hah!" he went on, handing me the bread-and-butter. "And air you a-going to Joseph?"

"In Heaven's name," said I, firing in spite of myself, "what does it matter to you where I am going? Leave that teapot alone."

It was the worst course I could have taken, because it gave Pumblechook the opportunity he wanted.

---

1. **watercress.** Plant with flavorful leaves used in salads, soups, and as a garnish

Words For Everyday Use

ab • sti • nence (ab´stə nəns) *n.*, act of voluntarily doing without something

clem • en • cy (klem´ən sē) *n.*, mercy

▶ Why is Pumblechook ready to be angry at Pip?

"Yes, young man," said he, releasing the handle of the article in question, retiring a step or two from my table, and speaking for the behoof of the landlord and waiter at the door, "I *will* leave that teapot alone. You are right, young man. For once, you are right. I forgit myself when I take such an interest in your breakfast, as to wish your frame, exhausted by the <u>debilitating</u> effects of prodigygality,[2] to be stimilated by the 'olesome nourishment of your forefathers. And yet," said Pumblechook, turning to the landlord and waiter, and pointing me out at arm's length, "this is him as I ever sported with in his days of happy infancy! Tell me not it cannot be; I tell you this is him!"

A low murmur from the two replied. The waiter appeared to be particularly affected.

"This is him," said Pumblechook, "as I have rode in my shaycart. This is him as I have seen brought up by hand. This is him untoe the sister of which I was uncle by marriage, as her name was Georgiana M'ria from her own mother—let him deny it if he can!"

The waiter seemed convinced that I could not deny it, and that it gave the case a black look.

"Young man," said Pumblechook, screwing his head at me in the old fashion, "you air a-going to Joseph. What does it matter to me, you ask me, where you air a-going? I say to you, sir, you air a-going to Joseph."

The waiter coughed, as if he modestly invited to get over that.

"Now," said Pumblechook, and all this with a most exasperating air of saying in the cause of virtue what was perfectly convincing and conclusive, "I will tell you what to say to Joseph. Here is Squires of the Boar present, known and respected in this town, and here is William, which his father's name was Potkins if I do not deceive myself."

"You do not, sir," said William.

"In their presence," pursued Pumblechook, "I will tell you, young man, what to say to Joseph. Says you, 'Joseph, I have this day seen my earliest benefactor and the founder of my fortun's. I will name no names, Joseph, but so they are pleased to call him uptown, and I have seen that man.'"

"I swear I don't see him here," said I.

---

2. **prodigygality.** Prodigality; wastefulness

Words For Everyday Use

de • **bil** • i • tat • ing (di bil´ə tāt´iŋ) *adj.,* weakening

"Say that likewise," retorted Pumblechook. "Say you said that, and even Joseph will probably betray surprise."

"There you quite mistake him," said I. "I know better."

"Says you," Pumblechook went on, "'Joseph, I have seen that man, and that man bears you no malice and bears me no malice. He knows your character, Joseph, and is well acquainted with your pigheadedness and ignorance; and he knows my character, Joseph, and he knows my want of grati-toode. Yes, Joseph,' says you,"—here Pumblechook shook his head and hand at me—"'he knows my total deficiency of common human gratitoode. *He* knows it, Joseph, as none can. *You* do not know it, Joseph, having no call to know it, but that man do.'"

Windy donkey as he was, it really amazed me that he could have the face to talk thus to mine.

◀ What does Pumblechook want to tell Joe? What exactly does Pumblechook claim to have done for Pip?

"Says you, 'Joseph, he gave me a little message, which I will now repeat. It was that in my being brought low, he saw the finger of Providence. He knowed that finger when he saw it, Joseph, and he saw it plain. It pinted out this writing, Joseph. *Reward of ingratitoode to his earliest benefactor, and founder of fortun's.* But that man said he did not repent of what he had done, Joseph. Not at all. It was right to do it, it was kind to do it, it was benevolent to do it, and he would do it again.'"

"It's pity," said I, scornfully, as I finished my interrupted breakfast, "that the man did not say what he had done and would do again."

"Squires of the Boar!" Pumblechook was now addressing the landlord, "and William! I have no objections to your mentioning, either uptown or downtown, if such should be your wishes, that it was right to do it, kind to do it, benevolent to do it, and that I would do it again."

With those words the impostor shook them both by the hand, with an air, and left the house, leaving me much more astonished than delighted by the virtues of that same indefinite "it." I was not long after him in leaving the house, too, and when I went down the High Street I saw him holding forth (no doubt to the same effect) at his shop door to a select group, who honored me with very unfavorable glances as I passed on the opposite side of the way.

◀ For what does Pip look to Biddy and Joe?

But, it was only the pleasanter to turn to Biddy and to Joe, whose great forbearance shone more brightly than before, if that could be, contrasted with this brazen pretender. I went towards them slowly, for my limbs were weak, but with a sense of increasing relief as I drew nearer to them, and a sense of leaving arrogance and untruthfulness further and further behind.

▶ *What does the return to the village remind Pip of?*

The June weather was delicious. The sky was blue, the larks were soaring high over the green corn, I thought all that countryside more beautiful and peaceful by far than I had ever known it to be yet. Many pleasant pictures of the life that I would lead there, and of the change for the better that would come over my character when I had a guiding spirit at my side whose simple faith and clear home wisdom I had proved, beguiled[3] my way. They awakened a tender emotion in me, for my heart was softened by my return, and such a change had come to pass that I felt like one who was toiling home barefoot from distant travel, and whose wanderings had lasted many years.

The schoolhouse where Biddy was mistress, I had never seen, but the little roundabout lane by which I entered the village for quietness' sake, took me past it. I was disappointed to find that the day was a holiday; no children were there, and Biddy's house was closed. Some hopeful notion of seeing her, busily engaged in her daily duties, before she saw me, had been in my mind and was defeated.

But the forge was a very short distance off, and I went towards it under the sweet green limes, listening for the clink of Joe's hammer. Long after I ought to have heard it, and long after I had fancied I heard it and found it but a fancy, all was still. The limes were there, and the white thorns were there, and the chestnut trees were there, and their leaves rustled harmoniously when I stopped to listen, but, the clink of Joe's hammer was not in the midsummer wind.

Almost fearing, without knowing why, to come in view of the forge, I saw it at last, and saw that it was closed. No gleam of fire, no glittering shower of sparks, no roar of bellows; all shut up, and still.

But the house was not deserted, and the best parlor seemed to be in use, for there were white curtains fluttering in its window, and the window was open and gay with flowers. I went softly towards it, meaning to peep over the flowers, when Joe and Biddy stood before me, arm in arm.

▶ *What kind of welcome does Pip receive?*

At first Biddy gave a cry, as if she thought it was my apparition,[4] but in another moment she was in my embrace. I wept to see her, and she wept to see me; I because she looked so fresh and pleasant; she because I looked so worn and white.

"But dear Biddy, how smart you are!"

"Yes, dear Pip."

"And Joe, how smart *you* are!"

"Yes, dear old Pip, old chap."

---

3. **beguiled.** Caused time to pass pleasantly
4. **apparition.** Ghost

I looked at both of them, from one to the other, and then—

◀ What good news does Biddy give Pip?

"It's my wedding day," cried Biddy, in a burst of happiness, "and I am married to Joe!"

They had taken me into the kitchen, and I had laid my head down on the old deal table. Biddy held one of my hands to her lips, and Joe's restoring touch was on my shoulder. "Which he warn't strong enough, my dear, fur to be surprised," said Joe. And Biddy said, "I ought to have thought of it, dear Joe, but I was too happy." They were both so overjoyed to see me, so proud to see me, so touched by my coming to them, so delighted that I should have come by accident to make their day complete!

My first thought was one of great thankfulness that I had never breathed this last baffled hope to Joe. How often, while he was with me in my illness, had it risen to my lips. How <u>irrevocable</u> would have been his knowledge of it, if he had remained with me but another hour!

"Dear Biddy," said I, "you have the best husband in the whole world, and if you could have seen him by my bed you would have— But no, you couldn't love him better than you do."

"No, I couldn't indeed," said Biddy.

"And, dear Joe, you have the best wife in the whole world, and she will make you as happy as even you deserve to be, you dear, good, noble Joe!"

Joe looked at me with a quivering lip, and fairly put his sleeve before his eyes.

"And Joe and Biddy both, as you have been to church today, and are in charity and love with all mankind, receive my humble thanks for all you have done for me, and all I have so ill repaid! And when I say that I am going away within the hour, for I am soon going abroad, and that I shall never rest until I have worked for the money with which you have kept me out of prison, and have sent it to you, don't think, dear Joe and Biddy, that if I could repay it a thousand times over, I suppose I could cancel a farthing of the debt I owe you, or that I would do so if I could!"

◀ What does Pip promise to do?

They were both melted by these words, and both entreated me to say no more.

Words For Everyday Use

ir • rev • o • ca • ble (ir revˊə kə bəl) *adj.*, that cannot be undone

"But I must say more. Dear Joe, I hope you will have children to love, and that some little fellow will sit in this chimney corner of a winter night, who may remind you of another little fellow gone out of it forever. Don't tell him, Joe, that I was thankless; don't tell him, Biddy, that I was ungenerous and unjust; only tell him that I honored you both, because you were both so good and true, and that, as your child, I said it would natural to him to grow up a much better man than I did."

"I ain't a-going," said Joe, from behind his sleeve, "to tell him nothink o' that natur, Pip. Nor Biddy ain't. Nor yet no one ain't."

▶ What does Pip ask of Joe?

"And now, though I know you have already done it in your own kind hearts, pray tell me, both, that you forgive me! Pray let me hear you say the words, that I may carry the sound of them away with me, and then I shall be able to believe that you can trust me, and think better of me, in the time to come!"

"Oh dear old Pip, old chap," said Joe. "God knows as I forgive you, if I have anythink to forgive!"

"Amen! And God knows I do!" echoed Biddy.

Now let me go and look at my old little room, and rest there a few minutes by myself, and then when I have eaten and drunk with you, go with me as far as the finger-post, dear Joe and Biddy, before we say good-bye!"

I sold all I had, and put aside as much as I could, for a composition[5] with my creditors—who gave me ample time to pay them in full—and I went out and joined Herbert. Within a month, I had quitted England, and within two months I was clerk to Clarriker & Co., and within four months I assumed my first undivided responsibility. For the beam across the parlor ceiling at Mill Pond Bank had then ceased to tremble under old Bill Barley's growls and was at peace, and Herbert had gone away to marry Clara, and I was left in sole charge of the Eastern branch until he brought her back.

▶ How does Herbert learn of Pip's investment?

Many a year went round, before I was a partner in the house; but I lived happily with Herbert and his wife, and lived frugally, and paid my debts, and maintained a constant correspondence with Biddy and Joe. It was not until I became third in the firm that Clarriker betrayed me to Herbert; but he then declared that the secret of Herbert's partnership had been long enough upon his conscience, and he must tell it. So, he told it, and Herbert was as much

---

5. **composition.** Settlement whereby creditors agree to accept partial payment of debt

moved as amazed, and the dear fellow and I were not the worse friends for the long concealment. I must not leave it to be supposed that we were ever a great house, or that we made mints of money. We were not in a grand way of business, but we had a good name, and worked for our profits, and did very well. We owed so much to Herbert's ever cheerful industry and readiness that I often wondered how I had conceived that old idea of his <u>inaptitude</u>, until I was one day enlightened by the reflection that perhaps the inaptitude had never been in him at all, but had been in me.

◀ *What does Pip realize about Herbert? about himself?*

Words For Everyday Use

in • ap • ti • tude (in ap´tə to͞od´) *n.,* lack of skill

CHAPTER 59

For eleven years I had not seen Joe nor Biddy with my bodily eyes—though they had both been often before my fancy in the East—when, upon an evening in December, an hour or two after dark, I laid my hand softly on the latch of the old kitchen door. I touched it so softly that I was not heard, and I looked in unseen. There, smoking his pipe in the old place by the kitchen firelight, as hale and as strong as ever, though a little gray, sat Joe; and there, fenced into the corner with Joe's leg, and sitting on my own little stool looking at the fire, was—I again!

▶ *Why do Joe and Biddy name their son Pip?*

"We giv' him the name of Pip for your sake, dear old chap," said Joe, delighted when I took another stool by the child's side (but I did *not* rumple his hair), "and we hoped he might grow a little bit like you, and we think he do."

I thought so too, and I took him out for a walk next morning, and we talked immensely, understanding one another to perfection. And I took him down to the churchyard, and set him on a certain tombstone there, and he showed me from that elevation which stone was sacred to the memory of Philip Pirrip, Late of this Parish, and Also Georgiana, Wife of the Above.

"Biddy," said I, when I talked with her after dinner, as her little girl lay sleeping in her lap, "you must give Pip to me, one of these days; or lend him, at all events."

"No, no," said Biddy, gently. "You must marry."

▶ *Why does Pip think that he will not marry?*

"So Herbert and Clara say, but I don't think I shall, Biddy. I have so settled down in their home that it's not at all likely. I am already quite an old bachelor."

Biddy looked down at her child, and put its little hand to her lips, and then put the good matronly[1] hand with which she had touched it into mine. There was something in the action and in the light pressure of Biddy's wedding ring, that had a very pretty <u>eloquence</u> in it.

"Dear Pip," said Biddy, "you are sure you don't fret for her?"[2]

"I am sure and certain, Biddy."

---

1. **matronly.** With the dignity and maturity of a married woman
2. **Dear Pip . . . her?** See "The Revised Ending of *Great Expectations*" on page 512.

Words For Everyday Use	**el • o • quence** (el´ə kwəns) *n.*, graceful expressiveness

It was two years more before I saw herself. I had heard of her as leading a most unhappy life, and as being separated from her husband, who had used her with great cruelty, and who had become quite renowned as a compound of pride, brutality, and meanness. I had heard of the death of her husband from an accident consequent on ill-treating a horse, and of her being married again to a Shropshire doctor who, against his interest, had once very manfully interposed on an occasion when he was in professional attendance upon Mr. Drummle, and had witnessed some outrageous treatment of her. I had heard that the Shropshire doctor was not rich, and that they lived on her own personal fortune. I was in England again—in London, and walking along Piccadilly with little Pip—when a servant came running after me to ask would I step back to a lady in a carriage who wished to speak to me. It was a little pony carriage which the lady was driving, and the lady and I looked sadly enough on one another.

"I am greatly changed, I know, but I thought you would like to shake hands with Estella, too, Pip. Lift up that pretty child and let me kiss it!" (She supposed the child, I think, to be my child.) I was very glad afterwards to have had the interview, for in her face and in her voice, and in her touch, she gave me the assurance that suffering had been stronger than Miss Havisham's teaching, and had given her a heart to understand what my heart used to be.

◄ *What has happened to Estella?*

The Revised Ending of *Great Expectations*

Dickens's original ending for Great Expectations, *which is used in this text, was considered by some to be too unhappy. At the urging of a friend, he changed the ending to be more sentimental and appealing. In the revised version, when Biddy says, "Dear Pip, . . . you are sure you don't fret for her?" (page 510), Pip replies, "Oh, no—I think not, Biddy." Then the following ending appears:*

▶ What is Biddy's concern?

"Tell me as an old friend. Have you quite forgotten her?"

"My dear Biddy, I have forgotten nothing in my life that ever had a foremost place there, and little that ever had any place there. But that poor dream, as I once used to call it, has all gone by, Biddy, all gone by!"

Nevertheless, I knew while I said those words that I secretly intended to revisit the site of the old house that evening alone, for her sake. Yes, even so. For Estella's sake.

I had heard of her as leading a most unhappy life, and as being separated from her husband, who had used her with great cruelty, and who had become quite renowned as a compound of pride, <u>avarice</u>, brutality, and meanness. And I had heard of the death of her husband from an accident consequent of his ill-treatment of a horse. This release had befallen her some two years before; for anything I knew, she was married again.

The early dinner hour at Joe's left me abundance of time, without hurrying my talk with Biddy, to walk over to the old spot before dark. But what with loitering on the way to look at old objects and to think of old times, the day had quite declined when I came to the place.

▶ What has happened to Satis House?

There was no house now, no brewery, no building whatever left, but the wall of the old garden. The cleared space had been enclosed with a rough fence, and, looking over it, I saw that some of the old ivy had struck root anew, and was growing green on low quiet mounds of ruin. A gate in the fence standing ajar, I pushed it open, and went in.

A cold silvery mist had veiled the afternoon, and the moon was not yet up to scatter it. But the stars were shining beyond the mist, and the moon was coming, and the evening was

---

Words For Everyday Use

av • a • rice (av´ə ris) *n.*, greed for riches

not dark. I could trace out where every part of the old house had been, and where the brewery had been, and where the gates, and where the casks. I had done so, and was looking along the desolate gardenwalk, when I beheld a solitary figure in it.

The figure showed itself aware of me as I advanced. It had been moving towards me, but it stood still. As I drew nearer, I saw it to be the figure of a woman. As I drew nearer yet, it was about to turn away, when it stopped, and let me come up with it. Then it faltered as if much surprised, and uttered my name, and I cried out:

◀ Who does Pip meet by accident?

"Estella!"

"I am greatly changed. I wonder you know me."

The freshness of her beauty was indeed gone, but its indescribable majesty and its indescribable charm remained. Those attractions in it I had seen before; what I had never seen before was the saddened, softened light of the once proud eyes; what I had never felt before was the friendly touch of the once insensible hand.

We sat down on a bench that was near, and I said, "After so many years, it is strange that we should thus meet again, Estella, here where our first meeting was! Do you often come back?"

"I have never been here since."

"Nor I."

The moon began to rise, and I thought of the placid look at the white ceiling, which had passed away. The moon began to rise, and I thought of the pressure on my hand when I had spoken the last words he had heard on earth.

◀ What does the moon rising remind Pip of?

Estella was the next to break the silence that ensued between us.

"I have very often hoped and intended to come back, but have been prevented by many circumstances. Poor, poor old place!"

The silvery mist was touched with the first rays of the moonlight, and the same rays touched the tears that dropped from her eyes. Not knowing that I saw them, and setting herself to get the better of them, she said quietly:

"Were you wondering, as you walked along, how it came to be left in this condition?"

"Yes, Estella."

"The ground belongs to me. It is the only possession I have not relinquished. Everything else has gone from me, little by little, but I have kept this. It was the subject of the only determined resistance I made in all the wretched years."

◀ What possession has Estella held on to?

"Is it to be built on?"

"At last it is. I came here to take leave of it before its change. And you," she said, in a voice of touching interest to a wanderer, "you live abroad still?"

"Still."

"And do well, I am sure?"

"I work pretty hard for a sufficient living, and therefore— Yes, I do well."

"I have often thought of you," said Estella.

"Have you?"

"Of late, very often. There was a long hard time when I kept far from the remembrance of what I had thrown away when I was quite ignorant of its worth. But since my duty has not been incompatible with the admission of that remembrance, I have given it a place in my heart."

▶ What did Estella come to realize about Pip?

"You have always held your place in *my* heart," I answered.

And we were silent again until she spoke.

"I little thought," said Estella, "that I should take leave of you in taking leave of this spot. I am very glad to do so."

"Glad to part again, Estella? To me, parting is a painful thing. To me, the remembrance of our last parting has been ever mournful and painful."

"But you said to me," returned Estella, very earnestly, "'God bless you, God forgive you!' And if you could say that to me then, you will not hesitate to say that to me now— now, when suffering has been stronger than all other teaching, and has taught me to understand what your heart used to be. I have been bent and broken, but—I hope—into a better shape. Be as considerate and good to me as you were, and tell me we are friends."

"We are friends," said I, rising and bending over her, as she rose from the bench.

"And will continue friends apart," said Estella.

I took her hand in mine, and we went out of the ruined place; and as the morning mists had risen long ago when I first left the forge, so the evening mists were rising now, and in all the broad expanse of tranquil light they showed to me, I saw no shadow of another parting from her.

Responding to the Selection

What has happened to Pip's great expectations? What has he suffered? What good has come to him? How do you feel about Pip at the end of the novel? Have your feelings changed since the beginning of the novel?

Reviewing the Selection

Recalling and Interpreting

1. **R:** What physical changes does Pip notice in Magwitch when he visits him in jail? What news does Pip share with Magwitch upon his deathbed?

2. **I:** In what ways, other than physically, has Magwitch changed? Does he fit his description as a criminal?

3. **R:** What happens to Pip upon Magwitch's death? In what way are Pip's anxieties manifested? Who takes care of Pip?

4. **I:** Explain whether the relationship between Joe and Pip has changed since the beginning of the novel.

5. **R:** What event occurs after Pip returns home? How does Pip react to this new development? What does he do after leaving Joe and Biddy?

6. **I:** Why does Pip decide to go abroad?

7. **R:** In the revised ending, why does Pip visit the site of Satis House? Whom does Pip meet by accident there? What do they remember about their last meeting in this place?

8. **I:** What is Pip's mood as he approaches the site of the old house? What details are used to show his mood? Which ending do you like best—the revised version or the original? Why?

Synthesizing

9. Magwitch serves as Pip's teacher. Identify and discuss the values Magwitch teaches him.

10. In the revised ending, what understanding and acceptance do Estella and Pip exchange in the ruins of Satis House? Do you think that they will live "happily ever after?" Explain why or why not.

Understanding Literature (QUESTIONS FOR DISCUSSION)

1. Effect. The **effect** of a literary work is the general impression or emotional impact it achieves. The effect of Magwitch's death scene is quite dramatic. Explain the effect of this scene and offer examples from the passage that reflect its emotional impact.

2. Symbol. A **symbol** is a thing that stands for or represents both itself and something else. A *conventional symbol* is one with traditional, widely recognized associations. Such symbols include doves for peace, morning or spring for youth, wind for change or inspiration and so on. Explain the meaning of the following symbols used in chapter 59:
• Estella's name (which is Latin for "star")
• Miss Havisham's destroyed property
• the moonrise and mists at evening

3. Ambiguity. An **ambiguity** is a statement that has a double meaning or a meaning that cannot be clearly resolved. At the end of the selection, Estella says that she and Pip must remain "friends apart," and Pip says, "I saw no shadow of another parting from her." In what different ways can this passage be interpreted? What particular word or words are used ambiguously? Do you think the author intended this ambiguity? If so, what effect might he have wanted the ambiguity to have? If not, which meaning did he intend?

Plot Analysis of *Great Expectations*

The Parts of a Plot

A **plot** is a series of events related to a **central conflict**, or struggle. The following diagram, known as Freytag's Pyramid, illustrates the main parts of a plot.

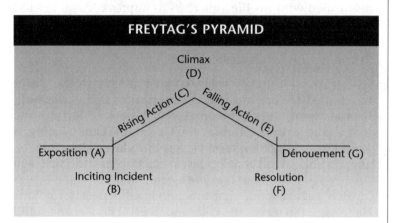

The parts of a plot are as follows:

The **exposition** is the part of a plot that provides background information, often about the characters, setting, or conflict.

The **inciting incident** is the event that introduces the central conflict.

The **rising action**, or **complication**, develops the conflict to a high point of intensity.

The **climax** is the high point of interest or suspense in the plot.

The **falling action** is all the events that follow the climax.

The **resolution** is the point at which the central conflict is ended, or resolved.

The **dénouement** is any material that follows the resolution and that ties up loose ends.

Exposition (A)

The reader first sees Pip as he stands alone in a churchyard at the graves of his parents and siblings. He is an orphan being raised by his surviving ill-tempered sister and her kind and simple husband, Joe Gargery. At the churchyard Pip is accosted by an escaped convict who demands Pip bring him food and a file to remove his leg irons. Greatly frightened, Pip supplies the convict with his requests.

Inciting Incident (B)

Pip lives a "common" life in the home of his blacksmith brother-in-law, to whom he plans to be apprenticed when he is older. Pip is offered work at Satis House, the home of the rich and eccentric Miss Havisham, and there he meets her young, beautiful, and proud adopted daughter, Estella. As a result of being exposed to the haughty Estella, Pip becomes dissatisfied with his life and vows to improve his status and become a gentleman.

Rising Action, or Complication (C)

After many unhappy years working at Satis House, Pip is indentured to Joe, and begins his training as a blacksmith. Joe's assistant, Orlick, becomes very jealous of Pip, fearing that Pip will replace him as Joe's assistant. One evening, a lawyer from London named Jaggers introduces himself to Joe and Pip and reveals that Pip has a secret benefactor, who will finance Pip's efforts to become a gentleman. Pip, and others in his village, assume that this unnamed benefactor is Miss Havisham. Pip leaves the village to live in London and fulfill his dream.

Climax (D)

Late one stormy night, several years after Pip has arrived in London, a coarse, older man appears at Pip's door. He identifies himself as Abel Magwitch, the convict whom Pip helped in the marshes years before. Magwitch has been a success in New South Wales, Australia, and reveals that he is Pip's secret benefactor. Pip recoils at having an association with such a man and vows to sever ties with him.

Falling Action (E)

Pip discovers that Magwitch is in danger because he has come back to England after being exiled, and feels responsible for Magwitch's safety. Pip, with his friends Herbert and Wemmick, plot to arrange for Magwitch's safe escape to Scotland. Meanwhile, Pip visits Miss Havisham and saves her when her clothes accidentally catch fire, injuring himself in the flames. Pip learns of Estella's true parentage. Pip is nearly killed by a vengeful Orlick but is saved by Herbert and others. At Wemmick's word, Magwitch, Pip, and Herbert set their plan to free Magwitch into action. They are thwarted by Compeyson, who has a grudge against Magwitch and has alerted the authorities to his presence in England. In the resulting confusion, Compeyson is killed and Magwitch is seriously injured.

Resolution (F)

Although seriously injured, Magwitch is made to stand trial, found guilty, and sentenced to death. Pip attends to Magwitch and reveals to the man on his deathbed that his daughter is alive and that Pip loves her. Pip is arrested for his debts and falls ill. He is nursed back to health by Joe, who also pays his debts and leaves unseen early one morning. Pip learns that Miss Havisham has died. He goes to visit Joe and Biddy, hoping to ask Biddy to marry him. Instead he finds it is Joe and Biddy's wedding day. He asks the two to forgive him for having neglected them while he lived his rich life in London, then leaves for Cairo, Egypt, to make a life for himself.

Dénouement (G)

Pip returns to England eleven years later, after meeting with some success, to find that Joe and Biddy have two children, one named after him. Pip decides to visit the empty site of Satis House, and there he discovers a much subdued Estella who has suffered much through her late abusive husband. The two leave together hand in hand.

Creative Writing Activities

Creative Writing Activity A: Obituary

Select one of the characters who dies in the novel—Mrs. Joe, Magwitch, or Miss Havisham—and write an obituary for this character. Before you begin writing, examine the kind of information generally included in an obituary by studying those in the local newspaper. Then skim through the novel to find information about the life of your chosen character. Before deciding which details to include and which to omit, remember that most obituaries list when, at what age, and how the person died, as well as some of his or her accomplishments and the person's surviving relatives. If you do not know some of these details, make them up, based on what you do know about the character. Also recall that most obituaries do not list a person's negative qualities. For example, a standard obituary probably would not include that Mrs. Joe mistreated Pip. However, you may wish to include some unusual details about your character in the obituary to make your chosen character "come alive" for the reader.

Creative Writing Activity B: Dramatic Scene

Dickens, like Mr. Wopsle, loved amateur theater. Try your hand as a playwright by selecting a scene or episode from the novel you particularly enjoyed and rewriting it as a dramatic scene. Dramatic scenes are composed of stage directions and dialogue. Except in some very rare cases, there is generally no narration, so a playwright must convey almost the entire action of a story through his or her characters' words and actions. Good examples of scenes to rewrite as drama include the scene when Pip first encounters the convict on the marshes, Estella's argument with Miss Havisham, Pip's meeting Magwitch on the dark and stormy night when he reveals that he is Pip's secret benefactor, Pip's revealing Estella's parentage to Wemmick and Jaggers and asking for information and advice from Jaggers, Wemmick's wedding, or Pip's meeting Estella again at the end of the novel.

Creative Writing Activity C: Point of View Experiment

Great Expectations is told from Pip's point of view, so his thoughts and perceptions color how the reader perceives events. Rewrite a scene or episode from the novel from another character's point of view. Choose the character whose point of view you would like to explore carefully, and think about this character's major personality traits to decide how this character would perceive events. You might, for example, rewrite one of the conflicts between Pip and Orlick from Orlick's point of view, write about the first encounter between Pip and Estella from Estella's point of view, write about Magwitch visiting Pip and announcing that he is Pip's secret benefactor from Magwitch's point of view, write the scene in which Jaggers verifies Magwitch's claim to be Pip's benefactor from Jaggers's point of view, or choose another particular scene and character's point of view to explore on your own. Consider how viewing that scene from a different character's perspective will affect the scene as a whole.

Creative Writing Activity D: Description

Dickens vividly describes many of his characters, but he does not describe Pip's physical appearance at length. Write your own description of Pip as you imagine him. Include such details as height, build, clothing, hair and eye color, posture, voice, special features and so on.

Creative Writing Activity E: Character Sketch

Dickens creates memorable and malicious villains in the characters of Orlick and Compeyson. Imagine your own villain and describe this person in a character sketch. Orlick is described as slouching and as appearing suddenly out of the mist, while Compeyson by all outward appearances is a gentleman. What does your villain look like? Is his or her appearance ominous or unsettling, or does your villain deceptively appear to be good-natured? What does your villain do that makes him or her a villain? What motivates him or her to act as he or she does? Freewrite answers to the above questions before writing your character sketch of a villain.

Critical Writing Activities

The following topics are suitable for short critical essays on *Great Expectations*. An essay written on one of these topics should begin with an introductory paragraph that states the thesis, or main idea, of the essay. The introductory paragraph should be followed by several paragraphs that support the thesis using evidence from the novel. The essay should conclude with a paragraph that summarizes the points made in the body of the essay and resolves the thesis.

Critical Writing Activity A: Theme—Goodness

A basic theme of *Great Expectations* is that goodness comes from inner worth and not from money or social position. Write an essay on the theme of goodness in the novel. In your essay, discuss the characters who exhibit true goodness, and how it is reflected in their words and actions. To demonstrate this theme, you may also wish to contrast the "good" characters with the characters who have money or higher social positions, but lack "goodness."

Critical Writing Activity B: *Bildungsroman*

Great Expectations is an example of a *Bildungsroman,* or a novel that tells the story of the growth or development of a person from youth to adulthood. What major changes does Pip undergo over the course of the story? What events or experiences create such changes? Discuss your responses to these questions in an essay. You may wish to refer to your responses to the Understanding Literature questions on *Bildungsroman* on pages 109 and 484.

Critical Writing Activity C: Comparing and Contrasting the Roles of Magwitch and Miss Havisham

Miss Havisham strives to make Estella into a lady. Magwitch works to make a fortune so that he can make Pip into a gentleman. How does each go about his or her task? Why are both Magwitch and Miss Havisham eager to change their young charges? Is either one successful? Why, or why not? Does the social status of Miss Havisham and of Magwitch affect their success? Use these questions as you examine the efforts of Miss Havisham and Magwitch. Then, in an essay, compare and contrast their methods, motives, and the results.

Critical Writing Activity D: Analyzing the Endings

Read both the original ending and Dickens's revised ending for *Great Expectations* (see page 512). Critics have made arguments for and against each ending. Which ending do you think is more fitting to the rest of the novel? Examine mood, tone, meaning, and effect in each ending. In what way does each element relate to the general or overall mood, tone, meaning, and effect of the novel? You may wish to review your answers to Synthesizing and Understanding Literature questions throughout the novel as you consider the novel as a whole. Then, in a thesis statement, identify which ending you think is more appropriate, and why. Then use examples from both endings and other parts of the text to support your decision.

Critical Writing Activity E: Theme—Justice

The life of a criminal pays a major role in this novel. Dickens vividly describes hunts for escaped convicts, visits to prisons, and court scenes. In what light are justice, the law, and those who represent criminals presented in the novel? What attitudes toward convicts and prisoners are represented? In what way do these attitudes contribute to or highlight major themes in the novel?

Critical Writing Activity F: Characterization

Choose one of the following characters or another character from *Great Expectations* whom you find interesting:

- Estella
- Miss Havisham
- Joe
- Wemmick

Examine the way this character is developed throughout the novel. In your thesis, make a claim about the character's main traits and why these traits are important to the story. Then, using descriptions of the character or examples of the character's speech or actions, discuss the development of the character and the character's role in the story.

Projects

Project A: Holding a Debate

Divide into small groups. Each group member should choose a character to represent. Select a character such as Uncle Pumblechook, Mrs. Pocket, Mr. Pocket, Pip, Joe, Orlick, Miss Havisham, Estella, Compeyson, Mr. Wopsle, Jaggers, Mr. Wemmick, Magwitch, Molly, or Mrs. Joe. Think about how your chosen character would feel about the values and lifestyles of other characters on your chosen panel. As preparation, you may wish to review sections of the novel in which your character appears. Conduct a debate so that each character can defend his or her lifestyle or values. You may wish to dress up as your chosen character or use a prop to represent that character. Try to speak in a manner appropriate to your chosen character, to state your values and ideals clearly, and to provide your chosen character's reactions to the values of others.

Project B: Enacting a Scene

Divide into small groups and enact and videotape an interesting or dramatic scene from the novel. Use dialogue from the novel and the settings that are described as the basis of your scene. You may wish to complete Creative Writing Assignment B before you undertake this project, so that you will have a script to work with. Assign roles to enact among your group, as well as assigning the task of videotaping your performance.

Project C: Drawing the Characters

Using the physical descriptions of the characters provided in the novel as well as your own imagination, draw a representation of at least three different characters. Select one of the following mediums for your illustration—chalk, paint, colored marker, or pencil. Think about which characters at which moments might be interesting to represent artistically. For example, you might choose to draw Miss Havisham viewing her rotten wedding cake, Jaggers washing his hands, or Magwitch as a convict hiding on the marshes.

Project D: Researching the Legal System

As you have read in "The Life and Works of Charles Dickens" on page vi, Dickens was familiar with the English legal system, having worked at a law firm and as a court reporter. Later in his life he was involved in a lengthy suit in the court of chancery when he sued publishers for a breach of copyright. Dickens used his own experiences in the legal system as the basis for much of the material in *Great Expectations* and other novels. Working in small groups, research the legal system in England during the Victorian period. Consider focusing your research on the training and qualifications of lawyers, the rights of the accused, the rules of procedure of a trial, the nature and severity of punishments, or the differences between courts of common law and courts of chancery. Compare the information you uncover to the information provided in the novel about the legal system.

Glossary

PRONUNCIATION KEY

VOWEL SOUNDS

a	hat	ō	go	ʉ	burn
ā	play	ô	paw, born	ə	extra
ä	star	oo	book, put		under
e	then	o͞o	blue, stew		civil
ē	me	oi	boy		honor
i	sit	ou	wow		bogus
ī	my	u	up		

CONSONANT SOUNDS

b	but	l	lip	t	sit
ch	watch	m	money	th	with
d	do	n	on	v	valley
f	fudge	ŋ	song, sink	w	work
g	go	p	pop	y	yell
h	hot	r	rod	z	pleasure
j	jump	s	see		
k	brick	sh	she		

A

a • based (ə bāsd´) *adj.*, degraded; lowered in value

a • bashed (ə bashd´) *adj.*, embarrassed

ab • er • ra • tion (ab´ər ā´shən) *n.*, mental derangement

a • bet (ə bet´) *vt.*, encourage and assist

a • bey • ance (ə bā´əns) *n.*, temporary suspension of activity

ab • hor • rence (ab hôr´əns) *n.*, loathing; hatred

ab • hor • rent (əb hôr´ənt) *adj.*, causing disgust and hatred

ab • ject (ab´jekt) *adj.*, miserable; wretched

ab • lu • tion (ab lo͞o´shən) *n.*, washing of the body

a • bom • i • nate (ə bäm´ə nāt´) *vt.*, feel hatred and disgust for; loathe

a • breast (ə brest´) *adv.*, side by side

ab • solve (ab zälv´) *vt.*, pronounce free of blame or guilt

ab • sti • nence (ab´stə nəns) *n.*, act of voluntarily doing without something

a • byss (ə bis´) *n.*, yawning gulf; huge gape

ac • ces • so • ry (ak ses´ər ē) *adj.*, helping in an unlawful act

ac • cord (ə kôrd´) *vt.*, give; grant; bestow

ac • cost (ə kôst´) *vt.*, confront

ac • cred • it (ə kred´it) *vt.*, authorize

ac • cu • mu • lat • ing (ə kyo͞om´yo͞o lāt´iŋ) *adj.*, growing in number

ac • cu • mu • la • tive (ə kyo͞om´yo͞o lət iv) *adj.*, collected; gathered together ac • qui • esce (ak´wē es´) vi., consent

ac • qui • es • cence (ak´wē es´əns) n., agreement without protest

ac • qui • si • tion (ak´wə zish´ən) n., acquiring; attainment

ac • quit (ə kwit´) vt., clear from a criminal charge

a • cute • ness (ə kyo͞ot´nəs) n., sharpness; intensity

ad • a • man • tine (ad´ə man´tin) adj., unbreakable; unyielding

a • dept (ə dept´) n., expert

ad • here (ad hir´) vi., stick; stay firm

ad • journ (ə jʉrn´) vt., move from one place to another

ad • junct (a´jʉŋkt) n., thing added to something else, but secondary or not essential to it

ad • ju • ra • tion (aj´o͞o rā´shən) n., solemn command; earnest appeal

ad • jure (ə jo͞or´) vt., appeal to earnestly

ad • mi • ra • tion (ad´mə rā´shən) n., regarding with delight and pleased approval

ad • mis • sion (ad mish´ən) n., giving as a right; entrance

ad • mon • ish (ad män´ish) vt., advise

ad • ver • sar • y (ad´vər ser´ē) n., opponent; enemy

af • fa • ble (af´ə bəl) adj., gentle and kindly

af • fin • i • ty (ə fin´ə tē) n., similarity

af • firm • a • tive (ə fʉrm´ə tiv) n., answer showing agreement

af • flu • ent (af´lo͞o ənt) adj., rich; prosperous

af • front (ə frunt´) n., open insult

a • ghast (ə gast´) adj., horrified

ag • i • tate (aj´i tāt´) vt., excite; disturb

ag • o • niz • ing (ag´ə nīz´iŋ) adj., distressing; tormenting

al • le • vi • ate (ə lē´vē āt) vt., make more bearable

al • lot • ed (ə lät´´d) adj., given or assigned

al • loy (al´oi) n., anything added that lowers value or purity

al • lude (ə lo͞od´) vi., refer in an indirect way

al • lu • sion (ə lo͞o´zhən) n., casual reference

al • ma • nac (ôl´mə nak´) n., book that contains information, usually statistical, on many subjects

al • ter • ca • tion (ôl´tər kā´shən) n., angry quarrel

al • ter • nate • ly (ôl´tər nit´lē) adv., by turns; following each other continuously

am • ble (am´bəl) vi., walk in a leisurely manner

a • men • i • ty (ə men´ə tē) n., attractive or desirable feature

a • mi • a • ble (ā´mē ə bəl) adj., good-natured; likable

a • mi • a • bly (ā´mē ə blē) adv., good-naturedly

a • miss (ə mis´) adj., wrong; faulty; improper

am • phib • i • ous (am fib´ē əs) adj., that can live both on land and in water

an • i • ma • ted (an´ə mā´təd) adj., lively

an • i • mos • i • ty (an´ə mäs´ə tē) n., feeling of strong dislike or hatred; ill will; hostility

an • te • ced • ent (an´tə sēd´´nt) n., previous happenings

a • pos • tro • phe (ə päs′trə fē) *n.*, words addressed to an absent or imaginary person

ap • pall • ing (ə pôl′iŋ) *adj.*, causing shock or dismay

ap • pa • ri • tion (ap′ə rish′ən) *n.*, unexpected appearance

ap • pease (ə pēz′) *vt.*, satisfy or relieve

ap • pend • age (ə pen′dij) *n.*, something that is attached

ap • praise (ə prāz′) *vt.*, decide the value of

ap • pre • hend (ap′rē hend′) *vt.*, understand

ap • pre • hen • sion (ap′rē hen′shən) *n.*, anxious feeling of foreboding; dread

ap • prise (ə prīz′) *vt.*, inform; make aware

ap • pro • ba • tion (ap′rə bā′shən) *n.*, official approval, sanction, or commendation

ap • pro • pri • ate (ə prō′prē āt′) *vt.*, take for one's own use

arch • ly (ärch′lē) *adv.*, mischievously

ar • id (ar′id) *adj.*, dry and barren; not interesting

a • ris • to • crat • ic (ə ris′tə krat′ik) *adj.*, having the tastes, manners, and other characteristics of the upper class

ar • ray (ə rā′) *n.*, fine clothes

ar • ti • fice (är′tə fis) *n.*, skillful trick

art • less • ness (ärt′lis nəs) *n.*, lack of deceit; innocence; naiveté

as • cer • tain (as′ər tān′) *vt.*, learn; find out with certainty

as • pi • ra • tion (as′pə rā′shən) *n.*, strong desire or ambition

as • sail (ə sāl′) *vt.*, attack with force

as • sail • ant (ə sāl′ənt) *n.*, one who attacks or assaults

as • sent (ə sent′) *vi.*, agree; consent

as • sev • er • ate (ə sev′ə rāt′) *vt.*, assert; state seriously or positively

as • si • du • i • ty (as′ə dyo͞o′ə tē) *n.*, diligence; constant attention

as • sume (ə so͞om′) *vt.*, adopt; pretend to have

a • sun • der (ə sun′dər) *adv.*, apart; into parts or pieces

at • test (ə test′) *vt.*, certify; declare valid

au • di • ble (ô′də bəl) *adj.*, able to be heard

aug • ment (ôg ment′) *vt.*, increase

aus • pi • cious (ôs′pish′əs) *adj.*, favorable

a • vail (ə vāl′) *vt.*, take advantage; make use

av • a • rice (av′ə ris) *n.*, greed for riches

av • a • ri • cious (av′ə rish′əs) *adj.*, greedy

a • veng • ing (ə venj′iŋ) *adj.*, retaliating; revengeful

a • verse (ə vʉrs′) *adj.*, reluctant; opposed

a • ver • sion (ə vʉr′zhən) *n.*, intense dislike

a • vow • al (ə vou′əl) *n.*, acknowledgment

B

badg • er (baj′ər) *vt.*, pester

base • ly (bās′lē) *adv.*, rudely

bas • est (bās′est) *adj.*, most contemptible; most despicable

bea • con (bēk′'n) *n.*, lighthouse

bear • ings (ber´iŋz) *n.,* position or situation relative to the circumstances

be • moan (bi mōn´) *vt.,* mourn over; express grief for

be • ne • fi • cent (bə nef´ə sənt) *adj.,* doing good

be • reaved (bē rēvd´) *adj.,* left in a state of loss and grief

be • reave • ment (bē rēv´mənt) *n.,* loss, as by death

be • reft (bi reft´) *adj.,* deprived; lacking something needed

be • siege (bē sēg´) *vt.,* surround with armed forces for a sustained attack

be • stir (bē stʉr´) *vt.,* exert or busy (oneself)

bland • ly (bland´lē) *adv.,* in a dull way

bla • tant (blāt´'nt) *adj.,* disagreeably loud or boisterous

blight (blīt) *vt.,* disappoint; frustrate; wither the hopes of

blight • ed (blīt´id) *adj.,* destroyed; with no growth or life

bliss (blis) *n.,* great joy or happiness

blithe (blīth) *adj.,* cheerful; carefree

blun • der • ing (blun´dər iŋ) *adj.,* clumsy; foolish

blus • ter • ous (blus´tər əs) *adj.,* noisy, swaggering, or bullying in manner of speech

boor • ish (boor´ish) *adj.,* ill-mannered

bram • ble (bram´bəl) *n.,* prickly shrub

breadth (bredth) *n.,* range; broadness; width

brood (brood) *vi.,* ponder in a troubled way

brute (broot) *n.,* person who is cruel and crude

C

cal • lous (kal´əs) *adj.,* unfeeling

can • did (kan´did) *adj.,* honest

can • dor (kan´dər) *n.,* honesty; frankness

ca • pa • cious (kə pā´shəs) *adj.,* roomy

ca • pac • i • ty (kə pas´i tē) *n.,* position in which one functions; role

cap • i • tal (kap´ət´l) *n.,* wealth

ca • pri • cious (kə prish´əs) *adj.,* changing without apparent reason; inconstant

cap • size (kap´sīz) *vt.,* overturn

cease (sēs) *vi.,* come to an end

char • ter (chärt´ər) *vt.,* authorize; commission

chasm (kaz´əm) *n.,* deep crack or opening in the earth's surface

chaste (chāst) *adj.,* pure; decent

chol • er • ic (käl´ər ik) *adj.,* bad-tempered; irritable

chron • ic (krän´ik) *adj.,* habitual

cir • cu • i • tous • ly (sər kyoo´ə təs lē) *adv.,* indirectly; in a roundabout way

cir • cum • stan • tial (sʉr´kəm stan´shəl) *adj.,* based on circumstances or evidence

clem • en • cy (klem´ən sē) *n.,* forbearance or mercy, as toward an offender

co • er • cion (kō ʉr´shən) *n.,* government by force

cof • fers (kô´fərz) *pl.n.,* funds

co • gent (kō´jənt) *adj.*, valid

co • her • ent (kō hir´ənt) *adj.*, clear, understandable

col • lect • ed (kə lek´tid) *adj.*, in control of oneself

com • bat (kəm bat´) *vi.*, struggle

com • mence (kə mens´) *vi.*, begin

com • mis • er • ate (kə miz´ər āt´) *vt.*, express pity for

com • mis • er • a • tion (kə miz´ər ā´shən) *n.*, feeling of sympathy for the distress of another

com • mit (kə mit´) *vt.*, make known the opinions or views of

com • mo • di • ous (kə mō´dē əs) *adj.*, spacious

com • mune (kə myo͞on´) *vi.*, have close rapport or communication

com • pass (kum´pəs) *vt.*, comprehend

com • pe • tent (käm´pə tənt) *adj.*, qualified; capable

com • pla • cen • cy (kəm plā´sən sē) *n.*, contentment; quiet satisfaction

com • pla • cent (kəm plā´sənt) *adj.*, self-satisfied

com • pla • cent • ly (kəm plā´sənt lē) *adv.*, with self-satisfaction; smugly

com • plex • ion (kəm plek´shən) *n.*, general character or tone

com • ply (kəm plī´) *vi.*, act in accordance with a command or request

com • pose (kəm pōz´) *vt.*, make calm

com • posed • ly (kəm pō´zid lē) *adv.*, calmly; tranquilly

com • po • sure (kəm pō´zhər) *n.*, calmness of mind or manner

com • pre • hend • ed (käm´prə hend´əd) *adj.*, included

com • pre • hen • sive (käm´pre hen´siv) *adj.*, large; extensive

com • prise (kəm prīz´) *vt.*, consist of; include

con • cede (kən sēd´) *vt.*, grant as a right or privilege; acknowledge

con • ces • sion (kən sesh´ən) *n.*, act of acknowledging as true

con • cil • i • ate (kən sil´ē āt´) *vt.*, win over; gain good will of

con • cil • i • a • to • ry (kən sil´ē ə tôr´ē) *adj.*, tending to reconcile; overcoming another's distrust

con • clu • sive (kən klo͞o´siv) *adj.*, that settles a question; final

con • course (kän´kôrs´) *n.*, open area where crowds gather

con • cur (kən kʉr´) *vi.*, agree

con • cus • sion (kən kush´ən) *n.*, blow; violent shock

con • dem • na • tion (kän´dem nā´shən) *n.*, pronouncement of guilt

con • de • scend (kän´də send´) *vi.*, lower oneself

con • de • scen • sion (kän di sen´shən) *n.*, willingness to descend to the level of a social inferior and bestow kindness, often in a patronizing way

con • duce (kən do͞os´) *vi.*, contribute; lead

con • fi • dence (kän´fə dəns) *n.*, something told as a secret

con • fine • ment (kən fīn´mənt) *n.*, restriction; restraint

con • fla • gra • tion (kän´flə grā´shən) *n.*, big, destructive fire

con • found (kən found´) *vt.*, confuse

con • ge • la • tion (kän´jə lā´shən) *n.*, solidifying or thickening by cooling or freezing

con • junc • tion (kən juŋk´shən) *n.*, combination; being joined

con • nu • bi • al (kə no͞o´bē əl) *adj.*, of marriage

con • sci • en • tious (kän´shē en´shəs) *adj.*, thorough; diligent; painstaking con • sign (kən sīn´) *vt.*, place in the care of another

con • so • la • tion (kän´sə lā´shən) *n.*, comfort

con • sol • a • to • ry (kən säl´ə tôr´ē) *adj.*, comforting

con • sort (kən sôrt´) *vi.*, keep company

con • ster • na • tion (kän´stər nā´shən) *n.*, great fear or shock that makes one feel helpless

con • sti • tu • tion • al • ly (kän´stə tōō´shən əl ē) *adv.*, by nature or temperament

con • strain • ed • ly (kən strā´nid lē) *adv.*, in a forced and unnatural manner

con • struc • tion (kən struk´shən) *n.*, interpretation

con • strue (kən strōō´) *vt.*, interpret

con • tam • i • nat • ed (kən tam´ə nāt´´d) *adj.*, infected; impure; corrupted

con • tem • plate (kän´təm plāt´) *vt.*, consider carefully

con • tempt • i • ble (kən temp´tə bəl) *adj.*, deserving scorn

con • temp • tu • ous (kən temp´chōō əs) *adj.*, scornful

con • tend (kən tend´) *vi.*, vie; strive in competition; argue

con • ten • tion (kən ten´shən) *n.*, argument

con • tig • u • ous (kən tig´yōō əs) *adj.*, adjacent; near

con • tin • gent (kən tin´jənt) *adj.*, dependent upon conditions or events not yet established

con • tract (kən trakt´) *vt.*, acquire

con • tract (kən trakt´) *vt.*, reduce in size; limit

con • trite (kən trīt´) *adj.*, showing remorse or sorrow

con • tri • tion (kən tri´shən) *n.*, remorse for having done wrong

con • triv • ance (kən trīv´əns) *n.*, invention; clever device

con • tu • ma • cious • ly (kän´tyōō mā´shəs lē) *adv.*, disobediently

con • ven • tion • al (kən ven´shə nəl) *adj.*, conforming to accepted standards

con • vert (kən vʉrt´) *vt.*, transform; change

con • vul • sive (kən vul´siv) *adj.*, marked by shakes, spasms, or jitters

co • pi • ous (kō´pē əs) *adj.*, plentiful

cor • dial (kôr´jəl) *adj.*, warm and friendly

cor • rob • o • rate (kə räb´ə rāt´) *vt.*, confirm; support

cor • ru • gat • ed (kôr´ə gāt´əd) *adj.*, wrinkled

coun • te • nance (koun´tə nəns) *n.*, look on a person's face that shows his or her feelings

coun • ter • part (koun´tər pärt´) *n.*, thing that goes with something else to make a set

cra • vat (krə vat´) *n.*, necktie or scarf

cre • dence (krē´dəns) *n.*, belief in a report of another

cre • den • tial (kri den´shəl) *n.*, written evidence of qualification

crest • fall • en (krest´fôl´ən) *adj.*, disappointed

cringe (krinj) *vi.*, shrink back with fear; act like a slave

cross- • ex • am • ine (krôs´ig zam´in) *vt.*, question closely

cul • mi • nate (kul´mə nāt´) *vt.*, bring to the highest point

cu • pid • i • ty (kyōō pid´ə tē) *n.*, greed

D

dan • dle (dan´dəl) *vt.*, play with

dazed (dāzd) *adj.*, bewildered

de • bil • i • tat • ing (di bil´ə tāt´iŋ) *adj.*, weakening

de • cant • er (dē kant´ər) *n.*, decorative glass bottle

de • cease (di sēs´) *n.*, death

de • cid • ed (dē sīd´id) *adj.*, definite; clear-cut

dec • la • ma • tion (dek´lə mā´shən) *n.*, loud and showy way of speaking

deem (dēm) *vt.*, judge

de • fer (di fur´) *vi.*, submit to the opinion of another

def • er • en • tial (def´ə ren´shəl) *adj.*, showing courteous respect

de • fi • ance (dē fī´əns) *n.*, open, bold resistance to authority

de • fi • cien • cy (di fish´ən sē) *n.*, defectiveness; lack of something essential

de • fi • cient (dē fish´ənt) *adj.*, lacking; incomplete; defective

de • ject • ed (dē jek´tid) *adj.*, depressed; in low spirits

del • e • gate (del´ə gāt) *vt.*, appoint

de • lib • e • rate (di lib´ər āt´) *vt.*, consider carefully

del • i • ca • cy (del´i kə sē) *n.*, tact in handling an issue

de • lir • i • ous (di lir´ē əs) *adj.*, raving wildly

de • lu • sion (di lo͞o´zhən) *n.*, false belief

de • note (dē nōt´) *vt.*, indicate; stand for

de • nounc • ing (di nouns´iŋ) *adj.*, condemning openly

de • nun • ci • a • tion (dē nun´sē ā´shən) *n.*, public criticism

de • pose (dē pōz´) *vi.*, bear witness

de • pose (dē pōz´) *vt.*, state or testify under oath, but out of court

de • pose (dē pōz´) *vt.*, remove from office or a position of power

de • pre • ci • a • tion (di prē´shē ā´shən) *n.*, belittling; lowering of value

de • pre • ci • a • to • ry (di prē´shē ə tôr´ē) *adj.*, belittling

dep • u • ty (dep´yə tē) *n.*, person appointed to substitute for another

de • ri • sion (di rizh´ən) *n.*, contempt or ridicule

de • ri • sive • ly (də rī´siv lē) *adv.*, with scorn

de • rive (di rīv´) *vt.*, trace from a source

de • scry (di skrī´) *vt.*, discover; detect; see

de • sign (di zīn´) *n.*, plan

de • sign • ing (di zī´niŋ) *adj.*, conniving; crafty

de • sist (di zist´) *vi.*, stop

de • spair (di sper´) *vi.*, feel or show hopelessness

de • spond • en • cy (di spän´dən sē) *n.*, loss of courage or hope

de • spond • ent (di spän´dənt) *adj.*, feeling hopeless

des • pot • ic (des pät´ik) *adj.*, like a dictator; tyrannical

de • ter (dē tur´) *vt.*, discourage from acting

det • ri • men • tal (det´rə men´t'l) *adj.*, harmful

de • vi • ate (dē´vē āt´) *vi.*, turn aside

de • vise (di vīz´) *vt.*, plan; contrive

de • volve (di välv´) *vi.*, be passed on or delegated

dex • ter • i • ty (deks ter´ə tē) *n.,* skill

dex • ter • ous (deks´tər əs) *adj.,* skilled in the use of hands or body

di • a • bol • i • cal (dī´ə bäl´i kəl) *adj.,* wicked or cruel

dif • fi • dence (dif´ə dens) *n.,* shyness

di • lap • i • dat • ed (də lap´ə dāt´id) *adj.,* shabby and neglected

di • late (dī´ lāt) *vt.,* expand

di • min • ish • ing (də min´ish iŋ) *adj.,* reducing; making smaller

dis • af • fec • tion (dis´ə fek´shən) *n.,* disloyalty; withdrawal of friendship

dis • cern • i • ble (di zʉrn´ə bəl) *adj.,* recognizable

dis • charge (dis´chärj) *n.,* firing

dis • charged (dis chärjd´) *adj.,* released

dis • close (dis klōz´) *vt.,* reveal

dis • com • fi • ture (dis kum´fi chər) *n.,* frustration; confusion; embarrassment

dis • con • cert • ed (dis´kən sʉrt´əd) *adj.,* upset

dis • con • so • late • ly (dis kän´sə lit lē) *adv.,* unhappily

dis • course (dis kôrs´) *vi.,* carry on conversation

dis • course (dis´kôrs) *n.,* speech; conversation

dis • cre • tion (di skresh´ən) *n.,* quality of being careful of what one does or says; good judgment; freedom to act on one's own

dis • crep • an • cy (di skrep´ən sē) *n.,* difference; lack of agreement

dis • dain (dis dān´) *n.,* scorn

dis • en • gage (dis´in gāj´) *vt.,* release from something that holds or entangles

dis • gorge (dis gôrj´) *vt.,* throw out

dis • par • age • ment (di spar´ij mənt) *n.,* anything that discredits or lowers in esteem

dis • par • i • ty (di spar´ə tē) *n.,* inequality or difference

dis • pel (dis pel´) *vt.,* drive away

dis • perse (dis pʉrs´) *vt.,* scatter

dis • pir • i • ted (dis pir´it əd) *adj.,* disheartened; depressed

dis • po • si • tion (dis´pə zish´ən) *n.,* nature; temperament

dis • pu • ta • tious (dis´pyo͞o tā´shəs) *adj.,* fond of arguing

dis • qui • et (dis kwī´ət) *n.,* uneasiness

dis • si • pat • ed (dis´ə pā´tid) *adj.,* unrestrained in the pursuit of pleasure

dis • so • ci • ate (di sō´shē āt´) *vt.,* separate

dis • tinct • ly (di stiŋkt´lē) *adv.,* clearly

dis • tor • tion (di stôr´shən) *n.,* misrepresentation; twisted information

dis • traught (di strôt´) *adj.,* extremely anxious; frantic; very troubled

di • verge (dī vʉrj´) *vi.,* depart

di • ver • sion (di vʉr´zhən) *n.,* something that distracts the mind and entertains

di • vert (də vʉrt´) *vt.,* distract attention

di • vest (də vest´) *vt.,* rid; dispossess

di • vine (də vīn´) *vt.,* guess or find out

di • vulge (də vulj´) *vt.,* reveal

dog • ged • ly (dôg´id lē) *adv.,* stubbornly; persistently

dole • ful • ly (dōl´fəl lē) *adv.,* mournfully; sadly

do • mes • tic (dō mes´tik) *adj.,* having to do with the home or house-keeping

do • min • ion (də min´yən) *n.,* governed territory or country

drawl (drôl) *vi.,* speak in a slow and lazy manner

driv • el • ing (driv´əl iŋ) *adj.,* slobbering

droll (drōl) *adj.,* amusingly odd

du • bi • ous • ly (doo´bē əs lē) *adv.,* doubtfully; with hesitation

E

ear • nest • ly (ʉr´nist lē) *adv.,* sincerely; with urgency

ec • cen • tric (ek sen´trik) *adj.,* odd or unconventional

ec • cen • tri • cal • ly (ek sen´trik lē) *adv.,* oddly; unevenly

ed • dy (ed´ē) *n.,* swirling current of air

ed • i • fy • ing (ed´i fī´iŋ) *adj.,* encouraging; heartening

e • gress (ē´gres´) *n.,* exit; way out

e • ject • ed (ē jek´tid) *adj.,* thrown out

e • lic • it (ē lis´it) *vt.,* draw forth; evoke

e • lix • ir (i lik´sər) *n.,* medicinal potion

el • o • cu • tion (el´ə kyoo´shən) *n.,* style of speaking or reading in public

el • o • quence (el´ə kwəns) *n.,* graceful expressiveness

e • lude (ē lood´) *vt.,* avoid; escape

e • man • ci • pa • tion (ē man´sə pā´shən) *n.,* freedom from bondage

em • bel • lish • ment (əm bel´ish mənt) *n.,* ornamentation; something that serves to make fancier

em • bod • i • ment (em bäd´i mənt) *n.,* ideal, visible form

em • i • nent • ly (em´ə nənt lē) *adv.,* remarkably

em • phat • ic (em fat´ik) *adj.,* expressed with emphasis

em • phat • i • cal • ly (em fat´ik lē) *adv.,* with emphasis

en • croach (en krōch´) *vi.,* trespass or intrude

en • cum • ber (en kum´bər) *vt.,* load or weigh down

en • deav • or (en dev´ər) *vi.,* make an earnest attempt

en • dowed (en doud´) *adj.,* provided with income or specified qualities

en • gag • ing (en gā´jiŋ) *adj.,* charming

en • gen • der (en jen´dər) *vt.,* bring about; cause; produce

en • sue (en soo´) *vi.,* follow immediately

en • ter • tain (en´tər tān´) *vt.,* hold

en • thrall • ing (en thrôl´iŋ) *adj.,* captivating; fascinating

en • treat (in trēt´) *vt.,* ask earnestly

en • treat • ing • ly (in trēt´iŋ lē) *adv.,* pleadingly; earnestly

er • rant (er´ənt) *adj.,* roving; wandering

er • u • di • tion (er´yoo dish´ən) *n.,* learning acquired by reading and study

es • teem (ə stēm´) *vt.,* value

es • teem (ə stēm´) *n.,* respect; regard

e • va • sion (ē vā´zhən) *n.*, avoiding or escaping by cleverness or deceit

e • va • sive • ly (ē vā´siv lē) *adv.*, in a manner characterized by avoiding

ev • i • dent • ly (ev´ə dənt´lē) *adv.*, obviously; clearly

e • vince (ē vins´) *vt.*, show plainly; indicate

e • voke (ē vōk´) *vt.*, call forth or summon

ex • act (ig zakt´) *vt.*, demand; require

ex • al • ta • tion (eg´zôl tā´shən) *n.*, being raised in status

ex • as • per • at • ing (eg zas´pər āt´iŋ) *adj.*, irritating; frustrating

ex • cres • cence (eks kres´əns) *n.*, abnormal or disfiguring outgrowth

ex • e • crate (ek´si krāt´) *vt.*, speak abusively; curse; denounce scathingly

ex • e • cute (ek´si kyo͞ot´) *vt.*, carry out; perform

ex • e • cu • tion (ek´si kyo͞o´shən) *n.*, act of carrying out

ex • em • pla • ry (eg zem´plə rē) *adj.*, serving as a model or example

ex • hort (eg zôrt´) *vt.*, urge

ex • on • er • ate (eg zän´ər āt´) *vt.*, free from a charge

ex • or • di • um (eg zôr´dē əm) *n.*, opening part of an oration or speech

ex • pa • tri • ate (eks pā´trē āt´) *vt.*, drive from one's native land

ex • pec • to • rate (ek spek´tə rāt´) *vt.*, cough up and spit out

ex • plic • it (eks plis´it) *adj.*, clearly stated

ex • po • si • tion (ek´spə zish´ən) *n.*, setting forth of meaning

ex • pos • tu • la • to • ry (eks päs´chə lə tôr´ē) *adj.*, reasoning with a person or objecting to his or her actions

ex • qui • site (ek skwi´zit) *adj.*, intense; acute

ex • tent (ek stent´) *n.*, range or limits

ex • ten • u • at • ing (ek sten´yo͞o wāt´iŋ) *adj.*, serving as an excuse

ex • tort (eks tôrt´) *vt.*, get money or goods from someone by violence, threats, or misuse of authority

ex • tract (eks trakt´) *vt.*, draw out by effort; pull out by force

ex • trav • a • gant (ek strav´ə gənt) *adj.*, given to excessive spending

ex • trem • i • ty (ek strem´ə tē) *n.*, extreme measure; severe or strong action

ex • tri • cate (eks´tri kāt) *vt.*, set free; release

ex • u • ber • ant (eg zo͞o´bər ənt) *adj.*, full of life

ex • ult (eg zult´) *vi.*, rejoice

ex • ult • ant (eg zult´´nt) *adj.*, triumphant

ex • ult • ing • ly (eg zult´iŋ lē) *adv.*, jubilantly; joyfully

F

fa • ce • tious (fə sē´shəs) *adj.*, witty

faint (fānt) *adj.*, weak; barely perceptible

fal • ter (fôl´ter) *vi.*, speak haltingly; stammer

fawn (fôn) *vi.*, act servilely; cringe and flatter

fea • si • ble (fē´zə bəl) *adj.*, likely; possible

feign (fān) *vt.*, pretend

fe • lic • i • tous (fə lis´i təs) *adj.*, appropriate

fe • lo • ni • ous (fə lō´nē əs) *adj.*, relating to crimes

fer • ment • ing (fər ment´iŋ) *adj.*, bubbling up

fe • roc • i • ty (fə räs´ə tē) *n.*, state or quality of being fierce or savage

fer • vent (fʉr´vənt) *adj.*, showing great warmth of feeling

fic • tion (fik´shən) *n.*, imaginary idea

fi • del • i • ty (fə del´ə tē) *n.*, faithfulness; trustworthiness

file (fīl) *n.*, steel tool with rough, ridged surface for grinding

flac • cid (flak´sid) *adj.*, weak; feeble

flaw (flô) *vt.*, spoil

flay (flā) *vt.*, strip off (the skin of)

flight • y (flīt´ē) *adj.*, crazy

flint (flint) *n.*, hard, sharp stone

floun • der (floun´dər) *vi.*, struggle awkwardly to move

flour • ish (flʉr´ish) *n.*, any motion done in a showy way

fol • ly (fäl´ē) *n.*, foolishness

for • bear • ance (fôr ber´əns) *n.*, self-control; patient restraint

forge (fôrj) *vt.*, make a fake document

for • lorn (fôr lôrn´) *adj.*, miserable; pitiful

for • mal • i • ty (fôr mal´ə tē) *n.*, observing of prescribed customs, rules, or ceremonies

for • ti • fied (fôrt´ə fīd) *adj.*, strengthened

for • ti • tude (fôr´tə tōod´) *n.*, firm courage and strength

for • tu • i • tous • ly (fôr tōo´ə təs lē) *adv.*, fortunately

fos • ter (fôs´tər) *vt.*, promote the development of; cultivate

fraud (frôd) *n.*, deception

fraught (frôt) *adj.*, filled

frayed (frād) *adj.*, worn or ragged

fri • vol • i • ty (fri väl´ə tē) *n.*, quality of silliness; amusement

frow • zy (frou´zē) *adj.*, untidy; sloppy

fu • gi • tive (fyōo´jə tiv) *n.*, person fleeing from the law

fu • ne • re • al (fyōo nir´ē əl) *adj.*, sad and solemn; gloomy

fur • rowed (fʉr´ōd) *adj.*, deeply wrinkled

G

gar • land (gär´lənd) *n.*, decorative wreath or woven chain of flowers or leaves

gen • er • ate (jen´ə rāt) *vt.*, bring into existence

ghast • ly (gast´lē) *adj.*, horrible; ghostlike

glad • i • a • tor (glad´ē ā´tər) *n.*, prizefighter; warrior

gloat (glōt) *vi.*, express malicious pleasure

goad (gōd) *vt.*, drive; urge on

god • send (gäd send´) *n.*, anything unexpected or needed that comes at an opportune moment, as if sent by God

grat • i • fi • ca • tion (grat´ə fi kā´shən) *n.*, satisfaction; pleasure

grat • i • fy • ing (grat´ə fī´iŋ) *adj.*, pleasing

griev • ous (grēv´əs) *adj.*, severe; serious

grope (grōp) *vi.*, seek or find (one's way) by feeling or searching about blindly grov • el • ing (gräv´ˈl iŋ) *adj.*, cringing; lowly

grudg • ing (gruj´iŋ) *adj.*, resentful

guile • less (gīl´lis) *adj.*, frank; without slyness and cunning

H

ha • bit • u • al (hə bich´o͞o əl) *adj.*, usual; customary; as a habit

hag • gard (hag´ərd) *adj.*, worn out; drawn

han • ker • ing (haŋ´kər iŋ) *n.*, craving; yearning

har • bor (här´bər) *vt.*, shelter

harp (härp) *vi.*, persist in talking or thinking continuously on one subject

hin • drance (hin´drəns) *n.*, obstacle

hoist (hoist) *vt.*, pull up

hom • age (häm´ij) *n.*, action performed to show honor

hom • i • ly (häm´ə lē) *n.*, sermon

hy • poth • e • sis (hī päth´ə sis) *n.*, theory

I

i • dle (ī´dəl) *adj.*, vain; pointless

i • dle (ī´dəl) *adj.*, not inclined to work

ig • no • min • i • ous • ly (ig´nə min´ē əs lē) *adv.*, shamefully; disgracefully

im • be • cil • i • ty (im´bə sil´ə tē) *n.*, stupidity

im • brue (im bro͞o´) *vt.*, soak or stain, especially with blood

im • pair (im per´) *vt.*, make worse, less, or weaker

im • part (im pärt´) *vt.*, make known; reveal

im • par • ti • al • i • ty (im par´shē al´ə tē) *n.*, objectivity; judgment based on reason

im • pede (im pēd´) *vt.*, hinder; block

im • pel (im pel´) *vt.*, force; urge

im • pend (im pend´) *vi.*, hang; be about to take place

im • pend • ing (im pend´iŋ) *adj.*, about to take place

im • per • cep • ti • ble (im´pər sep´tə bəl) *adj.*, barely noticeable

im • pe • ri • ous • ly (im pir´ē əs lē) *adv.*, urgently; in a domineering way; arrogantly

im • per • ti • nent (im purt´ˈn ənt) *adj.*, disrespectful; insolent

im • pet • u • os • i • ty (im pech´o͞o äs´ə tē) *n.*, impulsiveness; rashness

im • pi • ous • ly (im´pē əs lē) *adv.*, without due respect

im • pli • cate (im´pli kāt´) *vt.*, have a connection to a crime

im • ply (im plī´) *vt.*, indicate; suggest

im • port (im pôrt´) *vt.*, mean; signify an important action

im • pos • ing (im pō´ziŋ) *adj.*, impressive

im • pos • tor (im päs´tər) *n.*, one who deceives others by pretending to be someone or something that he or she is not

im • pre • ca • tion (im´pri kā´shən) *n.*, curse

im • pres • si • bil • i • ty (im pres´ə bil´ə tē) *n.*, tendency to be affected

im • pres • sion (im presh´ən) *n.*, idea

in • ac • ces • si • bil • i • ty (in´ək ses´ə bil´ə tē) *n.*, state of being unreachable or unattainable in • ap • ti • tude (in ap´ tə to͞od´) *n.*, lack of skill

in • censed (in sensd´) *adj.*, very angry

in • ci • den • tal • ly (in´si dent´ lē) *adv.*, by chance; as of little importance

in • cip • i • ent (in sip´ē ənt) *adj.*, in an early stage

in • cli • na • tion (in klə nā´shən) *n.*, tendency; preference; leaning

in • co • her • ent • ly (in´kō hir´ənt lē) *adv.*, illogically; irrationally

in • com • pat • i • bil • i • ty (in´kəm pat´ə bil´ə tē) *n.*, condition of not being able to exist in harmony; conflict

in • con • gru • i • ty (in´kän gro͞o´ə tē) *n.*, lack of consistency with what is appropriate

in • con • gru • ous (in käŋ´gro͞o əs) *adj.*, not in harmony with the surroundings

in • cred • u • lous (in krej´o͞o ləs) *adj.*, unwilling to believe; doubting

in • cur (in kʉr´) *vt.*, bring upon oneself

in • cur • sion (in kʉr´zhen) *n.*, coming in when undesired, as an invasion

in • del • i • ble (in del´ə bəl) *adj.*, that cannot be erased; permanent

in • dic • a • tive (in dik´ə tive) *adj.*, giving an indication or suggestion

in • dif • fer • ent (in dif´ər ənt) *adj.*, mediocre

in • dig • na • tion (in´dig nā´shən) *n.*, anger

in • dis • crim • i • nate (in´dis krim´ə nit) *adj.*, random; haphazard; confused

in • dis • pen • sa • ble (in´dis pen´sə bəl) *adj.*, essential

in • duce (in do͞os´) *vt.*, persuade

in • duct (in dukt´) *vt.*, formally admit

in • dus • tri • ous • ly (in dus´trē əs lē) *adv.*, busily; with earnest, steady effort

in • dus • try (in´dəs trē) *n.*, hard work; diligence

in • ef • fi • ca • cy (in ef´i kə sē) *n.*, inability to produce the desired effect

in • ex • pli • ca • ble (in eks´pli kə bəl) *adj.*, that cannot be explained or understood

in • fal • li • ble (in fal´ə bəl) *adj.*, incapable of error; never wrong

in • fer • ence (in´fər əns) *n.*, conclusion arrived at by reasoning

in • fir • mi • ty (in fʉr´mə tē) *n.*, weakness; feebleness

in • flam • ma • to • ry (in flam´ə tôr´ē) *adj.*, rousing excitement or anger

in • fuse (in fyo͞oz´) *vt.*, fill with a quality or feeling

in • ge • ni • ous (in jēn´yəs) *adj.*, clever

in • ge • nu • i • ty (in´jə no͞o´ə tē) *n.*, quality of cleverness; skill

in • grate (in´grāt) *n.*, ungrateful person

in • ju • di • cious (in´jo͞o dish´əs) *adj.*, showing poor judgment

in • junc • tion (in juŋk´shən) *n.*, command

in • quir • y (in´kwə rē) *n.*, question

in • scru • ta • bly (in skro͞ot´ə blē) *adv.*, mysteriously; in a way not easily understood

in • sin • u • a • tion (in sin´yo͞o ā´shən) *n.*, slight hint or suggestion

in • so • lent • ly (in´sə lənt lē) *adv.*, disrespectfully; arrogantly

in • sol • u • ble (in säl´yo͞o bəl) *adj.*, that cannot be solved

in • sur • mount • a • ble (in´sər mount´ə bəl) *adj.*, that cannot be overcome

in • tent (in tent´) *adj.*, firmly directed or fixed

in • ter • loc • u • tor (in´tər läk´yo͞o tər) *n.*, person taking part in conversation

in • ter • me • di • ate (in´tər mē´dē it) *adj.*, between two things, places, or stages

in • ter • ment (in tʉr´mənt) *n.*, burial

in • ter • min • a • ble (in tʉr´mə nə bəl) *adj.*, endless

in • ter • pose (in´tər pōz´) *vt.*, place between; introduce into a conversation

in • ter • po • si • tion (in´tər pə zish´ən) *n.*, intervention; placing between

in • ter • rog • a • tive (in´tə räg´ə tiv) *adj.*, questioning

in • ti • mate (in´tə māt´) *vt.*, hint or imply

in • ti • ma • tion (in´tə mā´shən) *n.*, hint

in • tri • ca • cy (in´tri kə sē) *n.*, quality of being complex

in • vei • gle (in vē´gəl) *vt.*, lure, deceive

in • vet • er • ate (in vet´ər it) *adj.*, firmly established

i • rate (ī´rāt) *adj.*, very angry

ir • rec • on • cil • a • bil • i • ty (ir rek´ən sīl ə bil´ə tē) *n.*, incompatibility; inability to be agreed upon

ir • re • pres • si • ble (ir´ri pres´ə bəl) *adj.*, impossible to control

ir • res • o • lute (ir rez´ə lo͞ot) *adj.*, indecisive

ir • rev • o • ca • ble (ir rev´ə kə bəl) *adj.*, that cannot be undone

J

jo • cose (jō kōs´) *adj.*, playful; humorous; witty

jos • tle (jäs´əl) *vt.*, bump; shove

jo • vi • al • i • ty (jō´vē al´ə tē) *n.*, playfulness; joyfulness

ju • di • cial (jo͞o dish´əl) *adj.*, carefully considering the facts

ju • di • cious (jo͞o dish´əs) *adj.*, wise

L

lac • er • ate (las´ər āt) *vt.*, wound

lair (ler) *n.*, hiding place; den

lamed (lāmd) *adj.*, made lame or injured

la • ment (lə ment´) *n.*, outward expression of sorrow

lam • en • ta • tion (lam´ən tā´shən) *n.*, outward expression of grief, especially wailing or weeping

lan • guor (laŋ´gər) *n.*, lack of vigor or vitality

lapse (laps) *vi.*, slip

lar • ce • ny (lär´sə nē) *n.*, theft

la • tent (lā´tənt) *adj.*, lying hidden or undeveloped (within a person or thing); inactive

laud (lôd) *vt.*, praise

lav • ish (lav´ish) *adj.*, extravagant; excessive

leer (lir) *vi.*, look at in a sly, lewd way

leg • a • cy (leg´ə sē) *n.*, money or property handed down to someone by a will

leg • i • ble (lej´ə bəl) *adj.*, readable

lei • sure (lē´zhər) *n.*, free or spare time

le • ni • ent • ly (lēn´yənt lē) *adv.*, not harshly or severely

le • thar • gic (li thär´jik) *adj.*, sluggish; drowsy

li • a • ble (lī´ə bəl) *adj.*, legally bound; subject

lib • er • al (lib´ər əl) *adj.*, generous

lib • er • al • i • ty (lib´ər al´i tē) *n.*, willingness to give freely

lib • er • ty (lib´ər tē) *n.*, action that is too free or too bold

liq • ui • da • tion (lik´wə dā´shən) *n.*, payment of a debt

lithe (līth) *adj.*, limber; flexible

liv • id (liv´id) *adj.*, grayish-blue from bruising

loi • ter (loit´ər) *vi.*, spend time idly; linger in an aimless way

loom (lo͞om) *vi.*, appear; take shape indistinctly as through a mist

lu • cid (lo͞o´sid) *adj.*, rational

lu • di • crous (lo͞o´di krəs) *adj.*, absurd; ridiculous

lu • mi • nous (lo͞o´mə nəs) *adj.*, brilliant

lus • trous (lus´trəs) *adj.*, bright

lux • u • ri • ous (lug zho͞or´ē əs) *adj.*, constituting richness, comfort, and extravagance

M

mag • is • te • ri • al • ly (maj´is tir´ē ə lē) *adv.*, authoritatively

mag • is • trate (maj´is trāt´) *n.*, civil officer empowered to administer the law

mag • nan • i • mous (mag nan´ə məs) *adj.*, noble in mind

ma • lev • o • lent (mə lev´ə lənt) *adj.*, wishing evil or harm to others

mal • ice (mal´is) *n.*, desire to harm another

ma • lig • nant (mə lig´nənt) *adj.*, evil

ma • lig • ni • ty (mə lig´nə tē) *n.*, quality of being harmful; ill will

man • gy (mān´jē) *adj.*, shabby and filthy

ma • ni • a (mā´nē ə) *n.*, abnormally intense desire

man • i • fest (man´ə fest´) *adj.*, obvious

man • i • fest (man´ə fest´) *vt.*, reveal; make clear

maud • lin (môd´lin) *adj.*, foolishly sentimental

maul (môl) *vt.*, injure by beating

mean (mēn) *adj.*, low in quality, value, or importance

med • i • ta • tion (med´ə tā´shən) *n.*, solemn reflection

mel • an • chol • y (mel´ən käl´ē) *adj.*, sad; gloomy

mend (mend) *vt.*, repair

mer • it (mer´it) *n.*, mark of excellence

me • trop • o • lis (mə träp´əl is) *n.*, main city, often a capital

met • ro • pol • i • tan (me´trō päl´i tən) *adj.*, of a major city

mis • cre • ant (mis krē´ənt) *n.*, villain

mis • de • mean • or (mis´di mēn´ər) *n.*, minor offense

mis • giv • ing (mis giv´iŋ) *n.*, feeling of uncertainty or apprehension

mite (mīt) *n.*, very small creature

mod • est • ly (mäd´ist lē) *adv.*, shyly

mod • i • fy (mäd´ə fī´) *vt.*, change or alter

mold • er • ing (mōl´dər iŋ) *adj.*, decaying

mol • li • fied (mäl´ə fīd´) *adj.*, less severe; appeased

mon • o • ma • ni • a (män´ō mā´nē ə) *n.*, mental disorder characterized by a preoccupation with one subject

mo • not • o • nous (mə nät´'n əs) *adj.*, going on in the same tone

mon • stros • i • ty (män sträs´ə tē) *n.*, something grotesquely abnormal

mor • bid • ly (môr´bid lē) *adv.*, gloomily

mo • rose (mə rōs´) *adj.*, gloomy; sullen

mor • ti • fi • ca • tion (môr´tə fi kā´shən) *n.*, shame; humiliation

mor • ti • fied (môr´tə fīd) *adj.*, humiliated

mor • ti • fy • ing (môrt´ə fī´iŋ) *adj.*, punishing or controlling by self-denial or fasting

mot • tled (mät´ 'ld) *adj.*, blotched

mute (myo͞ot) *adj.*, silent

mu • ti • ny (myo͞ot´'n ē) *n.*, revolt

N

nig • gard • ly (nig´ərd lē) *adj.*, stingy

nim • ble (nim´bəl) *adj.*, quick; agile

no • bler (nō´blʉr) *adj.*, loftier; grander

nom • i • nal (näm´ə nəl) *adj.*, very small

nook (no͝ok) *n.*, small recess or secluded spot

nur • ture (nʉr´chər) *n.*, upbringing

O

ob • dur • ate (äb´do͝or it) *adj.*, hardened; stubborn

ob • li • ga • tion (äb´lə gā´shən) *n.*, responsibility

o • blige (ə blīj´) *vt.*, do a favor for

ob • se • qui • ous (əb sē´kwē əs) *adj.*, showing too great a willingness to obey; fawning

ob • sti • nate • ly (äb´stə nət lē) *adv.*, stubbornly

ob • trude (əb tro͞od´) *vt.*, force upon others unwanted

ob • tru • sive (əb tro͞o´siv) *adj.*, calling attention to oneself in a displeasing way

ob • tuse • ness (äb to͞os´nəs) *n.*, stupidity; slowness to understand

oc • tag • o • nal (äk tag´ə nəl) *adj.*, eight-sided

o • di • ous (ō´dē əs) *adj.*, offensive; arousing hatred

of • fi • ci • at • ing (ə fish´ē āt´iŋ) *adj.*, performing the duties of an office

om • i • nous • ly (äm´ə nəs lē) *adv.*, threateningly, as of a bad omen

om • nip • o • tent (äm nip´ə tənt) *adj.*, all-powerful

oph • thal • mic (äf thal´mik) *adj.*, related to the eye

os • ten • ta • tious • ly (äs´tən tā´shəs lē) *adv.*, pretentiously; in a flashy or showy manner, as to display one's knowledge

P

pall (pôl) *n.,* covering of dark clouds

pal • lor (pal´ ər) *n.,* lack of color

pan • to • mime (pan´ tə mīm´) *n.,* dramatic representation played without words

par • a • lyt • ic (par´ ə lit´ ik) *adj.,* showing a helpless inability to act

par • cel (pär´ səl) *n.,* package

par • ox • ysm (par´ əks iz´ əm) *n.,* sudden attack; spasm

pa • tron • ize (pā´ trə nīz´) *vt.,* be kind or helpful to in a snobbish way

pen • ance (pen´ əns) *n.,* self-punishment done in repentance for wrong-doing

pen • i • ten • tial (pen´ i ten´shəl) *adj.,* expressing sorrow for wrongdoing

pen • i • ten • tial • ly (pen´ i ten´ shə lē) *adv.,* expressing a sin or regret

per • cep • ti • bly (pər sep´ tə blē) *adv.,* noticeably

per • cep • tion (pər sep´shən) *n.,* insight or intuition

per • for • ate (pʉr´ fə rāt´) *vt.,* pierce or punch holes in

per • il (per´əl) *n.,* exposure to harm or danger

per • ni • cious (pər nish´əs) *adj.,* causing great injury, destruction, or ruin

per • pet • u • al (pər pech´o͞o əl) *adj.,* continual

per • plexed (pər plekst´) *adj.,* confused

per • plex • i • ty (pər pleks´ə tē) *n.,* bewilderment; confusion

per • se • ver • ance (pʉr´sə vir´əns) *n.,* continued effort; steadfastness

per • son • age (pʉr´ sən ij´) *adj.,* person of importance or distinction

per • spi • cu • i • ty (pʉr´spə kyo͞o´ə tē) *adj.,* clarity of expression

per • u • sal (pə ro͞o´zəl) *n.,* thorough or leisurely reading

pet • tish • ly (pet´ish lē) *adv.,* with irritation; peevishly

phe • nom • e • non (fə näm´ə nən´) *n.,* unusual or extraordinary occurrence

pi • ous (pī´əs) *adj.,* coming from actual or pretended religious devotion

pitch (pich) *n.,* point or degree

plac • a • ble (plak´ə bəl) *adj.,* pacified, calm

plac • id • ly (plas´id lē) *adv.,* calmly; quietly

plain • tive • ly (plān´tiv lē) *adv.,* mournfully; sadly

ple • be • ian (pli bē´ən) *adj.,* characteristic of common people

plen • i • po • ten • ti • ar • y (plen´i pō ten´shē er´ē) *n.,* diplomat working as a representative of government

ply (plī) *vt.,* engage in diligently

poise (poiz) *vi.,* balance

poise (poiz) *vt.,* balance; keep steady

pom • pous • ly (päm´pəs lē) *adv.,* in a self-important manner

pon • der (pän´dər) *vt.,* consider carefully

pon • der • ous (pän´dər əs) *adj.,* very heavy or massive

por • ten • tous (pôr ten´təs) *adj.,* ominous

port • ly (pôrt´lē) *adj.,* large and heavy in a dignified and stately way

post (pōst) *n.,* position; job

prec • e • dence (pres´ə dəns) *n.,* first place

pre • ci • sion (prē sizh´ən) *n.,* quality of being precise, exact, or accurate

pred • a • tor • y (pred´ə tôr´ē) *adj.,* living by plundering or exploiting

pre • dom • i • nant (prē däm´ə nənt) *adj.,* superior; dominant

pre • fer • ment (prē fʉr´mənt) *n.,* promotion

pre • lim • i • nar • y (prē lim´ə ner´ē) *n.,* event that precedes the main event; step leading up to the main procedure

pre • mi • um (prē´mē əm) *n.,* reward; payment

pre • pos • ses • sion (prē´pə zesh´ən) *n.,* preconception

pre • pos • ter • ous (prē päs´tər əs) *adj.,* ridiculous

pre • sen • ti • ment (prē zent´ə mənt) *n.,* feeling that something unfortunate is about to take place

pre • side (prē zīd´) *vi.,* exercise authority; take control

pre • sume (prē zo͞om´) *vi.,* accept as true; take for granted

pre • tense (prē´tens´) *n.,* false appearance or action intended to deceive

pre • text (prē´tekst´) *n.,* excuse; false reason

pro • di • gious (prə dij´əs) *adj.,* of great size, power, or extent

pro • di • gious • ly (prō dij´əs lē) *adv.,* amazingly

pro • fess (prə fes´) *vt.,* affirm, declare; claim

prof • fered (präf´ərd) *adj.,* offered; presented

pro • fi • cien • cy (prō fish´ən sē) *n.,* skill; competency

pro • found (prō found´) *adj.,* very deep; intensely felt

pro • hi • bi • tion (prō´i bish´ən) *n.,* something that is forbidden

prom • i • nent (präm´ə nənt) *adj.,* noticeable; standing out

pro • pen • si • ty (prə pen´sə tē) *n.,* natural tendency or inclination

pro • pi • ti • ate (prō pish´ē āt´) *vt.,* cause to become favorably inclined

pro • pi • ti • a • tion (prō pish´ē ā´shən) *n.,* appeasing; winning a person over

pro • po • si • tion (präp´ə zish´ən) *n.,* proposal

pro • pound (prə pound´) *vt.,* put forth for consideration

pro • pri • e • ty (prə prī´ə tē) *n.,* accepted standard of behavior

pro • scribe (prō skrīb´) *vt.,* banish; exile

pros • e • cu • tion (präs´i kyo͞o´shən) *n.,* the state as the party that carries on legal proceedings against criminals

pros • pect (präs´pekt) *n.,* broad view; chance for success

pros • trate (präs´trāt´) *vt.,* make (oneself) lie flat on the ground

pro • verb (präv´ʉrb) *n.,* short, traditional saying that expresses some obvoius truth or familiar experience

prov • i • den • tial • ly (präv´ə den´shəl lē) *adv.,* fortunately

pro • vin • cial (prə vin´shəl) *adj.,* from a rustic area of the country situated away from the capital or national cultural center

pro • vok • ing (prə vō´kiŋ) *adj.,* irritating

pu • gil • is • tic (pyo͞o´jil is´tik) *adj.,* characteristic of a boxer or fighter

punc • tu • al (puŋk´cho͞o əl) *adj.,* appointed time; prompt

pun • gent (pun´jənt) *adj.,* producing a sharp sensation

Q

quell (kwel) *vt.,* bring under control

quer • u • lous (kwer´yo͞o ləs) *adj.,* full of complaint

R

raf • ter (raf´tər) *n.*, board that supports the roof

rak • ish (rāk´ish) *adj.*, dashing; elegant

ral • ly • ing (ral´ē iŋ) *adj.*, stirring

ran • kle (raŋ´kəl) *vi.*, cause resentment

rap • tur • ous • ly (rap´chər əs´lē) *adv.*, with great joy, pleasure, contentment

rav • age (rav´ij) *vt.*, destroy violently

rav • e • nous (rav´ə nəs) *adj.*, extremely eager for gratification

rav • e • nous • ly (rav´ə nəs lē) *adv.*, hungrily

rear (rir) *vt.*, raise; nurture; train

re • buff (ri buf´) *n.*, abrupt, blunt refusal of help or sympathy

re • cip • ro • cate (ri sip´rə kāt´) *vt.*, give, do, feel in return; return in kind or degree

reck • on (rek´ən) *vi.*, figure; calculate

rec • luse (rek´lo͞os) *n.*, one who chooses to live alone

re • coil (ri koil´) *vi.*, shrink back, as in fear or repugnance

rec • om • pense (rek´əm pens´) *n.*, repayment; reward

rec • on • cil • a • ble (rek´ən sīl´ə bəl) *adj.*, that which can be settled or brought to harmony

rec • on • noi • ter (rek´ə noit´ər) *vi.*, make a survey or exploration

re • cruit (ri kro͞ot) *vi.*, seek or enlist new members

re • deem • ing (ri dēm´iŋ) *adj.*, compensating

reel (rēl) *vi.*, stagger; move in an unsteady way

re • frac • to • ry (ri frak´tər ē) *adj.*, hard to manage

re • frain (ri frān´) *n.*, verse repeated at intervals throughout a song or poem

re • fur • bish (ri fʉr´bish) *vt.*, renovate; improve

reign (rān) *vi.*, rule

re • it • er • ate (rē it´ə rāt) *vt.*, say again repeatedly

re • kin • dle (rē kin´dəl) *vt.*, relight

re • lapse (ri laps´) *vi.*, fall back into a former habit

re • lin • quish (ri liŋ´kwish) *vt.*, give up; abandon; set aside

rel • ish (rel´ish) *vt.*, enjoy

re • miss • ness (ri mis´nəs) *n.*, carelessness; negligence

re • mon • strate (ri män´strāt) *vi.*, protest

re • morse (ri mors´) *n.*, deep sense of guilt

re • mote • ly (ri mōt´lē) *adv.*, distantly; faintly

re • mu • ner • ate (ri myo͞o´nə rāt) *vt.*, pay or reward for work

re • mu • ner • a • tive (ri myo͞o´nə rāt iv) *adj.*, paying

ren • der (ren´dər) *vt.*, cause to be or become

ren • der (ren´dər) *vt.*, give; present

re • nounce (ri nouns´) *vt.*, formally give up

rep • a • ra • tion (rep´ə rā´shən) *n.*, something done or paid to make amends

re • pent • ance (ri pen´təns) *n.*, feeling of sorrow for wrongdoing

re • pose (ri pōz´) *vt.*, place trust in someone

re • press (ri pres´) *vt.,* keep down; hold back

re • pressed (ri presd´) *adj.,* held back; stifled; controlled

re • proach (ri prōch´) *n.,* blame; disgrace

re • proach • ful (ri prōch´fəl) *adj.,* expressing blame

re • pu • di • ate (ri pyo͞o´dē āt´) *vt.,* refuse to accept

re • pug • nance (ri pug´nəns) *n.,* aversion; extreme dislike

re • pute (ri pyo͞ot´) *vt.,* regard; consider

req • ui • site (rek´wi zit) *adj.,* essential

re • quit • ed (ri kwīt´'d) *adj.,* paid back

res • o • lu • tion (rez´ə lo͞o´shən) *n.,* determination

re • sume (ri zo͞om´) *vt.,* take on again; continue after interruption

re • tal • i • a • tion (ri tal´ē ā´shən) *n.,* paying back injury for injury

ret • i • cence (ret´ə səns) *n.,* reserve; silence

ret • i • cent (ret´ə sənt) *adj.,* reserved; uncommunicative

re • tort (ri tôrt´) *vi.,* answer (an argument) in kind

re • trib • u • tive (ri trib´yo͞o tiv) *adj.,* in payment for evil done

ret • ro • spec • tive • ly (ret´rə spek´tiv lē) *adv.,* in a way that looks back on the past

rev • e • la • tion (rev´ə lā´shən) *n.,* revealing or disclosure of something

re • ver • ber • ate (ri vʉr´bər āt´) *vt.,* reecho

re • vert • ing (ri vʉrt´iŋ) *n.,* going back in action, thought, or speech

re • vive (rē vīv´) *vt.,* bring back to a healthy, vigorous, or flourishing condition

riv • et (riv´it) *vt.,* secure firmly

riv • et • ed (riv´it əd) *adj.,* firmly fixed or held

rouse (rouz) *vt.,* stir up

ru • di • ment (ro͞o´də mənt) *n.,* basic skill or need

ru • mi • na • tion (ro͞o´mə nā´shən) *n.,* thought

S

sa • ga • cious (sə gā´shəs) *adj.,* showing sound judgment; wise; shrewd

sa • ga • cious • ly (sə gā´shəs lē) *adv.,* wisely

sal • u • ta • tion (sal´yo͞o tā´shən) *n.,* greeting

sanc • ti • fy (saŋk´tə fī) *vt.,* set apart as holy; purify

san • gui • nar • y (saŋ´gwi ner´ē) *adj.,* bloodstained

scru • ti • ny (skro͞ot´'nē) *n.,* close examination

scuf • fle (skuf´əl) *n.,* rough fight

seared (sird´) *adj.,* burned

se • clu • sion (si klo͞o´zhən) *n.,* isolation

sed • a • tive (sed´ə tiv) *adj.,* tending to soothe or quiet

seize (sēz) *vt.,* take; capture

sel • dom (sel´dəm) *adv.,* rarely

self- • pos • sessed (self pə zesd´) *adj.,* in full control of one's feelings and actions

se • rene (sə rēn´) *adj.,* calm, peaceful, tranquil

ser • pen • tine (sʉr´pən tēn´) *adj.,* snake-like; evilly cunning or subtle

ser • vile (sʉr´vəl) *adj.*, too humble or submissive

sev • er (sev´ər) *vt.*, separate by cutting

se • ver • i • ty (sə ver´ə tē) *n.*, strictness; harshness

shud • der (shud´ər) *vi.*, shake, tremble suddenly

si • dle (sī´dəl) *vi.*, move sideways; edge along, especially in a nervous manner

sin • ew (sin´yo͞o) *n.*, tendon; muscular power

sin • ew • y (sin´yo͞o ē) *adj.*, tough; strong

slov • en • ly (sluv´ən lē) *adj.*, careless in appearance or manner; untidy

slum • ber (slum´bər) *vi.*, sleep

smol • der • ing (smōl´dər iŋ) *adj.*, with feelings of suppressed anger or hate

snare (snar) *n.*, trap for small animals

sneer (snir) *n.*, smile or expression that shows contempt

sniv • el (sniv´əl) *vi.*, make a whining, tearful display of false grief

so • ber (sō´bər) *adj.*, not bright or flashy; plain

so • lic • it (sə lis´it) *vt.*, ask or seek earnestly

sol • ven • cy (säl´vən sē) *n.*, ability to meet financial obligations

sov • er • eign (säv´rən) *adj.*, very effectual as a cure or remedy

spas • mod • ic (spaz mäd´ik) *adj.*, like a spasm; sudden and irregular; fitful

spec • ter (spek´tər) *n.*, ghost

spec • tral (spek´trəl) *adj.*, like a phantom or ghost

spec • u • late (spek´yə lāt) *vi.*, make guesses

spec • u • la • tion (spek´yo͞o lā´shən) *adj.*, guess; opinion or conclusion based on incomplete evidence

spon • ta • ne • ous • ly (spän tā´nē əs lē) *adv.*, having no apparent external cause

spu • ri • ous (spyo͞o´ē əs) *adj.*, counterfeit; fake

spurned (spʉrnd) *adj.*, rejected

stag • nant (stag´nənt) *adj.*, inactive; sluggish

staid (stād) *adj.*, resisting change; fixed; serious

steeped (stēpd) *adj.*, soaked; immersed

sti • fle (stī´fəl) *vt.*, smother

stip • u • late (stip´yo͞o lāt) *vt.*, specify as an essential condition

sto • lid • i • ty (stə lid´ə tē) *n.*, emotionlessness

strain (strān) *n.*, style; tone

strat • a • gem (strat´ə jəm) *n.*, trick or scheme

stren • u • ous (stren´yo͞o əs) *adj.*, requiring great effort

stu • pe • fied (sto͞op´ə fīd) *adj.*, stunned

sub • dued (səb do͞od´) *adj.*, softened; quiet; kept back

sub • lime (sə blīm´) *adj.*, noble

sub • mis • sive • ly (səb mis´iv lē) *adv.*, obediently

sub • orned (sə bôrd´) *adj.*, urged to do something illegal; bribed

sub • se • quent (sub´si kwənt) *adj.*, following in time, place, or order

sub • stan • tial • ly (səb stan´shə lē) *adv.*, amply; plentifully

sub • ter • fuge (sub´tər fyo͞oj´) *n.*, plan used to hide one's true intentions

suc • ces • sor (sək ses´ ər) *n.,* one that follows another

sul • ky (sul´ kē) *adj.,* dismal; sullen

sum • ma • ry (sum´ə rē) *adj.,* concise

sun • dry (sun´drē) *adj.,* various; miscellaneous

su • per • an • nu • at • ed (sōō´pər an´yōō ā´təd) *adj.,* too old or worn for further work

su • per • cil • i • ous • ly (sōō´pər sil´ē əs lē) *adv.,* scornfully; haughtily

su • per • flu • ous (sə pɥr´flōō əs) *adj.,* extra; unnecessary

su • per • sede (sōō´pər sēd´) *vt.,* replace; cause to be set aside

sup • pli • cant (sup´lə kənt) *n.,* one who makes a humble request

surge (sɥrj) *vi.,* move in a swelling motion

sur • name (sɥr´nām´) *n.,* family name or last name

sur • vey (sər vā´) *vt.,* examine or inspect carefully

sus • cep • ti • bil • i • ty (sə sep´tə bil´ə tē) *n.,* quality of being easily affected emotionally; sensitive nature

sus • pend • ed (sə spen´did) *adj.,* halted

sus • tain (sə stān´) *vt.,* undergo; suffer

swin • dler (swind´lər) *n.,* person who cheats or defrauds

sym • met • ri • cal (si met´ri kəl) *adj.,* well-balanced; orderly

T

tac • it (tas´it) *adj.,* unspoken; silent

taint (tānt) *n.,* trace of something that spoils or corrupts

taunt • ing (tônt´iŋ) *adj.,* sarcastic; ridiculing

teem (tēm) *vi.,* swarm; be abundant

tem • per • ate (tem´pər it) *adj.,* self-restrained; moderate in actions

ten • ure (ten´yər) *n.,* right of holding property

terse • ly (tɥrs´ lē) *adv.,* concisely; using as few words as possible

tes • ti • ly (tes´tə lē) *adv.,* irritably; with annoyance

the • ol • o • gy (thē äl´ə jē) *n.,* study of religion

thresh • old (thresh´ōld) *n.,* beginning point

thrice (thrīs) *adv.,* three times

tin • der (tin´dər) *n.,* dry, easily flammable material

tinge (tinj) *n.,* slight trace

trans • act (tran zakt´) *vt.,* carry on; conduct, as in business

trans • ac • tion (tran zak´shən) *n.,* business agreement

trans • fixed (trans fiksd´) *adj.,* made motionless with awe; fixed in one position

tran • spire (tran spīr´) *vi.,* take place

tra • verse (trə vɥrs´) *vt.,* pass over or through

trea • son • a • ble (trē´zən ə bəl) *adj.,* traitorous

trea • son • a • bly (trē´zən ə blē) *adv.,* like a traitor helping the enemy

trea • tise (trēt´is) *n.,* formal, systematic article or book on some subject

trem • u • lous (trem´yōō ləs) *adj.,* trembling; quivering

trench • ant (trench´ənt) *adj.,* forceful

trep • i • da • tion (trep´ə dā´shən) *n.,* fearful uncertainty

tri • fling (trī´fliŋ) *adj.,* frivolous; shallow

truc • u • lent (truk´yo͞o lənt) *adj.,* fierce; cruel

U

ul • te • ri • or (ul tir´ē ər) *adj.,* beyond what is openly made known

u • nan • i • mous • ly (yo͞o nan´ə məs lē) *adv.,* in complete agreement

un • cer • e • mo • ni • ous • ly (un ser´ə mō´nē əs lē) *adv.,* impolitely

un • con • scion • a • ble (un kän´shən ə bəl) *adj.,* unreasonable; without conscience

un • couth (un ko͞oth´) *adj.,* uncultured; crude

un • de • terred (un dē tʉrd´) *adj.,* not discouraged from doing something

un • gain • ly (un gān´lē) *adj.,* without grace; clumsy

un • re • mu • ner • a • tive (un ri myo͞o´nə rāt´iv) *adj.,* unprofitable

un • re • serv • ed • ly (un´ri zʉr´vid lē) *adv.,* without limits; without holding back

un • scru • pu • lous (un skro͞o´pyə ləs) *adj.,* not restrained by ideas of right and wrong

un • ten • a • ble (un ten´ə bəl) *adj.,* not defendable

un • wont • ed (un wän´tid) *adj.,* uncommon

ut • ter • ance (ut´ər əns) *n.,* that which is spoken; expression

V

va • cant • ly (vā´kənt lē) *adv.,* blankly; without expression

vac • il • late (vas´ə lāt´) *vi.,* waver in mind; show indecision

vain • glo • ri • ous (vān´glôr´ē əs) *adj.,* boastfully vain

val • e • dic • to • ry (val´ə dik´tər ē) *adj.,* said or done at parting

van • i • ty (van´ə tē) *n.,* futility; worthlessness

van • quish (vaŋ´kwish) *vt.,* defeat

ve • he • mence (vē´ə məns) *n.,* intensity of emotion, passion, or conviction

ven • er • a • ble (ven´ər ə bəl) *adj.,* worthy of respect or reverence by reason of age and dignity, character, or position

ven • er • ate (ven´ər āt´) *vt.,* look upon with deep feelings of respect; revere

ven • ture (ven´chər) *n.,* risky or dangerous undertaking

ven • ture (ven´chər) *vi.,* take a risk

ver • i • fi • ca • tion (ver´ə fi kā´shən) *n.,* confirmation; making sure

ver • i • ta • bly (ver´i tə blē) *adv.,* truly

ves • tige (ves´tij) *n.,* trace; bit

vi • car • i • ous • ly (vī ker´ē əs lē) *adv.,* as a shared participation in another's experience

vig • i • lance (vij´ə ləns) *n.,* watchfulness

vig • or • ous (vig´ər əs) *adj.,* strong; robust

vile (vīl) *adj.,* repulsive; low; most inferior

vir • tu • ous (vʉr´cho͞o əs) *adj.,* characterized by moral excellence, right action and thinking, or goodness

vis • age (vis´ij) *n.*, face

vi • sion • ar • y (vizh´ən er´ē) *adj.*, given to impractical ideas or fantasies

vi • va • cious • ly (vī va´shəs lē) *adv.*, in a lively way

vi • vac • i • ty (vī vas´ə tē) *n.*, liveliness of spirit

vouch • er (vou´chər) *n.*, statement of expense

vul • gar (vul´gər) *adj.*, common; crude

W

waive (wāv) *vt.*, set aside temporarily

wan (wän) *adj.*, sickly; pallid

ward (wôrd) *n.*, guard

wa • ver (wā´vər) *vi.*, show doubt or indecision

way • ward • ness (wā´wərd nəs) *n.*, quality of being unpredictable or erratic

weld • ed (weld´əd) *adj.*, united; fused

wind • fall (wind´fôl) *n.*, unexpected gain

wont (wônt) *adj.*, accustomed

wrath (rath) *n.*, anger

wrench (rench) *vt.*, pull out with force

Handbook of Literary Terms

Allusion. An **allusion** is a rhetorical technique in which reference is made to a person, event, object, or work from history or literature. In chapter 26 of *Great Expectations,* the narrator makes an allusion to the faces rising out of the witches' caldron in Shakespeare's *Macbeth.*

Ambiguity. An **ambiguity** is a statement that has a double meaning or a meaning that cannot be clearly resolved. In English, the word *cleave* is oddly ambiguous, for it can mean either "to cling together" or "to cut apart." Many literary *figures of speech,* including *metaphors, similes,* and *symbols,* are examples of intentional ambiguity in that they say one thing and intend another.

Analogy. An **analogy** is a comparison of two things that are alike in some respects but different in others. In an analogy, the comparison is direct, not implied. A *simile* is a type of analogy. See *simile.*

Aphorism. An **aphorism** is a short saying or pointed statement. An example of an aphorism is Matthew Pocket's observation about gentlemen: "no man who was not a true gentleman at heart, ever was, since the world began, a true gentleman in manner. . . . no varnish can hide the grain of the wood, and that the more varnish you put on, the more the grain will express itself."

Archetype. An **archetype** is an inherited, often unconscious, ancestral memory or motif that recurs throughout history and literature. The term is often used to refer to any element that recurs throughout the literature of the world. Thus the story of the journey, in which someone sets out on a path, experiences adventures, and emerges wiser, may be considered archetypal, for it is found in all cultures and in all times. See *motif.*

Bildungsroman. A ***Bildungsroman*** is a novel that tells the story of the growth or development of a person from youth to adulthood. *Great Expectations* is an example of a *Bildungsroman.*

Character. A **character** is a person (or sometimes an animal) who figures in the action of a literary work. A *protagonist,* or *main character,* is the central figure in a literary work. An *antagonist* is a character who is pitted against a protagonist. *Major characters* are those who play significant roles in a work. *Minor characters* are those who play lesser roles. A *one-dimensional character, flat character,* or *caricature* is one who exhibits a single dominant quality, or *character trait.* A *three-dimensional, full,* or *rounded character* is one who exhibits the complexity of traits associated with actual human beings. A *static character* is one who does not change during the course of the action. A *dynamic character* is one who does change.

Characterization. **Characterization** is the use of literary techniques to create a character. Writers use three major techniques to create characters: direct description, portrayal of characters' behavior, and representations of characters' internal states. When using direct description, the writer, through a speaker, a narrator, or another character, simply comments on the character, telling the reader about such matters as the character's appearance, habits, dress, background, personality, motivations, and so on. In portrayal of a character's behavior, the writer presents the actions and speech of the character, allowing the reader to draw his or her own conclusions from what the character says or does. When using representations of internal states, the writer reveals directly the character's private thoughts and emotions. See *character.*

Comic Relief. Writers sometimes insert into a serious work of fiction or drama a humorous scene that is said to provide **comic relief,** because it relieves the seriousness or emotional intensity felt by the audience. Paradoxically, a scene introduced for comic relief can sometimes, because of the contrast it provides, increase the perceived intensity or seriousness of the action around it. An example of comic relief in *Great Expectations* is the description of Mr. Wopsle's production of *Hamlet* in chapter 31.

Dialogue. **Dialogue** is conversation involving two or more people or characters. Plays are made up of dialogue and stage directions. Fictional works are made up of dialogue, narration, and description.

Dynamic Character. See *character.*

Effect. The **effect** of a literary work is the general impression or emotional impact that it achieves. Some writers and critics have insisted that a successful short story or poem is one in which each detail contributes to the overall effect, or dominant impression, produced by the piece.

Extended Metaphor. An **extended metaphor** is a point-by-point presentation of one thing as though it were another.

The description is meant as an implied comparison, inviting the reader to associate the thing being described with something that is quite different from it. An example of an extended metaphor is found in chapter 32 of *Great Expectations*. There Mr. Wemmick is described as a gardener and the prison as his greenhouse. The prisoners are the plants he is tending and a new prisoner is called a "shoot." See *metaphor*.

Falling Action. See *plot*.

Foil. A **foil** is a character whose attributes, or characteristics, contrast with, and therefore throw into relief, the attributes of another character.

Foreshadowing. **Foreshadowing** is the act of presenting materials that hint at events to occur later in a story.

Image. An **image** is a word or phrase that names something that can be seen, heard, touched, tasted, or smelled. The images in a literary work are referred to, collectively, as the work's *imagery*.

Imagery. See *image*.

Irony. **Irony** is a difference between appearance and reality. Types of irony include the following: *dramatic irony,* in which something is known by the reader or audience but unknown to the characters; *verbal irony,* in which a statement is made that implies its opposite; and *irony of situation,* in which an event occurs that violates the expectations of the characters, the reader, or the audience.

Irony of Situation. See *irony*.

Metaphor. A **metaphor** is a figure of speech in which one thing is spoken or written about as if it were another. This figure of speech invites the reader to make a comparison between the two things. The two "things" involved are the writer's actual subject, or the *tenor* of the metaphor, and another thing to which the subject is likened, or the *vehicle* of the metaphor. Personification and similes are types of metaphor. See *personification* and *simile*.

Motif. A **motif** is any element that recurs in one or more works of literature or art. A recurring image in *Great Expectations* is the mist rising from the marshes.

Motivation. A **motivation** is a force that moves a character to think, feel, or behave in a certain way. Pip's desire to be accepted by Estella motivates him to spurn Joe.

Narrator. A **narrator** is one who tells a story. The narrator in a work of fiction may be a central or minor character or simply someone who witnessed or heard about the events being related. Writers achieve a wide variety of ends by varying the characteristics of the narrator chosen for a particular work. Of primary importance is the choice of the narrator's point of view. Will the narrator be omniscient, knowing all things, including the internal workings of the minds of the characters in the story, or will the narrator be limited in his or her knowledge? Will the narrator participate in the action of the story or stand outside that action and comment on it? Will the narrator be reliable or unreliable? That is, will the reader be able to trust the narrator's statements? These are all questions that a writer must answer when developing a narrator. See *point of view.*

One-dimensional Character. See *character.*

Personification. **Personification** is a figure of speech in which an idea, animal, or thing is described as if it were a person.

Plot. A **plot** is a series of events related to a central *conflict,* or struggle. A typical plot involves the introduction of a conflict, its development, and its eventual resolution. Terms used to describe elements of plot include the following:

- The **exposition,** or **introduction,** sets the tone or mood, introduces the characters and the setting, and provides necessary background information.

- The **inciting incident** is the event that introduces the central conflict.

- The **rising action,** or **complication,** develops the conflict to a high point of intensity.

- The **climax** is the high point of interest or suspense in the plot.

- The **crisis,** or **turning point,** often the same event as the climax, is the point in the plot where something decisive happens to determine the future course of events and the eventual working out of the conflict.

- The **falling action** is all of the events that follow the climax.

- The **resolution** is the point at which the central conflict is ended, or resolved.

- The **dénouement** is any material that follows the resolution and that ties up loose ends.

- The **catastrophe**, in tragedy, is the event that marks the ultimate tragic fall of the central character. Often this event is the character's death.

Plots rarely contain all these elements in precisely this order. Elements of exposition may be introduced at any time in the course of a work. A work may begin with a catastrophe and then use flashback to explain it. The exposition or dénouement or even the resolution may be missing. The inciting incident may occur before the beginning of the action actually described in the work. These are but a few of the many possible variations that plots can exhibit.

Point of View. Point of view is the vantage point from which a story is told. Stories are typically written form a *first person point of view,* in which the narrator uses words such as *I* and *we,* or from a *third-person point of view,* in which the narrator uses words such as *he, she, it,* and *they* and avoids the use of and *we.* In stories written from a first-person point of view, the narrator may be a participant or witness of the action. In stories told from a third-person point of view, the narrator generally stands outside the action. In some stories the narrator's point of view is *limited.* In such stories, the narrator can reveal the private, internal thoughts of himself or herself or of a single character. In other stories, the narrator's point of view is *omniscient.* In such stories the narrator can reveal the private, internal thoughts of any character.

Satire. Satire is humorous writing or speech intended to point out errors, falsehoods, foibles, or failings. It is written for the purpose of reforming human behavior or human institutions. Dickens satirizes pompous, pretentious people in his portrayal of Mr. Pumblechook.

Scene. A scene is a short section of a literary work that presents action that occurs in a single place or at a single time. Long divisions of dramas are often divided into scenes.

Setting. The setting of a literary work is the time and place in which it occurs, together with all the details used to create a sense of a particular time and place. Writers create setting by various means. In drama, the setting is often revealed by the stage set and the costumes, though it may be revealed through what the characters say about their environs. In fiction, setting is most often revealed by means of description of such elements as landscape, scenery, buildings, furniture, clothing, the weather, and the season. It can also be revealed by how characters talk and behave. In its widest sense, setting includes the general social, political, moral, and psychological conditions in which characters find themselves.

Simile. A **simile** is a comparison using *like* or *as*. A simile is a type of *metaphor*, and like any other metaphor, can be divided into two parts, the tenor (or subject being described), and the vehicle (or object being used in the description). When Pip says that Estella's "calm face was like a statue's," the tenor is Estella's face and the vehicle is a statue's face. They can be compared because they share the quality of impassiveness. See *metaphor*.

Symbol. A **symbol** is a thing that stands for or represents both itself and something else. Writers use two types of symbols—conventional, and personal or idiosyncratic. A *conventional symbol* is one with traditional, widely recognized associations. Such symbols include doves for peace; laurel wreaths for heroism or poetic excellence; the color green for jealousy; the color purple for royalty; the color red for anger; morning or spring for youth; winter, evening, or night for old age; wind for change or inspiration; rainbows for hope; roses for beauty; the moon for fickleness or inconstancy; roads or paths for the journey through life; woods or darkness for moral or spiritual confusion; thorns for troubles or pain; stars for unchangeableness or constancy; mirrors for vanity or introspection; snakes for evil or duplicity; and owls for wisdom. A *personal* or *idiosyncratic symbol* is one that assumes its secondary meaning because of the special use to which it is put by a writer.

Three-dimensional Character. See *character*.

Tone. **Tone** is the emotional attitude toward the reader or toward the subject implied by a literary work. Examples of the different tones that a work may have include familiar, ironic, playful, sarcastic, serious, and sincere.